the air omen

academy of magical creatures book four

MEGAN LINSKI & ALICIA RADES

We the authors acknowledge that the United States of America is a country formed on stolen land. We respect and honor the indigenous peoples who have lived here for centuries, and we recognize there is still much work to do to make reparations and heal the damage caused to the many indigenous nations who were first here, both in the past and today.

May we remember the atrocities once committed, create a better world in the present, and look forward together for our future.

A special thank-you to our sensitivity reader Kris Riley of the Cherokee tribe for her invaluable feedback on indigenous life and culture, as well as her commentary on living with chronic illness.

This book features a character with Post-traumatic Stress Disorder (PTSD). PTSD is a mental health condition that develops in response to traumatic events, such as war, natural disasters, or sexual assault. It currently affects over 7 million Americans. Symptoms may include flashbacks, depression, anxiety, tiredness, and trouble digesting food.

ONE

Fifteen Years Earlier

"Do it again!"

Grandma and Grandpa lived in a cottage by the sea. The beach was their favorite place to be. Mine too. It was a sunny day and really hot. Grandpa stood in the ocean while his eagle Familiar flew circles overhead. Grandma weaved baskets on a bench in the sand and watched with a smile. We'd collected seashells this morning, and she was making the basket for me to take them home in.

Grandpa moved his hands in circles. The water in the ocean came out in two big strands and twisted together, creating loops and dips in the sky. The eagle flew through the loops and swirled in circles around the twisted strands. It looked like one really big rope. Grandpa was using so much water— much more than anyone else in the tribe could summon, even my Dad. Grandpa could do amazing magic. I could see fish swimming in the water high above me within the tunnels he had made. Grandpa lowered the rope, and out in the distance, a whale jumped out of the water and through one of the loops.

Grandpa made the water rope return to the sea. The water splashed past my knees, and waves crashed back and forth.

"Wow!" I said. "I want to do magic like that!"

"One day you will, my child. Be patient. You're only six." Grandpa raised his arm and called for his Familiar. Tinanco landed on Grandpa's forearm and shook his feathers.

I wrinkled my nose. "I'm seven now."

"That's right! I forgot." Grandpa winked. I think he was teasing me, but I worried he really had forgotten. Seven was much older than six.

Grandpa walked to a large rug spread out in the sand and sat down. I followed him. There were many bowls sitting on the rug, with strange powders of different colors in them. Beside the bowls was a large square piece of deer leather. Grandpa summoned water from the ocean and mixed it with the powder in the bowls. Tinanco jumped off his arm and stood on the blanket. His head tilted as he watched Grandpa mix the powders.

"Grandpa, why are we doing this?" I asked.

"Because this is our heritage. It's important you learn it before you become chief."

"But why?"

"You ask a lot of questions. A good chief stays silent, listens and learns. He rarely speaks his mind." Grandpa set the bowls in front of me. "Can you tell me what these are?"

I shook my head, and Grandpa said, "These are the sacred paints of our people. Red, white, blue, yellow, purple, and green."

"Why did you make red?" I scowled at the red paint. Red was for Koigni, and I didn't like them.

"A long time ago, before the tribes divided, we shared all the colors. We were one people and not four," Grandpa said. "Our tribe was not divided."

"It wouldn't be such a bad thing if things were like that again," Grandma said. Grandpa frowned like he was sad.

"Our paints are special, and they bestow powers and blessings onto those whom they are applied after they are prayed over," he said. "They are very sacred."

I got very serious. Grandpa uttered some prayers over the paints in our ancient language. I knew what he was saying, but it was hard to understand, because he used big words I didn't know.

When Grandpa was done, he said, "Each of the paints have a

different meaning. They were once used for battle, but now are mostly used for ceremonies. It is said that each of the paints have a symbolic animal guarding over them, which gives the wearer the protection of that animal."

"I like wolves best," I said eagerly. I howled like one and laughed. Grandpa smiled.

"I know you do. Some of our bravest warriors used to paint their faces white in battle, to gain stealth and bravery from the wolf."

Grandpa took a scoop of white paint with his fingers and started putting it on my face. It felt thick and grainy. "White was not just the color of Anichi. It was the color of the original Hawkei tribe. It represented all of us in one, the people of the Great Spirit in unity."

I couldn't see what Grandpa was doing, but it felt like he was making shapes on my face. "Certain symbols have power. It is said that when some designs are drawn with paint on the bodies of Elementai, their magic is enhanced by these symbols."

"What do all the different paints mean?" I put one of my hands in the blue paint. I smeared it across Tinanco's beak, and he chirped.

"Red is for war. Blue is for peace, and for weddings. Green is for new growth and new beginnings. Purple is a rare color, and shows abundance. The paint signifies our connection with the earth, with our ancestors and with the Great Spirit."

"What about the black paint?" I asked.

"We never use black paint. Black paint is only for those who mourn and seek revenge."

"And yellow?"

"Yellow is for warriors who are ready to give their soul up to the Great Spirit." Grandpa stirred the paints again. On the leather, he began drawing symbols. They looked like birds, dragons, and other magical creatures. "These are our talismans. Each one has a different meaning when used with the paint. You will learn them all. The Hawkei had our own written language before the colonizers came to our lands. Many of our people have forgotten, but some still remember the old texts."

"How *do we know* the Great Spirit is really up there?" I asked. "How do we know the ancestors are really listening?"

"My child, the Great Spirit will always be there to guide you, if you ask for his teaching. Our ancestors are all around us, and they are here to help us down our path. You need only to believe and listen. The proof that the ancestors and the Great Spirit love you will be in your magic, when it comes."

Grandpa seemed so sure. I wanted to be sure, too.

Grandpa had me draw many symbols on the leather with the paint. I tried to make mine as good as his, but they weren't. I didn't think I'd ever be as great a chief as he had been. There were so many stories and lessons to learn. I worried I couldn't learn them all.

Grandma asked me if I was hungry. I shook my *head*.

"Are you not feeling well, pawee?" Grandma brushed my hair back.

"Yes. My tummy hurts." It had hurt since this morning.

"Hold on. I might have a plant that'll help."

Grandma was a medicine woman. She always had something. Grandma went inside the cottage and came out a few minutes later. She gave me some coast buckwheat to nibble on, and I felt a little better.

My tummy was always upset. I felt tired sometimes and wanted to take naps, but I didn't anymore, because I was supposed to be big now.

When the leather was full of symbols, Grandpa looked over them. "Very good! You did well for your first time. Your father will be pleased."

"Dad is always busy. He doesn't have time for me." I dropped my head. I didn't want Grandpa to show Dad my symbols. They weren't good enough.

"Your chief training will begin in a few years' time, then you'll always be with him. Have patience," Grandma said sweetly.

Grandpa looked at me, then scooched over to give me a hug. "You'll be a wise chief someday. Your father knows it. He's already so proud of you." Grandpa shook me.

I shrugged my shoulders. "I guess."

Dad was the best chief ever. I wanted to be like him, but didn't think I ever would.

It was late at night and really, really dark when I heard a tapping on my sliding glass window.

I woke up right away and sat upright. I thought the knocking had been a dream, but it continued. It scared me. I pulled my blanket up to my nose. What if it was a monster? Dad said he'd gotten rid of the one under my bed, but maybe it had just moved outside?

"Liam! Liam, let me in!"

I knew that *voice*. "Jonah?" I got out of bed. Standing outside was Jonah. He was dripping wet and shaking from the cold. I opened the glass door to let him in.

"Jonah, how did you get here? And how did you climb up to my room?" I asked. We lived on an island, and my room was on the second floor.

"I snuck on a boat. I kinda got wet." He shivered. "And then I climbed up the vines to your window."

Mom grew twisting flowers outside that grew up the side of our house, but I didn't know it was safe to climb them. I wanted to ask Jonah why he was here, but I didn't. Jonah ran away from home all the time. He usually went to the treehouse my Dad had built for us back on the mainland, near Grandpa's cottage. He'd never made it to my house by himself before.

Jonah was Yapluma. I knew I wasn't supposed to be friends with people from other tribes, but I didn't care, because Jonah was cool.

"Do you have any dry clothes?" Jonah asked.

I nodded. Jonah was the biggest kid in my school and my clothes wouldn't fit him, but Mommy had bought some extra clothes for him and kept them in my drawer, just in case he wanted to sleep over one night. I gave him what Mommy had bought. He changed out of them, and I put the wet clothes in the corner.

"Can I stay here with you?" he asked. He wasn't shivering anymore, but he still looked cold.

I nodded. "Yeah. But we have to be quiet."

"Okay."

I turned on the TV in my room and put the volume really low. Jonah and I played with my new PlayStation before we got mad we couldn't pass the next level and decided to watch cartoons instead. There weren't many kid shows on this late at night. I wasn't allowed to watch some of the shows that came on, but Jonah said it was fine, because his mom and dad allowed him to watch whatever he wanted.

Jonah started snoring when the clock said the number three. I got tired and fell asleep beside him.

Jonah was up before I was. He started shaking me when the sun came up. "Hey, Liam, do you have anything to eat?"

I rubbed my eyes. I was really tired. "Yeah. Come on."

We went to the kitchen. The cereal was up really high, and I couldn't get it. Jonah moved a chair across the floor, but I still couldn't reach. He tried putting me on his shoulders but that didn't work, either. We both fell down and made a loud noise.

"Liam, what are you doing up so early?"

We'd woken up Mommy. She was carrying my little sister, Maddie, and wearing her robe. Mommy still seemed sleepy. Maddie was only three and was still asleep on her chest. Mommy's eyes widened when she saw Jonah. "Jonah, dear. I didn't know you were here."

Jonah blushed. She looked at the chair, and us on the floor. "How about I make you boys some breakfast?"

Mommy cooked us bacon and eggs. Maddie sat in her high chair. Jonah and I played swords with our forks. It wasn't too long before Ezra came downstairs. Ezra was my four year-old little brother, and he always got up when he smelled food. He tried to get between us and play swords, too.

I mostly pushed my food around, but Jonah ate his really quick. Mommy gave him seconds.

"Now, I'd love for you to stay, Jonah," Mommy began, "but I do have a lot of errands to run today. I'm sorry to say we're running low on groceries. Otherwise, you know I'd love to have you."

Jonah looked sadly down at his plate.

"Can I go over to Jonah's house? Please?" I asked. It sounded more fun than going shopping.

Mommy frowned. She didn't like me going over to Jonah's house and didn't tell me why. "Are your parents home, dear?" she asked Jonah.

He shook his head. "No, ma'am. My sister's the only one home until dinner."

"Well, I guess that's all right, then." Mommy sighed and picked up the phone. "I'll give her a call. Your father will be by to pick you up in a few hours, Liam."

"I want to go, too!" Ezra shouted.

"No, baby, you'll stay here," Mommy said. "Let your brother go alone."

Ezra started to cry. I was glad. He was always copying me. It was annoying.

Before we left, Mommy packed a lunch and told me to take it with us. Mommy always packed extra food whenever I went to Jonah's house, even if I already ate.

Menilly was Mommy's Familiar. She was going to take Jonah and I to the mainland, where Jenny was waiting for us. Menilly was on the beach when we walked out. She was a kelpie— a sea horse. She walked on four legs and had green scales all over. Her mane and tail were made of seaweed, braided with seashells, and her hooves were the color of pearls.

Menilly lay down in the sand so we could climb on her back. I got on front, and Jonah sat behind me. She waded into the sea, and I hung on tightly to the seaweed in her mane as she swam forward.

Kelpies were fast. Menilly swam in the sea like she was galloping on land. Dolphins tried to keep up with her as the water fanned out around us on either side. My hair blew backward, and the wind made my eyes water. Nobody was quicker than Menilly in the water.

Jenny was waiting for us on the docks. She was Jonah's older sister, and a teenager. She made a face as we got off of Menilly. Menilly bobbed her head, and the water dried out of mine and Jonah's clothes magically.

Jenny grabbed Jonah's hand sharply. "Come on. Let's go."

Menilly turned and dove back into the water. I hurried to follow Jenny as she pulled Jonah through the streets. She acted like I wasn't even there.

We took a carriage to the Yapluma neighborhood. Jonah lived in a really big house, but it didn't have much furniture in it. I didn't know why.

Once the *door was* closed, Jenny turned on us. "Listen, you little brats," Jenny started. "I have *a very* important piano recital tomorrow, and if I blow it, Mom and Dad are going to be pissed. So you guys stay out of my way, and keep quiet. Don't you dare bother me for anything."

We nodded. Jenny stomped her feet as she walked away. She always had to be perfect in everything. I heard the sound of the piano coming from the living room.

We went up to Jonah's room. Jonah still looked hungry. He ate the extra sandwich my mommy packed for him. I gave him mine, too, because I didn't want it.

"I'll save it for dinner," Jonah said, and he hid it inside his drawer. "My mom sometimes forgets."

I thought that was okay, because the last time I was over and Jonah and I wanted snacks, the kitchen was empty.

"What should we do?" I asked. Jonah didn't have a lot of toys to play with. His room had a bed and his clothes, and that was it.

"Let's play Hippogriffs and Dragons," Jonah said. "It's my favorite."

I liked that game, because Jonah always wanted to be the hippogriff and he let me be the dragon. "Okay."

Jonah made a chirping noise and jumped at me. I roared like a dragon and tackled him. We fought back and forth like animals. It was hard to wrestle when you were trying to be quiet, but the sound of the piano muffled most of our punches.

After an hour of playing, we got too excited. Jonah jumped off his bed and landed on me. We made a loud crashing noise *as Jonah* accidentally knocked his lamp off the nightstand. It didn't break, but it created a loud thump.

The sound of the piano stopped from downstairs, and I heard the front door open. I think I heard the voice of Jenny's girlfriend. "You kids better be quiet up there!" Jenny called.

Jonah and I stopped wrestling. We shut our mouths and stared at each other. I had the thought that Jonah's house wasn't very fun. It probably would be if his sister wasn't around.

"We should go to the basement," Jonah whispered. "She won't hear us down there."

"All right." We tiptoed down the stairs to the main floor, then took the stairwell in the kitchen down to the basement.

Jonah's basement was dark and creepy. It was concrete floors and concrete walls. There were a ton of boxes down here. The basement was stuffed full. Some of the things in here were creepy. There were weird statues and old dolls that I swear kept giving me weird looks.

In the middle of the room was a huge square, at least six feet tall. I couldn't really tell what it was, because it was covered up by an old white sheet. It was the only thing down here not covered in dust. I wanted to peek under it and see what it looked like.

I went to look, but Jonah said, "Don't touch. It's a painting my Dad just bought. He told me not to play with it."

The boxes were towered up high. It didn't seem like a very safe place to play, but where else did we have to go?

There were loud noises coming from Jenny's room. I didn't know what they were doing up there. I asked Mommy once, but she told me it was adult stuff, so I just ignored it.

"We should play hide-and-seek," Jonah suggested. "There are tons of places to hide down here."

That was a great idea. "I'll seek, you hide."

It was too easy to find Jonah. I played seeker for an hour, but he was so big and so bad at hiding that it didn't take me very long to find him, no matter how long I counted or what he hid behind. Jonah was too good at getting caught.

"It's my turn to hide," I said. "We've been at this forever."

"But I hate seeking," Jonah whined.

"No fair. It's your turn!" I yelled.

"Shh," Jonah said, with a quick look at the stairs. "Okay, fine. I'll seek."

Jonah started counting. I looked everywhere for a spot to hide that he hadn't picked, and found a tall wardrobe in the far corner. I ran toward it and shut myself inside.

"Ready or not, here I come!" Jonah started looking. I pressed my hand to my mouth so I wouldn't laugh. I didn't want him to find me.

Then something happened. The room got... colder. And darker. We had the light on, but the bulbs broke. I heard the sound of glass breaking, and the only light that came into the basement were from the windows on the ceiling's level. The sunshine from outside went away... like there was a storm coming. I swear I heard the crackling of thunder, and it shook the room.

"What the hell? Power's gone out," I heard Jenny say from upstairs.

I heard something else. A low growl. From a very, very big animal.

Panic made it hard to breathe. It felt like the air was filled with static — we'd learned about that in school. It made my hair get all frizzy. I could almost hear a kind of sizzling popping in the air. Large footsteps thumped on the ground only a few feet away. What if some sort of monster lived in the basement, and we'd bothered it? It was going to eat us up!

"Liam!" Jonah was nearby. I opened the wardrobe door to see that he was crouched behind a pile of boxes, looking scared.

"In here!" I whispered. Jonah crawled to the wardrobe. I opened it up so he could squeeze himself in. We held the doors shut and held our breath.

"What is it?" I whispered. Jonah was shaking so hard I was afraid he'd tip over the wardrobe.

He shook his head fast. "I don't know. I didn't see it. I was trying to hide. All I saw were really, really big paws."

I gulped. This wasn't good. How had a big magical creature snuck into the house and knocked out all the electricity?

"Liam, it's coming this way," Jonah squeaked. I gasped. Jonah and I held the doors shut as something bumped against the wardrobe, knocking it back and forth. We leaned onto the wooden walls so we wouldn't fall over. There was a sniffing sound— the creature was smelling us.

Then it went away. I heard the footsteps retreating. When it had been quiet for a moment, I dared to open the doors back up, and I saw that the light from outside had returned. There was no monster outside — just a few fallen towers of boxes that it had knocked over on its way out.

"Shit!" I said as we hopped out of the wardrobe. "That was scary!" I wasn't supposed to say bad words, but I liked how they felt coming out of my mouth, and doing things I wasn't supposed to was fun.

"Oh no," Jonah said, pointing. "The painting!"

I looked. I noticed the painting that had been leaning up against the wall from earlier was gone. It had been there when we'd been playing, but now, it had disappeared.

"The monster must've took it with them," I said. "Though I don't know what they'd want with a painting."

"This is really bad." Tears dotted Jonah's eyes.

"What's the big deal?" I asked. "It's just a painting. At least we didn't get eaten."

"You don't understand. When my dad brought it home the other day, he told me never to touch it, or I'd really get it. It was super important." Jonah sniffed. "Now it's gone, and he's going to think I lost it."

"But you didn't. That monster came and took it," I said, confused.

"It doesn't matter. He'll think it's my fault." Jonah was really scared that the painting was gone. He was almost crying.

"Maybe my dad can help," I suggested. He was the Water chief. I bet he was boss of all the magical creatures in Kinpago. He could find the monster who took the painting and force it to give it back.

Jonah opened his mouth to respond, but then the basement door flew open. Jonah sank down. I looked up to see Jonah's dad at the top of the staircase.

And he looked really mad. His teeth were clenched, and he was breathing hard. His boots made loud, thumping noises as he came down the stairs. "What are you doing? Didn't I tell you not to play down here?"

Jonah was shaking. I don't even think his dad *noticed* I was there. Jonah's dad looked at him, and then at the empty wall. His eyes bulged out when he noticed the painting *was* missing.

"What the hell did you do?" he yelled. "Where's my painting?"

Jonah's dad must've spent a lot of money on that painting. He was really angry.

Jonah looked up at his dad with and started bawling. "I'm sorry! I didn't mean it!"

"Are you fucking kidding me?" Jonah's dad shouted. Jonah started screaming and apologizing over and over. I didn't know what to do.

"I... I can rep*lace it*," I stuttered. I'd probably get grounded, but at least my family could pay for it, and Jonah wouldn't get in trouble.

"That painting was priceless, you little bastard! Where did it go!?"

Jonah's dad screamed. My lip wobbled. I wanted to cry, but didn't, because I was supposed to be brave for Jonah. I was the oldest, and Mommy told me the eldest always looks out for the younger ones.

"A monster came and took it," Jonah whimpered. Jonah's dad smacked him across the face, and he fell over. Jonah held a hand to his cheek and curled up into a ball *as* his dad stood over him. Jonah started to wail as a red welt formed across his cheek.

I was so shocked I froze. Jonah's dad wouldn't actually hurt us, right? My dad never hurt me.

When his dad raised his hand again, I ran to stand in front of Jonah. "He's telling the truth!"

Jonah's dad was shaking with anger. "I'll beat the truth out of you, you little shits!" Jonah's dad grabbed me by the shirt. He picked me up and threw me. I hit the ground hard. I think I scraped my elbow. Tears welled in my eyes, but I wouldn't let them fall. I had to be strong for Jonah.

Jonah and I looked at ea*ch other* in fear. What were we going to do? We were just kids, and he'd never believe us. That monster had gotten us into a lot of trouble.

"That is enough."

A voice scarier than Jonah's dad echoed through the basement. I felt relieved as I saw my father standing only a few feet away. He was here to pick me up. He must've heard Jonah crying and came downstairs. Jenny *stood* at his side, looking helplessly between him and her dad.

Jonah's dad straightened up. "I don't believe I allowed you permission into my residence, sir." It sounded really disrespectful.

"I am a chief. I need no permission of yours." Dad pushed past him. He bent down and picked me up, holding me on his hip. I put my arms around his neck and held him really tightly. I was still really scared, but I didn't need to be anymore. My dad would protect me. Jonah's dad couldn't fight him.

"What I do in my own house is none of your concern," Jonah's dad said in a mean tone. "I am handling my business."

"My child doesn't belong to you. You put your hands on my son again, I'll prosecute," Dad threatened.

Jonah's dad didn't say anything more.

Dad's voice was flat as he said, "There will be a welfare check made here by the Yapluma Elders in a few hours. Mark my words."

Jonah's dad's face got a little white. Jonah was taking his chance to sneak away. He ran past us, up the stairs and to his room.

Dad turned his back and carried me up the stairs. "Come, son. Let's go."

My dad's Familiar was waiting for us outside of Jonah's house. The grizzly bear rumbled a friendly hello as we approached. Dad put me on Tatum's back before he climbed on *beh*ind me. Tatum started walking through the Yapluma village at a slow walk.

"Did he hurt you?" Dad asked, looking down at me.

"I bruised my elbow," I sniffed. Now I wanted to cry. It was like the time after the scary part was worse than it actually happening. I showed him my elbow. My shirt was torn, too.

"We can patch it up at home. Come now, chiefs don't cry."

I let out a few sobs and wiped my face with my shirt. Dad patted my back, and I felt better.

"Dad, can Jonah come live with us?" I asked.

Dad frowned. "I don't think that's possible, son."

I ran my hands through Tatum's fur. "I hope I see him a lot."

"He can come over as much as he wants. But you can never go back over there. Do you understand?"

I nodded. I didn't want to. But Jonah was still stuck there.

One day, I wanted to be just as strong as my Dad was. Everyone respected him. Once I was a great chief, nobody would push Jonah and me around. I'd make sure everyone was safe, and I'd use my magic to slay all the monsters. I promised myself to listen more closely to Grandpa and his teachings next time.

"I know what'll cheer you up. How about we stop for ice cream?" Dad asked. Tatum gave a happy growl. He loved sweets.

Ice cream got my mind off of it. "Sure."

I had almost forgotten about the monster that had stolen the painting, but watching Tatum's big paws roam over the pavement reminded me. I wondered. Why had that monster taken the painting, and why had it been so important?

sophia

TWO

Stepping off the *Hozho* into Kinpago was supposed to feel like coming home. We'd spent the last two weeks in Europe on Imogen's dime, trying to recover from the riots that took place on New Year's Eve. But now, the *Hozho* seemed more like home than Kinpago itself.

I stood on the deck of the *Hozho* beside my friends. My sister, Amelia, was close by. She'd been working on the ship during our vacation. We could see the town square from our vantage point as the flying cruise liner descended into port. I was well aware of the destruction that took place that night— I'd been in the middle of it— but seeing it like this brought all that devastation back. One moment I was standing on the cruise ship's deck, laughing with my friends and my sister. The next I was back in the square the night of the riots, buildings crumbling and fire burning all around me.

"You okay, *pawee*?" Liam asked, draping his arm around me and pulling me close.

I swallowed the massive lump in my throat. "I'm fine," I lied. If he knew the kind of anxiety washing through me now like a flash flood, he'd spend the next semester making sure I never felt that way again. And I couldn't let him worry about me and neglect himself. He was already going through enough. I could handle this on my own. Esis snuggled in my arms, offering comfort— almost like he could feel my anxiety.

"I can't believe our trip is over already," Jonah complained. Squeaks huffed from beside him like she too was disappointed.

Our Familiars hadn't been allowed off the *Hozho* when we traveled, but they'd had a lot of fun onboard. We'd rented a huge suite big enough for the four of us. It had two levels and a floor-to-ceiling window with the most amazing views.

"I know," Imogen agreed with Jonah. "It sucks. I want to go back to Paris."

"And London," Jonah added. "And Amsterdam. Forget choosing. Let's go back to them all."

Imogen smiled, but it didn't quite reach her eyes. It was like we all shared collective disappointment.

"I'm glad you guys had so much fun," Amelia said.

"Are you staying in town for a few days?" I asked her. She was gone a lot for work, but she often got to visit when the *Hozho* came into port.

"I have to," she said. "I need to be sorted just like the rest of you."

Sorted. I didn't like that word. It suggested judgment— and if I knew the Elders, that judgment would be unfairly weighted.

After the riots, Elder Oleander had announced the Hawkei were doing away with the four House system, where you were placed at birth depending on your heritage. Now the Elders had replaced it with a two-part system. Defortai for whomever they deemed "strong," and Biyami for those they considered "weak."

It was a sick system if you asked me. I already knew it couldn't turn out good— and that didn't even consider the prophecy.

Fuck, I didn't want to think about the prophecy right now. We'd been avoiding talking about it the whole trip, but we had to discuss it sooner or later. The last piece— the Air piece— was our last hope to change everything, but we still had to find it.

The *Hozho* horn sounded, and the cruise liner came to a stop. The Nivita on board worked together to create a staircase out of the earth.

"I guess it's time to go," Imogen said sadly, grabbing her bags. Sassy took Imogen's purse in her mouth to help.

"Wait," I said quickly before anyone could move. Everyone eyed me expectantly. "Whatever happens, we stick together."

"Agreed," Liam stated firmly.

"Totally," Jonah added. "Squeaks and I would never leave you guys."

"Sassy or me neither," Imogen said.

Amelia looked between the four of us. "What you guys have here is really special. Just make sure you all stay safe, especially you, Sophia."

She pulled me into a hug.

"What do you mean by that?" I asked.

"I just love you is all," she said, but I sensed there was something she wasn't telling me. Maybe it was just my anxiety getting in the way.

Amelia drew away. "Anyway, shall we?"

We all started for the stairs. If we hadn't been here to witness the New Year's Eve riots, it would've been apparent by now that something had changed in Kinpago. Even the overcast sky seemed to sense the change in the town. As we descended the stairs, there was no longer the lively chatter filling the port. All the street vendors that'd been here last time were gone. The port was so quiet that all I heard was the whistle of the cold January wind. Apart from the Familiars of people exiting the *Hozho*, I saw no magical creatures.

A line of Task Force members stood at the bottom of the stairs. Each wore their masked helmets and carried noxite guns. Seeing them felt like we were being marched into a concentration camp or something. I wondered if any of them were the men we'd faced that night. They'd probably shoot us on sight.

At the bottom of the stairs, the Task Force ushered Hawkei officials to the right and all other passengers and *Hozho* employees to the left. My guts twisted as a Task Force member pointed us to join the group on the left.

"All Hawkei are hereby summoned to the square for public sorting," one Task Force member shouted to the crowd. "This is not optional."

"They're sorting us already?" I asked breathlessly, so only my friends could hear.

No one got a chance to respond before a Task Force member stepped in front of our group. "You three!" He pointed to Imogen, Amelia, and me. "This way."

"Wait, but—" I reached for Liam, but he didn't take my hand. Esis squeaked in protest.

"Do as they say, Sophia," Liam said sternly, giving me a look I knew I couldn't fight. "I'll see you soon."

What happened to sticking together?

My blood chilled as another Task Force member guided Jonah and Liam into a separate group, along with Squeaks. Esis crawled up my shirt and settled on my shoulder, hiding in my hair. I reached up and stroked his horns. They were several inches long by now and curling already.

Amelia took my arm. "It'll be okay."

I wanted to believe her, but I didn't know if I could. This wasn't the welcome we should've received. Who knew what else had changed? Or who else had died during the riots?

I'd checked in with my grandparents before we left for Europe. They were fine since they hadn't been there that night, and they were beyond relieved to see I was okay too. But there were so many other people, mostly professors, and peers, who I hadn't got to see yet.

I barely knew what was happening as I was ushered into a line between Imogen and Amelia, my luggage at my side. I tried to catch a glimpse of Liam, but all I saw was a Task Force member looming over him, trying to rush him into the line of men close by.

Imogen reached back and touched my hand. "This isn't any different than we expected," she reminded me.

I guess I'd been hoping that by some miracle Kinpago had decided to fix itself in the time we were gone.

The line began moving, and we were guided through the streets of Kinpago. I thought we'd begin to hear the normal chatter and feel the lively energy of the town as we entered the heart of it, but nothing changed since the port. I noticed a few people poking their heads out the shop doors or standing at the windows to watch us march through town like we were some sort of spectacle, but there wasn't a word spoken.

After the first block or two, I turned my eyes to my feet. I couldn't bring myself to look up, because I was afraid of the destruction we'd see.

I didn't know how much time had passed, but it seemed like we'd been marching for an eternity. The port was at the edge of town, several miles from the center square.

It wasn't until we entered the square that I finally lifted my gaze. The square looked totally different now. All the rubble had been removed, but buildings that once stood there had been completely demolished, making the square bigger than ever. All the statues were gone, and the only thing left of the big fountain was the base, which hadn't been refilled with water. The Blessing Tree, which had caught fire during the riots, wasn't there either. They'd even removed the stump, leaving the ground flush where the massive tree had once stood. The cobblestone had various cracks and lines running through it, though it looked like Nivita Elementai had leveled the areas that had been heaved or broken. Still, the pieces didn't quite fit back together properly, as if leaving behind scars in the earth.

The entire square just seemed... empty. All that was left was a large platform like a stage with a crowd of people surrounding it, though the crowd wasn't as big as it'd been on New Year's Eve. There were only a few hundred people here now.

We were guided toward the edge of the stage and given no other instructions than to set our bags aside and leave them there. Our line merged with another group of Hawkei who hadn't yet been assigned. I noticed Ezra enter the line not far behind Liam and Jonah. The men's line stood in front of ours, and it was so long that we could easily see the front of the stage. The stage was almost empty except for a burning fire in the center. The flames stretched high into the air for all to see.

Imogen and I scanned the crowd, looking for people we knew. I caught sight of Imogen's family. Her youngest brother, Levi, waved and took a step toward us, but Imogen's dad pulled him back and held him tightly.

I caught sight of my other friends— Lindsey, Miranda, Vanessa, and Bren, along with their Familiars. Vanessa's baby bump was still growing, and I'd almost forgotten how big she was getting, though she wasn't due for months. My grandparents were here, too, and they offered me a discrete wave. Not far from them, Maddie and Drew stood beside Liam's mom and his younger siblings. I didn't spot Liam's dad until someone in the crowd moved.

I noticed a circle of Elders sitting around a large drum below the front of the stage. They all wore their regalia— Liam's dad in his chief headdress. Elder Oleander straightened his spine and smiled out at the crowd like he had something to be proud of. Madame Doya sat beside him, her expression as stone-cold as ever. She caught my eye across the crowd, and I thought I saw a look of reassurance pass her features, but it was gone as quickly as it came.

Nobody moved. Nobody spoke. I didn't even breathe. The entire square went dead silent.

And then the click of heels came. Chieftess Annette climbed the stairs at the back of the stage and walked across. She wore elaborate regalia made of red fabric and glittering rhinestones that had feathers all over it. Her phoenix Familiar was at her side.

I furrowed my brow and leaned forward to whisper in Imogen's ear. "Should we expect a traditional Hawkei ceremony?"

Imogen gave me this look that said she had no idea. I spotted a hint of fear in her eyes.

Chieftess Annette raised her hands to the crowd. When she spoke, her voice rang out over the square from speakers set beside the stage. I noticed she wore a wireless microphone.

"Welcome!" she called, like this was a moment to be celebrated.

But no one cheered. In fact, I noticed a few scowls on people's faces. They weren't here to rejoice. They were only here to ensure the fair treatment of their loved ones.

Chieftess Annette cleared her throat. "Today, we complete the final Sorting Ceremony for our new tribe. May the ancestors bless us as we sort our fellow Hawkei according to the ancestors' will."

A drumbeat began, and the Elders started to hum a tune that was both beautiful yet melancholy. Chieftess Annette bent to pick up a bowl I hadn't seen before. She bounced on her toes in a traditional Hawkei dance as she circled the fire, singing along to the Elders' song. Her phoenix danced at her side.

The first Hawkei in line was ushered onto the stage. I didn't know him, as he looked a lot older than me, but he had a large wyvern at his side. The dragon-like creature was almost too big to fit on the stage.

Three guesses which house he'll be placed into.

Chieftess Annette continued to circle the fire, dancing and humming like she was having the time of her life. It was really weird to see her like that, but then again, this was the kind of thing that pleased her— watching everyone else crumble as she wiped their blood off the bottom of her pointed stilettos.

"Aiden Williams," Chieftess Annette said, addressing the man on stage. "The ancestors hereby assign you to..."

She reached into her bowl and pulled out a handful of red powder, then tossed it into the fire. The flames licked at least twenty feet into the air, roaring before quickly settling back down to their normal height.

"Defortai!" Chieftess Annette called.

A few people in the crowd cheered, and Aiden looked relieved, but the energy in the square was stale.

Aiden was quickly ushered off stage by a Task Force member, while another guy stepped up for his turn. He looked only a few years older than me, but was shaking in fear. At first, I didn't even think he had a Familiar, but then I noticed he was cupping something in his hands.

Chieftess Annette looked down at him, displeased. "Your name and your Familiar?"

I couldn't hear what he said from here, but I saw him open his hands. A small hamster with fluffy blue fur peeked out.

Chieftess Annette frowned but quickly returned to her dancing and humming routine. "Josiah Fisher, the Elders hereby assign you to..."

She tossed the powder, and the flames shrank so small that I could barely see them anymore.

"Biyami!" she shouted, like it was something to be proud of.

Josiah froze, and his eyes went wide. A Task Force member had to physically grab him to get him to move off stage since he was in so much shock.

My jaw was starting to hurt, I was clenching it so hard. I'd bet my ass the ancestors weren't doing shit to manipulate that fire. It was all Chieftess Annette's power.

The ceremony continued, and the line kept on moving. Most people were placed into Defortai, with a few Biyami thrown in here and there. I held my breath when Jonah got on stage. Squeaks was so nervous that she nearly tripped over her own hooves, but Jonah held his spine straight and confident.

"Jonah Chanee," Chieftess Annette said in a voice that sent chills down my spine.

Imogen held my hand so tightly that I lost blood flow to my fingers.

"The ancestors hereby assign you to..."

She threw the powder, and the flames died.

I gasped, as did Imogen beside me.

"Biyami!" Chieftess Annette called.

"Wait, what?" Jonah asked from onstage. "But I have a hippogriff Familiar. I won the Elemental Cup."

"It is not for the Elders to judge the will of the ancestors," Chieftess Annette said coolly. "The ancestors' decision is final."

I glanced around the crowd for signs of Jonah's family to see what their reaction was. I spotted his parents and sister at the edge of the crowd. His dad was staring at the stage with his arms crossed, but I swore he looked *pleased*.

Jonah tried to argue further, but a Task Force member raised a noxite gun at him. Jonah immediately shoved his hands into the air in surrender and followed them off stage. He'd already been shot by noxite once. He wasn't about to go through it again.

Liam was next. Though I already knew what was going to happen, I couldn't stop my knees from shaking. I held Imogen tighter, then reached for Amelia with the other hand. Esis buried his face into my hair, like he couldn't watch.

Liam didn't look scared at all— and I admired him for that. His expression was unreadable to most, but to me, that stone-cold resolve suggested he'd take whatever the Elders threw at him. He'd taken their shit plenty of times before.

"Liam Mitoh, the ancestors hereby assign you to..." Chieftess Annette threw the powder, and just as I expected, the flames died down. "Biyami!"

Liam nodded once, because it didn't come as a surprise. He quickly left the stage to join Jonah, where the two exchanged a brotherly hug.

Tears welled in my eyes. "I can't believe they're doing this," I whispered.

"There's nothing we can do about it," Amelia said.

I nodded, knowing she was right.

Ezra's assignment came soon after. Dyami followed him onstage, and the two of them looked confident beside each other.

"Ezra Mitoh, the ancestors hereby assign you to..." Chieftess Annette threw the powder, and the flames shot high into the air. "Defortai!"

I expected his ceremony to end there, but it didn't.

Chieftess Annette continued. "As the son of a chief and the next in line to take over your father's position, you are called upon to serve the tribe in this life and the next, in sickness and in health, by whatever means the ancestors deem necessary. Do you accept this responsibility?"

Ezra hesitated a moment as his gaze roamed over to Liam. Liam's expression was hard and pleading, like he wanted him to deny the chief hood so they could be together.

Ezra shook his head at Liam ever so slightly, then said, "I accept."

Liam started for the edge of the stage, where Ezra was making his exit, but Jonah grabbed him by the arm and held him back. The two exchanged words I couldn't hear, but they looked harsh.

The assignments continued, and I barely heard most of them until we'd made it all the way to the front of the line. Imogen picked up Sassy and climbed the steps, her gait a little stilted as she walked across the stage. I couldn't see her face from here, but it looked like she was taking deep breaths.

"Imogen Ahnild, the ancestors hereby assign you to..." Chieftess Annette tossed the powder, and I was shocked at what happened. The flames *shrank*. "Biyami!"

How could that be possible? Imogen was one of the best Nivita I knew. She could control the earth like nobody's business, and she studied harder than anyone. She understood our myths and legends better than most of our professors. And she had a freaking *kitsune* Familiar! It wasn't like that was a secret anymore, either. Imogen and Sassy should've been in Defortai.

Imogen rushed off stage, sobbing into Sassy's fur, but it wasn't until she reached the other side and turned to face me that I saw they were tears of relief. Jonah and Liam hugged her. She was relieved to be in the same House as them.

My body shook as I climbed the steps for my turn. *No matter what, we stick together*, I told myself.

I'd end up in Biyami anyway. I was sure of it, because the Elders still didn't know what Esis was. I'd effectively convinced Chieftess Annette I wasn't the prophesied one, so there was no reason for her to think I belonged in Defortai. Except...

She knew I could conjure lightning. Doya had taught me how, and that wasn't the kind of thing she'd keep from the Koigni Chieftess.

I guess it didn't matter anyway, since she was probably itching to get back at me for all the shit I pulled with Haley last semester. Esis clutched me tighter, and I reached up to where he sat on my shoulder to cradle him.

"Sophia Henley," Chieftess Annette said. I didn't like the sound of my voice coming from her mouth. "The ancestors hereby assign you to..."

She threw the powder, and the flames shot high into the air. A split-second passed where my heart dropped in my chest. I didn't want to be in Defortai, no matter how strong their house was. All of my friends were in Biyami, and I'd be damned if I wasn't going to stand at their side and fight with them.

But a moment later, the flames shrank, then went back to normal.

Huh? What did that mean?

Chieftess Annette looked totally taken aback. The surprise lasted only a second before she narrowed her gaze at me, like she was about to light me aflame. I completely froze, expecting the searing pain to come any moment now. It was clear she thought I'd tried to manipulate the flames. But I hadn't done anything.

"The ancestors have given Sophia a choice," Doya said without emotion from where she sat beside the drum.

Chieftess Annette turned her hard gaze to Doya. A moment later, her shoulders dropped, like she'd just remembered she was being watched by a crowd of angry Hawkei.

Chieftess Annette cleared her throat. "It's your choice, Sophia. Which House will you choose?"

For a moment, she looked pleased by this turn of events. I noticed something in her steel-hard gaze. She was curious to know if I'd choose power over my friends.

Not today, bitch.

I held her gaze and spoke with confidence. "Biyami."

The crowd gasped, like they couldn't believe anyone would make that choice. Chieftess Annette blinked a few times.

You heard me right.

She cleared her throat. "As you wish. The ancestors have hereby assigned you to Biyami."

I glanced at Doya and noticed a frown on her face. She was angry I hadn't chosen Defortai. Did she think that was where I belonged?

Or had she intended for me to be placed there, as if *she* was the one who'd manipulated the flames?

It didn't matter. I'd already made my choice.

I rushed off stage as fast as I could, my heart pounding. I ran straight into Liam's arms, slamming into him so hard it nearly took my breath away. Esis hopped off my shoulder and onto Liam's, hugging his face. We stood in a secluded group, far enough away from the Task Force members that they couldn't hear us.

"Sophia," Liam said softly, stroking my hair. "You didn't have to do that."

I buried my face in his chest. "I did. I told you, we have to stick together."

Imogen and Jonah joined us at our side. Imogen was about to say something until we heard Chieftess Annette's voice ring over the crowd again.

"Amelia Henley," she said.

We all turned to watch Amelia's Sorting Ceremony. She stood straight, with Kiwi perched on her shoulder, and didn't give her emotions away.

"The ancestors hereby assign you to... Biyami!" Chieftess Annette announced.

My stomach sank. I thought for sure Amelia would be put in Defortai. There was nothing weak about her.

But Amelia didn't seem to care— or at least didn't show it. She just walked across stage with a look of determination on her face, like she'd wear the Biyami label with pride.

"Am," I cried as she reached us. I threw my arms around her neck, nearly knocking Kiwi off her shoulder. "I can't believe you got Biyami. Aren't you upset?"

I drew away from her to try to get a read on her expression, but she continued to hide her feelings.

She shook her head. "I already knew where they'd place me. The best thing I can do now is to make sure they don't know how it affects me. They already think I'm weak. Well, I'm just going to have to surprise them with my strengths."

She smirked proudly, like she had something up her sleeve. I narrowed my eyes at her, but before I could ask anything about it, Jonah piped up.

"That's actually a really good strategy," he said.

"Yeah," Imogen agreed. "If we show our strengths and weaknesses, they'll know what to target us with."

"They already know how to target the four of you," Amelia pointed out.

"What do you mean?" Liam asked.

Amelia glanced between us, a frown fixed to her face. "You four are inseparable. If they hurt one of you, they'll hurt all of you."

Holy shit. She was right.

"Don't fool yourselves into thinking that they put the four of you into this House together by accident," Amelia warned.

My blood ran cold. Could that be true? Did the Elders put us in this House to see what we'd do together? To keep a close eye on us?

"You're right," I said. "Otherwise, why would Jonah and Imogen be assigned Biyami?"

Liam crossed his arms, and the crease between his eyebrows deepened. "Isn't it obvious? Jonah's parents wanted him here."

"Wait, what?" Imogen asked, looking baffled.

Jonah dropped his shoulders. He couldn't argue with the theory.

"Didn't you see them out in the crowd?" Liam asked. "With their kind of status, they were no doubt sorted into Defortai. They looked happy to see Jonah separated from them."

Jonah stared down at his shoes. "Guess it gives them a valid reason to disown me, huh?"

"Jonah," I sighed, feeling heartbroken for him. "Screw your family. They're assholes anyway. We'd never disown you."

"Never," Imogen confirmed.

Jonah offered a half-smile.

"I still don't get why Imogen was sorted into Biyami, though," I said.

Imogen scoffed. "Nivita hates my family, remember? Don't forget about the rumors that we're not *purebloods*."

"What rumors?" I said quickly.

She frowned but didn't look at me. "There are some Nivita who say my family's too white— too *Koigni*— and that we must be mixed House, since most Nivita have African or Latin American features."

"That's just wrong," I stated.

She obviously had *some* European blood in her, which was the group Koigni had bred with when they brought other cultures into the tribe. But it wasn't unusual to have mixed features throughout all of the Houses, since they interbred for hundreds of years before Anichi died out. For anyone to claim Imogen's family wasn't *pure* was ludicrous. No one was "pure" anymore anyway.

We were distracted from our conversation as the crowd began to disperse. We'd already reached the end of the sorting, and I hadn't even noticed.

Amelia nudged me. "I'll be right back, okay? I have to go talk to Trevor."

Trevor was Amelia's roommate when she was in town. They weren't romantically involved, but he had an apartment with a guest room where she slept when she wasn't working on the *Hozho*. She hurried over to him. I'd never met him before, but good Lord, I don't know why she *wasn't* dating him. He was a tall Toaqua with long black hair. There was a blue feline Familiar at his side, who had a large mane that shimmered like the ocean.

My attention was stolen away from the beautiful Familiar when I caught sight of a group of people pushing through the crowd. They quickly made their way over to us.

"Oh my ancestors, you guys!" Lindsey rushed forward and threw her arms around my neck. I hugged her back tightly. Medusa slithered around our feet, looking pleased.

Vanessa came up beside her and hugged me next. "How have you been? How was your trip?"

"It was great," I told them vaguely.

Bren and Miranda followed behind them, with Aisha and Kingston nearby. I noticed a kirin by Miranda's side and was pleased to see she'd bonded over break. It looked like a cross between a dragon and a deer, with both scales and soft fur. It had a long, beautiful mane like a lion's. I knew Miranda would have fun hairdressing her. I could tell it was a female because of the single antler in the middle of her head. It was really cool that she'd bonded with a kirin, because they were shy and unusual Familiars. Plus, they could control the weather.

Ezra came over to join us. He reached out to Liam to take his hand for one of those one-armed guy hugs, but Liam shoved him away. "You're a *fucking* traitor, you know that?"

Ezra sighed, like Liam was being ridiculous. "This isn't about you, bro."

"You had a choice up there," Liam insisted. He looked like he was ready to punch Ezra. "You could've said no and joined Biyami instead."

"It's not what you think," Ezra said quickly, lowering his voice. "We all wanted to go into Biyami— you know, to show the Elders they couldn't just push us around. But we talked and decided we'd take Defortai if we were offered so we could spy on them."

"Who do you mean by *we*?" Imogen asked.

"All of us," Ezra said, gesturing to the group. "Me, Bren, Vanessa, Lindsey, and Miranda. We're gonna fight this with you, bro."

Liam relaxed— I could tell by the look on his face he was embarrassed about being a jerk.

"What makes you think we're going to fight?" Jonah asked.

Ezra gave him a wide-eyed expression. "Because it's *you four*. You fought the Elders on interhouse relationships. Aren't you going to go after this, too?"

No one could really argue with that.

"We already have a few people in Biyami willing to help us out," Ezra said. "Maddie, Tabitha—"

"How is Tabitha?" I asked. She and Ben were close, and I knew she'd be devastated after hearing the news of his death.

"She's holding up," Lindsey said.

"Wait, Maddie got Biyami?" Liam asked.

"Yeah, since they don't know about her..." Ezra trailed off, as he quickly realized not everyone here knew Maddie was a *naderei*— a Hawkei who could see the future.

"What about your younger siblings?" I asked, breaking the awkward silence.

"They won't get sorted until they're of age," Ezra explained. "Honestly, though, there's no rhyme or reason to any of this."

"What do you mean?" I asked.

"Professor Baine got Biyami," Vanessa balked. "I mean, he used to be an Elder. How does that make sense?"

Liam thought about it for a second. "They must've put him there because he left the council."

"I guess that adds up," Vanessa admitted.

"Let me guess," I said. "Doya's Defortai?"

"Of course." Lindsey rolled her eyes.

Bren leaned in, like he was about to tell a very dark secret. "Okay, but get this. *Alric* got Biyami, too."

"Head Dean Alric?" Imogen's eyebrows shot up. "The master alchemist? With the *dragon* Familiar?"

"The one and only," Bren confirmed.

"He must've done something to offend the Elders," Jonah theorized.

Liam looked like he was calculating something in his head. Alric in Biyami definitely didn't add up. He drew a quick breath, like he'd suddenly realized something. The group pressed in closer to hear what he had to say.

"This never leaves this group, do you hear?" Liam demanded.

Everyone nodded in agreement.

He took a deep breath. "A few months ago, Sophia and I went to Professor Perot's office to talk to him, and we caught Alric coming out of Perot's apartment. What if Oleander knew Alric and Perot were in an interhouse relationship?"

Everyone inhaled a collective breath.

"Shut up," Lindsey said. "Alric and Perot?"

"That's what we saw," I told her. "Alric was in his pajamas and everything. I'm pretty sure they were seeing each other."

Lindsey's eyebrows were higher than I'd ever seen them. "Wow, my gaydar did *not* pick up on that one. Perot, maybe, but *Alric*?"

She kept repeating their names, like she couldn't wrap her head around it.

Liam leaned in even closer. "They must've legalized interhouse relationships as a way to bring people out and sort them into Biyami. They lured all those people into a false sense of security so they could tell who was more likely to go against their laws."

"There's definitely a pattern there," Miranda stated confidently. "Everyone we know who was involved in Jaymin's Interhouse Alliance was put into Biyami."

"That's partly because of the riots," Ezra pointed out.

"I'm guessing Jaymin got Biyami too," I said.

Lindsey and Miranda exchanged a glance, but it was Lindsey who spoke. "She never got sorted."

I inhaled a sharp breath. "What did the Elders do to her?"

"She was supposed to get a trial," Lindsey explained. "But she disappeared before it started. No one knows what happened to her."

Liam shared the same confused look I did. How did someone just go up and missing like that?

"Anyway," Ezra said, "you guys probably want to rest after your trip. We should head back to the castle."

"I'm going to talk to my grandparents first," I said, giving Liam's hand a light squeeze before I hurried off toward them and their Familiars.

"Sophia!" Grandma greeted brightly, holding her arms out to me. I wrapped her in a hug and inhaled her sweet vanilla scent.

"I missed you guys," I said as I drew away from her and moved to hug my grandpa.

He held on to me a little longer than usual. "We missed you, too. How was the trip?"

"Good," I told them. "How was your Sorting Ceremony?"

"We got sorted into Defortai," Grandma replied, but she sounded sad. "We're sorry your friends got put in Biyami."

It was obvious I picked Biyami because of them. I could tell she was sad I wasn't in her House.

"It'll be fine," I assured them. "Thank you for coming."

I glanced toward my friends to see they were walking across the square to get our bags. "I'll have to visit for dinner soon, but right now I think my friends are leaving."

"Okay," Grandma said. "We'll see you soon. We love you, Sophia."

Her words brought the smallest hint of a smile to my face. Kinpago felt a little more like home when I heard her say that.

"I love you, too."

I hurried off to join my friends, but before I got there, Amelia cut in front of me. "Hey, Sophia."

I stopped in my tracks. "Hey, Am. How's Trevor?"

"He's fine. It sounds like the *Hozho* is leaving port in the morning, so I'm not going to be able to stay in town long."

My heart sank. I'd just spent two weeks with her, but it wasn't enough. "Can't you skip this trip?"

She shook her head, then took my hands.

"What happens now that you're Biyami?" I asked. "Does that affect your employment options?"

She shrugged, looking down at our hands. "I'm probably going to end up with a pay cut, but I can't quit my job."

"Sure you can," I told her. "It's not like you need the money."

Amelia was loaded after betting on our team in the Elemental Cup.

She frowned. "I'd go crazy with nothing to do."

"Get a job here in Kinpago," I suggested.

She raised an eyebrow. "Where? Tons of businesses were just destroyed. Everyone's going to be flooding from those jobs into the ones that opened up from..."

She trailed off, but I knew what she meant. *From the people who'd died.*

I took a deep breath, trying to convince myself that this was for the best. At least Amelia would be safe and away from Kinpago.

"I need to do my job, Sophia," she said, like working on the *Hozho* was the most important thing in the world. I knew she loved it. "I'll come visit soon. I promise."

I nodded, choking down the lump in my throat.

"It looks like your friends are leaving," she said, glancing toward them.

"I love you, Am. I'll see you soon." I pulled her into a hug, not letting go for a good ten seconds.

"I hope so," she whispered. "Bye, Sophia."

"Bye, Amelia."

I made my way over to my friends and their Familiars. Esis was still sitting on Liam's shoulder, trying to braid his hair. I grabbed my luggage, and the group of us— now joined by Maddie, her Familiar, and Drew— started toward the castle. There were no taxi carriages in sight, which was weird, so we were going to have to walk all the way there. Thank the ancestors our luggage had wheels.

"Is everything okay?" Liam asked.

"Yeah," I replied with a nod, but it didn't sound honest, even to my ears.

The walk was long and silent. I could feel the tension in the air the closer we got to the castle, like the recent changes were more evident there. I guess it made sense, considering that's where everyone had fled after the riots and where Oleander had made the announcement on the two-House system.

When we stepped into the main hall, eyes began to swivel in our direction. People quieted, and they all watched as we passed through, like we were a spectacle in a parade. I spotted Renar on the second balcony, talking to some fuck boy that wasn't much more attractive than he was. He stopped mid-sentence to look at Jonah and turn up his nose at him. His arm cast had been removed, and his leg cast had been swapped out for a boot.

I continued to scan the hall, as if calculating how many students had survived the riots. That's when I spotted Haley. She sat in one of the big chairs near the fireplace, her head back in laughter— probably at some lame joke she made herself. She was surrounded by Kelsey and a bunch of Koigni guys, along with their Familiars. She caught sight of us and went dead silent, then shot up out of her chair and made a beeline for us.

She stopped at the front of the group, crossing her arms to block our path. But Imogen wasn't for it. She side-stepped Haley and continued forward, as did Jonah. Haley seemed shocked for a second, then stepped in front of me. I tried to step around her, but she followed me.

"I heard you got Biyami, *Loser Team*," she snarled.

Wow, news travels fast. Or she guessed. Either way, it wasn't like she was wrong.

"Reject Team," Jonah corrected her.

Our whole group had stopped, and they were closing in on her. She straightened and held her head up high. Her gaze flickered over to her group of Defortai and their strong Familiars, as if reminding us just how outnumbered we were.

"You're all *weak*," she snarled. "Defortai will beat you down to nothing. Have fun in the dungeons."

She pushed past us, returning to her squad, who'd stood like they were ready for a fight.

"What a bitch," Imogen said as soon as she was out of earshot.

"Well, she wasn't exactly wrong," Maddie said timidly.

"What do you mean?" Liam asked, sounding irritated.

Maddie chewed her lower lip. "Well, Defortai gets to keep their old dorms, in whatever House you used to be. But Biyami... it's probably best if I show you."

I didn't like the sound of this. We followed behind Maddie as she led the way. Liam's hand tightened in mine. Maddie led us down a maze of hallways and to a wide staircase big enough for even the largest of our Familiars— which was a tie between our resident dragon, Aisha, and Ezra's thunderbird, Dyami. The stairwell was dimly lit, with only a few flaming sconces lighting the way.

My hands started to shake. This had to be some sort of joke.

We reached the bottom and walked down a long, wide hall made of stone until we came to a huge doorway big enough for a dragon. Two iron gates were propped open, like they normally enclosed the area to keep in prisoners.

When we stepped inside the huge room, my jaw dropped. The room was as big as a gymnasium but with a lower ceiling. Endless bunk beds had been set up, with nothing more than a trunk at the base of each one for personal belongings. Students of all four Houses lounged on the beds and chatted. One group was playing a board game and using a trunk as a table. Another was crowded around a foosball table that looked like it'd been pulled from the dumpsters. Others were playing with their elements or tending to their Familiars.

My stomach dropped. Haley wasn't shitting us. We'd literally been thrown in the dungeons.

For as long as we were Biyami, this was our new home.

Liam

THREE

Goodbye Europe. Hello our new reality.

The break we'd gotten had been wonderful. Imogen had rented out the *Hozho's* biggest suite. It had multiple rooms, which meant that Sophia and I got to share a bed all to ourselves. My girlfriend and I stayed up all night talking and slept in late. We'd had a lot of amazing sex and cuddled just as often. When Jonah and Imogen were able to drag the two of us out of bed, we'd all gone out together and had fun experiencing the ship's waterpark, ice rink, and all the other stuff it had to offer.

While in Europe, Jonah had forced us into partying at all the best clubs in London before we disembarked in Paris and spent some time touring the city. It was nice being able to hold hands with Sophia and see the sights together without being stared at. People just acted like we were a regular couple. We'd gone to the top of the Eiffel Tower at night, and I'd kissed her. Sophia had nearly cried and told me she'd never felt so happy. That was before we got to Amsterdam and shit got really crazy.

And fun. Way, way fun.

On the last night, I'd been too tired to go anywhere, so the four of us stayed up late in the suite eating junk food and talking about really deep things— you know, the type of stuff you can only talk about with friends who are really, super close.

It'd been a nice little vacation. But I had the feeling all those good times were about to come to a quick end, and it was only amplified by the fact that we were now living in a glorified basement.

Sophia turned in a circle with an open mouth. Esis perched on her shoulder and pulled at his ears. Her expression was clearly horrified. "Are they kidding? Do they really expect us to *live* down here?"

"It's filthy!" Imogen said as she crossed the room with Sassy. She was right. There was a lot of water seepage, along with cracks in the walls. I bet it looked worse, but it was so poorly lighted it was hard to tell.

Jonah walked off for a minute and turned around the corner. Squeaks lay down on the floor, but she didn't look too happy about having her couch back in her old dorm replaced by cold stone.

Imogen dragged her suitcase to a bunk bed in the corner and said, "Here. Jonah and I will take this one, and you guys take the other."

Sophia and I immediately tested out the mattresses on our bunk. The top bunk was clearly more comfortable than the bottom. Esis bounced on both, but neither of them were very cushy, so he gave up on having fun and looked at us with sour faces.

I looked at Sophia. "You take top, I'll take bottom."

"No. You're not going to get a damn bit of sleep on that thing, and you need it for your health," Sophia said sharply. "You take top."

I shook my head. "Not a chance. I can handle being on bottom."

Sophia snickered, and I added, "That's not what I meant. But I'm not taking the top bunk."

"Then I'll sleep on the floor."

"*Sophia.*"

Sophia gave me a steely look and said, "We'll switch off every night."

I knew that was the best I was going to get. "Agreed. It's a good compromise."

Jonah came back around the corner with Squeaks and said, "The showers are communal, guys. There's like, no privacy, separated by sexes. Which normally, I'd be okay with, but this is a school, not a fricking barrack."

"Are you kidding me? We have to shower in front of *other people?*" Sophia complained.

"Yeah." Jonah frowned. "There are students here who aren't comfortable with that sort of thing. I can't believe they're allowing this. It's a total violation of personal boundaries."

Imogen sighed and flopped onto her mattress, but I heard her say, "*Ow.*" It was probably like falling on concrete. "This sucks," she complained. "I didn't come to college so I could relive summer camp."

Sassy climbed on top of her and curled up on her back, where she finally seemed comfortable. Imogen groaned.

"Come on, guys. We've been through worse," I suggested. "We can make it work."

"*Worse?* Hun, you've got to be joking. My designer pumps are going to get soaked down here," Jonah rebutted.

"Next thing you know, Liam will be taking out a harmonica and playing it in this prison," Imogen jibed. Sassy yipped in agreement.

"I mean, we're all together now, right?" I said. "It's not like we're in separate dorms anymore. Now we can hang out whenever we want."

Sophia raised an eyebrow. "What's up with your brand new positive attitude? It's kind of... scary."

I shrugged. "I don't know. But we've already been through hell and high water. We can get through this."

"You're only saying that because you're *graduating* this semester," Jonah shot at me.

"Not true," I said, but he did have a point. A few months from now and I wouldn't have to sleep in a bunk bed.

"It'd be better if you weren't leaving us," Imogen teased. "You should fail this semester so you can come back again next year."

"No chance," I told her. "I have total senioritis. I'm getting out of here. Four years was more than enough."

"Aw. Our boy's getting his diploma!" Jonah faked a few tears and wrapped his arm around my shoulder.

"I'm going to miss you." Sophia seemed sad. "Orenda Academy won't be the same without you here."

"I'm sure you'll see me plenty," I said, and I nudged her playfully with an unrevealing smile.

Sophia seemed curious. I hadn't talked about it with her yet. But I had plans the moment I graduated to buy a house in Kinpago and take her with me, close enough to the school so she could walk to classes every day. I didn't want her sleeping in these bunk beds longer than she had to. I didn't have much in my savings after the court settlement from my trial took it all, but Dad had told me he'd give me a loan if I promised I'd work hard on finding a job before I left school.

I also planned to ask Sophia something else, *before* graduation— but I still needed to make sure now was the right time.

And with the way things were going around Kinpago... shit, I didn't know if it would ever be the right time. I hoped this semester would be a lot better than the hell the last one had proven to be, but signs were already showing that wasn't going to be the case.

We started putting our things into the trunks beside the beds. I was able to get most of my stuff in pretty quickly, but Imogen ran out of room for her books and was forced to put some on the wet ground, while Jonah's trunk was overflowing with shoes, feather boas, and ancestors only knew what else. He and Squeaks tried to shove everything in and climb on top of the trunk in order to shut it.

I moved most of the water on the floor away from our bunks, but I couldn't push it too far away, because other people would get pissed I was maneuvering it into their area. Sophia carefully took her camera out of her suitcase and looked around, but no one was glancing our way.

"Make sure you hide that," I told her in a low breath. "Everything's out in the open here. If people know you have it, they'll probably steal it. There's no privacy in this dorm."

"Right. I'll hide it *upstairs* once I get a chance." Sophia nodded as she mentioned the Anichi dorms, and tucked her camera underneath a bunch of clothes. She shut her trunk and noticed that I had been watching her ass as she was bent over putting clothes away. Esis gave an annoyed sigh, like he'd been putting up with our horniness for far too long and was just done with it.

Sophia leaned over and whispered to me, "You know, having sex in here is going to be impossible."

"Not necessarily," I said. "We'll just have to get creative. Just don't go looking at all those naked girls in the communal showers." I winked and nudged her.

Sophia blushed before she rolled her eyes and laughed. "Seriously, Liam, I would never. Can't say I'm not gonna look at you, though."

That sent a thrill through me. I wanted to grab her and start making out with her, but I didn't want to make anyone else feel uncomfortable, as we were out in the open and there were at least a dozen other people in here.

My mind wandered to other things. "On the serious side... we're not on vacation anymore," I said lowly. I hated to draw the conversation away from sex, but there were important matters to attend to. If we kept flirting, Sophia and I would probably sneak off to fool around instead of getting business done.

Sophia's face became impassive. "I know. Prophecy stuff," she whispered. She turned around and said, "Im, Jonah, we need to go for a walk."

Imogen and Jonah weren't listening. They were currently arguing about who was getting the top bunk.

"Jonah, look, I can handle sleeping six feet off the ground," Imogen said. "I *really* think you should sleep on the bottom. So the top bunk doesn't collapse and I don't get squished."

Jonah was currently on the top bunk, which was bowing under his weight. His legs hung off of it as the wood strained to support him and the mattress dipped down. Squeaks eyed Jonah, like she was considering climbing on top of him in order to get off the soggy floor, which would *definitely* break the entire thing.

"Im, I'm an *Air Elementai*. You're an Earth Elementai. It makes sense for me to be up here and you down there!" Jonah argued. He waved his hand, and the bunk creaked again. I winced as I heard something crack.

"You're too damn big! Look how much it sags!" Imogen shouted. Squeaks lifted a hoof to join Jonah on the top bunk, and Sassy began an array of loud barks.

Jonah grinned and quipped, "You wanna know what *else* that sags?"

Imogen facepalmed, and Sophia stepped in. "Guys, we need to

focus. There are *other things* we need to talk about. Preferably *right now*."

Their faces cleared. "Uh... right," Imogen said. "Let's go."

We were more than happy to leave the Biyami dorms behind and go back upstairs to the light and warmth of the main castle. The basement didn't seem a part of Orenda Academy at all— Orenda was magical, and safe, and home. It was nothing like where we'd come from, but maybe we could make the basement our home, too.

Task Force members were walking throughout the school in higher numbers than they were before. Some students didn't seem bothered by it, but others kept their heads down and pressed to the walls with their Familiars so they'd go unseen. We took some of the lesser-used passages around the school to get to the Anichi tower. Thankfully, the area around the tower's entrance was void of police, so we were able to slip in and out without being seen.

The Anichi dorms were the one place that didn't seem touched by all the new changes around Orenda Academy. It looked the same as it had when we'd left it the night of the riots.

Sophia stepped into the room and looked around. She wrapped her arms around herself and rubbed them slowly, as if she was cold. Esis, who was at her feet, pressed himself against her leg in a hug.

"Hey. You okay?" I asked. I laid my hands on her shoulders and squeezed.

Sophia nodded. "Yeah. It's just... a little unsettling coming back."

I got what she meant. Last time we were here to hide. But we weren't hiding anymore. We needed to start fighting back. I didn't know what we were fighting— the Elders, the Task Force, time... but we had to start somewhere.

It was cold in here, so Sophia lit the fireplace and we collapsed in the couches around it. Imogen came out of one of the dorm rooms with a cork board on rolling legs. Pinned to it were all the bits and pieces we knew of the prophecy so far. Imogen kept all the information we knew on the prophecy in one specific bedroom, and kept it locked with a key only she had. No one else knew the Anichi dorms were here, besides the people we'd hidden inside on the night of the riots, but we couldn't be too careful. If someone broke in, by accident or on purpose, we needed a fallback plan.

"All right. So where are we with this bullshit?" I started.

Imogen tapped the cork board. "So far, we have three pieces— Fire, Water, and Earth. We need the last piece of the prophecy— the Air piece."

"What's the wording of the prophecy again?" Jonah asked as he leaned against Squeaks, who'd gladly sprawled on the couch. "I'm a little short on memory."

Imogen huffed, and Sassy waved her tail in annoyance. Imogen opened her mouth and began to recite.

"The fated Koigni child, born in the Summer Solstice in the Year of the
Dragon,
Shall bring glory to the greatest House.

The prophesied one will bring death beyond comprehension.
It is she who shall cause Toaqua's darkest hour.

The future of the tribe is in Nivita's hands.
No Hawkei shall survive if the weakest refuse to bend."

"Did you memorize that?" Jonah asked, impressed.

"Someone had to," Imogen said. "The thing is, I'm not sure it makes sense this way. I've thought about it over and over, and something seems out of place."

There was silence for a moment, before Sophia said, "I think we're overlooking something. The pieces we have might not go in the order we got them."

My eyes widened. "I think you have a point."

"Ooh, good one, Sophia." Imogen scribbled a note and stuck it on the cork board. "That *would* change things."

"The first part has to be Koigni's," Sophia said. "I haven't brought glory to my House yet, but it talks about my birth, so that has to come before everything else."

"Toaqua's darkest hour hasn't happened yet, or we'd know. It'd be obvious," I said. "So I'm betting that's probably last."

"And Nivita already chose their side. They chose to side with Elder Oleander and diffuse the four tribe system," Imogen speculated. "That has to come second."

"So all we need to find out is if Yapluma's part of the prophecy is coming up, and we can turn this all around!" Jonah said in excitement.

"Depending on what it says." I leaned forward, thinking. "It's hard to tell if we don't have it."

"Guys, I just realized something," Sophia said, and our gazes all turned to her. "The prophecy talks about the strong and the weak. The *naderei* who made the prophecy... Showana Harjo... said things can be interpreted differently. Maybe we're looking at this all wrong. Maybe Koigni isn't the *greatest house* that the prophecy talks about. What if... what if it's Defortai?"

"Oh my gosh, ew," Jonah said, and Squeaks screeched in revulsion. "I really hope that isn't it."

"It *has* to be," Imogen said. "Think about it. Showana Harjo specifically said that the weakest need to bend to the strong. Doesn't that sound like Biyami submitting to the will of Defortai?"

"If I have to bring glory to Defortai, I'm gonna hurl," Sophia said. Esis patted her cheek.

"We're trying to prevent that," I reminded her. Sophia didn't respond. She looked downtrodden... as if she'd already accepted there was no possible way to save the tribe.

I didn't like that. I needed my brave Sophie back. We wouldn't be able to do this if she gave up now.

"So what do we think Yapluma's role is in all of this?" Jonah asked. "If we had to speculate?"

"I don't know. Did you manage to get anything out of Renar when you told him we were looking for pieces?" I asked, crossing my arms.

Jonah had accidentally told Renar, his piece of shit ex-boyfriend, that we were trying to stop the prophecy after Renar got him drunk one night and started asking questions. Originally, it'd made us all freak out because Renar's dad was on the Air Council, but so far, nothing had come of it.

Yet. There was always a yet attached to these things.

Jonah blushed, and said, "Um... kinda."

"Kinda? Jonah, that's not an answer," Imogen said.

"Renar told me the Air Council *knew* it. I mean, they *had* it," Jonah blundered.

"Knew?" Sophia asked.

"*Had?*" I added.

Jonah laughed nervously. "They... uh... heh-heh... see, thing is, with the Air Council and the prophecy piece, they... uh... they lost it."

"*What?*" All three of us shouted at once. Jonah threw his hands up in a "don't-turn-on-me" gesture.

"How can you *lose* a prophecy piece?" Imogen moaned. Sassy lay down and put her paws over her eyes. Esis sat on the couch cushion besides Sophia and gave me a look like we should've seen this coming.

"We're the carefree House," Jonah said lightly. "We probably didn't think it was that important."

"Fucking Yapluma," I cursed under my breath. Sophia reached out and stroked Esis, her expression more troubled than before.

"They didn't write it down or anything?" Imogen asked. "Not even half of it?"

"You see, Yapluma doesn't really do *books*," Jonah argued.

"Or intelligence," I added.

Jonah shot me a glare. "All I'm saying is, Renar told me that the Air Council misplaced their piece of the prophecy years ago. None of our Elders know what it is, and he said for sure they didn't write it down. It was probably forgotten about in the memory of a passed Elder years ago."

"Renar was probably making the whole thing up," I said. "Why wouldn't he? He loved to torment you."

"Liam, you don't get it. Renar's a horrible person, I know. And this doesn't excuse him, but he had it *bad*," Jonah said.

"Oh, please." I made a skeptical noise and rolled my eyes. Jonah said nothing.

"How do you know Renar wasn't lying? He could be feeding you information to misguide you," Sophia said.

"Renar didn't lie. And I'm not sticking up for him." Jonah's expression grew cold as I opened my mouth to speak. "He was as drunk as I was that night. Say what you want about him. He was abusive, he cheated on me, and I would never take him back, not even if my life depended on it."

Jonah's eyes dimmed. "But— and this is a huge but— he did trust me. I've gone over that night in my head a million times, and I always knew when he was lying to me— even when I didn't want to believe it. I got a feeling in my gut. That time... I know he wasn't."

Squeaks gave a loud squawk and shook her feathers. Jonah added, "Squeaks says that she agrees with me, though I know you guys can't hear her."

Squeaks nodded, and that was enough confirmation for me. If Squeaks was certain Renar was telling the truth— and she despised Renar— it was clear. The Air piece was gone. Yapluma had truly lost it.

"Jonah, why didn't you tell us this sooner?" Sophia asked. Her mouth was a thin, stern line— I'd seen that expression elsewhere, but I couldn't tell from where. "You knew this information months ago."

"Last semester was *hard*, guys," Jonah said. "You and Liam had that court case, there was the plague, Imogen got attacked, and then Cade..."

The room got deathly quiet at the mention of Imogen's lost love. Imogen's face became drawn and pale. Jonah cleared his throat and said, "There just never seemed to be a good time to bring it up. And I didn't want to let everyone down again. Like I always do."

Jonah hung his head. Imogen's angry expression faded, and she laid a hand on Jonah's shoulder.

"You didn't let anyone down, Jonah," I said softly. "There's still time to turn things around."

"We hope," Jonah said lowly. "I just pray we don't screw it up, like we did last semester."

Imogen and I shared a guilty glance. We had screwed up. It wasn't like we had a lot of control over it, but we'd failed to stop the prophecy once already. Nivita had chosen to side with Oleander. And that was causing devastating consequences for the tribe now.

Sophia was barely listening. She was staring into the fire, completely immobile. Esis had moved to her lap and curled up into a ball on her legs. She sat so still I didn't think she hardly breathed. It was like her eyes were haunted... replaying something the rest of us couldn't see.

What was up with her lately? It was like she was in a whole other world.

"We need to focus," Imogen said. Sophia tore her eyes away from the flames and sat straight up, like Imogen had gotten her attention. "Is there anywhere we can start looking on how to recover this piece, if it still exists?"

"I decided to look through the Air Elders' scrolls to find out who the Yapluma Elders were at the time the prophecy was made," Jonah said. "I've got a few names."

"We can start there. Research may turn up something." Imogen seemed relieved they had a starting point, though I wasn't sure if it would amount to anything. A couple of names from history scrolls wouldn't mean much if they didn't lead somewhere, and we had to find that next piece— fast.

"Is there anything else we should cover?" Imogen suggested.

Sophia shrugged. "I wanted to research the *Azaimperiai*— the weapon that's supposed to control the ancestors— but I don't even know where to begin."

"I don't think it exists, Sophia," Imogen said quietly. "I've searched everywhere, and there's nothing on it, not even in the ancient tomes or Elders' scrolls. It has to be an old Hawkei legend. Just a story to tell around the fire."

"Is it ever just a story, though?" I asked.

Imogen sighed. "No. It never is."

I clasped my hands together and put my elbows on my knees. "There's something I need to tell you guys."

"What is it? Oh, ancestors, if you're coming out, I'm not interested. I don't do friends with benefits," Jonah said.

Esis had opened his blue eyes to stare at me, and his ears perked, though he didn't move from his curled-up position on Sophia's lap. "Oleander wanted those riots to happen," I said. "Separating the tribes was something he had in mind from the start of his inauguration on the Toaqua Council."

"What do you mean?" Sophia asked. Everyone was on the edge of their seat, looking at me.

I bounced my leg nervously. "There's some stuff Dad told me before we left on the *Hozho*. He told me to keep it to myself, but I don't think I can."

"If your Dad told you, maybe it's best to keep it private," Sophia said gently.

"No. You deserve to know." I took a deep breath. "Last semester, Oleander was taking advantage of the plague. He was coercing and threatening the other Elders to replace the ones who died from the illness with people *he* wanted— which we guessed, but there's more. The night of the riots, he never consulted the other Elders about making the two tribes system. He already had this planned for weeks. There were people in the government waiting on his orders. He was just looking for the perfect time. The chaos and death that night created a perfect storm for him to implement his final solution without opposition from the tribe. All the other Elders who would've opposed him were either dead, injured, or being bullied into submitting to him."

I dropped my head. "Like my father."

"Liam, why would your dad tell you all this?" Sophia asked. "It had to be hard for him to admit."

"He wanted me to be prepared for anything," I said. "He's made it pretty clear that we can't trust anyone. And being the son of a chief isn't enough to protect me anymore."

Imogen turned to stare at the cork board, her eyes wandering over all the clues. "Jonah and I will get a head start on researching those names. Maybe with time, we'll get a lead."

"Maybe," Sophia said, but her voice was tinged with doubt. It was hard to hear— Sophia wasn't the kind of person who allowed herself to be uncertain.

Though I understood where she was coming from. Time was something we just didn't have.

Master Toaqua Magic was my first class of the semester. It was held early in the morning, like always, so I was up before most of the other people in the dorm were. It'd been hard sleeping the night before with dozens of people around me. You could hear everything. People went to sleep at different times, which meant you never knew if the lights were going to be on or off, and there was always noise.

I hoped I'd get used to it. Sophia was sound asleep when I left, with Esis tucked in next to her legs. She had class, but I didn't want to wake her, as she needed rest. I think she'd stayed awake most of the night, as I could hear her tossing and turning.

The first day of Water class was held on the beach, as it always was at the start of the semester. But when I got there, something was really weird. The class was only a third of the size it usually was. I didn't see a lot of the people I'd had in my Toaqua class in the years prior. There were only ten other people in here. The rest of my class looked similarly confused. It was time to start, and most of our normal group wasn't here.

"Wyatt, what's going on?" I asked. His walrus Familiar lounged lazily on the sand and flopped his flippers, like he didn't care who showed.

Wyatt shrugged. "I don't know, dude. Maybe people dropped out?"

"This many?" It was rare for someone to flunk out of Orenda Academy.

"Settle down, people." Professor Baine emerged from the woods and entered the beach. He looked even more scruffy than he usually did. His hair stood up on one end, and there were deep purple bags under his eyes. I'm pretty sure his shirt was stained, though I didn't look closely enough to check.

Well, good morning to you too, Baine. He was clearly in a mood.

Lira raised her hand, and Baine's beady eyes flashed to her. "What, Lira?"

I was taken aback for a moment. Baine didn't talk like that to his students. Lira seemed similarly surprised. She hesitated for a moment before saying, "I'm sorry, sir, but where is everyone? Most of the class isn't here, and—"

"The Defortai students have been reassigned to another Toaqua teacher," Baine said. "I am only the instructor for the Toaqua students who've been sorted into Biyami, as I was assigned to that tribe myself."

Geez, no wonder he was irritable. He'd gotten demoted.

Baine clapped his hands together and rubbed them. "Let's get down to business, shall we? Master Toaqua Magic. At this point in your magical education, there's no room for playing around. What I am about to teach you is very advanced. Either pay attention, or squander your potential. Makes no difference to me."

Ancestors, couldn't he lighten up a little? He was starting to act like old-me. Or like Madame Doya, barking orders. As much as he annoyed me, I kinda wanted regular, weirdo Baine back, not this crabass.

"All magic comes from a primal source in the earth, which is constantly in motion and cannot be destroyed. It was created by the Great Spirit, and is able to be used by those who have magic in their blood— supernaturals who've been born or gifted with power," Baine began. "Each supernatural race is able to manifest this power in a different way. Elementai in particular have a strong connection to the natural world, which enables us to bond with our creatures and manipulate the elements. But there are other ways that Elementai can increase their power beyond their normal limits."

Baine motioned to the water. His sea serpent Familiar, Thalassa, wiggled onto the sand. She was just as big and gorgeous as ever, with her shining blue scales, webbed feet, and pointed horns. I never got tired of looking at her— though that didn't seem to be the case for Baine.

Baine didn't acknowledge her when she came upon shore, just crossed his arms and gave a haughty turn away. Thalassa huffed, and sea water came bursting out of her nostrils. It soaked Baine in snot and salt water. He gave her a resentful look before he magicked it off himself. She growled, showing her teeth for a moment before settling.

What the hell? They seemed to be fighting. Why? I didn't get the drama.

But she wasn't the only creature that emerged from the sea. Beside her, another form splashed out of the waves. A sea turtle the size of an elephant floated to the surface, with giant black eyes and flat flippers that skimmed the surface. She was green in color, but on her back grew all kinds of seaweed and coral that was pink, purple, and blue. She looked like a mini-island that belonged underwater. She was a special kind of turtle— a zaratan.

On the zaratan's back were hundreds of tiny green frogs nestled in the seaweed, with bat wings and long reptile tails. They were called water leapers. As they came out of the sea, the water leapers beat their tiny wings and rose into the air, fluttering around the area. Students oohed as they tried to snatch the water leapers out of thin air and failed.

I was patient. I put out my hand and waited. A water leaper came down and landed on my open palm, where it croaked. I stroked the back of the water leaper with my finger and listened.

"All Elementai can harvest strength from their Familiars," Baine began. "But what many Elementai don't know is that they can also harness power from their element itself, and any magical creatures in the area that are connected to that particular element— even if those creatures are not bonded to you. Observe."

Baine turned toward the water. He raised both hands over it, and the water pushed back, creating a wall that was fifty feet wide and just as high. I expected him to stop there, but he didn't. Baine increased the size of the wall until it was just as tall as a skyscraper— three hundred feet or so.

People gasped in surprise. Even I was impressed. Baine shouldn't have been able to make such a towering structure of water on his own, even though I knew he was talented. What was the catch?

"My Familiar is with me, but I'm not drawing power from her. I am concentrating on drawing my energy from the life of the ocean itself," Baine instructed. "I am also harvesting energy from the zaratan beside me."

That made sense. The ocean provided a massive source of magical energy, and I bet the zaratan had power as well. Baine let the wall drop back down slowly, and the ocean rocked violently as its large source was returned to the depths.

"Elementai have to be very careful when drawing energy with their elements," Baine instructed. "Nivita who take too much power from the forest have been known to destroy all the trees. Yapluma who draw too much magic from the skies have been known to poison the air. Koigni can ruin a fuel source's ability to create fire. We as Toaqua have to be especially careful. If we take too much of a water body's life force, the marine habitat within the water will perish, and eventually, the water body itself will dry up, leaving nothing more behind than a desert wasteland that can never be replaced."

"Has that ever happened before?" Lira questioned.

Baine raised an eyebrow. "There are many places in the United States that weren't always deserts."

Muttered conversation grew around the classroom, but Baine ignored it and continued. "Drawing power from something other than your Familiar is extremely difficult. You must master a deep connection to the earth and to nature. All magic is an endless, flowing connection. If you find yourself becoming one with nature around you, you'll be able to channel the ability of the earth to your will."

Baine waved his hands. "Take the water leapers in the air. I ask that each of you try to harness the power inside of the little creature and use it to perform magic that's outside your normal capabilities. Magic is an endless, flowing substance— once you can tap into it, the possibilities become endless."

I looked at the water leaper in my hand. I concentrated on staring at it for a moment while the students around me tried to force the magic to come. There were splashes of water and alarmed shouts all around me, but I didn't pay attention to it. I just tried to focus on the waves, and the sand, the smell of the ocean, and the croaking of the tiny winged frog in my hand.

One guy had been trying so hard to get energy out of the water leaper that his own magic had backfired and killed the creature. He was a big, muscular guy who could've been on the soccer team, but he looked near tears.

"I'm sorry, little guy," he said. He stroked the water leaper's belly. Lira laid a hand on his shoulder.

"Don't try too hard!" Baine bellowed. "If you overexert your potential, there can be consequences. This is something that has to be given, not forced! Allow the earth to gift you the power!"

He was barking a lot of instructions that wouldn't make sense to most people. But not me. I got it. It was a lot like basket weaving. You had to let yourself go and be consumed by the ability of just existing.

I felt an energy flow through my hand from where the water leaper sat. It was different from my own. I moved my hand over the ocean, and a tall column rose. I could usually only make them about a hundred feet or so, but I pushed it fifty feet higher. The water leaper's power slowly zapped as the column grew, and I backed off, letting the column crash back into the sea.

"Well done, Liam!" Baine said. "You've got it!"

I changed my attention. The water leaper flew off, and I directed my focus on absorbing power from Thalassa and the zaratan instead. I was surprised to see that when I connected with Thalassa, I could feel Baine's magic too, moving through his body.

I cut off my tie to Thalassa. It was rude to draw from someone else's Familiar, and I wanted to prove to Baine I didn't need his magic to improve my own. The zaratan observed me with calm eyes as I forged a stronger tie to her.

At first, it hurt. It was too similar to what I experienced with Nashoma. I'd forgotten what it felt like to have a Familiar. You could constantly feel a push and pull of magical energy between you and your creature, whether you noticed or not. The zaratan's connection to me wasn't even close to what Nashoma's was. But it was a close enough memory that it made me choke up for a moment.

The connection began to fade, and I refocused. I needed to center myself on the earth. Thinking about myself would make the spell fail.

I felt the zaratan's power absorb into my body, and it was almost overwhelming. All that magical energy had to go somewhere. I thrust my hands at the water, and a twisting corkscrew emerged, two times as big as the ones I'd ever created. It rose like a rollercoaster to the sky, hundreds of feet wide.

My mouth dropped open in awe as I moved the corkscrew without breaking a sweat. It wasn't like when I'd moved the river during the riots. That had been all me, and it'd taken all my energy to do. Because I was pulling energy from the zaratan, I could create monstrosities of Water magic with ease.

By the end of the class, I was the only one who could do it. A couple of people gave me jealous looks, but the majority of students clapped and cheered.

"Liam, that's beautiful magic," Lira breathed as she came up beside me, looking upward.

"Thanks." I'd changed the corkscrew into a vortex that twisted off into several different veins. The vines wrapped around each other and flowed in an infinity pattern, an endless loop that fed itself as the water churned within the tunnels over and over. I didn't even feel tired. I returned the water to the sea, and it was like nothing ever happened.

I understood that this type of magic wasn't meant to change things. It was meant to keep the ecosystem as it was.

"Why'd you get sorted into Biyami? With that kind of power, you definitely should be Defortai," Wyatt said. His tone clearly held admiration, though I didn't want it.

I turned away from him and stared at the ocean. "You know why."

Wyatt and Lira's eyes averted at the obvious. Why was I Biyami? Pick a reason. I had no Familiar. I was sick. I was in an interhouse relationship. Any one of these reasons would be good enough to make me Biyami, and I had a triple whammy.

Baine waved us off. "That's enough for today. Wednesday we'll move on to other matters. I suggest you keep this lesson between us. Class dismissed."

Lira, Wyatt and I gave each other weird looks as Baine climbed onto Thalassa's back and sailed off into the ocean.

"Okay, that was totally weird," I said. "Wasn't it?"

"Yeah..." Lira's eyes narrowed. "It was like he didn't want us spreading around what his lecture was about."

"That's ridiculous," I started, before I paused. "Right?"

"I don't know," Wyatt said carefully. "What he taught today, it wasn't on the syllabus. Or in our textbook. I know, because I looked before class. Baine specifically said that only extremely powerful Elementai could draw energy from something other than their Familiar. He knew most of us would never be able to master it. Why did he bother instructing us on it if we can't use it?"

"Because he wanted to sort out who could," Lira said, with a meaningful look at me.

I wasn't about to take the bait, so I said, "It doesn't matter. He said we're moving on to another lesson anyway. This was just a one-time thing."

"I have a feeling Baine *wasn't* supposed to teach us that. It gives us more power as Biyami," Lira said in a low voice. "I bet Oleander will have a fit when he hears."

"Let him. He's not king of this school. Alric is. He's still Head Dean," I said harshly.

"Alric is Biyami now, though," Wyatt whispered. "How long is that going to last?"

I wasn't sure. But Alric wasn't a pushover, either. He was a master alchemist, had a dragon Familiar, and was just as strong a Koigni as Chieftess Annette was. Even Oleander couldn't just knock him off his post.

"Alric's going to maintain control," I said. "We need to trust Alric knows what he's doing."

Lira and Wyatt shared a doubtful glance before Wyatt said, "I guess."

I wasn't willing to talk more about it. Alric had things handled. Oleander had control of Kinpago, but Orenda Academy was still outside his control. He wouldn't get his hands on this school.

Alric would make sure he didn't.

I DIDN'T HAVE another class until after lunch. I planned to meet up with Jonah, Sophia, and Imogen in the dining hall, as was our usual tradition, but when I got there, I found the dining hall had been completely transformed. The tables and booths had been moved up against the walls, and I heard the buzzing of tattoo machines. Hundreds of students were standing in long lines. What exactly was going on here?

"Get in line!" a Task Force member barked. She shoved a few students into place before threatening them with a noxite gun. People moved quickly to get out of her way, faces marred with fear.

I saw my friends and their Familiars collected in a corner. I hurried over to them, clearly feeling lost. "Hey. What's going on?"

"We're being *ordered* to get identification tattoos on our right forearm," Imogen said, with gritted teeth and clenched fists. "To show we're Biyami."

"What the fuck!?" I was totally appalled. "You can't be serious."

"It's a mandate," Sophia said. "They dropped them off this morning."

Sophia handed me an orange sheet of paper. On it were orders that every Biyami in Kinpago report to a station to be given their identification tattoos. As we were students, that area was the dining hall within the school. If a Biyami didn't show up for branding, they were instantly to be considered an enemy of the tribe and arrested.

The tattoo itself was a design of an unfinished circle with a broken arrow in the center. The arrow tip was pointed downward, and the two halves lay side by side next to each other, the half with the feathers above the half with the arrow head.

During war, the ancient Hawkei would take the arrows of their enemies and break them to show dominance over the defeated. An incomplete circle was also a sign of being inferior.

I frowned before I folded up the paper and tucked it into my pocket, "Well, if it's what we have to do, so be it."

"You can't be serious. We can't just allow this to happen! We have to fight back," Imogen hissed.

"What choice do we have?" Jonah asked. His eyes nervously skirted around the room. A few students had tried to run away, but the Task Force had blocked off all exits except the one I'd come in. I was pretty sure that they'd done this at lunch time on purpose— because most people would be heading this way regardless. People who hadn't gotten the mandate would end up walking into a trap.

"We don't have a choice." My brow furrowed, and I dropped my voice. "Listen. I know you guys want to fight back, but this isn't the right way. Not yet. It's just going to get us hurt, or worse."

"Liam, you're not supposed to get tattoos." Sophia's face was full of concern. She was right. I was supposed to avoid any open wounds, because there was a much higher chance that they'd get infected. Tattoos were a part of that category.

"I don't think they care about that, Soph."

One girl was screaming that she was petrified of needles. Four Task Force members forcibly held her down on the floor as she screamed and cried while the tattoo artist got to work on branding her arm.

They were going to tattoo me whether I made a scene or not, so I figured I might as well get it over with. The four of us joined a long line of Biyami in front of the tattoo machines. I made sure to go first.

Sophia let out a sigh of relief as our line progressed and she got a glimpse of the tattoo artist. He was a guy in his thirties that had tattoos all over his skin, though he didn't look like a Task Force member.

"What is it?" I asked.

"He's the guy who did my daisy tattoo. He's good. His name's Luca," she said. "His Familiar does the tattoos. He'll make sure it'll heal well."

Well, at least that was a relief. When it was my turn, I sat across from the artist. He seemed pretty miserable.

"Sorry, man," Luca whispered under his breath. "I don't want to do this."

"It's fine," I replied back. "Just do what you gotta do."

I laid out my forearm on the table. The tattoo artist's scorpion Familiar crawled onto my skin, and I resisted a shiver. I wanted to cringe every time the scorpion's pincher dug into my skin, but I kept my expression blank. I wouldn't give the Task Force the satisfaction of seeing me suffer.

By the end, my arm was throbbing, and the skin around the tattoo was irritated and red. I was really freaking out that I'd get sick from it, but it was too late now to do anything. Luca wrapped up my new tattoo and called for the next person in line.

Sophia took the tattoo like a champ. Esis sat on the table next to her as Luca adorned her skin. She didn't even flinch, just looked straight ahead and talked with Luca as if this was her choice. I knew it was to piss off the Task Force.

Imogen was harder to watch. She had a mini-freakout before a Task Force member forced her into a chair. Tears beaded her eyes, but they vanished once the scorpion touched her arm. Sassy licked her face, and Imogen's tears faded.

Jonah took the tattoo easily and joked around with the tattoo artist that he'd always wanted to get some ink anyway. The artist lifted a smile, but it dropped when he saw a Task Force member scowling at him. Squeaks lifted her tail at him as she walked by. She had a venomous expression that clearly said if Jonah would let her, she'd rip the cop's head off.

When we were done with the tattoos, none of us were very hungry. Nobody wanted to return to our crappy dorm, so we headed to a large sitting area off the dining hall where people usually studied. It was usually quiet in there, so we hoped we wouldn't be disturbed further. Our Familiars gathered around us. Sassy yowled, and Squeaks snapped her beak at anyone who got too close.

Esis laid his tiny paws on my arm. I felt the tattoo beneath the bandage begin to mend slowly, until most of the pain dulled and I was left with an almost-healed tattoo. Esis ran amongst the group, healing each of our tattoos as quickly as he could.

Jonah broke the silence. "I mean, we talked about getting squad tattoos in Europe," he joked. "At least now we all match."

Sophia stared off into space. She'd told me she wanted to get another tattoo to complement the daisy on her shoulder, but I was pretty sure the identifying mark for Biyami wasn't what she had in mind.

"Hey everybody, if I get blood poisoning from this thing, can someone dig a hole and throw me in?" I waved my arm in the air and tried to force a laugh, because death humor was always appropriate for changing the mood.

"We'll throw you out back in a ditch beside the castle," Imogen cracked.

The three of us chuckled, though Sophia didn't even crack a smile. At least we could laugh about it. Because if we didn't, what other alternative was there?

A hush fell over us as a Second Year approached. A mass of blonde curls stuck out around a bitter, frustrated face full of tears. Taylor Meyers, a Koigni. Sophia and I had her in our Medical Care of Familiars class a little over a year ago. Her new identification tattoo shone out in harsh black ink against the exposed, raw skin. She gave us a harsh glare that was difficult to endure.

"Can I help you?" Imogen snapped. She clearly was in the mood for no shit today.

Taylor's nose wrinkled. "It's *your* fault," Taylor accused, pointing at me and Sophia. "You two went up against the Elders and forced them to make interhouse relationships legal. That's why all this is happening."

"We didn't *force* them to do anything," Sophia replied coldly.

"Oleander had this planned for a long time, Taylor," I said calmly. "This wasn't something any of us could control."

"I don't believe that for a second," Taylor snarled.

"Leave off it, Taylor." Levi, her older brother, stepped in front of her. He too had a new Biyami tattoo on his skin. "It's not their fault."

He tried to put a hand on her arm, but Taylor wrenched it away. She sneered and said, "I'll never forget I'm in this because of you. I hate all of you for stirring up trouble. You should've just learned your place."

Taylor stomped away, curls bouncing. Levi tilted his palms up and gave us a helpless expression. "I'm sorry. My sister— she's just upset."

He took off after her. Imogen had the nerve to lift a middle finger in farewell, though the rest of us did nothing.

Taylor was just looking for someone to blame— just like the tribe was trying to blame Biyami for all the problems in it. I didn't blame her. I knew she was upset and looking for a way out. But accusing others wasn't the answer. It was that kind of thinking that had gotten us all here.

The sound of a scuffle on the other side of the room caught our attention. Two large boys, both with hyena Familiars, had cornered a girl against the wall. She was shaking as they advanced on her. With a sinking feeling, I recognized her as Isabella... the Nivita girl who was the first to have her Familiar go missing last year. She'd gotten her Familiar, Essarae, back, but it looked like they were still in trouble. The tiny glowing horse with little wings hovered over Isabella's shoulder in a mad panic.

"Please, stop," Isabella pleaded. "I didn't do anything!"

The fucker standing over her grinned. "You don't *have* to do anything. This is just for fun."

I heard Sophia gasp as one of the guys raised a fist and punched Isabella across the face. All four of us stood up at once. Isabella crumpled to the ground, and the two guys started kicking her in the gut.

Essarae couldn't protect Isabella. The filly-pixie looked like a tiny glowing ball as the Familiars of the Defortai tossed her back and forth between them. It was like a game to them, though Essarae was screaming in pain.

I caught a flash of the Biyami tattoo on Isabella's arm. Of course poor Isabella had been sorted into Biyami. Her Familiar wasn't very strong, and she was related to an old Elder who'd died while on the council. That made her a target.

I felt a wave of rage well up inside me and threaten to explode at the surface. Isabella's Familiar had already been kidnapped and taken away from her last semester. Hadn't she suffered enough?

I moved forward to interfere, but a Task Force member raised his gun and pointed it at me in a clear threat to back off.

I didn't care. Let them shoot me. I couldn't just stand here and—

A hand on the back of my shirt held me back. "Liam, don't," Sophia begged. "Stand down."

I was shocked to hear those words come out of her mouth. Sophia was the *last* person who'd stand down when someone needed her. She'd always protect those who couldn't protect themselves.

But that was exactly what was happening now. It was completely out of character for her. Yet it was happening, and I didn't know how to react to it.

"I don't want you getting hurt," she pleaded. Her words were desperate. She truly believed that if I did anything, I'd end up just like Isabella.

I couldn't go against her. Not when she was begging me like that. I held back, though the sights of the noxite gun were still fixed on me.

"We need to stop this," Imogen protested. She went to go forward, but Jonah reached out and snagged her arm to hold her back.

It was a definitive move that I think shocked us all. For the first time, we weren't getting involved.

Someone near the fight— I think it was Isabella's friend— tried to step in and use her Earth magic to drag the Defortai off Isabella. But a Task Force member nearby stopped her. They put a hand on her shoulder and forcibly shoved her to the floor. They told her to stay down and shoved a noxite gun in her face while the Defortai students continued to kick and punch Isabella, obviously getting enjoyment out of her torture.

"We can do nothing," I said emptily, realizing how horribly true it was. If we tried to help, the Task Force members would either force us to back off or shoot us with noxite.

Or worse. We'd end up getting beaten next.

Not all the Defortai in the room were getting enjoyment out of this. It was clear only a few were getting pleasure from the torment. There were a lot of students from the so called stronger house that looked disturbed, but they just turned away, or left the room. It was obvious they were too scared to take a stand.

They were cowards. They had actual power to do something, but they ignored Isabella's cries for help.

The door opened, and I felt relief. Professor Bates strode into the sitting area and caught sight of the beating. A teacher could stop the beating. He'd replaced Professor Fawn over the break, and was Nivita. He wouldn't let this happen to Isabella.

"Professor, please do something!" Isabella's friend cried from the floor. Her comment earned her a hard hit in the mouth with a butt of the gun.

Professor Bates maintained a void expression. He looked down his nose at Isabella curled into a ball on the floor, and said, "If she wasn't so weak, she could defend herself."

Cold horror crept over my bones and settled there. Esis had his paws over his mouth. He looked like he longed to run to Isabella and heal her, though Sophia clung to him with all her might.

The Defortai boys looked to Bates for approval, and he said, "She deserves to be punished. This just proves that the Biyami aren't equal to us."

Without another word, Bates strode off. The guys continued their beating with increased vigor. It went on for minutes, though it seemed like hours. I felt sick, but eventually, the sickness faded away to be replaced with a kind of desensitization that I hated. I was getting *used* to it.

I couldn't stand this. I wanted to reach out and comfort Sophia, put an arm around her, but I couldn't even move. I had totally frozen.

Eventually, the Defortai got bored. They walked off with their hyena Familiars, laughing and high-fiving.

Isabella struggled to get off the ground. As she got to her feet, her lip was bleeding and she walked with a limp. She was covered in bruises. She stooped down to pick up her filly-pixie, who had a bent wing. Her lip trembled as she left the room with as much dignity as she could muster. Blood dripped down the tattoo on her skin.

I managed to move. The first place my eyes went to was Sophia.

I expected her to be crying, but she wasn't. Sophia's body was rigid and still as she hugged Esis. She appeared a statue. Her face was pale, and although fear was written across it, her eyes were far, far away. It was like she'd completely dissociated from what was happening around her.

She wasn't my brave Sophia anymore. And that scared the hell out of me.

I didn't want to believe something like this could happen at Orenda Academy, but I'd seen it with my own eyes. We could no longer hide that we were Biyami. These brands made sure everyone knew.

Society had proclaimed us to be a problem. There'd be consequences to pay— and none of us would be able to do a damn thing about it unless we did something *now*.

Trying to reverse the prophecy wouldn't be enough. We needed a new plan.

We needed to fight back.

sophia

FOUR

Over the next week, the incident with Isabella stuck with me. I knew I should've let Liam step in, but I just couldn't stop picturing what would happen to him— to any of us— if we did. Bloody images like the night of the riots invaded my thoughts. We had to fight back, yes, but not physically. The riots had proved that violence solved nothing.

It was still in the back of my mind as I headed to my Introduction to Parenting class the week after, clutching Esis close to my chest. I did my best to push it out of my head so I could focus on my studies. I met up with the rest of the class near the bus-sized carriage at the front of school. Last week, we'd covered the syllabus and our introduction unit. This week, we got to meet our "kids" for the first time.

The class was split into two parts. The first was our lecture once a week, and the second was interacting with the kids who lived at the Kinpago group foster home. We got to be their "big brother slash big sister" for the semester.

"Everyone in," Professor Maynard called, gesturing to the carriage. She was a short, plump Toaqua woman without a Familiar at her side, which probably meant it lived in the ocean. She had a hard gaze, like she didn't really want to be teaching this class.

It was like that with a lot of professors this semester. Many of our old ones had died during the riots. Others had resigned and been replaced by new teachers who were often underqualified. But it wasn't like the school had any other choice. They had to fill the positions somehow. I didn't know what had happened to my child development professor, Professor Ambika. She was supposed to teach this parenting class as well, but like many of the other teachers, she left the school after the riots. I'm not sure anyone knew where they'd gone.

The ride to the group home wasn't long, as it was close to the school. We stopped in front of a brick building that reminded me a little of a church and followed Professor Maynard inside. We were introduced briefly to the director in the foyer. Her name was Miss Evangeline. She was an older Nivita woman with a hummingbird Familiar at her side. We hung our coats on hooks in the entrance, then she gestured for us to follow her down the hall.

We entered a large room with wood flooring and tall windows, toys everywhere. Children ran around and played with each other. Various baby Familiars played as well. A baby hippogriff with a missing wing jumped on a bean bag chair, while a little monkey helped one of the toddlers build a block tower. The room was filled with laughter and chatter.

I made a quick assessment and guessed there to be about twenty kids in total, which made one for each of us. The youngest orphan was a newborn, which was in a nurse's arm as she rocked him in a chair near the play area. The oldest I guessed to be around twelve.

"Children," Miss Evangeline called.

The room quieted quickly as the children's eyes turned toward us. They quickly got excited and rushed over.

I noticed one child didn't leave the play area. It was like he hadn't heard her. He looked around four years old and was facing the wall, organizing blocks by color. The nurse who held the baby glanced to him, but she didn't tell him to go join the rest of the group. He looked kind of lonely.

"Shh..." Miss Evangeline held her finger to her lips, and the kids went silent. "As you all know, students from Orenda Academy will be coming in once a week to visit with you. Today, we will start with some play time. Next week, you will be partnered up with your official *friend* for the semester. So everyone have fun."

A girl at the front around eight years old quickly grabbed one of my classmate's hands and said, "I want to be with *you*. Your dracavern is beautiful!"

Sandy laughed and pulled the cave dragon off her shoulder to show the girl. "You can pet her. She's very friendly."

Sandy was in my Elementai Explorations class last semester. She had bonded with a dracavern shortly after we'd explored their cave.

Children quickly paired up with students, mostly raving about their Familiars. I expected someone to come up and ask to pet Esis, but since I was in the back, most of the kids didn't notice me. They all paired up so quickly that I was left standing on my own. I looked around the room stupidly.

"Sophia," Professor Maynard said. "Why don't you go play with Adriel?"

She pointed to the little boy who was organizing the blocks on his own. I nodded and made my way over to him. I sat on the rug next to him, feeling a little awkward.

"Hey, there," I forced out. The boy didn't look up at me. I was starting to wonder if maybe he was deaf.

"I'm Sophia," I tried. "Is your name Adriel?"

At the sound of his name, he turned to me. He kept his head low and wouldn't meet my gaze, but he acknowledged me by holding a yellow block out in my direction.

I took it. "Thank you. Does this one go here?"

I placed the block next to the other yellow ones.

He nodded, then turned back to the blue ones and started organizing them in a straight row. Esis hopped out of my arms and began doing the same with the yellow ones.

"No! No!" Adriel shouted, pushing Esis away. He shoved him so hard that Esis stumbled and fell onto his back.

"Adriel," I scolded, scooping up Esis into my arms. "That's not very nice."

"No!" he screamed again, even though Esis was far away from the blocks. Adriel started flapping his arms and swatted at Esis.

Instinct took over. I set Esis aside and reached for Adriel's hands, holding them gently but firmly in place. Sternly, I said, "We do not hit."

Adriel squirmed, and tears sprang to his eyes as he started to scream bloody murder. The little hippogriff without the wing rushed over to us, as if he could comfort the crying child.

"Adriel, look at me," I instructed calmly, but he didn't. He wrenched away and threw himself onto the ground, kicking his legs and covering his ears while he cried.

Then it hit me. I'd spent enough time in the campus daycare to know this wasn't normal behavior for a child his age. I turned to the nurse in the chair, though she wasn't paying attention to us— as if she did her best to block Adriel out.

I cleared my throat. "Excuse me?"

It took her a second, but she finally tore her gaze off the kids surrounding the dracavern.

"Is Adriel on the autistic scale?" I asked.

"Yes, he is," she replied. "How did you know?"

I shrugged. "Instinct, I guess."

The nurse went back to ignoring us, even though Adriel continued to throw a fit. I got to my knees and inched across the carpet to Adriel's side. I placed a gentle hand on his back and leaned down so he could hear me.

"Adriel, we're going to go outside," I told him. "Can you follow me?"

"No! No!" he screamed, still kicking his feet.

"It's not going to help," the nurse said dryly.

"He's overwhelmed," I snapped back. "He needs to go someplace he deems safe."

I didn't know what else to do, so I grabbed Adriel around the middle and carried him into the hall. The nurse watched my curiously but didn't do anything to stop me. Esis and the little hippogriff, which I decided to call Baby, followed behind me.

As soon as I set Adriel down, he melted back onto the floor with his hands at his ears. I felt hopeless. I didn't know how to fix this. Esis reached out like he could help heal him, but it didn't work that way.

"Esis." I shook my head, and he backed off. I knelt down beside Adriel. "Hey, watch this."

In one hand, I conjured Fire. The brightness of the flames illuminated the wall next to us. Using my other hand, I made shadow figures on the wall. Esis saw what I was doing and quickly joined me, creating a butterfly with his hands, then morphing his paws into more complicated designs like a dolphin and a unicorn.

"A long time ago..." I started a story, even though Adriel didn't seem at all interested. "The ancestors gifted us elemental powers. Magical creatures rained down from the skies, creatures they called Familiars."

I created a dog-like shadow with my hands and pretended like it was flying down from above. Esis used the shadow of his ears to pretend he was a dragon, then used his tail for a sea serpent. Baby stood in front of the flames and pretended he was a giant bird.

Adriel caught sight of the moving shadows. It quickly caught his attention, and he quieted.

I continued my story as Esis made more shadow puppets on the wall. "Soon, Elementai began bonding with Familiars. They were our souls, the half we'd been missing from birth."

Esis stepped up to Adriel, so close that his fur brushed Adriel's arm. Adriel jerked away before reaching out his hand to pet Esis' fur.

"This is Esis," I introduced. "Is it okay if he plays with you?"

Adriel pushed himself to a sitting position and pulled Esis onto his lap. He reached upward and waved his hand, creating his own shadow on the wall.

"There you go," I encouraged. "You got it."

He started to laugh, and soon, we were making up our own stories. Before I knew it, over an hour had passed. The door to the main room opened, and Miss Evangeline stepped outside. She looked to us where we sat on the floor.

"Your class is getting ready to leave," she said lightly. "Thank you so much for entertaining Adriel today. It's been a long time since he's taken a liking to one of the students."

"It's no problem, really," I told her.

I killed the flames in my hand and turned back to Adriel. "I'll be back next week, okay?"

Adriel didn't look me in the eye, but he nodded. Then the most unexpected thing happened. He threw himself forward and *hugged* me. For one brief moment, my heart felt full as I hugged him back.

He drew away, then pointed to himself. "Adriel."

"That's right," I told him, smiling. "That's your name."

He pointed to my chest and said my name, separating each syllable carefully. "So-phi-a."

"Good job, Adriel!" I praised.

He stood, his face at my level since I was still sitting. Then he leaned over and pressed his cheek to mine before turning around and racing back into the open doorway. Baby followed quickly behind him.

I lifted my hand to my cheek, my skin warming where he'd touched me. It wasn't a kiss, exactly, but it felt like his version of one.

"He likes you very much," Miss Evangeline said. "You'll make a great mother someday."

My stomach sank, but she didn't notice, because she turned and headed back inside before she could catch the look on my face. Either Miss Evangeline didn't follow the news, or she didn't realize what she was saying, because everyone knew that Liam was sterile and we'd never have kids.

No matter how much I still wanted them.

WE RETURNED to our classroom shortly afterward, my mind still on what Miss Evangeline had said.

"Before you go, remember to pick up your dragon egg!" Professor Maynard called to the class. "As we discussed last week, hatching a baby dragon takes great care, much like parenting. This project will be worth a quarter of your final grade."

She started passing out the eggs on our way out the door. Each was placed in a basket and wrapped in white fabric. They were bigger than my fist, all different colors, and covered in what looked like dragon scales that shimmered beautifully in the light. The one she held out to me had red scales and a purple shimmer.

"Take good care of it," Professor Maynard warned.

I nodded. "I will."

Esis jumped into the basket beside the dragon egg and snuggled right in. I didn't mind, since dragon eggs had to be kept warm to incubate. I held the basket close to my chest as I started down the hall.

I should've been thrilled about the egg. It was, after all, going to be one of the best assignments I'd had at Orenda Academy. I had to warm it in the sun for two hours per day, sing to it at night, and clean it once per week.

But it was also going to be torture. Every moment spent caring for this egg was nothing more than a reminder of what I'd never have. This parenting class was a huge slap in the face. Pressure built up in my eyes, and I bit down on my lower lip. My jaw started to hurt from clenching it so tightly.

I didn't want to go back to the Biyami dorms, so I found my way to a secluded study area on the second floor. I set my basket on my lap and ran my fingers over the dragon egg. It was so smooth and warm, like a real dragon. Esis saw what I was doing and started stroking it, too.

"Sophia?" Liam's voice came from above me.

I was so out of it that I hadn't heard his approach. I forgot I was supposed to meet up with him after class. I quickly straightened. "Oh, hey. What's up?"

"I was looking for you." He sounded worried as he sank beside me. "Sophia, what's wrong?"

"Nothing," I lied, ducking my head. "Just nurturing this dragon egg."

Liam eyed me skeptically, but he leaned over to get a better look. "For your parenting class?"

I nodded.

"How'd it go?" he asked.

"It was... all right, I guess." I shifted in my chair.

"Soph." He frowned, then reached out to take my hand. It was cool in mine, but it made my stomach twist. "Tell me what's wrong."

"Nothing's wrong," I insisted. "Why do you think so?"

He kept his eyes on our hands as he ran his thumb over my skin. "You haven't been acting like yourself lately. And you seem... I don't know. Upset."

"I'm just..." I shrugged. "Not feeling well."

Liam frowned. "I've known you for a long time, *pawee*. I think I know when you're hiding something from me. No secrets, remember?"

Aw, fuck. Couldn't I just have one?

But he was right. We agreed to that when we got back together.

"No secrets," I agreed with a sigh. "The thing is, Liam... I still want kids."

A look of guilt crossed his face— like he thought it was all his fault. He opened his mouth to say something, but I cut him off.

"I know that we can't," I said quickly. "And I stand by what I said before. I would give up having kids for you. I know we can't have kids the *traditional* way..."

It was heartbreaking to say. Somewhere deep inside of me, I still wanted to carry a baby. I wanted to feel it kick and go through the joys and wonder of welcoming a child into the world. I knew logically it'd never happen between us, but part of me still couldn't accept that.

"But," I continued. "Maybe we can still have them somehow."

Liam furrowed his brow. "What are you suggesting, Sophia?"

I straightened up in my chair as the possibilities of our future started coming at me full-speed. "We could adopt."

Liam's eyes brightened for a second, but the light in them quickly faded as his lips turned down into a frown. "I don't know if the tribe would allow that, *pawee*."

Tears pricked at my eyes. "But interhouse relationships are legal now. Why wouldn't we be allowed?"

Liam looked me in the eyes with heavy sorry. "Because, Sophia. We're Biyami."

The word felt like a slap in the face. I hadn't considered it, but the way things were going, Liam had a point. We'd already been branded for what we were. To think the Elders would approve us for an adoption was ludicrous. But then again, we once thought the tribe would never let us be together, and we'd made it happen.

"We'll have to change that, then," I said.

Liam's lips tightened. It was hard to read his features— like he was holding back his reaction.

"We already changed the Elders' decision on interhouse relationships," I pointed out. "We can change this, too."

He sighed and squeezed my hand tighter. "People died in the name of interhouse relationships, Soph."

The reminder was like a stab to the gut. He didn't have to finish what he was saying for me to get it. *How many more will have to die for this?*

Tears sprang to my eyes before I could stop them. I quickly dashed them away, but it was too late. Liam leaned in closer and wrapped an arm around my shoulder. His scent surrounded me, making me feel just a little less alone.

"I'm so sorry, *pawee*," he whispered.

"It's fine," I said quickly, my voice cracking.

"It's not fine." He took my chin and forced me to look at him. "This clearly matters to you."

I swallowed the lump in my throat as I stared him in the eyes. "It's not your fault, though. There's nothing you can do. Nothing *we* can do."

"Can I at least cheer you up?" he asked.

I sniffled and wiped the tears away, then nodded. "What did you have in mind?"

Liam glanced down to the dragon egg in my lap. Then he stood and held his hand out. "Follow me."

Liam led me outside the castle. It was the end of January and cold, but I still had my coat on from earlier. Light flurries of snow coated the ground. I carried my basket close to me as we walked. Esis sat on top of the egg, keeping it warm as chill wind blew his fur around. Liam didn't seem to mind the cold, since he was so used to the ocean.

"Where are we going?" I asked as we started up a hiking trail.

"Do we need a destination?" Liam replied.

I shrugged. "No, I guess not. It's good to just get out sometimes. Thanks, Liam."

He smirked from beside me. "Don't thank me yet. It just so happens that we *do* have a destination today. So, tell me about your dragon egg."

I looked into the basket and pulled the cloth tighter around the egg. "I don't know much about it yet. We're supposed to take care of them until they hatch at the end of the semester."

"Have you given it a name yet?" He nudged me with his shoulder.

I offered a slight smile. "I just got it less than an hour ago. You're rushing me."

He playfully held his hands up in surrender. "No rushing. Just curious."

"I bet it's a fire dragon, though," I said. "Since the egg is red. In Dragonology, we learned they could be any color, but that's just my instinct."

"You have good instincts," Liam complimented. "So I bet you're right."

I blushed. "How much farther?"

"Not far."

The farther we climbed the mountain, the colder it got, until it started snowing. And these weren't the small, flurry snowflakes like the ones down at the castle. They were so big that I could see the unique design of each one as they floated through the air. It was usual in this part of California. The path began to disappear as smooth mounds of snow overtook the ground. The forest quickly turned into a winter wonderland. Snow rested on evergreen trees, and icicles hung from their branches. Everything was covered in white and glittered like diamonds. It was like something straight from a Christmas movie.

"Are you doing that?" I asked Liam as I gazed around the forest in wonder.

"Doing what?" he asked.

"Turning the water in the air to snow." I reached out and caught a snowflake. Esis turned his nose toward the sky and tried to catch the flakes on his tongue. "This seems magical."

"It is, but I'm not the one doing it," Liam stated confidently, like he knew exactly where the snow was coming from.

Then I spotted them. The trees parted, giving way to a wide clearing filled with snow. Straight in front of us was a cave opening twenty-feet tall with long icicles hanging down from it. But the most beautiful part of it were the dragons.

Ice dragons of all different sizes frolicked through the clearing. Each had white or blue scales, and some had purple horns. Baby dragons chased each other around and stumbled through the air, barely able to fly. Other smaller ice dragons blew streams of snow at each other playfully. The largest ones sat near the tree line, looking completely at peace as they watched their children play. There must've been at least thirty dragons in this one clearing.

I drew a breath and held it, unable to focus on my breathing as I took in the wondrous sight. "Liam, they're beautiful."

"Remember Eirakari, Maddie's Familiar?" he asked.

I nodded.

"This is where she came from." Liam beamed as he pushed a branch of an evergreen aside and led me into the clearing. "Do you want to know the sex of your baby?"

My body tensed. "What?"

He looked horrified for a second, as if he'd just realized what he said. He quickly glanced down to the basket in my hand.

"The baby dragon," he clarified. "The ice dragons can tell. They hold their own gender-reveal ceremonies for their clan. If it's a male, they'll turn their heads up to the sky and blow snow to celebrate. If it's a female, they'll create an ice wall around the egg to protect it."

"That sounds really cool."

"Come on." Liam held his hand out to me, and we stepped fully into the clearing.

Around us, the dragons turned their heads and slowed, keeping a close watch on us. They didn't seem afraid, though— just curious. Esis waved as we made our way through the snow toward the largest dragon of them all. He looked old, with a wisdom in his eyes and blue horns larger than all the others. He kept his eyes on us the entire time, but seemed relaxed as he lay casually beside the cave.

Liam bowed his head when we stopped in front of the elder ice dragon. I did the same, as I'd learned in my Dragonology class. The ice dragon bowed back, accepting our arrival.

Liam didn't say anything, so I followed his lead and remained silent. I knelt in front of the creature and set my basket down, then pulled Esis out of it and placed him on my shoulder.

The dragon bowed his head to sniff the egg. He eyed it carefully, assessing it with great care. All around us, the other dragons closed in as they watched curiously. The moments ticked by slowly as the cold air seeped into my bones. I hugged Esis tighter and brought my Fire to the surface of my skin to warm myself.

"How long does it take?" I whispered to Liam.

"Shh..." he replied gently.

Minutes passed. Just when I thought the ice dragon had given up, he turned his head toward the sky. A beautiful sound came from his mouth — it was a lot like a roar, but in joy. Snow shot from his nose and fluttered down all around us. The other dragons in the clearing started dancing and kicking up snow, sharing the same roar-like sound.

My heart warmed, and a smile spread across my face. "It's a boy!"

"It is." Liam beamed. He turned back to the ice dragon and bowed again.

The ice dragon nodded once, like he understood Liam and accepted his gratitude.

"Thank you," I told the dragon, before bending to retrieve my basket and dragon egg. Liam and I left the clearing. I was grateful to be back to warmer trails.

"Thank you for taking me, Liam," I said as we walked. "That was really cool."

Liam looked proud. "What are you gonna name him?"

I took a deep breath, contemplating the question. There was a name I'd had picked out for years, but I'd been saving it for my own son. Now that I knew that was never going to happen, it seemed a shame to waste.

Part of me was happy the dragon was a boy. The girl's name I'd picked out for my own daughter was too precious to give away.

I looked up to Liam. "His name is Julian."

"Julian," Liam repeated thoughtfully. "I like it."

I offered a shy smile, but deep down, giving away the name felt like a betrayal.

❦

I WAS surprised at how quickly I warmed up to Julian. He hadn't even hatched yet, and already I felt an attachment to him. It was the name. It had to be.

Esis seemed just as pleased. He slept in the basket that night and hissed at anyone who got too close to the egg. Imogen tried to touch the egg in the Biyami dorms, and Esis nearly bit her hand off. He was still a child himself, and already he was acting like a dad.

The next day, I placed Julian inside my backpack, because he was easier to carry around that way. Esis protested and tried to unzip my bag so he could sit beside the dragon egg. Eventually, the only way to calm him was to open the bag and let him sit inside with his head poking out the opening.

I had Fundamentals of Familiar Magic that morning and Intermediate Koigni Magic that afternoon. Like every semester, I wasn't looking forward to Koigni Magic, but this year was worse. Unlike Liam's Water class he'd told me about, there weren't enough Koigni sorted into Biyami to have a separate class. Instead, we sort of formed our own group, since the rest of the class looked down our noses at us.

Doya didn't say anything about it. She acted as if the sorting never happened, but we could feel the tension from our other classmates.

There were only three of us— Taylor, Tabitha, and me. Taylor still blamed me for the whole dual-House system, which meant Tabitha was stuck in the middle of us trying to keep the peace, since Taylor refused to team up with me. Doya must've caught on, because she started teaming people up deliberately so no one would be left without a partner.

That day, Doya had paired up Haley and Taylor. Haley bossed her around the entire time and bitched about how she was doing it wrong. We were supposed to work with our teammate by transferring flames from one log to another. Taylor completed the task before Haley, which only pissed her off.

"You can't seriously think I believe you did that on your own," Haley snarled. "You didn't transfer the fire. You just killed it and started a new one on the other log. A total simple task, though maybe not for a *Biyami*. It doesn't surprise me you cheated, considering how weak you are."

By the end of class, Taylor was almost in tears. My stomach sank for her as we gathered our bags at our desks. We were the last two left in the room.

"Hey, Taylor," I said gently.

She didn't even look up as she shoved her books into her bag. She ducked her head, letting her curls mask her face.

"Haley's not worth it." I tried to be reassuring.

She swung her bag over her shoulder and flipped her hair. She tugged her long sleeve down over her tattoo. "Thanks, but I think I can handle myself."

My chest felt heavy. I was only trying to be nice. "Well, if you ever need help, don't hesitate to ask, okay?"

Taylor looked at me like she didn't take the offer seriously. "Got it."

She turned and headed out of the room. I stayed close, because we were both headed back to the Biyami dorms. As we rounded the corner to the next hallway, Taylor slowed as she caught sight of Haley standing there around her posse. Haley noticed us and turned her lips into a sneer.

"Move along, Biyami losers," she said, waving her hand at us.

Taylor kept walking but mumbled under her breath, "Screw you."

"*What* did you just say to me?" Haley yelled it so loud that everyone in the crowded hall quieted to look at her. Even the Task Force members took notice, but they didn't move forward to do anything. Haley didn't care that all eyes were on her.

Taylor whirled around, fuming. "I said, *screw you.* You think you're better than me because you're Defortai?"

Haley crossed her arms, looking amused. "No, bitch. I *know* it. There's a reason you're called the weaker House."

"That is *it!*" Taylor screamed. She lunged for Haley, her nails aimed straight toward her face.

Haley was quick to fight back. She threw a fireball at Taylor's head, and when that missed, shoved her fingers into Taylor's curls and started tugging. Taylor shrieked.

Esis clung tightly to my back from where he sat atop my bookbag. I glanced around, waiting for the Task Force members to step in, but they kept their distance. Haley's posse had surrounded the fight, and Kelsey had begun a chant to fight.

A few onlookers had scattered, but most had stopped to watch. Fire heated my skin, but I couldn't bring myself to move. I stood frozen in place, watching the scene in horror. It barely felt like I was in my own body.

I didn't even notice my friends and their Familiars had entered the hallway until I felt a pair of hands on my shoulders, shaking me.

"Sophia!" Liam's face came into view, blocking my line of sight. Screams continued to fill the hall. "What happened?"

I shook my head, unable to answer.

"Should we step in?" Imogen sounded nervous. Jonah looked just as conflicted beside her.

Before any of us could move, the sound of footsteps pounding down the hall reached us. We all turned to see Levi racing toward Haley and his sister. Levi grabbed Haley by the shoulder and dragged her off Taylor. Blood dripped down Taylor's face as she clutched her nose, and a red burn mark marred her cheek.

"Get off her!" Levi shouted to Haley as he shoved her.

Haley went stumbling backward into her friends, her dark hair a wild mess around her. Three Koigni guys caught her. Another stepped up to Levi, cracking his knuckles. Kelsey's jaguar Familiar growled at Levi. Haley's phoenix, Anwara, flapped her wings in protest, but Haley shoved her Familiar back with her foot.

"It's cool, guys," Haley said, holding up her hands to her friends. "I've got this."

She whirled on Levi, who was helping Taylor to her feet. "Who the hell do you think you are?"

"Me?" Levi snapped. "You're the one picking fights with my little sister."

Haley crossed her arms. "She thinks she's so tough? Why can't she defend herself?"

"I can!" Taylor quickly formed a fireball in her hand.

Levi stepped in front of her and signaled her to calm down.

Haley's features darkened. "Looks like she *was* sorted into the right House, considering she needs her big brother to step in to save her."

"That's what family does," Levi growled. "Seems to me that makes us stronger than you. You don't know how to stick with anyone."

Haley narrowed her eyes. She was on the brink of exploding. "Then why do I have more friends than you?"

She gestured to the group of Koigni behind her.

Levi scoffed. "Please. You think they actually *like* you? You're too selfish, Westfenix. All you care about is yourself. It's why I broke up with you. It's why you killed your teammates in the tournament."

That was the moment Haley lost it. "Fuck you, Levi!"

She shoved Levi hard in the chest. He went stumbling backward and tripped over Taylor. They both fell onto the ground. Haley swung her foot into Levi's gut, and he grunted in pain.

"You couldn't... get me off... anyway!" Haley snarled between every kick.

"Stop it!" Taylor cried— literally *cried*. She'd gotten to her feet, and tears streamed down her face.

Three of Haley's guys had surrounded Levi and were helping her beat the shit out of him. Kelsey cheered from the sidelines, along with several other Defortai onlookers. Taylor tried to make a move on Haley, but Haley signaled to her posse. The three guys turned and aimed fireballs at her in warning. Taylor took a step back, unable to do anything to save her brother. My whole body shook as I watched helplessly. It was like watching the night of the riots all over again.

"Get up, Levi!" Haley leaned over him and taunted. When he tried to push himself to his elbows, she slammed her shoe into his face. A dark bruise began to form below his eye. "I thought you were strong! Prove it!"

He rolled over, groaning in agony, and aimed his palms up at her. Before he could summon a fireball, she shot her own Fire at him. He shrieked as the flames spread across his clothes and overtook his body.

Taylor's knees buckled beneath her, and she fell to the ground shaking. "You bitch!"

Haley didn't even notice. She leaned over Levi, taunting him as he screamed in pain as the Fire enveloped his form. Why weren't the Task Force stepping in? What the fuck was going on in this school?

I couldn't watch. I turned my face into Liam's chest, and he wrapped an arm around me. But even when I tried to pretend it wasn't happening, the screams continued.

"A real Koigni can't die by Fire!" Haley yelled above the agonized cries of Taylor and Levi. "Fight back, Levi! Prove how strong you are!"

I didn't know how long it took. It seemed like forever yet, only one moment. But at some point, Levi's pained screams ceased, and Taylor's cries turned into wails of grief. Liam's arms shook around mine. I wasn't sure I even knew what happened until the chanting stopped and the hall went dead silent.

Blinking, I lifted my face from Liam's chest. Had he not been holding me up, I would've crumbled to my knees. Levi's body was charred to the bone— so much that it barely looked like a body anymore. His features were completely unrecognizable as red and black skin hung off his bones.

Haley stared down at his burnt, unmoving form in shock. It was clear she hadn't intended to actually kill him. She slowly took a step back, distancing herself from her crime. When it hit her that this was real— that she'd murdered Levi— she looked up at the crowd, as if calculating how many witnesses had seen.

Her eyes met the Task Force members, who hadn't moved an inch since it all began. She relaxed. She knew she'd get away with it, because she was Defortai and he was Biyami.

She cleared her throat. "Fuck him. He should've been strong enough to save himself."

Then she turned and strolled away. Her entourage hesitated, glancing between Haley and Levi. Even Anwara didn't move right away.

"Let's go!" Haley snapped.

They all quickly followed behind her, looking terrified. They just left the body sit there... like it didn't matter.

"I hope you burn in hell, Haley!" Taylor screamed across the hall.

Haley whirled back toward her. "Watch your mouth, Taylor, or you'll be next."

Taylor's mouth snapped shut, and Haley walked off, looking proud of herself. The rest of the crowd slowly started to leave, and whispers filled the hall.

Taylor crawled over to Levi's body and reached out for him. Her hand just hovered there. She couldn't bring herself to touch her brother's body.

"Should we do something?" Jonah asked softly.

I nodded, holding back the lump in my throat. Liam dropped his arms from around me, and I stepped forward to place a gentle hand on Taylor's shoulder. She shrugged me off, barely acknowledging I was there.

I knelt beside her. "Taylor."

She wiped the tears from her cheeks, but they kept on coming. I glanced to the Task Force members, who had finally started moving again. They were talking amongst themselves, as if discussing a course of action.

"Taylor, the school officials will be here soon," I told her.

"It all just happened so fast," she said with a sniffle. "I— I can't believe..."

She trailed off as sobs took over.

My friends came up behind me, looking as broken as ever.

"I meant what I said, Taylor," I told her. "If you need anything..."

Taylor nodded. "I— I need to go somewhere safe. Where Haley can't find me."

My friends and I all exchanged a glance. I knew we were all thinking the same thing. *The Anichi dorms.* Before we could say anything about it, a voice came from down the hall.

"Everyone out of the way!" Alric rushed through the crowd with a group of Task Force members behind him. One of them carried a body bag. Alric knelt on the other side of Levi's body, looking horrified. It took him a second to find his voice.

"I'm going to have to ask the five of you to step back," he told us.

"No," Taylor said firmly. "This is my brother!"

"This is a tragedy," Alric reminded her softly. "We will do everything we can to honor your brother, Miss Meyers. But he's gone to the ancestors now."

I helped Taylor to her feet. She barely seemed like she was paying attention to where I was leading her as she watched her brother's body being moved into the bag. Alric seemed distressed. Liam motioned to me, and I began dragging Taylor away.

"We need to get Taylor *somewhere safe*," Liam stated firmly, once we were far enough away from the Task Force.

I looked up to him. "Are you sure we want to take her there?"

"We don't have a choice," Jonah said. "It's the only place."

"What are you talking about?" Taylor asked through her tears.

"You'll see," Imogen whispered. "Keep walking."

Sassy and Squeaks hurried on ahead, leading the way to the third floor. Ahead of us, Imogen and Jonah whispered quietly.

"What's up with Sophia?" Imogen hissed— like she thought I couldn't hear her.

"Beats me," Jonah replied. "I thought Haley was her one exception."

"I know. Usually she'd go berserk over this kind of thing," Imogen said.

The lump in my throat grew bigger. They were right. I'd never been afraid to confront Haley before. I didn't know what was wrong with me.

Jonah turned to Taylor while we walked. "We'll keep you safe. But in return, you have to keep this a secret."

Taylor was still shaking. "I'll do anything."

The third-floor hallway was empty, so we slipped into the Anichi tower without being seen.

"I thought this tower was off-limits," Taylor said as we climbed the twisted staircase.

"It is," I said. "Which makes it the perfect place to hide someone who doesn't want to be found."

Taylor looked amazed as we entered the common room. Her gaze flickered up to the high ceiling, then over to the beautiful windows and across the ornate fireplace. "Ancestors. It's the Anichi dorms."

"See why we keep it a secret?" Imogen asked.

Taylor stopped in the middle of the room and glanced down to her knotted hands. "Thank you, guys, but I don't think I can stay here."

"Why not?" Liam asked. "Haley won't find you here."

Taylor's bottom lip trembled. "Yeah, but what about in class? Sooner or later, Haley will find some reason to do to me what she did to my brother."

"What are you suggesting?" I asked. "That you leave Orenda Academy?"

Taylor's fearful eyes met mine. "I need to leave Kinpago all together."

I gaped at her. "But what about your Familiar? You still haven't bonded. And your parents?"

She dropped her head. "My parents died during the riots. Levi was all I had left."

My heart sank. "Taylor, I'm so sorry."

Liam looked concerned. "Where will you go?"

Taylor wiped at her eyes. "I have an aunt who lives in Southern California. I'll visit her for a while. I just need to get out of the castle."

"Okay." I was completely on board with her decision. It was the best option to keep her safe. "We'll get you a carriage and—"

"No." Taylor's hand shot out. She grabbed my arm, squeezing it hard. Esis growled at her from my shoulder. "I can't go back down there. If Haley sees me, she might... she might..."

Sobs broke out in Taylor's chest again.

"Then we'll wait until nightfall," Liam suggested.

Taylor wiped at her nose. "With the Task Force roaming the halls?"

"How else are we going to get you out, Taylor?" I asked. I wasn't sure exactly what she wanted from us. "And what about all your stuff?"

"Honestly, I don't need anything." She gestured to her backpack. "I have everything I need."

Squeaks was stomping her hooves and shaking her head, shooting a pointed expression at Jonah. He exchanged a glance with Imogen, and they both looked a little guilty.

"What is it?" Liam asked. It was clear they were hiding something from us.

"Well..." Imogen twisted her skirt fabric around in her fingers. "We might have another way."

I furrowed my brow. "Another way?"

Imogen looked to Jonah again, like she was uncertain. "We're not sure if it'll work, but we should at least try it."

"Try what?" Liam demanded. He sounded irritated that they were keeping something from us.

Jonah sighed. "A few months ago, while Imogen and I were up here cleaning by ourselves, we found a secret passageway in one of the dorm rooms. We never got to see where it led, but maybe..."

"Maybe it leads out of the castle," Liam finished for him. "Then we have to try it. Show us."

"I want to get out of here as fast as I can," Taylor added.

Jonah nodded. "Follow me."

He led us down a long hallway off the common room. We hadn't cleaned up all the dorm rooms, so some places were still covered in a thick layer of dust. Jonah led us into a room with a tall wardrobe against one wall and a small wooden door beside it.

I stared at the door. "Why didn't you guys tell us about this?"

Jonah shrugged. "It was just cool at the time. We didn't think it'd be important."

"Come on." Imogen cocked her head. "Let's go."

Behind the door was a long, dark hallway. Taylor and I both lit flames in our palms to light the path. The hall ended at another doorway. Taylor reached for the handle and jiggled it, but it didn't open.

"Step back," Jonah warned.

We all did as he said. He backed up a few paces, then went running at the door full-force. His shoulder slammed against it, but nothing happened. He groaned and clutched his shoulder.

"Maybe we should look for a key," Liam suggested.

Jonah waved his hand. "Nah, bro. I got this."

He ran for the door again. This time, the lock gave way. Jonah flew through the doorway, screaming in surprise. I expected to hear him hit the ground on the other side. Instead, I heard several thumps, one right after the other.

I rushed forward to see what had happened, only to come upon a narrow, twisted stairwell. Jonah lay with his head on one step and his legs propped uncomfortably on the wall beside him.

"Ow," he groaned breathlessly as he tried to right himself. He finally got to his feet and rubbed his sore neck. "Let's see where it goes."

Squeaks promptly followed behind him, but Jonah paused as he eyed the darkness in front of him.

"I'll go first," I offered, pushing past him. Jonah didn't like tight spaces. The least I could do was light the way. Everyone else followed behind me.

The stairwell wasn't large, just big enough for one person at a time.

But the stairs seemed to never end, constantly twisting like a corkscrew as we descended.

"Maybe this goes down to the dungeons," Taylor theorized after a few minutes.

Behind me, I could hear Liam breathing heavily. These stairs were obviously taking their toll on him.

"I guess we won't know until we reach the bottom," I said.

It seemed like we never would, though. Several minutes passed by, and there was still no end in sight.

"Is this creeping anyone else out?" Jonah asked in fright.

"Of course not," Imogen said. "It's an adventure."

Jonah grumbled, "I'm a bit sick of adventures."

At last, I spotted a level surface at the bottom of the stairs. "I think we've reached the end."

Jonah breathed a sigh of relief. At the bottom, we came to another long hall, but instead of being lined with stone like the staircase was, there were rocks and dirt all around us. It reminded me of the caves I'd explored in my Elementai Explorations class last semester. The passageway stretched far back, turning into nothing but darkness beyond the light of my flame.

"What is this?" Imogen asked in wonder as she reached the bottom.

I touched the rocks along the dirt walls curiously. From my shoulder, Esis reached out and ran his paws across them, too. They were cold and a little slimy.

"I think this is part of the cave system that runs under Kinpago," I said.

Imogen looked upward, then stepped near the wall. She placed her hands on the rock and closed her eyes to concentrate. We all held still while she did so.

Finally, she opened her eyes. "I'm not sure. We're definitely underground, but this feels different. I can't feel this passageway connect to any other tunnels."

"We should check anyway," Liam said. "If we find another tunnel, we can get Taylor out through one of the caves."

Jonah looked nervous. "Or we can just go back upstairs? Come up with Plan B?"

Taylor stepped forward. "Sorry, but no. If this tunnel gets me out, I'm taking it."

Well, we couldn't argue with that.

I cocked my head. "Let's go, then."

The tunnel seemed to go on forever. Five minutes of walking turned into ten, then twenty.

"Guys, I don't think this is going to work," Jonah complained. "There's nothing here. We could be walking for days."

"Or there could be something a hundred yards up," Taylor shot back.

Jonah stopped, and the rest of us slowed. "If you want to keep walking, fine. But I can't stand this anymore."

He turned, but Imogen stepped in front of him and placed a hand to his chest. Beside her, Squeaks huffed at him in protest. They stared each other down for a moment.

Jonah didn't look pleased, but he finally said, "Fine. But the rest of you are paying for my therapy."

We continued on for another ten minutes until the tunnel suddenly ended. There was a huge boulder placed right at the end. I glanced around for tunnels branching off, but I didn't see any.

"That's weird," I observed.

"See?" Jonah sighed. "Useless. Time to go back."

"Hold on," Imogen insisted.

"What the hell?" Taylor whispered, trying to calculate it all in her head. "Caves don't just end like this. They have to go somewhere."

Liam pressed a finger to his lips, thinking. "It's like this tunnel was put here deliberately, instead of naturally formed."

Imogen stepped up to the stone again and placed her hands on the rocks. She drew in a sharp breath.

"What?" Jonah asked quickly. "What is it?"

"We're really close to the surface, guys!" She sounded excited. "I mean, we could basically dig our way out."

I glanced upward, and that's when I saw it. Several boards had been placed in a neat row above the massive boulder— like they'd been put over an opening. The boards were at least twelve-feet long, making the opening big enough for even some of the largest Familiars to fit through.

"Look!" I pointed. "It's a trap door."

"Thank the ancestors." Jonah pushed past me and climbed onto the rock. There was only enough space between the rock and the ceiling of the cave for him to kneel. He placed his hands firmly on the trap door and pushed. Nothing happened.

He sighed and dropped his arms. "It's super heavy. I bet it's grown over."

Imogen swatted at him to get down. "Here, let me try."

Jonah frowned, but he climbed off the boulder anyway. "Sweetheart, if I can't lift that thing, you can't either."

Imogen ignored him and climbed up anyway. Sassy jumped onto the boulder behind her. Imogen closed her eyes again and placed her hands flat above her head onto the boards. We waited in silence for several seconds, then she stood straight up. The door moved with her, flipping open to give way to a chill breeze and bright sunlight. There were two doors that met in the middle, like the entrance to a cellar.

Jonah's jaw dropped. "How'd you do that?"

Imogen knelt back down to look at us and shrugged. "There were roots in the way. I used my magic to move them. Come on."

Imogen crawled out of the hole, then reached down to help Sassy out. Jonah was quick to climb onto the boulder behind her, and he and Squeaks hurried into open air. Taylor followed, then me and Liam. Esis took a deep breath once we were outside.

I glanced around. We were in the middle of the forest. It was quiet, and a small dusting of snow layered the ground. I didn't recognize the area, so I had no idea how far away from the castle we were.

Taylor breathed a sigh of relief. "Thank you all for helping me."

"Will you be all right on your own?" Liam asked.

"I'll be fine," she assured him. "I can hitch a ride and be to my aunt's by the end of the week. I'm just glad to be getting out of here."

"Stay safe," I told her.

She nodded. "I will. And... Sophia? I'm sorry I blamed you for the tribe dividing. I know it's not your fault. I just..."

She choked up again.

"I know," I said quickly. "I get it."

She sniffled, then nodded. "Well, I guess it's time for me to go."

"Yeah," I agreed. "You get out of here, Taylor. Run, and never look back."

"Believe me, I don't plan on it," she said.

And that was it. Taylor waved, and she was off, running through the forest without so much as a glance back at us— just like I told her to do.

When we could no longer see her, I felt like I could breathe again. It wasn't much in this war against the Elders, but at least we managed to save one person. That filled me with a sense of pride.

Liam turned to the trapdoors and rounded them, inspecting them from every angle. There was moss and dried leaves caked onto the doors, completely hiding the wood. If we shut them, no one would even notice they were there. The only way we'd find them again would be from the big boulder that sat close by.

"Guys, I think we can use this," Liam said, still staring down at the doors.

Imogen furrowed her brow. "What do you mean?"

"These doors are concealed incredibly well," he pointed out. "I bet no one could find them even if they tried."

"And?" Jonah raised an eyebrow.

Liam stopped pacing and looked up to us. "We saved Taylor, but what if she's not the only one who *needs* saving?"

I got what he was saying instantly. I stepped up to stand beside him. "I agree. If anyone else needs a way out, we'll help them. And this is how we do it."

"Agreed," Imogen said immediately.

Jonah nodded. "I'm in... as long as I don't have to escort them through that tiny tunnel."

I slipped my fingers into Liam's. He gave me a firm nod, like we'd just come up with something incredible. And we had.

Somehow, without realizing it, we'd just launched our first mission in a smuggling operation we never intended to create.

iam

FIVE

The Anichi dorms had become our way to fight back. We couldn't stand up to the Elders in public. But we could defy them in secret by smuggling people out of the school, before they were brutally killed.

It was only a few days after we'd helped Taylor escape. No one else had needed our help just yet, but still, I felt confident. We'd actually made a difference, and we could do it again. If anyone needed a way out, we'd have one. Now it was just a matter of identifying those students who were most likely to become targets, and getting them out before anything bad happened to them.

Screw Oleander, the Task Force, and anyone else who wanted to put the Biyami in their place. We weren't going down unless we were taking them with us.

Around three o'clock on Wednesday, I headed to Hawkei Art to find Jonah, Sophia, and Imogen already there. They'd already pushed our four desks together to make our usual cluster in the middle of the room.

We'd all signed up to take Art together, because it was a blow-off class and the last chance for us to hang out together before I graduated. Jonah and Imogen were currently debating on if nipple piercings were "in" or not. Sassy sat on Squeaks' head and preened her feathers. Squeaks' eyes were half-closed, as if she was enjoying the experience.

On the other side of the desks, Sophia played with Esis and mostly stared off into space. I sat beside her and gave her shoulder a squeeze. She grimaced back. Esis shook his fluffy tail and scowled, as if to tell me whatever he was doing to try and cheer Sophia up wasn't working.

"Hello, everyone! I am *so* pleased to have you all here on this beautiful rainy evening!" Professor Amber sang as she spun into the room. The hippie beads around her neck jingled as her tiered skirt billowed all around her. Today, she was wearing so many bangles on her arms I wondered how she lifted them.

Professor Amber had been sorted into Biyami, obviously. The Defortai didn't want to touch her.

She gave me a huge grin as she passed my desk and patted my head. "Liam! I am exceptionally pleased to see that you've made it into my den of desire! Thank you for joining us today on our trek of awareness and understanding."

As if I didn't show up every day. Imogen and Jonah giggled. Even Sophia managed to lift a smile.

Professor Amber was thrilled to have me, as I'd taken all of her Basket Weaving courses. I was probably her favorite student. Her orangutan Familiar was currently flinging paint on a canvas at the head of the classroom, a beret on its head. The painting looked like a lot of random lines to me, but hey, I was no art critic.

"Are you *sure* Professor Amber doesn't want to fuck you?" Jonah asked under his breath as Amber trailed away from our table.

This had become a thing in our group over the past month, debating on if Amber wanted to screw me or not. "I've told you guys, she's just weird," I hissed back.

"Weird for you," Imogen added, and Jonah cracked.

Sophia wasn't even listening. She continued to stare at the chalkboard, as if she didn't even hear us.

It hurt me to see. She couldn't even join in on the joke. *Please, Sophia, don't go there.*

But she already was. I felt like she was lost to me lately. She'd been even more distant since Haley had murdered Levi. It'd really taken a toll on her. I mean, you didn't get over seeing someone being burned alive in front of you, but the rest of us were at least trying to cope with it as best we could.

Sophia was imploding.

Professor Amber blew one note on a wooden flute before she said, "Once again, I am thrilled to see you all enter into this cavity of pleasure. I hope we can travel together through this experience of enlightenment." Professor Amber beamed.

"I'm not letting her into *my* cavity of pleasure," Jonah whispered, and Imogen snickered.

"This is the biggest Hawkei Art class I've ever had. I'm gleeful to be able to share my wealth of knowledge with you." Amber paused before she said, "Though I know for some of you, it was not an option."

A chorus of mumbles uttered lowly around the classroom. All of us had been sorted into the weaker tribe. It was clear that Art had been defined as a Biyami subject. It wasn't the only one. All the literature, creative writing, history, music, and liberal arts courses were deemed "weaker" subjects only taken by the Biyami students. The Defortai were trying to push things like advanced magic, technology, math, and sciences for their tribe. They considered those higher subjects, and more important.

Amber tapped the chalkboard with her flute. "Everyone, please gather your painting supplies and begin to design your work of truth. As you paint today, I will be giving a lecture on the importance of Spirit Art to our culture."

That was weird. Professor Amber never gave lectures. She kinda just threw materials at you and expected you to make something out of it while she walked around, sang songs, and made up bullshit. Even if you did a shit job, she didn't care. It was all about *the journey* to her.

The whole class got up to gather paint, brushes, and canvases from the cabinets lining the walls. Imogen was trying to do a watercolor scene of a forest, while Jonah was working on some ugly Expressionist art that looked like a copy of *The Scream*, except the man was screaming at a dude in a trench coat who was obviously flashing him. Very mature.

I worked on painting a smiley face, because it was all I felt like doing and all I really could do. My talent with art went as far as basket weaving and ended at that.

"Really, Liam?" Imogen said as she caught notice of my painting. "What a work of art."

"It counts." I scowled at her before I glanced down and caught sight of Sophia's painting.

Sophia was the most talented artist out of us all, so her painting actually resembled what her scene was supposed to look like. At first glance, it appeared to be a painting of a giant flame, a mixture of red, orange, and yellow paints.

But if you looked closer, the flames themselves dissolved into shadows and images of people, reaching their hands toward the sky and crumbling into torturous, fiery deaths. The expressions on their faces were clearly ones of horror and pain. Sophia painted the image with a blank expression, though her eyes said something different.

I didn't like her painting. It scared me. *She* was scaring me.

Sassy dipped her tail into the paint and streaked it across her canvas. Squeaks tried to help by drawing designs in the paint with her hoof, but Sassy growled at her, so Squeaks resentfully started to stomp all over her own painting.

Amber gasped as she came near our desks. She pointed at the floor and said, "Jonah, your Familiar has created the most beautiful piece of art! It's so... tortured and extreme!"

Squeaks' painting resembled nothing more than a crushed, wet mess, but the hippogriff seemed to glow with pride. Jonah patted her shoulder and said, "That's my girl."

Sassy hung her head low and shot resentful glances at Squeaks. Amber hadn't even noticed her complicated Chinese watercolor painting.

Professor Amber clapped her hands and said, "Very well. Spirit Art, the topic of today's class. When you create a piece of art— whether it be a painting, a drawing, a poem, or a basket— you are putting part of yourself into that artwork. If an artist cares enough about their work, the creation of that work can actually take a piece of that person's soul, creating Spirit Art."

I stopped painting for a second. That was interesting. I'd never heard of such a thing before. Apparently, neither had other people, because many paused what they were doing to look up and listen.

Brittney— a Toaqua girl with a pink alicorn Familiar who'd been sorted into Biyami— raised her hand. Amber nodded to her, and Brittney said, "So if you're really, *really* into what you're doing... say, making a drawing... that drawing can actually take a piece of you and preserve it forever?"

"Precisely!" Amber said. "It is a way of retaining an eternal piece of yourself on this earthly plane, even after your spirit joins the ancestors."

"Could someone summon that piece of a person's spirit from the artwork after they're dead?" Brittney asked curiously.

Amber's eyebrows knitted together. "I'm unsure what you're asking."

"Well..." Brittney blushed before continuing. "My grandmother used to make quilts. She loved them. She put so much effort into every stitch. Before she died, she made me a quilt of my own. I... I was just wondering if there was a way to bring that part of her spirit out of the quilt. You know, so I could talk to her."

I felt bad for Brittney. It was clear she missed her grandmother very much. Still, it was a valid question. I bet everyone in this room had someone that had passed on they wanted to bring back. Could Spirit Art do that?

Amber paused, seeming puzzled. "No one has ever asked that question before. But I suppose that in order to contact a spirit through their art, you would have to be considered worthy. Being related to them wouldn't be enough to summon them. Though even if it did happen, it would be considered exceptionally rare."

Brittney frowned and looked down. It wasn't the answer she was looking for.

"I don't think that's the right question." Sandy, a Nivita girl, spoke up. "What I want to know is how someone can tell whether something is a work of Spirit Art, like a book for example, rather than a regular old novel someone wrote just to make money."

"It's not something that can be known, only felt," Amber explained. "Not all pieces of art are created with the heart and the soul. But some special pieces are, and you can feel it when you experience or see them. Some of the most famous artworks of all time are clearly Spirit Art. It's something our soul recognizes."

"Is it something only Elementai can do?" Sandy asked.

Amber shook her head. "This isn't exclusive to Hawkei. Every magical race has the ability to create Spirit Art. Even non-magical humans can do so, though accidentally, if they put enough love and passion into what they're creating."

"What you're saying is that if you want a piece of your spirit to live forever, you just have to make a painting, put some love in it, and call it good?" some guy in the back asked.

"It doesn't work that way. Spirit Art isn't something that's made intentionally." Amber shook her head. "It just happens during the process of creation itself. Through passion for the craft."

Professor Amber gave me an intense stare right then that made a shudder roll down my spine. I couldn't explain it. She'd never given me such a direct look before.

It was... bizarre.

"The best works of art are created without the destination in mind. Rather, it is the joy of the process that makes the piece special," Professor Amber finished, and her gaze drifted away from me. "For now, let us continue our work in peaceful harmony."

Professor Amber sat at her desk and began playing a quartz singing bowl for ambiance. Jonah and Imogen chatted lowly, though I was deep in thought. Sophia's brows knitted together as she put her entire concentration into painting her ominous scene.

Around five o'clock, we finished up our paintings, and Amber dismissed us. We put them on the racks to dry before it was discussed we should go to the Commons, to see if anyone else wanted to join us for dinner.

Esis was covered in paint. He'd gotten all kinds of colorful splotches all over his white fur. I think he'd done it to try and get Sophia's attention, but it hadn't worked. His paws reached up for her as he sat in her arms, and she didn't even notice.

"I've got you, buddy." I took Esis from Sophia and put him on my shoulder. He put a paw on my cheek, and I felt his healing magic begin channeling through my body. I was glad for that, because my back had really started to hurt.

When we made it up to the Commons, we saw Ezra playing air

hockey with Lindsey. Vanessa and Miranda were gathered around them, cheering for Lindsey to win. Dyami, Medusa, and Miranda's kirin Familiar, Evelyn, watched the puck as it whizzed back and forth on the table.

Air hockey had become the new favorite around campus. Nobody really played ping-pong anymore since Cade had died.

Lindsey sank a goal, and she and Miranda high-fived. Ezra rolled his eyes and groaned, then saw me coming.

"Hey bro," he said lightheartedly. "You wanna play a game? Lindsey is kicking my ass."

"Maybe," I said. "We came to see if you guys wanted to come eat with us."

Ezra went to answer, but before he could, a Task Force member came between us and shoved Ezra and I away from each other. He turned his noxite gun on me. "Defortai students are strongly advised not to associate with those from Biyami," the Task Force member said in a monotone voice.

"He's my brother," Ezra said flatly. His fingers curled, as if he was thinking of summoning a water ball any minute and smashing it into the cop's head. By his side, electricity zapped off of Dyami's feathers. This guy was walking on thin ice.

"Tribal lines are deemed to be thicker than blood, and therefore more important," the Task Force member replied.

Ezra went to say something, but I cut him off. "It's fine, Ez," I told him. "We can just go over there." I gestured to our usual spot in front of the fireplace.

"Biyami students are not allowed to be in the Commons," the Task Force member stated. "Take your business somewhere else."

"We're not even allowed to hang in the Commons anymore?" Jonah said with disgust. "Where *are* we allowed to go?"

"Biyami students are confined to their specific classrooms, a section of the dining hall, certain areas of the gardens, and their dormitory," the Task Force member rattled off. "Defortai students have run of campus as they see fit, though they are discouraged from entering into areas specifically designated for Biyami."

This was total bullshit. They were separating us even more. Ezra put a hand on the Task Force member's chest and said, "I'm going to be the chief of Toaqua. You don't tell me what the fuck to do."

Dyami snapped his beak, and I could see a ball of lightning forming within. This could get ugly quickly. Miranda, Lindsey and Vanessa stood behind him, ready for a fight.

"I suggest you take your hand off me, sir," the Task Force member said calmly. He didn't move to turn the noxite gun on Ezra, though it was clear he meant business.

I didn't want Ezra to get shot. "Never mind," I said bluntly. I backed off. "You guys want to find us, you know where we'll be."

The cop would think we were talking about the Biyami quarters, but I meant the Anichi dorms. The four of them got the hint. Ezra's eyes widened, and he nodded. He stepped away from the Task Force member and turned to the girls. They returned to the air hockey table, huddling together and talking in low voices. Jonah, Imogen, Sophia and I left the Commons and headed downstairs to the dining hall.

"I'm glad soccer season is over," Jonah said glumly as we descended the stairs. "I'm Biyami. I would've been cut from the team. There's not a chance of me getting on the roster next year."

"Don't say that," I said. Yapluma's team went on to win the season last semester, and Jonah had been one of their star players. They wouldn't refuse to let him back on the soccer team because he was Biyami, right?

I had a feeling I was forcing myself to be optimistically naive. I'd been through more than most anyone. I knew how these things went.

"Are there even four soccer teams anymore? Seeing as how the four Houses were split into two?" Sophia asked.

"As far as I know, everything is running mostly like it was. If you're in Defortai, you're still in the same dorms as before," Imogen said. "It's only if you're Biyami that things have changed."

The Biyami section of the dining hall was shit. It was shoved in the corner and composed of all the broken chairs and sticky booths that were in the dining hall. We grabbed one of the better ones before we got our food. It took us over an hour, because we had to let all the Defortai students go ahead of us before we could get anything to eat.

By the time we sat down, I noticed two figures sitting in a booth on the Defortai side of the dining hall. I recognized them instantly— Renar and Mallory, Cade's ex-girlfriend.

Mallory had bonded over break. Her Familiar was a horrible thing. It had green and brown fur that looked like moss that hung limply on its skinny form. Two gray horns took the place of eyes. It had a wide mouth, and a row of jagged fangs still glistening with blood from its meal. It was easily the size of Alvarice, Renar's cockatrice.

A bunyip. They were swamp dwellers. They liked to hide in the murky depths before they came out of the water, sunk their teeth into unsuspecting prey, and dragged them downward to drown. When I watched it walk, it moved in a twitchy way, like a spider.

The bunyip snapped playfully at Alvarice. The cockatrice hissed and preened his feathers. It was the nicest I'd seen the monster act since Renar had bonded with it. The two of them made a creepy pair.

Renar and Mallory were acting all cuddly in the booth. Mallory was practically on Renar's lap, running her hands through Renar's greasy hair. Imogen and Jonah both looked up at the same time, and that's when Mallory decided to kiss Renar.

On the mouth. Tongue and all.

Holy shit. This couldn't be happening. Cade's ex and Jonah's ex, *together*? What a nightmare.

Jonah's hand turned white around his fork, and Imogen gagged. When Mallory finally wrenched her face away from Renar's, she saw us looking and gave a sickly grin. She got up from her booth and deliberately walked over to us. Sassy growled, and Squeaks hissed as Mallory approached. From across the dining hall, Renar watched with an obvious expression of glee written all over his ugly mug.

"Nice to see that the trash has finally been taken out," Mallory said. "I'm glad you four have finally been put where you belong."

"I thought the Elders didn't approve of interhouse relationships," Imogen spat. "Why are you and Renar Defortai? You should've been sorted into Biyami."

"We're not in an interhouse relationship, loser. We're just fucking on the side. The Elders don't care about a little bit of fun," Mallory sneered. "It's clear that both of us are a better lay than Cade and Jonah put together."

Imogen jumped out of her chair, but Sophia grabbed her arm to hold her back.

"Whatever, bitch," Jonah said. He rolled his eyes as he took a sip of his drink. "You can have him. Have fun getting crabs."

Mallory narrowed her eyes, but she didn't have a good enough response, so she walked off. She rejoined Renar in the booth, and she didn't look happy. She yelled at him and shoved his chest while Renar threw his hands up in a bewildered way. It was clear she was interrogating him about having a sexually transmitted infection.

"Cade never even slept with her," Imogen snarled. "She's totally lying."

"She's just trying to get to you, Im. Don't let her," Jonah said darkly. But it was clear he was fuming about Renar, too. He wrenched his gaze away and stabbed his food with more force than was necessary.

Sophia played with her salad for a moment before she stood up. "I need to go for a walk."

She'd barely eaten. "Okay," I started. "Do you want us to come with you?"

"No. I just want to be alone right now." Sophia picked up her tray and dumped the remains in the trash before grabbing her bag and the dragon egg.

She didn't even take Esis. She'd left him with me. He stood on the table and watched Sophia go with a tilted head, confused at why he'd been left behind.

"It's okay, buddy." I picked up Esis and put him into the crook of my arm. "She just needs some space right now. You can hang with me."

His ears flattened against his head. Esis whimpered pitifully and snuggled his head into my chest. Sassy and Squeaks both peeped noises of encouragement.

I stood up to leave, too. I had a meeting with Baine tonight about graduation. I didn't get two steps away from the table before Imogen reached out and grabbed my arm.

"Liam, hold on." Imogen sent a nervous look at Jonah, and both of them stood. "We need to talk to you."

I groaned and whirled around on my heel. "Okay. What about?"

"Your girlfriend," Jonah started. "She's been acting a little..."

"Off? Yes, I've noticed," I said, a twinge of irritation entering my tone. I was probably the first one who had. "So what?"

"*So what?*" Imogen repeated, like she couldn't believe I was being so casual. "Liam, how Sophia is acting is *not normal.*"

"Yeah. Last semester, Haley called Imogen a mean name and Sophia beat the shit out of her," Jonah pointed out. "Now Haley kills Levi right in front of her, and she doesn't even make a move to stop it? It's not like her, Liam."

"There are more consequences now, guys. She can't get away with going after Haley like she did before. It could actually get her killed this time," I said.

"That didn't matter to her during the Elemental Cup," Imogen pointed out. "Or during your trial, or about a million other things she's done since she got here. There have been a dozen situations where Sophia could've lost her life and it didn't matter to her. She always went with what she believed, no matter what the consequences ended up being."

"It's not the same." My voice was nearly a growl. I didn't like how we were talking about Sophia behind her back. I got that they were worried, but they should know better. I'd defend Sophia no matter what, and this was a touchy subject on multiple levels already.

"Liam, I get we're all looking to stop this together, but we. Need. Her." Imogen smacked her hand into her open palm, like she was trying to make a point. "Sophia's the prophesied one. Without her, all of this falls apart."

"Yes, but she doesn't *want* to be," I said harshly. "I'm not going to force her to do something she's not ready for."

"You don't have a choice," Jonah said firmly. "She can't fall apart now. Like it or not, Sophia's the only way we're going to turn this all around. If she goes the way the prophecy says she's going to, Liam, we're all fucked."

I was pretty much fuming by this point. It took all my self control to not shout at them in the middle of the dining hall. "You're her best friend. Why don't you say something?" I asked Imogen.

"She's closer to *you*, Liam. If I try to ask her if she's okay, she'll just shrug me off. It's the same thing she did when you guys were broken up," Imogen said. "She likes to pretend she's strong, but she's breaking, Liam. I've never seen her like this before."

I knew they were right, but it didn't change my mind about my original course of action. "So what do you want me to do?" I asked bluntly.

"Talk to her!" Jonah burst. "She's gotta open up to you! If not, who?"

I took in an impatient breath. "Look. You guys don't know what she's going through. *I do*, because I've been there, and I know what it's like. When she's ready to talk about it, she'll come to me. So back off."

I didn't give them any more time to speak up, because I fucking left. They didn't get it. What Sophia was experiencing right now was fucking hell. And I wasn't going to push her to do something about it until she was ready. Right now, I didn't even think she wanted to admit it. Shit, she still needed time to *process*.

I'd already talked about this to my therapist a few times, and she assured me I was doing the right thing by letting Sophia come to me. When she wanted to talk, she would. I'd just be there for her until then.

"Settle down, people," Professor Baine said as I entered into his Toaqua classroom. There were at least ten Biyami packed in here from Toaqua, plus Familiars. Esis squeaked as I sat down in the back and placed him on top of a desk.

Someone slid into the seat beside me. I looked up and saw blood. It was Wyatt, but he was barely recognizable. He had a black eye, and blood dripped down his face from several cuts and bruises. His face was so swollen it was hard to tell it was him. He held an ice pack over the other eye. At his feet, his walrus Familiar bore several scrapes and marks that were just like his.

"Dude, what the hell happened?" I leaned in to whisper as Baine started distributing papers, blabbing on about ordering caps and gowns.

Wyatt grimaced as he held the ice pack to his face. "You know Micah and I don't get along. I caught him smacking Mia around. Again. They were fighting about wedding plans."

"That son of a bitch." I hadn't seen Mia since I'd lost my shit on Micah last year. I was pretty sure Micah had forbidden her from talking to me. He'd isolated her from almost everyone now.

"I tried to put a stop to it, and he and his Familiar ganged up on me,"

Wyatt said. "You know he's got that... *thing*. And he's Defortai now, so he can get away with whatever he wants. We didn't stand a chance."

Baine glanced at Wyatt's face as he walked by, but he put our papers down and didn't say anything. White-hot rage flooded through my body from my core. How could Baine not do something? We were his students. He was supposed to protect us. I longed for him to make a stand and stop being so passive.

If Baine didn't do something, I would. "That asshole. I'm gonna kill him."

"You go after him, you'll be next." Wyatt moaned as he removed the ice pack to reveal another black eye.

Esis reached out to heal Wyatt, but I snatched him up and stuffed him inside my jacket. Esis meeped uncomfortably. I felt bad for him, but even though Wyatt was a friend, too many people knew about Esis' healing powers already, and Wyatt's injuries weren't bad enough for me to warrant exposing him further. We had to be extra careful now.

"I couldn't help myself, man," Wyatt rattled on. "I just saw her crying, and I had to step in. How can he treat her like that? I could never do that to a girl."

"Me either," I mumbled. I'd rather lose my arms than hit Sophia. It was unfathomable to me.

Wyatt always had a thing for Mia, even when I was dating her. He never made a move, though, because he was my friend. Unlike Micah, the royal asshole. I had the thought quite a few times that Wyatt and Mia should hook up, but as long as Micah was in the way, hell would freeze over first.

I had a thought, and I leaned in closer. "Hey, Wyatt... if you need a way out, you only need to ask. Just let me know."

"You mean... leave the city?" Even though his swollen eye, I caught a glimmer of surprise.

I nodded. "I can get you out of here without being noticed. If that's what you want."

Wyatt hesitated, then shook his head. "I'm not dropping out a few months from graduation just because some prick blacked my eye. I'm staying."

I had a feeling Wyatt was staying for Mia, but I said, "Fine. But if you know anyone else who needs a safe place to go… let's just say I have connections."

Wyatt thought for a moment before he replied, "I don't want to leave. Orenda Academy's my home, and I'm staying until they force me out."

Then his voice dropped to a serious note. "But if you need help with whatever you're doing, I want in. I want to do something to get back at these bastards."

My heartbeat picked up. We were discussing treason, but it needed to be done. If we didn't stand up, who would? "There's not much more I can say right now. Just be ready to move when I need you."

Wyatt nodded, and his Familiar mimicked the movement. "Trust me, Liam. I will be."

&

AFTER THE MEETING, I returned to the Biyami dorms, because there really wasn't anywhere else for me to go. As I walked in, I heard a couple of cheerful shouts. Maddie and Drew were playing a game on the crappy foosball table. Eirakari observed the game in interest while a dog romped at her side. It was only a puppy, with big paws and pointy ears. I guessed the breed had to be German Shepherd. The puppy chewed on a tennis ball before it tossed the toy at Maddie's feet and barked. Maddie laughed as the dog licked her ankle.

"Ace, down," Drew told him, and the dog lay on the floor, his tongue lolling. He had to be Drew's new Familiar. Maddie and Drew laughed as the game increased in intensity. They started rocking the table as they spun the handles. Ace scattered, and Eirakari lifted her wing so she could tuck him against her side.

At least Maddie and Drew were having fun, because it didn't look like anyone else was. Imogen turned the pages of a magazine in boredom, while Jonah played a game on a handheld system he'd snuck in. Everyone else was either talking, trying to nap, or messing around with their Familiars listlessly.

I saw that Sophia had come back, thank the ancestors. She was sitting on the bunk bed, doodling on a sketchpad with some drawing pencils. When she saw me getting close, she snapped the sketchpad shut so I couldn't see what she was drawing.

Okay. That was a little hurtful. I sat beside her on the bunk and brought Esis out of my jacket. "Esis missed you."

Esis crawled from my lap onto Sophia's. He made a purring noise, and his eyes grew wider as he observed her. Sophia stroked his ears and said, "I missed him, too. It wasn't a very fun walk."

"I can't imagine it was." I wanted to put my arm around her, but I didn't know if she wanted to be touched right now, so I held back.

There was a shrieking noise, and both Sophia and I jumped. Imogen had been the one that had screamed. She'd gotten down from her bunk bed to go to the bathroom, only to find a creature in her path.

"Eep! Holy ancestors, it's a giant snail!" Imogen screeched.

It was. Somehow, someway, a snail the size of a small dog was inching its way around the Biyami dormitory. It left a long path of green slime behind it and made slurping sounds as it continued its mindless trail, eye stalks wavering.

"Yuck! Get it out of here," Jonah said in disgust. He held up his dance shoes, which had been slicked full of slime without him noticing. The snail slithered toward him, and Jonah curled up on the bed to avoid it. Squeaks put her beak out to nudge it, and the snail tipped over.

Where had the creature come from? It showed up out of nowhere.

"Don't hurt him!" I heard footsteps as a boy, Second Year probably, came running into the dorm. He was breathless and sweating. "I've been trying to find him all day!"

"How the fuck do you lose a snail?" I wondered aloud. The boy bent down and picked up the giant snail, which made a suctioning noise as it left the stone. Ew. Fucking gross.

"Hudson?" Sophia got off the bunk bed. "What are you doing here? I thought you were sorted into Defortai."

He had to be from Sophia's Koigni class. Hudson turned red and said, "I, uh... I got re-sorted."

"Re-sorted? Can they even *do* that?" Jonah asked.

"Why would they re-sort you?" I narrowed my eyes at Hudson, thinking this was some sort of trap. They'd probably sent him down here to spy on us or something.

"Because of him." Hudson held up the giant snail, which dripped mucus on the floor in thick, nasty globs. "I bonded with him and brought him back to the Koigni dorms, but he kinda made a mess. Chieftess Annette said my assignment was a mistake and I had to move down here."

"What's the snail's name?" Sophia asked.

"Gooby," Hudson said without batting an eye.

"*Gooby*. Are you fucking serious?" I asked scathingly.

"Leave him alone! He said it was his name!" Hudson yelped, and he hugged the snail to his chest like it was something precious.

Never mind. Hudson had been re-sorted because he was freaking annoying and he had a lame-ass Familiar. Looking at Gooby, I was starting to wonder if there really was a difference between Defortai and Biyami.

"Ugh! Gooby!" Imogen had slipped and fallen in one of the snail trails. Jonah got off the bed, tip-toed around the goo and reached out a hand to help her up, while Sassy licked the slime off the floor.

Living in such close quarters with no privacy was starting to wear on everyone, and it was only the start of the semester. I glanced at Sophia. "You wanna get out of here?"

"Please." Sophia shoved her sketchbook under a pillow. She left her dragon egg behind on the floor, though Squeaks, who'd taken a particular liking to the egg, curled up around it to keep it warm. Esis perched on Sophia's shoulder as we walked up the stairs. We could hear Hudson apologizing for Gooby all the way to the first level.

"Where are we going?" Sophia asked.

"There's a place I've been meaning to take you. It's in the Toaqua village," I said.

"Are you sure we're allowed to go there?"

A lot of places in Kinpago had been restricted to Biyami now. We weren't permitted into most public places anymore.

"Over half of Toaqua was sorted into Biyami, so we won't get in trouble there," I said.

"That's weird, considering Oleander is running the show, and he's Toaqua," Sophia mused.

"I... don't think he has any loyalty to his House," I said slowly. "The way Dad tells it, he was never really treated well by Toaqua. Making them all Biyami is his way of revenge. Nobody from the Water tribe really liked him."

"Wonder why," Sophia mumbled.

We took a peryton carriage to the edge of Kinpago. I held Sophia's hand as we walked through the streets. Both of us made sure to keep our heads down and our tattoos pressed closely to our sides. Nobody bothered us, thankfully, but we also didn't dawdle.

On the beach was a large glass dome, connected to the water. A large sign on the top of the building said *Totlissh Station*. People were coming in and out of the building carrying briefcases with Familiars in tow. As we entered the dome, there was the sound of the announcer calling out arrival and departure times over the intercom system, mingled amongst chatter and frequent footsteps. The floors were marble, and stone benches were placed here and there next to a long embanking platform. The platform itself was next to a large glass tube that looked like some sort of tunnel, with a railway in the middle. It stretched out in both directions and went out the left and the right side of the station.

"We'll be safe now." I let go of Sophia's hand and started toward the ticket booth.

"What is this place?" Sophia asked, looking around. Esis poked out of her jacket.

"It's an underwater subway system," I explained. "The train is called the *Totlissh*. It's how most Toaqua get to work from the village, though a lot of people from other Houses ride the train just for the experience. I thought we could get dinner."

"We already ate," Sophia protested. Esis grumbled, as if saying that eating three times a day wasn't nearly enough.

"You didn't eat dinner. You barely took three bites. And I didn't eat, either, because I was busy watching you," I countered.

Sophia withered under my stern stare. "Well... I guess I am hungry."

"That's my *pawee*."

In Kinpago, most places had been separated by Defortai and Biyami — with signs on many stores proclaiming *No Biyami Allowed*. I was relieved to see that the station wasn't like that. It still had only one line to buy tickets and seemed integrated. I wondered how long Toaqua would be able to keep that up before the Elders forced them to change things.

"I need two tickets for the *Totlissh*. Round-trip, presidential cabin," I said. Sophia's eyes widened when I said the word *presidential*.

"Of course." The attendant typed something onto her computer, then handed me two tickets as they came off fresh from the printer. "They're always free for you, Mister Mitoh." The attendant handed me the tickets with a big smile.

"*Aheas ve.*" I took the tickets with a courteous nod, then led Sophia to the embankment platform. The next train was coming in about five minutes or so.

"What did you say to her?" Sophia asked curiously.

"I just told her thank you." I leaned in. "Also, most of the people on this train speak strictly Hawkei, so if you want something, you're probably going to have to ask me to translate."

"Can't they speak English?" she asked.

"Of course they can, but this is *our train*. Toaqua don't like speaking English unless they're talking to other Houses."

"I see." Sophia looked to the left. "I think it's coming now."

There was a loud whooshing noise as a gigantic subway train came hurtling through the large tube. The subway itself was completely made of glass and steel. It had large windows in all the cabins so travelers could look out into the ocean. Doors in the glass tunnel slid open as the subway train came to a screeching stop by the embankment platform.

Sophia went to enter into one of the normal doors, but I stopped her and shook my head. "No, we're over here."

I took her to a different door at the front of the train. There, the conductor stood waiting for us. As we came on board, he reached out to shake my hand.

"Mister Mitoh. Pleasure to have you on board again," the conductor said. "I'll lead you to your cabin."

Sophia gave me a weird look as we entered further into the train. The floor was royal blue carpet, with silver embellishments on the walls. At the end of the hallway were two large double doors, where the conductor was leading us to.

"Everybody seems to know you," Sophia said under her breath.

"This station is run by Toaqua. You forget who I am." I gave her a playful nudge.

The conductor opened the silver doors to reveal the presidential cabin. It was decorated in a very modern way, with marble floors, white furniture, and a mini-bar. There was already a bottle of champagne waiting in a bucket of ice. A dining table had been lit with candles for ambiance, while soft music played on the speaker overhead. Inside, there was a small kitchen, a living room, and a bedroom with its own door attached for privacy off to the side. Sophia's mouth dropped open as she entered the cabin, taking it all in. She took her jacket off and placed it on a chair as she turned in place to observe. A huge window along one wall reached from the floor up to the ceiling.

"Is there anything else I can get for you two? More wine, chocolate, a couple's massage?" the conductor asked.

A couple's massage sounded fantastic, but Sophia shook her head.

"We're fine. Thank you," I said.

"Very well. I hope the two of you enjoy your dinner. Miss Henley."

The conductor bowed to her as he turned on his heel and left. Sophia seemed uncomfortable. She put Esis down on the floor and said, "Does he know me because of the trial, or because I'm connected to you?"

"I mean, I'm the son of the chief, and you're my girlfriend, so..." I shrugged. "I don't know. You've got perks."

Esis scrambled across the tile floors. He ran into the bedroom, jumped on the bed, and grabbed the TV remote. The sound of people screaming at each other and throwing things blared from the speakers.

"He's obsessed with MTV lately," Sophia said, tossing Esis a strange glance as he watched the program with wide eyes. "I don't know what's up with him."

"He's hitting his teenage phase," I joked. Thank the ancestors, she cracked a smile.

Sophia walked around the room. "Bring any other girls here?" Sophia asked with a coy grin.

"I took Mia once, but it wasn't very fun. We fought the whole time."

I shrugged. "She was on her phone a lot. I figured out she was texting Micah."

"Ouch." Sophia winced. "She still hasn't left him, has she?"

"No," I said. "But she will. She'll get tired of his crap eventually."

Sophia seemed doubtful, but she didn't say anything more about it. She stumbled as the train began to move, and I caught her.

"Watch it," I told her. "Don't lose your balance."

I could feel her heartbeat thudding against my chest. Her breasts were pressed up against me, and they were almost falling out of her shirt. Her large brown eyes sucked me in and held me there as she placed her hands against me to steady herself.

My dick jerked in my pants. We hadn't been able to have sex in a while. There was no privacy in the Biyami dorms, and most of the spots in the castle that were secluded enough to mess around in were typically preoccupied with other Biyami couples who had the same idea we did. We'd considered the Anichi dorms, but seeing as how that was supposed to be our new smuggling base, we didn't want to go there unless we absolutely had to.

Dammit, I just wanted to rip her clothes off of her and screw her hard and fast right now...

Nope. Don't get horny now. Not the right time.

I put my hands on her arms instead of her breasts and set her gently on the couch, which was placed next to one of the large windows. I sat beside her, but I couldn't resist letting my fingers trail up and down her thighs. I was a man, not a fucking superhero.

Sophia turned to watch as the water raced by. There were lights on the side of the train that lit up the water as the subway rushed through the open ocean. They illuminated the schools of colorful fish, hundreds of which were in the water. Schools of dolphins swam by, tossing a blown-up pufferfish between them. Sea turtles, giant and regular size, rested on the ocean floor, while sharks swam in circles, waiting to descend on their prey. Sea serpents twirled in the distance, passing by megalodons, kelpies and hippocampi.

A harmonious sound shook the train as a group of humpback whales swam by, singing their song. A baby whale beat its fin to catch up with his mother, and Sophia teared up.

"It's so beautiful," Sophia said. "The sea creatures are all around us."

I ran a hand through her hair. "Look over there." I pointed to a pair of sea serpents, one purple and the other green, and watched as they twirled around each other in the distance. "They're performing a mating ritual."

"Wow," she whispered. "This is better than any movie."

Sophia gasped as a large eye took up most of the window, but I put a hand on her shoulder to tell her it was all right. The eye shrank as it pulled away, revealing a giant squid that had come up to investigate. It was pink in color and at least a hundred feet long. It waved a tentacle in farewell as the train began pulling the other way.

"Liam, this is such an amazing experience," Sophia breathed as she watched a rainbow-scaled fish the size of a dragon swim by.

"I knew you'd like it." I put an arm around her and lounged back against the couch. "Most people are amazed when they take the *Totlissh* for the first time. Even Koigni."

Sophia put a hand against the glass as she watched a seal perform several loops. "You know, Liam, Ancestors' Day is coming up again," Sophia said. "You can talk to Anna. There isn't anything holding you back this time from speaking with your ancestor. She might have answers about your illness, since she went through it herself."

I looked out the window. "I know. It's been on my mind. Now that I have a name for my disease, I can start putting the links together. She might be able to give me some information that'll help find a cure. Or at least make it easier to live with."

"I hope we find a cure." Sophia leaned into me. "I don't want to see you suffer like you do."

"I don't need a cure. I can manage it. All I need is you." I kissed the top of her head.

Ancestors, she smelled so good. I was going to have to wrestle my dick to the floor at this rate.

"We should make a plan this year to celebrate," Sophia said. "I don't want you missing a single moment of the holiday." She paused. "And maybe I can speak to my spirit guides, too. They might have some insight on the prophecy that we're missing. I don't want to skip out on Ancestors' Day again."

"We won't," I promised. "Not this time."

Our server came a short time later. Esis insisted on ordering both a pizza and a hamburger for himself. Sophia ordered scallops, while I got the salmon, as well as strawberries with melted chocolate for dessert. We popped the champagne while we waited for food to arrive.

"I'm not very fancy," Sophia said. "I don't think I've ever been to a place that's this high class before, and I'm wearing jeans." She giggled.

"Simple is nice. It's not complicated." We clinked our glasses together and downed the first glass.

Alcohol didn't help my *little problem*. I was more aroused than ever. Sophia had definitely noticed I was hard, though I'd tried to hide it. She pressed her legs together and wiggled on the couch. I bet she'd already soaked through her panties.

"You look pretty uncomfortable there. Want me to relieve you of your stress, Miss Henley?" I teased. I fingered the edge of her panties inside her jeans. When I tried unzipping her pants, Sophia smacked my arm.

"Stop it." Sophia snickered. "We have to wait. You want the server to walk in on you banging me on the table?"

"I couldn't give a damn at the moment. All I want right now is me buried deep inside of you," I replied.

Sophia blushed. "What about the windows? Some poor whale is going to look inside and be traumatized."

"I've already got a plan for that," I told her. "Just wait."

We watched the sea creatures until our meals arrived— though it wasn't easy to keep our hands off each other. Once the food got here, Esis took his tray and waddled back into the bedroom. He slammed the door shut and clicked the lock behind him. I could hear the volume of the TV increase about ten levels.

"Okay, definitely teenage phase." Sophia laughed out loud as we sat down to eat.

"You shouldn't be bummed. At least now we can get some privacy from the kids," I cracked.

Sophia froze, and instantly, I wish I could punch myself in the face.

Shit. Why did I say that? She'd been so depressed lately about us being unable to have children. She was obsessed with adoption even though we both knew it'd never be possible. I'd allowed her to get her hopes up, because I couldn't bear letting her down. Then I had to go and make a stupid comment like that. I was *such* a great boyfriend.

But Sophia seemed to shrug off my mistake and said, "You know, we've been spending a lot of time with your family lately. When the semester is over, we should go to Utah together, so you can visit mine."

"That's not a bad idea. Though I don't figure your parents would like me much," I said. "Considering the first and only time I met them, I threatened to take you away, report them to the Elders, and throw them in jail."

"Well, first impressions aren't always correct." She took a bite of scallop and wiggled her eyebrows.

"What *do* your parents think about me, anyway? They weren't at the trial," I said.

She shrugged. "I can tell they're a little bitter that you took me away, but they support me. They understand that this is my choice and want me to be happy."

"Do they now?" Hm. If I wanted to make this permanent— in a really, *really* permanent way, I was going to have to patch things over with the in-laws.

Sophia caught sight of the tray of strawberries and snickered. She put her hand over her mouth as she struggled to contain an obvious fit of laughter.

"You know, strawberries are an aphrodisiac," I said. "Though I never got what you and Imogen are giggling about whenever they come up. Or... pineapple for that matter."

Sophia's smile widened, and she said, "It's just an inside joke."

"Well, I plan on finding out what it means tonight," I told her. "Even if I have to force it out of you."

Sophia squirmed in her seat and said, "You can try."

The server came and took our plates away, though he left the straw-berries and melted chocolate, as we hadn't started on them yet. I moved them to the kitchen counter and started running hot water out of the kitchen faucet.

"What are you doing?" Sophia asked.

"I'm giving us some privacy," I told her. I waved my hand, and the room began to fog— I moved the condensation to the window, so that it fogged over and hid us from the outside world. "Take your clothes off."

"Are you really going to try and tell a Koigni what to do?" Sophia got up from her seat and leaned against the table.

"You can take them off yourself or I'm ripping them off you. Your choice."

"Well, if that's the case." Sophia began to strip, and my heart pounded faster. I greedily observed her beautiful form and her full breasts, then started toward her. I picked her up by the hips and hitched her around my waist. Her legs wrapped around me as I pushed her back against the wall.

"Hey, not fair," she protested. "If I'm naked, you have to be, too."

"Those aren't the rules." I took her mouth in mine and surged my tongue against hers. She opened her mouth hungrily to let me in as we began to make out furiously. She tangled her hands in my hair as we kissed, hips moving upon me as if she was trying to make herself come right there.

"Nuh-uh. You're being a bad girl." I swung her off the wall and onto the table. She lay backward, her legs hanging off the end. Her hair spread out all around her as she looked up at me.

"The table thing was supposed to be a joke," Sophia gasped. She was already panting.

"It was a good idea." I raised my hand, and an ice cube rose out of the champagne bucket and into my hand.

"Whoa, wait a minute, what are you doing with that thing?" Sophia stuttered.

I didn't answer. I put the ice cube between my lips and leaned down. Sophia gasped as I dragged the ice cube over both of her nipples, which hardened instantly. I left a trail as I ran the ice cube over her breasts and down her navel. I slowed to an agonizing pace, trailing the ice cube around her thighs, and eventually, to her apex. I held the ice there as she cried out before I caressed it over her lips, then shoved it inside of her with my tongue.

Sophia yelped in a combination of pleasure and surprise, her body writing on the table. I watched her with a deep satisfaction. I liked watching her squirm. It was *so* fucking sexy.

As she was still recovering from the ice cube, I grabbed a strawberry. I dipped the strawberry in chocolate, then I held it over her body. The chocolate dripped down onto her breasts and coated her stomach in slow droplets. I began drawing weaving lines in the chocolate with the fruit. Her chest heaved as I drew closer.

I drifted the strawberry across her lips, and she opened her mouth to take a bite. I fed her the strawberry before I ducked down and delicately began licking the chocolate off of her. Sophia's body moved with desire and want the more places my tongue touched. She reached out to grab my dick through my pants, but I pushed her hands away. When she couldn't get away with that, she reached down to try and pleasure herself, but I pinned her wrists to the table and didn't allow her to move until every bit of chocolate was gone.

I moved myself to the end of the table, between her legs. The look in Sophia's eyes was different now. She'd come back to me. She was my Sophie again. That scared look, that distant and ever present fear, was gone. She was truly living in the moment, because I wasn't giving her any other choice.

But I knew once this was over, she'd go away again. She'd cease to be herself and become something else.

I only had these small moments with her. I wanted to make them last as long as possible.

Sex sure as hell couldn't fix everything. But it had a healing all its own, and right now, Sophia needed that healing. It could make things better, even just for a little while.

I unzipped my pants and dropped them just enough so that I could place my dick against Sophia's entrance. I rubbed myself up and down over top of her, and she was dripping. I coated myself in her as I began drawing circles around her most sensitive areas.

"Is this what you want? Or you want me to stop?" I dipped the head inside her for just a moment before I pulled sharply back. Sophia moaned, and her back arched on the table.

"That sounds like you want me to continue," I breathed. I continued rubbing her with soft, fluid motions, though I didn't go in yet.

"Fuck you, Liam Mitoh, for teasing me," she growled.

"What, like this?" I entered her as slowly as was humanly possible. She shuddered as I began to stretch her insides and fill her up. I went as deep as I could before I nestled myself there, enjoying the feeling of her clenched around me, though I didn't make a move.

"What are you doing?" Sophia gasped. "Screw me, damn you."

I snickered. "Not unless you beg for it."

"Liam!"

I gave one long stroke and surged it back into her before I paused again. "Beg."

Sophia's body trembled. "Please, Liam. I'm begging you."

Okay, I couldn't hold it anymore. I was tormenting myself as much as I was torturing her. I began thrusting, slowly at first, but then hard and fast. Sophia moaned as if she'd been waiting for this all along. She grabbed the table and screamed her release. I grabbed on to her hips for leverage and allowed myself to experience the feeling of *Sophia* all around me. I stroked her for long minutes before I came, flooding into her, and it was one of the most powerful orgasms I'd ever experienced. It was hard to stay standing, though I forced myself to keep awake and not pass out now.

Fuck if the whole train hadn't heard us. Sophia was lying listlessly on the table, reaching out for me. "Liam. I just want you to hold me."

I staggered before I reached down and picked her up into my arms. I fell onto the couch, and she curled up against me, burying her face in my hair and whispering my name.

"I want us to be like this forever," she hushed, and I shivered as I felt her lips brush my neck.

"We will be," I promised, and she nestled closer into me. The gears were turning in my head. Emotions were flooding through me as I cradled the woman I loved. An uncontrollable well of passion threatened to burst through and ruin me right then and there.

Vanessa was still having a baby. Mia was still getting married to that shithead Micah. Despite the fact that the world was falling apart, people were still going to school and falling in love, going to work and continuing on with their lives just like they always had. The fact that Kinpago had fallen under a dictatorship didn't stop people from following their basic instincts, and creating a family.

Life went on. Even though it felt like the world should stop turning when terrible things happened, it didn't. It never would.

I still loved Soph, and she loved me. That would never change— no matter what was to come. The world could burn up in flames tomorrow, and it wouldn't make a difference as to what I'd chosen to do.

I decided that now was the right time. I couldn't bear waiting any longer. Before I graduated from Orenda Academy, I was going to ask Sophia Henley to marry me.

sophia

SIX

Being with Liam made me forget everything that had happened to us— if only for a moment. One beautiful, blissful moment.

But a single moment couldn't last forever.

I listened to lectures in class, but I didn't really hear what my professors said. I walked the halls without looking where I was going. One moment, I was headed out of the classroom, and the next I was in the Biyami dorms without knowing how I'd gotten there. It happened to me again on my way to Intermediate Koigni Magic on Tuesday. I left Fundamentals of Familiar Magic that morning, auto-piloted my way through lunch, and made it to Doya's classroom before I realized it.

Lindsey and Miranda were the first ones there. They waved me over, and I slid to the desk beside them. Esis hopped down from my shoulder and reached out to touch Evelyn's nose.

"Hey, Sophia," Lindsey said. "Have you heard from Taylor?"

I froze as images from last week invaded my mind— the flames, Taylor's cries, the dark tunnel below the school...

"Sophia," Miranda prodded, calling me back to attention.

"Why would she contact me?" I asked, not really answering Lindsey's question.

Lindsey shrugged. "I don't know. Because you live in the same dorms. Maybe she told you why she missed class on Friday."

Miranda leaned in and lowered her voice, even though we were alone. "No one's seen her since Haley... you know."

I tried to blink away the images, but I couldn't get the sight of Levi's burnt body out of my head. I forced myself to look past it, but Lindsey and Miranda swam in front of me like they weren't really there. The memory of Levi's corpse and the scent of burnt flesh seemed more real in that moment.

Lindsey's face fell, and Miranda frowned. They looked really worried.

"What if someone hurt her because she's Biyami?" Miranda theorized. "What if Haley got to her?"

Lindsey chewed her lower lip. "Or what if she hurt herself after what happened to her brother?"

"She's fine," I blurted.

They both gave me a quizzical expression. I decided I could trust them with the truth. At least it would ease their minds, and I knew they'd keep the secret safe.

I glanced toward the door to make sure we were still alone, then whispered, "Taylor left Kinpago."

Lindsey's brow furrowed. "How do you know? Did she tell you?"

I lowered my voice even further. Even though no one was around, I decided not to tell them about the smuggling operation yet, not until we were someplace safe. So I kept my confession vague. "I helped get her out. But you can't tell anyone."

"Absolutely," Miranda said firmly. "Our lips are sealed."

"Right," Lindsey agreed. "If she left for her own protection, we wouldn't want to compromise that. We won't tell a soul."

I relaxed a little. "Thanks, guys."

The sound of heels clicking hit my ears, and I turned to see Haley walking into the room, swaying her hips like she was on a runway. Kelsey and her Familiar followed close behind, carrying Haley's bag for her. Anwara flew overhead and circled near the high ceiling.

Haley caught sight of us, and her proud smile quickly turned into a scowl. "Ew."

She tossed her hair over her shoulder and took a seat far away from us. She made a show of eyeing the three of us up and down with a disgusted look on her face.

Lindsey's hands curled into fists, then she shot to her feet. Medusa startled from where she lay curled on the floor. "You have a fucking problem?"

"Lindsey," I warned under my breath, but she didn't hear me. Provoking Haley wasn't going to do any good. She'd already shown us what she was capable of— and how much she could get away with.

"Yeah, I have a fucking problem," Haley snapped.

Kelsey froze from beside her, but Haley leaned forward in her seat, not even bothering to stand to challenge Lindsey— like she barely saw Lindsey as a threat.

"You're Defortai," Haley stated. "What are you doing hanging out with a Biyami reject?"

Finally, she got the name right.

A fireball instantly formed in Lindsey's hand. "Watch your mouth, Westfenix."

Haley pursed her lips in amusement. She spoke as if Lindsey was a child. "Or what? You'll throw a fireball at my head? It'll barely leave your hand before I light you up in flames. Burn, baby, burn."

"Oh? You mean like you did to Levi?" Lindsey asked calmly.

Haley snapped. She shot up out of her chair and started for Lindsey, but Kelsey threw herself in front of her.

"You can't. Lindsey's Defortai," Kelsey hissed, and Haley backed down.

"Not for long, I'm sure," Haley sneered, narrowing her eyes at Lindsey. "As long as she's hanging out with a Biyami loser, she is one. The Elders will see it soon enough."

Lindsey never got a chance to respond, because a group of people entered the room just then. The fire in her palm disappeared, and Lindsey sat back down. Haley whirled toward Kelsey and started talking to her in hushed whispers.

Vanessa came into the room and sat beside us, rubbing her belly. Aisha was at her side. She lowered her voice and shot a glance to Haley. "What happened?"

Lindsey rolled her eyes. "Haley and I were just about to have a showdown. Too bad. I would've liked to—"

"Everyone in your seats," Madame Doya barked as she breezed into the room, Naomi by her side.

Haley either didn't hear or didn't care, because she was still talking to Kelsey without moving an inch. Kelsey shot a nervous glance to Doya, who was making her way to the front of the classroom.

Doya whirled around, her velvet dress swirling at her ankles. "Miss Westfenix."

Haley didn't even acknowledge her. She kept on talking to Kelsey.

"Miss Westfenix!" Doya snapped.

Haley finally looked at her, a bored expression on her face. "Can't you see I'm busy?"

"I don't give a dragon's ass what you're doing," Doya said coolly. "You're in *my* classroom, on my time. You'll do what you're told to."

The entire room had gone so silent that all I heard was a low growl bubbling out of Naomi's throat.

Haley crossed her arms and tilted her chin up at Doya, like even Doya didn't scare her now. "You can't talk to me like that. You know who my mother is."

"I'm well aware," Doya shot back. "I'll be sure to tell her of your constant disrespect in my classroom."

Haley gaped at her. "My mother's a chieftess!"

"And I'm an Elder," Doya reminded her. "I'll gladly show your mother the respect she deserves. As for you, until you become an Elder — and there's no guarantee you ever will— you will treat me as your superior. I'm not going to tell you again, Miss Westfenix. Sit. Down."

Haley's jaw hung slack. I bet no one ever talked to her like that before in her entire life. Slowly, she sank into her chair, her wide eyes on Doya the entire time. Kelsey quickly sat behind her, looking terrified, though I wasn't sure if she was scared of Doya or Haley.

Doya looked pleased. She turned and started for the whiteboard. She wrote a few words while the rest of our classmates entered the classroom. It was obvious they could feel the tension in the air the second they entered, because each one of them quieted as they took their seats.

Doya seemed to sense when everyone had arrived, because she

looked at us and began lecturing. "Now, can anyone tell me which of the four Elementai are the strongest?"

She pointed to the board, where she'd written out the names of the four Houses.

Haley piped up without raising her hand. "Koigni, obviously."

Doya ignored her and locked her eyes on Hudson, who had his hand raised sheepishly. From beside him, I could tell that Tabitha knew the answer, but she didn't raise her hand because she was Biyami. People like Haley didn't like it when Biyami showed them up. Hudson looked unsure if he should answer, since he'd just been sorted into Biyami from Defortai.

"Yes, Hudson?" Doya called on him.

"Koigni is strongest," he stated.

"Correct. But why?" Doya asked.

Hudson looked a little unsure. "B— because fire is the most destructive of all the elements."

Doya raised an eyebrow. "Is it?"

Hudson hesitated.

"If a Toaqua was strong enough to create a tidal wave, could it not destroy Kinpago more quickly than a fire?" Doya challenged. "The same damage could be done by a Yapluma who's created a tornado, or a Nivita with an earthquake, or a landslide."

Hudson sank a little in his chair, holding his giant snail close to him. Doya turned her gaze from Hudson and glanced around the room. "Does anyone have a guess as to what makes Koigni Elementai stronger than the others? Miranda?"

Doya called on her without Miranda even raising her hand.

Miranda sat a little straighter in her seat. "Is it because of our status in our society?"

"No," Doya answered. "Anyone else?"

I racked my brain trying to think of the answer she wanted to hear. Fire *was* stronger than other elements in many ways, but the others outperformed us, too. We couldn't use our Fire to lift ourselves into the air like Yapluma. We couldn't kill by rushing blood to the heart like Toaqua. We couldn't build like Nivita.

Then it hit me. Doya wasn't asking about our element. She specifically asked about Koigni Elementai. But our magic wasn't any different... what could we do that the others couldn't?

I realized it as soon as I asked the question. Doya must've seen the look on my face, because her eyes stopped on me.

"Sophia?" she called.

I cleared my throat. "We're the only Elementai who can create our element from nothing."

I might've been mistaken, but I swore I saw Doya smile a little.

"Precisely," she said.

Haley shot me daggers from across the room. Of course, a *Biyami reject* couldn't have the answer.

Doya continued her lecture, teaching about how the other Houses needed earth, water, and air to already exist around them and could only manipulate it, while Koigni could create fireballs and sustain them magically without requiring fire to be there first.

"Koigni magic works by manipulating the chemicals around us," Doya explained. "We create heat by speeding up the vibrations of the molecules in our environment, and ignite fires across distance by creating a combustion reaction. But as we all know, fire requires three things: oxygen, heat, and fuel. How, then, are we able to create Fire from nothing?"

Doya looked around the room but was only met by blank stares. Her eyes stopped on me. I hoped she'd move on, but she wouldn't stop staring. "Sophia, any ideas?"

I cleared my throat. "I suppose there has to be a fuel source of some sort, even if it's magical."

Doya smirked and turned to write a word on the board. "When the ancestors gifted us our powers, they bestowed upon Koigni a unique power. Our bodies contain a magical fuel source called ithane."

She stabbed her marker under the word *ithane*.

"When you create a fireball in your palm, you are also forming ithane," she explained. "This is why we can't create fire mid-air, because there is no fuel to sustain the flame. Fire creatures like Naomi produce the same fuel source."

Naomi stepped forward and demonstrated. Her entire body lit up in flames.

"This is also how dragons are able to breathe fire, as they produce the ithane chemical as well within their stomachs," Doya continued. She nodded to Naomi, and the flames on her fur died. She took a step back.

"Ithane is an unlimited, renewable resource," Doya said. "But you can only produce so much in one go. By understanding the limits of the ithane in your body, you can create larger fires and sustain them longer. Otherwise, your fireballs will burn out as soon as they leave your hands. Everybody up. We're going to practice producing ithane and creating long-lasting fireballs."

Creating ithane came naturally, as we'd all been doing this for some time without knowing it. But it was easier to create stronger Fire when we knew the theory behind it. By the end of class, Haley was loudly telling Kelsey how she was going to brag about this lesson to their Defortai friends over dinner. I gathered my things and placed Esis on my shoulder. I turned to follow my friends out of the room, but Doya stopped me.

"Sophia?"

I turned to see her watching me expectantly.

"Can I have a word?" she asked. Naomi purred at her side.

"Catch you guys later," I said to Lindsey, Miranda, and Vanessa. I walked up to Doya's desk. She stood in front of it, leaning back against it.

"Sophia," she said gently, which was weird. I mean, this was *Doya*. She wasn't a gentle woman. "You knew the answer today. Why didn't you raise your hand?"

I dropped my head. "I'm Biyami now. I thought I should give a Defortai student the chance to speak up."

It was partially true, but there was another part of me that just didn't want to participate anymore.

Doya pursed her lips. "Biyami or not, it's unlike you, Sophia. The Sophia I know would challenge these new social norms."

My voice got so small I hardly recognized it. "Things have changed."

The words resonated so true that my body gave a shudder. It wasn't that things had changed. *I* had changed, and I didn't particularly like who I was becoming. It was hard to admit that I was losing myself, since I'd just found who I was a few short months ago. I wished that I could pull her— Kyra Koignichi— back, but it wasn't that simple.

I was no longer *Blazing Firespirit,* and didn't know if I ever could be again.

"Our society is in a constant state of change," Doya pointed out. "No day is the same as the last. You'll have to learn how to manage these changes and stay strong in the midst of them if you ever hope to become chieftess."

My spine instantly straightened at her words. "Chieftess?"

Doya looked confused at my shock. "Yes. I was under the impression that you'd be seeking a leadership role within the tribe after your trial. You challenged the Elders. I assumed you'd like to become one and begin calling the shots."

Her assumptions were freaking me out a little. When did I give her the impression I wanted to become an Elder?

"I think you should," Doya stated when she noticed my blank expression.

"You think I should...?" I trailed off, trying to wrap my head around the conversation. Why was Doya being so nice to me? Was this some sort of manipulation tactic? I wasn't in the right mindset right now to read her well enough.

"I think you should petition to become Koigni chieftess," Doya said simply. "When all of this is over, of course."

My mouth hung agape. I had so many questions and didn't know where to start.

"You don't think the two-House system is permanent?" I asked.

Doya shook her head. "Not if the prophecy is to be believed... and fulfilled."

She gave me a knowing expression. Despite convincing the other Elders I wasn't the prophesied one, Doya still believed I was. I wasn't sure why.

"Even if that happens, I can't become an Elder," I reminded her. "I'm not descended from one."

Doya frowned, like something I said had bothered her. "There are other ways to become an Elder, Sophia."

I furrowed my brow. "How?"

"Should you do something noble for your tribe, or show great power, the Elders can vote you onto the council," she told me.

For whatever reason, I still couldn't bring myself to believe her. She had to be playing some sort of game with me. I mean, yeah, if I got a seat on the Elder Council, I'd have to take it. It'd give me a chance to make a difference.

But it was never going to happen. Especially not the chieftess position.

"Even if the Elders voted me on, Haley's first in line to be chieftess," I pointed out.

"First in line, yes," Doya confirmed with a nod. "But she'd have to be confirmed by the council. And I don't believe she has what it takes."

"And I do?" Was she serious? I didn't know anything about being a chieftess. Haley had been groomed for it her whole life.

Doya took a breath and stood up straight. "Do you remember when I paired you and Haley up last semester to practice sharing your magic?"

How could I forget? Haley had burnt my hands to a crisp. If I hadn't had Esis to heal me, I'd have spent weeks in the infirmary gaining my range of motion back.

I nodded.

"I saw what you did, Sophia," Doya said.

The breath left my chest. I'd caught Haley's fireball and pretended like it didn't hurt, just so we could finish the assignment. But Doya had never said anything about it. Why had she let us pass?

Doya reached out to pet the top of Naomi's head. "A true chieftess makes sacrifices for her people, Sophia. Haley would never do that."

The way she said a *true chieftess* made it sound like she was making a jab at Chieftess Annette— like she had something to do with Oleander's plan.

"One day, my generation of Elders will be gone," Doya said. "I won't leave without knowing the tribe is in good hands. I will do *whatever* it takes to make sure that happens."

The way she said it chilled me to the bone. It was clear she'd resort to anything— be it manipulation or murder— to get me that spot. But I didn't believe for a second she wanted it for the good of the tribe. I bet she thought she could get me the position and use me as her political puppet, so I took the fall for all her mistakes.

"Think about, Sophia," she encouraged. "When the time comes to refill the council seats, I hope that you will be sitting in one of them."

I swallowed the lump in my throat. "I'll think about it."

"Good." Doya turned away and rounded her desk, which was my signal to leave.

I walked into the hall, still trying to process what Doya had said. When I turned the corner, Esis chittered in my ear and tugged on my ponytail, pulling me back to attention. He pointed to a girl down the hall. Her filly-pixie was flying beside her, trying to scare away the guy who was following her like a creep.

Isabella.

She clutched her books tightly to her chest and kept her head ducked. She wore a cute plaid skirt that fell to her knees and a button-up top.

The guy trailing behind her was a big upper-class Koigni named Logan, and he had a large lion Familiar at his side. Other than them, the hall was silent.

"Come on," he teased, reaching out for her. "Daddy wants some sugar."

Logan grabbed for the bottom of her skirt and lifted it, showing off her panties to the empty hallway. I froze and backed away into the shadows, unable to believe what I was witnessing. Esis protested by tugging hard on my ear.

Isabella squealed and twisted away from the predator. Essarae swooped down at his hand, but he just swatted the creature away. The tiny frilly-pixie was knocked off course and slammed into the wall. Isabella gasped and stopped in her tracks. She bent to scoop up Essarae.

"Leave me alone," she begged as she checked Essarae's wings to make sure they weren't broken.

"You can't tell me what to do," he snarled. "I'm Defortai. You're Biyami. You have to do whatever I want. Now, why don't you show me what's under that pretty little skirt of yours?"

"Stop!" she cried.

Logan lifted her skirt again. When she tried to run, he grabbed her ass and pinned her front up against the wall. She dropped her books.

They just lay there, forgotten. Nausea rolled around in my gut. I wanted to move, but I stood frozen in place.

I didn't know what was wrong with me. It was like it'd been with Levi— like I was watching it from above without actually being there.

"No," Isabella whimpered. "Please don't do this."

He shoved his hips into her backside and leaned in close to her ear, though he spoke loud enough that I could hear. "I could take you right here in this hallway, and no one would say a damn thing."

"Someone will see you," she warned in a wavery tone.

"What will they do?" Logan asked, trailing his lips down the side of her neck. "Haley killed a Biyami bastard the other day. This is hardly murder."

He pushed her skirt up further and ran his hand down the front of her panties.

"Help!" Isabella screamed, trying to struggle away. "Someone help!"

The sound of her pleas snapped me back to my own body. It suddenly occurred to me that I was alone. Unlike with what happened to Levi, there was no crowd, no one else around who could possibly step in. And yeah, this jerk could hurt me, because he was Defortai and I was Biyami, but wasn't this what Doya had just been talking to me about? I was the kind of person who made sacrifices for my own. Isabella was Biyami like me, which meant I had to step up for her.

I stepped out of the shadows. "Hey, asshole!"

I was surprised by the harsh tone of my own voice.

Logan's gaze snapped up to mine. He paused for a second before realizing he was looking at a Biyami.

"Go away," he demanded, turning back to Isabella. A look of sheer terror crossed her face as tears began to streak her cheeks.

"Like hell." I marched straight up to him and grabbed him by the shoulder. "Get off her!"

I yanked on him hard enough that he went stumbling backward. His lion Familiar planted his feet firmly and growled at me. Esis bared his teeth from where he sat on my shoulder. I threw myself in front of Isabella, protecting her from Logan and his lion.

Logan smirked. "What is it, babe? Want a piece of this? There's plenty to go around."

Two red-hot fireballs formed in my palms. "Back. The fuck. Off."

He chuckled, then quickly turned serious. Fire formed in his hands as he prepared to face off with me.

"You think your Second Year training is enough to go up against a Fourth Year?" he taunted.

"I don't know. Why don't we see?" I found myself playing along. I didn't know why, because in that moment, I didn't feel like myself. All I knew was that I couldn't watch what had happened to Levi happen again.

Logan shot a fireball straight at my head. I threw my hand up and caught it, letting it sear my fingers before I threw it to the ground and stomped it out. Esis would heal me later, so I didn't care. The pain actually felt good— like a reminder that I was still living and breathing.

It was enough to get Logan to pause. In that brief moment where I had the advantage, I formed a long string of Fire in my hand like a whip. It seemed to take on a solid form as I snapped it at him. I didn't even know how it happened. It was as if the rage within me had manifested in the physical world.

The Fire whip slapped across his cheek, leaving behind a red-hot welt. He stumbled back a step, clutching his face. "You bitch!"

His lion lunged at me before he could react. Without hesitation, I threw my hands forward and shot Fire directly at the creature. The lion let out a pained whimper and twisted in the air. It landed in front of me, writhing in pain as the flames consumed it. This lion wasn't like Naomi. It didn't have Fire power the way she did.

Logan's eyes went wide as he realized what I'd done. He quickly aimed his hands at his Familiar and killed the flames. The creature's fur had been burnt off, and its skin was covered in blisters.

Logan knelt down beside him, assessing his injuries. His nostrils flared, and his eyebrows lowered deep over his eyes. Slowly, he lifted his gaze to mine. "You're going to pay for this."

"*Mister Melborne!*" The sound of Madame Doya's sharp voice echoed down the hall. Her heels clicked against the tile as she made her way over to us.

Logan looked terrified, and Isabella shrank further behind me.

Doya stopped next to us. Naomi growled at the other lion at her feet. It was as if they'd had run-ins in the past and she wasn't too fond of him.

Doya stared down at Logan with utter disdain. "You *dare* fulfill that threat, I will personally see to it that the Elder Council prosecute you for it."

"But she's Biyami!" he was quick to point out.

"Are you questioning me, Mister Melborne?" she asked with a raised eyebrow.

"N—no, ma'am," he stammered.

"Return to your dorm room. Before I personally escort you there," Doya instructed him.

Logan scampered to his feet, helping his lion as he limped along. He shot several glances back at us, but he looked utterly terrified of Doya. I didn't think he'd be following through on his threat.

"You two," Doya snapped, turning to us.

She looked conflicted... like she didn't know whether to yell at us or help us. Her voice softened to an unusual steady tone. "Take care of her, Sophia."

Then she turned on her heel and was gone, Naomi trailing behind her. I breathed a sigh of relief and quickly turned to Isabella. She was leaning against the wall, trying to steady herself. Essarae flew around her, blowing cool air into Isabella's face with her wings.

"Are you okay?" I asked. Esis tugged at my sleeve, trying to pull my hand up so he could heal it. I lifted it to him but kept my eyes on Isabella.

She pushed her hair away from her face. Tears streaked her cheeks, and her eyes shimmered when she looked to me. She seemed to contemplate the question, then slowly shook her head. Her voice broke when she spoke. "No, I'm not. Logan might not come for you again, but he'll come for me. I know it."

"Isabella," I said gently, hoping to offer some words of comfort. But there was nothing I could say in this situation.

She wiped her face and sniffled. "He's been following me around for a week. Every time, it just gets worse. If I stay here any longer, he'll—he'll—"

She choked up, and heavy sobs shook her body. I quickly reached out and wrapped my arms around her, pulling her close as she buried her face in my shoulder. Her entire body shook.

"It will be okay, Isabella." I ran my hand up and down her back, forcing down the thick lump in my throat.

Isabella was Nivita, and I was Koigni. We weren't even in the same year. We hardly knew each other, but somehow, it felt right to comfort her.

"No... it... won't..." she cried between sobs. Finally, she pulled away and wiped her tears. "My mom died from the plague. I was sorted into Biyami. Now there's a sicko out there who wants to rape me. This stupid society can't possibly get any worse."

I placed a hand on her shoulder. "Then we'll get you out."

She furrowed her brow. She'd stopped crying, and Essarae was perched on her shoulder. "Out of Kinpago?"

"Yes," I told her gently. "You can't stay here."

"This is my home," she argued.

"Where people are trying to hurt you," I pointed out. "It's no longer safe."

She looked like she was considering it. "But what about the Task Force? They patrol all entrances to the school. They'll notice me leaving with my bags. I can't just climb on the *Hozho* without someone spotting me."

I glanced up and down the hall to make sure we were still alone, then lowered my voice anyway. "There's another way."

Her eyes lit up with hope.

Isabella and I returned to the Biyami dorms, where I told her to pack the absolute essentials and leave everything else. She went over to her trunk, while I headed to the back corner of the dorms. There I found Liam sitting on the lower bunk, working on an essay. I was a little surprised, since I usually wrote his essays for him, but for some reason he'd decided to do this one on his own. He stared down at his paper, the tip of his tongue stuck out in concentration.

Esis hopped down from my shoulder and ran over to Liam.

His head snapped upward when he noticed our approach. He quickly set his homework aside and stood. "*Pawee*, what's wrong?"

I glanced to Imogen and Jonah's bunk. The top bunk was neatly made, while the bottom was a mess of sheets and blankets. "Where are Imogen and Jonah?"

"They're, uh, working on their routine for class... in the dance studio." I could tell by the way he said it that they'd gone to the Anichi dorms to practice instead of the actual dance studio on the third floor.

"Good," I said. "We need to meet them there. Now. Isabella's coming with."

Liam became instantly alert. "Wait. What?"

I gave him a light nod so the other Biyami nearby wouldn't notice. "She needs our help."

"Okay. Let's go." Liam didn't even ask what had happened.

While we wove through the maze of bunk beds, I lowered my voice and said, "By the way, you might want to steer clear of Logan, from your old Hawkei Leadership class. I pissed him off big time."

Liam eyed me. "What'd you do?"

I bit my lower lip as we came beside Isabella's bunk, where she was adding belongings to her bag. "I, um... lit his Familiar up in flames."

Liam's eyes practically bulged out of his skull. "You *what?*"

"I—"

"She saved me," Isabella interrupted as she stood and swung her bag over her shoulder. Essarae pushed the top of the trunk with all her might, and it fell closed. She flew over to settle on Isabella's shoulder.

"You did, huh?" A hint of a smile touched Liam's lips, though I wasn't sure why. I'd just told him I attacked someone else's Familiar, and he thought that was amusing. I guess he hated Logan even more than I thought.

I nodded, then turned back to Isabella. "If you have anyone to say goodbye to, now's your last chance."

She shook her head. "No. I don't want anyone to come after me. I'll be fine on my own."

Liam leaned in and whispered so nobody else could hear. "We can get you out of the castle undetected, but after that, you really are on your own. Are you sure you'll be okay?"

She nodded. "I have a plan."

"What kind of plan?" Liam asked.

"Don't ask," Isabella warned. "The less you know, the safer you'll be."

I reached for Liam's hand. "She's right. No questions. Not with Isabella. Not with anyone."

Liam searched my eyes for something, though I wasn't sure what. Finally, he nodded in agreement.

"Let's go," Isabella said.

We led her out of the dungeons until we reached one of the main hallways. There were a lot of people passing through, including various groups of Task Force members. I noticed Head Dean Alric speaking with Dean Hestian of Nivita, who had a white stag at his side.

Alric glanced our way as we passed, and his features changed. I couldn't explain it, other than a hint of surprise. One second it was there, and the next it was gone. He gave a polite nod, but kept on talking to Dean Hestian.

There was something strange in the way he looked at us. It was like a sort of thank-you for Liam and I keeping his secret about him and Perot. Which apparently had gotten out anyway, since he'd been sorted into Biyami.

I ducked my head and kept walking. It felt like all eyes were on us as we led Isabella through the hallways and up the stairs. It shouldn't have felt weird, because we were all Biyami and allowed to hang out, but I felt like any moment a Task Force member would turn on us and yell at us for what we were doing. At one point, I thought I heard footsteps behind us, but when I glanced back, nobody was there.

We reached the third floor tower safely. The coast was clear, so we opened the doors and slipped inside. Isabella tilted her head back to take in the magnificence of the twisted staircase.

"You might've heard this tower is off-limits to students due to compromised structural integrity," Liam said as he started climbing the stairs. It was like he'd rehearsed a speech to explain it to anyone new we introduced to the dorms. "That's a lie meant to keep students out. In reality, this is the site of the Anichi dorms. We're going to get you out through a secret passageway."

Isabella nodded and followed behind, still staring up at the ceiling that seemed to go for miles. When we stepped into the common room,

Jonah and Imogen were indeed there, dressed in their dance attire and practicing their routine. They stopped dead when they noticed Isabella. Jonah rushed over to turn the music off.

"Is everything okay?" Imogen asked in a rush.

I shook my head. "Isabella needs help getting out of the castle."

"Well, what are we waiting for?" Imogen came forward and took Isabella by the hand, like they were best friends. "Let's show you the way out."

Everyone came along except Jonah and Squeaks, because according to Jonah, he'd only go back down there if it was *over my beautiful dead body.*

"You can thank *me* for the whole operation," he'd said before we left. "If it weren't for me, we never would've found this tunnel in the first place."

"This is amazing," Isabella said as she ran her hand along the wall of the tunnel. "How did you find it?"

"It was an accident," Imogen told her, before diving into the story about how Esis had found the dorms, and then later how she and Jonah had discovered the tunnel when moving furniture.

"We're here," Liam announced as we reached the end.

I climbed on top of the boulder, since Liam looked a little worn out, and opened the trap door.

"Thank you so much, Sophia," Isabella said once we were out of the tunnel and into fresh air. "How can I ever repay you for helping me?"

"Just stay safe," I told her. "It's the only thing you can do."

She nodded. "I will." She scampered out of the trapdoor, and soon the sound of Essarae's wings beating faded away.

It was a long walk back to the Anichi dorms. When we returned, Jonah was pacing the hall at the top of the stairs. He looked half relieved and half scared to see us. He hadn't changed out of his dance leotard yet, and I knew he kept a stash of clothes in one of the bedrooms. Weird. Squeaks was stomping her feet and shaking her head.

The blood immediately drained from my face. It was obvious something was wrong.

"Jonah, what is it?" Liam asked in a rush.

Jonah chewed his lower lip and picked at his fingernails. "See, the thing is... I didn't know he was here, and..."

"Jonah, what are you talking about?" I demanded.

"Well, he just... you know..." Jonah stammered.

Imogen marched straight up to him and shook him by the shoulders. "Spit it out!"

"Head Dean Alric found our hideout!" Jonah blurted.

The dark hall went dead silent. We all exchanged a glance. What did this mean? That our smuggling missions were over? That we had to find a new place to hide our research on the prophecy?

"Come on," Jonah said, gesturing for the group to follow him. "He wants to talk to us."

Liam grabbed for Jonah's shoulder and whirled him around before he could get far. "Jonah, what'd you tell him?"

Jonah's eyes went wide. "Nothing! I mean, something. Not everything. Now, come on. He's waiting."

We followed behind Jonah, but our footsteps seemed to tap in an unnatural rhythm. I didn't know about everyone else, but my heart was pounding fiercely in my chest. Alric would make us board up the dorms for sure.

When we reached the common room, Alric sat on one of the couches facing us, his back straight and one ankle rested on the other knee. A dragon's cry came from far above. I glanced upward to see his dragon Familiar, Valda, flying high above the glass ceiling outside.

Alric placed both feet on the ground when he saw us, then stood. He gestured to the couches around the fire. "Students, please have a seat."

Nobody said anything as we shuffled further into the room and did as he said. We filled the couches, but Liam remained standing with his arms crossed— like he was ready to defend our territory at any cost.

Alric cleared his throat once we were all seated. "I think it's time that I officially commend you for your bravery."

"*Commend* us?" Imogen balked. "You're not kicking us out?"

Alric shook his head firmly. "Precisely the opposite, Miss Ahnild. I've known you four have been coming here for quite some time, though I wasn't sure why."

Liam's jaw dropped. "How did you know?"

Alric shot a glance to the fireplace, then looked upward. It was clear what he meant. The smoke from the chimney had alerted him someone was in the tower. "You have not been as careful as you think."

"And you... approve?" Liam asked. "Of what we're doing here?"

Alric looked a little confused. "Why wouldn't I?"

"Wait," Imogen insisted. "What is it you think we're doing?"

Alric held his head confidently. "Mister Chanee tells me you're using a secret passageway to smuggle students out of the castle."

All eyes turned to Jonah, who had a look of utter guilt on his face. "Come on, guys. What was I supposed to do? He followed us and *saw* the passage."

It didn't sound like Alric knew anything about the prophecy pieces we'd been collecting. Which was a relief.

"Never mind that," Alric said with a wave of his hand. "Mister Chanee did nothing to betray your confidence. It's true I followed you into the dorms. And I want to help."

"You want to smuggle people out with us?" I asked.

Alric nodded. "Gather all the people you can trust with one hundred percent certainty. We will meet back here at six o'clock tomorrow night."

Alric checked his watch, then said, "If you'll excuse me, I have somewhere to be. I'll see you all tomorrow."

And that was it before he turned on his heel and left the room. We didn't even get a chance to ask him any questions. The dorms were silent for several long seconds as we all looked between each other.

Imogen sighed. "Well, it looks like our hideout isn't much of a hideout anymore."

My shoulders fell. It was nice to have this place to ourselves for a while.

"No," Liam said, looking deep in thought. "It's still our hiding place. The only thing that's changed is that our group has expanded."

Imogen cracked a smile. "I guess you're right."

"Come on," Liam said, nudging Jonah. "Let's gather the troops."

THE NEXT NIGHT we were all sitting in the Anichi dorms, waiting for Alric to arrive. We'd explained about our smuggling operation to our friends, as we wanted them to hear it from us instead of Alric. We were all here— everyone who'd escaped with us the night of the riots. Maddie and Drew were camped on the couch beside me and Liam, while Lindsey and Miranda were sitting cross-legged on the floor. Our Familiars all crowded around us. The only person here who hadn't been here the night of the riots was Wyatt. He stood close to his walrus Familiar and leaned against the arm of the couch.

"It's a trap," Ezra said for the third time as he paced back and forth in front of the empty fireplace. He cracked his knuckles and kept his lips tight.

"Bro," Liam started. "It's not a trap. Alric wants to help us."

"Or kill us," Ezra insisted. "This could be the council's way of luring out the traitors."

"Alric's Biyami," Bren pointed out. He sat between Imogen and Vanessa on one of the couches. One arm was around Vanessa's shoulder, the other on her belly as the baby kicked. "Besides, he's not even on the council."

"He could be playing both sides," Ezra theorized. "I mean, I know he was getting it on with Perot, but this is *Alric*. He never should've been in Biyami in the first place. Maybe Oleander offered him a deal, a pardon for being in an interhouse relationship if he spied on us."

"We can trust Alric," Jonah promised. "He wants to help."

Ezra stopped pacing and narrowed his eyes at the rest of us. "How can you be so sure?"

Just then, the sound of footsteps on the stairs caught our attention. We all turned. Liam got to his feet and stood beside Ezra, as if he was going on the defense just in case. Alric strolled into the room, but he wasn't alone. Baine walked in behind him. It seemed as if we all held our breath as they moved across the common room.

"Students, I'm so glad you all could join us today," Alric greeted kindly. He stopped between the couches and gestured to Baine beside him. "I've invited Professor Baine here because he believes in this cause as much as I do. I also know that several of you had him as your mentor during the tournament. If he can get you through the tournament, he can get us through this, too."

Alric continued. "I've asked you all here today because I want to create an alliance. Though many professors have chosen to step away from Orenda Academy, Professor Baine and I stayed because we believe we can fight what's happening in a peaceful, democratic way. The other teachers left because they wanted to use violence to change the situation here, but I believe in the power of our tribe. We can use other methods to stop what's happening."

Everyone stared up at him in admiration, except Baine, who nodded his head along while he listened carefully.

Alric was right. I'd snapped enough times to know violence was merely a quick fix. But quick fixes didn't work on an entire society.

"What kind of methods are you talking about?" Imogen asked.

Alric looked pleased by the question. "We can put people in positions of power. We can speak out and use our voices. We must trust that the people will rise up and not allow these heinous acts to continue. We must stand as examples to reunite the Hawkei."

Alric's voice grew stronger the more he talked. "In the meantime, we must do what we can to protect our fellow Hawkei until they wake up and make a stand. I want you to continue what you're doing. When a student needs help, you smuggle them out. It's the only way some of them will remain safe. I believe in the good of the tribe. The ancestors will never let the evil in the hearts of the few to pervert the entire nation. We can overcome this, but we must be diligent in our values. We must stand as a firm example of the Hawkei's unity. Peace. Harmony. The elements as one!"

Hope filled my chest as Alric spoke. If anyone could help us stop the prophecy, it was Alric and Baine. I noticed the same hope begin to fill everyone else's eyes. Even Ezra had relaxed.

"Things are bad," Alric continued, "but I assure you that if we go about this in the right way, we can reverse what has become of Kinpago."

Liam stepped forward, holding his head high in confidence. All eyes turned to him. Liam was our leader, and so we waited for him to speak first. "Then we will stand with you."

Baine gave a nod of approval. "I knew you would make the right choice."

Alric smiled at us. "You're all on board then?"

Ezra stepped up beside Liam. "If Liam believes this is the right way, then I'm in."

"Me, too." Jonah stood to join them.

"And me." I got to my feet, and Esis cheered from my arms.

Soon, everyone had joined in, both Elementai and Familiars alike. Within moments, everyone was standing and cheering for Alric.

As soon as the cheers quieted, Liam asked, "What's the plan?"

"We need to gain information," Alric said. "We need to encourage the people to take a stand. I want you all to be my eyes and ears around the castle. If you see injustice, you stand up. Violence must only be used as a last resort to defend yourself."

"How can we fight against this without violence, though?" Ezra asked curiously, his tone softer than before.

"We must take every alternative precaution," Alric stated. "We can't become like them, or we become the animals."

Animals. That's what people like Haley and Logan had become. And I wouldn't become like them— or let any of my friends, either.

I was ready to make a stand. Alric would show us the way.

"Okay," I said. "Tell us what you need us to do."

Liam

SEVEN

lric's speech had stirred up hope in me that I didn't know was there. The tribe wasn't doomed to this two-House system. It couldn't be. The ancestors would protect us and restore things back to normal. We just had to wait out the storm and do what we could to help people until that happened.

Alric was right. We didn't need to use violence to stop Defortai. We could change the hearts and minds of the Elementai by sticking to our morals. As long as we stayed together and remained consistent in our message, eventually, things would change.

There was another way to do this without going to war. We could spy, we could smuggle people out, and no one would get hurt. The Hawkei would only let things go so far before the people revolted. Oleander would be overthrown, along with all the other corrupted Elders. Then balance would be restored.

This wouldn't last forever. It couldn't. There was just no way something like this could continue to happen in Kinpago. It was crazy that it had started at all.

We'd be okay. Things were bad, but they weren't horrible yet. All this was going to stop. It had to.

Because I had faith in Alric, I was willing to sit back and let someone else take the lead for a change while I focused on other things. He was planning our first big smuggling operation for the end of the week, and we'd all planned to be there. It was the first time we'd be sneaking out a group of people instead of just one at a time, and to say that I was nervous was an understatement. What we were doing was against the law, but the law wasn't always just or right. It was worth the risk to get people out.

Meanwhile, I was focused on one of the most important tasks of my life— asking Sophia to marry me.

I still had to get the ring. Sophia had Intermediate Koigni Magic for two hours on Tuesdays, starting at one o'clock. I didn't have War and Negotiation until four that day, and that little gap was pretty much the only time I had when Sophia wouldn't notice me sneaking off. If I wanted to buy this ring, I needed to hurry.

My tournament winnings were gone, but I still had some money left in my savings. I'd been keeping it for this moment.

As I was making my way out of the castle, I was cornered by none other than Jonah and Imogen. I rounded the corner near one of the towers and nearly ran into them. They stood there with crossed arms and narrowed eyes. Imogen was trying to appear intimidating, though she wasn't very scary, being all of five feet tall. Sassy and Squeaks backed them up, Squeaks with ruffled feathers and Sassy raising her tail. Jonah looked like a bouncer as he kept his brawny arms tight.

"Guys, can you get out of the way? I'm kind of in a hurry," I said.

Jonah and Imogen said nothing. Neither did their Familiars make a sound. Instead, they pressed in around me until I was forced to step away. The four of them made a semi-circle and marched inward. I backed up until I was pinned against a wall.

"Um, okay," I said. "Good afternoon to you, too."

"We have some *questions* to ask you," Jonah said, and Squeaks snapped her beak.

"Liam, what is *this?*" Imogen shoved a magazine in my face. It was wrinkled up and crumpled, because I'd shoved it under my pillow when I saw Sophia coming yesterday. It must've fallen out this morning, and Imogen had discovered it.

She acted like she'd found a Playboy hiding under my bed. I felt like

I was getting interrogated by the Task Force. "It's just a jewelry catalog. What of it?"

"Nuh-uh. That's an *engagement ring* catalog, from Lux's Fine Jewelers in Kinpago," Jonah countered.

"There are *notes* on it!" Imogen hissed.

"Yeah," Jonah added, before he said, "except we couldn't read them. Because your handwriting is awful."

"It *is* your handwriting, isn't it, Liam?" Imogen poked me in the chest. "Tell us the truth!"

"He can't handle the truth!" Jonah shouted.

"No, Jonah, you're doing it wrong," Imogen said. "That's not how it works."

Sassy barked. Jonah cocked out a hip and said, "Either way, we're not letting you out of this corner until you tell us what's going on. Spill the deets."

Their inquiring eyes were all I needed to know that they'd wait until the end of time to get good gossip. I sighed. "All right, fine. You caught me. I'm going to ask Sophia to marry me."

They stared at me with open mouths for a moment. Then huge smiles lit up their faces, and they both screamed so loud I thought my eardrums would shatter. The two of them hugged each other and jumped up and down. Sassy rose up on her hind legs and hopped in a circle around them.

"'I'm going to be a bridesmaid!" Imogen squealed.

"Oh my gosh! We get to plan a *wedding!*" Jonah sang. Squeaks danced in joy beside him and ended up falling on her face.

"You know, Sophia and I would like some input, if you two don't mind," I put in sourly.

"Liam, why didn't you tell us? This is only, like, the biggest deal of your life!" Imogen exclaimed.

"Because you two can't keep a secret like this!" I hissed. "You're being so loud I'm sure the whole castle has heard."

The two of them immediately dropped their voices. Imogen said, "Liam, I am seriously *so* happy for you guys. Jonah and I want to be there for everything. What do you need from us?"

"Yeah. You can't seriously be thinking of asking her and keeping us in the dark," Jonah said.

Of course they'd decide to butt in and get involved. "If you guys really want to help, fine, you can help me pick out a ring. I haven't bought it yet, and I was going now."

"Of course we're coming. This is *so* much better than dance class. I'm in," Jonah said.

We proceeded out of school and down the path to Kinpago. Imogen was skipping instead of walking. "Sophia's going to make *such* a gorgeous bride. I can't wait to help her pick out a dress."

"I get you're excited. But seriously, you guys can't breathe a word of this to Sophia. Not even a hint. She's too smart. She'll figure it out," I said.

"We aren't going to say a thing, honey, I promise," Jonah vowed. Squeaks cooed in agreement behind him.

I was putting that promise on lasting two days, at most.

There was no way to get to town without going over the bridge. Which really kind of sucked. Every time I crossed that bridge, I was reminded that I'd tried to toss myself over it.

I wasn't that person anymore, but it was always going to be a part of my past, and something I never really could escape from.

Things had turned around so fast. A few months ago I'd tried to kill myself, and now, I was getting married. Well, hopefully married. I didn't know if Sophia would say yes yet.

Imogen noticed I was a bit bothered and rushed to distract me. "So when are you planning on having the wedding? Sometime next year?"

"Um, I wanted to have it in the fall," I said. "Maybe late summer? Before Sophia goes back to school, anyway."

"This fall? Holy ancestors, you can't plan a wedding in a *few months*. Everything's booked up!" Imogen argued.

"Why not?" I asked. "We'll make it work."

"Clueless," Imogen quipped, shaking her head.

"He's a total man." Jonah rolled his eyes. I scoffed at that, because it wasn't like he wasn't a man, too. He had a dick dangling between his legs just like I did.

When we got to Lux's Fine Jewelers, there were large yellow signs on the windows advertising everything at fifty to seventy percent off. There was a lone shopkeeper, peddling around boxes that were scattered all around the store. It looked like he was packing up. A mole Familiar stood on one of the displays, putting away rings into a cardboard box.

"Why is everything on sale?" I asked, looking around. The jeweler was selling diamonds at half price. There were some killer deals here.

"I'm closing up shop, son," the shopkeeper told me. "Elder Oleander just made a decree that Biyami cannot own businesses. I have until the end of the week to pack things up, before the Defortai come to take it over."

I frowned. The Biyami couldn't be in business anymore? How did they expect people to provide for themselves if they couldn't work?

Even more worrying was how I was supposed to find a job after graduation, especially with a new wife to provide for. No Defortai would hire me.

Guess I'd worry about that later. I had to propose first. While the shopkeeper kept packing, Jonah, Imogen and I scanned the glass containers for what I hoped would be the perfect ring.

"Black's totally not my color. Or gold. Silver. Silver is good," Jonah said, pressing his face up against the glass as he surveyed the men's rings with barely-contained envy.

"I want an emerald. It's more unique than a diamond," Imogen went on. "Something square-cut on a gold ring."

"You guys are supposed to be helping me pick out an engagement ring for Sophia, not be looking for yourselves," I mumbled. I crossed my arms. Why had I brought Imogen and Jonah along? I could've done better on my own.

While they were bickering, something caught my eye. Below me was a thin silver ring, a pear-shaped diamond in the middle that was surrounded by tiny sapphires and garnets. It was simple, but really elegant.

Toaqua and Koigni. The ring was a representation of our relationship. It was perfect.

"I see you like that ring," the shopkeeper said. He abandoned the boxes and walked over. "Do you want to see it?"

"I'd love to."

The shopkeeper took the ring out of the box and handed it to me. It felt small and light. When I held it up close, the gemstones sparkled.

"It's a completely original piece. I handcrafted it myself," the shopkeeper said. "I watched your trial on TV, son, and I had the idea for that ring afterward. I just knew I had to make it. Let's just say you inspired me."

"Wow, really? That's amazing." It was like fate or something.

"It comes with a bridal set as well," the shopkeeper said. He handed me a silver women's band that matched the engagement ring, then brought out a men's band that was silver and plain. I liked it, because it wasn't too fancy and looked like something I would wear.

"The women's rings are size six, men's size eight," he said. "It seemed like the right thing to do at the time. Both of them are immune to all elements— including a Koigni's Fire."

They were the perfect size. Esis had helped me by sneaking next to Sophia and wrapping a string around her ring finger when she was sleeping so I could check her measurements. I tried on the men's ring and it slipped on flawlessly. Now that it was on, I didn't want to take it off. I liked how it felt on my hand. It was like it belonged there.

Regretfully, I took the ring off and put it back in the box. "Guys, come look at this," I said. Imogen and Jonah huddled around me as I held the engagement ring up to the light. "What do you think?"

"Ooh, good choice, Liam," Imogen said. "She's gonna freak when she sees it."

"I still don't think it's big enough. How is that little ring supposed to prove his love?" Jonah asked.

"Sophia likes simple things. She wouldn't want something gaudy," Imogen argued.

"Right," I said. "Besides, it's not like I'm asking *you*, Jonah. We all know that the man who asks you to marry him has to buy a diamond that's bigger than your huge head."

"Bigger, honey. Even bigger," Jonah said.

I paid for the rings, then pocketed them as we walked back up the road to school.

My thoughts were going a million miles an hour. Holy shit. I was actually doing this. I was going to ask Sophia Henley to marry me.

Ancestors, I hope she said yes. What if she said no? I think I'd die. Yep, probably die. No other alternative.

"So when you gonna pop the big question?" Jonah asked.

"Um, I don't know," I said, thinking. "Maybe tonight?"

"Tonight? No, no, no. You have to have a *plan*," Imogen said. "Do you have a plan?"

I blinked at her. "Uh... no. Should I?"

"Ancestors." She rolled her eyes and looked at Jonah. "He obviously needs our help."

"Obviously." Jonah shook his head. "This is a proposal, Liam Baby. You have to make it *special*. It's the only one she's gonna get."

"Hopefully," Imogen added.

"Sophia's not one for huge gestures, guys," I said. "I was just going to ask. Maybe on a hike or something."

"By the ancestors! You're not putting in any effort at all. Do you want to *insult* her?" Imogen exclaimed.

I hesitated. No. I really didn't want to do that. I'd done romantic stuff before, but those were only dates. I'd been too excited about proposing that I didn't put much thought into how. Maybe that was a mistake.

"What do you guys think I should do?" I asked. I couldn't believe I was asking them for advice, but they knew more about this stuff than I did, didn't they?

"Leave it to us," Imogen said confidently.

"Yeah." Jonah slung an arm around my shoulder. "By the time Im and I are done, we'll have come up with a proposal that Sophia *can't* say no to."

I hoped they were right. Because at the moment, I was just hoping asking them for help didn't blow up in my face.

ON WEDNESDAY, I walked from Master Toaqua Magic and to the library, as I needed to pick up a book for Hawkei Art later that evening.

As I walked in, I saw Mia sitting at a table with a bunch of books, doing homework. Her canine Familiar, Taryn, lay at her feet. It seemed like she was taking a nap.

When Mia noticed me come in, she waved me over. I cringed. I'd been trying to avoid her since last semester ended, but it was hard, seeing as how we had a class together. She was still with Micah, and she had been sorted into Defortai, so I hoped that would be enough to stop her from reaching out to me. But guess not.

"We're not supposed to associate," I whispered under my breath as I approached her. A Task Force member had his back to us, but if he turned around, we'd be in his direct line of sight.

"Not here," Mia said. She rose up from the table and gestured for me to follow her behind a bookshelf.

"What's going on?" I asked as we ducked out of sight. I was being so quiet I'm surprised she heard me.

"I just thought you should know something, before it gets out. The Elders are starting to pull people out of the academy who they suspect are mixed House," Mia whispered. "The Elders don't want interhouse children running around."

"But most people aren't," I argued. "I know there were a lot of inter-house couples in hiding before, but the majority didn't have children because they knew the consequences."

"Doesn't matter." Mia shook her head. "They're trying to get rid of any opposers any way they can. If they can't accuse people of being interbred, they make it sound like you stole your Familiar from another Elementai."

"What the fuck? You can't *steal* your Familiar and force them to bond with you." The idea was outrageous.

"The Elders are saying you can." Mia shrugged her shoulders. "Do you remember Maddox, from Yapluma?"

"Yeah. He was in my Hawkei Leadership class last year." He'd been the one person to stick up for me, although he'd caved under pressure and agreed when my other classmates insisted I didn't deserve to live because I was sick. I had mixed feelings about him.

"Remember his Familiar, the white lion with the wings? Well, Maddox saw a Biyami getting pushed around by a Defortai in the hallway, and he stepped in. The next day, he was reassigned to Biyami and his lion got taken away. The Elders said that he'd stolen him from a Defortai. No one knows where his Familiar went."

"Are you fucking serious?" That was insane. It was practically unbelievable.

"Yep." Mia's words had taken on a hardened tone. "Things are really getting bad around here."

If what Mia said was true, my little sister Maddie was a huge target. She was Biyami, but she had a powerful ice dragon for a Familiar. The Elders could very well target her next. "Thanks for telling me this, Mia."

"No problem." Mia sighed. "I just wish there was something I could do about this, you know? It isn't right."

I paused for a moment. There was something Mia could do. She could help us with the smuggling operation.

The more Defortai we had on our side, the better. They could go places we couldn't and had more authority. Bringing Mia in would be a risk. Expanding the operation farther than our little group always brought on the chance that we'd be found out.

But Mia was a good person. She had a good heart. I felt it in me we could trust her.

"There is something you can do," I started, and Mia leaned in. "But you have to swear not to tell anyone. It's life or death."

"I promise, Liam. I won't tell a soul," Mia vowed. "What is it you had in mind?"

§a

Valentine's Day this year wasn't anything like last year. Typically, there were all sorts of decorations around the school, but this year the castle remained void and barren. Instead of exchanging gifts out in the open, couples hurried to private places to hide in order to avoid attracting attention. I think people got the notion that if you let it be known publicly that you loved someone, they could be used as a target against you later.

Sophia and I didn't have that problem, because everyone already knew we were together. We met up in the evening in the Great Hall. It was pretty empty this time of day, but come to think of it, most of the castle looked like a ghost town these days, even though the number of people who attended here hadn't decreased.

"Hi." Sophia rose up on her tiptoes and gave me a quick kiss. "I missed you today."

"I missed you, too." I wrapped an arm around her and gave a tight squeeze. Esis was sitting on Sophia's shoulder. He had on a pink t-shirt with a red heart that looked like it'd been made for a doll, along with a headband with tiny heart antennas. At least Esis was stubborn enough to keep celebrating the holidays.

"I'd really like some alone time." Sophia leaned against me. "Do you have anything in mind?"

I seconded that. Privacy was impossible to come by in the Biyami dorms. "Mom's having a family dinner at home. She invited everyone. I figured we could go there and spend some time at my house. It's about the only place we won't be watched."

"Dinner with your parents sounds lovely."

We left the Great Hall and ventured into the chilly winter air. As we were passing through the gardens, I said, "I don't want to bring up… *business*… today of all days… but I think I've found someone else who's willing to help us with what we're doing."

"Really?" Sophia sounded curious, but her voice had taken on a tone of nervousness.

"You're not going to believe this, but it's Mia."

Sophia come to a halt. She let go of my arm and almost slipped in the snow. Her face turned pale white as she gasped, "Excuse me, *what?* You told *Mia* about what we're doing?"

"Yeah," I said. "Is that a problem?"

"This can't be happening." Sophia's expression bordered on the edge of panic. She took deep breaths, like she was forcing herself to calm down. Esis fanned her face frantically with his tail.

"Soph, calm down. It's not that big of a deal—"

Sophia yanked me behind a statue of a rearing unicorn. She pulled us further into the hedges until we were completely concealed from view. "You didn't say anything about the hidden passage, did you?" Sophia asked. She was nearly out of breath.

"No. I said she could help us by keeping an eye open and looking for anyone who might need to escape. We need all the help we can get," I said.

"What exactly did you tell her?" she hissed.

"All I told her was we were trying to smuggle people out of the castle. I didn't tell her about the Anichi dorms, or where or how we were doing it," I said.

Sophia put her hands on the sides of her face. "That's a small comfort when people start looking! Sooner or later, they're going to put two and two together like Alric did."

"Not unless Mia says anything, which she won't," I said.

"She will! And Liam, it'll be your fault when it happens!"

That stung. Sophia wasn't one to ever place blame. She wasn't one to freak when secrets got out, either, but apparently that had changed.

I knew she wasn't herself right now, which meant I was the one who needed to keep calm. I steadied my temper. "We need Defortai on this job. The more, the better."

"Defortai we can *trust*, not her. She cheated on you! She already betrayed you once. Who's to say she won't do it again?"

Esis crossed his arms and nodded. I hardened my tone. "Look. I know Mia. I grew up with her. She wants to stop what's happening just as badly as we do."

"Your feelings are compromised. You trust her because you slept with her!" Sophia flung at me.

That was a total slap to the face. "That's not fair. I've told you I don't even remember what that was like! I'm not hung up on her anymore."

"I know that. You love me, but you have a history with her. That's always going to make things difficult. You can't think clearly when it comes to her," Sophia growled. "It's like you have a weakness for saving toxic people, just like Jonah."

"Don't compare me to Jonah. This isn't the same thing. She just wants to help." It was hard keeping my voice down, but we had to stay quiet.

"Micah is in Oleander's pocket. Her loyalties are divided." Sophia's hands became fists at her sides. "As long as Mia's still engaged to Micah, she's on their side, not ours."

"She's gonna leave him, Soph. I just know it. She's gonna get tired of his bullshit, and—"

"Liam, how many times does that actually *work?*" Sophia crossed her arms. "How do you know that once she leaves, she won't just change her mind and go back to him? Nothing he's done so far has made her want to escape this relationship."

I couldn't argue that one. "You make it sound like we should give up on her."

"I'm not saying she's hopeless, but she can't be trusted. Not with something like this," Sophia snapped.

"I can't believe she's a lost cause."

"You have to. There's no other choice," Sophia insisted. "We have to pick and choose who we want to survive in this war, and Mia's already made that choice for us. If she stays with Micah, she's a goner. That's just how it is. We can't save her. And by trying, you're putting this whole operation at risk."

"That's pretty dramatic, seeing as how I just asked her to keep an eye out," I said scathingly. I couldn't believe Sophia was taking it this far.

"Bottom line. There are only a few people we can trust. Mia should be *nowhere near us!*" Sophia shouted.

I shushed her so she'd bring her voice down. Sophia took a few more deep breaths. Her anger... or should I say, her paranoia... faded away to sadness as tears welled up in her eyes.

Now I felt like a dick. Involving ex-girlfriends in anything was always a certain recipe for trouble. "Aw, Soph, come here."

I took Sophia in my arms and held her there. I embraced her super tight, so she'd feel more secure and safe. She was overreacting. Nothing bad was going to happen because I'd told Mia we were helping people. She had to believe that.

I rubbed her back. "It'll all be fine. You'll see."

Sophia looked up at me, and our eyes connected. "Liam, you're such a wonderful man." She laid her hands on my chest. "But you try too hard to see the good in people. Even when it's not there. And I'm terrified that someday, it's going to come back to bite you."

It was hard to respond to that, because I didn't know what to say.

But I was saved by a rustling in the hedges. Both of us jumped back a few feet when Baine's head popped through the leaves. Esis peeped in surprise.

"Ah, there you two are. I thought I heard Miss Henley shouting," Baine said. He looked like he was out of breath. "I'm sorry to interrupt your Valentine's Day, but we are in urgent need of your help."

"Um... does this regard the *thing*? Because we have dinner with my parents tonight," I told him.

"It does. I've already spoken with your father and told him I needed you and your siblings here, though I didn't specify for what," Baine said. "I wasn't sure if you wanted him to know."

"He's safer if he doesn't, for now." Dad was already having trouble keeping the little power he did have as Water chief. I didn't want to put any more stress on his shoulders knowing three of his kids were involved in illegal operations.

"Let's go, then." Sophia let go of me and strode out of the hedges. She wore a deep frown and a stern look in her gaze. We weren't having a very good record with Valentine's Days in general.

The group of us walked in silence. I think Baine felt the need to say something, because he took a deep breath when we began climbing the stairs.

"That was a very good spot, by the way," Baine told us as we ascended to the Anichi dorms. "The hedges make it particularly seclusive for romantic endeavors. I ventured there in my youth one or two times, myself."

Fucking. Ew. As if I *ever* wanted to know where Baine used to screw girls. Sophia turned pink and put her hand over her mouth, as if she couldn't believe Baine had just said that.

"I do beg your pardon. I didn't mean to intrude, but it did sound like you were arguing," Baine rambled on. I was sure he was just talking to talk. "If I may offer a piece of advice, I believe the best sort of relationships have the most *passion*. Make-up sex is always the best kind, I would say. The anger leads to more fun."

"Oh my gosh," Sophia squeaked. My mouth dropped open at the audacity of this conversation.

"Now, Miss Henley, don't be so crude. We are all adults here, and this is college," Baine went on. "I have no issues discussing relationship matters among my students. I have quite the wealth of experience, if you're so curious. Could give you a few pointers about your... uh... unique situation."

Could Baine just fucking shut up? Why was he trying to give us advice right now like he was some sort of love expert?

"We're here!" Sophia announced loudly, and she flung open the door to the Anichi dorms in a desperate effort to cut Baine off.

Ezra, Lindsey, and Miranda all looked up at the same time. Wyatt was having a conversation with Jonah and Imogen in the corner. Vanessa and Bren weren't here— I'd heard that Vanessa had been having issues with the pregnancy and put on bedrest. Bren was probably tending to her.

"Where's Alric?" I asked, expecting him to be here.

"Alric will be bringing along the refugees shortly," Baine said.

"How many are there?" Wyatt asked.

"Twenty or so, not counting Familiars," Baine said. "The operation will be a bit different this time. Once they're through the trap door, we'll be escorting them to the beach, where a boat will be waiting to take them out of the area. There are too many people this time to risk leaving them in the woods to be discovered. I'll be leading the route."

Great. Baine was liable to give me and the rest of the crowd here the birds and the bees talk all the way down to shore.

"What are our jobs?" Imogen asked.

"We'll be doing it in sections this time," Baine instructed. "Alric needs Lindsey and Miranda with him on the third floor, to watch for Task Force patrols so we can bring the students up to the tower. Once we leave, their job will be to make sure that the Task Force on campus stays put."

"We're already on it." Miranda and Lindsey went back down the stairs with Medusa and Evelyn.

"Imogen, you can wait at the end of the tunnel, to lift the trapdoor and move the roots with Sassy's help. I need Jonah and Squeaks in the forest surrounding the trapdoors to provide security. Wyatt, we need you and Tuskin to stay in the Anichi dorms and alert us if there are any intruders. And take them out if necessary." Baine dug around in his pocket and handed him a two-way radio.

"I'll be ready to knock some heads if any Task Force show up." Wyatt cracked his knuckles. Wyatt's walrus Familiar, Tuskin, gave a low bellow.

"Ezra, you'll be providing support from above," Baine said. He handed Ezra another two-way radio. "You're to fly above Kinpago upon Dyami and let us know if the path is clear or if we need to find another way. Sophia, Liam, you're with me. Our job is to get these students out of Kinpago safely. And protect them, if it comes down to that."

"Hold on. Where are Drew and Maddie?" I asked.

"They have the most important job. They're creating a distraction on the other side of campus," Baine said. "They're ready to go on Alric's signal."

Baine scowled. "I must inform you all that this mission is very important. Twenty people don't just up and disappear overnight. Once these students go missing, security *will* crack down around the school. It'll be even more difficult to sneak people out from this point on. But we have no other choice. The boat can only make one trip, and that's tonight."

"We can handle it," Sophia said. "But before we do, I think there's something we need to talk about."

Sophia sent a direct look at me. I stepped forward and said, "I told Mia about what we're doing. She said she wants to help find people who need to leave."

"Miss Imikayi was informed of this?" Baine asked. His eyes widened in shock.

"Bro, you can't be serious." Ezra's voice was flat and strained. He despised Mia with a blazing passion.

"Oh, dude." Jonah slapped his head. "Bad move."

"What?" I looked at Wyatt. "You know her pretty well. Don't you think we need her?"

"Uh..." Wyatt hesitated. "Maybe you should've kept your mouth shut."

Geez. If even Wyatt was uncertain about bringing Mia on— and he had a major crush on her— that was a pretty big sign I might've made a mistake.

But I couldn't believe that. Mia would help us. I was sure of it.

"How big do we want this operation to be? Any larger and we risk exposing ourselves," Imogen said.

"If we haven't already," Ezra chipped in with a glare at me.

"I think it should be a rule that if anyone wants to bring more people into this operation, then we all have to vote them in first, as a unanimous decision," Sophia said. "Someone *everybody* trusts."

There was a mumble of agreement around the group. I felt like a major dick. Baine said, "We'll discuss it later. Everyone's minds needs to be on the mission."

We waited in the Anichi dorms until midnight, at which point Alric showed up. Behind him was a collection of Orenda Academy students. Most of them were freshmen. The majority of them had Biyami tattoos, though I picked out a couple of Defortai in there as well. None of them had particularly strong Familiars, if they were bonded at all. They carried things like toads, small birds, and forest mammals that could fit in your hand, along with backpacks or tiny suitcases.

All of them seemed so scared. I'd do whatever it took to get them to safety tonight, even if it was the last thing I ever did.

"This is all of them. Valda is currently flying the perimeter," Alric said. "I'll be staying on campus, to play actor to our distraction. You have one hour."

Baine nodded. Ezra climbed on Dyami. Jonah opened up the glass ceiling, and the thunderbird took to the air through the exit. Jonah then got on Squeaks' back to follow, so he could go to the forest, find the boulder where the trapdoor was hidden, and wait there.

"Let's go." Baine led the group to the dorm room with the passageway. Sophia lit the way with a ball of fire in her hand down the long and dark tunnel.

Dammit, I hated these stairs. There were so fricken many of them. I got winded every time we did this.

My heart began to pound as nervousness took over me. If we got caught, we were fucked. Like really, really, fucked.

When we got to the end of the tunnel below, Imogen moved the roots for us and widened the holes by the trapdoor so we could get more people out faster. It took some time, but eventually, everyone had clambered out of the tunnels.

"Good luck," she whispered before closing the doors. She was the only one left inside as the trapdoor was shut.

Jonah was pacing the area around the trapdoor. In the distance, I could see Squeaks looping around the forest on high alert, her sharp eyes looking for any intruders.

"So far there's nothing to see here," Jonah said. "We'll trail you guys until the tree line breaks, to make sure you aren't followed. Then you'll be pretty exposed until you get down to the beach."

The only sound that could be heard in the darkness of night was heavy footsteps and shallow breathing. The feeling of a noose slowly tightening around our necks enveloped the group. One girl behind me was crying, but she kept her sobs low. A boy beside her looped his fingers with hers and held them tight.

When the trees ended, Jonah held back. "This is as far as I go," he said. "I'll meet you guys back at base."

This was the scariest part of all. The path from here to the beach was wide and open. There was a good chance we'd be seen walking to the docks. Baine got on the two-way radio. "Thunderbird, do we have clearance?"

I heard my brother's voice as it emerged from the radio, along with the flapping of Dyami's wings. "All is clear for now, but you better get a move on. A Task Force patrol is coming your way."

"Dammit!" Baine swore. A couple kids started to panic. They were making noise, squeezing their Familiars and speaking in anxious tones.

"We're not gonna let anything happen to you guys," I said lowly. "Just keep your voices down and trust us to get you there."

The noise quieted, but the fear in their eyes didn't go away. They were absolutely terrified.

"Everyone follow me, and hurry." Baine ducked down and began moving forward as quickly and quietly as he possibly could. The rest of us followed. Sophia and I both took a side, so we could keep our eyes open and react if we spotted any Task Force members.

Sophia had a determined look on her face, which was matched by

Esis. There was a fire back in her eyes that was all too uncommon these days.

I was pretty proud of her. Despite what she was going through, she was staying strong and keeping her mind on the mission.

That path seemed like the longest walk of my life. I had taken this road before, and it was less than half a mile, but every step stretched on into eons. It felt like I was being strangled as I surveyed the area around us. There was nowhere to hide if we were spotted. The trees were too far away to slip behind in time.

"Professor! Task Force, on your left!" Ezra shouted through the radio.

Everyone's heads yanked to the side. A Task Force member, alone and on patrol, came out ahead of us onto the path where it forked onto the way to Kinpago. He was carrying a noxite gun and moving in a leisurely manner. He hadn't seen us yet, but if he turned around, he would.

Sophia reacted before any of us did. Before the Task Member saw us, she ran forward and jumped on his back. He struggled to throw her off, though Sophia and Esis both clung on.

I reacted the moment I saw that Sophia was in danger. I was over there so fast I hardly remember moving my legs. I yanked his helmet off and punched him with as much strength as I could muster, from the back so he didn't see my face. The Task Force member crumpled, and Sophia and I stepped back.

"Drag him behind the bushes. He won't be out for long." Baine's tone had an edge of anxiety to it. He was starting to lose control. Sneaking out people was one thing, but we were attacking Task Force members now.

There was a row of bushes alongside the road. Sophia and I moved the body out of sight, and the group made a break for it. We abandoned secrecy and broke out into a full-out run. Baine did his best to try and keep the group together, though a few kids left the group and went on ahead.

Finally, the blissful sight of the beach ahead came into view. I saw a medium-sized boat waiting on the docks there, manned by someone from Toaqua. The students ran onto the boat without waiting for us. A freshman started sobbing in relief as he flung himself onto it. Sophia and

I stood on the docks, watching for other Task Members, while Baine spoke to the boat captain. "You know where to take them."

"Yes, Professor." The captain gave a nod and started up the boat. He turned it slowly. Students waved goodbye and thanked us as they left the docks and ventured into the safety of open waters.

"Where are they going?" Sophia asked as we watched the boat sail into the ocean.

"It's best if you don't know," Baine replied. "All that matters is that they're going to be safe."

I nodded. We were just sneaking people out. If we knew where everyone was going, and the Task Force members found out about our operation, they could interrogate us until we admitted where Alric was hiding people. The less we knew, the better.

"We need to return. Before anyone notices we're missing," Baine said.

We made way for the end of the docks, but a lone figure standing in the shadows blocked our way.

And it was an Elder.

Madame Wells, from Toaqua, stood on the entrance to the docks with her arms crossed. Her braid waved in the slight wind, and her young face appeared stern and harsh in the moonlight.

Shit, shit, shit. Madame Wells had caught us. This was all over.

Madame Wells narrowed her eyes. "I figured I'd find you here tonight."

Though she'd seen what we'd done, Baine remained calm. "I had no idea you'd be here."

"You weren't informed." Madame Wells proceeded toward us. "Elliot, I think it's best if I speak with these two alone. You need to leave." Madame Wells fixed her gaze on Sophia and I, and I felt a shiver run up my spine.

"Of course. Do what you must." Baine ducked around Wells and left the docks.

What the hell, Baine? Was he really gonna abandon us right now? Baine high-tailed it along the beach and took a separate path from the one we came back to Kinpago.

"Did Baine sell us out?" Sophia bunched her hands into fists while

Esis growled from her shoulder. "Liam and I will take the fall, but you're not gonna get a word out of us about where we're hiding people."

"Calm down, Miss Henley," Madame Wells replied. "I'm only here to help."

Madame Wells fished in her dress. She held out her hand and unfurled beautiful fingers. Within her palm was a small totem, decorated with the symbols of the five Houses.

"The Spirit Totem," Sophia whispered. Esis peeped in surprise.

"I acquired it during your trial, if you so remember. When it was in Elder custody, I stole it back, and kept it hidden from the other Elders. I had them believe it was lost during processing," Madame Wells said. "I believe this belongs to you."

Madame Wells pressed the Spirit Totem into Sophia's hands. Sophia herself was too shocked to speak.

I managed to string a couple of words together. "What the hell? You're on our side?"

"I've always been on your side, Mister Mitoh. You are on the right side of history," Madame Wells said, turning to me. "I am the last of the Toaqua Elders that is still loyal to your father. I believe the rest of them have become Oleander's puppets. We are doing what we can from within the Elder ranks to stop this, although it's been extremely difficult. We are very much outnumbered, and therefore outvoted."

A loud note came from the ocean. I turned my head to see a killer whale jump out of the water and splash down into the sea, causing a major wave.

"My Familiar," Madame Wells said with a smile. "Surely you remember my orca, Mister Mitoh."

I did, but this still didn't make any sense. "Why do you want to help us? You're an Elder yourself. Wouldn't it be easier to go with what everyone else is doing, and better your position?"

"I know more than most why freedom is so important. Every creature deserves to forge their own path. It is something I am willing to die for," Madame Wells said strongly.

Her eyebrows knitted together. "When I was young— twelve or so— my grandfather told me I needed to see what the colonizers did to the creatures of the earth for money. So he took me somewhere I wished to never venture to— a theme park that profited off the suffering of marine animals."

I drew in a breath. Elementai hated zoos and aquariums. It was just in our nature. Animals didn't belong in cages.

"I was appalled by what I saw. So many poor creatures, doing tricks for food and trapped in containment centers that could never replace or imitate their habitat." Wells shook her head. "I didn't know how people could enjoy the pain of sea creatures, until I realized that all of them were unaware this was wrong. Or just didn't care."

Wells' voice trembled as she continued. "I believe the worst was the orca tanks. I stepped up to the glass, and immediately, my eyes connected with a large orca male. He had the darkest eyes, and a large scar across his side. I knew upon instinct— in my heart— that his name was Tsoen. He told me. I heard his mournful song wrap all around me and lift me up in that moment. It was the most horrible thing, seeing a beautiful orca trapped in such a small tank."

Wells' eyes shone with tears as she recounted the story. "The colonizers were so cruel that they put his tank right next to the ocean, only yards away, so that he could see it through the glass but never experience it like he had before they'd stolen him away from his pod. I put my hand against the glass and stared at him. It was like I could feel all the pain and sadness he'd stored up in him from years past. And so, I knew I had to do something. After my grandfather and I left the park, under the cover of night, I came back. I snuck inside the theme park, so I could return to see Tsoen."

Wells shook her head. "I wasn't supposed to be able to do it. But I was so angry about what they were doing to him. I wanted to change it. I felt my magic swell up within me as I came near him. I harnessed all the water out of that tank and levitated it into the air, along with Tsoen. I carried him and the water to the ocean, where I placed him back within the sanctity of the waves, where he belonged. It took all my strength. Nearly killed me. But I knew that even if it did, I had to set him free."

"At twelve?" I said, astonished. "You shouldn't have been able to do that. Or bond at all."

"No. But I did," Wells said. "Once Tsoen was in the sea, my body gave out and I crashed into the ocean. The waves carried me away from the beach. I thought I would drown.

"I expected him to swim away. But he didn't. Tsoen swam under me and carried my body through the waves. He brought me many miles away, to an island in the middle of the sea. When I woke up, I could see his fin bobbing as he soared through the waters. I knew then that we were bonded. And that we were destined to make this world a better place."

Madame Wells faced Sophia. "That is why I desire to help you, Miss Henley. I don't believe what the prophecy says about you. I think you're destined to save the tribe, not destroy it. And to do that, you need that Spirit Totem. And you need to learn how to use it properly."

Sophia nodded solemnly, and Esis copied her. "Thank you, Madame Wells. I won't let you down."

"How much have you told my dad about what we're doing?" I asked. "Baine said he didn't know."

"Your father is still in the dark, but I suggest you tell him soon. These missions are only going to get more complicated, and the Chief of Toaqua would be able to pull strings no one else could," Madame Wells said.

"How much power do the chieftains still have?" Sophia asked. "I thought Oleander was basically running things."

"The chiefs and chieftesses still have supreme power, but they cannot enact decrees without a majority vote from the rest of the Elders. And Oleander currently controls the council, along with his followers," Madame Wells said. "He's currently in the process of trying to get the Elders to vote him to the position of High Chief, so he has ultimate ruling power over each of the four Houses. A High Chief needs no support or majority vote to enforce his laws. Chief Mitoh and I, along with a few others, are working to delay the vote, but we can only keep postponing it for so much longer before Oleander forces our hand."

"Are you kidding me? There hasn't been a High Chief since Anichi ran things," I said. "It's a Soul House position."

"If Oleander gets his way, there will be one again."

I shook my head. "By the time Ezra becomes chief, Oleander will have total control of everything. Being Chief of Toaqua, or any of the other Houses, won't even matter anymore. Oleander could overrule anything that comes through if he's High Chief. It'll be a total dictatorship."

"Yes. Which is why we cannot allow that to happen," Madame Wells said.

Madame Wells fixed her eyes on Sophia. "Miss Henley, I speak directly to you. The outcome of this war is entirely in your hands. People are looking to you. I swear that I will do whatever is in my power to be of service in your time of need. You need only ask for my aid."

Madame Wells clapped a fist to her chest and bowed before turning on her heel and striding off the docks.

I looked to Sophia. "Hey, no pressure, right?"

"I can handle it." Sophia held the Spirit Totem tightly to her chest and looked out at the water. Esis put a paw to her cheek, but it was like she barely noticed.

She was somewhere else entirely. A place I couldn't reach.

sophia
EIGHT

There was blood. Blood everywhere. The fires blazed somewhere behind me, and the screams echoed throughout the square. But all I saw was the blood. The couple lay side by side on the cobblestone, their intestines spilling out of their slashed abdomens. The twisted organs entwined together.

I didn't know what compelled me to inspect the gruesome scene, but I found myself bending and reaching out for the entrails that lay between them. My fingers sank into their soft, gooey guts. Tears streamed down my face as I tried to separate his intestines from hers. But the more I tried to untangle them, the tighter they twisted together— until I realized that there weren't two sets of guts here.

There were two bodies, but they shared the same intestines, like one twisted rope connecting their bodies together. I stood and took a step back, my entire body shaking. And that's when I noticed their faces.

Ben and Marcee.

A TERRIFYING SHRIEK startled me from my sleep. It was bloodcurdling and cold. It sounded like a woman was being brutally murdered— like she was being tortured from the inside out.

"Sophia!" Liam's voice came to me from a distance. Cool hands settled on the side of my face, but it was so dark that I couldn't see anything.

"Sophia, calm down." His voice was closer this time. I felt his finger touch my lips, and the screaming instantly died down. It was in that moment that I realized I'd been the one crying out.

All around the Biyami dorms, people groaned and stirred. A few lights turned on— some were flashlights and others were flames from Koigni bystanders.

"What's going on?" someone asked from the middle of the room.

Imogen's voice came from the upper bunk beside me. "I saw a spider."

"Ancestors, you woke us up for a spider?" another voice groaned. "No wonder you're Biyami."

"Mind your own damn business and go back to sleep, dipshit," Imogen snapped through the darkness.

My breath finally began to slow, and my eyes adjusted to see Liam next to my bunk. Esis snuggled into my lap, trying to offer what comfort he could. Imogen's brows came together in concern, and she lay with one elbow propping her up. Sassy was wide awake and alert, her ears perked up. Jonah and Squeaks had stirred but were barely processing what was going on.

"Sophia, what's wrong?" Liam used his thumb to wipe the tears from my cheeks. I hadn't even realized I'd been crying.

I blinked a few times as utter mortification overtook my body. My hands shook, and I had a hard time speaking as the images of the dream assaulted me.

"It was just a bad dream," I whispered as soon as I found my voice.

"What was it about?" he asked gently.

I shook my head, like that might get rid of the images. "Nothing," I lied, before quickly remembering that we'd agreed not to lie to each other anymore. I just didn't know if I could recount the details. "I mean, it was nothing new. It was the riots."

An ache filled my chest as I thought about it.

"Are you going to be okay, Sophia?" Imogen asked.

Liam turned to her and said, "Go back to bed, Im. I've got this."

I couldn't really see Liam through the darkness, until he started climbing the ladder onto the upper bunk.

"What are you doing?" I whispered so quietly that we wouldn't disturb anyone in the silence.

"I'm sleeping by you," he said simply.

I didn't protest as he crawled under my sheet and took me in his arms. It felt so good to lay my head on his chest. It felt warm and safe there. We didn't fit well on the bed together, but I didn't care. I just wanted to be next to him. Esis curled up on our legs so he was touching both of us.

"Do you want to tell me about your dream?" Liam asked.

I shook my head lightly. "Not really."

He kissed the top of my head. "Okay."

We lay there in silence for several minutes, but I could tell by the rate of his breathing that he wasn't going back to sleep anytime soon. I certainly wasn't.

I took a deep breath and focused on the rhythm of his heart under my ear. I was so lucky to have him here by my side. I never wanted to lose him.

I snuggled in closer, until the front of my body was completely pressed against his side. "Thanks for staying with me tonight, Liam."

"You don't have to worry, *pawee*," he whispered. "I'll always be here."

THE FOLLOWING DAY WAS SATURDAY. I was excited to be meeting up with my grandparents for lunch to show them that I'd gotten the Spirit Totem back. Grandpa knew how it worked, since he used to catalog ancient artifacts. Maybe he could teach me more. I mean, Madame Wells gave it back for a reason. She had so much faith in me. The least I could do was figure out what to do with it.

"Sophia!" Grandma sang as she invited Esis and me into the house. She pulled me into a hug. "Lunch is almost ready."

I followed her down the hall and into the kitchen, where it smelled of roast beef and potatoes. "Wow. That smells amazing."

"Wait until you taste it," Grandpa raved as he gestured for me to sit beside him. "Tell us, Sophia, what happened this week?"

I set Esis on my lap and paused momentarily. There was so much I could tell them, and so much I still had to keep secret. I couldn't tell them about the smuggling operation for sure. Though I trusted them, I didn't want to put them in danger.

Grandma must've noticed the troubled look on my face. "Has there been drama?"

I chuckled lightly. "When *isn't* there drama? I mean, Liam and I had a little fight, but it's not a big deal."

I wanted it to be the truth, but it was a lie. I was really bothered that he'd confided in Mia.

"An argument, or a fight?" Grandma asked.

I shrugged. "What's the difference?"

Grandma sighed and brought the plates over to the table. She sat, and we began dishing up our food. Esis licked his lips as he watched me place the potatoes on my plate.

"Every couple argues," Grandma said. "No one agrees on everything. But when you're throwing punches, that's when you know it's a real fight."

I could tell by the way she said it she didn't mean it literally. I'd thrown an emotional punch or two at Liam when I found out he'd told Mia, so I guess that fell into the realm of a fight. Which sucked, because I hated fighting with Liam. I thought we were past that.

"It was a fight, I guess," I admitted.

Grandpa tilted his head, looking sympathetic. "Sophia, I'm sorry. But you two are good now, right?"

I popped a potato in my mouth and answered vaguely. "We will be."

"I really do like Liam," Grandpa said. "I hope you two can find balance in your relationship."

"What do you mean?" I asked.

Grandma mashed her potatoes on her plate. Esis was already scarfing the smaller ones down whole. "He means that every relationship takes work. Even ours."

"Really?" I asked skeptically as I cut my meat. "You two seem perfect together."

Grandpa laughed. "It wasn't always that way. We had a bit of a bumpy ride there, especially in the middle."

"Why?" I asked. "What happened?"

They seemed to ignore my question. Instead, Grandma said, "We're Koigni, so we're both very head-strong. We don't break down our walls so easily, and we don't swallow our pride."

"But we had to," Grandpa said. "To make things work. It was the decision between our pride and our love, and our love won out."

Grandma gazed to him like she was falling in love with him all over again. "Eventually, we had to put our pride aside and listen to where the other person was coming from. Once we understood each other, we learned how to compromise, in ways where we were both satisfied with the outcome."

That's what I should've done with Liam. Instead of lashing out when he told me about Mia, I should've let him explain to me why he trusted her. Maybe I could learn to trust her, too. *Maybe.*

I took a deep breath, and my shoulders relaxed. "Thanks. I'll keep that in mind."

Grandpa popped another piece of roast beef in his mouth. "Is that all that happened this week?"

"No." I reached for the string around my neck. Grandpa gasped when I showed him the totem. "I got the Spirit Totem back."

He took it in his hands and gazed down at it like he was seeing a ghost. "But the Elders... they took it during your trial."

Grandma froze and stared at the totem in shock. "How ever did you get it back?"

"It's probably best if you didn't know," I told them.

Grandpa's eyes went wide, like he was imagining the worst.

"Don't worry," I said quickly. "I didn't break any rules."

He relaxed and ran his fingers over the delicate artwork. His ram Familiar, Ernesto, sniffed it. "You're still interested in practicing with it, I presume?"

I nodded. "Yes. I was hoping maybe you knew more?"

Grandpa pressed his lips together. "I have some theories. Some things we weren't able to test last time."

"What kind of theories?" I asked curiously.

Grandpa handed the totem back. "Why don't we eat first?"

It was like he was keeping me in suspense on purpose, but I agreed anyway.

❦

AN HOUR LATER, I was standing in the woods with my grandparents and our Familiars. We were far off the main pathway, so no one would see us. Whatever Grandpa wanted to test with the totem was obviously too much to try in the house.

Esis ran around a tree, chasing my grandma's white cat, Thelma, while Grandpa's fire-horned sheep lay lazily at the base of a tree beside them.

"Let's sit," Grandpa suggested.

Though it was mid-February and still cold out, the area around us warmed to a comfortable temperature as Grandpa manipulated the heat in our secluded area of the woods. The ground was comfortable and dry when I sat. Grandma sat next to me until we formed a triangle.

Grandpa took a deep breath before he spoke, like he was enjoying the nature around us. "Ever since the Spirit Totem was taken from you, I've put some thought into how it works. You said that the totem helped heal Liam in the caves, correct?"

"Oh, um..." I bit my lower lip and glanced to Esis. I'd forgotten my grandparents believed that lie, since I'd told the Elders that during our trial to protect Esis. I couldn't let my grandpa keep believing that, or it could change everything we knew about the totem. Plus, I knew they'd keep Esis' healing abilities a secret. I trusted my grandparents with my life.

"That's what I said," I admitted. "But it was a lie."

Grandpa furrowed his brow. "Why would you lie about that, Sophia?"

I sighed. "I did it to protect Esis. He's the one with the healing powers."

Grandma inhaled a breath and looked to Esis, who was panting as he chased the ruby-eyed cat. "He's a Soul creature?"

I nodded. "He's a kurble, possibly the last of his kind. I'm not sure. All I know is that he can heal."

Grandpa pressed his lips together in thought. I expected him to act a little more shocked at the information, but it looked as if he was placing it into some calculation in his head.

"What is it, Alan?" Grandma asked.

He snapped out of it and looked up to us. "This makes perfect sense."

I tilted my head. "What does?"

He nodded, still thinking. "Yes, I think my theory is correct."

"What?" I prodded. "What did you realize?"

Grandpa straightened. "You see, when you spoke of the Spirit Totem healing Liam, I realized that it never should've worked like that. Spirit Totems don't contain their own power like other artifacts. They enhance what's already inside of you. The Elders believed what you told them because there are some Anichi artifacts that can heal on their own — since the power is inside them. But at the trial, I already knew it was a Spirit Totem, so that got me thinking..."

"What?" I demanded. "Grandpa, tell me what you know."

He pressed his lips together. "What I don't get is how the Spirit Totem works for you at all, since you're Koigni."

I shrugged. "I guess the ancestors want it to, since they've chosen me as a Spirit Warrior."

"That could be," he agreed. "But there's never been a Spirit Warrior outside of Anichi. I looked deeper into Spirit Totems after the Elders took yours, and there's something that doesn't quite add up."

I furrowed my brow. "What's that?"

Grandpa took a deep breath. "Only someone with the power of Spirit should be able to use a Spirit Totem."

"Are you sure?" I asked. It didn't make any sense. "The ancestors can do whatever they want, can't they?"

He shook his head. "Even the ancestors have to abide by the physical laws of our world— and our magic."

I touched the totem around my neck. "So, how can I use it? It *is* a Spirit Totem, isn't it?"

"Yes." He held his head high. "Sophia, I believe you have Anichi power within your blood."

I recoiled a bit. *That,* I was not expecting. "You think I'm Anichi *and* Koigni?"

Grandpa nodded, while realization crossed Grandma's face. "Somewhere within your lineage must be an Anichi ancestor. They were probably one of the last alive. Otherwise, you wouldn't be as connected to Anichi as you are."

"What do you mean?" I asked. "Connected to Anichi?"

"Well, you bonded with an Anichi Familiar," Grandpa pointed out.

I looked to Esis, who was sprawled out on the ground, his limbs pointing straight out as he tried to catch his breath.

"But people cross-bond all the time, don't they?" I pointed out.

I'd seen plenty of students with Familiars who didn't quite match up with their House— Nivita with aquatic Familiars and Toaqua with land mammals. I'd even seen a Koigni with an ice dragon.

"Yes," Grandpa confirmed. "But Anichi creatures have all but gone extinct. There must be a reason Esis sought you out."

Was that what made me special? Is that why Showana chose *me* for the prophecy? Because I was the last remaining Elementai with Anichi blood, and I was the only one who could control the Spirit Totem? It had to be.

"That's why I'm the Spirit Warrior," I said aloud. "Because I'm part Anichi."

Grandpa nodded.

"Who was my ancestor?" I asked, suddenly intrigued. "How many generations have passed? One of my parents must've had Anichi blood, too. Do you think it came from your side?"

Grandma raised her hands and spoke gently. "Not so fast, Sophia."

She exchanged a glance with Grandpa, like he could come to her rescue.

"It must be from your father's side," he said quickly, though there was something in his tone I couldn't quite read. It was like he wasn't quite sure.

I guess that made sense, since everyone I knew from his side was already gone, including my paternal grandparents.

I took a deep breath, still trying to process it all. "So if I'm part Anichi, can I heal?"

Grandpa pressed his lips together in thought. "I wondered that myself, but I can't say for certain. I think with so little Anichi blood, your Soul powers only work when you have the totem. That was my initial theory— that together your Anichi blood and the totem helped heal Liam in the caves, but that obviously wasn't the case. Still, I don't see why you wouldn't be able to heal with the totem's help."

"What else does it do?" I asked. "It amplifies my Koigni powers, but you make it sound like it only works with Spirit."

"I believe you are able to access it through your Anichi blood, and it then amplifies *all* the power inside of you, including your Koigni magic," he explained. "I'm not sure yet if you'd be able to heal, because we don't know how much Anichi power you possess. But Anichi is capable of more than that."

"They are?" I asked in shock.

Grandpa stood and held a hand out to me. "Yes. Let's see how much Anichi power you have."

Grandpa made me stand between two trees while he stood a few feet in front of me. Grandma went to sit beside our Familiars to watch.

"You trust the totem, correct?" Grandpa asked.

I nodded firmly. We'd gone through that lesson already. I knew that if the totem wasn't working, it wasn't the fault of its powers but fault in my faith in it. I knew it would work as long as I trusted in it. "Yes, I believe in it."

"And in yourself?" Grandpa asked.

"Yes," I told him. I'd proven myself too many times to doubt my magic anymore.

"Among Anichi's powers, they are able to create light," Grandpa explained.

"Out of nothing?" I asked. It basically went against what Doya had taught in her lesson. Then again, none of our professors considered Anichi in their lessons.

"Yes," Grandpa said. "It's a magical type of light that originates inside of you. The Anichi used it to send signals or to blind their enemies."

I nodded along as he explained, trying to wrap my head around the idea that I was part Anichi and could possibly create beams of light before the day was through.

"I want you to relax and picture a beam of light aimed right here." He pointed to the center of his chest.

"How do I differentiate it from my Koigni magic?" I asked.

"The same way you differentiate the different types of Koigni magic — heat versus Fire," Grandpa said. "There should be another type of magic inside of you, one that's untapped, one you've never touched."

"I never felt anything else, though," I told him.

"Have you looked?" Grandpa challenged.

The truth was, I hadn't. I'd never known to look for something else.

"Close your eyes, Sophia," Grandpa encouraged. "Focus on your inner magic, and find that piece that you've never touched before."

I closed my eyes and took a deep breath. All around me, the forest seemed to still. The air around me was warm, and the trees were quiet. Esis had stopped panting, and everything else remained quiet. It was peaceful and serene.

I turned my focus inward. I could feel my Koigni magic at my heart. It was like a warmth that was always there, twisting slowly through my chest while waiting to be used. I knew its energy signature like I knew the sound of my own voice.

I pulled my attention away from my Koigni magic and searched by body for other energy signatures. I could feel the thump of my heart in my chest and noticed the rhythm of my breath, but I felt nothing else.

"Use the totem if you must," Grandpa suggested.

I reached my hand to my chest and curled my fingers around the totem. The Fire in my chest warmed, as if begging to escape, but I commanded it to calm while I searched for the Spirit magic within me. I mentally explored every inch of my body, from my toes all the way up to my head and down to my fingers. As I reached my fingers curled around the totem, I noticed something. It was a softer, smoother energy where I touched the totem. It wasn't hot like my Fire, but bright and melodic. I couldn't see or hear it, but that's how it *felt*. It was my Spirit magic that connected me with the totem. Grandpa was right. I had Anichi blood.

Taking another deep breath, I focused inward again, searching for the source of that beautiful magic. I found it buried deep within my abdomen. It swirled there like a gentle pool. Unlike my Koigni magic that moved like a raging river, the Anichi magic didn't beg to escape. It awaited my command. That was why I'd never noticed it before.

"I found it," I announced to my grandparents.

"Good," Grandpa said. "Now open your eyes and aim your light straight at me."

My eyes opened, but I didn't lift my palm right away. "What if I hurt you?"

Grandpa shook his head. "You're not going to."

"How do you know?" I asked.

"Because you trust in the totem, Sophia," he said simply. "And I trust in you."

I took a deep breath and held it for a moment, then slowly let the air out through my nose. "Okay."

I lifted my right palm and aimed it at my grandpa. Bypassing the Koigni magic in my chest, I dug deep into my belly and tugged the Anichi magic upward. My Koigni magic protested, as if it were a jealous child pushing my Soul magic out of the way. I willed my Fire to calm as my Soul came to the surface.

I expected the light to burst from my palm like my Fire often did, but it didn't. It came out smoothly, as if I were controlling it with a dimmer switch.

"That's it!" Grandpa cried.

I could hardly believe it! Grandma looked proud from the sidelines, and Esis cheered.

"Keep going," Grandpa instructed.

I pulled more magic to the surface, and as I did, the light in my palm brightened until it was nearly blinding. I narrowed my focus and aimed it so that it was a circle on Grandpa's chest.

Grandpa let out an excited cry. "Look at you, Sophia! You've done it."

A lump rose within my throat. I was thrilled, but there was something touching about learning I was something more— and that my grandpa had helped me realize it.

"Excellent, Sophia," Grandpa said, stepping toward me. He clapped me on the shoulder. "I think you're ready for round two."

"Round two?" I asked.

"Force fields," he said simply, like it was an everyday thing.

My eyebrows shot up. "Anichi can create force fields?"

"Yes," Grandpa said as he began walking away from me. "I want you to take that beam of light and form it into something solid. Use it to protect yourself."

"Protect myself from what?"

I barely got the question out before Grandpa whirled on his heel and shot a fireball at my head. Instinct overcame me, and I flung my own fireball at it, intercepting its path. The two collided and exploded mid-air.

Grandma gasped. "Alan! You don't have to be so aggressive."

"How else is she going to learn?" Grandpa asked.

"It's fine, Grandma," I assured her. "He's right. I have to learn somehow."

"Koigni magic is off limits," Grandpa stated. "Use your Soul magic. Again."

He shot a fireball at me a second time. I tugged on my Soul magic and aimed it at the Fire whizzing through the air, but instead of some force field forming around me, a beam of light glowed out of my hand. I ducked at the last second before Grandpa's fireball flew by my head and landed behind me. A few dry leaves lit up in flames, but they died out within seconds. Again and again we went through this routine, but each time ended with the same result.

"Maybe my Anichi magic isn't strong enough for force fields," I theorized.

"We don't know that yet," Grandpa said. "We've only just begun. It's time to push you."

"Push me how?"

Grandpa didn't answer. Instead, he formed a fireball and drew it back. I expected him to throw it at me like he had with the others, but instead, he twisted at the last second and sent it straight at Esis. Esis squealed as his eyes went wide, but he was too frightened to move.

I did the only thing I could. I jumped in front of the fireball.

I landed hard on my shoulder, my hands aimed out in front of me. I squeezed my eyes shut, awaiting the impact of the flames. But when I opened them, I saw that the fireball was gone. I glanced behind myself, expecting the ground to be on fire or there to be scorch marks somewhere, but there weren't.

Grandma gazed down at me in amazement. "Sophia, you did it."

Esis hopped onto my back and squealed in delight.

"I did?" I looked around. I barely had a chance to take anything in before Grandpa was barking orders again.

"Keep going, Sophia!" Grandpa instructed. He threw another fireball at us. I flinched, but it slammed into an invisible barrier a few feet away from me. Something tingled within me, like I could feel the attack on my magic.

Then I saw it. Next to the explosion, something white shimmered in the air, like the bubbles I played with as a kid. I looked upward, and I noticed the shimmering at all angles. I'd created a dome that encompassed me, my Grandma, and our Familiars. The force field seemed to cut through the trees, keeping parts of them inside the protective barrier.

Grandpa threw another fireball, then two more after that in quick succession. I knew what I had to do. Esis jumped off of me while I rose to my feet. I dug deeper into that Anichi magic and aimed it out through my hands. The force field around us grew bigger as more and more fireballs rained down on us. Grandpa tried to penetrate my barrier, but he couldn't.

He took a step back as my force field grew, stretching ten yards wide, and then twenty. It reached high above our heads, until it went past the tall trees and encompassed some of them entirely.

Grandma clapped in delight. "Go, Sophia!"

The three of our Familiars were on their feet, watching the shimmering grow through the forest. Esis stuck his fingers in his mouth and let out a shrill whistle. He was thrilled.

By the time my force field grew to thirty yards across, I was struggling to push it anymore. I felt as if I pushed it any further, I might collapse. My limbs were shaking, and sweat had broken out across my brow. I couldn't hold on any longer. I dropped my hands, and the shimmering disappeared. I fell to my knees and breathed a sigh of relief.

Grandpa ceased his assault of fireballs immediately and rushed to my side. Grandma was already beside me, a gentle hand on my shoulder. I inhaled deep breaths to regain my strength.

"That was amazing, Sophia," Grandma complimented.

"Truly amazing," Grandpa agreed. "I'm so proud of you."

I wiped the sweat off my forehead and looked to him. "I'm basically still in shock. I can't believe I'm part Anichi. Thank you for teaching me how to use the totem, Grandpa."

I threw my arms around his neck, and he hugged me back.

"This is only a start, Sophia," he reminded me.

"I know, but it was a good start," I said.

He nodded. "I can't wait to see how much you can do with the totem. You, my girl, are extraordinary."

I found Jonah, Imogen, and Liam in the Anichi dorms that evening, along with their Familiars. Liam was lying on one of the couches with a wet washcloth on his head and a bucket clutched in his arms. A thick blanket was wrapped around his shoulders, but he was still shivering.

"Ancestors," I cried as I rushed into the room. "Liam, what happened?"

I hurried over and knelt beside him. Imogen was already there, sorting through various potion vials. Jonah sat on the other couch, looking a little helpless.

"My immune system's shit," Liam complained. "That's what happened."

"It's just the flu, right?" I asked in a rush. I hoped to the ancestors it would pass.

Liam shook his head. "Same old illness. Just a bad day."

"That's good," I said. "We can fix this."

Imogen set her vials aside. "I was looking for something that would help the nausea until you and Esis got back, but I've got nothing."

"I'll be fine—" Liam's face paled, and he leaned over his bucket and made awful gagging sounds, though nothing came out. Finally, he lifted his head and gestured to Esis. "Come on, buddy. What do you say to a treatment?"

I held Esis firmly in my lap. "Wait."

All eyes turned curiously toward me.

I cleared my throat. "I want to try something first."

I told them about what had happened in the woods with my grandparents today, and how I'd learned that I had Anichi blood. They all looked stunned at the news, and at the fact that I could channel light and create force fields.

"Whoa," Imogen said breathlessly. "I didn't think it was *possible* to exhibit two types of powers, even from mixed parents."

"My grandpa thinks that the only way I can access my Anichi power is through the Spirit Totem," I explained. "So I don't think I could without it."

"And you want to try healing me?" Liam asked. He didn't sound apprehensive at all. He sounded curious to see the result.

I nodded. "If that's okay with you."

He set his bucket aside and shifted on the couch. "I don't see why we shouldn't try. I trust you, Sophia." He reached out and took my hand in his, then placed my open palm on his heart. "Let's see if it works."

Liam closed his eyes, awaiting my powers. I was acutely aware of all eyes on me, but I tried to pretend like they weren't there as I focused inward and pulled my Soul magic to the surface. I guided it out of myself, but instead of flowing into Liam, it manifested in a bright glow, so bright that it lit up Liam's chest.

"Holy ancestors," Imogen breathed in amazement. Sassy's eyes went wide, and Squeaks ruffled her feathers like she couldn't believe what she was seeing.

"That's amazing," Jonah said.

Liam opened his eyes and glanced down to take in the white light. I felt his chest rise beneath my palm as he turned his head back up and closed his eyes again. "Keep trying. I believe in you, Sophia."

My chest felt lighter when he said that. But it didn't seem to matter, because no matter how much I tried to channel my Anichi magic into him, it didn't help. Maybe I was doing it wrong. Maybe healing magic worked differently than I thought.

"I don't feel anything," Liam said.

"Do you want me to stop?" I asked.

He shook his head. "Keep trying."

But it didn't help. After a good twenty minutes of sitting there waiting for something to happen, we gave up.

I dropped my hand. "Sorry, Liam."

"It's okay, Sophia," he said as Esis crawled into his lap. Almost immediately, I noticed color return to his lips, and his eyes seemed brighter. "We'll try again next time."

I chuckled lightly. "So, basically, tomorrow?"

Liam laughed. "Yeah, probably."

Imogen cut in and reached for Liam's bucket, washcloth, and blanket. "Here, let me clean this up."

Jonah jumped to her side and helped fold the blanket, then they went off into one of the rooms to return everything.

Liam already looked so much better. He took my hand and guided me onto the couch. He put one arm around me and pulled me close to cuddle. I rested my head on his shoulder.

He placed a warm kiss on my head. "Thanks for trying."

"At least we have Esis," I said.

"Yeah." Liam scratched Esis behind the ears, and he purred. "He's a real life saver."

I sat there for several seconds, enjoying the rise and fall of Liam's chest. It felt so good to be in his arms, but there was something I had to say.

"Liam," I whispered. "I'm sorry about the other day."

He laid his head on top of mine. "What do you mean?"

"When I yelled at you about Mia. I know you were only doing what you thought was right. I don't want to fight."

Liam let out a soft breath. "I'm sorry I told her without asking you first. I don't want to fight either, *pawee*."

Jonah and Imogen returned then.

"Aw..." Imogen sang. "I love how you call her *pawee*. *Cherished one* is so fitting, don't you think, Jonah?"

The two of them sat on the couch across from us, and Sassy jumped up to cuddle in. Squeaks tried to sit next to Jonah, but she was basically on his lap.

He slapped her ass. "Squeaks! You're going to suffocate me."

She huffed and got off to sit on the floor beside him, appearing insulted.

Jonah turned to Imogen and wiggled his eyebrows. "Yeah. I think *pawee* is just about perfect."

They exchanged this knowing smile that suggested they were talking in code or something.

I narrowed my eyes at them. "What's going on? Liam calls me *pawee* all the time, and you guys have never said anything."

"Nothing," Imogen insisted, but her voice sounded higher than normal. "I'm just saying, you two make the perfect pair. Hey, Sophia. Have you ever considered what you'd wear to a formal event?"

I furrowed my brow at her. "I wore that blue dress to the Elemental Ball."

"Yeah, but what about your hair?" Imogen asked. "I'm thinking a nice braid with blue flowers—"

"Oh!" Jonah chimed in. "And maybe a few roses to match the—"

"Guys!" Liam snapped so loud that it startled me and Esis.

Imogen turned bright pink, and Jonah wore an innocent look on his face. What was going on?

Liam cleared his throat. "Since I'm feeling better, maybe we should go do something. You know, get out of here, where you won't be tempted with this *small talk.*"

Obviously he knew something I didn't. This was going right over my head.

"What are we supposed to do?" I asked. "We're not allowed in the Commons anymore, and the Biyami dorms suck."

"We could go into town and pick up some booze," Jonah offered. "Party in the Anichi dorms?"

Liam groaned. "Can't we get out for once? Like we used to?"

"Where are we going to go without getting in trouble?" I asked. "I bet we can't even party on the beach anymore without the Task Force sending us back to the castle."

"I have an idea!" Imogen exclaimed, bouncing a little in her seat. "We could go visit my tarot card reader."

Jonah pressed his fingers to his eyes. "Ancestors, Imogen, not this again. Tarot cards aren't real."

"So what?" Imogen shot back at him. "It would still be fun, wouldn't it?"

I couldn't say I wasn't intrigued. "I think it's a good idea. We should go."

Liam shrugged. "If it gets us out of the castle, I'm all for it."

"Fine," Jonah groaned. "But we're taking a carriage."

We snuck out of the Anichi dorms and down to the stables. The sun was just setting, leaving enough light to lead us down the path.

When we got to the stables, though, something was different. Usually you could walk right up and sign out one of the unicorns, or take a carriage for the day. Now, there were signs on every carriage that read *For Defortai Only.*

Liam's hands curled into fists. He walked straight into the stables and got one of the worker's attention. "Hey, what's going on? Biyami can't rent out transportation anymore?"

It wasn't until the worker lifted his gaze to us that I realized I recognized him. His name was Sam. He used to play ping pong with Cade in the Commons. He had an alicorn Familiar who'd gotten sick with the plague last semester before we'd brought Kinpago the cure. I'd seen him around the Biyami dorms.

Sam's shoulders fell. "Liam, I'm sorry. We didn't make the rules. If it were up to us, we wouldn't put a label on anything."

Sam gestured around to the other volunteers. There were half a dozen of them who were cleaning the stables and feeding the creatures before bed. "We're all Biyami here. Even we can't sign the creatures out anymore."

Imogen stepped forward. "Then why are you still volunteering?"

Sam sighed. "Someone has to take care of the unicorns. The Defortai who used to volunteer for extra credit dropped out when Professor Azalea called the stables *Biyami work.* She oversees the stables and has convinced the Deans to require Biyami in certain majors to work here. If we don't, we won't pass."

Imogen frowned. "Sam, I'm so sorry."

He shrugged. "It is what it is. Sorry you couldn't get a carriage. I hope you can still get to where you're going."

"We will," Imogen said. "Thanks for letting us know, Sam."

"No problem," he replied. "See you guys around."

We waved, and Imogen led us back along the trail. She walked a little faster than normal. "Well, that just pisses me off."

Worry knotted in my gut. Biyami were being singled out for so much crap lately. How far would Defortai take it?

"We can still get carriages from town, right?" I asked.

"I would think so," Imogen answered, "but we can walk. Her place isn't far. I just want to forget about this Defortai-slash-Biyami crap for the night, if that's okay with you guys."

"Totally," Jonah agreed.

"I'm in," Liam said.

We continued along the path, while Sassy, Squeaks, and Esis chased each other around ahead of us. They looked like they were having a good time. Jonah tried lightening the mood by making dick jokes, and Imogen played off him with nasty jokes of her own. Liam and I strolled side by side with our fingers entwined, laughing at the two of them.

"So tell me, Im, what's the deal with this tarot card lady?" I asked. "Aren't *naderei* the only ones who can tell the future?"

"Tarot cards aren't about telling your future," Imogen informed me. "They're more like a roadmap about the path that you're on, which you can always change. They're different from prophecies. Anyone can read them, not just an oracle."

"Then why do we need to visit someone? Couldn't we just buy a deck ourselves?" I questioned.

"Because she actually knows how to read the cards," Imogen stated flatly.

I chuckled. "Good point."

"It's just for fun," Jonah insisted, like it wasn't real.

"It is not," Imogen shot back at him. She turned to me to explain. "Look, you can't tell anyone I told you this, all right? The Elders don't know."

I pretended to zip my lips. "My lips are sealed."

"You guys, too." Imogen gave the guys a pointed look.

"Agreed," Liam said.

Jonah replied, "Your secret's safe with me."

Imogen took a deep breath. "She's not entirely Hawkei. She's also part witch."

"Part witch!?" Jonah practically screamed. "Like from the Miriamic Coven? The bastards who gave us the plague?"

Imogen reached up to slap her hand over his mouth, which was basically as high as she could reach. "Shh... You don't need to announce it to all of Kinpago. If anyone knew, they might think she started the plague. She could be sentenced without a trial just for being associated with the Miriamic Coven."

I eyed Imogen skeptically. "To be honest, Im, it sounds kind of sketchy. How do you know she wasn't involved?"

Imogen's hands balled into fists. She looked a little irritated. "I've been going to her for years. I trust her entirely. She didn't start the plague."

"Okay," I said, a little taken aback by her harsh tone. "If you trust her, then I trust her."

Imogen relaxed. "Anyway, all witches can read tarot. Hattie does it to stay in touch with her witch side, since she's not really able to use her other magic here in Kinpago. It would give her away."

Liam wore a nervous frown. "I hope you know what you're doing, Im."

"I do." She looked forward again, and her eyes lit up. "We're here."

We turned down a narrow path with trees on all sides. A tiny brick cottage came into view. Ivy grew up the sides, and there was a little fountain out front that trickled with water. Smoke billowed from the chimney, and the air smelled crisp and clean. Fortune Fairies fluttered around the front lawn, lighting it up in a beautiful display of twinkling lights. It was like something straight from a fairytale. It looked so peaceful and homey.

"Wow," I remarked. "It's beautiful."

Esis' mouth turned into a perfect O as he gazed up at the Fortune Fairies. He swatted them playfully as we approached, and Sassy chased one around in circles.

Imogen led us straight up to the front door and knocked. A few moments later, the door swung open, and an old lady poked her head out the door. She had deep age lines across her face and long white hair that fell to her waist. Though she hunched over and used a cane to walk, she had a young look in her eyes. She had mostly European features, with a little bit of Hawkei mixed in.

"Imogen," she said brightly. "It's been a while."

"It has, Hattie," Imogen said. "Are you available for a reading?"

"Of course!" Hattie opened the door wider. "Come in, come in. Who are all your friends?"

Hattie shook each of our hands as we stepped inside.

"These are Jonah, Sophia, and Liam," Imogen said. "And their Familiars, Squeaks, Sassy and Esis."

Hattie looked delighted to have us. The cottage was small, with beautiful natural textures like stone and wood. A large area rug lay on the other side of the couch in the living room. It'd been woven with various colors of thread in the traditional Hawkei artform. All around, I noticed Hawkei influences. Arrows hung above the stove, and a dream catcher hung in the doorway to the bedroom. A round table sat in the middle of the room, close to the burning fireplace. It was set with a beautiful carving of a wolf as the centerpiece. In the kitchen, endless herbs grew in the window, and other plants were placed around the room. If I had to wager a bet, Hattie was Nivita.

I glanced around for a Familiar and didn't see one, until a gray wolf stepped out from behind the couch. She had a grace about her, but she looked ancient and moved slowly. Hattie held her hand out, and her Familiar come over to nuzzle against it.

"Please, sit," Hattie invited, gesturing us to join her around the table.

There were only four chairs, so Jonah sat on Squeaks' rear to get up close to us. Liam sat on my right and took my hand in his, while Esis perched on my lap and peeked up over the edge. Hattie opened a drawer on a small table by the door and pulled out a deck of cards. She walked slowly to her chair and sat down, her Familiar at her side.

Hattie began shuffling. "What brings you here today?"

"We needed to get out," Imogen said. "We thought a tarot reading would be fun."

Hattie nodded in understanding. "It is, indeed. I will pick three cards for each of you— your past, present, and future— and one card for your Familiar. Your Familiar will go first."

Hattie fanned the cards out toward Squeaks, and she pulled one from the middle with her beak. Hattie took the card and flipped it over.

"The Seven of Swords," she said curiously. "This is the card of betrayal, deception, and trickery. Your Familiar feels betrayed, Jonah. You must work with her to resolve these feelings."

Jonah's face paled. Clearly, he and Squeaks were still having issues since their fight over Renar. He reached out to pet her, and Squeaks gave a low coo.

Hattie put the card back in the deck and set the deck in front of Jonah. "Your turn. Slice the deck, please."

Jonah looked a little skeptical, but he reached out and cut the deck in half anyway. Hattie positioned the lower half on top of the upper and pulled the first card.

The whole time, my heart beat wildly in my chest. I didn't know whether to believe in this stuff or not, but I'd seen so much since coming to Orenda Academy. I knew this could be as real as elemental magic. I only feared what Hattie might tell us.

Hattie placed the top card face up. It depicted a man upon a throne, holding a large gold coin with a star on it. "The King of Pentacles," Hattie announced. She turned a curious eye to Jonah. "You had great wealth in your past."

Jonah shifted uncomfortably. "Well, yeah. We won the Cup, so I had some money for a while."

Hattie turned over another card. This one depicted a man holding two swords, with three others on the ground. Two figures faced away from the man, as if they'd been betrayed.

"Mm..." Hattie mused, eyeing the cards.

"What?" Jonah sat up straighter and leaned into the table. He suddenly didn't seem so skeptical anymore.

"Have you lost your financial abundance?" she asked. "This card represents conflict and disagreements. You've had a falling out over this, haven't you?"

Jonah's brows fell over his eyes, like he couldn't figure out how she knew. Everyone knew we won the Cup, but only a few people knew he'd lost all his winnings to his parents. "Yeah. How did you know?"

She shook her head. "I know nothing but what the cards tell me. The Five of Swords suggests that in walking away from this situation, you are experiencing sadness and loss."

Jonah's face fell. "Well, yeah. They're my family."

Hattie nodded. "The cards urge you to make amends, and to move on, Jonah. Now is not the time to dwell on the past. You must accept what you lost, and learn from it."

Jonah's eyes widened, like he was starting to get a little freaked out. "What about the future? What does that card say?"

Hattie turned over another card. This one showed a couple with two children standing in front of a rainbow with ten cups. "The Ten of Cups," Hattie said, more to herself than to anyone else. "Should you follow the advice of the Five of Swords and move on from your loss, you shall experience love beyond measure. Your relationships— your family — will live in bliss and harmony."

Jonah eyed her skeptically. "That doesn't sound like my family."

Hattie offered a small smile. "This card speaks of the future, Jonah. Perhaps your family of the future is not your family of the past."

Jonah seemed extremely hopeful. His eyes shone with the possibility that he'd be able to have a family of his own someday. With that, Hattie gathered the cards and began to reshuffle, leaving Jonah plenty to think about. She fanned the cards out toward Sassy, who sat on Imogen's lap. Sassy nudged one of the cards with her nose, and Hattie pulled it out of the deck and flipped it over. The card showed a woman petting a lion.

"Strength," Hattie said. "A very fitting card for Sassy. This card indicates that Sassy is full of courage and compassion. Sassy is persistent and determined, and she can overcome any obstacle in her way."

"Wow. That's crazy accurate." Imogen scratched Sassy behind the ears. "Isn't it, girl?"

"Imogen, please split the deck." Hattie placed the deck in front of her, and Imogen cut the deck down the middle. Hattie flipped over her first card. It showed a figure standing in front of a collection of cups in the sky. Each one held a different item, like a snake and a pile of jewels.

"The Seven of Cups?" Imogen asked. "What does that mean? I never got that one before."

"This is the card of opportunity," Hattie explained. "But it can also signify illusion. There's a bigger picture that you're not seeing. The answer to your deepest pain is right in front of you."

Imogen tilted her head to the side, looking unsure of what that meant.

Hattie pulled another card. This one had the gold coins again— and a lot of them. "The Ten of Pentacles. This suggests you have much wealth and financial security."

Imogen nodded. "I'm the only one with my Cup winnings left."

Hattie placed another card on the table for Imogen's future. It depicted a naked woman pouring water out of two pots, with a large star above her. She smiled brightly. "The Star."

Imogen's eyes brightened. "The Star?"

Hattie nodded. "You will go through many challenges, but in the end, they will be worth it. This is the card of hope, Imogen. The ancestors have a plan for you, and you will be greatly rewarded when your period of turmoil is over. At the end of your spiritual journey, you will find yourself, and your life will settle as calm energy surrounds you and embodies you."

"Wow," Imogen said. "I like the sound of that."

Jonah nudged her. "We both got good ones."

Hattie reshuffled and had Liam cut the deck next. When she placed the first card, my blood ran cold. It showed a skeleton man riding on the back of a white horse.

Death.

I gasped, but Liam's expression remained stone cold.

"That one's obvious," Liam stated. "Everyone knows my Familiar died."

"The death card is vastly misinterpreted, Liam," Hattie explained. "It does not signify literal death, but a metaphorical death— moving from one stage of your life to the next. In this case, yes, it could've been marked by your Familiar's death, but only because that set off a domino-effect that led you on your new path."

She wasn't exactly wrong. When Nashoma died, the tribe shamed Liam. It was the reason they'd sent him to escort me to Orenda Academy in the first place. He'd hoped to gain some favor back with the tribe. If Liam hadn't come to get me, things would be very different now.

Liam seemed unsettled by the Death card, even though he didn't seem sure he really believed in all of this.

Hattie drew another card, which showed a woman sitting in front of two pillars, one light and one dark. "Your present aligns you with the High Priestess. She represents your intuition and subconscious mind. You should be listening to your intuition now to guide you on your path, Liam."

He nodded. The way he looked at her with unmoving eyes suggested what she said resonated with him. It was almost like he believed it.

She flipped over his card for the future. It showed a man on a throne holding a sword. "If you follow your intuition, it will lead you to the King of Swords, where truths will be revealed to you. This is the card of authority and mental clarity. Though you have suffered loss in your past, you will rise to serve as a great leader and a source of knowledge to many."

"That sounds just like Liam," I said.

"Yeah," Imogen agreed. "It really does."

"Totally you, bro," Jonah said.

Liam pressed his lips together. It looked like he was trying to decide whether he agreed or not. "Yeah, I guess so."

Esis was next. Hattie shuffled and fanned out the cards, and Esis pointed to one. Hattie flipped it over. The card depicted a woman floating in the sky and dancing inside a wreath. I didn't know what it meant, but it looked like a good card.

"The World," Hattie announced, carefully studying the image. "This is the card of achievement and success. You, Esis, are meant for great things, and you are close to fulfilling your quest."

The way she said it made the hair on the back of my neck stand up, though I didn't know why. Before I could question what she meant by that, she turned to me. "Cut the deck, please."

I took a deep breath before touching the cards. It was like if I cut them at the wrong location, I'd get a bad reading. I didn't go in half. I only took a few cards off the top, then set them beside the others.

Hattie gathered them, then flipped over the first card. It showed a man sitting beside a tree, with three cups in front of him and another being offered to him by an invisible hand. He crossed his arms and refused. "The Four of Cups is a card of contemplation. You've had opportunities come to you, but have said no to them."

I couldn't argue with that. I'd put a lot of energy into trying to find a way out of the prophecy when I'd contacted Showana.

Hattie turned over another card, and my guts twisted. The card showed a man and woman bound by chains around their necks. A man twice their size stood between them. He had curved horns growing out of his head and bat-like wings.

The Devil.

I didn't know what the card meant, but I knew it couldn't be good.

Hattie drew a sharp breath. She looked a little flustered as she rushed to explain. "The Devil represents your dark side— the parts of yourself that are holding you back from your true potential, things like addiction, negative thoughts, and destructive behaviors." Her voice grew stronger as she spoke. "You feel trapped. You feel as if you have no control over your situation. But you do, Sophia. You must face your dark side, become aware of it, and break free from these negative influences."

She sounded like she knew exactly what she was talking about, which sent a shiver down my spine. How could she know what was happening to me when I barely knew it myself? It was obvious the riots had left permanent damage. Was I making it worse by pushing my emotions away instead of facing them?

But she was right. I didn't feel like I had the power to change it. I couldn't go back and erase the riots.

Hattie fixed her gaze on me. I kept my head down, because I felt like if I looked her in the eye she'd know what I was thinking— that I wasn't sure I could do what she was asking.

Hattie placed a gentle hand on mine. "Nowhere does the card suggest you have to do this alone."

I swallowed the lump in my throat and forced the tears back. Liam squeezed my hand tighter. "Okay," I whispered. "What about the future?"

Hattie turned over my final card. My stomach plummeted to my toes. All my friends had gotten good cards for their future, telling them they would thrive once all of this was over. I didn't need Hattie to tell me what this card meant, because it was clear by the image.

Heartbreak.

"Three of Swords," Hattie said solemnly.

The card showed a red heart floating in the sky during a storm with three swords pierced straight through it. My breath wavered.

Hattie swallowed. "This is the card of heartbreak. Soon, you will make a sacrifice that will take your life."

My hand shot over my mouth. Hattie couldn't be any clearer.

Sooner or later, the day would come when I would die for the Hawkei.

Liam

NINE

Fuck those tarot cards. Sophia wasn't going to die on me. No fucking way.

I got that we were trying to save the Hawkei from certain extinction, but I'd sacrifice the entire tribe as long as it meant keeping Sophia alive. There wasn't anything I wouldn't do for my people, except give up the love of my life.

Not her. That was one line that I refused to cross. I understood that Sophia had promised the ancestors she'd give her life to save the Elementai if it came down to it. She had forced me to agree that if she needed to, I wouldn't stop her.

I didn't know if that was a promise I could keep. If what we were doing was eventually going to lead to Sophia's death, I was willing to let the world burn just to save her life.

I'd tried to push the reading out of my mind— though I couldn't deny that it'd been really accurate for all of us. I knew the moment I pulled the Death card that there was more magic involved than I wanted to admit.

But who could trust witches, anyway? Not fucking me. Hawkei needed to stick to their own kind. I didn't agree with magical races mixing, especially not Elementai. There weren't enough of us in the

189

world already to keep our culture going, especially not with the bullshit the Elders were currently pulling. We needed to keep our bloodline pure and resist watering it down with other supernatural races—including colonizers like the Miriamic Coven.

Yet... that was the same kind of thinking that led the Defortai to treating the Biyami like crap, and I realized that. Not to mention it wasn't very different from the kind of hatred Sophia and I experienced as interhouse.

Maybe I was the bigoted one. Who the fuck knew.

Head Dean Alric summoned us to the Anichi dorms late Friday evening. My symptoms had been flaring off and on for the past few weeks, so I ended up getting there last. It took me forever to climb the stairs and drag myself to the couch.

Alric and Baine stood near the fireplace, where everyone had gathered around in a semicircle. Imogen and Jonah were squeezed together on one of the armchairs, while Squeaks lay on the floor with Sassy on her back. There were plenty of chairs, so I didn't know why Imogen and Jonah felt like sharing one, but I'd stopped asking long ago why the hell those two did anything.

Lindsey and Miranda were talking in low voices with Maddie in the corner. Drew was nearby, and he seemed left out next to Ace, Eirakari, Medusa, and Evelyn. Ezra was leaning up against Dyami and appeared deep in thought.

Wyatt and his Familiar weren't here. I didn't know where they could be. Bren had shown up with Kingston, but Vanessa was still missing.

"Vanessa all right?" I asked Bren when I passed him.

He didn't answer right away. "I'm not quite sure," he confessed. "She's been okay, but the baby's been taking a lot out of her. She's had to miss a lot of class."

"Are you sure you don't want to go home?" I asked.

Bren shook his head. "No. She told me I needed to be here. Aisha will watch over her."

I hoped so. I didn't know how Bren held it together. If Sophia was pregnant, I'd be freaking out all the time.

But that would never happen. You know, because I couldn't give Sophia her dream.

Sophia was sitting on the couch and playing with Esis. When she looked up at me, she immediately caught on to the fact that I didn't seem well, though I was trying to hide it.

Guess that was one of the things about being in a relationship. Your significant other always knew.

Esis immediately scurried over and sat on my lap, placing his paws on my abdomen. I felt his healing power work almost instantly, though it didn't immediately take away most of the pain like it normally did.

Esis scowled, like he could sense his magic wasn't working as well as it used to. It made me think about how my ancestor Anna had died young despite the Anichi doing what they could to save her. I didn't want to end up like that, and it was freaking the hell out of me. If Esis' magic stopped working, I didn't exactly have a lot of options.

"Are you okay?" Sophia asked.

I cleared my throat, which felt thick. "I'm fine, *pawee*."

Her eyebrows knitted together. "Fine never means *fine*."

"I'll be okay." I didn't want her to worry more than she already did, and with the smuggling operation well underway, I was under a lot of stress lately. It didn't leave a lot of time for me to take care of myself.

My brother must've noticed I looked pale, because he stood up and crossed the room.

Ezra tossed me a water from the mini-fridge, and I snatched it out of the air. I gave him a nod to say thanks.

The conversation quieted as Alric stepped forward. Alric took a deep breath and said, "I think it's important to address some issues that have come up. The Elders and the Task Force have taken notice of the disappearances. They know that students are leaving the school, though they don't know how. We can expect a crackdown in surveillance here very soon."

"But does anyone really *care* that people have gone missing? I mean, they're Biyami. The Defortai just want us gone," Jonah said.

"Yes and no," Alric began. "Oleander's main goal is ethnic cleansing. But for the meantime, the Biyami are still useful for menial tasks and jobs that the Defortai don't want to do. They're an easy source of slave labor."

"I hate being called one of them," Ezra said spitefully.

"Me too," Lindsey chimed in. Miranda hung her head in agreement.

"Right now, Defortai outnumbers Biyami three to one," Baine said. "We can expect things to continue on like they have been for a few months more, but the real concern is whether or not Defortai will start executing people soon, and on a mass scale."

"Things won't ever get that far," Alric insisted. "The ancestors will intervene, I'm sure of it. Nothing like that could ever happen within the tribe."

Baine grimaced and said nothing. I knew what he was thinking. Something like this *had* happened before. Anichi had been wiped out because of it.

Still, I didn't want to challenge Alric and speak up. We needed to have faith in him.

"So how do we need to change things?" Sophia asked.

"We've been sloppy. That can't be allowed to continue," Alric said. "I believe it's best if we keep sneaking students out one by one, so that their disappearances aren't as noticed. That way, we avoid arousing more suspicion."

"I disagree," Baine said. "I think we need to start smuggling out as many people as we can. Before it's too late."

"Elliot, you're putting this whole operation at risk," Alric snapped. "We nearly risked exposure the last time."

That much was true. Smuggling twenty people out of the castle hadn't been easy. The Task Force had definitely noticed. If they caught on that any of us had been involved, it wouldn't be too long before they'd start watching us and piece together what we were doing.

"This mission can't go on forever," Baine said, a low tone of warning to his voice. "We'll eventually need to stop doing this, before we're discovered, so we should save as many lives as possible in the meantime."

"I have no intention of stopping," Imogen spoke up. "We've barely begun."

Many of us nodded in agreement. I didn't intend to stop helping people escape until we were found out. Too many Biyami needed us.

"Forgive me, Miss Ahnild, but you're being unrealistic," Baine said, before he turned to us. "As are all of you. I understand that you're young and optimistic, but we're putting our lives on the line for an impermanent solution. And we can't help anyone if we're dead."

"I'm telling you that the people won't allow it," Alric said. His tone was so harsh that it surprised me. Alric never lost his temper. He always maintained control at all times.

"Caspian, you need to think of the *long term*," Baine said through clenched teeth. He quickly glanced at Sophia before setting his eyes forward.

Alric cleared his throat. "We will continue the operation as we have previously," he said. "We will sneak out students one by one unless it is necessary to smuggle out a large group all at once. Does anyone else have any questions?"

Baine made an angry noise and shook his head. I raised my hand. "I have a question, actually," I said.

Alric and Baine glanced at me. I was pretty bold for doing this, but I had to have answers.

"Where did Professor Perot go? Along with all the other professors," I stated. "He left a letter behind for me, but it's not enough. Most of the staff has been replaced. Can anyone tell me what happened?"

Baine and Alric held a glance with each other. It was like they were trying to figure out what exactly was safe to tell me. The two of them were keeping secrets from us. I just had a feeling.

Alric sighed. "Shortly before the riots, a secret meeting was called between all the teachers, by Professor Perot himself. Many of them knew where society was going and had heard rumors of the two-House system before Oleander revealed it. Obviously, most of the staff did not want any part in this. Multiple teachers turned in their resignation papers to me that day and left quickly during the night. Very few decided to remain behind."

"But where did they go?" I asked. "They must've went somewhere."

"That I cannot tell you," Alric said. "If I knew where, I would be there myself. That is a piece of information Jacques decided not to share with me."

Alric's voice was very sad. It was obvious he really missed Perot. I believed him when he said that he didn't know where Perot went, because if he did, he'd be there with him.

Baine stepped in front of Alric and said, "The teachers who left scattered. They're probably all hiding in different places. But that doesn't matter, because they're not here. And we can't rely on people who aren't here to help us stop what's coming."

That much was true. No matter how badly we needed Perot, and people like him, to help us, he'd decided to dip. The people in this room were the best we were going to get.

The room was quiet. Lindsey and Miranda shifted uncomfortably in the corner, and Alric said, "I won't be calling any more meetings unless they're absolutely necessary. Everyone needs to keep their guard up. From this moment on, all of us need to be extra careful."

❧

Saturday morning, I headed to the library to meet up with Jonah. Biyami students were still allowed in the library, but we were confined to a corner behind a group of shelves where most people couldn't see us. That was fine by me, as I didn't want anyone noticing what we were doing anyway.

Jonah was supposed to be doing his homework, but his books were spread out in front of him and he wasn't paying attention to them. Instead, he was goofing around, floating around a balled-up piece of paper while Squeaks tried to snatch it from mid-air. Every time she got close, he yanked the ball away. Squeaks let out a low, irritated tone while Jonah snickered.

"Do you and Imogen have everything ready for tonight?" I whispered as I came up beside him.

"It's all ready to go," Jonah said. "Here's hoping you don't lose your nerve."

"Yeah." Ancestors, I was so nervous I felt like I was gonna throw up. "Shit, Jonah, what if she says no?"

"You should've gotten a bigger ring."

"Fuck you."

Though the library was supposed to be quiet, loud slurping noises broke the silence. Footsteps came around the corner. I leaned around the shelf to see Renar and Mallory.

They were making out in a rather disgusting way, which accounted for the nasty noises, but I nearly vomited when I saw that Mallory's skirt was hiked up around her middle. Her legs were wrapped around Renar's waist as he slammed her up against a bookshelf. I tried to avert my gaze, but Renar caught it first, and he grinned at me like he was proud.

He was literally fucking her right here in the library. I mean, I didn't have any room to talk, because I'd messed around in here too, but damn. He'd seen us and not even cared. Could Defortai get away with whatever they wanted these days?

I averted my eyes and tried to block out what was going on. We could hear Mallory's moans coming out from behind the shelf. Jonah kept his eyes down on his books. He ignored the spectacle like it wasn't even happening. After a few seconds, the moans died off, which I took to mean that Renar had a top record of lasting ten seconds or less.

Mallory's giggles faded as she and Renar ran off somewhere else. Squeaks clacked her beak in a displeased way.

"It doesn't matter, Squeaky. I don't care about him anymore," Jonah said, but his tone was slightly depressed. Even though Jonah had ceased to have feelings for Renar, it was obvious he felt lonely.

"I wish you'd broken both his legs, so he couldn't walk at all," I growled.

Jonah shook his head. "I lost my temper that night. I never want to do anything like that ever again."

"You were protecting Imogen. That bastard deserved it." I slunk into the seat opposite him.

"Who are you and I to make that call, though?" Jonah asked. "Believe me, I wanted to kill him that night he hurt Im, but what held me back was the thought that if I did, I'd be just like him."

"Who cares? It doesn't matter," I argued.

"Yes, it does. There's no justice in violence or war. There's no reason for it," Jonah said. "The Hawkei could avoid all this suffering in the first place if we sought peace instead of power. If we don't hold ourselves to a higher standard, this is never going to end."

"War isn't avoidable," I said quietly. It was one of those things my dad had drilled into my head during my chief training. No matter how hard people tried to resist their inner nature, some fuckheads would always come along to ruin things for everyone. Then others would have to rise up to stop them, and that always required sacrifice.

"It has to be. Otherwise, what are we even doing this for? Just for another war to start again somewhere down the line?" Jonah asked.

"Forget about the future. We're in the middle of a war right now," I reminded him. "Sometimes violence is the only way. For survival."

"I don't believe that. Alric says there's another way, so it has to be true," Jonah said. "I don't believe in hurting people or taking lives. It's not right."

"Being a pacifist is only going to get you hurt in these kinds of situations," I said, before I added, "Or killed."

"Fine, then. But I won't compromise my morals," Jonah said.

He made a scoffing noise and said, "I'm not some kind of a monster like my dad."

"You could never be your dad. He's on a whole other level," I said. "But that doesn't mean that you can't protect your own."

"Liam, I want to be a teacher because I want to help kids. I want to show them there's a better way," he said. "Someone has to stop the cycle."

"I guess." I got that Jonah was into philosophy and psychology, and we could debate this all day, but regardless it'd always come down to the same point. Until the tribe changed... which I wasn't sure it ever would... I didn't think Jonah's dream of a peaceful world was possible.

Jonah shook his head. "If people don't change, we're just going to end up making more people like Renar. He's a product of his environment."

"Why do you still stick up for him? It's obvious he's a piece of trash," I said.

"I don't stick up for him, but I understand him," Jonah said. "I know why he's the way he is."

I made a skeptical noise. "There is no excuse for how that asshole behaves."

"No," Jonah said quietly. "But I do wish he'd gotten a better chance."

"Jonah, what the hell do you mean?" I put an arm on the table.

"You're always saying how Renar had it bad, but how can I believe you after all he's done to you?"

Jonah hesitated. He eyed Squeaks for a moment before she gave a chirp, and he said, "Squeaks says that you should know. But you have to promise not to tell anyone. This isn't my story to tell."

"I won't say a thing," I said. "But I think I need some answers if I'm going to understand where you're coming from."

Jonah took a deep breath. "There were a lot of things wrong about Renar and I, but he did trust me. He told me stuff that he never told anyone. Stuff I couldn't save him from."

"Like?"

"His dad abused him," Jonah started.

"Okay," I said slowly. "Your dad hit you, and you're not a huge jerk, so—"

"I mean he was molested."

The confession almost knocked me out of my chair. "What?"

"His dad sexually abused him. He told me everything when he got really drunk one night. He started crying and everything. I just... the way his voice sounded, I knew he was telling the truth. His dad's a pervert, Liam. It didn't stop until he was almost in high school. His mom knew about it and didn't do anything, because she didn't want to lose the marriage."

I was so shocked that it was hard for me to come up with words. I always felt like there was something bad about Elder Raviro, but I could never figure out why. Now I knew. The sick fuck molested his own son.

Jonah reached out and stroked Squeaks' feathers. "That's why he's the way he is. He can't escape what happened to him in his past. I tried to change him, but I didn't realize back then that only he could change himself. And he didn't want to change."

I forced myself to say something. "As sad as that is... Jonah, that doesn't give Renar the right to hurt other people. There are plenty of people in this world who are abused that don't grow up to be complete dicks. And it doesn't give him the excuse to do the same to you."

Jonah's hand froze on Squeaks' feathers. It was a weird reaction, because I was talking about emotional abuse, but a lump formed in

Jonah's throat. He got this distant look, like he was remembering something that happened a long time ago.

Wait. No.

"Jonah, is there something you're not telling me?" I asked as a feeling of dread suffocated my chest.

Jonah's hand buried in Squeaks' feathers. "It was... it's in the past, Liam. I don't want to talk about it."

"Talk about what?" I felt like I was croaking out the words, my throat was so tight. Ancestors, this couldn't be what I thought it was.

Jonah put his other hand in his hair, like he was trying to force the memories out. "A few weeks before we were in the Elemental Cup... Renar and I were hanging out in his dorm. Squeaks wasn't there, because Renar wouldn't let her come in. I'd sent her back to my room. It was really late— I was a bit intoxicated. Renar wanted sex, but I wasn't sure, because I'd never done it before. He tried to talk me into it, but I was thinking about leaving. Before I did, Renar handed me this drink... I didn't know what was in it, or what it tasted like. I can't remember. He said it would loosen me up."

My mind was blank. It was so hard to process this information. I didn't want to believe it was true.

"I chugged it down, and everything afterward was a blur," Jonah said. "All I knew was that when I woke up, my clothes were gone and I didn't know where I was. Renar was gone. I managed to get dressed and stumble to my dorm, but I just knew... Renar had done something to me."

Squeaks let out a low coo and nibbled at Jonah's hair. My entire body had gone cold. If there was something to say or do, I was at a loss.

"I wanted it, right? I wouldn't have been his boyfriend afterward if I didn't," Jonah babbled. "That doesn't make any sense. He talked me into it. I basically said yes. I was the one who took the drink."

"There was no consent, Jonah." Ancestors, this was a nightmare. I couldn't comprehend that Jonah had been violated in such a way.

"But I ran right back into his arms," Jonah insisted. "I didn't need to be drugged the next time I had sex with him. Or the time after that, or the time after that. I slept with him willingly. I chased after him with an obsession."

"Not the first time," I told him. Renar had played on Jonah's desire to be loved, and used it to get what he wanted. It was just sick.

"I'm... I'm not a victim," Jonah said. "Nothing happened to me. I just don't want to talk about it."

Jonah fell quiet. I knew what the real truth was, even though Jonah didn't want to admit it. I could see it in Squeaks' eyes.

I thought my next words through carefully. "Have you told anyone else about this?"

Jonah let out a long breath. "No. Not a soul. I think Imogen suspects, but she hasn't asked. I want to keep it a secret."

"Well, thank you for telling me," I said. "I won't say anything to anyone. Not even the girls."

"Thanks for that, bro." Jonah sighed. "I'd rather leave it where it belongs. In the past."

"For sure, buddy." I hesitated. I didn't want to offend Jonah by asking him this question, and I knew it was a bit insensitive, but I felt like I had to. "Do you think you should report him?"

"Who would believe me? He's Defortai, and I'm Biyami," Jonah said. "Who would've even believed me *before* the two-House system started? People think stuff like that isn't supposed to happen to men. Whenever women come forward, they're always treated like shit. People make it out to be their fault. Society never takes the side of the victim... not that I'm a victim, because I'm not. I just don't want to relive the whole thing."

"Yeah," I said. "I get that."

Sadly, if you ever told anyone you were assaulted, the way it worked in our world is that people found out ways to make it seem like you wanted it. They never blamed the rapist, and if they did, they always got off easy. Jonah speaking up would just put him through more pain, and at the end of the day, Renar would still get away with it. Just like he got away with attacking Imogen.

"Anyway." Jonah stood up and started gathering his things. "Imogen and I will be there tonight. Be ready to be an engaged man, lover boy."

"Yeah. See ya."

I waved goodbye to Jonah as he walked off with Squeaks. I was still trying to gather my bearings and bring myself back to earth. My limbs felt like they were made of lead, while my head buzzed with a fogginess that was hard to clear.

I was still in shock. Renar had tried to kill Imogen, and he'd raped Jonah. Whatever had been done to him in the past by his dad was no excuse for the monstrous actions he'd taken against my friends.

I wanted to kill him. It wouldn't be hard. I'd done it before. It was effortless for me to rush the blood to Professor Fawn's heart, and that was a mercy killing. I had so much anger stored up in me right now that I wanted nothing more than to see Renar's lifeless corpse before me. What people didn't understand is that once you took a life, it was all too easy to do it again.

I'd never be found out. No one would guess what happened. They wouldn't think a Toaqua student would be powerful enough to kill someone that way. It was something only masters could do. They'd chalk it up to a freak accident, and Renar would finally get what he deserved. If society wouldn't do its job and take out the trash, I was all too willing to do so.

But that's not what Jonah wanted, and Jonah was the one who'd been hurt. It was his decision what happened to Renar, and he wanted to do nothing. He wanted the world to be at peace. The last thing he wanted was for someone to die of violence because of what had happened to him.

I'd honor Jonah's wishes, but Renar was going to get his one day. And I hoped to the Great Spirit the ancestors didn't spare any mercy for him when the time came.

I DID my best to push the earlier events of the day out of my mind as I prepared myself for Sophia and I's date tonight. This was it. This was the day I was going to ask her to marry me.

I was so nervous I hadn't eaten anything all day in preparation for this moment. It was a warm day for February, no snow, which was perfect for what we were doing.

I only hoped things would go according to plan, though Imogen had sworn up and down earlier that she'd rather "die than mess this up."

"Any particular reason you wanted me to wear a ponytail?" Sophia asked when I met her in the Great Hall. She was wearing jeans, tennis shoes, and a jacket. Esis sat on her shoulder and ran his hands through her soft hair like it fascinated him.

"You'll see," I said. I felt like I was going to jump out of my skin. My whole life had practically led up to this moment.

"I think it'd be nice if you told me where we were going, considering that you were very particular about what I should wear," Sophia said.

"It's a surprise."

Sophia laughed softly. "You and your surprises."

As we reached the edge of the grounds, I heard someone call my name. A groan nearly made its way out of my mouth when I saw who it was.

Motherfucker. Not now, Mia! This couldn't be worse timing. I didn't want to deal with her on a day like today.

Sophia frowned, but she didn't say anything. Esis' hair stood on end as Mia approached.

"What is it?" I asked. "Better make it quick, before someone sees us associating."

Mia seemed out of breath. She swept her hair away from her eyes, leaned in and dropped her voice. "There's a Biyami Third Year from Toaqua. Her name is Yvonne Yanaha. Her parents went missing and she doesn't have anyone left but her little brother. He's a First Year. They need somewhere to go."

"I'll get in contact with her," I said. "Thanks, Mia."

"Any time." Mia gave us a wink and hurried off. Esis tilted his head after her as she ducked back inside the school.

"See? She's not so bad," I told Sophia. "There's nothing to worry about."

Sophia nodded. "You're right. She can help us. Sorry I freaked out. Guess I was wrong about her."

"Don't mention it. It's not a big deal." I nudged her with my shoulder, and she smiled slightly.

The peryton keeper, Jones, stood at the entrance to the grounds with two of the flying deer themselves. I'd paid Jones extra to have them waiting for us. He'd managed to keep the perytons running, even if

Biyami couldn't rent carriages anymore, though I didn't know how long that would last.

"Good evening, Mister Mitoh," Jones said as he approached with the perytons. "Special evening, isn't it?"

"That it is, Jones," I said in a flat tone, indicating he should shut up. Luckily, he didn't say anything more. I helped Sophia onto the peryton's back before climbing on the other myself, and we took off into the sky.

The sun was starting to fall around this time, painting the sky a deep red. I told my peryton to climb higher as we soared toward the mountain range. Esis was perched on one of the peryton's antlers, letting the wind blow back his fur.

Eventually, the perytons landed on one of the tallest mountain tops. I assisted Sophia off the peryton by putting her hands on her hips and lifting her off.

"Your hands are shaking. You must be nervous," Sophia commented as I set her on the ground.

I let out a hoarse laugh. "Wait till you see what I have planned."

Esis jumped off the peryton and launched himself on Sophia's back. We wound up the mountain path until it ended, and Sophia stopped dead in her tracks. "You've got to be kidding me."

"I'm not," I said with a wide grin. "You ready to jump off a mountain?"

At the path's end was a small building, a metal platform built off the side of the mountain's ledge. A couple of workers were setting up harnesses by the platform's edge.

Yep. Bungee jumping. One of the few extreme sports I hadn't yet done.

I'd purposefully planned to do something extreme to conceal my anxiety about asking her to marry me. I wanted Sophia to think I was freaking out about bungee jumping rather than she get suspicious about something else.

Sophia held back warily. "I can't believe this is what you had planned. Are you really going to make me do this?"

"I'll never make you do anything you don't want to," I said. "But you've gotta admit, it would be pretty cool."

Sophia paused for a moment, then her face broke into a smile. "You know what? Why not."

"I thought you'd say that." I put an arm around her shoulder as we walked to the platform. The company was run by Defortai, but our tattoos were covered up by our sleeves, so they couldn't tell we were Biyami.

We signed the forms and went through a quick instructional process before being told it was time. I tied my hair back, and the workers fitted the body harnesses around us. Esis sat far enough away from the platform that he wouldn't accidentally get knocked off when we jumped, but that he could still watch.

"We'll be jumping in tandem," I told her. "Better hold me tight."

Sophia didn't say anything. I think she was too afraid to speak. Her face was pale white. Shit. I hoped I didn't make a mistake by picking this for my proposal.

Once everything was in place, the workers told us to step closer to the edge. The line was attached to our ankles as Sophia and I shuffled to the gap where the platform ended and air began. We were so high up we couldn't see the cliff's bottom. The drop had to be at least two hundred feet. A brush of cold wind slipped past our faces, and Sophia shivered. Our toes were hanging off the edge.

"Are you ready?" I asked. I put my arms around her and squeezed tight. She nearly suffocated me when she wrapped her arms around my middle, and I gasped.

"Sorry," Sophia squeaked out. "I'm ready."

"Have fun," the worker told us, and he gave a smirk as he gently pushed us over the edge.

Sophia screamed as we dove downward headfirst. Her screams were muffled by the wind and went silent as an adrenaline rush surged through our veins. I was laughing. There was nothing like that bottomed-out feeling your gut gave when you were falling through the air, completely weightless. It was completely liberating.

Sophia kept her eyes open. The fear left her gaze as she took in the amazing world around us as we dropped, almost in slow motion.

Then she looked at me, and our eyes connected. Her hold around me tightened as she pressed her lips to mine and kissed me deeply as we fell. It was the most exhilarating feeling. I'd never felt such a rush in my entire life.

Finally, we got to the end of the jump, and the cord surged backward. We bounced up and down a couple of times as the cord eventually lost its momentum. Sophia was giggling by this point as we swung back and forth over the ground.

"Worth it?" I asked breathlessly.

"Yes!" she exclaimed. "So worth it."

After the jump ended, we were gently lowered to the ground below, where there was another team waiting to take off the harnesses. The perytons were already there at the bottom, Esis on one of their backs. He was clapping and cheering loudly as Sophia approached.

"Okay, this is the best date ever. You're never going to be able to top *that*," Sophia said as she picked up Esis and whirled him around. Some of the joy seemed to have come back to her. My plan was working.

"You shouldn't put the cart in front of the unicorn," I said. "Wait until the end of the night to see if you feel the same."

"There's another surprise?" Sophia asked. Her eyebrows shot up.

"Yep. It's at my parents' house," I said. "Come on."

We climbed back on the perytons, and they flew us over the mountains and in the direction of the island where I lived. When we landed on the beach outside my house, it was dark, though the outside lights were on and a string of lights had been set up over the porch. Mom was bustling around, putting food out on a long table. On the side of the house was strung a big banner that said, *Congratulations!*

Squeaks and Sassy were outside, relaxing in the sand as they watched Mom peddle around. My little brother, Jackson, was most likely inside the house sleeping.

I wanted to do something really big, get the whole family involved. Imogen and I tried to reach out to Amelia so she could be here, but we couldn't get in contact with her. She was still working on the *Hozho* and was rarely in Kinpago. It was like she'd disappeared off the map since she'd become Biyami, and wanted it that way.

Dad was helping Mom set the table. He glanced up once and remained impassive as I dismounted the peryton. Tatum bellowed a friendly hello before going back to sleep.

Dad didn't necessarily approve of all this— thought I was jumping into things— but when I pointed out he and Mom had gotten married when they were my age, he came around.

Mom, however, was a different story. She had almost been as bad as Imogen and Jonah when I told her about the proposal and wanted to get started on the wedding planning right away. She kept sneaking glances at me as she bustled around, as if counting the seconds down to the right moment.

"What's all this?" Sophia said as she slid off the peryton, looking around. Esis jumped out of her arms and ran onto the table, where he promptly began nibbling on a biscuit.

"We just wanted to put a little something together for you, dear," Mom said quickly. "We never truly celebrated you two winning your court case."

I was surprised how smooth the lie came out. However, it was barely restrained. Mom was practically bursting with the need to tell Sophia the surprise.

Her eyes flickered downward to my arm. The Biyami tattoo was covered up by my jacket, but she still asked, "How's that healing?"

"It's fine, Mom." The tattoo had gotten infected, like I feared, but Esis had cleared it up before it'd gotten too bad.

"Hm." Mom slammed a plate down a little harder than she should. "Barbarians, the lot of them."

"Haloke," Dad said, and Mom didn't say anything more about it, but there was a bothered look in her eyes as she continued getting things around. It was clear that she wanted to stand up and do more to stop what was going on, but with Dad on the Elder Council, it was obvious she had to keep up appearances and pretend she was okay with what was happening. If she didn't, it would put the rest of the family in danger.

"Jonah's in the house, darling, if you want to talk to him," Mom said.

"Sure. I'll be a minute," I told Sophia. I touched her on the arm, then left her outside. Since we were going bungee jumping, I entrusted Jonah to keep the ring safe for me until we got back to my house.

"Where's the ring?" I asked Jonah the minute I saw him in the hallway.

"I gave it to Squeaks," Jonah said. "The Task Force stopped me as I was leaving the Biyami dorms. They've started searching people and confiscating anything that looks of value. I thought if I gave it to my Familiar instead, she could hide it and they wouldn't search her. I was right."

"They've started searching people now?" This was getting beyond ridiculous.

"Yeah. But don't worry, bro. Squeaks is waiting on your signal. Just let her know when it's the right time," Jonah said.

"It'll be any moment now," I said. "Where's Imogen?"

"Setting up the fireworks. It's all you from this moment on."

Fireworks weren't exactly *legal* in California, but magical ones made by Koigni were permitted inside the Hawkei reservation— for now, at least, until the Elders decided to ruin even more fun by banning them.

"All right." I was freaking shaking. "It'll be any moment now, once everyone's there."

"I'll get it on camera," Jonah said. He waved his smartphone around, and I nodded. One less thing to worry about.

I went to the bathroom for a moment, tried not to gag, and splashed my face with some cold water before I forced myself to go back out there. I felt like I was being overdramatic, but at the same time, I just wanted to get this over with.

There were sounds of raised voices coming from the kitchen. When I entered, the tense conversation fell silent— it had been Dad and Ezra. They glanced at me guiltily, though there was obviously something going on between them.

"Hey, I'm ready," I told them. "So if you want to watch, I suggest you head out there."

Ezra gave me a grin, but it was forced. "You sure you're ready for this?"

"Surer than anything," I said. "Now hurry up, before I wimp out."

"Hey dude, feel free to tie yourself down with the old ball and chain," Ezra said. "I'm single for life."

"I'll have you married off by the time you're twenty-five," Dad grumbled.

"You can try," Ezra shot back. He was playing around, but there was thinly concealed note of resentment in his tone. He wasn't all kidding.

"The tribe needs an heir to the chief hood," Dad complained.

Ezra smirked. "You don't need to be married to make heirs."

Dad broke. "Legitimate heirs, you do!"

I quickly left the room and ducked out of the conversation. This was such a common argument between Dad and Ezra that it was starting to get old. Ezra had never been gung-ho about being chief in the first place, but since Cade had died, he'd gone full-on rebellious. He was digging his heels in as much as he could about being chief, and it was really weighing on Dad.

The old guilt settled in, and I thought about Nashoma. If he was here, this wouldn't even be an issue, because the chief hood would still fall to me. *I wish you were here, buddy. You should be with me today.*

I passed my little siblings, Christian and Katie, in the hallway. It sounded like they were bartering.

"Ten bucks she says no," Christian said to Katie.

"You're on," Katie replied. I heard the sound of dollars being exchanged.

"Hey, you two, get outside," I snapped at them. "And not a word."

Katie wrinkled her nose, and Christian stuck his tongue out at me, but they did as I said. I took a deep breath and held it as I entered onto the porch. Maddie had shown up and was talking with Sophia. The minute she saw me, my sister's gaze lit up.

Almost everyone was on the porch, save for Squeaks, Sassy, Imogen, and Jonah, who were waiting on the beach. Everyone was staring at me with anticipation. Talk about pressure.

I let out the breath I'd been holding and said, "I have an announcement to make, everyone. But before I do, I suggest we turn our attention toward the beach."

Sophia tilted her head in interest, and I walked forward. Without an explanation, I grabbed her hand and led her off the porch and onto the beach.

The plan was for the fireworks to go off, Squeaks to slip me the ring, and for me to get down on one knee while they were exploding above us.

Jonah and Imogen insisted it was the only way to do it. It was a bit flashy, in my opinion, but whatever.

I faced her and took both of her hands in mine. "Soph, there's been something I've been meaning to ask you," I said quietly.

"What is it?" Her eyes widened. She had no idea what to expect.

I looked for Imogen. She and Jonah were nearby, running away from the batch of fireworks they'd just lit.

I realized they had set up the fireworks too close to the house as it was too late to do anything about it.

"Guys," I started, but the sound of my voice was drowned out by the explosion. Dozens of fireworks went off all at once in a giant inferno. Some went up into the sky and detonated as expected, but one veered off course and went careening toward the porch.

"Oh no!" Imogen screamed as one of the fireworks collided with the banner, setting it ablaze. Katie and Christian screamed in terror as the banner fell onto the side of the house in a blazing inferno. Most of the Familiars ran around in a blind panic, except for Tatum, who continued sleeping.

Dad immediately moved to put the fire out before it consumed the whole house. He used his magic to make a wave rise up from the ocean's waters and drench the flames that were about to creep up the siding. Ezra copied him, and they were able to put the fire out before any major damage had been done, though a couple of boards were black and needed to be replaced.

"I'm so sorry, everyone!" Imogen squealed. Her face was tinged with red. "I didn't mean to do that."

Sophia had let go of my hands and was looking at the charred area of my house with an open mouth. I was currently trying to gather my bearings.

Okay. Okay, a little fire wasn't anything to worry about. Just a small sidetrack in the plan.

Squeaks was still waiting nearby, the ring box in her beak. I gestured for her to hurry up and get over here. Squeaks walked toward me. I held my hand out so she could slip it to me, but Squeaks being Squeaks, you can guess what happened.

She tripped.

She *fucking tripped.*

And as she tripped, falling head over hooves, I watched the ring box slip down her throat.

Squeaks. Ate. The ring.

Squeaks peeped in alarm. Both of my hands tangled in my hair.

This couldn't be happening.

Almost everyone had been watching me, save for Sophia, so there was a collective gasp around the porch. Mom's hands flew up to her mouth. Imogen and Maddie gaped. Even Dad's eyes widened in surprise.

Ezra, fuck him, was barely concealing that he wanted to die laughing.

As I tried not to have a meltdown, Maddie did damage control. "Sophia!" Maddie shouted. She ran off the porch and onto the beach. Sophia turned her way, and Maddie grabbed her wrist. "There's, uh, something I need to show you!"

"Um, okay," Sophia said, bewildered. Maddie dragged Sophia into the house, and Eirakari stampeded after. Once the door was closed behind them, Jonah rushed forward, and Squeaks opened her mouth wide. She gagged a few times as he stuck his hand inside.

"It's gone, dude," Jonah said hoarsely. "I can't get it back."

I sunk to the sand and put my head in my hands. Ezra came up beside me.

"I can't believe it. The ring was eaten by a hippogriff," I moaned.

"Hey, look at it this way, you'll get it back eventually," Ezra said. He couldn't resist letting a snicker slip by. I threw my hand forward, and a five-foot wide stream of water came out of the ocean and knocked him over.

"Maybe something a little more private next time," Mom said, laying a hand on my shoulder. "Though I knew this meant a lot to you."

"It's fine, Mom. I'll just have to try again." Ancestors, I had to do this *again.* In another way, with an entirely different plan. Kill me now.

Eventually, Maddie brought Sophia back out, and we ate dinner underneath the stars. I was too grumpy to really consume much. This plan had taken weeks to set up. I didn't know how soon I could come up with and execute another proposal.

It was near midnight before the party died down. The little kids had long since gone to bed, and the rest of us had congregated around a bonfire on the beach.

"It's getting rather late," Mom said as she leaned against Dad. "I think we should all be turning in."

"Please don't make us go back to those bunk beds tonight," Jonah begged. "I'll die, Mom."

Jonah called my mother "Mom," too, which was fine by all of us, as she was a better mother to him than his own had certainly ever been.

"You're all more than welcome to stay the night," Mom said. Her face became troubled at the mention of the Biyami dorms. If Mom had her way, none of us would be sleeping there, but the decision wasn't up to her. The Elders would make sure we knew our rightful place as Biyami.

"Liam, I'm a little tired, too," Sophia said, and she yawned. "I think I'm going to turn in."

"Go on. I'll be there in a little while," I said. Sophia sauntered off to bed, with Esis following. Once she was safely in the house, I said, "This was a disaster."

"Well, that's what you get for allowing Jonah to help you," Dad said.

I groaned and looked to Maddie. "Can you tell me if I'm going to get it right next time?"

Maddie gave a nonchalant shrug. "What, you want me to give you all the answers to life? I told you I know what *happens* to you, not how it's going to go down. You could ask Sophia a million more times before you get an answer, for all I know."

There was a hacking sound behind me. I didn't bother to look. Imogen let out a triumphant squeal, and Sassy barked a few times.

"Hey, Liam, we got the ring!" Jonah said. He held out the box, which was covered in sticky hippogriff spit. "Squeaks coughed it up."

I jumped out of my seat and snatched it out of his hands, ignoring the goo coating my fingers. The ring itself didn't look like it'd been harmed, but I was going to have to get a new box.

"Well, that's a relief," Imogen said. "Now we just have to work on a plan for next time."

"No. No, no, *nope*, you guys aren't getting anywhere near this again," I said. "Let me do it on my own."

Imogen let out an offended sound, and Jonah sniffed. "Very well. It's clear that you don't want our *superior* help."

"Unless I want my house burned down? No thank you."

Dad chuckled behind me. I shoved the ring in my pocket and seethed. Okay, so *this time* hadn't worked out very well, but *next time* it'd be perfect. Sophia was totally going to fall for my next plan.

If it didn't self-destruct halfway through. This proposal thing was a lot more complicated than I thought.

sophia
TEN

"Whose idea was the fireworks?" I asked Imogen on Monday after class. I'd met up with her in the dungeons, and we were on our way to the Anichi dorms. Imogen said she had something to talk to us about, but this was the only time I'd gotten her alone since the celebration dinner that nearly sent Liam's house up in flames. It was half shocking, half hysterical to say the least. Maddie and I shared a good laugh afterward. It felt *so* good to laugh.

"Ugh," Imogen groaned. "You're still on that?"

"Well, yeah," I said, stroking Esis in my arms. He snuggled into me with his arms wrapped protectively around the dragon egg. "I haven't had a chance to grill my best girl about it. So, who thought it was a good idea to burn the Mitoh's house down? You or Jonah?"

Imogen hung her head and answered in a small voice. "Me."

I snickered. It felt good, but odd at the same time— like I shouldn't be laughing with everything else going on. "I knew it. It was a little over the top, though, don't you think? I mean, we were just celebrating our trial win. It's not like it was our wedding or something."

Imogen pressed her lips tightly together. Then her eyes brightened, like she'd just remembered something. "Hey, guess who has a date."

My eyes widened. "Imogen, seriously?"

She shrugged. "It's not a big deal. I'm not even sure it's a date. Sam asked if I wanted to get dinner with him to catch up, since we haven't talked much since Cade…"

She trailed off. "Anyway, I said yes because, well, it'd be rude not to. And like, I'm really sick of the cafeteria food."

I nudged her playfully in the side and sang, "Imogen and Sam sittin' in a tree. K-I-S-S—"

"Can you not?" she asked, pressing her fingers to the sides of her temples. I suddenly felt bad for teasing her. She looked up and breathed a sigh of relief. "Oh, good. We're here."

Two Task Force members were walking by, so Imogen stalled by bending to adjust the bow around Sassy's neck. As soon as they rounded the corner, we snuck into the Anichi dorms. The guys were already there when we arrived, playing video games on Jonah's TV.

"Get him! Get him!" Jonah shouted as he pummeled a button on the controls. Liam was sitting up straight, his tongue stuck out of his mouth in concentration. "Get him!"

"I'm trying!" Liam growled.

We heard the sound of an explosion, then saw animated body parts flying toward the camera.

"Ew," Imogen complained. "Do you *really* have to be playing that? What is it with guys and their fascination with gore?"

Jonah hit pause on the game and tossed his controller aside, then lounged back on the couch casually. "Hey, if you want me to play something else, use some of those Cup winnings you have sitting around and buy me some games. This is basically all I have. Unless you want me to play boxing, but it's all tall girls with big boobs. I'd rather see me some muscle."

Imogen rolled her eyes and shoved his shoulder. "Move aside. It's time to get serious."

Liam turned off the TV, and I sat beside him. Esis jumped out of my arms to sit next to Liam. When Liam tried to pull Esis onto his lap, he slapped his hand away and insisted on sitting on the couch like a big boy. He set Julian between his legs and ran his paws along the outside of the egg.

"What's up, Im?" Liam asked.

Imogen reached into her bag and pulled out a stack of papers. "Well, I think I might've found something."

"About the prophecy?" Jonah looked a little shocked, like he thought we'd reached a dead end.

Imogen nodded. "Here's what I could find from the Air Elder scrolls Jonah got for me. Since the prophecy was made, I found three mentions of it. But none of the records say what it was, only that they discussed the prophecy during their council meeting."

"How does that help us?" I asked.

"I *might* have a lead." Imogen sounded a little uncertain, but she straightened and cleared her throat. "I went back to the last mention of the prophecy in the scrolls, then cross referenced who was serving on the Elder Council at the time. Almost all these guys died shortly after, since they were so old. But there was one guy on the council who was a lot younger. His name was Emmett Chang. I went through all of his meeting notes. After the other Elders died, he never spoke of the Air piece to new inductees, according to the scrolls. Which makes him the last person to know the Air piece, as far as we know."

Liam's brow furrowed. "I still don't get how that gets us any closer to the prophecy."

Imogen shuffled her papers. "Well, he only died about twenty years ago. I looked into whether he had kids or grandkids, thinking he might've left the prophecy to them, but he didn't. So my other thought is that maybe he left a clue. We could hunt down parts of his estate that were sold off when he died."

Liam pressed his fingers to his eyes and sighed. "Im, that sounds like a lot of work that could lead nowhere."

Imogen chewed her bottom lip. "I know, but we have to at least try, right?"

Jonah looked hopeless. A sinking feeling entered my gut. It didn't seem like a lot to go on.

"Look," Imogen said. "I know if anyone was going to lose their piece of the prophecy, it'd be Yapluma. But I just don't get that vibe from this guy. He would've left something behind."

Jonah scrunched up his nose. "How can you get a vibe from a dead guy?"

"For one, I read the scrolls," Imogen pointed out. "Two, you can just see it in his eyes."

"His eyes?" Jonah asked.

"Yeah," Imogen said simply. "There's a picture of him."

Imogen flipped through her papers and handed one to Jonah. He stilled as he took the paper in his hands and stared down at it. Squeaks peeked over his shoulder.

"What?" Liam asked, rushing over to look at the paper.

I rose to my feet and looked, too. It showed a painting of a guy with long, dark hair wearing traditional Hawkei regalia. He sat with his back straight. He wore a soft expression but had strength in his eyes. Behind him was a clouded sky, and in the corner, a thunderbird flying through a streak of lightning.

"This makes sense," Jonah said thoughtfully.

"What do you mean?" Imogen asked.

Jonah shrugged and handed the paper back to Im. "Of course he was the last person trusted with the prophecy. He was the last Storm Lord."

Imogen, Liam, and I all exchanged a glance. It was obvious no one knew what he was talking about. "Um... Storm Lord?" I asked.

Jonah looked at us like we were idiots. "Yeah, the Storm Lord. You've never heard of him?"

"No, we haven't," Liam stated flatly. He sounded like he was getting annoyed.

Jonah just sat there without responding, as if astounded we didn't know.

"Um, a little more info would be nice," Imogen pressed.

Jonah snapped to attention. "Right. The Storm Lord. So there's a Storm Lord once a generation. They're an exceptionally talented Yapluma who's gifted extra powers from the ancestors. They can create and control lightning, which is why they bond with thunderbirds."

My brow furrowed deeply. "That can't be right."

"What can't?" Jonah asked.

I quickly shuffled through my memory, trying to recall what Doya had told me about conjuring lightning. "Well, Doya told me only Koigni could create lightning. We superheat the air to create plasma— or something." I didn't remember all the scientific details.

"Well, Doya's wrong," Jonah stated. "Koigni might be able to create lightning, but so can Yapluma."

"No, *you're* wrong," I accused. "How does a Yapluma create lightning anyway?"

Jonah looked at me like I was stupid. "Do you even know how lightning's created? It's because of the air. When cold air and warm air meet, it creates thunderstorms. The ice crystals in the cold air bump into the water droplets in the warm air, which creates an electrical charge. When the charge gets strong enough, it lets out energy that results in lightning."

We all stared blankly at him.

"Dude," Liam said. "How do you know that?"

Jonah shrugged. "I pay attention in *some* of my classes."

I eyed him quizzically. "If all it takes is some air manipulation, why can't all Yapluma make lightning? I mean, didn't the Yapluma Elders create a thunderstorm during the Elemental Cup?"

"Yeah, but that was five Elders *together*," Jonah pointed out. "Same with the twister. Anyway, the science behind it doesn't really matter. Even if a Yapluma can create a thunderstorm, they can't *control* lightning, and most can't manipulate the air from that far away anyhow. But the Storm Lord isn't just Yapluma. He's a category all his own. If there was a House for lightning, he'd be it— a single Hawkei chosen by the ancestors to rule the skies."

"How do you even know about the Storm Lord?" Imogen asked, like she couldn't believe Jonah knew something about the tribe that she didn't.

He shrugged. "I don't know. It's a story all Yapluma grow up knowing, like your Earth legend. Plus, my dad had that same portrait of the Storm Lord in our house when I was a kid."

Liam narrowed his eyes a little, like he was thinking hard. "Wait, Jonah. You mean the exact same one? Like, the original?"

Jonah leaned away from Liam a little, like he was being interrogated. "It's a long story."

"So tell us," Imogen insisted. "If we want to find this Air piece, we need to know everything."

"It's really not a big deal," Jonah said.

Imogen grabbed him by the shirt and got up close, until their noses were nearly touching. "Tell. Us. Everything."

Jonah brushed her off and sighed. "Fine. So when I was a kid, my dad had some debts he couldn't pay off. The guy he owed money to took him to court, and the Air Elders ruled against him. My dad wanted to get back at them, so he stole this painting that hung in the council chambers. It was really expensive, because the Storm Lord had painted it himself. Dad was going to sell it to pay off the debts, but before he could..."

Jonah trailed off. Beside me, Liam looked thoughtful— like he was remembering something important.

"The beast came for it..." Liam whispered, so softly that I barely heard him.

"Beast?" I asked as a shiver traveled down my spine.

Jonah dropped his shoulders and groaned. "I don't know what it was, honestly. Maybe someone's Familiar. It came, it took the painting, and it left. Liam can tell you. He was there."

All eyes turned to Liam. "When did this happen?" Imogen asked him.

"Ages ago," Liam said. "We were kids, playing in Jonah's basement. I never saw the beast. I was hiding in the wardrobe."

The gears were turning in Imogen's head. "Guys, this painting could be the answer."

"What do you mean?" I asked.

"What if Emmett didn't trust anyone with the prophecy and that's why it never came up again in the scrolls?" she questioned. "What if the only way to hide the secret was with himself?"

I tried to understand what she was getting at, but it took me a few moments. Then something clicked. "You think he hid the prophecy in the painting? Like Spirit Art?"

Imogen's eyes brightened. "Exactly! Guys, if we could get our hands on this painting, maybe we could summon the piece of his soul he put into it."

"I thought you couldn't do that," I said. "Didn't Professor Amber say that wasn't possible?"

"It depends," Imogen reminded me. "You can if you're worthy."

"That means one of us has to be worthy," Jonah pointed out. "And we're not."

"What about Sophia?" Imogen asked. "The prophecy's about her."

"Im, I don't think—" I started, but Jonah cut me off.

"No, no. When I think of *worthy*, I think about Elders," he said. "Oleander's got all the Air Elders wrapped around his little finger. They're not going to help us."

"Unless we could ask someone else," Liam cut in.

"Who else?" I asked.

Liam took a breath. "What about another Storm Lord? I bet they'd be worthy."

"Yeah, that'd work," Jonah replied. "But where are we going to find one of those?"

"You said there's one every generation," Liam reminded him. "So who's the new Storm Lord?"

Jonah rolled his eyes. "I don't know. It's not like we crown one. That said, there are only two people we know in Kinpago bonded to a thunderbird."

"Ezra is one, but he's not Yapluma," I mused. "Who else?"

"Dean Alizeh," Jonah said. "She's Yapluma and she has a thunderbird. That means she has to be the new Storm Lord."

Imogen slapped her knees and stood. "Then it's settled."

Jonah's eyes followed her. "What's settled?"

She pointed to Jonah. "You're going to tell me everything you know about this beast, then I'm going to do some research and see if I can find where it took the painting. And *you*." She pointed to Liam. "You're going to help Jonah talk to Dean Alizeh and figure out if she'll help us."

"What about me?" I asked.

Imogen eyed me for a moment. "You? You can just... relax."

My jaw dropped. Was she suggesting I couldn't handle this?

... *Of course* she didn't think I could handle this. I'd been falling apart lately. I could barely keep myself together. I didn't blame her for wanting to leave me out of this one.

Imogen turned back to Jonah and Liam and clapped her hands. "Chop chop, people. That prophecy piece isn't going to wait around forever."

"Actually, it might," Jonah said. "It's in a painting, you know."

Imogen rolled her eyes. "Yeah, well, *we* can't wait much longer."

❧

I HADN'T HEARD any more about the prophecy until Wednesday, when I'd asked Liam in Hawkei Art if they'd made any progress. Today, the chairs and easels were set up in a circle, with a small platform in the middle.

"Dean Alizeh is really busy. It's hard to get a meeting with her," Liam told me.

"Class," Professor Amber called softly as she strolled into the room. "If I could have your attention, please."

The room quieted, and all eyes turned toward her. I was surprised when I looked up to see Lindsey standing next to her in a silky red robe. Medusa was wrapped around her shoulders.

"Today, we'll be studying the art of the human form," Professor Amber said brightly. "Miss Andrews has volunteered to be our model for the day. Take all the time you need to get comfortable with the curve of her body as your pencil moves across the paper. Let your sexuality flow into the drawing."

My jaw dropped. Was she serious? *Please don't tell me this was what I think it is.*

"Miss Andrews." Professor Amber nodded to her, then gestured toward the platform in the middle of the room.

Lindsey stepped up to it, then just as I feared, she tugged on the strap of her robe, and her clothing fell to her ankles. She stood stark naked, her boobs and ass on full display. Lindsey winked at one of the guys across the circle from me, who was already drooling, then lowered herself to strike a pose on the platform. Medusa slithered around her body, somehow making the pose even more sexual.

I averted my gaze and moved my head so my easel blocked the view of her naked form. I noticed Imogen and Jonah shooting me matching smirks. They thought this was hilarious.

Liam leaned over and chuckled lowly. "Awk-ward."

Honestly, it wasn't as awkward as I expected. I didn't feel anything for Lindsey anymore. I was worried about what was going through Liam's head. Like, was he concerned I'd be sitting here all class with a lady boner? Because I wouldn't. I reserved all my sexual energy for him and only him.

"If this is too weird, I can go," I said quickly. "I'll skip class for the day."

Liam crinkled up his nose. "Nah, stay. Unless it's weird for you."

Okay. Liam didn't seem bothered by it, so why should I?

"Well, Lindsey and I dated," I said, like he needed the reminder. "You probably don't want me staring at her for the next two hours."

Liam shrugged. "I'll be staring at her, too."

"Yeah, but not like *that*," I pointed out.

At least, I hoped not. Oh, God. Did he find her attractive?

He shook his head. "No, not like that. I only have eyes for you, *pawee*."

I smiled, but it was forced. I didn't think Liam understood how serious Lindsey and I had been. If Liam hadn't wanted me back, I'd probably still be with her. Not that I still liked her, because I didn't, and I was happy she was with Miranda now. I just expected it to bother Liam more than it did.

"Same here, Liam," I told him honestly.

He leaned over and kissed me, then we got to work on our drawing. The more I focused on drawing, the less I focused on Lindsey, until she became just a prop in my mind and not a sex object. But even then, the thought that I was drawing my naked ex kept creeping in. My racing mind caused me to go slower than everyone else. By the time class finished, everyone was done with their drawings except me.

Professor Amber came around to inspect everyone's drawings. Her orangutan Familiar followed behind, placing a gold sticker on every drawing to indicate who passed the assignment. "Very good, Miss Ahnild. Mister Chanee, that extra touch you've added is very unique."

I glanced over to see he'd drawn a penis where Lindsey's vagina should be. I face-palmed, and Liam groaned beside me.

"A dick, Jonah?" I asked. "Really?"

He shrugged. "She told me to channel my sexuality."

Professor Amber came to Liam and I next. "Miss Henley, you didn't finish."

I blushed and ducked my head. "Yeah, I couldn't get this part right."

I gestured to the general chest region. I'd done great drawing Medusa, though I couldn't bring myself to draw Lindsey.

"Take all the time you need," she encouraged.

She moved on to Liam next, and her orangutan placed a gold sticker on the bottom side of his drawing. I peeked over at it and saw that it wasn't half bad.

Lindsey came up to us as Professor Amber moved on. She was wearing her robe again. "How was it, guys? Did I do okay? It was hard sitting still for that long."

"You did great," Jonah told her.

"Did you really draw me with a dick?" she asked curiously.

Jonah beamed. "Sure did."

Lindsey's eyes lit up. "Let me see."

She squeezed between two art easels and came to look at Jonah's drawing while the rest of the class packed up their stuff. Lindsey took one look at it and threw her head back in laughter. "Oh my ancestors, Jonah. I love it!"

He took the paper off his easel and held it out to her. "Here, take it."

Her eyes widened in gratitude. "Are you sure?"

"Absolutely," he said. "We all need a little dick in our lives."

Lindsey burst into laughter again. "Yeah, not all of us."

Imogen snickered beside them, then said, "So, *Lindsey*. I didn't know you were modeling."

Lindsey leaned in like she was about to tell a secret. "Hell yeah. Do you know how much money models make? Professor Amber offered me two hundred bucks for this gig."

"Wow." My jaw dropped.

"I mean, it's only temporary," she said quickly. "It's not like I'm going to graduate and rock the porn industry or anything."

Jonah laughed. "But you could, babe. You could."

Lindsey tossed her red hair over her shoulder for show, then struck a pose. "You think?"

"What do you think about starring in a cabaret show?" Jonah asked. "I'd *love* to host one."

Imogen swatted him in the shoulder. "You would not."

"I totally would," Jonah said as he stood and gathered his things.

Liam sat silently beside me, rolling his eyes while I continued drawing.

Imogen turned to me and Liam. "Are you guys coming?"

"I'm going to stay here and finish," I said. "I didn't get my sticker yet."

Liam shook his head. "I'll stay with Sophia."

"See you later, losers," Jonah quipped as he slapped Squeaks' ass to get her moving. Esis climbed out of my lap to go with them, but I told him to stay.

"Bye," Liam said to our friends. He turned back to me as soon as they left the room. The door shut behind them, leaving us entirely alone. Even Professor Amber had left to go back to her office on the second floor.

"I hope it's okay I stay. I don't need to hear about Jonah's cabaret show again," he mumbled.

"So it's a thing?" I asked.

"When was it never *not* a thing?" Liam joked. His eyes turned to my paper. "You okay?"

I sighed and set my pencil down. "I don't want you to think this is about Lindsey, because it's not. It was a little awkward at first, yeah, but I'm over her. We're just friends."

"I believe you," Liam said. "But if that's the case, why aren't you finished? You're the best artist out of all of us."

I dropped my shoulders. "I don't know. I was worried what you'd think."

Liam stared me straight in the eyes. "If you say you're over her, you're over her. It's fine, Sophia. It's just an art class."

I relaxed, but when I placed my pencil back to the paper, I paused.

"What is it?" Liam asked.

I sighed. "We've been doing so much artistic realism lately. My creativity needs a break. I want to paint something crazy."

"Okay." Liam shrugged. "So paint."

"Huh?" I asked.

"If you want to paint, go paint," he repeated. "We've got all the supplies for it."

A small smile began to form across my lips. "You wouldn't like it."

"Like what?" he asked.

"You wouldn't like what I want to paint."

"Is it a dick?" he groaned.

I chuckled. "No, it's not a dick. I'm in the mood for abstract. Chaos."

He looked a little unsettled, but quickly relaxed. "Okay. Chaos it is. Show me."

Esis followed behind us as Liam and I headed to the back room where extra painting supplies were kept. I pulled a big sheet of paper out of the roll in the storage room, then spread it across the floor as a barrier. I took another smaller sheet and placed it on top, which would serve as my canvas.

"Here." I handed Liam a paintbrush, then turned to fill a styrofoam cup with blue paint. I handed that to him as well.

"What are we painting?" he asked.

"Whatever you want," I replied with a shrug as I filled my cup with red. I took my own paintbrush and dipped it into the thick liquid, then flung it at the paper below us. The paint splattered over it.

A wide smile spread across Liam's face. "Ah, I see. Chaos."

Liam dipped his paintbrush into the paint and splattered blue color over my red. The two bled together to create a gorgeous purple. Esis jumped into the wet paint before I could stop him and ran across the paper, leaving little footprints along it.

I groaned. "Esis, you really shouldn't—"

It was already too late. He dipped his paws into the glops again and brushed the color across his fur. I rolled my eyes. "Fine, but don't whine when I give you a bath later."

As we continued splattering the paper, my mood lifted. I couldn't resist asking Liam, "So, what'd you think of class today? Did you *let your sexuality flow onto the paper*?"

He shook his head, looking amused. "There was nothing sexual about it. I already told you, I only have eyes for you."

I scoffed playfully as I flung another glob of paint onto the paper. "Like I believe that. Her boobs are bigger than mine."

"And your ass is nicer than hers." Liam stepped behind me and squeezed my ass. He was so close I could feel the heat of his breath across my neck. It was kind of hot, and his touch was starting to turn me on—until I felt a cool liquid seep through my pants and onto my skin.

I squealed and jumped away from him. "Liam!" I exclaimed as I turned to look at where he'd touched me.

"What?" His eyes went wide, and he sounded concerned.

"You got paint on my jeans!" I cried.

Liam bit his lip guiltily. "Woops. This stuff is washable, right?"

"Yeah, I think so," I said.

"Then no big deal, right?" He laughed.

"Yes, big deal," I told him.

He crinkled his nose. "*Is it*, though?"

Just as he said it, he wiped blue paint across my cheek, then jumped out of the way as I reached out to swat him. My jaw dropped dramatically, and I drew in a breath.

"Jerk," I teased as I flung my paintbrush at him. Red paint splattered all along the frontside of his shirt.

He gasped and stared down at the damage. "Sophia Henley. How dare you?"

"How dare *me*? How dare *you*?" I shot back.

Liam sighed. "We're going to have to do something about this."

"Like what?" I challenged.

Before I could react, Liam threw his arm out. The entire contents of his cup flew out and landed on my face. I froze as thick blue paint dripped down my chin. I didn't want to move and get it in my eyes.

"Liam!" I screamed. "It's down my shirt!"

Liam rushed forward and tugged at the bottom of my shirt. I didn't know how it all happened, because it was so fast, but I must've instinctively shot my hands into the air to help him get it off. One second I had a paint-soaked t-shirt on, and the next my torso was exposed to the storage room while Liam wiped my shirt across my face and down my chest to stop the paint from dripping.

"I'm sorry," he said quickly. "I didn't think there'd be so much."

"You didn't think...?" I rolled my eyes, confident that he'd cleaned enough paint off my face for me to open them again. "Liam, it's an entire cup of paint. What did you think would happen?"

"I don't know. That—"

Liam cut off as the cool red liquid of my own paint cup dumped over the top of his head. I jumped away from him, snickering. I was proud of myself that I'd got him before he noticed my hand moving.

Liam wiped his eyes, looking baffled that I'd dare try something like that.

"Now we're even," I said lightheartedly.

Liam narrowed his eyes at me, then grabbed me by the wrist and dragged me forward. He used his other hand to wipe red paint down my arm.

"Liam, no!" I cried, but I was laughing too hard for it to sound serious.

Liam joined in on the laughter. The second he let me go, I darted across the room to grab another bottle of paint. Liam saw what I was doing and reached for his own bottle. I whirled toward him and aimed, but nothing came out when I squeezed. Liam's, on the other hand, squirted with precision, landing directly on my bra.

"Wow," Liam said in a serious tone. "He was *very* happy to see you."

I stopped in my tracks and gave a look of disbelief. Liam looked like he was trying to hide a laugh.

"Oh, no," I said in a playful voice. "What am I going to do? I guess I'll just have to... take it off."

Liam's eyes widened as I set my paint bottle down and reached for the hook of my bra. It fell onto the floor, leaving glops of green paint on the paper and exposing my breasts to the cool air.

Liam's eyes locked on my boobs. He didn't move an inch as he drank me in. It was enough of a distraction that he didn't notice me grabbing for another full bottle of paint. I popped the top off and shirted it at him, but there was an air bubble inside that made my aim a little short. The yellow paint landed right on top of his dick.

Liam looked surprised, but I threw my head back in laughter. I couldn't contain myself. I laughed so hard that I had to grab the countertop for support. Nearby, Esis had stopped pushing paint around long enough to laugh with me.

"Liam..." I sucked in a heavy breath between laughs. "You've got something... just there..."

I pointed to his dick, but he didn't look amused. The dead serious face he gave me only made me laugh harder, until I literally couldn't keep myself on my feet. I fell to the ground on top of the paper, clutching my stomach and laughing as hard as I possibly could.

"I can't leave here looking like this," Liam stated flatly. "I guess I'm going to have to throw these away."

"Do it," I challenged him.

Liam smirked and kicked off his shoes, then began unbuttoning his pants. He pulled his paint-splattered shirt over his head and stood there in nothing but boxers.

"My pants have paint on them, too," I reminded him.

"Oh, no," he feigned. "What will we do about that?"

I lay on the ground looking up at him and shrugged playfully. Already, my heart was trying to beat its way out of my chest. I was *so* turned on right now.

Liam lowered himself to his knees and reached for my zipper. Tingles spread across my skin where he touched me, and heat pooled between my thighs.

Liam stripped off my pants, but forgot about my shoes. I kicked them off before he pulled my pants the rest of the way down my legs.

"It's a shame," I said.

"What is?" he asked.

"You're still wearing boxers." I stuck my thumb into a glob of paint, then wiped it over the fabric.

Liam looked down at the paint and frowned. "Well, *damn*. Now these have to come off, too. Oh well."

He stripped off his boxers until he was sitting there naked, his dick totally ready for me.

"What about mine?" I teased. I was so wet I was probably leaking through my panties by now.

Liam looked down at me and pretended to inspect my underwear for paint. "I don't know. You look pretty good."

"Take my damn panties off," I growled.

Liam laughed. He leaned over and swiped a bit of paint off the paper, then pressed it into my panties, straight over my clit. I arched my back and gasped.

"I don't know," Liam said. "I guess now they're ruined. Should we get rid of them?"

"Take them off and fuck me!" I cried.

Liam was having far too much fun teasing me. He snickered, then slowly slid my panties off. I was already writhing on the floor, needing him. I couldn't wait any longer. If I didn't get relief now, my thighs were going to light up in flames. It was so fucking hot down there.

"Come here," I demanded as I sat up. I wrapped my arms around his neck, then pulled him close. Our lips connected, and his tongue slid inside my mouth. I drew a deep breath and held it, pressing my breasts against the front of his chest. Red-hot tingles spread throughout my body, lighting up every nerve within me. I wanted him. Right here. Right now. Screw the mess.

Quite literally.

Liam shoved his hands into my hair, even though they were covered in paint, and I did the same to him. My hands roamed his body, getting even more paint everywhere, but I didn't care. I actually found it kind of sexy. He gently cradled my back as he lowered me onto the paper so I was lying down again.

"Liam," I said breathlessly as I pulled away. "Fuck me. Now."

Liam didn't waste any more time teasing me. He pressed inside of me without having to guide himself. We'd become so accustomed to each other's bodies now that our movements became natural —synchronized.

Liam pounded me from above, making my body come to life with every thrust. I moaned as he kissed me all over—along my jawline, down my neck, and to my breasts. My heart pounded fiercely as my back spread the paint across the paper.

"Oh, God, Liam," I moaned.

He silenced my moans with more kisses, twisting his tongue inside my mouth in a way that turned me on even more. I couldn't stand it. I grabbed hold of him and wrapped my legs around his middle and forced him to roll over. Liam gasped as cold, wet paint touched his back.

"No, Sophia," he said, forcing me to continue rolling. "I'm top."

I made him roll another time. Esis squealed and jumped out of the way before we squashed him, then ran over to the other side of the paper to continue painting.

"Screw that," I said, tossing my hair over my shoulder. "*I'm* top today."

I straightened my back and ran my hands all along his muscles as I moved my hips back and forth. My clit pressed against him, and his dick hit me in just the right spot inside. Liam tilted his head back and moaned as I rode him. His hands came up to caress my breasts. There was so much paint now, mixing into a beautiful rainbow of colors on the canvas and our bodies. I sighed in delight. Liam took it as an invitation to increase the heat. He took my nipples between his fingers and pinched them. It sent a wave of pleasure downward. He thrust upward one more time, and that was it for me.

The sexual pressure that had been building up inside of me exploded into a glorious orgasm at the same time he came. All the energy drained out of me as a euphoria took over. I slumped on top of him, and he wrapped his arms around me, cradling me close.

"Fuck, *pawee*," he whispered. "That was great."

"Yeah," I breathed, closing my eyes and resting the side of my face on his chest.

"Sophia," Liam said softly. "I... I..."

"You what?" I asked.

He took a deep breath. "I wanted to know..."

He paused. Liam was being kind of weird right now.

I finally opened my eyes, and instantly noticed the mess we'd made. There was paint all over the paper, but it was actually kind of pretty. A wide smile spread across my face, and I sat up to look at it.

Our painting was beautiful. It wasn't chaotic like I'd said I wanted. It was soft and gentle, with areas that were rough and fierce, just how sex should be. It was a painting of passion, with every color of the rainbow mixed seamlessly into a beautiful work of art.

"What's wrong?" Liam asked.

I shook my head, keeping my eyes on our painting. "Nothing's wrong. I think Professor Amber would be proud."

Liam shot upright and glanced down at the paper beneath us to see what I was talking about. He let out a light chuckle. "Yeah, she would be."

Esis tapped me on the leg. When I looked down, he was holding my paint-stained panties up to me. My face heated as I reached down to take them. "Thanks, buddy."

He chittered, then bounced away like it was nothing.

"We should probably get dressed," I suggested.

"Yeah," he agreed, but he sounded disappointed.

Liam and I cleaned up and got dressed. He pulled me into his arms once we were fully clothed again. I leaned into him and inhaled his ocean scent.

"I love you, *pawee*," he said into my hair.

"I love you, too." My eyes were fixed on the floor. When I pulled away from him, I suddenly realized something.

"What is it?" he asked as I stared down at the painting.

"Liam," I said breathlessly. "I think we just made Spirit Art."

❧

"Mm..." Jonah stood with one arm across his chest and his chin rested on the other, eyeing our painting like he was an art critic. We'd brought the painting back to the Biyami dorms and hung it between our bunks. "It's... It's..."

"It's *unique*," Imogen said.

"Yes," Jonah agreed quickly. "That's the perfect word for it. Unique."

Liam and I shared a look. We were both trying not to burst out in laughter. I wondered how long it'd take them to get it. Esis stood in front of the painting proudly, pointing at the parts where he'd left paw prints. Squeaks stood behind Jonah. She narrowed her eyes and tilted her head, as if she was trying to make out what it was. Sassy was on the bed and had a similar look of confusion on her face.

"You don't like it?" I asked with amusement in my voice.

"No, no," Jonah rushed to deny. "I just don't really... get it, you know?"

"There's nothing to get," I said. "It's just art."

"Yeah, but art *means* something," Jonah argued. "This is just... *intense*."

By now, Liam was biting his bottom lip to keep from laughing.

"It's great," Imogen assured us. I noticed her eyes moving between the painting and mine and Liam's stained clothes. "Just because Jonah doesn't get it doesn't mean—"

She stopped in her tracks and inhaled a deep breath. Her voice fell flat, but she didn't blink. "Oh. I think *I* get it."

"Get what?" I asked innocently. "It's just a painting."

It hit Jonah a moment later. He gasped and pointed to a corner of the paper. "Great ancestors! Is that a dick print?"

Liam's face fell, and he glanced around the room to make sure no one else heard. "What? No."

I looked closer at what Jonah was pointing to. "That's Esis' tail. Jeez. Get your mind out of the gutter."

Jonah ignored me and started snickering. "Wow, Liam. You're really gifted, and I don't mean artistically."

"Dude, it's not a dick print," Liam insisted.

Imogen laughed. "I don't know about that, but *that* is definitely an ass print."

Imogen pointed toward another spot toward the middle. I pressed my lips together tightly as my face turned a deeper shade of pink.

Imogen leaned back a little to check out my backside. "Yep. Definitely Sophia's ass."

"Maybe," I admitted sheepishly.

"Ooh," Jonah sang. "You guys are so *bad*. How much do you want for it? A grand? Ten?"

"What are you talking about?" Liam asked.

"This work of art is brilliant," Jonah said. "One day, it'll be worth millions."

I rolled my eyes at him. "Jonah, you literally didn't like it until two seconds ago."

"Hey, I'm allowed to change my mind." Jonah plopped down onto the bed beside Sassy. "What do you say, Im? Chip in ten grand for it now and resell it for a million when they die?"

Imogen went rigid. "Oh, I, uh... no."

"What do you mean?" Jonah said, like he didn't notice her discomfort. "The value goes up when the artist dies. And you're loaded from the Cup winnings anyway. What's wrong with a little investment?"

"Nothing," Imogen said in a small voice. She joined him on the lower bunk and began to pet Sassy's fur. She wouldn't meet any of our eyes.

"Im, what's wrong?" I asked.

"It's nothing," she assured me, but I didn't believe her. I had to get to the bottom of this.

"Hey, Im," I said quickly. "Can you help me clean up Esis? He's going to put up a fight."

She finally looked to me, then nodded.

Liam shook his head when Imogen stood and we started toward the bathrooms together. "What is it with girls and going to the bathroom together?"

Jonah shrugged. "It's a social thing. You wanna go take a piss together?"

"Ew, no." Liam declined with a frown.

I cornered Imogen as soon as we were in the privacy of the girl's bathroom. It was a lot like a locker room, with a few bathroom stalls and a shower area. Everything was always wet in here, and kind of gross. Luckily, we were alone.

"What's going on, Imogen?" I demanded.

Imogen walked to the sink and started running her fingers through her hair as she gazed into the mirror. At her feet, Esis began grooming Sassy.

"Nothing's wrong," she insisted.

"Im, we're best friends. I can tell when you're lying. Was it something Jonah said? About how Liam and I would die? You know there's a possibility of that. We're fighting a war."

"It's not that." It sounded like she was telling the truth.

"Then what?" I pressed. "Something Jonah said about the money?"

Imogen turned to me and sighed. "Look, Sophia. I know we tell each other everything, but some things I just need to keep private, okay? I need you to trust that if there's something I'm not telling you, it's for a reason."

My stomach sank. Imogen *was* keeping something from me, and it definitely sounded like it was about money.

I furrowed my brow and spoke lowly. "Imogen, are your Cup winnings gone?"

She turned back to the mirror, avoiding my gaze. "Like I said, I need you to trust me, Sophia."

My eyes widened. How could *all* our Cup winnings be gone? I couldn't possibly imagine where Imogen's had vanished to... unless she spent them already. Which wasn't likely, because Imogen was practical. Whatever she spent her money on must've been important. The fact that she wouldn't tell me suggested it was a pretty big deal.

And that worried me to my very core.

Liam

ELEVEN

I wasn't a big fan of art, but the painting Sophia and I had completed together was a true masterpiece. I got a cocky grin every time I looked at it, hung on the wall near our bunk. So what if it had dick prints and ass prints? As far as I was concerned, Da Vinci himself couldn't have done a better job.

Da Vinci didn't have as much fun painting his pieces, either. I couldn't stop thinking about how fucking hot Sophia looked with paint smeared all over her naked body... along with other substances.

But life at Orenda Academy wasn't all good times and hot sex. We'd gotten one step closer to finding the Air piece, but to do so, we needed a Storm Lord— and that Storm Lord would be Dean Alizeh. I met Jonah in an alcove near the Biyami dorm entrance on the first floor. He was leaning against Squeaks with his arms crossed and looking tense.

"Let's do this." Jonah began climbing stairs, up to Dean Alizeh's office on the third floor. It'd been difficult to get a meeting with Alizeh, but we'd finally gotten one scheduled. Jonah had to slow down for me a couple of times, because I had no energy lately. Esis had been giving me healings on a daily basis, but they weren't working quite as well as they should be. I chalked it up to winter ending and ignored the pains my joints gave me. It was nothing unusual for me to feel like shit, anyhow.

Jonah knocked before we entered into Dean Alizeh's office. I'd never been in here before. The ceiling was exceptionally high, the room itself over thirty feet tall. She had the skeleton of a thunderbird hanging from the ceiling, and hundreds of feathers were suspended around it, twirling in mid-air. Alizeh was grading papers at her desk and looked up when she saw us coming. Her thunderbird sat on a large perch behind her desk and slept with his head under his wing.

"Hello, boys," Dean Alizeh said, a large smile brightening her face. "What brings you here today?"

Dean Alizeh had been sorted into Defortai, but she had a soft spot for Jonah, which I hoped would help us today. Jonah and I slowly sank into the two chairs in front of her desk. I planned to be back-up and let Jonah do most of the talking.

"It's kind of an important issue," Jonah said. "We wouldn't be asking your help if we had any other choice."

"Is it a project? I assure you though I'm very busy, I always take time to help out my favorite students," she replied.

"No..." Jonah drew out his words. Squeaks chirped, and Jonah finally forced out, "We need a Storm Lord."

Alizeh stopped scribbling on her papers. Her thunderbird woke up and brought his head out from underneath his wing. I watched the blood drain from Alizeh's face. "What?"

"The Storm Lord," Jonah repeated. He sank lower in his seat. "We... think you could be it?"

"Jonah!" The chair scraped back as Alizeh rose to her feet. She pointed at me. "You've told a *Toaqua* about our traditions? How dare you! The Storm Lord is a protected Yapluma secret!"

I cringed. This wasn't exactly the reaction we'd been hoping for.

"I know that, but there was no other way," Jonah said. He'd moved on to pleading now. "We figured that you have a thunderbird, you're a powerful Yapluma... you're the only rational choice."

"Why do you need a Storm Lord?" Dean Alizeh's voice rose. I'd never seen her like this before— she was the calmest Dean out of all the Houses, but I swore the wind in the room was picking up as her fury raged unbound. The feathers floating above my head bounced up and down in an angry display. The suspended thunderbird skeleton swung on its chains.

Jonah and I glanced at each other. We didn't know how much to reveal without getting ourselves in trouble, but we'd agreed we wouldn't tell Alizeh about the prophecy unless she was on board with helping us.

"We think it could be a way to stop this war," Jonah floundered out.

Dean Alizeh's hands clenched into fists. "If you think I'm prepared to rise up against the current administration, you're highly mistaken, Mister Chanee."

My mouth dropped open. Dean Alizeh didn't want to oppose the Elders and stop this?

"You don't disapprove of what's going on?" Jonah peeped. His resolve was getting smaller by the minute. Squeaks' eyes widened in disbelief.

"Of course I do! But it is the way of things now!" Dean Alizeh hissed. Her eyes flashed toward the door, as if she was afraid of being overheard. "If I make a move against the Elders, I will lose my head! If they believe I'm the Storm Lord, do you know what they'll do to me?"

"I... I..." Jonah stuttered.

"We're looking for a painting," I began, hoping it would help. "If we don't find it—"

"I know very well what you're looking for, but I can assure you I have no idea where said painting is," Alizeh said finitely, though her words sounded like a lie. "I suggest you give up whatever you're trying to do and focus on saving yourselves."

"We *have* to find it, though," Jonah barely spoke up now.

Dean Alizeh shook her head and pointed at the door. "Out. Get out. I can assure you I am not the one you are looking for."

"But—"

"*Get. Out!*"

A gust of wind so strong blew from Dean Alizeh's hands that it knocked Jonah and I out of our chairs. We scrambled to get up as her thunderbird rose off his perch and spread his wings, electricity bouncing off his feathers. The thunderbird flew after us as Jonah, Squeaks and I made a run for it. We barely got the door closed behind us before we heard a crackle of thunder boom from behind.

"That didn't go well," Jonah gasped. He was bent over his knees and heaving.

"Like shit, actually." It took me longer than usual to catch my breath. When I finally rose to my full height, I was a bit dizzy, and had to put a hand on the wall to steady myself. "Though her behavior was a bit suspicious, wasn't it?"

"Yeah." Jonah ran a hand through his hair. "I don't know why you'd act like that unless you were the person we were looking for."

"So that makes it clear. Alizeh's the Storm Lord," I said.

"Fine, but what good does that do us?" Jonah snapped in frustration, and Squeaks bristled her feathers. "She doesn't want to help."

"She doesn't want to help because she's scared," I noted bluntly. "I bet if we give her some time, she'll come around."

"She's not just scared. She's fucking *terrified* of the Elders," Jonah said. "She's not all wrong, either. If she was the Storm Lord, Oleander would consider her a threat. She'd be executed by element the moment he got word."

"We just have to convince her," I said. "It doesn't have to be today. We still need to find out where the painting is. We'll keep asking, and eventually, she'll crack." *If she doesn't report us first*, I thought.

"You're probably right." Jonah wiped his brow with the back of his sleeve. "Imogen and I are going to focus on locating the painting, and figuring out what exactly took it."

"Do you have any leads?"

"There aren't as many Yapluma texts as there are from the other tribes. It'll take time to sort through them all, but eventually we'll get some answers."

I sure fucking hoped so. We were running out of time, and we needed that last piece.

But our chances of getting it seemed dismal at this point. Even if we did figure out where the painting was and what was guarding it, all of this would be useless without Dean Alizeh. The piece of soul trapped in the painting wouldn't speak to us without another Storm Lord present.

Jonah huffed. "Are there any other options?"

"The only other person who has a thunderbird that we know of is Ezra, but he's not Yapluma. It wouldn't make any sense for him to be the Storm Lord," I argued.

"It can't hurt to look into," Jonah said. "Let's just double check with him as a last resort."

It was a stupid plan, but the Reject Team was all about stupid plans. Ezra and I didn't live in the same dorms anymore and weren't supposed to talk in the first place, but I got lucky when I saw him walk past before lunch.

"Ezra," I called. "I need to talk to you."

He didn't ask questions, just ducked after me into an empty classroom. Dyami shut the door behind him with his foot, and Ezra said, "What do you need?"

I took a deep breath. "So, this is going to sound crazy, but there's this Yapluma legend. It's about an exceptionally powerful Air Elementai bonded to a thunderbird. He's called the Storm Lord. And... well, we need him. You might be who the legend refers to."

"Me?" Ezra raised a skeptical eyebrow. "And you think I'm the Storm King—"

"Storm Lord," I corrected.

"Whatever. You think I'm this guy because I have a thunderbird?" Ezra asked.

"It's the only thing that makes sense, right? Otherwise, it's gotta be Dean Alizeh," I said. "I know you're Toaqua, but is there a chance it could be possible?"

Ezra crossed his arms. "Why do you want to know? You're acting pretty suspicious."

This was the part I was worried about. I knew Ezra would press for answers. But I wasn't going to hesitate to tell Ezra the truth. He was my brother. I trusted him with my life.

"We're hunting prophecy pieces," I said.

Ezra's eyes widened. "For real? You mean, the one about Sophia?"

"Yeah. We've got a piece from each of the tribes, except Yapluma. The Air piece is the last part we're after, and the one we think is coming up next. We figure Toaqua's piece is last, and Ez... whatever it means, it's not good."

Ezra bit his lip and stared at Dyami in contemplation. "So you're trying to figure out what happens before it does."

"Yes. It's the only way to stop what's coming."

Ezra scratched Dyami under his chin, and the thunderbird cooed in relaxation. "All I can tell you is that I'm definitely not the Storm Lord. Thunderbirds might be Air creatures, but they also have a close affinity to Water. I'd have to have Yapluma blood to be who you're looking for, and you know as well as I do our bloodline is pure Toaqua. I've never been able to summon Air in my life."

"I figured as much." I felt deflated. Getting Ezra to help us would've been a lot easier than Dean Alizeh.

"But," Ezra subbed in, "I *can* tell you that if I'm not it, Dean Alizeh has to be."

"Why's that?"

"Because when I bonded with Dyami, I was required to sign up with the Protected Familiar Registry," he said. "Thunderbirds are a critically endangered magical species, and everyone who bonds with an endangered magical creature has to sign up for the PFR."

"So what does that have to do with Dean Alizeh?"

Ezra leaned in and dropped his voice. "When I went to register, Dean Alizeh was the only other person on the list who had a thunderbird— that's still alive, anyway. So unless someone in Kinpago is hiding one, she and I are the only people bonded to that species."

"Could someone bond with a thunderbird, then just not inform the Elders?"

Ezra shook his head. "You can, but it's a tribal felony, because they're a protected species. And I don't think anyone's stupid enough to risk breaking the law these days unless they have to."

I nodded. "That makes sense."

"I think the Registry was originally created to make sure the people who bonded with these creatures was taking care of them, but now it's become a way to keep tabs on who owns what," Ezra said.

"Basically, you're saying if I want to find out if anyone else owns a thunderbird, I should look at Tribal Headquarters."

"Yep." Ezra bobbed his head, and Dyami copied him. "That'd be the way I'd do it."

"Thanks, Ez," I told him. "This helps a lot."

"Don't thank me." Ezra wrinkled his nose. "I'm just doing what I can."

We separated then, because a Task Force squadron walked by and we didn't want to get harassed. I planned to look into the Protected Familiar Registry, but I didn't expect to find anything.

Our only hope seemed to be Dean Alizeh. And she had convinced herself she wanted no part in this.

❦

THE NEXT DAY, Jonah and I went back to Dean Alizeh's office, but when we knocked she didn't answer. We could hear her working inside, but when Jonah tried to turn the knob, a gust of wind from the other side pressed against the door and turned the lock shut.

Clearly, she didn't want to speak with us. We agreed to give her some space for a few weeks and try again later.

I was early to class that evening, because I wanted to make a good impression. War and Negotiation was taught by Professor Cheveyo, my old Hawkei Leadership professor. I was one of only three Biyami in this class, including Wyatt and Lira, and I didn't want to get kicked out. I was pretty sure the only reason I was in his class was Professor Cheveyo had fought for me, which I felt honored by. He could get in trouble for sticking up for a Biyami. The least I could do was prove I deserved his support.

"For your grade, you are required to maintain some sort of internship position until you graduate," Cheveyo announced. "I will be assigning them tonight. The first position up for grabs is an administrative assistant at Tribal Headquarters in Kinpago. Any volunteers?"

The room remained quiet. Nobody wanted the administration internship. It was the worst one. You'd be running around getting coffee all day and fixing printers instead of learning from the Elders first-hand.

But this internship would get me into Tribal Headquarters, which was exactly where I needed to go. I had to double check if Alizeh was the only Yapluma with a thunderbird. "I'll do it," I said, raising my hand.

"Excellent, Liam." Professor Cheveyo seemed pleased I'd taken the hard job. "If you're interested, you can start tonight. They need a custodian at eight."

"Fine by me," I said. Eight o'clock was late enough that no one would catch me going through the Protected Familiar Registry.

"Suck up," Logan whispered. A couple of people laughed. I curled my fingers around a pen and didn't say anything.

Sitting by Logan was pretty much torture. Sophia had told me what he'd done to Isabella, and it took everything in me not to punch him in the face every time I saw his smug mug. No doubt he'd moved on to terrorizing other Biyami girls now that Isabella was gone.

"Of course the Biyami becomes the pencil pusher," Courtney cracked. "I think menial labor suits him. Puts him in his place."

Normally, I'd sneer at her or give her the finger, but I was trying to rise above all that shit now. I mean, we were practically graduated. We were becoming adults. It was time to stop acting like we were in fucking high school.

"Calm down, everyone," Cheveyo said sternly, before he returned to his list. Even though he was Defortai, he couldn't be seen sticking up for me. I guaranteed Courtney would report him for it.

I had dinner with the group, and told them what I was up to before I left. Tribal Headquarters was a huge concrete building near the center of Kinpago. It'd been damaged during the riots, but was repaired before any of the other structures in town. Cheveyo had given me a keycard so I could enter without having to go through security. Inside, the building smelled musty, and it was dimly lit. It looked like any office building, except the paintings on the walls were of old Elders that had passed on, and the grey carpet was starting to curl at the edges.

Most people weren't at the Tribal Headquarters this late at night. The halls were practically empty, save for a couple of secretaries finishing up. I headed to the administrative section, where I was supposed to report to the night clerk.

The guy waiting at the desk gave me a nasty look when I stepped into the room. I looked around for his Familiar, but didn't see one.

"Hi," I said. "I'm here about the internship?"

The clerk rose from his desk slowly. His keycard hung from a clip on the side of his pants. "Show me your arm."

"What?"

"Your arm."

He wanted to check if I was Defortai or not. This was fucking humiliating. I rolled up my sleeve and shoved my forearm in his general direction. His lip curled when he saw my tattoo, but he said nothing else. "Follow me."

His footsteps stomped heavily on the floor as he led me down the narrow hallway. He opened a door. It was a meeting room, but it was a total mess. Coffee spills, crumbs, and papers were spread all over the table, and had even amassed on the floor. The printer was smoking, and a bunch of computer parts were lying disregarded. Most shocking was a scattering of red feathers collected in a bloody spot on the carpet.

Shit. Someone had thrown a laptop. Not to mention it looked like a couple of Familiars had gotten into it.

"The Elders had a long meeting today," the clerk began. "This needs to be cleaned up. I expect it spotless by the time you leave tonight."

"You could say please," I snapped. Damn, shouldn't have said that. Couldn't get away with that kind of stuff now.

The clerk narrowed his eyes at me. "Dirty Biyami," he hissed. The clerk shoved past. My shoulder throbbed from where he rammed me, but I ignored it.

Thank the ancestors he'd left me alone. Now I could get down to business. It'd take me forever to clean up the mess left in the conference room, but I'd worry about that later. I made sure to wait until the clerk was gone, then abandoned the conference room behind me.

I knew a bit about Tribal Headquarters. I'd been in here a few times before the chief hood had been reassigned to Ezra. Records were on the third floor. I took the elevator up, so I didn't pass out on the stairs, and was happy to see that the records area was completely empty when the doors opened.

There was a problem, though. My keycard wouldn't get me through to the records area. I had no clearance.

Good thing I'd swiped the night clerk's ID off of him when he'd shoved into me. Fucking dickhead.

I swiped the keycard, and the door to the records area opened. I moved quickly and sat at the nearest computer. I was able to get into the record files, miraculously, with another scan of the keycard. I wonder whose ass this guy had to kiss to be granted this type of clearance. He had to have access to all areas of headquarters for security purposes, sure, but I was surprised further privileges had been granted.

There were thousands upon thousands of files in the computer's hard drive. I found the Protected Familiar Registry pretty quickly, and although there were hundreds of people bonded to endangered Familiars, when I narrowed the search down to thunderbirds, only two names popped up.

Ez had been right. The only people registered to thunderbirds in Kinpago were him and Alizeh. That meant Alizeh was our Storm Lord for sure.

I went to log out, but before I could, my eyes spotted something. *Registry of Biyami.*

That was new. I didn't have a lot of time, but my fingers itched to click on the button. I opened the registry and as an experiment, typed in my own name.

A new window on the screen popped up, outlined in red. There was a photograph of myself, one I'd never seen of me walking in Kinpago. A ton of text was attached to the file. I leaned forward to read.

"Liam Mitoh, Toaqua, Familiar deceased," I read aloud. "Projection: Code Red, highly dangerous. In an interhouse relationship with a Code Black. Monitor until further instruction."

Didn't know what a Code Black was, but it didn't sound good. Below was a giant paragraph on the trial, as well as the classes I took at school, how powerful my magic was suspected to be, and my medical condition. They even had a slot on what I did in my free time and that I'd gone bungee jumping recently.

Shit. These goons had a lot on me. They'd been following me around. Probably knew more about me than I did. It was ridiculously unsettling.

I searched Jonah's name. He came up as a Code Green, which was listed as *not a threat.* They didn't have a whole lot in his file, save for a few pictures and that he'd been bonded to Squeaks.

When I searched Imogen's name, I got a jolt when I saw her file was listed as a Code Yellow: *proceed with caution.*

"Suspected mixed House," I read aloud. "Familiar is a kitsune, most likely stolen from a Defortai. Familiar Removal scheduled for March fifteenth."

What the fuck? They were going to steal Sassy away from Imogen? Not a fucking chance. I looked for a section on where to edit files, and miraculously, I found one. I changed Imogen's file to a Code Green, and deleted the information about Sassy being a kitsune completely. I took out the part about Sassy being removed from Imogen and changed her species to a common fox.

There. Fuck these assholes. They weren't messing with my friends.

I didn't want to search Sophia's name, because I was worried about what I would find. But that's why I had to. Sophia's file popped up, outlined all in black. It had a giant bold heading on the top of it.

WARNING: CODE BLACK. EXCEPTIONALLY DANGEROUS.

I skimmed the rest of the file quickly. There was a small section on the trial, but more on how Sophia had been stolen as a baby, raised outside our culture, and brought back in as an outsider.

"Showed abnormal abilities during the Elemental Cup. Bonded to an Unidentified Familiar Species. Prophesied to bring about a major tribal change. In contact with several Code Reds," I mumbled.

I did a quick look through the Biyami Registry, and although there were quite a few Code Reds, no one else had a Code Black. Sophia was the only one.

Sophia's file was fucking scary. The more I read, the worse it got. I found out her sister was categorized as a Code Red, too, as well as her adoptive parents.

All that was missing from her file was an order to kill on sight. I didn't know how much longer it would take for the Elders to make that decision— or what was holding them back in the first place.

I had to get off of Sophia's file before I had a panic attack. I surveyed the registry closely. Maybe this could be a tool for figuring out who the Defortai were targeting next. I narrowed the search to a list of Biyami students at Orenda Academy who were listed as Code Red and came up with twelve names. I memorized as many names as I possibly could, and then logged out before someone found out what I was up to.

I walked back to the conference room with a lot on my mind. We had to get those twelve kids out of the school, before the Elders decided to do something about them. I was almost thinking of going back to the academy and gathering up people now, but I didn't want to blow my cover, so I had to finish up the job for the internship first.

I groaned when I walked back into the messy room. This was going to take forever. I started throwing pieces of the broken laptop into the trash. Every part of me was tense. I couldn't get my mind off of what I'd seen. Sophia and I were being more closely watched than ever...

The door cracked open behind me. "Liam?"

I jumped about five feet in the air. I whirled around, expecting to toss a water ball into someone's face, but I let out a sigh of relief when I saw it was just my dad.

He looked unkempt. His tie was undone, and his suit was rumpled. I noticed for the first time Tatum's muzzle was starting to grey. I wondered if it was from stress.

"Dad, you nearly gave me a heart attack," I complained. I rubbed my chest and tried to breathe. Fuck, I was on edge. "What are you doing here?"

Dad's main office was at Serpent Assembly back within Toaqua tribal lines, but he had another office here for when the Elders from the different Houses all had to convene. He'd been here more than he'd been at the offices back home lately.

"Sorry. I've been taking care of some... things." He glanced around. "What are *you* doing here?"

"I landed an administrative internship. This was my first job," I said.

"I see." He sighed as he stepped into the room. "I remember my internship. Not exactly glamourous."

"It's work. I'm fine with it," I said.

"Let me help you," Dad said. "It'll go quicker with the three of us."

"Dad, you don't have to do that. You're chief," I objected.

"Nonsense. A chief isn't above a bit of cleaning," he insisted.

I didn't object, because I really didn't want to be alone right now. I was kind of freaking out. Dad began wiping down the conference table while I tried to lift the stains out of the carpet with my magic. I got the coffee to come up, but the blood just wouldn't lift. Tatum gathered the red feathers into a pile with his paws and grumbled something under his breath, but I obviously didn't know what, because I couldn't speak bear.

"You'd think they'd let Christian and Katie loose in here, with how it looks. Such a disaster." Dad shook his head and sighed. "The meeting didn't go well today. As I'm sure you can see."

"What happened?" I asked. I stopped trying to lift the blood. I wasn't getting anywhere.

Dad dug in his pocket and placed a silver orb on the table, one that pulsated and shot out thin bands of light. I tilted my head in confusion. I'd never seen such a thing in my life.

"It's an illusion charm, from the Arcanea sorceresses," Dad explained. "I purchased it some time ago. Anyone listening in on us from the outside will only hear dull conversation instead of what we're actually talking about."

"That's really clever," I marveled. I wanted one of my own, but I bet objects like that were rare.

"I wish I had another for you, but magical artifacts are being tightly monitored by the Elders these days. I barely managed to sneak this one in." Dad pocketed the orb again. "What you need to understand, son, is that the council is heavily divided. There are very few of us left from the old days. And the ones who aren't in Oleander's pocket are in Chieftess Annette's. Koigni isn't willing to give up power so easily. That often results in fights."

I glanced at the blood stain on the floor. "I thought Chieftess Annette was on Oleander's side?" I asked.

"Far from it. She goes with him because she has to. The two-house system was Chieftess Annette's idea all along," Dad said. "She had the idea to make herself High Chieftess after the new order was complete, and then groom her daughter so Haley could take over. She's been in the process of changing the tribe for years."

"But... I'm guessing Oleander got there first."

"Precisely." Dad nodded. "He stole her plan, and modified the council so that the vote was in his favor. Obviously, Annette is furious. But she can't go against Oleander at the moment, because this was her idea in the first place, and showing her hand would put her in an unfavorable light. Very few Elders understand why she's so upset."

"It should be obvious. Oleander stole her power. She's been working forever to try and get the title of High Chief, and he's about to come in and take it away from her." I couldn't believe the other Elders were so stupid. They didn't realize what was right in front of them, but most of them were Oleander's lackeys. I doubt he put anyone of intelligence on the council that might be a threat to him.

"Annette and Oleander are currently in a battle for power," Dad said. "Whoever wins the title of High Chief will have control of the tribe. And at this point, I'm not sure who is worse. The council is currently locked in a perpetual state of disagreement. We can't decide on anything."

Tatum moaned and rubbed his head, as if just mentioning it gave him a headache.

"It can't stay that way forever, can it?" I asked.

"No." Dad shook his head. "It cannot. Sooner or later, there will be assassinations. And the council will swing one way or the other."

I paced the room. "There must be a way to stop it. Right, Dad?"

"My plan is to undermine them both," Dad said. "They're so focused on fighting each other they're not counting on being overthrown from the outside. If that means we have to start taking people out... yes, Liam, I'm willing to do it."

I paused before I said, "This is why you wanted me to kill Sophia, isn't it? Because you thought it would undermine Annette's attempts to become High Chieftess by keeping Koigni from rising to power."

"Unfortunately, yes," Dad said. "But that obviously was the wrong move, seeing as how Sophia's practically been abandoned by the Koigni Council, and she's about to become my daughter-in-law."

I grinned. "Yeah. Didn't expect that one, did you?"

"You probably didn't either." Dad laughed.

I shook my head and parted my hair back. "No. I really didn't."

I wanted to ask Dad more about the Biyami files, as I was sure he'd know about them, but I didn't want him knowing I was sneaking around in the records system. I'd get a lecture I was being too risky. I had the thought so long as Dad was on the Elder Council, Sophia and I were safe, so I put it in the back of my mind... as much as I could, anyway.

Cleaning up the conference room took until midnight, but we eventually got it done. I said goodbye to Dad before I hit the street, and picked up the pace on the road back to school. I tossed the clerk's ID into the river when I passed it and watched the water carry it away to the ocean. I kept glancing over my shoulder every now and then, getting the feeling someone was watching me, but there wasn't anyone around.

I expected to find the group back in the Biyami dorms, but they weren't in the bunks. I trekked to the Anichi dorms and found Jonah, Imogen, and Sophia gathered around the fireplace, sharing hot chocolate. Esis was on the coffee table, shoving marshmallows down his trap like no tomorrow. Squeaks tried to balance a tower of marshmallows on her beak and kept letting them drop.

"Guys, we can't keep hanging around here like this," I said as I sat next to Sophia. She handed me my own hot chocolate, and I took a sip. "This place has got to be a base only. If people notice we're always gone, they'll suspect we have a hideout somewhere."

Jonah pouched out his lip. "But this is the only cool place we can still chill!"

"Liam's right." Imogen set her hot chocolate down with a sigh, and Sassy jumped up to curl on her lap. "We're coming up here too much. We need to lay low for a while."

Sophia put a hand on the small of my back. "So, how'd your internship go? Did you find anything?"

With a glance at Sassy, I remembered what I'd found in the Biyami files. "I went through the Protected Familiar Registry," I said. "Dean Alizeh is the only person in Kinpago who has a thunderbird except Ezra. The Storm Lord's gotta be her."

"That's not all you found, was it?" Sophia asked. Her tone had a slight measure of dread.

"Believe me," I started. "It gets worse."

I told them what I'd found in our files in the Biyami Registry. Their eyes grew wider and wider as I recalled everything I could remember. I told them the names of the Code Red students at the school, and Imogen wrote them down.

When I got to the part about Sophia being a Code Black, she squeezed my hand tightly. I hated putting more stress on her— wondered if I should tell her at all, really— but I had no choice in the matter. She deserved to know what the Elders had pegged her as.

"I can't believe they were going to take Sassy away! I would never steal her!" Imogen shouted. The tip of Sassy's tongue dangled out of her mouth as Imogen squeezed her for comfort.

"Well, with luck, they won't now. All record of her being a kitsune is gone. I deleted it," I said.

"Good riddance," Jonah grumbled. He had his head in his hands and was looking at the floor with narrowed eyes. Jonah had taken it as a personal insult he'd been labeled a Code Green and not considered a threat. The rest of us would've loved to take his place.

"Exceptionally dangerous." Sophia's voice was hollow. "That's really funny."

"It's not without reason," I said lowly. "You scare them."

"I'm not a threat to anyone anymore. I'm useless," Sophia said quietly. She brought her legs on the couch and wrapped her arms around them, propping her chin on her knees.

Jonah and Imogen sensed we needed space. Imogen got up and said, "Let's get to bed. It's been a long night."

Jonah nodded and stood. As Squeaks shut the door behind them, the only sound that could be heard was the crackling of the fire. Esis had so many marshmallows stuffed into his cheeks he looked like a squirrel hoarding nuts.

"You're not useless. You saved Isabella," I pointed out.

"I had no choice," Sophia said. "If I didn't do something, no one would. I couldn't let her be raped in front of me. Seeing her get beat up was bad enough. And I couldn't stand to watch someone get hurt again — not after Levi."

The flames in the fireplace began to change shape. Sophia was manipulating them to look like people, dancing in the shadows.

"Levi wasn't your fault."

"You can say that over and over again, but I'm never going to believe it." A dancer rose up in the fire before she spun out and fell into the flames. "The truth is, I would've never stood for that a year ago. No matter what rules were in place, I should've stopped it."

"You aren't the same person now." I twirled a few strands of Sophia's hair around my fingers. "And just because you couldn't save Levi doesn't mean that you didn't help other people. You were the one who got his sister out."

"But what good does it do, Liam? We can save one person, but so many more can't be saved. It's a useless endeavor." The flames climbed in intensity, and I felt the temperature in the room increase.

"We can't make a difference for everyone. That's just not possible. But we made a difference for those people we helped escape."

Sophia turned her head away, and her hair fell out of my fingers. "I don't know if the Hawkei deserve to be saved. Not after what I've seen. I don't even know if humanity has the right to exist."

"We don't. That doesn't mean life has to be wiped out," I said softly.

"I *hate* them for what they've done to me." Sophia's voice shook with fury. "They've turned me into a coward. I used to be brave. Now I think I was just naive. I was a stupid girl who didn't know how the world really worked."

She gave a skeptical noise. "I know now."

"You were never stupid. Too optimistic, but so what? It worked," I said. "You accomplished things nobody could just because no one ever told you it was impossible to do them. How many times did we walk away from situations we should've died from? Too many. And your faith never wavered. The Elemental Cup is the biggest example."

"We only survived that tournament because I had the totem," Sophia spat. "I can't summon lightning without it anymore. I tried and failed during the riots. Everything that makes me special comes from that totem. I'm nothing without it. Average at best."

"You told me you could use Anichi powers. You can project light and make a force field. That's anything but average."

"Yes, because I have an Anichi object!" she yelled. "It's not coming from *me*. My Koigni powers aren't even that strong if I can't use the totem. Why the ancestors think I'm special is beyond me. I wish they would've picked anyone else. They probably would've gotten the job done by now."

"That's not true. Sophia. Look at me." I reached out and turned her head gently toward me. "Ancestors don't pick whoever they want. They pick the person best suited for the job."

"I'm not anymore," Sophia whispered. "Why can't you all see that?"

"Why can't you see what a miracle you are?" I whispered. "Ancestors, Soph, you're killing me here."

She swept her hair back from her face. Esis held out a marshmallow for her, but she ignored him.

He frowned and shoved the marshmallow back in his fur. Sophia and Esis were on totally different levels lately. It was difficult to witness, seeing as how they used to be so in sync.

"You have to believe the ancestors are leading you down the right path," I continued. "It's not over yet."

"How can I believe? I've found myself, but I'm having trouble holding on to who Kyra Koignichi *is*," Sophia said. Her words sounded more like a lonely echo than her actual voice. "There's just nothing but... empty. Not *emptiness*. That's a different feeling. To feel emptiness you have to be something else. And I'm not anymore. There's just nothing there. You can't understand."

"Sophie, if there's anyone on this planet who can understand how you feel, it's definitely me." I knew exactly what it was to be empty.

Her eyes cleared with the truth of that statement. "I guess that's true. I didn't mean to be insensitive."

"It's okay. I've been dealing with it a lot longer than you have."

"You seem to be getting better."

"Therapy helps. But to be honest, I'm still depressed, though it's a hell of a lot better than it used to be." I shrugged. "What are you gonna do, though?"

Sophia took a deep breath. "It's hard not to be depressed in this fucking society."

That got a laugh out of me. "Touché."

"I don't know how to describe how I feel. It's so complicated." Sophia rubbed her eyes, and the dark circles beneath them became more pronounced in the firelight. "It's like there's this big black hole inside me, sucking everything up. I never believed in ghosts— I suppose they must exist, because other magical things do, too, but I didn't realize you can be a ghost and still be alive. It's like I'm this shell walking around, and if you open me up, there's nothing there."

"You're incredibly sad and numb at the same time," I said. "You feel everything in the world, and nothing all at once. And it never stops."

Sophia blinked in disbelief at me.

"See? I told you that I knew," I said.

"Liam, you have to understand that I'm tired," Sophia said. "I'm tired of fighting. I don't want to anymore. I'm not suicidal and I don't want to die, but I'm exhausted constantly. It's getting to a point where I hardly care what happens anymore, with the tribe or otherwise. I just want to return to a time when things were simple and I didn't have to think so much."

She inhaled a sharp breath. "And you can't imagine how sick I am of being scared. I am terrified *all the time*. It's twenty-four seven. It never stops. Even when I'm happy, or when I'm laughing, I'm still scared. It even gets boring, being so frightened. But it never goes away. I get tired of looking over my shoulder, waiting for the next catastrophe to happen."

Sophia put her head in her hands. "I want to give up. Maybe if I just stopped caring, everything would get better."

"You can't give up. What if I had given up on that bridge? I wouldn't be here now," I said. "What if you give up? What's going to happen to the tribe? What's going to happen to Jonah and Imogen? Hell, what's going to happen to us?"

Sophia raised her head. "That's the only thing keeping me holding on. You and me. I feel like if I didn't have you I'd just fade away into the paint on the walls."

"You were my anchor to this life for the longest time. Now it's my turn to be yours," I said. I opened up my arms. "Sophia, I need you. Come here."

Sophia crawled across the couch and sat in my lap. I enclosed my arms around her tightly. She nestled into my chest, and I laid my chin on top of her hair.

"I'm sorry it happened to you," I whispered. "I wish I could take it all away."

Sophia pressed herself into my chest. "I need you to be present with me now.'"

"Always."

She gave a hopeless laugh. "Sometimes I want to press into you and disappear."

"That wouldn't work." I gave a grim smile. "All of me would go with you."

There wouldn't be anything of me left to give.

"I'm glad we got a second chance. I could never replace you," Sophia hushed. "I don't care what people say about getting back with your ex. I swear we're gonna make it."

"We'll find a way no matter what. I'll be here to take care of you until my heart bursts," I said. "And probably long after."

She turned to face me and threaded her fingers between mine. As Sophia pushed forward, I leaned backward until I was spread out on the couch and she was on top of me. She started kissing me slow. The movements were gentle and tender.

This was a secret moment in time tucked away for her and me. In these few seconds, the rest of the world didn't matter. This was a safe place where everything would be okay. At least until tomorrow.

When she pulled her mouth away from mine, I said, "Soph?"

"Hm?"

"Just don't ever tell me you're fine," I spoke gently. "Because I never was."

Tears dotted her eyelashes. "I won't, Liam. I promise."

sophia

TWELVE

I was lying to myself. For weeks I thought things were getting better. Then Liam told me about my file— how closely the Elders were watching me— and that gaping wide hole in my belly split open to swallow me. I couldn't stand watching my back at every moment, wondering when the Elders might finally cave and hurt me— or worse, Esis.

I felt like a shell of a human being. Liam decided to cheer me up Wednesday after Hawkei Art by taking me to the group home to play with Adriel, my foster kid for my parenting class.

"This is really sweet of you to come with," I told Liam on our way. We walked along the road hand-in-hand.

Liam shrugged. "You talk about him so much that I wanted to meet him. You two seem really close."

The kids were passing through the main foyer after dinner when we arrived. Adriel spotted me and ran over screaming, "Sophia!"

He didn't hug me, because he didn't like being in close contact with people, but he leaned his head close to me, which was basically his version of a hug.

I bent to his level on one knee. "Adriel, how are you?"

"Okay," he replied, but it came out sounding like a jumbled mess. He wasn't very good with language yet, though the nurse had told me he'd been working with a speech therapist and had been getting better since I started coming to see him.

"Adriel, this is my friend, Liam," I said. "Can you say hi?"

"Hi, Adriel," Liam said kindly as he knelt beside us.

Adriel didn't look him in the eye, but he held his hand up to wave.

I chuckled. "I think that means he likes you."

"Play! Play!" Adriel cried.

I stood and noticed Miss Evangeline's eyes on us. She smiled lightly as she watched Adriel interact with me.

"Is it okay if we join?" I asked her.

"Of course, Sophia," she said. "You're always welcome."

We followed the other kids to the play room, and Adriel immediately went to the blocks. He looked back a few times to make sure I was following him. Esis knew the drill by now, and he started helping Baby—the group home's hippogriff— gather the blocks and put them in piles next to Adriel.

Liam sat on the ground and started reaching for blocks. "What do we have here? Are we building a tower?"

Adriel snatched a blue block from Liam's hands and started a pile next to the red ones.

"Adriel," I scolded. "That wasn't very nice."

Adriel tucked his chin in and crossed his arms. He mumbled something incomprehensible.

"Next time, ask politely," I told him, before picking up a block and offering it to him.

His eyes brightened as he took it out of my hand and piled it on top of another green block, making certain their edges were lined up.

I smiled, then glanced to Liam, only for my cheeks to flame red. He was looking at me with this dreamy look in his eyes. "What?" I asked innocently.

"Nothing," Liam said, but I could definitely sense there was *something*.

As we continued playing, Adriel took a liking to Liam. When he placed a block in Liam's hand, I nearly jumped for joy. This wasn't something Adriel normally did, and it was a huge step in his development.

Liam didn't even notice. He just placed the blue block on top of the others. "How's that? Is that where it goes?"

Adriel shook his head and resituated the block so that it was in perfect alignment with the others.

"You're right," Liam said in a light voice. "It was a little crooked. It looks much better now. Thanks for fixing it for me, bud."

The more Liam interacted with Adriel, the heavier my heart got. Liam used water from a water bottle to create small magical creatures that galloped and jumped around Adriel. Adriel laughed as he watched the water elephant play with the griffin.

I wanted this for us *so badly*. Seeing Liam play with Adriel made me think of what we might've had together someday— if Liam weren't sterile. I wanted to sneak away with Liam and fuck him as soon as we got back to the castle. My ovaries were about to explode with how cute it all was.

But I could never say that to Liam. Because the fantasies in my head were just that...

Fantasies.

❦

THURSDAY MORNING, I woke to a light tap on the side of my face. I'd slept on the bottom bunk that night, since Liam insisted we had to switch off. My eyes shot open to see Esis standing on my chest, peering down at me. I blinked him into focus. "What is it, buddy?"

He peeped and held up a sheet of paper. I took it to see that it was nothing but a bunch of scribbles. He pointed to my trunk, then to his chest proudly. I looked over to see that my sketchbook and colored pencils had been pulled out of the trunk and were scattered on the floor between the bunks.

I set Esis beside me and pushed myself to a sitting position. My head nearly grazed the underside of the top bunk. "Esis, did you draw this?"

He nodded, then started pointing at it like he was trying to explain what it was. He pointed to a red scribble, then to me. He touched the blue scribble, then pointed upward. After touching the yellow scribble, he placed his paw on his chest. Finally, he pointed out a purple circle, then pointed to Julian sitting in the basket at the foot of the bed.

"Is it me, Liam, you, and Julian?" I asked.

He bobbed his head up and down. A warmth entered my chest. Esis was obviously trying to make me feel better. He was saying we were a family.

I scratched him behind the ears. "Thanks, buddy."

I glanced around the dorms. They were pretty much empty. Jonah and Imogen were already gone. I could hear Liam stirring from above me, but he didn't have class until late that afternoon. Judging by how quiet the dorms were, most people were already in class, which meant I'd slept in a little longer than I meant to.

"We should probably get ready for class, huh?" I asked Esis.

He nodded and hopped off the bed, taking the drawing with him. He tried to stick it to the wall next to our painting, but it just fell to the floor.

I chuckled as I stood and picked the paper up off the ground. "We'll hang it up later, okay?"

After cleaning up my trunk and getting dressed in the girl's bathroom, I packed Julian in my bag and hoisted it over my shoulder. I wanted to give Liam a kiss for the day, but he looked peaceful sleeping there. I didn't want to wake him. I nudged Esis to give him a quick treatment before we left.

My first class of the day was Fundamentals of Familiar Magic. So far we'd covered a lot of things I already knew, like how we drew magic from our Familiars, and that was why our magic got stronger when we bonded. Professor Curt taught this class. I'd had him for Dragonology my first semester. He was Koigni sorted into Defortai, and bonded to a red dragon named Kalina. He was one of the few professors left since the riots. I took a seat toward the back of the class.

"Welcome, class," Professor Curt said, folding his hands in front of himself at the front of the room. "Last week we finished our unit on Koigni Familiars. Before we get into Nivita magic, I'd like to talk about Anichi Familiars."

My stomach twisted, and I shifted uncomfortably in my chair. I hoped Professor Curt didn't say anything about kurbles.

At the front of the room, someone raised their hand. It was Riley, a guy from Yapluma I didn't know very well. He had a hawk Familiar that stood on the desk in front of him. "Aren't all Anichi Familiars extinct?"

"Yes," Professor Curt replied.

I breathed a sigh of relief. Esis was safe— for now.

"However, that doesn't mean we can't learn from them," Professor Curt added. He turned to his projector screen and pressed a button on his remote. A slide came up showing a collage of drawings of various Anichi Familiars. My gaze roamed over beautiful white deer, large dragons, small bats, and creatures I'd never seen before— a sheep with wings, a koala-like creature with a mane around its face, and lemurs with piercing sapphire eyes.

Professor Curt began his lecture. "These are some of the Anichi Familiars we know once existed. As you can see, Anichi had a wide variety of species connected to their House."

He used his laser pointer to call attention to a small lizard. "Reptiles."

Next, he pointed to a creature that looked a lot like a opossum, but with a shorter nose and bigger ears. "Marsupials."

He pointed out a rabbit Familiar next. "Lagomorphs."

He ran his laser pointer along a snake-like creature that looked like it had fins. "Water creatures."

He turned back to the class. "Though the Anichi Familiars differed in appearance, they all had one very important thing in common. They all shared magical characteristics known only to the Soul House. They could create beams of light, protect their Elementai in times of war with shields, and yes, in rare species, even heal."

A girl at the front of the room raised their hand. "How did the Anichi die if their Familiars could protect them?"

Professor Curt's face fell, and he took a deep breath. "That's a question best suited for your history professors, but as I understand it, there came a point in the Great War when Anichi were separated from their Familiars. In effect, this weakened their magic. As Familiars died, so did the Anichi."

Nausea twisted in my stomach. It was clear what Professor Curt was saying, though he didn't go into detail. There was a dark look on his face that suggested he didn't want to admit what had really happened, because then he'd have to face the fact that it was happening all over again. I'd bet anything that back in the Great War, Koigni forced the separation of Elementai from their Familiars and executed all the Soul creatures they could find— to weaken Anichi's magic. They were probably too stupid to realize it'd kill the entire House off.

My hands curled into fists. Koigni was better than this. I knew because of people like Vanessa, Lindsey, Miranda, and Bren. My grandparents had been the ones who'd showed me Koigni weren't all bad— it was just those in power who thirsted for more.

And they were doing it all over again. There wasn't a damn thing I could do about it, either, until we had that Air piece— and knew what came next.

Riley raised his hand again. "Could there still be Anichi creatures out there, even though the Anichi Elementai are gone?"

Professor Curt frowned. "If you're asking if Soul creatures could survive without Elementai, the answer is yes. There are more magical creatures in our world than there are Elementai, and many go their whole lives without bonding. But there are no Soul creatures left. Everybody knows that."

Professor Curt left it at that and changed the slide, diving into the various classifications of Anichi Familiars. Meanwhile, I couldn't get my mind off what he said. I stared down at Esis and stroked his fur.

He was wrong about the Soul creatures being extinct. Esis was one of them, and he had to come from *somewhere.* He couldn't be the only one.

So the only question was, where were the other Anichi Familiars hiding?

WHEN I RETURNED to the dorms after class, Liam was still lying in bed. It was almost lunch time, and he was normally up by now. My stomach sank in worry.

"Liam?" I nudged him a little, but he didn't move. I nudged him harder and spoke his name louder.

Liam stirred and rolled over. He didn't open his eyes as he moaned, "Go back to sleep, *pawee*."

"Liam, it's almost noon," I stated. "What are you still doing in bed? It's time for lunch."

He swatted me away. "I'm not hungry."

"Liam," I snapped.

Liam's eyes fluttered open, and he lifted his head slightly to look at me. Immediately, my eyes went wide. Liam's face was pale, and his lips had turned a bluish tint. His breath came in shallow heaves, and his forehead was covered in a sheen of sweat.

"You look awful," I breathed.

He shook his head, though it looked strained. "Nah, *pawee*, I'm fine—"

Liam's words were cut off as he started coughing. It sounded like he was hocking up a lung. He covered his mouth with his hand, but it didn't help stifle the sound. The few people who were here between classes looked our way. Esis jumped off my shoulder onto the top bunk.

"Ancestors!" I exclaimed. I rushed to grab a bottle of water Jonah had left sitting on top of one of the trunks, along with Liam's inhaler. I held the bottle up to Liam, but he declined as the coughing fit continued.

Esis ears fell as he worked his healing magic, but nothing happened.

Finally, Liam's coughing slowed. He pulled his hand away from his mouth and looked down at it, then curled his hand into a fist.

"Liam, show me," I demanded.

He sighed. "*Pawee,* I said I was fine."

"You're not," I insisted. "You're lying to me. Now show me your hand."

Liam hesitated, then unfurled his fingers. Inside lay a ball of dark phlegm. *Fine, my ass.*

"Okay, that's it," I stated firmly. "We're headed to the infirmary."

"What? No," he protested.

"You don't have a choice." I shoved his inhaler into his hand, then started gathering clothes from his trunk. I lowered my voice as I leaned in to hand them to him. "Liam, your magic is getting weaker. There's only so much Esis can do. It's time to get modern medicine involved, because no matter what, I will *not* lose you."

Liam's expression didn't give anything away as he stared back at me. "It's not going to help."

I shrugged. "Fine. Prove me wrong."

Liam groaned. "Just let me sleep it off, *pawee*."

I sighed. He was so stubborn. "I'll make you a deal. If you make it to class, you don't have to go to the hospital. But if it doesn't get better, you're headed up there the moment you wake."

"Deal," he agreed. He used his inhaler once before handing it back to me.

I relaxed and softened my tone. "Can I get you anything?"

"Nah," he said as he rolled over. "I'm okay."

Liam's message was clear. He was far from okay, but he didn't want to do anything about it. I'd give him a pass now, but next time, I was dragging him to the infirmary myself.

I stayed in the Biyami dorms to keep an eye on Liam, even though I hated it down here— we all did. I worked on homework while Esis snuggled up to the dragon egg and took a nap. Liam had managed to drag himself out of bed to go to class like we agreed, but he went back to sleep the moment he returned.

It was late before Jonah and Imogen entered the dorms, along with Sassy and Squeaks.

Imogen looked like a walking disaster. Her hair was in disarray, and there was a sticky stain all over her lavender dress. The bow on Sassy's tail had been crushed, and the fur on top of her head stuck straight up. I instantly set my homework aside.

"It couldn't have been *that* bad," Jonah insisted.

Imogen's eyebrows shot up. "Believe me, it was."

"What was bad?" I asked.

Imogen groaned. "My date with Sam."

I furrowed my brow. "What happened?"

Imogen started counting off on her fingers. "Well, we were denied service at three different restaurants. One said it was going to be a two hour wait, even though we could see empty tables. Another obviously lied to us about an *E. Coli* breakout. We finally covered up our tattoos and the fourth place let us in, but I ended up spilling my lemonade all over my dress, so they moved us to another table. Let's see... what else? The soup was cold. Zaria stepped on Sassy's tail, and I'm pretty sure it's *still* bruised. Sam lost his wallet, and I only had my card on me, which got declined at the register, so I had to run to the bank while he stayed at the restaurant. *Then* we ran into Sam's ex-girlfriend in the square. She wanted to *hang out* with us. Ew. I told her we were on a date and to get lost. What else? He bought me a flower at a street vendor, but it had a bee in it that ended up stinging him. Guess who's allergic to bees? He's in the infirmary now, and he's okay, but he can barely talk through the hives."

Imogen took a long-winded breath.

"Is that all?" Jonah asked flatly.

Imogen crossed her arms and scrunched up her nose. "Is that not enough?"

"At least you got a good story out of it," Jonah pointed out.

Imogen shrugged. "If you can call it that. I don't think there's going to be another date. I'm not really into Sam, anyway."

Jonah frowned. "Is it because of Cade?"

Imogen crossed her arms. "So what if it is?"

My heart fell. "Im... it's been months."

"You don't think I *know that*, Sophia?" Imogen snapped. She quickly softened her tone, but tears welled in her eyes. "I just need more time to get over him. Okay?"

Jonah's face fell. "Take all the time you need, Im. But girl... eventually, you'll have to move on. So you can be happy again. We don't want to see you suffer like this."

Imogen's tears threatened to spill over. "I know," she practically whispered.

I felt so bad for her. Imogen was my best friend, but I couldn't cure the worst pain she'd ever felt. I couldn't bring Cade back, nor could I make it better. The best thing I could do was be here for her, and it would never be enough.

Jonah shot a look to the top bunk where Liam was sleeping. "He okay?"

I shook my head. "He's not feeling well."

Imogen set her bag on Jonah's bed and sat down. "Again?"

I raised an eyebrow. "You mean still."

Jonah groaned and plopped down on my mattress beside me. "Ugh. I bet it's the stress. Everything's going to shit lately."

Imogen swung her leg out to kick him lightly, but her legs weren't long enough. "We all know."

"At this point, we might as well leave," Jonah complained.

It wasn't meant to be a real suggestion, but Imogen and I both froze.

"Do you really think we could?" I asked.

Jonah lowered his voice. "I don't know. Honestly, what are we even staying for? We're going to get ourselves killed the longer we stay."

"I mean, where would we go?" I questioned, glancing around to make sure no one heard us. "Maybe my parents' house, but the Elders are watching us. I don't want to drag my family into any more conflict. There's nowhere for us to hide. We can't just pick up and leave when we don't have anywhere to go."

Or any money to do it. All of our Cup winnings were gone.

"Besides," I added, shooting a glance upward to the top bunk. "I don't know if Liam would make it."

"What do you mean?" Jonah asked.

I face-palmed. Did Jonah not understand how *bad* Liam's condition was? "Me, you, Imogen... we could all handle being homeless. But Liam? He needs medical care, and that's not something he can get if we're on the run. Even if we got a car or something, I don't think he could handle sleeping in it for weeks on end until we found a place to live. He won't survive on the streets."

Jonah's brow furrowed. "But we have Esis."

"And clearly his condition is getting worse anyway," I pointed out.

Jonah's shoulders dropped. "Yeah, I noticed."

"We can't go," Imogen stated. "We have a lot left to do. We have to help people, or no one else will."

It was obvious she was talking about the smuggling operation, though she wouldn't dare say it out loud. She probably meant we had to find the Air piece, too.

"We can't leave. I have to help my dad." The sound of Liam's voice above us shocked me. I thought he was asleep. I went still, hoping he hadn't heard what I'd just said. He'd make a big deal about how he didn't want us to worry about him and how he could handle it.

Jonah stood to look at Liam, like we hadn't just been talking about him. "Help your dad with what?"

I was curious, too, so I got to my feet beside Jonah. Liam had his head rested on the edge of the mattress as he stared down at us. "Not here. But it's important."

I nodded, understanding that he'd tell us all later.

"It's something we can consider," Imogen said. "But as a last resort. I don't want to leave my parents or my brothers behind."

"I don't want to leave my grandparents, either," I added.

"My family needs me, too," Liam said.

"So it's settled," I said. "We don't leave Kinpago unless we have no other choice. For now, we're going to stay and fight, and hope things turn around."

Jonah's face fell, but he held his shoulders back, like he was trying not to let it show. He didn't have anyone left he really cared about except us. "I'm staying as long as you guys are. Nothing can break apart the Reject Team."

❧

Saturday morning when I woke, I rolled over and felt a piece of paper crinkle beneath me. I sat up in bed and used my Fire to create a small flame so I could see through the dark dungeon. My heart leapt when I saw the curved letters of my name on the outside of an envelope.

Amelia. Kiwi must've snuck in last night to get me a message.

I instantly became alert as I tore the envelope open and read Amelia's letter.

Sophia,
> *Today's my only day in town. Breakfast at* Dragon Bean?
> *Amelia*

I'd never been to *Dragon Bean* before, but I'd passed it in Kinpago. It was a cute little coffee shop on the edge of town close to the school.

I kicked off my covers, which stirred Esis awake, and climbed down from the top bunk.

"Sophia?" Liam groaned from where he slept.

"Shh..." I told him, glancing around at all the other Biyami who were sleeping in. "My sister's in town. I'm going to have breakfast with her."

Liam rubbed his eyes. "Okay. You want me to come with?"

I could tell he still wasn't feeling well. Anxiety knotted in my gut.

"No," I whispered. "I'll be fine."

Esis helped me pick out my clothes for the day, then followed me into the bathroom to shower. He grumbled when the water sprayed his fur, but he didn't seem to mind when I told him he could give Julian a bath. Esis carried the dragon egg to a puddle in the shower room and started scrubbing the outside of the egg while humming a soft tune.

After a quick shower, I dried off, dressed, and threw my hair into a ponytail. I couldn't get out of the castle and to the coffee shop soon enough.

The morning sunlight was a warm welcome to the dark, dank conditions in the Biyami dorms. I was actually feeling pretty good as I walked into town.

When I stepped inside *Dragon Bean*, I spotted Amelia right away. She sat in a booth, reading the paper and sipping on her coffee. Kiwi sat on her shoulder and looked interested in the pictures on the page.

It was quiet in here, with only a half dozen patrons. It looked like a normal coffee shop, except with dragon decorations everywhere. Different colored eggs had been placed on shelves above all the tables. They must've been reconstructed after the dragons hatched, because I didn't think anyone would just leave dragon eggs lying around like this. The light fixtures were even made from dragon scales. It was all very colorful and reminded me of a kaleidoscope.

Amelia heard the sound of the bell above the door and turned. Her eyes lit up when she saw me. She squealed and stood with her arms out wide.

"Sophia!" she sang.

I pulled her into a tight hug. She was so warm and familiar that it took my breath away. I just wanted to squeeze her for hours. "Amelia, it's so great to see you."

She drew away and took my hand. "Let's get you something to eat. On me."

"Am, really, I can pay for myself," I protested. I only had a couple dollars, but it was enough for breakfast.

"I'm the one with the job. Remember?" she said.

Amelia dragged me up to the counter and told me to order whatever I wanted. I chose a strawberry smoothie and a blueberry muffin. Esis tugged on my ear until I ordered a second muffin for him.

"How's work been?" I asked once we sat. Esis perched in my lap, happily eyeing the muffin I was unwrapping for him.

Amelia shrugged. "Could be better. I was demoted to the laundry department. I didn't think you could be demoted from maid, but apparently you can. I just wash and fold laundry all day, because apparently it's *bad* if passengers see Biyami making their beds."

My shoulders fell. "I'm sorry, Am."

She shrugged. "It's fine."

She had that same tone in her voice that Liam always got when he said that. Translation: things were *totally not fine*.

"Do you at least get off the *Hozho* at port?" I asked. I knew one of the reasons she'd taken the job was to travel.

"Here and there," she said, staring down at her second cup of coffee.

It was clear she wasn't being treated well on the *Hozho* and didn't want to tell me. I had this horrible image in my head of her wearing rags for her uniform and eating lunch in a tiny corner behind the washing machine. I didn't get why she wouldn't quit.

"Anyway, how's Kinpago been?" Her tone brightened.

I swallowed a piece of muffin. "Not great, to be honest. The Biyami have basically been thrown in the dungeons, and people are getting their Familiars taken away."

She frowned. "I heard. Is it really as bad as they say?"

I nodded. "I watched someone get murdered in front of me at school, and nobody did a thing to prosecute the bitch."

My harsh tone got a few people to look our way, so I lowered my voice. "I'll tell you about it later."

Amelia had this wide-eyed look of terror on her face, but she quickly said, "Yeah, that's probably best. Why don't we go for a walk?"

We gathered our take-out cups and left the coffee shop. Neither of us spoke until we veered off the main road onto a narrow hiking path in the woods.

"So, what's been going on?" Amelia asked.

I dove into the story of how Haley killed Levi. I hadn't really talked about it since, though it was always hanging on the edge of my mind. I was surprised at how good it felt to tell her— like I was finally making some sense out of it. Once I started talking, I couldn't stop. I told Amelia about the scene I'd witnessed with Logan and Isabella, and how I'd stepped in to stop it.

"Good," she said firmly. "I'm glad you stood up to him. The Biyami need people like you to protect them."

I burned to tell Amelia about our smuggling operation, but I didn't think it was fair after I'd chewed Liam out about Mia. It was supposed to be a unanimous decision to tell other people, even though I trusted Amelia with my life.

Eventually, we reached the beach, and Amelia and I sat on a big rock. I curled my arms around my knees, since there was a chill in the air. Esis and Kiwi sniffed each other, until Kiwi started pecking Esis' horns. Esis hissed and cowered behind me.

"It's okay, buddy," I said, pulling him into my lap. "Kiwi's just playing."

Kiwi never did like me much— probably because I was Koigni and he was bonded to a Toaqua— but he'd started warming up to me since I came to Kinpago.

Amelia stared out into the ocean, looking deep in thought. The wind breezed through her dark hair. I noticed the waves grew the more she stared at them. Thoughts were racing through my own head— things I'd been wanting to ask her for a while.

"Am," I said softly.

She tore her gaze from the water to look at me. "Yeah?"

"I'm curious. Why do you think the Elders put you in Biyami? You're not a threat to anyone. You wouldn't hurt a fly." I dropped my gaze. "Do you think... it's because of me?"

Her face fell, and she looked deeply hurt by the suggestion. "Sophia, no. Even if that's the case, it's not the only reason."

I furrowed my brow and searched her face for an explanation. She gave nothing away. "What do you mean? How could the Elders hate you—?"

My question halted in its tracks when I realized something. The day I learned of my powers, Naomi had been prowling the hiking trail in Utah where Amelia and I had spent our afternoon. I never knew why, and Amelia had dodged around the question when I'd asked before. Had Amelia done something to get herself in trouble with Madame Doya— with the Elders?

My tone hardened. "Am, what'd you do to Doya?"

Amelia scoffed. "That bitch? Nothing."

"It doesn't sound like nothing," I asserted.

She shook it off. "I promise, I didn't do anything to Doya."

I crossed my arms. It annoyed me when she closed me off like this. "Well, she seemed pretty interested in you. Enough to send her Familiar two states away to spy on you."

"How do you know she wasn't spying on you?" Amelia shot back.

"Because no one knew where I was until *you* exposed me," I snapped.

Amelia went so still that she didn't even breathe. She looked like a wax figure, until tears began to rise to her eyes. Shock riveted through me. Amelia *never* cried.

"I'm sorry about that." Her voice cracked. "I just wanted you to bond. If I could go back and do it all over again, I'd never let you get involved with this mess."

"Amelia," I said softly. I leaned over and pulled her into a hug.

When we drew away from each other, Amelia wiped at her eyes.

"I'm so sorry, Am," I said, "but that's exactly why I need to know. I'm involved now, and you can't change that. So please, don't lie to me."

Amelia took a long, deep breath, like she was stalling. Finally, she lifted her gaze to meet mine. "Okay. I'll tell you."

I resituated myself on the rock to face her head-on. My pulse quickened as I waited to hear her story.

"During my senior year at Orenda Academy... something happened..."

"What happened?" I asked when she paused.

Amelia hesitated. "My friends wanted me to rise up against the Elders. I didn't know if I wanted to or not."

"Did you do it?" I questioned.

Amelia sat rigid. "Most of them ended up dead in the tournament. The ancestors chose a different path for me."

I furrowed my brow. "What path?"

She took a deep breath. "When I was trying to figure out what I wanted to do, I prayed to the ancestors to help guide me. It was the longest meditation of my life— even longer than my Naming Ceremony... even longer than yours."

Amelia swallowed. "When my ancestral guides finally arrived, they showed me a vision of the totem."

Amelia's gaze flickered down to my shirt, where the totem was safely tucked inside. I pulled the totem out from under my shirt so she could see it. "You knew I had it?"

"I've known you had it since your Naming Ceremony," she admitted. "I saw it around your neck when you changed in the woods."

I'd forgotten about that. "Right, but I gave it to the Elders during the trial."

"I saw the string around your neck," she said. "I assumed."

"So the ancestors wanted you to find it and... what? Give it to me?" I asked.

She shook her head. "No. They wanted me to put it somewhere where you'd find it— in the cave."

I gasped. "*You're* the one who put it in the cave? Where'd you get it from?"

"In my vision from my ancestral guides, I was climbing a mountain, up the tallest peak in all of Kinpago," Amelia explained. "When I went to climb the peak for real, the totem came to me."

"Came to you?" I asked.

She nodded. "From the sky. This bright light came down from the clouds, and the totem was there, floating straight into my hand. I knew the ancestors had brought it to me."

I couldn't explain what I felt when Amelia told the story. A warmth spread throughout my chest. I couldn't believe the totem had come straight from the Ancestral Lands.

"Once I had it, I followed my vision to the cave," Amelia said. "That's where I left it until you found it."

"Wow," I breathed. I lightly touched the totem, still trying to process it all. "What does any of this have to do with Doya?"

Amelia took a deep breath before continuing. "I think Naomi must've seen me praying to the ancestors, because she started following me around afterward. Doya must've sent her to trail me to Utah because she thought the ancestors gave me information."

It was a lot to take in. I thought Amelia was innocent in all this, but she was a lot more involved than I'd assumed.

"But I showed the totem to Doya, and she didn't think anything of it," I said.

Amelia shook her head. "I'm not sure that's what she was looking for."

What was it Doya wanted from Amelia? Theories were going wild in my head, and none of them were good. Was Doya looking for some kind of weapon? She'd mentioned something to me about finding an object long ago.

"Doya must've realized I didn't have what she wanted, because Naomi stopped following me after that," Amelia said.

I took a long, deep breath as I processed everything Amelia had said. When I exhaled, I finally spoke again. "So, what happened to the rest of your friends? The ones who didn't die in the tournament? Do they still want to rise up against the Elders?"

The muscles in Amelia's jaw tightened, and she got a dark look in her eyes. "That's a road you don't want to go down, Sophia."

When I opened my mouth to protest, she quickly added, "It's for your own safety."

A heavy weight settled on my chest. "Am, if there are people out there rising up against the Elders—"

"Sophia," Amelia snapped. "Don't ask me questions you don't want to know the answers to. I don't want to have to lie to you."

There was something in her eyes that suggested she'd already lied. My jaw clenched. "I don't like being kept in the dark."

Amelia took my hands in hers and looked me straight in the eye. "I need you to trust me on this. Just knowing could put you in danger."

Tears pricked at the corners of my eyes, and Amelia let go of my hands. "Look, I have to leave for a few days, but I'll be back at the end of next week. There's more I want to tell you, but..."

Amelia shot a glance around the beach. Even though we were alone, she looked nervous. "Not here. I'll send Kiwi. Next week, Friday the thirteenth. We'll meet after you're done with class. I promise I'll explain everything."

"Okay," I agreed, because I didn't know what else to say.

I only hoped by then Amelia would be honest with me. I didn't believe her when she said her friends had died.

Amelia was lying, and if we were going to win this war, we both needed to tell each other the truth.

Liam

THIRTEEN

Jonah and I were doing everything in our power to try and get Dean Alizeh to talk to us, but it was going about as well as a bag of limp dicks.

She literally ran away every time she saw either of us coming. I hadn't managed to get within ten feet of her since the last time she'd thrown us out of her presence. Jonah had Alizeh as his advisor for his major, but after every Psychology class she immediately left the room so that Jonah couldn't speak with her.

"It's maddening, dude. She won't even look at me," Jonah told me the second Monday in March. I'd just gotten out of Master Toaqua Magic, and he'd caught me on my way back to the Biyami dorms.

Jonah was holding a massive coffee, which Squeaks kept guzzling from. Her feathers were ruffled, and she looked stressed. She kept snapping her beak at Familiars who dared to get too close as they walked by. Some of the ones from Defortai gave her warning signals, but she made angry noises and clearly made it known she didn't care.

Jonah took a deep breath. "I tried bringing it up during my advisory meeting, but Alizeh told me she didn't want to hear it and blew me out of her office." He shook his head. "Maybe we should think about getting someone else to ask her."

"I don't—" I broke into a coughing fit. The sound was thick and wheezing. I had to gasp for breath a few times before my chest finally settled. It'd been bad enough to make my eyes water.

"Dude, you sound horrible." Jonah's eyes narrowed in concern.

"I think I'm good." It was kind of a lie, and Squeaks caught it. She clacked her beak and let out a high-pitched note.

"Haven't you been sick for a while?" Jonah questioned.

"Yeah, like the past two years, every fucking day," I snapped.

"That's *not* what I meant. I mean like this," Jonah's tone was blunt. "Whatever you caught clearly isn't getting any better. This has been going on for weeks."

"So it's lasted a bit longer than usual, so what?" I didn't get why everyone was so concerned. I literally got a cold like, every month. It wasn't anything newsworthy.

Jonah paused for a moment. "There's like, a crap ton of mucus in your lungs. I can fucking feel it," Jonah started. "You're breathing like shit."

"I always breathe like shit."

"Not like this." Jonah's mouth became thin. "You need to go to the doctor."

"Fuck no. I'll be fine." I was sick of going to doctors. This wasn't serious. I hardly noticed a difference from what I felt like every day. I'd get over this random virus eventually.

"I'm going to tell your girlfriend on you," Jonah started.

"If you do that, I'll never forgive you." Sophia had nearly dragged me to the hospital wing last week. But we'd had a deal. If I went to class, I didn't have go to the infirmary, and so far I was keeping up with that bargain. I had to be getting better. Jonah didn't know my body. I did.

I cleared my throat again. "Anyway, I don't know if asking someone else to help us with Alizeh would work." We'd talked about getting the girls involved, but doubted it would do any good. Everyone on campus knew the four of us were glued at the hip. If Alizeh saw Imogen or Sophia coming at her, it'd be the same situation.

"No, I mean, someone else that isn't us," Jonah said.

"Then we'd have to tell them about what we're doing." I didn't want anyone else knowing we were hunting prophecy pieces. Ezra already knew, and although I trusted him, this kind of information would put people in danger.

"Do we really have a choice?" Jonah pointed out. "We're running out of options, here."

I went through the list of people we could trust in my head, and something clicked. "Maddie," I said. "She has Dean Alizeh for one of her classes. She'd be the perfect fit."

Jonah's eyes cleared. "Yeah. She's a *naderei*. It'd be the best solution."

"Keep your voice down," I snapped. I glanced around to make sure no one had overheard before I noted, "Her next class doesn't start for another hour. We can ask her now."

The Biyami dorms were mostly empty when we entered. Sophia and Imogen, along with everyone else, were probably still in class. The only people inside were Drew, Maddie, and Ezra, who were hanging around the foosball table with their Familiars. Ezra wasn't supposed to be down here, but he'd clearly decided to fuck the rules and sneak in as often as he could in order to hang with us.

Ezra was playing a game against Drew. He scored three goals in a row and gave high-fives to Maddie. Drew wrinkled his nose and cast worried glances at Maddie, like he was worried he was doing bad at impressing her.

Ezra scored another goal, and laughed. "That's game, dude. You're done."

Drew sighed. "Man, I suck at sports. Even tabletop ones. If it doesn't have a controller, I can't win it."

"You'll always be a winner to me." My sister giggled. Maddie rose up on her tiptoes to give Drew a kiss on the cheek.

Drew's face went completely red, and a few flames flickered around his fingertips. At his feet, his German Shepard Familiar wagged his tail, tongue lolling out of his mouth.

Ezra sent me an obvious look, and I nodded back. Maddie began gathering her things from her bunk. She piled several gigantic books into Drew's hands and said, "Would you mind taking these to Dean Alizeh's classroom for me? They're so heavy. I can't carry them."

Maddie batted her eyelashes, and Eirakari gave a delighted noise. The ice dragon reached out and ruffled his hair gently with her breath.

Drew gulped. "Yes, Maddie. Whatever you want."

Maddie beamed. "Perfect. I'll meet you there."

"Okay." Drew struggled to carry the books toward the Biyami staircase. It was comical, watching the scrawny dude waddle under the weight of all those books.

She had him totally whipped. It was clearly time to do the big brother thing and start interrogating this guy.

Ezra moved before I did. As Drew rounded the corner, out of the sight of Maddie, Ezra and I honed in and blocked his way forward.

Drew immediately knew what this was before either of us said anything. His eyes contracted, and he visibly gulped. "Hey, guys," he started. "What's up?" His Familiar, Ace, whimpered on the floor.

"Hey there, bud. Let's talk." Ezra took the books out of his hands and set them on the floor. Although they were nothing for Ezra to carry, Drew sagged when the heavy tomes left his arms.

"Wha— what do you want to t-talk about?" Drew stuttered. The kid was already losing his nerve.

"We just want to know what your intentions are with our little sister," Ezra began, and he crossed his arms. Dyami ruffled his wings and let out an intimidating noise.

"In— intentions?" Drew squeaked.

"She obviously likes you," I said. "So do you like her back, or what?"

Drew hesitated for a minute. "I— Maddie's great. I mean, she's amazing. I like her— but in a friend way. And in a more than that way, too. And she's really hot, I mean beautiful, I mean…"

Drew drifted off awkwardly. His German Shepherd had settled for lying on the floor and putting his paws over his eyes.

"And that's fine and all, but *we're* here to make sure you don't mess up." Ezra gestured between himself and me. "Or take advantage of her."

"I would never!" Drew burst. "I haven't even—"

Drew went even redder as he cut himself off at the last minute. I rolled my eyes. No shit Drew was still a virgin. It was obvious the kid never had sex.

Except now with Maddie, that was totally a possibility. Though it kind of made me want to beat him up to think about him screwing my sister, I also wanted Maddie to be happy. And she could do a hell of a lot worse than Drew. He was a nice kid.

"I know you don't like me, because I'm not Toaqua," Drew mumbled. His eyes went downward and remained glued to the floor.

"I don't give a shit if you're Koigni. I'm in an interhouse relationship myself, with a Fire girl mind you," I said.

"Yeah," Ezra added. "We just want to make sure you don't break her heart."

"Or we'll break your face," I finished.

Drew cringed. "Okay, I'm just gonna level with you," he started. "I like Maddie, but I'm kind of scared to ask her out. I mean, she's *her*, and I'm... me." He let out a long sigh. "She's totally a ten. I'm more like a two."

Couldn't argue with that analysis. But I knew Maddie cared about him. I wanted her to be in a healthy relationship, and though Drew might be a total nerd, I could tell he was a good guy.

"It's not the looks that matter, bro," Ezra said, but he was kinder than I was. "She likes you for you."

Drew snorted. "Yeah, right. If I asked her to be my girlfriend, she'd say no."

"She wouldn't turn you down. She's head over heels for you," Ezra said.

Drew's eyes gleamed with hope, and it was both endearing and sickening to watch.

"We just want to make sure that this isn't going to be a problem," I subbed in. "So, is it?"

Drew shook his head so quickly I'm surprised it didn't go flying off. "No, sir. It won't be."

"Good." I waited for a moment before I said, "We don't want to be dickheads to you, but Mads... she's sensitive. You get what I'm saying?"

I didn't want to add that a breakup would devastate her. She wouldn't be able to handle it.

Drew nodded. He suddenly grew very serious as he said, "I know how she is. She's told me some... things. Stuff she'd never say to anyone else."

Our eyes connected with a mutual understanding, while Ezra's remained curious. Maddie had told Drew that she used to cut herself? That was a big deal. If Maddie had opened up to Drew like that, she really loved him. Drew seemed to care about keeping Maddie's heart safe just as much as Ezra and I did.

And Eirakari seemed to favor him. Familiars didn't do that with significant others unless they truly were a good match.

Ezra looked to me for approval, and I gave it with a nod of my head. "Fine. You've convinced me," I said. "Just don't mess it up."

"And use condoms," Ezra said. "Or else."

Drew gave a meep that sounded like it came from Esis. "O— kay."

"Good talk." Ezra reached down and put the books back into Drew's arms before he clapped him on the back. Drew wheezed as he began to climb the stairs with the collection of books in his arms, the dog jumping around his legs.

"I think he's a decent one," Ezra said. "We don't have to worry about him."

"He's a good guy." *Ancestors, what a dweeb though.*

Ezra's watch went off. "Shit, I'm gonna be late," he told me. "Catch you later, bro."

When I left the stairwell to talk to Maddie, she was sitting on her bunk with her arms crossed. She'd clearly known what Ezra and I were doing. Jonah stood a few paces back, waiting for the explosion.

"*Seriously!?*" Maddie burst once I was within earshot. "Can you guys stop harassing Drew? We're just friends."

"You want to be more than friends," I pointed out, and Eirakari chortled.

Maddie's cheeks flashed pink before she said, "That's none of your business! It is totally sexist and outdated for you and Ezra to question Drew about what's between us. I can speak for myself!"

"Fine, but if you think I'm going to be slacking on my duties as a big brother, you obviously don't know me that well," I said.

The tone in my voice made it clear the argument was over. I was the eldest, and in our society, there was a chain of command to follow.

Maddie rolled her eyes and snorted. "Whatever. You guys are impossible."

"We actually wanted to talk to you about something." Jonah stepped in. Maddie's gaze grew interested as he and Squeaks approached.

"What about?" she said. "If this is about the... thing... I'm ready whenever you guys are."

She was obviously talking about sneaking students out.

"It's not," I said. We hadn't smuggled anyone else out of the castle in a while for fear of getting caught, but we'd have to do another mission soon.

Jonah crouched down, and I sat beside Maddie on her bunk. Jonah dropped his voice. "It's about the prophecy," he began.

"The one about Sophia?" Maddie whispered. Eirakari cooed and lowered her head. "I'm sorry, but I can't help you guys with that. I'm not the one who made it."

"We know. But maybe you could offer some insight," I started.

I went to say something else, but I broke into another coughing fit again. Fucking dammit, this was annoying. It was like I couldn't speak without hacking something up.

Jonah glared at me, and Maddie said, "Liam, you're really sick. You need to go in."

How many people were going to harass me about this? I was fine. "Leave me be."

"If you wait too much longer I'm going to tell Mom and Dad," she shot at me.

"Mads, I swear to the ancestors, you keep your mouth shut," I growled.

She flashed her eyes toward the ceiling and shook her head. "You're so stubborn. But regardless, what did you want to ask about the prophecy?"

"Well..." Jonah cast a glance at me as he began. "For the past couple of semesters, we've been looking for *all* the pieces of the prophecy— one from each House."

"There's more than just the part from Koigni?" she asked in surprise.

"Yes," I said. "We've got one from Nivita and Toaqua as well."

"What about the Yapluma piece?" Maddie asked.

"That's the problem," I began. "We need Dean Alizeh to help us with it. We think she's the Storm Lord... some kind of legendary

Yapluma... and that only she can help us gain access to where the last piece is hiding."

"But she won't help us," Jonah said. "She wants nothing to do with any of it. She's too scared of what the Elders might do."

Maddie tapped her chin with her index finger. "Okay. So you want me to convince Dean Alizeh to help you find the Air piece of the prophecy, so you can understand it better?"

"Not exactly," I said. "We've been putting the prophecy together so that we can stop it."

Maddie's mouth dropped open. It hung there for a moment before she whispered, "That's impossible."

My heart skipped a beat. Maddie knew about this kind of stuff. But she couldn't be right about this, could she?

"Well... why not?" Jonah asked. "Is there a problem?"

"Prophecies can't be changed once they're made," Maddie said adamantly. "Whatever they say will come to pass, one way or another."

"That can't be true," I began. I leaned forward. "A year ago, the four of us contacted Showana Harjo on Ancestors' Day at the Anichi temple. She's the one who made the prophecy. She told us that the future can be changed."

"You guys didn't understand what she meant. She may have told you that prophecies can be misinterpreted," Maddie said. "If Sophia doesn't fulfill the prophecy, some other Koigni child will, in some other way, but the prophecy will come true regardless. There are a million ways *how* the prophecy can be fulfilled, good or bad, but stopping whatever's coming is a futile effort. It will always be."

"I have no idea what you're getting at," Jonah said. "You're making no sense."

Maddie breathed a harsh gust of wind out her nostrils. "Okay. So it's like this. For example, if I prophesied that you were going to... I don't know, have an event tomorrow that would change your world forever, so many different things could happen. You could meet the love of your life, or you could end up losing your best friend. Both are insanely different, with totally different emotions behind it, but it came to the same result. Your life changed."

"So what you're saying is that the prophecy will always come true, but it doesn't have to be negative?" I asked.

Maddie nodded. "Exactly. There are so many different paths to take, but the destination is always the same. The individual actions and choices will determine the outcome, but the outcome came full circle either way."

Maddie turned to me. "Can you tell me what you have so far? I might be able to interpret."

I went to speak, but I ran out of breath before I could and coughed again. Jonah subbed in for me.

"The fated Koigni child, born in the Summer Solstice in the Year of the Dragon,
Shall bring glory to the greatest House.

The future of the tribe is in Nivita's hands.
No Hawkei shall survive if the weakest refuse to bend.

The prophesied one will bring death beyond comprehension.
It is she who shall cause Toaqua's darkest hour."

Maddie's expression was pale when he finished reciting. "It's always up for interpretation, but... that's pretty clear to me what's going to happen."

"That's why we have to stop this!" I took a few deep breaths and added, "We can't just let this go on!"

"You guys don't understand how any of this works. I'm a *naderei*. Prophecies aren't just words on a piece of paper about the future, they're an *experience*," she said. "Whenever supernaturals tap into prophetic powers— either through tarot cards, or meditation, or by using their powers that were naturally gifted— all they're doing is gaining insight into a journey that has to be taken. But you can't go back once the journey has started. And if things have already come true, that means the journey has begun. I'd figure you guys are coming to the end of it now. There's nothing else you can do but ride it out."

"Mads, if we don't stop this, Toaqua is going to face its darkest hour. It might already be here. Do you want to doom our tribe?" I pleaded.

Maddie hesitated. It looked like I was going to change her mind before she shook her head. "No. This goes against everything I know as a prophet. It's against the *naderei* code. I can't interfere with this."

"But Maddie—"

"Don't, Liam." Maddie shook her head. "I get what you're trying to do, but you don't know how these things work. I would help you if it was for anything else, but I can't with this. You're tampering with things you shouldn't be messing with. Trust me."

She got up and swung her bag over her shoulder. Eirakari dove after her as they ran up the stairs. I gave Jonah a frustrated glance. He gave a hopeless one in return.

"Do you really think this is a futile effort?" he asked quietly. Squeaks dropped her head behind him.

"Like hell. We're not giving up," I growled. "If Dean Alizeh can't help us, we'll do it ourselves."

Jonah rubbed his left arm. "I guess. Imogen and I will work on locating the painting in the meantime. And figure out what kind of monster took it."

"It's all we can do right now." We needed a Storm Lord to speak to the painting, but that was a useless effort if we didn't know where it was in the first place, or what was guarding it. We'd figure out a way to convince Dean Alizeh to help us later.

Maddie could believe all she wanted that changing the prophecy was a lost cause. But I was never very good at giving up on lost causes.

And I'd be damned if I started now.

❦

At six o' clock on Tuesday evening, I reported to Tribal Headquarters for my internship. I was only working for two hours, which I was glad about, because I really did feel like shit. All I wanted to do was go to bed, but I had to suck it up. I had plans for later tonight, anyway, and I wasn't about to break them.

I moved at a crawl as I vacuumed and dusted the main offices. The internship wasn't as bad as I thought. I mostly worked nights cleaning up people's messes, and everyone left me the fuck alone.

I was leaning against a wall, trying to stop the vertigo when I heard footsteps. My eyes flew open. The grumble of a bear greeted me as Dad and Tatum walked into the office I was cleaning.

Dad's gaze searched me up and down. I didn't move to get off the wall. "Are you all right?"

"I'm fine, Dad." I'd recently decided I wouldn't say that to Sophia anymore, but my father? Absolutely.

Not that he looked convinced. But he didn't question further. Instead, he moved closer. "We need to talk."

He showed me the illusion orb in his pocket— the one from the Arcanea that manipulated conversations if anyone overheard. I nodded and followed him down the hall to his office.

This office wasn't as nice as the one at Serpent Assembly. It was small and cramped, and both the desk and chair were broken. They'd obviously given him the poorest of conditions.

"What's going on?" I sat in the worn armchair closest to the desk and wished the room would stop spinning. Tatum sat beside me and eyed the jar of honey my dad always kept for him on his desk.

"I've been thinking." Dad leaned against the desk and crossed his arms. "You know I've been attempting to overthrow Oleander and Annette both. To do that, I need intel. Unfortunately, my people have come under a lot of surveillance lately. We can't do anything without the Task Force tailing our every move. If we're going to stop what's happening, we need someone to get that information for us. So we can make our move."

"So you need a spy," I said.

"Yes," he began. "I wouldn't ask anyone else if there was another option, but there isn't. I hate putting you in this position again. But you're the only one who can gain access to Tribal Headquarters this late in the evening without looking suspicious."

"Whatever you need, I'm here for," I said. "This isn't like last time."

Dad frowned. "I regret asking you to kill Sophia. I'd promised that I would never force my son to endanger himself again."

"You aren't forcing me, I'm willing. You wouldn't ask if you didn't have to. As for danger, I can take care of myself," I said firmly. "What is it you need?"

Tatum grumbled. Dad handed him the honey pot, and he began digging his claws in it as Dad continued, "Madame Wells and I have decided there's only one way to solve this. Oleander and Annette have to go."

"I figured as much. You just need to sort out the details," I said.

Dad nodded. "Correct. What we need to figure out is where, when and how. We've gotten some information that shows Annette is planning an attempt on Oleander's life. If she succeeds, we'll have to be there to make sure she's next."

"I could just stop her heart," I said. "It'd be easy."

Dad's eyes widened. "Ancestors, son, I'd never ask that of you. You're not a murderer."

I scoffed. "Yeah, well, too late for all that."

He gaped at me, as if he couldn't believe what I'd just told him. "Are you saying...?"

"I did what I had to do during the riots," I said. "And I'd do it again to protect the tribe."

Tatum looked up from his honey pot. Dad ran a hand through his hair tiredly... as if he felt broken at my confession. The motion was something I did all the time, too.

Dad sighed. "Regardless of what you're willing to do, I'm afraid that's not possible, either. We can't use Toaqua magic to stop her heart. Something like that in a woman her age would be strange. It'd show up during the autopsy, and suspicion would point right back on us. No other House has the ability to do something like that."

He was right. If I killed Annette like I had Professor Fawn, we'd be key suspects. "Okay. So we take her out another way."

"Not until Oleander is dealt with. Both of them need to go at the same time in order to prevent a takeover," Dad said. "But just in case Annette's plan fails and Oleander survives, we need a backup."

I thought about it. "The easiest way to deal with Oleander is to take out his Familiar."

"You'd be right. But there's a problem. We don't know where it is— or what." Dad began to pace. "I've already reviewed the tapes from his

Cup year. He went through the entire competition by himself with his teammates, without a Familiar. It never showed up once. I've spoken with people he attended Orenda Academy with, and none of them ever remember him bonding, or recall seeing a creature with him."

"He's Toaqua. His Familiar has to be in the ocean," I said.

"That's his excuse as to why it's never here," Dad said. "I called him out on it this morning. He claims it's too far out for him to just summon on a whim, but I don't buy it. He's hiding something, I'm sure of it."

"He has to have a Familiar. Otherwise, he wouldn't be alive," I pointed out.

"I think we're overlooking the obvious. I'm sorry to bring this up, son, but you're still here," Dad said. "Maybe Oleander is another anomaly."

A pang entered my chest at the mention of Nashoma, but I shook my head. "No. I think we'd know if he was like me."

Dad laid a hand on Tatum's head. "Either way, we need answers. I need you to get that information for me. So we can find out where his Familiar is, and target it before Oleander suspects what we're up to."

I stood up. My knees wobbled for a moment, but I remained on my feet. "I can sneak into Oleander's office tonight. Maybe there's something I can discover."

"Report back to me if you find anything," Dad said. "But make sure no one follows. I'll be at home waiting."

"Got it." I headed out of Dad's office and toward the elevator. Oleander's office was on the fifth floor, and no frickin way was I taking the stairs.

When I got there, I was shocked to find that his door was unlocked. Was Oleander so arrogant that he didn't think anyone would be stupid enough to try and snoop in his stuff? Or was this some kind of trap?

Either way, it wasn't going to stop me. I walked in slowly and closed the door behind me. Of course Oleander had the fanciest office in the whole damn building. It was decorated like he was some sort of king, and was the size of my parents' living room. A large window behind the expansive mahogany desk displayed all of Kinpago below it, and the mountain range beyond.

Oleander probably sat up here and thought about how great it would be once he was High Chief and could lord over everybody. Not on my watch. There wasn't a computer in here— Oleander must have a laptop that he took with him.

I started rifling through drawers. I found a bunch of files, but on a quick skim through, I saw that they were just minutes on council meetings.

All of this was stuff that my dad already had access to. It wouldn't help us.

The shelves were filled with books on Elementai law. I rifled through them, just in case he was hiding something inside, but nothing there. I checked underneath the desk, behind statues, even under the rug, but came up with nothing.

Geez. No wonder the guy left his office unlocked. There was nothing in here. All the incriminating shit was probably at his house.

I was just about to give up when I tripped on something. I tumbled backward and landed on my ass. Fucking ow. When I sat upright, I noticed that my shoe had caught on a floorboard that was slightly raised.

Huh. That was interesting. I slid forward and lifted the board out of its place. Bingo. Underneath was a wooden chest, about the size of a shoe box. I lifted it out of the hole in the floor— it was really freaking heavy— and opened it. Inside was a small book, like an instruction manual, and a large silver collar, one that was large enough to fit a dragon, or some other giant creature.

The collar glowed a dark red. I tried touching it, but it burned my skin. I gasped. I had a few blisters on my fingers as a result.

The collar had to be magical. Didn't think it was Elementai. Not sure what supernatural race it was from, really, but that part didn't matter right now. Carefully, I moved around the collar and took out the instruction manual, quickly skimming it.

Words leapt out at me immediately from the page, terms like *Familiars* and *mind control*. This was a device for controlling magical creatures.

My thoughts raced as I tried to think of what Oleander would possibly want with a magical collar that could control a Familiar's mind. I didn't get it. It'd be useless on your own bonded creature. Familiars did what you told them to, most of the time. They had no trouble obeying orders... as long as it was from their Elementai. Why would Oleander need magic to make his Familiar listen?

The answer rang clear. Because the creature he was trying to control wasn't his.

Oleander had accused other people of stealing Familiars from the start. Was it possible that he'd stolen his own? Had he bonded with a weak Familiar years ago, and been ashamed of it? Was that enough for him to imprison it somewhere while he looked for an alternative, a creature that would be impressive and intimidating? One he could use magic on to bend to his will?

If Oleander's real Familiar was out there in hiding, Oleander didn't have to worry about it being killed, and losing his own life in the process. He could flaunt whatever monster he found as his own while keeping his true soul under tight security. He'd be harder to kill that way.

Dad could use this information. I had to get it back to him as soon as possible. I had planned to take Sophia out tonight— once we were done, I'd head back home and tell him then. I put the instruction manual back, replaced the wooden chest and the floorboard. I left everything in the office as it was when I entered.

A fresh bout of confidence flooded through me as I proceeded toward the exit. This was the right way to win a war. Not by winning battles, but by outsmarting your opponent. Alric was right. We didn't need to take unnecessary lives in order to turn things around.

As I left through the main entrance, I heard a crashing sound. I rounded the corner. Outside near the dumpster, Haley was standing on Logan's shoulders and trying to climb in through a window. They'd knocked over a trash can as she put her foot in his face.

"Higher, you dumbass! I can almost reach it!" Haley hissed. Logan tried lifting her up, and nearly dropped her.

What the hell was Haley doing here with Logan, trying to sneak into Tribal Headquarters this late at night? Had Chieftess Annette assigned her to be a spy, just like my Dad had with me? I had a gut feeling I was right.

I tried to slip away, but Haley fell down, and Logan went with her. As both of them looked up, they noticed me standing there. Too late to run now.

Haley sneered as she got to her feet. "Spying on me, Mitoh? That's fucking typical. Your daddy probably put you up to it."

"I was just leaving work, Haley," I told her. "By the way, the front door is open, if you want to try using that. But I guess with whatever you're doing, you don't want to be caught going through security."

Haley flushed. "Fuck you, Mitoh. Why don't you go jump off a bridge?" Haley's mouth widened into a cruel smile, and she said, "Oh, *right*. I forgot you already tried to kill yourself. My bad."

Logan laughed loudly, but I didn't flinch. The comment stung, but only a little. I'd stopped giving a fuck about what Haley said to me long ago.

"Whatever you say," I replied, with as little emotion as possible.

Her right eye twitched. Haley seemed bothered her jibe hadn't gotten to me.

I heard the sound of flames igniting behind me, and I turned around. Imogen and Sophia were standing right there. Esis had his teeth bared from Sophia's shoulder, and at Imogen's feet, Sassy was growling. Giant fireballs glowed from Sophia's hands.

Oh, fuck. Sophia had overheard. I'd asked the two of them to meet me in Kinpago after I got done with work, and it looked like they'd gotten here early. Perfect fucking timing, as usual.

Sophia went to move forward to slam a fireball in Haley's face, but Imogen grabbed her by the arm. "Sophia, don't," Imogen said. "You're putting yourself at risk."

Sophia hesitated, but only slightly. The decision whether to attack Haley or not warred behind her eyes.

At the sight of Sophia's rage, Haley's wicked sneer returned. She was totally getting a kick out of this. "Anyway, Mitoh, I'm sorry you didn't succeed," she added loudly, her eyes locking with Sophia's. "Everyone else hates you just as much as you hate yourself. We'd all be happier if you were dead."

Fuck off, Haley. She was purposely antagonizing Sophia. And damn if it was working. The fireballs in Sophia's hands swelled to an enormous size.

"You'd better apologize," Sophia said lowly. I could feel the heat radiating off her as fire began to swirl around her legs.

"Or what?" Haley's grin grew even bigger. "I make the rules now, Henley. I can say whatever I want and do whatever I want. So you'd better watch your mouth; otherwise, there will be consequences."

"What the hell are you gonna do? Kill me?" Sophia snarled.

"I could!" Haley's voice grew louder. "I could turn you into a pile of ashes right now, and nobody would do a fucking thing, *Biyami.*"

"I'd like to see you try," Sophia spat.

Flames began licking at the tips of Haley's fingers. I stepped between them. "This isn't the time or place."

"Liam, move out of the way," Sophia said. "I'd love to get my chance at frying this bitch."

Haley blanched a little. A fireball that was forming in her hand slowly began to fizzle out as she observed the flames that were gathering around Sophia's form.

Logan grabbed her arm. "You can't do anything now. People will know we were here," he hissed.

The fire in Haley's palms died out. She flipped her hair over her shoulder and rolled her eyes as she turned to leave. "Just watch your back, Henley. Before you find a fucking knife in it."

Haley strolled away, rocking her hips back and forth in a deliberate way. Logan followed. He slammed into me as he passed, but I didn't bother to retaliate. It wasn't worth it.

Sophia's chest was heaving with fury. I blocked her view of Haley by stepping in front of her. "*Pawee*, you can't lose your temper with Haley like that anymore," I said gently. "She has the power to really hurt you now."

"Suicide jokes aren't fucking funny," Sophia raged. "She shouldn't be saying that to you."

"Never mind her. She's not worth our energy," I said. I took both of her hands in mine. "I want to take you out tonight. Just the two of us. What do you say we get a break from all this drama?"

Sophia's expression slowly cleared of its anger, and a soft smile caressed her beautiful face. "That sounds perfect, Liam."

"Then let's go." The ring was in my pocket. I'd been planning to propose once work was over. Time for round two of operation Get Sophia to Say Yes.

Imogen's eyes glittered as she gave us a wink. "Have fun, sweethearts. I'm meeting up with Jonah in town. We're looking at locations for his *cabaret.*"

When Sophia's back was turned, Imogen mouthed, *Good luck,* and scampered away with an excited giggle, Sassy skipping behind her.

"Why is everyone acting so weird lately?" Sophia asked as we walked through town. "It's like they're all... giddy."

"Maybe there's something to celebrate." I couldn't resist dropping hints.

"Well, no one told me." Sophia scowled. Esis slipped down from her shoulder and slid inside her shirt. He stuck his head out of her collar and gave a delighted trill as he cozied up to her chin.

"I'd be lying if I said I'd shown you everything in Kinpago. There's so much to explore." I took her hand in mine and intertwined our fingers. "There's a full moon tonight. I wanted to show you something really special, something that only happens once a month."

"Then show me." Sophia's eyes glimmered. We walked from the edge of town back toward school. A couple of Task Force members passed us by, but they seemed to be in a hurry to get somewhere. They didn't harass us, thank the ancestors.

Spring was starting to show, and the nights were getting less brisk. A fresh wind of clean air blew past, cooling my face.

"Liam, you're a little warm," Sophia said. "Are you sure you're okay?"

"Would I be walking?"

"Uh..."

"Exactly."

We left the path and entered into the woods. This was a part of the forest Sophia had never been to. I felt a little faint as we maneuvered around rocks and plants, but chalked it up to the late hour, and continued on. My vision faded in and out several times, but hey, I was just nervous. This was the biggest moment of my life, after all.

As we neared a clearing, I told Sophia to hush. Esis pressed a paw to his lips, and I pulled aside a branch.

Before us in a circular clearing were a collection of animals. There were all kinds, from deer to lions, unicorns to bears. Wolves, bears, badgers, foxes, horses, and others had joined together to perform what looked like a complicated dance.

They didn't look like regular creatures, though. They shone with a silver light, and were transparent. You could see through them as they hovered over the ground and glided upon streams of silver light that suspended their bodies over the grass. The creatures moved delicately, as if they were made of air. Their eyes shone like sapphires, and collectively, the white light they emitted made it seem like daytime. Silver owls soared in swirling circles above glowing dragons and shining manticores. Beaming griffins moved in complicated patterns around see-through hippogriffs. A music, much like the one that arrived when the ancestors came, played from the area, though it wasn't clear where the music came from.

"They're beautiful," Sophia breathed. "What are they?"

"They're called lunar-fauna," I said. "They're magical creatures that gain power from the light of the moon, like Star Beasts use the power of the galaxies."

"That's incredible. Why are they all here?" Sophia hushed.

"They gather once a month under the full moon to dance under it. It's how they gain their magic. They only look like this once the moonlight hits them. In the daytime, they're disguised as regular creatures." Carefully, I emerged from the trees and led Sophia into the clearing.

A few lunar-fauna scattered, but most remained at a cautious distance. As we entered the center of the circle, the lunar-fauna resumed their dance. They ventured closer, pressing in around us as the music swelled to a louder volume.

"Speak quietly. If you're gentle, they won't run away," I whispered.

Sophia reached out a hand. A lunar-fawn stretched her head out and brushed it against Sophia's outstretched fingers. Sophia shivered when they touched. "They're so cold."

Esis wriggled out from Sophia's shirt and jumped on the ground. He held out his hands to a lunar chimera, but it snorted at him and knocked him over.

A couple of the lunar-fauna gave trills of delight. Silver streams of magic ventured out from underneath their feet and wove around us. The moonlight ribbons wrapped around Sophia and I and forced our bodies together. We squeezed each other tightly as the lunar-fauna cheered and began to dance more furiously. A thrill of exhilaration went through me as the moonlight ribbons tightened around our form before dissolving into the air.

"What are they doing?" Sophia let out a laugh.

"It's an old Hawkei tradition," I said. "Years ago, couples used to leave the tribe together in search of the lunar-fauna. If they found them, and the lunar-fauna tied them together with ropes made of moonlight, it was said that the couple was meant to be."

"Did you make that up?" Sophia asked in a teasing way.

"Nope. It's one-hundred percent true," I said. "They're harder to find now, so people don't do it anymore, but I've spent a couple of weeks looking for them, just for you."

"Oh, Liam. That's so sweet." Sophia's eyes became watery with happy tears. "I can't believe you did that for me."

"I did it for us."

This was the moment. The lunar-fauna were dancing all around, everything looked pretty and magical, and Sophia was awed. It was time. My hand entered my pocket to grab the ring.

And at that exact second, my limbs became water.

I thought I was getting down on one knee, but all I was really doing was *going down*. I vaguely realized that I was in the process of passing out before my head smacked against the ground. I heard Sophia call my name, and everything went black.

"LIAM! LIAM, WAKE UP!"

Sophia was shaking me. The stars came into view first, and then her face. Esis was sitting on top of my chest. Both of his paws were placed over my heart, and his eyes were tightly closed in concentration.

The lunar-fauna were gone. They'd run off after I fainted, making everything dark again, and the music had vanished. If it weren't for the light of the full moon, we wouldn't be able to see anything.

Unfortunately, it *was* a full moon, and so there was no way to disguise my dazed demeanor. I felt like someone had taken a wooden board and smacked it into my face.

"Why are you grabbing at your pants like that?" Sophia looked down, expression baffled. I realized my hand was fishing in my jeans. The ring was still in my pocket. She hadn't found it. Thank the ancestors.

Except now it probably looked like I was jacking off. I mumbled something that was incoherent— because I don't even know what I fucking said— and she helped me sit up. Esis scuttled to my thigh and perched on it, making chirping noises that sounded very alarmed.

"Where is your head at right now?" Sophia asked. Her tone was full of worry. My eyes lolled in the back of my head, and I almost passed out for the second time. Sophia flung her arms around my torso and caught me at the last second.

"Okay, deal's off!" she snapped. "You're going to the hospital right now!"

Couldn't argue with her this time. I didn't have the strength.

Sophia dragged me back up to the castle and to the hospital wing. The staff took one look at me and put me in an emergency room immediately. I stumbled inside, and the nurse asked, "It says here that you have a pre-existing condition. What's your diagnosis?"

"Combined Magical Suppression Syndrome," I said, before launching into another set of coughs. Fuck, I could hardly breathe. And things were fading in and out again.

"What's that?" The nurse's gaze was blank. She had no idea what I was talking about. Her pegasus Familiar took my temperature, and of course it was off the charts.

"It's in his medical file," Sophia blurted out. I wavered again, and vaguely heard the nurse mutter something else before she left the room.

"God damn you, Liam." I felt Sophia pull my shirt over my head before she fiddled with the button on my jeans. She yanked my pants down to my ankles and pushed me into a chair as she ripped off my shoes. Kinky.

"Hey, now's not the time for sex," I slurred. This was all out of order. I was supposed to ask her to marry me first, *then* rock her world with my dick. I was doing it all wrong.

"I'm not screwing you, jackass, I'm helping you into a gown." Sophia removed my jeans from my ankles and picked them up off the floor. I was terrified that she was going to look into the pockets, but she folded my pants up and put them safely on the counter with my shirt.

Whew. Crisis averted. It'd be no good if she found an engagement ring while she was currently stripping me down for a medical diagnosis.

Esis watched us from a chair and pulled on his ears. It was clear he was frustrated.

"It's not your fault, Esis," Sophia said fiercely. "Liam knows your magic won't work if he doesn't take care of himself. He should've went in weeks ago."

Esis pouched out a lip, and his blue eyes watered. I reached out and patted his head, giving a giggle. Sophia bit her lip before she yanked me up and slipped a hospital gown over my arms. She started tying it in the back. I jumped when her fingers brushed the ties near my ass.

"Don't touch my butt." I snickered again. I don't know why, but everything seemed funny right then.

"Oh, Liam." Sophia helped me into bed. She lifted the covers over me, and I sighed when my head hit the pillow. I could barely keep my eyes open.

The doctor came in at this point. Usually, at hospitals, you waited forever, but I must've been bad enough they wanted to look at me right away. His Saint Bernard Familiar walked to my bed immediately and began sniffing my arm. He gave two barks, to which the doctor frowned.

"I think we can narrow this down fairly quickly," he said. "Even with the little we know about his condition. His primary care is listed as Jaques Perot. Is there a way to get in contact with him?"

I snorted. "Ha. That's funny."

The doctor and Sophia glanced at each other. Sophia said, "I think he's a little delirious."

"He's definitely dehydrated." The doctor glanced at his clipboard again and said, "Let me run some tests and get back with you."

I wasn't even aware nurses were shoving IV's in until I tried to move my arm and found it hooked up to a line. Sophia sat in a chair with Esis on her lap, her foot bouncing nervously. My eyes drifted to my jeans, where the ring lay waiting.

I was taken back for some x-rays and a CAT scan. An hour later, the doctor returned, and he didn't look happy.

"You have double pneumonia, son, in both of your lungs," he said. "If we can get you started on antibiotics, we could have the infection cleared up within a week, but you'll need to be admitted. And some of the symptoms are going to linger for a while. That is, *if* we can get this under control now."

My heart sank. Another week in the hospital. That was if I was lucky and the antibiotics actually worked, which, with the way my body acted, wasn't a sure thing.

"You should gather some of his things, along with his homework, if he has any. It's going to be a long stay for him," the doctor said. He smiled grimly at Sophia. "He's lucky to have someone like you. A few days longer and things wouldn't have turned out good for him."

As the doctor left, Sophia's eyes narrowed at me. "I'm going to kill you."

I gave a halfhearted chuckle before I forced out, "If this doesn't first."

"That's not a joke, Liam! This is serious!" Sophia shouted.

"I know, I know." I didn't need a lecture right now. Another proposal, blown up in my face. Though this one was definitely my fault this time.

"You promised me you'd take care of yourself when we got back together," Sophia accused. "Was that a lie?"

"No! Ancestors, Sophia, there's just been a lot going on lately." I rubbed my eyes. "I promise I won't do this again."

She sent me a heated glare before she added, "It *won't* happen again. Because I'm going to make sure of it."

Sophia took Esis in her arms and rose to her feet. "I'll get some things from the Biyami dorm for you. Is there you anything you want?"

"Can you send my dad?" I still needed to tell him about what I'd found out on Oleander.

Sophia's eyebrows knitted together in confusion. "Why? I can tell your family you've been admitted."

"It's not about that." I took a deep breath. "My dad's asked me to spy on Oleander and Annette for him. If he has intel, he can... get rid of the problem."

Sophia sucked in a breath, and Esis copied her. "So that's what you meant about helping your dad."

"Yeah. And I found out something. I snuck into Oleander's office today. I think he's hiding his real Familiar, and trying to steal a more powerful one, so he can bolster his place on the council."

"That makes sense." Sophia grabbed my hand. "But should you really be doing this? I'm so worried about you, Liam. I don't want you to take on more than you can handle. We're already doing this smuggling thing. Look where you've ended up."

"Due to my own stupidity." I squeezed her hand back. "I can handle it, *pawee*. I'm sorry this happened. I should've listened to you and taken better care of myself."

"You should've." She parted a strand of hair back from my face and smiled. "But now you're in a place where you're forced to do that, so I can worry a little less. Try to get some sleep."

Sophia squeezed my fingers before she left the room. Esis pointed at me from her arms, as if telling me to stay put. My head slammed back onto the pillows as the door closed behind her, and I let out an aggravated groan.

"Fuck you, lungs. You couldn't keep your shit together for *five more minutes*, could you?" I complained.

Of course, they gave no response, except to make me hack up another huge globule of phlegm.

Sexy. Being disabled was neither romantic nor glamourous. But hey, it was life.

This espionage thing was working out, but my plan to ask Sophia to marry me was going fucking nowhere. I was striking out. Was the rest of my life going to be nothing but failed and humiliating proposals?

Hopefully, the third time would be the charm. If I ever got out of this damn bed.

sophia
FOURTEEN

I woke to the feeling of Liam stirring beside me. I lifted my head to see that I'd fallen asleep, slumped over the side of his hospital bed. Esis slept in the crook beside Liam's neck. I'd snuck back into his room after his dad came to visit. Liam had already been asleep by that time.

Liam's eyes fluttered open. "*Pawee?* What are you doing here? Shouldn't you be in class?"

I checked my watch. I still had twenty minutes until my parenting class. "I have some time. How'd it go with your dad last night?"

Liam coughed, but he sounded better than yesterday. I reached for the cup of water on the table beside him and practically forced the straw into his mouth. Liam took a sip, then relaxed back onto the pillow.

"Forget that," he said. "How long have you been here?"

I shrugged. "A couple of hours. So, your dad?"

Liam frowned at my insistence. "Dad took the news about Oleander well. Said it made a lot of sense and might give him an edge in going up against him, but..."

I raised an eyebrow. "But?"

He took a deep breath. "But he wasn't really happy to see me in the hospital. Again. He kind of chewed me out for not coming in sooner."

"Good," I stated firmly.

Liam rolled his eyes. "Do we have to do this again, *pawee*?"

I crossed my arms. "Liam, you scared me last night."

"Look at me. I'm all right." He gestured down to his body. "We agreed if I go to class, I don't have to be here. We have Hawkei Art at three. I'll be out of here by then."

"No." I pushed on Liam's shoulder as he started to sit up. "You're staying at least another night."

"Bullshit," he said, though it was lighter than usual.

I leaned over and looked him straight in the eye. "Liam. You have pneumonia. I know you don't care about your health, but I do. I've been on the verge of losing you too many times, and you're not going out by some stupid infection because you wouldn't take care of yourself. So if you're not going to do it, I am. You're staying until the doctors say you can leave."

Liam searched my eyes, as if looking for signs that I was screwing around. I wasn't. I wouldn't let his pride get him killed.

He hesitated, then finally backed down. "Okay, *pawee*. I'll stay."

I breathed a sigh of relief. "Good. Now, I brought you some things."

I lifted a shopping bag I'd brought back from Kinpago last night. Inside were various things I hoped would help him feel better, like painkillers, bath salts, and chocolates. I bet a bath in his hospital room would feel great after months of cold showers in the Biyami dorms. I pulled out a small paper bag with three donuts inside. Liam didn't like his glazed or stuffed, so they were just plain. I pulled one out of the bag and handed it to him. "Breakfast?"

Liam's shoulders fell. "*Pawee*, you didn't have to—"

"I did. Eat up," I told him, shoving the donut in his direction.

Liam took it and began nibbling on it. While he ate, I scooted my chair to the foot of his bed and pulled out the painkilling lotion I'd bought. I pulled the sheets up over his feet and began massaging the tender areas in his toes and ankles.

"Mm, *pawee*," Liam said, tilting his head back in delight. "That feels sooo…"

He sank deeper into the bed as I rubbed my thumbs into the arch of his foot. By now, Esis had stirred awake, and he was copying me by kneading on Liam's belly.

The room went silent for a few moments, until Liam whispered, "Thank you, *pawee*. But you should really get to class now."

I huffed. "Fine. But only because I need to go find Jonah and Imogen and tell them what happened. We'll come visit you this afternoon."

"Well, you'll know where to find me," he said. "I'm not going anywhere."

I shot him a skeptical look. "You better mean it, Liam. Because if you discharge yourself before you're ready—"

"I won't, *pawee*," he assured me. "Now get to class."

He shot me a smirk, and I walked to the head of the bed to kiss him. He grabbed my hand and held me there a while longer. "See you later, *pawee*."

"Bye, Liam."

Esis jumped into my arms. As much as I didn't want to leave, I forced myself to step out of the room. I knew if I didn't go to class, he'd make a big deal out of me skipping for him.

I suffered my way through Introduction to Parenting, but I could hardly concentrate when I knew Liam was up in the infirmary waiting for me. After class, I headed to the cafeteria to find Imogen and Jonah. They were seated in a dark corner sectioned off for Biyami only.

On their plates were only a piece of bread and a slice of meat that looked more processed than bologna. Imogen was poking at her food, but not eating, while Jonah leaned across the table and held her hand. A big rainbow-colored bow like the ones she usually wore in her hair sat beside her plate.

My eyebrows knit together as I approached. "Hey, guys. What's up?"

Imogen immediately straightened at the sound of my voice. When she looked up, I saw that her eyes were red and bloodshot. She wiped at them and sniffled. "Nothing. What's up with you?"

I sat beside her and ignored her question. Esis hopped down to sit beside Sassy, who was lying with her chin on her paws glumly.

"Imogen," I pressed. "What happened?"

She waved her hand and wiped her eyes again. "It's nothing. It's dumb."

"Im, it's not dumb," Jonah assured her softly. "It's cruel."

I glanced at him. "What is? Imogen, please tell me."

Imogen dabbed at her eyes with the sleeve of her dress. "It's Haley..."

My hands curled into fists. If she touched one hair on her head...

Imogen sniffled again and softened her voice. "I was walking with Sam in the hall after class, and Haley walked by. And she's like... she's like..."

Imogen choked up. I looked to Jonah for explanation. He had this sad, fallen look on his face.

Imogen wiped her nose. "She's like, 'Imogen, I never took you to be so heartless.' And I'm all like, 'What the fuck are you talking about, bitch?' But like, nicer, you know? And she's like, 'You're moving on so fast after your boyfriend died in the tournament. You must've not *really* loved him.'"

Imogen's shoulders started shaking. "If Jonah hadn't shown up, I would've... I would've..."

"Strangled the bitch?" I finished for her.

Imogen threw herself onto the table, her face buried in the crook of her elbow. She spoke in a muffled voice, I could hardly tell what she said. "No one knows how much I loved Cade. And now he's gone." She lifted her head and looked me straight in the eye. Tears streamed down her face, and her cheeks were red with fury. "He's gone, Sophia! And I just can't... I can't..."

Imogen shot up out of her chair and grabbed her bag. She made a beeline for the door, covering her mouth with her hand as she went. Jonah and I both ran to catch up with her, but she whirled around and held a hand up to us. "Please don't follow me, you guys. I need to be alone right now."

Jonah and I stood there as she and Sassy left the dining hall. Squeaks tried to give chase, but Jonah held her back.

I turned to him once she was out of sight, my features tight with worry. "Should we go after her?"

Jonah shook his head. "I think Im means it. She hasn't had any time to grieve since the tournament."

"Aren't you worried about her?" I demanded.

"Of course I am," Jonah said, like he was offended. "But if Imogen wants space, that's what we need to give her."

I nodded. "Okay, but there's something I need to tell you. Liam's in the hospital."

I didn't think it was possible, but the sadness in Jonah's features deepened. "What happened?"

Tears welled in my eyes. "He passed out last night, and I wouldn't take no for an answer. He has pneumonia."

"He'll be all right, won't he?" Jonah asked.

"As long as he does what the doctors say," I told him. "I was hoping you, me, and Imogen could visit him after class, but if Imogen's not up for it—"

Jonah placed a gentle hand on my shoulder. "I'll let her know. We'll be there."

I swallowed the lump in my throat. "Okay."

I grabbed a plate of food, and Jonah and I returned to our table. I tried to eat, but I didn't have much of an appetite with everything going on lately. I was worried about Liam and Imogen. Eventually, we had to head off to Hawkei Art, though I considered skipping because I didn't want to deal with it. But I knew what kind of lecture I'd get from Liam if I did.

Imogen wasn't there, but Jonah said he knew where to find her. He went looking for her while I headed back up to the hospital the minute class ended. When Esis and I arrived, the head of Liam's bed was propped up at an angle, and he was reading a book. I noticed all the donuts from earlier were gone, and it looked like he'd finished off the orange juice I brought him, too. He set his book aside when I walked in.

"Hey, *pawee*," he said weakly, but at least he didn't cough up a lung. "How was class?"

I shrugged. "It was class. What are the doctors saying?"

"They want to keep me for more monitoring, to see if the medications are working." Liam scratched behind Esis's ears as he hopped onto the bed. "They are, thanks to this guy."

"That's because you're finally taking care of yourself," I pointed out. Liam frowned at that.

Just then, a knock came at the door. Liam and I both turned to see

Jonah step inside, with Squeaks behind him. I waited for Imogen to come in after him, but I didn't see her. Before I could ask where she was, Jonah cleared his throat. "May I present to you... the new Imogen!"

Imogen walked into the room, swaying her hips like she was on the runway. When I saw her, my jaw dropped. Imogen's outfit was even crazier than normal. Total eighties neon, with one of those skirts that was really short in the front and long in the back. It had long feathers attached to it that reminded me of a peacock. The shoulders on that thing were so pointed they could poke someone's eyes out. Sassy strutted behind her, wearing a matching dress, her fur spiked at the top of her head.

But it wasn't the outfit that caught my attention. It was Imogen's hair. Instead of her strawberry blonde hair falling in waves to her shoulders, it'd been completely chopped off— buzzed on the sides, and spiked in the front.

Liam spoke before I could find my voice. "Wow, Im. It suits you."

Imogen touched the side of her shaved head. "You think?"

A smile spread across my face. Liam wasn't lying. It was *so* Imogen. "It really does. I love it."

Imogen began to tear up. "Thank you. I just thought, you know, with Cade gone... it was time..."

Jonah turned to me to explain. "In Hawkei culture, we cut our hair after experiencing a great loss."

"Well, I think it looks great," I said.

"Thanks, Sophia." Imogen looked touched. She spread her arms out and pulled me into a hug. When she drew away, she turned to Liam. "Sorry, I didn't mean to make this all about me. How are you?"

"I'm—"

"*Fine*," we all finished for him in unison. Everyone shared a quick glance before we all started laughing.

"Seriously, though," Liam said. "I'll be back to normal soon. I should be out of here by Friday."

My face fell. I almost forgot about my meeting with Amelia this Friday.

"What?" Liam asked in alarm. "Soph?"

I took a deep breath. "Well, I had something I wanted to ask you guys. But..."

Everyone was already dealing with so much already. I didn't know if now was the time.

Liam reached over and took my hand. "What is it?"

I sighed. "Well, I'm supposed to meet with my sister on Friday. And I was just wondering... I trust her with all my heart, but I know we agreed to a unanimous vote. And we should probably ask everyone else, too. But... do you guys think I should tell her about what we're doing?"

The room got really quiet. It made me uncomfortable.

Jonah was the first to speak. "I don't know, Sophia. I mean, I know you trust her, but the more people we get involved, the riskier it is."

"Amelia has friends who wanted to go against the Elders," I blurted. "If we got them involved too, we could be stronger."

"It could put her in danger," Imogen pointed out.

I chewed my lower lip. "I know but... I think Amelia might already be in trouble."

"What kind of trouble?" Liam asked.

"Like, *our* kind of trouble. She wouldn't tell me," I said.

Liam squeezed my hand. "We'll bring it up in the next meeting. We've got your back."

Imogen and Jonah gave nods of agreement. I knew they trusted my judgement.

I just wasn't sure if everyone else would.

THAT NIGHT, I took a walk into Kinpago to visit Vanessa. She and Bren lived in this cute apartment complex with a pool, large trees and adorable buildings that looked like fairy-tale houses. It was way better than the Biyami dorms. I was kind of jealous. I knocked on the door, and Bren answered.

"Hi, Sophia," he said. Bren was wearing an apron and covered in flour.

"Cooking?" I asked.

Bren glanced down to his apron. "This? No. Vanessa likes when I wear it during sex."

My face paled.

"Oh my gosh, Bren!" Vanessa protested from somewhere inside the apartment. "He's lying, Sophia!"

Bren chuckled and stepped aside to invite me in. "She wanted apple pie."

"Aw, that's so sweet," I said as I stepped inside.

Their apartment was huge, with a tall ceiling and industrial architecture. It was big enough for Aisha to fit through the balcony doors. The dragon lay curled up in the corner next to the couch, where Vanessa sat with her legs propped up on a pillow on the coffee table. She was dipping strawberries into a container of French onion dip balanced on her belly, which was getting really huge. Kingston was nearby, each one of his three heads digging into a different food dish lined in a row.

"Sophia, it's so good to see you," Vanessa said brightly, patting the cushion beside her.

I sat, while Bren returned to the kitchen. Esis bounded to Aisha and snuggled up beside her.

Vanessa was watching some reality TV drama, but she hit pause on the remote. "What's up?"

"You weren't in class yesterday, so I wanted to check on you," I said.

She frowned. "Yeah, my doctor's got me on bedrest. Apparently my blood pressure is scary low."

I gasped. "That doesn't sound good."

"I'm fine as long as I don't get up and walk around." Vanessa popped another French onion-covered strawberry in her mouth.

I nearly gagged. "So, how are those pregnancy cravings?"

Vanessa glanced at the dip and laughed. "No judging, okay?"

"I'm not," I assured her. "I brought you something."

Vanessa sat up straighter. "Oh?"

I reached into my bag and pulled out a blue onesie complete with tiny sweatpants, itty bitty socks, and booties so small they could fit Esis.

Vanessa threw her hand over her mouth, and tears rose in her eyes. It must've been her hormones, but seeing her like that made *me* want to cry.

"You said you're having a boy, right?" I asked.

Vanessa nodded and took the clothes from my hand. She peered down at them like they were made of gold or something. "Sophia, you didn't have to."

"Of course I did. It's not like I'm going to be able to shop for my own..."

I choked up, but quickly cleared my throat before Vanessa noticed. "I'm going to be cool Aunt Sophia. I'm starting early."

Vanessa chuckled. "You totally are. Do you want to feel him kick?"

My eyes lit up. "He's kicking?"

Vanessa set her food aside and took my hand, then placed it on her belly right below her ribs.

The strangest sensation traveled over my palm. It wasn't a sharp jab, like you'd expect a kick to be. It was more like he was running his foot along her ribs and doing somersaults inside of her. I tried to imagine what it would feel like to have a baby inside of me, but that just made me sad.

"It's like you have a little alien in there," I joked.

Vanessa laughed. "Some days it feels that way. I can't wait to meet him."

"Yeah. It'll be the best day of your life," I said.

"I'm thinking of decorating the nursery with dragons," she said brightly. "What do you think? Too cliché?"

I glanced over to Aisha, but inside, my guts sank. Vanessa was acting like there wasn't a war going on outside— like people weren't rioting on the streets and getting their Familiars taken away. I wish life was that simple.

"No," I finally said. "Not too cliché."

Bang!

I jumped at the sound of a slamming door. Vanessa sat up straighter and shot a look at Bren. He'd gone still in the kitchen.

"Do you think that's them?" Vanessa whispered.

My gaze darted between the two of them. "Who?"

Bren hurried to the door and looked out the peephole. He frowned as he turned around. "It's just her sister again."

"Who's sister?" I asked Vanessa. "What's going on?"

Vanessa's face fell. "A few days ago, the Task Force came and arrested our neighbor across the hall. We heard the whole thing."

"*Arrested* her?" I balked. "For what?"

Vanessa shrugged. "We don't know. I can't imagine her doing anything wrong. She was such a sweetheart. The Task Force kept saying they had a warrant, but wouldn't say for what. She was a single mom with two kids. We haven't seen the kids since, just her sister coming every now and then to pick things up."

My jaw dropped. "Well, is she coming back?"

Vanessa shook her head. "I have no idea."

My stomach sank. "I hope the kids are okay. Maybe they're staying with her sister."

Bren leaned against the counter and crossed his arms. "They aren't. I ran into her in the hall yesterday and asked how they were doing. She said she hasn't seen them."

Bren leaned forward and lowered his voice. "Personally, I think they won't let her see them because she's Biyami."

The word *Biyami* had never sounded like more of a curse than in that moment. Kids were being kept from their families now just because they'd been sorted into the wrong House?

How much more of this could we handle before we finally left?

I woke Friday morning expecting to find a note from Kiwi in my bed like last weekend, but my bed was empty. There'd been no meeting with Alric and the others yet, and he hadn't been in his office when I'd gone looking for him. It looked like I wasn't going to get permission to tell Amelia about our operation before I saw her.

I dragged myself out of bed, showered, and headed to Hawkei Artifacts. I spent the whole day on the lookout for Kiwi, but by the time I finished Intermediate Koigni Magic, I still hadn't heard from him.

It's only three o'clock, I reminded myself. There was still plenty of time in the day to meet up with Amelia. I just wished she'd send Kiwi already.

I headed up to the hospital after class. When I entered Liam's room, the curtain was pulled around his bed, and the room was quiet.

"Liam?" I asked.

The curtain moved, and Liam poked his head out. He shot me a bright smile. He looked amazing. "*Pawee*, I'm just getting dressed."

"You're getting discharged?" I stepped behind the curtain with him, and Esis jumped out of my arms and onto the bed. Liam wore only a pair of jeans. I couldn't help it when my eyes traveled down his bare chest.

"I am," he said. "I told you I'd be out of here by Friday."

"Isn't that a little... soon?" I asked.

He shrugged. "Once I got the drugs in me, Esis did most of the work."

I reached out for Liam and gently ran my hands down his sides. He wrapped an arm around me and pulled me closer, then placed a soft kiss on my lips.

"You look like you're doing a lot better," I said as we drew away from each other.

"Yeah. Thanks, *pawee*."

I gazed into his eyes, and my insides turned to mush. "For what?"

"For helping me get better," he said. "I wouldn't have if it wasn't for you."

I shrugged and grabbed the shirt that was lying on the bed, then handed it to him. "All I did was make you come to the hospital. I did what any girlfriend would do."

Liam slipped his shirt on. "You did what the *best* girlfriend would do."

I blushed slightly. I'd expected him to be in the hospital longer. Liam was acting like he'd been cured in a matter of days. I wondered if it was all an act just to get out of here.

Liam sat on the bed and looked up to me. "You know, I'm not officially discharged. I still have this room for a while. And I'm feeling great, so..."

I nudged him in the shoulder and snickered. "Liam. A nurse could walk in at any time."

"Then we'll have to be quick about it—"

"Knock, knock." The sound of a woman's voice cut him off.

Liam grumbled and got to his feet again, then pulled the curtain aside. "I'm decent."

A nurse stood in the doorway with a stack of papers in her hands. "Here are your discharge papers, Mister Mitoh. You're free to go."

"Ah, freedom." Liam placed his hand over his heart for show.

I smiled. It was great to see him doing so much better.

The nurse left the room, and Liam sat on the chair to pull his socks on. "How'd it go with Amelia?"

I frowned, my bright mood instantly crushed. "I haven't seen her yet."

He furrowed his brow. "I thought you were meeting with her today."

"Yeah, but she didn't tell me what time or where. She said she'd send Kiwi, and I haven't heard from him yet."

A hint of worry crossed Liam's eyes, but it was gone as soon as it came. "Well, it's still early. Maybe she'll meet you for dinner."

Liam pulled on his shoes, then stood and took my hand. "Come on. I'm dying to get out of here."

Esis hopped on my shoulder, and we left the hospital. I knew Liam probably didn't want to head straight back to the dungeons, but I didn't want to wander around where Kiwi couldn't find me, so we headed back to the Biyami dorms anyway.

When we got there, Tabitha was sitting on one of the nearest bunks, sobbing. Beside her, Hudson rubbed her shoulder with one hand while cradling his giant snail in the other. A large crowd had gathered around them, including Imogen, Jonah, and Maddie. We rushed over to them.

"What happened?" I whispered lowly to Imogen. She was wearing another crazy outfit today, one that had an attachment behind the neck that looked like a giant fan.

She lowered her voice to explain. "Tabitha had a run-in with the Task Force in the library. Someone saw her knitting. I guess they thought her needles looked like a weapon. They confiscated all her supplies."

My face paled. "Can they do that?"

Jonah crossed his arms and huffed. "They're the Task Force. They can do whatever they want."

Tabitha sniffled and wiped her nose. "They were my grandmother's knitting needles. She taught me how to knit..."

She sobbed again before catching her breath. "I was making a baby sweater for my Hawkei Home Ec class. It was supposed to be... for my... niece."

Tabitha broke into a full-on sobbing fit. My stomach sank, and heat rose to the surface of my skin. I couldn't believe the Task Force would just take her personal belongings like that.

No, scratch that. I *could* believe it. It was the kind of abhorrent thing they would do.

I couldn't stand to watch her cry like this. I pushed between Jonah and Imogen and knelt in front of Tabitha.

"It's going to be okay," I assured her. "We can all pitch in to buy you new supplies."

Tabitha sniffled, but her sobs slowed. "But what if they find them again?"

"We'll talk to your Home Ec professor," I suggested. "Maybe they'll let you keep your supplies in the classroom."

"You... you think they'd allow that?" she asked timidly.

I shrugged. "Why not? It's for an assignment."

Tabitha wiped her eyes. "Thanks, Sophia, but it's not going to get my grandma's knitting needles back."

"I know," I said softly. "I'm so sorry."

Tabitha took a deep breath, but tears continued to fall down her face. "If you guys don't mind, I'd really like to be alone right now."

"Well, if you need anything, we're all here for you," Maddie said.

Tabitha offered her a light smile. "Thanks."

Everyone dispersed. My friends and I headed to our corner of the dorms.

Imogen checked her watch. "I know it's still early, but does anyone want to go get something to eat?"

"I'm fine," I said. "I'm waiting for Kiwi."

"I already ate," Liam told her.

Imogen looked to Jonah, and he shrugged. "Squeaks and I could eat."

Imogen and Jonah headed off with their Familiars, leaving Liam,

Esis, and me alone. I pressed my face into my hands as I sat on the lower bunk.

"What's wrong?" Liam sat beside me and wrapped an arm around me.

I took a deep breath and looked up to him. "I'm getting so sick of waiting, Liam."

"For Amelia?" he asked.

I shook my head. "For this war to end. I feel like we're living in constant fear of when the next riots will break out. I feel like I'm counting the days until I lose one of you."

Tears welled in my eyes. I didn't even want to think about that.

"Hey," he said softly. "We're not going to die. You and me? We're going to grow old together. Imogen's going to own her own fashion line, and Jonah's going to party until his walker gives out."

I chuckled as an image of Jonah twerking with his walker entered my mind. The image quickly faded when I noticed that Squeaks wasn't there in my imagination. If she died in this war, so would Jonah.

"Liam, please don't make promises you can't keep," I whispered.

"It's not a promise," he said. "It's just something I feel. Right here."

Liam pressed a palm to my heart.

I forced a light smile. "You're not a *naderei*."

"No, but I know I could never love you this hard if I was only going to lose you."

I blinked a few times to hold my emotions back. Esis placed a paw on my hand to calm me.

"Come on, *pawee*." Liam wrapped his arms around me and guided me to lie down on the bed.

Being in his arms made me want to cry— like it was okay to let my emotions flow. I curled into him and focused on my breathing. I didn't want to keep crying all the time. Liam ran his hands through my hair, which soothed me until eventually I fell asleep.

I woke to the sound of a crash next to my bed. Liam's arms were still around me, and he startled awake, too.

Jonah was standing beside us with a shocked look on his face, while Squeaks was trampling over a pile of bangle bracelets that had spilled from the box Jonah dropped. "Whoops."

I sat up, and Esis rubbed his eyes from where he slept at my feet.

"Blame Squeaks," Jonah said quickly. "She's the clumsy one."

"Jonah, I watched you drop that," Imogen said as she started helping him gather his jewelry.

"How long have you guys been back?" I asked, pushing my hair out of my eyes.

Imogen shrugged. "A few hours?"

Hours!

I checked my watch, and it was already almost nine o'clock. My guts sank. Amelia should've sent Kiwi by now. What if he'd been caught by the Task Force?

I quickly looked around the bed for signs of a note, but there wasn't any. "Did Kiwi stop by?"

Imogen's face paled. "No, we didn't see him. You still haven't heard from your sister?"

I shook my head as worry knotted in my gut. "No. She was supposed to send her Familiar today so we could meet up. Guys, I'm getting really worried. What if something happened to Kiwi?"

"Maybe she's waiting until after dark," Liam suggested as he sat up, but he didn't sound so sure of himself. "Before we make any assumptions, we should go check on her."

I relaxed a little. "Okay. We'll start at Trevor's apartment and see if she's there."

Everyone quickly gathered their things, and the four of us left the dorms with our Familiars. We avoided Task Force members as we left the castle and snuck off school grounds.

Amelia's friend Trevor, who she stayed with when she wasn't on the *Hozho*, lived in an apartment complex near the town square. I'd never been there, but Amelia had given me the address my first year at Orenda.

My hands shook the whole time we walked, and the hairs stood on the back of my neck. I could sense something wasn't quite right.

When we arrived, I raised my hand to knock on the door. On the first knock, the door swung open an inch, as if it wasn't latched. My guts turned hollow, and I shot a quick glance to my friends. They all shared the same look of worry.

Slowly, I pressed on the door while I called out, "Amelia?"

Something caught in the way, and I pressed harder. "Amelia, it's Sophia—"

Whatever was blocking the door shot out of the way, and I stumbled inside. When I saw what was there, I completely froze. My friends went still behind me.

Trevor's apartment was totally trashed. Pots and pans had been ripped out of the cupboard, and broken dishes littered the floor in the small kitchen. The coffee table was overturned in the living room, and posters had been ripped from the wall. An acoustic guitar lay smashed in the corner, and all the gaming consoles below the TV were lying in a heap on the floor.

I stepped further into the apartment, and something crunched beneath my shoes. I looked down to see shards of glass in the carpet from some glasses that'd been thrown off the counter. Esis clung tighter to me.

"Careful," I warned. "There's glass everywhere."

I went to the first bedroom, which looked just as bad as the living room. The sheets were in disarray, and clothes had been yanked out of their drawers and strewn all over the floor and on top of furniture. The doors on the closet had been pulled off their tracks, and contents of various storage containers had been dumped everywhere.

"Bathroom's clear!" Jonah called from the other room.

"Bedroom, too," Liam replied.

"Second bedroom is empty," Imogen said.

We all returned to the living room with hopeless looks on our faces.

"What do you think happened?" Imogen asked.

I shook my head. "I don't know."

I was imagining the worst. What if Task Force members had come to imprison Amelia and Trevor? What if they took their Familiars away?

Liam held his hand out. "Jonah, I need your phone. I'm calling my dad."

Jonah dug into his pocket for his phone and handed it over. While Liam dialed his dad's number, I inspected the apartment for any signs that Amelia had been there. I poked my head into the guest room, but it was pretty much empty. There was a bed and a dresser, but the dresser drawers were empty. Everything else looked like Trevor's belongings from the closet.

Imogen came up beside me and must've noticed the thoughtful look on my face. "What is it?"

"Well, Amelia was supposed to be staying here," I said. "But I don't see her bag anywhere. Or her clothes or anything."

The only thing I noticed was an abandoned pile of bird seed in a dish next to the bed.

"Maybe she wasn't here when it happened," Imogen said thoughtfully.

"Then why hasn't she contacted me today?" I pointed out. "If something happened to her roommate and she was fine, she would've said something."

Deep down, I knew whatever happened here involved Amelia.

Liam stepped into the guest room behind us. He pressed a button on the phone, then looked up. "My dad said there's no record of an arrest for Amelia or Trevor, but that he's going to send a team to investigate. We should leave before they get here."

"But we haven't had time to do an investigation of our own!" Imogen protested.

"We don't have time," Liam said. "Every second we stay, we risk someone spotting us and somehow twisting this like it was our fault."

"Who does he think did this?" I demanded. "The Task Force? Someone else?"

Liam looked unsure. "He doesn't know. He says it's possible the Task Force is doing things for Oleander, but it could've been anyone. Which is another reason why we have to go, in case they're still hanging around."

I shot another glance around the room. Liam was right, but I was hoping to find some sort of clue or something. If only Amelia had left me a note, like when we were kids...

I inhaled a sharp breath and rushed over to the bed.

"What is it, Sophia?" Imogen asked quickly.

I shoved my hand beneath the mattress and felt around. "When we were kids, Amelia and I used to leave secret notes for each other under our beds. What if she— yes!"

My fingers curled around a piece of paper, and I ripped it from beneath the mattress. I quickly unfolded it and scanned the words.

Little Dweeb,

I can't tell you where I've gone, but I can tell you that Kiwi and I are okay. Mom and Dad are with me. I'm sorry I had to leave like this, but there wasn't any other option.
    We will come for you when it's safe.

Big Dweeb

My eyes teared up at the nicknames on the page. Relief washed over me, but at the same time, I was angry— angry that I didn't know what had happened to my family, and angry that they'd left me behind. Had the Elders forced them to leave, or had then chosen to leave on their own? I didn't know, and even though Amelia said they were okay, I wasn't sure whether to believe it.

I was vaguely aware of a hand tugging on my elbow as I read the note through a second time. I thought I might find some code in it— like Amelia had explained where she was, or that the Elders had forced her to write it, but nothing stood out to me.

"Come on, *pawee*," Liam pressed. "We have to go."

I swallowed the lump in my throat and folded the note up. I slipped it into my pocket so I could study it more later. "Okay, let's go."

We snuck out of the apartment complex. Kinpago was quiet tonight, and we didn't think we'd been seen, but it was kind of hard to miss four kids with a hippogriff Familiar who walked like she was stomping on drums.

When we got inside the castle, the first thing we heard was the sound of screams coming from the dungeons. Everyone's faces paled in unison. No one said anything before we were all racing toward the Biyami dorms together.

When we got there, we saw that the place was packed with Task Force members. Biyami students were screaming and crying as their possessions were ripped out of their hands. A Task Force member snatched potion vials from Maddie, and she fell to the ground sobbing. Our group rushed over to her.

Liam knelt to her level. "Maddie, what's going on?"

Tears streamed down Maddie's face. "They say they're investigating and taking away anything that could be deemed a weapon, but Liam, they're taking everything!"

Liam's face fell even further. "Everything?"

"Yes." Maddie grabbed Liam's shirt and looked him straight in the eye. "Hurry, Liam. They haven't gotten to the back yet. Hide your stuff before they get there."

Liam was quick to spring into action. He helped Maddie to her feet, and the five of us— along with our Familiars— pushed through the crowd to the back of the dungeons.

Liam flung his trunk open and grabbed his prescriptions. He frantically looked around for a place to hide them. He looked on the verge of tears as he struggled to find a hiding spot.

"Here." I reached out and grabbed the pill bottles, then shoved half of them at Imogen. "We'll hide these."

Imogen followed my lead and shoved the pill bottles down her dress and between her bosom. She could hide more than me, since her boobs were bigger. I handed Maddie a bottle, then shoved the rest deep in my backpack next to my pads and tampons. Liam only had his inhaler left. He quickly shoved it in his pocket.

My heart pounded, and I was breathing heavily when two Task Force members arrived between our bunks. They aimed noxite guns at us.

"Open your trunks," one of them demanded.

Everyone moved to their trunks to open them. My hands were shaking. Esis was hiding beneath my ponytail.

"We have nothing," Jonah stated confidently.

"We'll see about that," one of the Task Force members snarled.

They came to my trunk first. Instead of doing a quick glance, they shoved me aside and started pulling out all my clothes. At the bottom of the trunk, they found my sketchpad and colored pencils. One of the men held my pencils up to the other, and he nodded. They tossed my collection of coloring supplies into a cart filled with other odds and ends they had confiscated.

My stomach plummeted to my toes.

"Hey!" I cried, but Liam held me back. "You can't do that!"

"These could be used as a weapon," a Task Force man said firmly.

"But I have art class!" I argued.

"Then you can use the approved supplies in the art room," he snapped. "These things have no place in the dorms."

They went to Jonah next, while another group of Task Force members came up to inspect Imogen's trunk. The dorms were chaotic and out of control. Everyone was crying as Task Force members yelled at them. It all happened so fast that I could hardly process it.

On one end of the bunks, Jonah was arguing with a guy about his costumes. Even when Jonah assured them they couldn't be used as a weapon, they claimed it was "unnatural" for a man to possess them, and that they were going to conduct an investigation into the "unusual" material.

"My soccer stuff!" Jonah exploded. "You can't be serious!"

The Task Force threw his cleats into the cart.

"Hold on," Liam demanded, stepping in front of a Task Force member who held Jonah's soccer ball. "You can't really think we'd use a *soccer ball* as a weapon."

The Task Force ignored him. "Out of the way, *Biyami*."

He shoved him aside, and Liam caught himself on the edge of the bunk. My entire body heated in rage. I just stood there shaking, trying to keep my Fire from exploding out of me. There was literally nothing we could do that wouldn't make everything worse. I calculated in my head which belongings we had left and which were at risk. The blanket Liam had given me was still at his house, so that was safe. I was sure I'd left my camera upstairs in the Anichi dorms, but nausea rolled in my gut as I wondered if I'd accidentally left it in my trunk. Liam didn't have much, thankfully, since most of his prized possessions were at his parents'.

"Man, please," Jonah begged. "Not my makeup. Take the brushes. Leave the eyeshadow."

They didn't even respond as they tossed his eyeshadow pallet into the cart. The top popped open, and broken bits of pressed powder went everywhere.

Meanwhile, Imogen was sobbing as they took all her hair bows away, claiming that the pins in them could hurt someone. My features were knitted so tightly that I was starting to get a headache.

"I need those books!" Imogen screeched.

One of the Task Force members pulled out a stack of library books from Imogen's trunk. They were all about magical creatures and crypto-zoology.

"These aren't required texts," the Task Force member informed her.

"No, but they belong to the school!" Imogen belted.

"Exactly," he snarled. "I bet you *stole* them."

Imogen sobbed harder as they took the books away.

"No!" Liam shouted.

I turned to see him reaching for the bottle of pain relief lotion I'd gotten him as a present a few months ago. The Task Force member yanked it away from him. He popped the top open and sniffed it beneath his helmet, then made the guy beside him smell it.

"Could be lethal," the second one said.

"I swear," Liam pleaded. "It's just what it says on the bottle!"

They didn't respond as they continued searching his trunk. I threw my shaking hands over my mouth to keep from yelling obscenities at them. Everything they took from Liam was something I'd given him. They took his headphones and mp3 player, which they seemed to think was some sort of radio to contact people outside the castle. On top of that, they piled his heating pad, wrist braces, and the stuffed wolf I'd bought him.

"Those were gifts!" I shouted.

They didn't give a flying shit about it.

Fuck you! Fuck you all! I wanted to scream.

But the Task Force members outnumbered us, and each of them had a loaded noxite gun on them. Lashing out wouldn't get us our stuff back.

I watched in horror as they took everything from us— everything but our clothes. They took our razors and our toothbrushes, as if they thought we'd file them down into prison knives, and our soap, like we'd use it to make bombs or something. They even took our deodorant. By the time the Task Force members had abandoned my trunk, all I had left besides my textbooks and schoolwork were my clothes, an extra blanket, and a comb. Everyone else looked to be in the same boat.

"Open your bag," a masked man demanded.

I was so stunned he'd stepped up to me. "Wh— what?"

"Open your bag," he snarled as he raised his gun on me.

I quickly grabbed my backpack from the bed and pulled the zipper open, holding back the lump in my throat. Red-hot rage burned my eyes, and my Fire begged to escape.

The Task Force member riffled through my bag and pulled out anything he deemed a threat— pens, pencils, and a spiral-bound notebook. He thankfully avoided my feminine products, which hid Liam's pills, but he snatched up my dragon egg. I was on the verge of exploding as he held it up carelessly. Esis growled at him.

"What's a Biyami like you doing with a dragon egg?" he snarled.

"It's for a class," I stated firmly. "We're to take care of them until they hatch at the end of the semester."

He held Julian up a few seconds longer, until deciding I must've been telling the truth. He tossed the dragon egg back on the bed. Esis screamed as it flew through the air, then he bounded over to cradle the egg protectively.

"I'm all done with you," he growled at me. "But you!"

He turned to Imogen and pointed a finger at her. She whirled around with a whimper, as she was watching another Task Force member look through her bag.

"That thing you're wearing!" he snapped. "Take it off."

Imogen's eyes sparkled with tears. "My... my clothes?"

He stomped over to her and pointed to the rigid fan-like structure behind her neck. It was something the Queen of Hearts might wear.

"The ribbing in your dress could pose a danger," he insisted. "Take it off."

Imogen stared wide-eyed at him. "But I'm not... I'm not wearing anything under it."

He was obviously getting really angry. He swung the strap of his gun over his shoulder so fast the barrel nearly hit me. "I said, take it off!"

He grabbed for Imogen, and she screamed.

"Stop!" I cried, but it barely sounded like anything past the heavy weight on my chest.

He took her dress in one hand and tugged as hard as he could. The Queen of Hearts piece ripped halfway off and hung there. Sassy yipped and howled at his feet, but he ignored her as he tore the other half off.

Imogen sobbed. "That was... brand new!"

He tossed her ripped piece of dress into the cart, then held his gun up at her again. "You do as you're told, Biyami. Next time, I won't be so forgiving."

Imogen struggled to find her breath. "Yes... yes, sir."

He turned from her and looked up to our painting between the beds. "Let's see what they're hiding behind here."

"No!" I screeched. But it was too late.

He and another Task Force member stomped up to the painting. The four of us gasped in unison as they reached up and tore it off the wall. The sickening sound of tearing paper resounded through the dungeons. Nausea slammed into my gut like I'd just been punched.

That was when I lost it.

"You crazy fuckers!" I cried, rushing toward them. Fire was ready in my palms.

But I never got to use it. A sharp pain entered my ass, and the room spun around me before it all went black.

I woke up to the darkness of the dorms. Things were quieter now, like the Task Force had left, but I could still hear the sobs of fellow Biyami students. I struggled to push past the dizziness swirling around in my head as I sat up. "What happened?"

Liam sat beside me, his eyes bloodshot in the little light we had coming from nearby Koigni flames. "I'm sorry, Sophia. We tried. We really tried."

I furrowed my brow. "Tried what?"

Imogen and Jonah stood from the bunk across from me with sad looks on their faces. Even Squeaks and Sassy looked melancholy beside them. Esis's ears drooped from Liam's lap.

"We tried to fix it," Imogen said sadly.

She leaned down and lifted mine and Liam's painting from the ground. Jonah helped, and they held it up. A huge tear ran through the middle of the painting, but there were pieces missing on the end— like the Task Force had ripped it up.

My whole body shook as I took it in. "It's just a painting," I said in a choked voice, though it wasn't true. It was *our* painting. It was special. "At least no one got hurt."

Imogen frowned. "Well, you got shot."

I shrugged. "It's happened before. I'll recover. Did anyone save anything good?"

Jonah sighed and lowered the painting. "Luckily, most of my good stuff isn't here."

I knew he was talking about his makeup and costumes in the Anichi dorms.

"It could've been worse," Imogen stated flatly.

"Drew managed to save a few Star Trek action figures," Liam said. "And Maddie hid a couple potions. We saved a bow for Sassy, and they didn't get Squeaks' stash of mice."

I breathed a sigh. It made me feel a little relieved to know they'd managed to salvage a couple of things.

"I think the worst is going to be the razors," Imogen said with a frown. "My pits are going to be awful."

"You can braid them," Jonah joked. "Like they do in France."

"Shut up." Imogen swatted at him. "No one *braids* their pit hair."

Liam chuckled lightly, and I couldn't help but join in. It was nice that those two could still joke about things at a time like this. It hurt, but it also gave me hope.

The scuffle of footsteps approached, and we all looked up. Maddie was making her way over to us. She crouched down between our bunks and whispered in a low voice. "I just got word from Alric." She shot a glance around the room, but no one was close enough to hear. "After what happened here tonight, he wants to move up the date."

Maddie didn't say it, but I knew she was talking about the next smuggling operation, the one with the twelve people Liam had found labeled *Code Red* in the Biyami database.

"We're meeting tomorrow at nightfall," Maddie said.

"Okay," Liam replied. "We'll be there."

As promised, we met in the Anichi dorms the following day at dark. Everyone was still on edge after what happened in the dorms yesterday, so it was quiet as we climbed the stairs. Liam carried our rolled-up, torn painting. We planned to hang it up here, where the Task Force couldn't ruin it.

Most of the group was already there when we arrived, including Maddie, Drew, and Wyatt. Lindsey and Miranda didn't quite look like themselves. Lindsey's red hair was tied into a messy bun, and she wasn't wearing any makeup. Miranda's wild, dark curls were all over the place. They were surrounded by their Familiars and a couple of dracavern, tiny little cave dragons who were perched on the back of the sofa.

"Hey." Lindsey stood as we came into the room. Miranda followed as she made her way over to us. "I heard about what happened last night. How bad was it?"

I rubbed my ass where I'd been shot by a noxite dart. By now, the effects had worn off, thanks to Esis. "Well, I got shot, so it was pretty bad."

"Don't worry," Imogen said proudly. "They didn't get everything."

Today, she was wearing an even crazier outfit than the day before. It was all sequins and ruffles, and a pointed hat that was two feet tall. It was her way of getting back at the Task Force for tearing apart her dress.

"What about you guys?" I asked, eyeing Lindsey and Miranda. "How's it going as Defortai?"

"Better than Biyami, for sure," Miranda said.

Liam tilted his head to the side. "You two look very..."

He trailed off, and Lindsey placed a hand on her hip. "Very what, Mitoh?"

"Great!" Jonah quickly subbed in. "You look great."

I rolled my eyes at him. "You look stressed."

Lindsey's hands were shaking— like she was nervous about this meeting or something.

I eyed her curiously. "What does Alric have you guys doing?"

Lindsey and Miranda shared a look, and Miranda's eyes darted over to the dracavern.

Miranda gave a nervous giggle. "Nothing. What makes you say that?"

I crossed my arms and raised an eyebrow. "The fact that it sounds like you're lying."

They didn't get a chance to answer before Alric and Baine entered the room, with the twelve students we were smuggling out behind them. I noticed a dracavern perched on Alric's shoulder. What was up with that?

"May I have everyone's attention, please?" Alric called across the common room.

I turned back to Lindsey and Miranda and whispered under my breath. "Will you tell me later?"

Lindsey shook her head as a look of regret crossed her face. "Sorry, Sophia, but you need to stay out of this. There are things we can't tell you."

My shoulders fell. Why did it seem like everyone was keeping things from me?

FIFTEEN

The Task Force didn't take our things to disarm us. They took our things to *break us*.

Morale seemed permanently low in the Biyami dorms after the Defortai stormed in and stole everything. What laughter and joy that had been there was completely gone. People were quiet now and kept their heads down.

They'd dehumanized us, and no one knew how to deal with it. We didn't feel like people anymore. We felt like property.

On Monday, I had to go to the pharmacy to pick up a refill of my inhaler. I headed up to the medical ward and found it oddly quiet. The pharmacy itself was almost empty. Usually, it was packed in here.

I asked for my prescription at the counter, and immediately got a sick feeling in my gut when the pharmacist took too long to give it to me. I was standing there for fifteen minutes before she finally returned from the room she'd been in.

"There's nothing here for you, Mister Mitoh," she replied. "All of your prescriptions have been cleared."

"Nothing there? No, that's impossible." I shook my head. "I get a refill of this inhaler every three months."

The pharmacist's eyes narrowed as she read my file on the screen. "Notes from the doctor that treated you said you made a miraculous recovery from pneumonia last week. You obviously don't need anything to help you recover."

Shit. I *knew* using Esis was going to lead to some consequences. People didn't have double pneumonia and walk out of the hospital four days later. I should've been in there at least a month. I'd definitely raised some suspicion about my condition.

"I'll pay the cost of the prescription outright," I told her. It was expensive, but I needed it.

"I'm sorry, but the notes in your file specifically state you are no longer permitted to use this medication," the pharmacist replied. "Have a good day."

Her cold and informal tone left no room for argument. She was staring at me in a way that made me feel ashamed and want to curl up inside. It was like she didn't consider me worthy enough to have medical care.

Inwardly, I was panicking. I needed that inhaler. I couldn't breathe most days without it, and I was still recovering from having pneumonia. I'd go backwards if I didn't have medicine.

What if they started restricting all my other medications as well? I had enough of a supply to get by... for a while... but after three months I'd be totally screwed.

When I walked out of the pharmacy, there was a Nivita guy hanging outside the door. His Familiar was a tiny bird that sat on his shoulder. It looked like a sparrow with pointed cat ears. The sparrow was losing feathers, and its head hung lowly. The guy himself had huge bags under his eyes, and looked tired.

"They refuse to give you your pills, too?" he asked. The tattoo on his arm marked him Biyami. I think I knew him— he was in one of my classes freshman year. His name was Darren.

"Yes," I said. "I think they've stopped refilling everything. What do you have?"

"Cancer," he replied. "They're holding my chemo drugs."

"Holy shit, dude. I'm so sorry," I said.

Darren coughed. "They're saying my insurance doesn't cover it anymore, but my parents are already paying so much in premiums. I think they've just restricted medical access to Biyami now."

Horror infected my core. They were slowly killing us. Denying medical care was an easy way to get rid of the disabled. I should've considered myself lucky I was allowed to be treated at all last week.

"Do you need to get out of here?" I asked him.

Darren shook his head. "My parents are taking me to a cancer treatment center at the end of the week. But I'll have to leave Julianna behind."

Darren stroked the sparrow on his shoulder, and she let out a sad peep. I felt terrible for him. He had to be separated from his Familiar in order to get treatment elsewhere, all because the Elders had to be dicks.

"That really sucks. I'm sorry." It seemed like sorry was all I could say, and I wish there were alternatives, because ancestors knew how much I hated people giving me sympathy. "Take care of yourself, man."

Darren coughed again. His exhausted face stayed with me all the way back to the Biyami dorms. I really hoped he pulled through, but I knew he wasn't the only Biyami in Kinpago who was sick and needed drugs to get by.

Including me. Fuck, I was totally screwed.

Sophia immediately noticed something was wrong when I walked in the door. "What's up?" she asked when I joined her, Imogen and Jonah near our bunks. Squeaks was leaning against Jonah, while Sassy and Esis chased each other around on the floor.

"They're refusing to refill Biyami prescriptions," I told her. "I can't get any of my meds."

"Seriously!?" Sophia shouted. The color drained from her face.

"Yeah." I nodded. "I have enough to get me by for a while, but I'm totally out on my inhaler."

"Is it the red one?" Jonah asked.

"I mean, yeah." I took it out of my pocket and showed him. "Why do you ask?"

Jonah got a hard look on his face. "I'll see you guys later. Come on, Squeaks."

"Where are you going?" Imogen asked.

"I'm not going to let Liam suffocate," Jonah said harshly. He and Squeaks left without another word.

"What does he think he's going to do, bang on Oleander's door and get him to change his mind?" I asked.

Imogen shook her head. "I don't know. He's been acting strange lately."

Sophia nervously ran her fingers through her ponytail. "You need those pills, Liam."

"I'll be okay," I said, though that was an outright lie. Good thing we'd hid what I had from the Task Force when they'd stormed in here.

"Maybe the Elders will reverse the ordinance," Imogen said, though her tone was full of doubt.

Sophia checked her bag. At first, it was a casual browse through, until her motions became more frantic.

"Fuck. I'm out of my birth control, too," Sophia said. "I was going to pick it up tonight."

"It's not like we need it," I said. I hated bringing up the obvious, but my swimmers had permanently retired.

"Yeah, but it was helping my period cramps." She frowned. "Oh, well. It's not as important as you getting what you need, anyway."

"We'll figure something out." I had no idea what. I checked my watch. "We're going to be late for art class. Come on."

Jonah didn't show up during Hawkei Art. The three of us kept looking around, expecting him to walk in any minute, but he never did. We returned to the Biyami dorms after class, but he wasn't there, either.

"Do you think something's happened to him?" Imogen asked anxiously. She was petting Sassy, her brow furrowed and mouth downturned.

"I don't think so. He acted like he had somewhere to be." I checked my watch. "I've got to get to my internship. See you guys later."

Tribal Headquarters was still busy when I got there. People and Familiars both were rushing around like chickens with their heads cut off. It was like everyone was preparing for something big, though I didn't know what. I kept my head down and refilled the copy machines like I was asked, until I was assigned a new task.

"There's a water leak in the women's bathroom on the first floor," my supervisor told me harshly after I was done banging on the same printer for the eightieth time. "I want it repaired by closing time."

Like I knew how to fix that, but okay. The floor in the women's bathroom was coated in a thin layer of water when I got there. I stepped inside and immediately sensed the problem. The water leak was coming from a busted pipeline beneath the floor. I could feel the water rushing through it beneath the ground, seeping upward as it overflowed over the foundation.

I couldn't fix it, but I could redirect the water so it didn't soak through the tiles anymore. If they wanted anything more than that, they'd have to hire a plumber.

As I was working on it, I heard voices in the hallway outside. "Hurry. This is the only place we can speak without fear of being overheard."

That sounded important. I ducked inside a stall and closed the door shut behind me. Then I flattened myself against the wall as two women walked inside. Claws and hooves trailed behind them as their Familiars followed. None of them seemed to care about the water that had overflowed the bathroom.

"We should've gone back to your residence," a woman spoke. "It would've been safer."

"There's no time," another responded. "We need to discuss this now."

Koigni Elders. If I had to guess, it sounded like Madame Wright and Madame Locklear. They were new. I'd heard them on TV sometimes when they gave speeches on the news. They were hasty replacements for Madame Chavis, who'd died of the plague, as well as her twin sister, who'd been killed in the riots. I'd heard Annette had a difficult time filling spots after her council had been decimated and Oleander took over.

Locklear's heels clicked on the tile and sent water splashing everywhere. "There's nothing we can do. The council has already decided."

"Nonsense. I have no great love for Biyami children, but this has gone too far," Wright argued.

"It's what is necessary!" Locklear hissed. "Those children don't belong here. They and their families are a threat to our way of life. They must be dealt with."

"By removing them and putting them in detainment camps?" Wright snapped. "Be reasonable."

"The extraction process has already begun. The construction of the camps are complete. You can't possibly expect us to turn back now," Locklear argued.

A shivering chill quaked up my spine. The Elders were detaining children from Biyami parents and putting them in concentration camps? What kind of world were we living in? This couldn't be real.

"We need to roll back on detainments. This is happening too quickly," Wright said.

"Roll back? We need to step them up," Locklear spat. "The Biyami take our jobs. They take resources from the tribe and leech off the system. The Defortai need to be concerned about taking care of our own people before we help everyone else. Our society isn't a charity. The Defortai come first."

"Yes, but *children*? This isn't what I signed up for when Annette asked me to be an Elder," Wright said.

"If you're so concerned, open up *your* home to them. What the tribe should really do is send them away. Get them to go back to where they came from," Locklear said.

Where we came from? The Biyami were born and raised right here in the tribe! This lady was acting like we were some kind of outsiders, instead of Hawkei just like they were.

"I've heard about these camps. The conditions are terrible. There's no food, little water. They're abusing those kids," Wright argued.

"So? Why is it our responsibility to take care of them?" Locklear asked. "Reports of the camps and their poor quality is greatly exaggerated. It's a Biyami trick. They'll do anything to gain sympathy."

"You don't understand where this is going. It doesn't stop here." Wright sounded worried. She began pacing, and her Familiar followed her around the room.

"They aren't our problem. If their parents didn't want them to be detained in camps, perhaps they should've been strong enough to defend themselves." Locklear's tone was harsh. It was clear she believed every word she said.

"What if they come for *our* children next?" Wright argued.

"That's impossible. The Defortai children won't be touched. Such things can never happen in a *civilized* society." Locklear sniffed. "You must be insane to believe that would happen in this day and age. We aren't living in World War II."

Wright stopped pacing. "I don't know. All of this makes me very nervous."

"Nothing is going to happen. I don't see what the big deal is about a bunch of Biyami brats being held somewhere due to their parents' wrongdoing." Locklear's tone was disgusted.

"Are they all criminals, truly?" Wright questioned in a soft voice.

"Of course! We need to take their children *somewhere* while their parents are being questioned. We can't just allow Biyami children to run wild in the streets."

"But what about the parents who are released? I've heard their children aren't being returned to them after questioning," Wright said nervously.

"Do people who put their own children in danger really deserve to be parents?" Locklear asked. "Paperwork takes time. Defortai can't spend endless resources on reuniting families."

This was all Oleander's way of dividing the tribe further. Biyami parents wouldn't unite and fight back if they didn't know where their kids were. The paperwork process was just an excuse.

"But these kids... I've heard stories, and they're not good. Some don't have blankets. They're fighting over food," Wright whispered.

"We shouldn't even be helping the children of criminals. They aren't our problem. The fact that we're giving them shelter at all is something they should be grateful for. So what if it's not a five-star resort? We're doing the best we can for those kids while their parents are in jail," Locklear replied. "If you ask me, we're doing too much for them already."

Locklear sounded like she considered Defortai a saint for taking care of these kids' basic needs. It made me sick.

"The tribe hasn't even noticed," Locklear continued. "Biyami are being removed by the day, and the Defortai have said nothing. Everyone is content to move on with their own lives."

There was a bout of silence before Wright whispered, "What are we going to do about Oleander?"

"We don't have to do anything," Locklear said. "Annette's assassins will take care of him."

"Yes, but when? Annette can't be High Chieftess unless he's out of the way."

"Patience. Annette's people are working on something. Once they find an opening, the old man is done for. They're trailing his every move as it is."

"I don't like this. I don't like it at all."

"Grow a backbone," Locklear sneered. "It's only a matter of time before Oleander is taken care of."

"He's got people after us as well."

"Let him. I'm not afraid."

Heels clicked again on the tile floor. "Come on," Locklear said. "It's time for us to save face."

The two Elders and their Familiars left the bathroom. I remained hidden in the stall for five more minutes until I was sure they wouldn't return.

My heart was pounding in my chest. The Elders had gone too far this time. The Elemental Cup was one thing, but now they were removing children from their parents, and they didn't care what happened to them after. People were disappearing left and right. What was the council's ultimate goal? To get rid of the Biyami for good?

I didn't bother to clock out. My dad needed to hear about this. He wasn't in his office, so I planned to head back home, until I saw him standing in the street outside the square. Kinpago was crowded today— I had to maneuver around a large group of people, who were looking around and acting like they were waiting for something.

"Dad!" I ran to him. He looked up, and Tatum grumbled a hello as I skidded to a stop beside him. I dropped my voice and said, "I overheard Madame Wright and Madame Locklear. Is it true that the council is taking Biyami kids away from their parents?"

He nodded solemnly. "I've heard about the camps, son. I voted against them, but was obviously outnumbered. What else have you discovered?"

I lowered my voice and told him about Annette's assassins. Dad nodded, and he said, "Then we need to be prepared. Either Oleander or Annette will be taken out within a few weeks, or less. We need to look at methods to get rid of whoever's left without drawing suspicion to ourselves."

"Then that's what we'll do." My eyes skimmed the crowd. "Why are there so many people here? Is there something going on?"

Before he could answer, a colossal roar shook the skies. I spun around. Oleander had wandered into the middle of the square, and a shadow fell upon him as a monstrous creature slithered up beside him.

So this is what everyone was preparing for. The unveiling of Oleander's Familiar.

It was a dracash— a dragon hybrid. The monster had a long body like a snake's, with enormous bat-like wings on his middle and five heads sprouting from his shoulders. The monster was scarlet in color and three hundred feet long. His tail ran all the way down the street and out of sight. The creature opened his mouths and bellowed an intimidating cry, and the sound shook the earth below my feet.

I'd never seen such a large Familiar in my life, except for Thalassa. This thing was massive. All the other creatures in the square were cowering at the sight of him. Oleander's grin was wide and mocking, daring anyone to come forward and challenge him.

Something about the creature didn't quite seem right. If Oleander was bonded to a dracash, why hadn't he shown it off until now?

Then I spotted it. I noticed the same collar that I'd discovered last week around the middle neck of the dracash as he roared.

So my earlier theory was correct. This wasn't Oleander's true Familiar. He had hid it somewhere. The creature he was showing off now was under his control.

"I would like everyone to meet Skylis, my Familiar," Oleander boomed. "He is very eager to serve the tribe."

Smoke filtered out of Skylis' nostrils. The creature bared his fangs, which seemed to be stained red by blood, and the sun glinted off of them.

Dad's expression was grim. "This doesn't bode well for us. The rest of the council will be even more wary about going up against his rulings."

"Doesn't work out for Annette, either." Good luck on getting her assassins close to Oleander when he had that thing skulking around.

Skylis growled as he narrowed his heads, and Dad said, "Get back to school. It's not safe for you here."

Not safe for me there, either, but with a dracash crawling around, I got his point. I left the square and headed up the road back to Orenda Academy.

Wasn't but five minutes after I entered the Great Hall that I met my brother. "Hey, Liam." Ezra grabbed my arm. "I need to talk to you."

Ancestors only knew what this was about. "Okay, what is it?"

He took a deep breath. "Alric wanted me to tell you to watch what you say in the Biyami dorms. The Task Force is secretly setting up microphones and recording devices down there, so they can incriminate people without them knowing. Don't do or say anything that could be used against you."

"Wow. That's over the top."

"Yeah. Just be on your guard," he said heavily.

I took a moment to observe my brother— *really* see him. He looked tired, like he'd been up all night, and his clothes were wrinkled and worn. His hair was a mess, like he hadn't combed it. Weird, considering he was just as vain as I was and was obsessed with how he presented himself. Dyami matched him. His feathers were rumpled, and the thunderbird looked around as if afraid we'd be overheard.

I hated how Ezra looked nowadays. Used to be you couldn't wipe a smile off the kid's face. He was always optimistic one-hundred percent of the time. Carefree was his middle name.

Now he seemed perpetually worried. He barely talked, and his eyes were constantly calculating... like he was strategizing or something.

I realized I hadn't seen him sneaking around the castle with a girl in some time, which was crazy to think about. "Hey, Ez, when's the last time you went on a date?" I asked.

"What? Why is that important?" His eyebrows knitted together.

"Never mind." My heart sank. If Ezra had lost interest in chasing girls— one of his favorite hobbies— there really was cause for concern.

He caught my meaning and said, "I'm not depressed, Liam. I'm just stressed out. There's a lot on my mind."

"Like what? The operation?" I asked.

"It's not just that." He was avoiding my eyes now.

"Okay, you can tell me. Whatever's on your mind, I can help with."

"You can't," he objected. "Not this time."

His refusal was like a punch in the gut. Suspicion rose in my mind. "Do you know something I don't?"

"Liam, please, don't press for answers." Ezra was begging me. "I can't tell you anything."

"Why? What's the big secret?" I tried to control my temper, but dammit, I didn't like people hiding things from me. Especially my own family.

"It's my burden to bear. I can handle it. You guys just concentrate on staying safe, all right?" Then, because he knew I'd press him for answers, he wandered off with Dyami behind him.

As if I needed any more reason to hate the Elders. This war was robbing my brother of his college experience. And he refused to let me help him. Which just about drove me nuts.

Sophia was waiting for me on a stone bench outside the Great Hall. Esis was in her lap, combing his fur out with a small pink brush and chittering, like he had gossip. Sophia was hardly paying attention to him.

"Hey. Jonah found us. He said to meet him in the Anichi dorms," Sophia whispered.

"Good, because I have stuff to tell you guys," I replied.

When we got to the Anichi dorms, Imogen was already there, sitting on a wooden chair and poring over texts that looked like they had to be the Yapluma Elders' scrolls. Sassy was on the table, munching on a pile of berries.

Jonah stood by the fire, a bag in his hand. Squeaks lay on the rug beside him. Her eyes were closed, but it didn't look like she was sleeping.

Jonah saw me coming and stomped toward me. "Here." He shoved the bag at me.

I looked inside. My mouth fell open when I saw my inhaler lying at the bottom. "How'd you get your hands on this?"

"I broke into the pharmacy after hours. Squeaks and I stole your inhaler," he said. "I would've gotten your other prescriptions, but I couldn't remember what they were."

I was speechless. Stealing drugs was a federal offense, not to mention prohibited by tribal government. Jonah had risked everything to help me. "Jonah... thank you."

"Don't thank me. You shouldn't have had to deal with this in the first place." Jonah turned away. He seemed... moody, but not necessarily at us.

"Liam says he's got news," Sophia announced. All eyes looked to me. I told the three of them about what I'd overheard from the Koigni Elders, as well as about Oleander's new "Familiar," and what Ezra had told me.

Imogen was strangely quiet. She hadn't moved from her chair. Esis was currently packing all the berries he could in his mouth, while Sassy yelled at him to stop.

Squeaks remained on the floor, though one of her eyes was currently open. She prodded Jonah's ankle with her beak, as if she wanted him to say something.

"Well, it's obvious what we need to do next, isn't it?" Jonah said darkly.

"What do you mean?" Sophia asked.

A shadow fell over Jonah's face. "We have to leave Orenda Academy as soon as possible."

Imogen's head snapped up. A moment of shock passed through the room before I said, "You want to leave now? I'm graduating in a couple of weeks. I'm not going to throw that away."

"Dude, fuck graduation. It's better to be a college dropout than to end up dead," Jonah said scathingly.

"Jonah, why do you want to leave?" Sophia asked. "You've brought it up before, but it's not like things have changed since then."

"Of course things have changed. It's gotten worse. They're taking people from their homes. Children are being put in fucking camps. What is it going to take before you guys figure out we need to get the hell out of here?" Jonah said.

Imogen rose so quickly from her chair I'm surprised she didn't knock it over. "I'm not leaving!" she shouted. "I'm not going to be a coward and run away while people lose their lives!"

"Imogen, I love you, but taking revenge against the Elders isn't going to bring Cade back," Jonah whispered.

Imogen's eyes watered. She wiped tears away with the palm of her hand before she exclaimed, "No, but it'll save some other girl the heartbreak of experiencing what I did! I never want another person to have to go through losing their brother, or the love of their life. That's why I'm staying. Because someone has to stand up and fight. If we don't, who will?"

"This is way bigger than us. We can't control what happens anymore," Jonah argued.

"Are you saying we can't make a difference?" Imogen asked.

"Yes! This is beyond our control! We need to focus on saving ourselves," Jonah hissed.

Imogen's voice wavered. "Let me tell you something, Jonah. I don't give a damn what happens to me anymore. I haven't since I lost Cade. The only thing I've thought about since that night is bringing the Elders down, and saving as many people as we can along the way."

"We're trying. But that's getting harder and harder every day. Eventually, we're going to be next," he said.

"We still have to find the Air piece. This isn't over." Sophia broke in, her voice elevating above Jonah's.

Jonah angrily tore at his hair. "Oh yeah, I forgot, the impossible fucking task. Newsflash, Imogen and I haven't found anything on the Air piece since we started looking. Figuring out the prophecy is getting us nowhere."

"So you want to just give up?" I asked. "That wasn't part of the plan."

"Fuck the plan! We're being stupid by sticking around!" Jonah bellowed.

"We can't just pick up and leave! I'm not going to abandon my parents and siblings while we go and hide!" I protested.

"Then get everyone to leave with us. Convince them somehow," Jonah insisted.

"My dad is one of the few people left who has enough power to turn things around. He's not going to leave his people now," I argued.

"It's too late to turn things around!" Jonah kicked the end table, and it skittered to the side. "Don't you guys get it? They're barely feeding us! How long before they start taking people out in a systematic way?"

"That's not going to happen. Alric said it wouldn't," Sophia said, her voice growing in intensity.

Jonah made a scoffing noise. "Have you guys been paying attention? Alric is clearly hiding something from us. Him, and everyone else! There's some big secret going around that Alric's told everyone not to let us in on."

"You're speculating. You don't know that for sure," Imogen rebutted.

"Open your eyes!" Jonah rubbed his face in frustration. "Lindsey, Miranda, *everyone's* sneaking around, giving us information on a need-to-know basis. Hell, even Ezra can't tell Liam the truth. That's his own brother!"

"Leave Ez out of this," I snapped. I was starting to get pissed.

"You know it's true." Jonah's eyes were getting desperate. "Our friends keep telling us that there's stuff we don't need to know. And when we go to pry, everyone lies, or makes up excuses. Something's up. Why aren't we being involved?"

"What reason would Alric and the rest have to keep a secret from us? We're the ones who started the smuggling operation in the first place," Imogen said.

"Really? What *reason* do they have for not telling us stuff? Gee, I wonder why," Jonah said sarcastically, with a sideways glance at Sophia. Her expression hardened, and her mouth flattened into a stern line.

"You think they're keeping secrets from me?" Sophia asked harshly. She was daring Jonah to say yes.

"No offense, Sophia, but it's *always* about you," Jonah said. "And everyone else knows that the three of us are close to you, so they're keeping us out of the loop so we don't tell you whatever they don't want you to know."

"You think they're using me?" Sophia said viciously.

"I didn't say that," Jonah argued. "But they've probably got some big plan for you. Otherwise, why not let you in on what's going on?"

"You're reaching. You don't have facts to prove any of this," Imogen said.

"I can feel it in my gut," Jonah responded.

"Gut feelings aren't good enough! We need absolute proof," Imogen insisted.

I stepped forward. "You guys can go if you want, but I have to stay no matter what. My dad needs me to gain intel on Oleander and Annette."

"Liam, being a spy for your dad isn't going to make up for losing your chance at being chief," Jonah said roughly.

His words were like a kick to the balls. Sophia noticed the crushed look on my face and stepped in. "Jonah, if we can't trust Alric... if we can't trust our friends... this war is already over. We have to put our faith in the people we've allied ourselves with."

"You want to know who I trust? The people in this room, and no one else," Jonah shot at her. "We should've kept what we were doing between us. There's something going on that's just not right here."

I hated that Jonah had a point. I knew Ezra was keeping something from me. I saw it on his face earlier. But it was too difficult to admit that my little brother was hiding shit behind my back.

When we were quiet for too long, Jonah barked out, "You guys know something's not right. I know you do. So what are we going to do about it?"

"Jonah, we *can't leave*," Sophia said firmly. Her voice had taken on a pleading note. The three of them shared a glance, and I knew without anyone having to say anything that she was talking about me.

It wasn't a big secret I wouldn't last long on the road. I had Esis, sure, but I didn't know if his magic would be enough to keep me alive as we were on the run. I had pills... doctors appointments... fuck, it was up in the air somedays if I could make it across the castle without getting out of breath. I can't imagine how I'd keep up with the group if we had to jump from location to location for an extended period of time.

But I hated the fact that Sophia wanted to stay here because she feared she might lose me if we took our chances and left school. I wanted her to be safe. No matter what consequences that brought me.

I shook my head. "You guys don't have to hide anything. If you decide to go, I'm staying behind. I already know I'd slow the group down."

"We aren't leaving without you," Sophia snapped.

"We aren't *leaving* at all," Imogen said viciously.

"Im, don't tie yourself to this sinking ship just because your boyfriend went down with it," Jonah whimpered.

Imogen snapped. "You don't know how I feel! *None* of you do!" she screamed. The room shook— dust fell from the ceiling and scattered on the floor. "You don't know what it's like to wake up every morning and realize that the man you love died for *nothing*!"

"We're all going to die for nothing if we keep this up. I love you guys! You're the only family I have left!" Jonah was getting emotional. His hands balled into fists as he stepped forward and shouted, "If you guys are dead, I'll have no one! I'd be devastated if I lost a damn one of you. And I get more and more worried every day that I will."

"No one's dying, Jonah," I said. I tried to make my voice steady and calm.

"Yet," he shot at me. His eyes dampened, but he held it in.

"I'd gladly give my life if it meant the tribe could change," Imogen said, but her anger was fading. She was worried about Jonah now. Her voice had sunk to a quiet tone, and her mouth slightly opened as she saw Jonah's lip tremble.

"I don't care about the tribe anymore. Imogen, if I lost you, that's something I'd never get over," Jonah choked out.

I needed to calm everyone down. This was getting out of hand, and I was leader here. I felt responsible for everybody. And we couldn't fall apart now, not when we needed each other the most.

"Let's try to clear our heads," I said. "Nothing's happening right now. We need to think for a moment."

"There's nothing to think about. The right thing to do is clearly in front of us," Jonah said.

"We'd need a plan. We don't have one yet," I argued.

"Look, Liam. Your family is well off, and so are Sophia's grandparents. We could figure out a way to make it work," Jonah pleaded.

"What about *my* family? My parents, my brothers?" Imogen demanded.

"We can hide them, too. We can hide all of us," Jonah said, but his voice was getting weaker and weaker.

"Where, Jonah? Where are we going to go?" Sophia asked. "You're asking to move a large group of people to nowhere. You think the Elders aren't going to notice? They'll send people to find us. We're safer here."

"Where do you think Alric is sending all those people we've been smuggling out? They have to go somewhere," Jonah said.

"Most of them have families outside Kinpago. We don't have that option," Imogen said.

Jonah hung his head. "It's pretty clear that you've made up your minds. I won't leave without you. I just pray to the ancestors I'm wrong."

A quiet moment of silence passed. I broke it as a thought crossed my mind. "We can compromise," I said. "We can think about leaving eventually."

"That's not good enough. We need to make an agreement," Jonah said harshly. "If things don't get better, and soon, we have to get out of here. It's not an option anymore."

Imogen was still seething. Sophia said nothing— instead, she looked to me.

I took a breath. "Fine. We'll consider leaving. But only if there's no other choice, and... hear me out... there's absolutely no chance of getting the Air piece. That has to be our first priority."

Jonah's expression was hard to read. "Done. I need some air."

He left, and Squeaks got up to follow. After he slammed the door, Imogen collected the scrolls in her arms.

"He's just scared," she told us. "We'll figure out the Air piece eventually."

Her words didn't hold any form of confidence. Even Imogen's faith was failing her. I didn't blame Jonah for being scared. I was scared, too. For my family, for my friends, Sophia...

For all of us.

THE GROUP DIDN'T TALK MUCH over the next few days. Jonah seemed to be avoiding us— he went to class, and skirted off by himself whenever he didn't have somewhere to be. Imogen surveyed the Yapluma Elders' scrolls over and over, but she didn't find anything.

Sophia and I kept to ourselves. We didn't want to take sides, and at the moment it was easier to get lost in our own little world then to try and deal with everything that was going on outside of our relationship.

By Thursday night, Jonah seemed to be in a better mood, which I was thankful for. Such a good mood, in fact, he insisted on dragging me into Kinpago to do some shopping, though for what, he didn't say.

"Jonah, where exactly are you taking me?" I asked. We were in the gay district, in an alley I'd never been in. We passed under a rainbow flag hanging from the rooftop, and window displays of mannequins wearing... ancestors... leather spiked bras, with matching panties.

"We're here!" Jonah announced. Squeaks let out a happy chirp. I stepped inside the store, and a feeling of dread rose from the bottom of my feet all the way to the top of my head.

"Oh, no." Jonah had dragged me into a *sex shop*. I should've known he'd do something like this. Lingerie hung from racks next to shelves full of vibrators, erotic novels, and sex board games. There were dozens of displays on bath products, massage oils, and every lubricant you could imagine. Costumes and wigs were stocked next to condoms and pheromones. There were anal beads, cock rings, and about a million other things that I didn't know the purpose of. The room smelled like incense, and girly music played in the background.

And dildos. They were fucking dildos everywhere, in every shape, size, and color. I couldn't imagine how so many people had different preferences in dick size and shape. Hell, some of these even fucked you themselves. I wondered why some women wanted a man, with these high-powered devices they made nowadays.

Jonah skipped around like a kid in a candy store. This was like the time he'd forced me to go to a strip club. Why didn't I start asking where we were going *before* we actually went?

A woman with spiked hair and tattoos ran the counter. Her Familiar was a pink miniature deer, with a long oxen tail and a singular horn sticking out of its head. When the deer moved, little hearts bubbled out of its tail and popped against the ceiling. The worker smiled at us as we walked by. "This the one you're talking about, Jonah? He's cute. What are you two looking for today? I have a new comfort gel that really does the trick."

I nearly gagged. She thought I was screwing Jonah. And that I needed comfort gel for my ass.

Jonah waved his hand and said, "Oh, he's just a friend, Junine. I'm here for myself today."

"Yeah. Just here to look for stuff for me and my *girlfriend*," I said firmly.

Junine scratched her Familiar's ears. "Hm. Does she have any particular kinks?"

I didn't know. We hadn't been sleeping together that long. We certainly weren't getting bored, but it might be fun to try something new. "Um... I think I need some time to look around."

"I can make a few suggestions. Come to me if you need any help," Junine said.

I skirted to Jonah's side and lowered my voice. "Dude, what the hell? You couldn't have told me we were coming here?"

Jonah eagerly proceeded to the BDSM section. "Would you stop whining? I need this stuff. Besides, you can pick up something for yourself while you're here."

"You think I'm into..." I read a nearby box of what looked like a torture device for your dick. "*Male chastity* cages?"

"I *meant* you and Sophia. Monogamy doesn't have to mean monotony, you know."

I guess that was true. I'd never been in an adult novelty store before. But there was just so much here. I don't even know what she'd like, or where to start.

Jonah started taking whips down from the wall and comparing them. He checked out a pair of handcuffs and a ball gag before shaking his head. "I just don't know what... ah, here we go."

He reached out and took down a spreader bar from the display on the ceiling. "Just what I was looking for."

"Why are you even here, Jonah? You're single," I said.

"That doesn't mean I'm celibate." He eyed the spreader bar eagerly. "Besides. I can do all kinds of things by myself. Sex included."

"You aren't telling me you're using that on yourself," I argued.

Ancestors, why was I even asking these questions when I clearly didn't want to know.

"No. I have a date on Friday. It's best to be prepared," he stated.

"Are you going out with Caleb again?" I asked, hoping I got the name right. He was some Biyami kid that Jonah had barely known a few days before they'd hooked up. Before that was some other guy that I didn't know, and couldn't remember the name of. Jonah had messed with him once or twice before moving on. Myself— and everyone else in the bunks— knew about him, too, though they'd tried to keep quiet.

Jonah made a disgusted face. "No. I already slept with him last week. He's old news. Aiden and I are meeting up at his apartment at the end of the week. He graduated last year, remember? ... Or was his name Aaron? Oh, I don't know. It's not like it matters. I'm not dating him."

I opened my mouth to say something before I thought better of it. I didn't approve of Jonah sleeping around with a bunch of random guys, but we all had our methods of coping to get by these days. I wasn't going to judge him for it when he just needed an escape.

"I totally need this." Jonah put down the spreader bar and held up a male-enhancement pump. "My old one broke."

"Ancestors, Jonah." I had to get away from him. I walked to the opposite side of the store and started browsing, trying to figure out what Sophia would like. Nipple clamps would be fun. But it'd probably be best if we started out with something a little more vanilla. I nearly got a hard-on picturing her in some of the lingerie that was hanging around the room, but that was more for me, not for her.

"What about this size?" A familiar female voice could be heard from not so far away.

"Oh, no. Liam's *much* bigger than that. Eight inches, at least."

I rounded the corner and saw none other than Imogen and Sophia, comparing dildos and laughing. Sassy was batting a dildo around on the floor with her paws, while Esis looked in the mirror and fluffed up his chest fur, as if pretending he had boobs.

I snuck up from behind Sophia and tickled her sides. She let out a tiny scream when I poked her. She turned around, and her mouth dropped open in shock. "Oh my gosh! What are you doing here?"

"Let's just say I did not come here of my own free will," I said. "Although I'm not opposed, either."

Sophia giggled. "Imogen and I came in on a whim. I'm definitely not disappointed."

"Look. At. This!" Imogen lifted a giant purple dildo into the air, one that looked like it was made of a gelatin substance and sparkled in the light. It was at least ten inches long. "It's huge!"

Sophia's eyes bulged out of her head. "Holy crap, that's the largest dick I've ever seen!"

"Besides your boyfriend's," Imogen teased, and both of them snickered.

Imogen eyed the lingerie racks on the other side of the room. "Sophia, I think you need to try some stuff on."

"What? Me?" Sophia squeaked. "But I—"

"No buts." Imogen gave a teasing glance at me, then dragged Sophia across the store by her wrist. Imogen started yanking items off the rack. When Sophia had at least ten garments in her arms, Imogen shoved her into a dressing room. My heart rate picked up when I heard Sophia slip out of her jeans, and the rustling of plastic hangers.

"Can I see?" I asked, hoping Sophia would crack the door open just a peek.

"No!" Imogen said. "You'll ruin the surprise!"

Talk about getting blue balls. "Not fair," I complained.

Imogen dropped her voice so Sophia couldn't hear and said, "You can wait until your honeymoon. The only reason I brought her here was because she needs something for your wedding night."

"We haven't even set a date," I argued.

"It's good to be prepared. What do you expect her to do, grow three sizes by the time you get married?" Imogen shot back.

"What are you two talking about out there?" Sophia called over the door.

"Nothing!" both of us responded at once.

Imogen smacked the purple dildo into her hand, and the package bent. "I think I need to get this. *For the bachelorette party,*" she hushed. Her eyes lit up when she saw the multi-colored wigs. "Ooh! I want a green one!"

Sophia didn't come out with anything, but there was a soft smile on her face as she exited the dressing room.

"Like anything?" I prompted.

"Oh, yes, but you don't get to see me buy it," she teased. "I'll come back and get it when you aren't looking."

I moaned and rolled my eyes. "You're killing me, *pawee*."

She ran her fingers down my chest and gave the bulge in my pants a squeeze, biting her lip in a mischievous way. "I just want to see you squirm from anticipation."

What the fuck? Did she just grab my dick in the middle of the store? Count me turned on. Nobody else had seen, but at the moment, I hardly cared if they did.

At the opposite end of the store, Jonah was trying on thigh-high platform shoes. Imogen waltzed up to him, adorned with a green wig. "Those are some pretty rad pumps," she said in admiration as Jonah laced up the obnoxious heels.

"You know it, babe." Jonah winked, and Imogen gave him a thumbs-up. Looks like they had made up after that fight, which was a relief. They weren't the kind of friends who could stay mad at each other for long.

"Sophia, try these on!" Jonah pleaded, and he tossed a pair of six inch heels her way. "I think you'd look mad sexy in them."

"I'm gonna break my leg," Sophia grumbled as she ducked down to untie her sneakers. Once she had the heels on, she had to hold on to Imogen to keep from falling over. Imogen and Jonah insisted she try on another pair, "just in case she needed them for something *formal*," while Sophia argued that flats were the only way to go.

Esis hid himself inside one of the heels, while Sassy wore a boot on her head. Squeaks was currently moaning that her hooves wouldn't fit inside a pair of pumps that were just like Jonah's.

While they were bickering, something grabbed my attention. A blindfold hung from a display rack not far by.

Perfect. It was small, but it'd do the trick. While Sophia was distracted, I nabbed the blindfold, and something else I'd caught her eyeing on the way to the dressing room.

Junine grinned as she packaged up the items. "Good choice. That's one of my personal favorites. Your girlfriend's going to love it."

I hoped so. Sophia's eyes lit up when she saw me walking toward her with the bag. "What's that there?" Sophia asked. She tried to peek inside, but I yanked it away from her.

"No peeking," I told her. "Though you can have a hint."

I took the blindfold out of the bag. "So my mom asked me to watch the house tonight," I told Sophia lowly. "Apparently, Dad and the kids are going somewhere."

"Really? Where to?" Sophia asked, smiling lightly.

"I'm not sure." I didn't ask questions. I'd been too excited about getting the house to myself. "I was thinking. How about you get that corset out of the closet?"

"The one I wore to piss you off last semester?" she said coyly.

"Yes. And this." I pressed the blindfold into her hand. "I'll be there around nine. I expect to find you dressed and ready to go."

"Yes, Mister Mitoh." She gave me a wink. Esis took the blindfold from her and put it over his own eyes, until she snatched it back.

The four of us got dinner at one of the few Chinese places left that allowed Biyami in, and everyone picked on me for only ordering brown rice. Imogen and Jonah split up from us in order to see a burlesque show on the other side of town with their Familiars. Sophia went back to school to get her corset. It was at the bottom of her trunk, and thankfully, one of the few things the Task Force hadn't found during their raid.

Jones was still giving us peryton rides, as he was a friend of Baine's, so Sophia would be able to make it to the island by herself. I worried how much longer the Elders would allow that to continue.

Mom had left the boat on the docks for me to take back home, as well as given me a list of groceries to pick up before I got home. I threw things into the cart and practically flipped the boat over on my way back to my parents' house.

Hey, what could I say? I wanted to see Sophia in that corset again as fast as possible.

Esis was on the couch watching TV when I got there. More reality television. A bag of cheese balls sat in his lap, and his fur was covered in orange dust. He took a giant gulp of the soda at his side before waving me upstairs carelessly.

Ugh. Totally a teenager. At least he wouldn't bother us. I put the groceries on the counter and vowed to put them away later before I hurried to the stairs.

I cracked open the door to my bedroom. Sophia had done as I'd asked— she was sitting on the edge of the bed, the blindfold over her eyes and waiting. Her hair was in a low ponytail, and she'd put on a bit of perfume that I could smell from here. The black corset lined with red lace pushed her breasts upward so that they swelled above the fabric. Now that we were back together, I could appreciate the corset in all its beauty, instead of being jealous that she was wearing it at all.

Instead of leather shorts, Sophia had on a thong that matched the color of the corset. It was mesh and see-through. They held nothing to the imagination.

Good. Oh, this was going to be fun.

I slipped off my shirt and crept up behind her, but she heard my footsteps coming and slightly turned her head. I crawled onto the bed before I reached out and grabbed her ponytail. I twisted it in my hand and gently pulled it to the side, exposing her neck. I then bent down and pressed my lips to the nook where her shoulder ended and her neck began. I caressed my lips up and down the skin there, while using my free hand to massage the top of her breasts.

She smiled and let out a happy sigh as my lips moved down her shoulders. I made little patterns with my mouth, lingering on small spots where she gasped. Her skin was blushing pink, and I was really, really enjoying this.

I left a few hickeys on her shoulders before I pulled her hair once again so her head was tilted back. I looked down at the tiny bruises starting to form— I liked seeing that. It was a way of saying she was mine.

Course, I belonged to her a hundred, thousand times more. I did since the day I walked into her house to bring her to Orenda. I couldn't get enough of Sophia. A thousand years with her would feel like five minutes. If she wanted me to be her slave, I would become it— gladly. She meant everything to me. I thought I'd been gone forever when I lost

Nashoma, but I wasn't. The missing piece of me that was still living on was inside her.

I leaned forward and took her mouth, pressing it against mine. She accepted eagerly, groaning a little, and I brushed my tongue against hers. Ancestors. She tasted so good.

We made out for a few blissful moments before I took her hands in mine. She went to take off the blindfold, but I snatched her fingers. I sucked her fingertips onto my mouth before I leaned forward and drug my lips across her ear.

"Leave it on," I whispered. "I like the mystery."

She giggled. I swept her into my arms, and she let out a yelp as I tossed her onto the middle of the bed. She landed on a pile of pillows, and I began dragging my lips over her legs and her wanting middle. She'd stopped gasping now and was making these tiny little sounds that I thought were really cute and turned me on.

I stopped worshipping her body for a moment so I could rustle through the bag from the sex shop. I put the batteries in. Sophia froze and tilted her head.

"Liam? What are you doing?" she asked as I clambered back on the bed.

I didn't answer. Instead, I turned the vibrator on, and pressed it against her clit. Her body immediately jolted, and her back rose off the bed as I began moving the vibrator over her.

"You like it?" I whispered. Sophia didn't respond but to moan loudly. I took that as a good sign. I turned up the intensity, and Sophia gasped. She sniffled, body writhing, as the vibrations sent her into a state of delirium.

"Liam, it's almost too much," Sophia pleaded. She sounded on the verge of tears. This thing was worth every penny I'd paid for it.

"Do you want me to stop?" I asked.

I pressed the vibrator down harder, and Sophia whimpered. "Emm... no," she finally breathed. "Keep going."

I turned the acceleration up again. At this point, Sophia's hands were bunched in the sheets, and her legs were shaking. Her mouth opened slightly, and I could tell she was about to come. Once she was at the point of climax, I took the vibrator away and gently eased it into her.

Sophia moaned. I moved the vibrator in and out of her body at a consistent speed. Fuck, this was *so* turning me on. I'd had fantasies of using one of these on her for ages. She was practically water in my hands.

Then Sophia did something she never had before. She screamed in pleasure. I dove the vibrator in faster, and tears leaked from behind the blindfold as Sophia came again and again. Eventually, she lay boneless on the bed, her body quivering and gasping for breath.

Seeing her orgasm like that, I couldn't get my clothes off fast enough. I yanked off my jeans and boxers and tossed them to the floor. I maneuvered to my knees in front of her hips and put her ankles on my shoulders so that her legs were lying against my torso. I reached down to move the string of her thong aside so I could thrust in.

Sophia moaned again as I moved within her, and I reached out to grab the vibrator. I ran it along her erect nipples as I continued to thrust. I surged forward so I was fully inside of her, and her spine arched. She dug her nails into the covers and held on as I rammed into her body at a high speed.

We'd never fucked like this before. And I said *fucked* intentionally. This wasn't making love. We were going at it like animals.

"I want you to make me sore tomorrow," Sophia breathed out.

"Wish granted," I gasped. We were being really rough. But damn, both of us wanted it. Sophia let go of the covers and reached out to claw at my arms. She held on as our bodies collided, and stars burst in front of my eyes as I came like I never had before.

I fell to the side. Sophia pushed the blindfold off her eyes— she still looked dazed.

We lay there panting for a few moments. I had to take a few breaths before I asked, "So... are you going to be sore?"

She snickered. "Let's just say I hope I can walk to class."

There were few things that made a man prouder than his woman acknowledging that he'd done a stellar job in bed. A glowing feeling in my chest spread as Sophia lifted the blindfold away. "Next time, you're wearing this thing."

"Fine by me." It gave me a thrill to imagine the kind of stuff Sophia would do to me when it was my turn to be blindfolded.

Sophia played with the ends of my hair. "I want things to be like this forever between us," she said. "I hope our feelings never change."

"They never will," I promised. "For better or for worse."

I let that last part slip out, but Sophia didn't notice anything unusual about it. She smiled and rolled into my chest. I put an arm around her and rested my lips against her forehead.

I wanted things to be like this forever, too. Sophia was my catalyst. She was the one thing I was told I couldn't have, and the one thing I needed to keep breathing.

But I'd gladly take my last breath, as long as it was for her.

As GREAT AS the night before had been, Friday was a long. Fucking. Day.

Communing with the Ancestors started at noon, and already, I was *this close* to skipping and throwing in the towel in favor of an early weekend. I don't know why, but nothing went right. Mom and Dad didn't show up until after ten, making Sophia late for Hawkei Artifacts. I realized I was behind on a project for War and Negotiation, and it was due next week. Not to mention I'd fallen in a puddle of slime left behind by Hudson's giant snail after I'd gone to get my bag back in the Biyami dorms, and ruined my shirt. Freaking gross.

Yep. It was a day where nothing could go right. But I knew I had to suck it up. Communing with the Ancestors was a two-hour long class, but it wasn't hard. I could sit through it. Maybe my luck would turn around.

We'd mostly been learning about different rituals, herbs, and incenses that you could use to heighten spirituality and deepen your connection with the ancestors. I'd been taught most of this during my chief training as a kid, but still paid attention, as there was a lot of stuff in the material I'd forgotten.

Professor Kinrah's Familiar was a creature that had horse hooves, a fiery mane and tail, but a wolf's body and head. The tone of her fur was blue, and antlers grew from between her ears. I never got tired of looking at her, as she was one of the most beautiful creatures I'd ever seen. She perched on Kinrah's desk and watched as he began writing down some main points on the board. Professor Kinrah himself was a new teacher—fairly old, a replacement for one of the professors that had resigned. He was a Religions professor and used to work for the museum in town, if I'd heard correctly. Despite being one of the new hires, he wasn't bad. Just super old, and maybe on the verge of having dementia. Didn't mean he wasn't brilliant, though. The guy knew his stuff, and he didn't seem to care he was teaching a classroom full of Biyami.

Kinrah tapped the board with a piece of chalk. "For today's lesson, we're going to start with something a bit unconventional." He moved his glasses up with a trembling finger. "Many of you have been taught that only chieftains and their first-borns can summon the ancestors, along with some Elders. I am here to inform you that is a misconception. The blood of the ancestors runs through all our veins. Any of us can summon them at any given time."

Surprised murmurs whispered throughout the classroom. Someone near the front raised their hand. It was Sam— the kid who Imogen had gone on a date with. "But sir, I don't know how such a thing is possible. I've never seen anyone but a chieftain and a first-born summon their ancestor, unless it's on Ancestors' Day."

"You misunderstand. Chieftains and first-borns have the ability to make the ancestors *appear* before a great number of people. But just because a Hawkei who is not a chieftain or a first-born calls upon the ancestors and cannot see them, it doesn't mean they are not there. The idea that only a few chosen can summon their ancestral lines is an illusion, a misconception spread by those in power wishing to force the masses to submit," Kinrah stated.

Sam still looked confused. "Then why is Ancestors' Day so important? It's supposed to be the only day of the year you can speak directly to your spirit guides and talk to other Hawkei who aren't in your ancestral line."

"It is true that it is easier for Hawkei to connect with their departed kin on Ancestors' Day. However, this wasn't always the case." Kinrah shook his head. "In previous ages gone past, the Hawkei didn't need a special day of the year to speak or gain wisdom from their ancestors. Elementai were able to contact and ask the ancestors for help whenever they needed guidance. Now, this didn't always mean that the ancestors spoke— or could even be seen by those whom they were called upon. But they were always there to aid the one who requested their appearance. Name-finding ceremonies are another example of common Hawkei being able to speak with their spirit guides. The arrival of the ancestors and their guidance is dependent on the situation, not the individual."

That made sense. Sophia had told me her spirit guides had led her to Esis when they were separated during the Elemental Cup, and guided her back to me when I was dying. Nashoma had come to me when I asked last year before Sophia and I got back together. It seemed the ancestors did arrive, in certain situations.

"So how come things are different now?" Lira, the girl from my Toaqua class, had a note of uncertainty to her voice. "Why can't we talk to our ancestors like we did hundreds of years ago?"

"Many things have changed since the ways of our ancestors. The more years that pass, the farther we get away from our tribal roots. The modern world and technology have dulled our senses to the way things used to be," Kinrah said. "Some say you cannot speak with your ancestors unless you are pure of heart, and worthy of their acceptance— another misconception. Anyone, regardless of who they are or what they've done, can reach out and speak with their ancestors. Whether they choose to guide you or not is up to them."

"And does that happen?" Sam asked. "Do the ancestors become silent if they no longer wish to guide you?"

Kinrah took a deep and heavy sigh. "It is... very rare for an ancestral line to abandon their kin." His expression became serious. "One would have to be considered so evil that the ancestors would consider banning your soul from entering the Ancestral Lands after death."

I gave a shiver. That would be the worst fate ever. To be banished from the eternal land of our people, and forced to wander *Aiya Nocshun* — the Mighty Darkness— forever.

Kinrah shuffled around the room slowly. "We connect with our ancestors a variety of ways. Fasting is one. Prayer is another. War paints are a way for us to reach out to our ancestors without having to summon them directly. The point is to make yourself vulnerable, and be willing to open your soul up to the Great Spirit, having faith that he knows what's best for your life path."

Lira crossed her arms. "I wouldn't say the ancestors and the Great Spirit *always* know best," she said critically. "I mean... look what's going on. They aren't even interfering."

Kinrah gave her a kindly gaze. "Speaking with the ancestors often requires sacrifice. You must show you are willing to make yourself humble and learn from their wisdom, and the wisdom of the earth. Trust in their guidance is critical. With time and patience, you'll be able to feel the ancestors guiding you along your life path without even having to hear them speak. Even if your life becomes incredibly difficult, and you can no longer understand their plan."

He moved toward the center of the room. "Turn to page three-hundred-and-sixty in your textbooks. You'll find terminology there. I expect a full written report on the lecture today, due by the end of class."

I tried to work on my essay, but what Kinrah had said was eating away at me. If there were more ways than we'd been taught to contact the ancestors, maybe deciphering the prophecy wasn't as difficult as we were making it.

Though a small, angry voice in my head hatefully agreed that Lira was right. The ancestors didn't know what was best for us. If they did, why were they allowing people to suffer? They didn't want to help. They wouldn't even if we asked.

Not that we deserved it, anyway. Look what the Hawkei had done to their own people.

Had the ancestors abandoned the tribe to their fate? Or had we merely grown so proud they now refused to hear us?

sophia
SIXTEEN

That night with Liam was the most fun I'd had in months, but when we returned to school, it was back to tiptoeing around Defortai in the halls just in case you set one of them off. The Defortai were getting worse by the day. I'd heard some douchebag had thrown Lira and her Familiar into a tar pit and didn't even get a slap on the wrist. They'd survived, luckily, but both of them acted scared of everything now.

According to Tabitha, five guys had jumped Riley in the Atrium on his way back to the dorms a few nights ago, and left him and his hawk Familiar bleeding out on the path. A group of Biyami found him the next morning. I hadn't seen him to confirm the rumors, but I'd heard he was refused treatment at the hospital and sent home to recover because his injuries weren't "life threatening."

I was starting to question whether Jonah had a point about leaving. But I wouldn't— not at the expense of Liam's health, not until we smuggled everyone out we could, not until we were at our breaking point.

I worried we didn't have much longer.

Imogen walked me to my Hawkei Artifacts class on Friday, though she didn't have to. It'd become an unspoken rule to stick together whenever there were Defortai nearby. At least I felt comfortable once I got to class. Everyone here was Biyami, since all the Defortai dropped. Apparently, this subject wasn't *important* enough for them.

Baine walked into the room after everyone was seated. He carried a small drawstring bag with him. Baine wasn't originally meant to teach this class, but the deans had rearranged his schedule after he'd been sorted into Biyami. Apparently, they worried what parents would think of a Biyami teaching advanced Defortai classes. But at least Baine knew his stuff.

"Today, we'll be working in groups," Baine announced. "If everyone will please sort themselves by House."

All thirty of us glanced around the room at each other. We were all Biyami— all from the same House now. Baine stared back at us blankly, not understanding our hesitation.

"Quickly, students," he said. "We have much to cover today. Koigni, up in the front, Toaqua in back, Nivita on the left side and Yapluma on the right. Let's go."

Everyone scrambled to join their respective groups. I sat in front by Tabitha, Hudson, and three other Koigni I didn't know well. Our group was the smallest.

Baine began to walk around the room while he spoke. "I want each of you to take a moment and study what I'm about to hand you. Let each group member hold it and see if you can feel anything."

Baine reached into his bag and handed Tabitha a polished purple stone that fit in the palm of her hand. She tested its weight and flipped it over a few times before passing it off to Hudson. He did the same.

Baine continued around the room. He handed Nivita a red stone, Toaqua a green one, and Yapluma a blue. I noticed none of the colors matched up with our Houses, but I wasn't sure what that meant.

Baine didn't give any more instruction. He returned to the front of the room and leaned against his desk as he watched the groups discuss what they felt.

"I don't feel anything," Hudson said as he eyed the stone in his hand.

He handed it to a First Year, and the stone continued its way around the circle until it reached me. I took the rock in my hand and looked it over, but I couldn't figure out what Baine was getting at. Esis reached out for it and ran his paw over the polished surface. He tried to take it from me. I just knew he was itching to add it to his collection.

"No, buddy," I scolded. "We can't keep it."

"What's our theory?" Tabitha asked the group.

"I thought it was... maybe a little cold?" the First Year girl said.

I rolled it into my other hand. "It feels warm to me, but we've all been touching it."

"Maybe it's a little heavier than it's supposed to be?" Hudson suggested.

"I didn't feel anything out of the ordinary," a Koigni guy named Nicholas said.

I glanced up to Baine, and he had a light smirk on his face. "Maybe that's the point," I said thoughtfully. "Maybe it *is* just an ordinary stone."

"Then what's the point of the lesson?" Tabitha pointed out. "It has to be something special."

Baine's voice sounded from the front of the room. "Once you've finished examining your stone, please pass it to the group beside you."

We gave ours to the Nivita group and started passing around the blue stone Yapluma had given us. It was exactly the same as the last— nothing out of the ordinary. Same with the green stone we received next.

When I took the red stone from the Yapluma group, I gasped. This one felt different. It was warm in my hand, but not from everyone touching it. This was a different kind of warmth— a fiery glow akin to my own magic. It buzzed like it, too.

"What is it?" Tabitha asked, sensing the wonder in my features.

"I don't know, but it's definitely different." I handed her the stone, then looked around to the other groups. They shared similar looks of wonder, and the chatter in the room began to rise. Whatever was happening had everyone excited— not just us. I was watching a Toaqua girl toss the blue stone into the air when it hit me. We were all lined up with our own colors. Whatever we were feeling with the stones could only be felt by specific Houses.

"What do you feel now?" Baine asked the class. "Do these stones feel different to you?"

A Nivita girl held up their rock. "The green one feels magical!"

"So does the purple," a Yapluma guy said.

"But we didn't feel anything with those ones," a Toaqua First Year argued.

Baine eyed the class curiously, as if waiting for it to click.

I decided to play along and announce my theory. "There must be magic in the stones that resonates with each House. Like we can't feel the Toaqua stone because we don't have Toaqua magic."

Baine smiled proudly and stood up straight. "Precisely, Miss Henley. These stones have been infused with elemental magic, much like the ancient artifacts we've been studying this semester. However, just because magic has been infused into an object doesn't mean all Elementai are capable of harnessing it, or transferring the magic."

"Wait," Hudson said. "So if this stone has Koigni magic in it, any Koigni could use it to enhance their powers?"

"Yes," Baine said. "It can be very helpful if you need an extra boost, or if your magic becomes fatigued."

"Like in times of war?" Tabitha questioned.

She said it casually, like she was honestly curious, but the suggestion sent a shiver down my spine. Is this what we would have to resort to if things came down to it: using our magic or dying?

Baine cleared his throat, like he was uncomfortable with the suggestion. "Yes. Like in times of war."

My hand shot into the air before I could stop myself. Baine's eyebrows rose. "Miss Henley?"

"If we can infuse magic into objects like this, then why don't we use these all the time?" I asked. "I mean, why isn't everyone walking around with an artifact as a back-up power source? Why aren't these things sitting on every street corner?"

If this was how Anichi put Soul magic into my totem, why was this one so special? Why weren't there hundreds all around Kinpago?

"To be perfectly honest, they're not often needed," Baine said. "We each have enough magic to serve our purposes, and that magic can be restored over time. It is only in times of great excess that objects like these are needed. But more than that, Miss Henley, transferring your magic into an object— or moving it from one object to another— is a very difficult, very advanced process. Most Elementai die without ever mastering the process. Most who try are unable to stabilize their magic enough so it can be harnessed. But should you be strong enough— and start practicing the art *now*— it may just give you an edge when you need it."

My blood ran cold with the look Baine gave me. He stared directly at me as he spoke, a heavy weight in his gaze. It was like Baine was trying to tell me something— trying to *challenge* me.

He held my gaze a moment longer before ripping it away to call on another student with their hand raised. I didn't hear what they said, because I was still trying to decipher the message in Baine's stare. He couldn't say it out loud, but I was pretty sure I knew what he meant. He wanted to use these artifacts as weapons.

And he wanted us to start building our arsenal now.

I TOLD my friends about Baine's lesson when we met in the Anichi dorms that night. We were seated around a study table that was covered in Imogen's open textbooks.

"I don't know, guys. It was like... like he was trying to tell me something," I told them.

Imogen inhaled a sharp breath, and her eyes went wide. "He must think you can do it!"

"That can't be," I said quickly. "Baine said it's really complicated, and he didn't teach us how to do it or anything."

"Maybe he wants you to figure it out for yourself," Jonah suggested.

"*Pawee*, you've conjured lightning," Liam pointed out. "I bet this isn't half as difficult."

"Yeah, but I had instruction," I argued.

"You know what?" Imogen grabbed for one of her books and flipped through the pages. "I was researching Spirit Art, and I think I saw a section on transference. Ah! Here it is."

Imogen dropped the heavy book onto the table and began reading. *"Transference is a complicated technique that works by stabilizing magic within an object. It is executed using crystals, although in rare cases, it can be performed on everyday objects."*

Imogen's eyes brightened, and she reached into her bag. "You should try it, Sophia. Baine wants you to."

I shook my head. "I don't even have a crystal."

"Yes, you do." Imogen pulled a cloth bag from her purse and poured a collection of small crystals over the table. Jonah, Liam, and I stared down at them. Esis tried to grab for them, but I held him back.

"What are you doing walking around with crystals?" I asked.

Imogen shrugged. "I got them from Hattie. She said they're supposed to soothe the soul and stuff."

"Im, I'm not ready for this," I insisted.

"What will it hurt?" she pressed.

I bit my lip nervously. "I could burn down the dorms?"

"Psh, you will not," she insisted.

"I'm not that strong," I argued.

Imogen crossed her arms. "Then why would Baine want you to do it?"

"*Pawee*, that's a lie," Liam started. "We all *know* you're strong. You did some amazing things during the tournament, and several times afterward. Don't say it was because of the totem, because it's not. You're a strong Elementai. You just don't want to admit it."

Their stares bored into me. I caved. "I don't know," I said. "But if I'm going to do this, you should all try it with me."

"Fine." Imogen passed a crystal to each of us, then turned back to her book. "It says here that you need to visualize your magic becoming one with the crystal. Funnel it into the object like you're putting it into a box. Let the crystal work on your magic, not your magic on the crystal."

"That makes no sense," I stated.

"Sure it does," Jonah replied.

I frowned. Did Baine seriously expect me to figure out this advanced magic without him?

Imogen sighed. "Tell you what, Sophia. Let's make a bet."

"What kind of bet?" I asked skeptically.

"Obviously, you need some motivation." Imogen reached into her bag and slapped the giant purple dildo she'd bought from the sex shop onto the table.

"Ancestors, Im! You're still carrying that around?" I squeaked.

Liam found it funny. He covered his mouth and snickered. Jonah didn't bother covering his mouth. He flat-out belly laughed so loud I thought someone might hear him.

"If you can get transference before any of us, I'll walk around school holding this thing for a full day," Imogen offered.

My mouth went dry. "And if I *don't* get it?"

Imogen leaned forward and leveled me with a challenging gaze. "Then *you* have to walk around with it for a full day."

I groaned. "Imogen, no. I'm not doing that."

Imogen stomped her foot under the table for show. It startled Sassy at her feet. "Sophia, come on!"

"I'd take it," Liam said with a smirk. "I mean, you're the strongest out of all of us. Imogen's going to lose. Don't you want to see her walk around with that thing?"

An image of Imogen walking into the dining hall waving the dildo above her head entered my mind. I started laughing.

"Plus, public humiliation is a great motivator," Jonah pointed out. He eyed me up and down. "Well, for you, at least."

"Yeah. I'm sure you'd love this," I giggled.

Jonah shrugged innocently. "What can I say? I like me some dick."

I got serious again. "Is there a time limit on this bet?"

Imogen shook her head. "Nope. Whoever gets it first."

"So, when we're like eighty and I figure it out, you'll walk into Orenda Academy carrying *this* dildo," I challenged.

Imogen nodded. "Absolutely."

Now the image in my head was even more hilarious. Imogen would be in her wheelchair rolling into the Great Hall with a giant dildo all like, "*I'm here, bitches!*"

"We'll all take the bet. The three of us against you," Liam said. "If any of us gets it before you do— you lose the bet."

The odds weren't in my favor, but everyone had a point. I hated being the center of attention. If anything would make me master transference, this was it.

"Okay," I agreed. "You have a deal."

Imogen and I shook on it. I turned my attention to the crystal and got to work. I tried to envision my magic entangling with the crystal, but all that happened was I made it kind of hot. I asked Imogen for her book so I could reread the passage, but all it talked about was visualizing your magic. It was a lot like what Doya had taught me about conjuring lighting. I guess it made sense, since magic was inside of you. You couldn't just wave a wand and make it work.

Across the table, Jonah had his eyes squeezed tightly shut. He looked like he was going to shit himself. Well, at least I didn't have to worry about *him* getting it before me. Meanwhile, Liam sat there calmly with his crystal in his hand. He too had his eyes closed, but his features were unreadable. He looked like his mind was somewhere else. Imogen was concentrating hard and narrowing her eyes at her crystal, like it might work through sheer will.

Esis had taken one of the extra crystals and was trying to chew on it, though it was too big to fit in his mouth. Squeaks took a crystal in her beak and closed her eyes like she was trying to do it too. Sassy sat quietly watching Imogen.

It was silent for a long time as we all focused— until finally, Jonah's voice cut through the quietness. He tossed his crystal onto the table and wore a proud smile on his face. "And that's how it's done, ladies and gentlemen!"

He leaned back in his chair and made a crude gesture toward his junk, then crossed his arms proudly.

"You did not," I accused, eyeing him curiously.

Jonah raised an eyebrow. "Oh, really? Wanna bet?"

"I thought that's what we were already doing," I pointed out. "You just want me to carry that thing around." I gestured to the dildo that was still lying on the table.

"I'm serious," Jonah insisted. "Here, check it."

He shoved the crystal in my direction, but I leaned back. "I can't. I'm not Yapluma."

Liam's eyes had gone wide. "Did you really do it, Jonah?"

Imogen had an equally shocked expression on her face.

"I really did!" he cried. "I can feel the magic inside of it."

I couldn't tell if Jonah was lying or not. He sounded dead serious, but I knew he could put an act on when he wanted to.

I crossed my arms. "We're going to have to confirm that."

Jonah nudged Squeaks in the side, who'd come closer to look at the crystal he'd apparently just infused with Yapluma magic. "Tell 'em, Squeaks."

"No," I stated firmly. "We need an impartial Yapluma."

Jonah shrugged. "Okay, so we'll go find one. Follow me."

We gathered our things and hurried behind him out of the dorms. The third floor corridor was pretty bare, so he led us down to the first floor in the direction of the dining hall, where students roamed the halls. Jonah stopped the first Yapluma he saw, an upperclassman named Maddox who'd been resorted into Biyami. His Familiar was nowhere to be seen, as it'd been taken away. Maddox seemed sad, and kind of out of it.

I couldn't blame him. If Esis was taken from me I didn't know what I'd do.

"Hey, Maddox, my man!" Jonah said as we approached him.

"What's up, Jonah?" Maddox asked in a friendly tone. He eyed Liam for a minute, then quickly averted his eyes.

"Can I get your expert advice on something?" Jonah asked, then added, "It's for a class."

Maddox's eyes brightened, like being asked for *expert advice* meant something important. "Sure, man. What's up?"

Jonah cocked his head, and we all followed him down a quieter hall. Jonah pressed his crystal into Maddox's hand. "Can you tell me if you feel anything?"

Maddox held up the crystal to inspect it in the light. He pressed his lips together and hummed through them. "I definitely feel something. Yapluma magic for sure."

I gasped. Liam and I exchanged a glance, like neither of us believed Jonah could do it until now. Had he been holding out on us?

"Dude, where'd you get this?" Maddox asked as he handed it back to Jonah.

Jonah shrugged. "My professor. Told you, it's for a class."

"Well, don't lose it," Maddox warned. "These things are pretty powerful. Good luck on your assignment."

Maddox clapped Jonah on the shoulder before heading back toward the main hall. Nobody spoke until Maddox was out of sight.

"Holy shit, Jonah!" I smacked him on the shoulder. "You seriously did it? How's that possible?"

Squeaks huffed, like she was offended, but Jonah just smirked at me. "Hey, you're not the only one with decent powers."

"Yeah, well, you could've told us you were *amazing*," Imogen joked.

Jonah made a duck face. "Honey, open your eyes. I've *always* been amazing. Who wants dinner?"

Jonah snapped his fingers and walked off swaying his hips, like this whole transference thing was nothing. I just stood there blankly, watching him go. Liam and Imogen were stunned beside me.

"Did *you* know Jonah could do that?" I asked them.

Liam shook his head. "No. I guess he's been held back."

"Well, good for him," Imogen said. "And just so you don't forget, Sophia..."

Imogen pulled the dildo from her bag and handed it to me. "Your punishment starts tomorrow."

❦

THE ONE PERK to losing this bet was that it was Saturday, so I didn't have to walk to my classes carrying a giant dildo. But Imogen also wasn't letting me stay in the Biyami dorms all day.

"Come on, Sophia," she begged. "Sassy needs a walk, and she's not leaving without Esis."

I groaned and joined Imogen for a walk around campus, holding the dildo in one hand and Esis in the other. I blushed a bright pink as a group of Biyami passed us on our way out of the dungeons. Luckily, no one took notice.

"Im, this is ridiculous," I hissed. I hid the dildo behind my back as a few Task Force members passed.

"Nonsense." She beamed, obviously loving this. Her eyes darted from person to person, waiting for someone to notice the dildo in my hand.

Nobody did. People were too absorbed in their thoughts. When she started to get impatient, she led me toward the dining hall.

"Imogen," I protested. "I'm not eating breakfast holding *this*."

I waved it in her face.

It was at that moment that I heard a gasp from down the hall. I looked up to see Doya and Baine talking next to her classroom. Baine had spotted the dildo, and his face had gone pale. He looked like he was going to have a heart attack.

Doya snapped her fingers in front of his face. "Elliot, pay attention!"

Her gaze followed his, and she caught sight of the dildo before I shoved it behind my back. The corners of her lips slammed downward into a frown, and Naomi growled. "Miss Henley, what is the meaning of this?"

I immediately got flustered. "It's, um, not mine. It's... it's Imogen's!"

I shoved the dildo in Imogen's direction, and she snickered. "We share custody."

The blood drained from my face, but Baine looked worse for wear than I was. "L-ladies, perhaps it's b-best if you put that thing away."

Imogen and I were both trying not to laugh. "Yes, sir," I said.

"*Now*, Miss Henley," Doya snapped.

"Ancestors," I mumbled as I shoved it into my bag. Imogen and I continued on down the hall. "What a prude."

"I heard that, Miss Henley!" Doya shouted so loud it made me stop. She stomped over to me and lowered her voice. "The Elders are coming to visit the school today. I suggest you keep that thing where it belongs— *out of sight*! If I didn't have enough on my plate today, I'd be giving you detention."

I was mortified, and for totally different reasons than showing off my latest sex toy. Esis buried his face in my elbow. "Yes, Madame Doya," I answered in a shaky tone. Damn. Her mood swings were giving me whiplash.

Doya whirled around, obviously done with me.

"Don't listen to her," Imogen whispered as we entered the dining hall. "A bet's a bet."

"Imogen," I complained. "You heard what she said. Elders are coming."

"Well, they're not here yet, are they?"

Imogen forced me to bring the dildo back out and leave it on our table while we ate breakfast. Today, it was gross scrambled eggs that tasted like they came from a box. Most of the meal was fine, until someone noticed the dildo sitting on our table and pointed it out. Soon, a bunch of people were looking our way and whispering. Some Koigni jackass even pointed and loudly announced it to his friends.

"Imogen, I think I've been humiliated enough. Can I put it away now?" I begged.

"Nope." She smiled. She was obviously having way too much fun with this.

After breakfast, Imogen and I headed toward a nearby study area. I had a paper to write from Fundamentals of Familiar Magic, and Imogen was working on a design for her fashion major. But when we reached the study area, the chairs were already filled with Defortai students who were laughing about something I didn't hear. Imogen and I turned around right away, but not before one of them spotted us.

Logan— the douchebag Koigni who'd attacked Isabella— jumped up from his chair and followed us. His Familiar stayed put with the other Defortai. Scars ran through the lion's skin from where I'd burned him, creating ugly patches of fur.

Imogen and I tried to ignore Logan, but he hurried in front of us and cut us off. "Sophia. We meet again."

My fingers tightened around the dildo. We were far enough away from the study area now that the other Defortai couldn't see us. "What do you want, Logan? I thought Madame Doya told you to stay the fuck away from me."

"I was never good at following rules." He smirked and glanced down to the dildo in my hand. "I saw your toy at breakfast. You and Mitoh break up again? Looking for a replacement?"

"In your dreams," I spat. My Koigni Fire hovered just below the surface. What was this asshole's deal? Didn't he know by now not to mess with me?

Logan's eyes traveled down my body. "I'd be lying if I said I hadn't dreamt about it. You're hot, Henley."

Ew! Gross!

Imogen took charge. "Get lost, Logan."

"Why don't *you* get lost, chubster?" Logan snarled back.

"Don't even fucking start," I snapped. "What do you really want?"

"Hey, I'm just making an offer," he said.

"Like hell," I shot back. "Last time we talked, I nearly lit your ass on fire. Besides, I'm Biyami, and you're Defortai. I don't believe for a second you'd want a piece of me."

Logan chuckled. "Then you don't know me at all, Henley. I've been screwing Biyami chicks all semester. You're the first to tell me no."

I gasped. I didn't believe it for a second. He'd probably done the same to them as he tried to do to Isabella.

I narrowed my eyes. "You can fuck right off. I'd never sleep with you."

Logan's featured darkened, and his lips turned into a sneer. "I said you'd pay for what you did to my Familiar, Henley. Nobody tells me no."

Logan reached for me, and I yelped as he grabbed hold of my wrist. I yanked back. Thinking quickly, I swung my arm and brought the dildo down on his face as hard as I could. Logan's eyes rolled back into his skull, and he slumped to the ground.

I stood over him, taking shallow breaths as my heart pummeled against my rib cage. A red welt in the shape of a dick was starting to form on Logan's forehead.

"Shit, Imogen!" I cried. "I've killed him!"

"You did not." Imogen grabbed my shaking hand. "We have to go."

I glanced behind me to see Logan's lion Familiar charging at us. I quickly gathered my wits and raced behind Imogen, clutching Esis tightly in my arms. We ran back to the main hallway, only to smack straight into Madame Doya and Chieftess Annette. Doya shot a look down at the dildo in my hands.

"Miss *Henley*," she snarled between gritted teeth.

"We— we were attacked," I said quickly before I could stop myself. My heart was still pounding, and I wasn't thinking straight.

"Attacked?" Annette laughed, like the idea was ludicrous. Her phoenix squawked from beside her. "In broad daylight?"

"It was Logan," I told Doya, ignoring Annette's accusation.

Annette's laughter quickly died down, and she shot me daggers. I bet she was still pissed about all the shit I got away with between me and Haley last semester. She was probably plotting her revenge.

Doya's lips pressed into a thin line. "In my classroom. Now."

Imogen and I practically raced to her classroom and each took a seat at one of the desks.

"Stay here," Doya told us, then she and Annette breezed out of the room with their Familiars.

I didn't know where they had gone or what they were doing. Imogen and I sat in silence for what must've been at least fifteen minutes. It might've been shorter, but I was so on edge that it seemed to take forever. Esis and Sassy got bored and started chasing each other around in the training area next to the fireplace. Eventually, I heard the sound of Doya's heels clicking on the floor outside her room.

"Listen to me, Eleanor," Annette snapped before they'd made it back to the room. "I don't know why you think so highly of this little snake, but you can't protect her forever."

Snake? I was a snake now?

"What do you want me to do, Annette?" Doya replied in a harsh tone. "Let some idiot like Logan kill her?"

"Who cares?" Annette said. "She's Biyami."

Doya gasped, as did I. Imogen's jaw dropped from beside me.

"What are you suggesting, Chieftess?" Doya demanded. "You don't care if we make *murderers* out of our own children?"

My jaw dropped so far it was comical. It was an obvious jab at Haley.

Annette let out a laugh that sounded more evil than anything. "If we have to, yes."

Doya huffed. "You do what you must, Annette, but Sophia Henley isn't getting hurt on my watch."

I could practically hear the smirk in Annette's voice. "The clock's ticking, Eleanor. One of these days, your watch is going to end, and when it does, Sophia Henley isn't going to last very long."

My hands quivered as I heard the sound of Doya's heels once more. I snapped my gaze away from the door, pretending as if we hadn't heard. Doya and Naomi entered alone. "Logan's been taken care of," she started.

"Wait... that's it?" I asked.

"That's it," Doya stated. "You can go now."

Doya looked at me with an indifferent expression. I didn't know why she pretended like she didn't care, when it was obvious that she did. I didn't know *why*— considering I was Biyami and she didn't need me anymore. Maybe she thought I was still useful to whatever plan she was concocting on her own.

Or maybe— just maybe— there was a part of her that still had a heart.

I saw Logan in the hall that afternoon on my way back from the Anichi dorms. He still had the imprint of the dildo on his head, and his hand was wrapped in bandages. I didn't know why, since his hand hadn't been hurt when I left him passed out in the hall. Something told me it had to do with whatever Doya had said or done to him to scare him off. One glance my way and he curled in on himself, like he was terrified.

I continued on my way down the hall. I was alone, no one but Esis with me. He was perched on my shoulder. In my arms, I clutched my mother's scrapbook. I'd hidden it in the Anichi dorms. After the way Doya stuck up for me today, I thought she might appreciate it as a thank-you.

Doya wasn't in her classroom, so I headed to her office and knocked on the door.

"Who is it?" A harsh voice came from inside.

I cleared my throat. "It's Sophia."

"Come in." Doya's tone was bored.

"Hi, Madame Doya," I said timidly as I opened the door. "Can I talk to you?"

Doya looked up from her desk. "If this is about Intermediate Koigni Magic, Sophia, you can visit me during my office hours on Monday—"

"It's not," I said quickly, clutching the book tighter to my chest.

She glanced downward and noticed it for the first time. "Then what is it?"

I stepped further into the room and closed the door behind me. "I found something I wanted to show you. If you have time."

Doya rarely showed emotion other than bitterness and rage, so I was surprised to see curiosity rimmed around her eyes. She stood and gestured to the couch. "I have time."

I sat, and she came to sit beside me on the couch. Naomi didn't move from where she was curled up under Doya's desk.

I ran my hands over the cover. "My grandparents gave me this. It was my mother's."

A look of recognition crossed Doya's features as she gazed down at the book. I couldn't meet her eyes, because I was afraid of how she might react to my request. "I thought maybe... maybe you could tell me more about her?"

Doya's voice came out softer than I'd ever heard it before. "May I see?"

I nodded and handed her the scrapbook. She flipped it open to the first page, and her eyes softened.

She swallowed as she flipped the pages, running her fingers over the faces in the photographs. Holy shit. Was Doya actually showing emotion?

"It's true that Lucy and I were friends," Doya said, though I couldn't read her tone. "I don't know what you expect to learn from me, Sophia."

"Do you have any stories about her?" I asked. "Or my dad?"

The corners of Doya's lips twitched as she stared down at a picture of the three of them in front of the castle. I wasn't sure if she was trying to hide her smile, or didn't know how to smile anymore.

"I have many, Sophia, but to revisit them..." She hesitated, never taking her eyes off the scrapbook. "I can't."

"Well, how'd you two meet?" I asked.

She shook her head, as if trying to push bad memories from her mind. But for whatever reason, she didn't shut me down like I expected. "We knew each other since we were kids. We grew up in the Koigni village together. My father died when I was young, and so my mother would send me over to Lucy's house whenever she needed someone to watch me. But my mother..."

Doya trailed off as she stared down at another picture. She and Lucy were in the Koigni common room dressed in their pajamas. Lucy was bent over with her hand to her mouth and a fake look of shock on her face, while Doya pretended to slap her butt.

"Your mom what?" I asked gently.

Doya took a deep breath and flipped the page. She spoke like she was repeating facts, but her eyes remained on the photos as a hundred memories flickered behind them. "My mother died before I came to Orenda. We had been very close. After she passed, Lucy and her family were all I had."

"So my grandparents... they were like a surrogate family to you?"

Doya nodded.

"What kinds of things did you two do together?" I asked. "Did you have any hobbies? Did you go on double dates?"

Doya's face fell, but she didn't look at me. "No, Lucy didn't approve—"

She stopped in her tracks. I wanted to ask what Lucy didn't approve of, but the dark look in Doya's eyes suggested she wasn't going to tell me.

I looked down to the scrapbook. She'd stopped at a picture of her and Baine. Doya was holding up a certificate and looking up at him in admiration.

Doya's eyes glossed over. She didn't seem to see the picture on the page. After a moment, Doya slammed the book closed and shoved it back in my direction. I thought I caught a glimpse of tears rising to her eyes, but it must've been a trick of the light.

Doya turned away from me to return to her desk, her voice strong. "I'm sorry, Sophia, but there's nothing more I can tell you about your parents."

She turned back to me. "Lucy was a very kind, strong woman. You're very lucky to call her your mother. Now, if you'll excuse me, I have work to get to."

I still burned with questions. I stood on shaky feet. Esis clung tightly to my shoulder. "Madame Doya... what happened?"

Her lips pressed into a thin line. "What do you mean?"

I gestured down to the scrapbook, my hands trembling. "You look so carefree in all these pictures. What changed?"

Doya's eyes darkened as she narrowed them in my direction. "I grew up, Sophia. Eventually, so will you."

My blood ran cold. There was no getting an answer out of her. Doya would never let it show, but I sensed that I'd made her uncomfortable. I thought she might appreciate this— I was wrong.

"Yes, Madame Doya. Sorry to bother you." I started for the door.

Doya muttered something, but it wasn't meant for me to hear. I could've sworn, though, that I heard her say, "It was no bother at all."

&

WHEN I RETURNED to the Anichi dorms to put my scrapbook away, Imogen was bawling. I dropped the book onto the nearest table and rushed to her. Liam and Jonah sat on either side of her and tried to calm her down. Sassy was rubbing her nose on Imogen's face, but Imogen sobbed so hard that nothing anyone did seemed to work. Esis jumped off my shoulder as I knelt in front of Imogen and took one of her hands in mine.

"Ancestors, Im," I cried. "What happened?"

"T-they're g-gone," Imogen sobbed.

"I'm sure they're okay," Liam said gently.

"Who? What's going on?" I demanded.

Imogen ignored my question and opened her other hand to reveal a piece of paper crumpled up inside. "Does it sound like they're fine to you? *Imogen, if you find this, we're safe. Don't worry. Mom and Dad.*"

"Wait." My breath stalled in my chest. "Your family is gone, too?"

Jonah pressed his lips together. "And you guys wouldn't believe me when I said people were hiding shit from us. First Amelia and Sophia's parents, now Imogen's family. Where's everyone going, and why are they leaving us behind?"

I shook my head. "Jonah's right. That doesn't sound like them."

"They must have a good reason," Liam argued.

Imogen sniffled. "Yeah, like the Task Force got them and forced them to write these notes."

"I don't think they'd do that," Liam said, rubbing Imogen's back. "And if they did, your families would've left some sort of code, wouldn't they? To let you know something wasn't right."

"This isn't right!" Imogen waved the letter in front of Liam's face.

"My family wouldn't just leave me behind without saying goodbye! Mom, Dad, Levi, Quentin, Soren, Roland... they're all gone!"

"Imogen, where did you find this?" I asked.

Sobs bubbled up in her throat again. "While you were doing your t-thing, I t-took a peryton to the Nivita village to grab some books from our library. But the house was empty, and this was on the t-table."

Imogen let out a high-pitched wail again, and Sassy nuzzled even closer to Imogen. My hands curled into fists as I watched her break down. Jonah pressed his fingers to his eyes, then shot to his feet in a fit of rage. He stomped across the room toward the door.

I stood in alarm. "Jonah, where are you going?"

He whirled back toward us. "We can't just keep sitting around while everyone around us keeps leaving. We're staying for the Air piece, right? Well, it's time we got it so we can fucking leave this place. I'm not taking no for an answer."

Jonah's heavy footsteps echoed throughout the room, and Squeaks' hooves clicked behind him. I shot Liam a worried look, and he quickly said, "I don't know what he's planning, but we should probably go after him."

Imogen wiped her tears, and the three of us hurried down the stairs behind Jonah. He was pretty far ahead of us now. Liam was having a hard time keeping up.

"Jonah, stop!" Imogen cried down the hall. He just kept walking. "Where are you going? Please!"

Jonah didn't stop until he was standing in front of Dean Alizeh's office. He landed a heavy fist to the door over and over again until it popped open and Dean Alizeh stuck her head out.

Her face fell. "Not you again."

Jonah stuck his foot in the door before she could slam it in his face. "I know what you're going to say, but here's the deal. People are disap-pearing off the street, and if we don't do something about it, all the bloodshed in this war is going to be on *your* hands. So I'm going to ask you one last time to help us, or so help the ancestors, I will rain down the wrath of Jonah Chanee on your ass so hard even the ancestors won't show mercy."

"Jonah," Imogen protested with a groan.

"Imogen, I won't stand for this!" Jonah cried. "Your family is gone. Who's next? We can't keep dragging this out."

Dean Alizeh's brow knitted tightly, and her lips pressed into a thin line. "Mister Chanee, you are way out of line! I've told you many times, and I won't repeat it again. *I. Am. Not. The. Storm. Lord.* Even if I wanted to help you, I couldn't. So I suggest you leave me alone, or I will flunk you."

"Go ahead," Jonah said, calling her bluff. "I know you're lying. So I'm going to sit here until you decide you want to actually help the Hawkei."

"Fine with me," she snapped. "Make yourself comfortable."

At that, Dean Alizeh shoved Jonah's foot out of the way and slammed the door. We heard the sound of the lock slipping shut behind her.

My shoulders fell. "Well, that didn't go well."

Jonah crossed his arms and slumped to the ground. Squeaks plopped down beside him. "I mean it. I'm not leaving. I won't let these disappearances be in vain."

Imogen knelt beside him and placed a gentle hand on his knee. "Jonah, I really appreciate that, but I don't think she's going to help us."

"Then what do we *do*?" Tears rose to Jonah's eyes.

Imogen sighed and sat next to Jonah, leaning her head against his shoulder. He wrapped her in his arms, and the two rocked back and forth together.

"I don't know anymore," Imogen whispered before a fresh wave of tears began to streak her cheeks. "I just want this to be over with."

Jonah squeezed her tighter. "Soon, baby doll. Soon."

I spent all night trying to calculate the similarities between my sister's and the Ahnild family's disappearance. They happened too close together, and were too similar to write off as a coincidence. Had her family been pushed to leave by the Task Force, like Amelia and Trevor had been? Is that even what had happened to my sister?

I didn't know. I didn't know anything. Why hadn't anyone given us more information? Why hadn't they asked us to come with? Were they both so rushed that they didn't have time to come get us? Or was there really some underlying conspiracy and they were all in danger? I didn't even know where to start to get answers.

Liam seemed to notice my unease the next day, because he suggested we go visit Adriel to get my mind off things. I agreed, mostly because I wanted to get away from the castle.

The group home was a welcome change to the darkness surrounding Orenda Academy. The kids here didn't seem to have any idea what was going on outside these four walls, so they were happy and energetic when we arrived. It was play time, so after Miss Evangeline greeted us, we went over to play with Adriel in his favorite spot by the blocks.

"Sophia. Blue." Adriel held up a blue block.

"Good job, Adriel," I praised.

Baby, the hippogriff, ran up when he saw us and started nipping at Esis's tail. Esis jumped down and chased him around.

"Aminals. Aminals!" Adriel cried to Liam.

Liam chuckled and unscrewed the cap on his water bottle. He'd brought it along just in case Adriel asked him to show him the water animals again. Adriel giggled as Liam made images of birds in the water, and had two lion cubs chase each other around on the carpet.

"Miss Evangeline White," a voice boomed across the playroom.

Liam and I startled, and the water creatures he'd created melted into puddles on the floor. Adriel let out a disgruntled scream, while the rest of the room had gone quiet. We turned to see at least a dozen Task Force members step into the room.

Miss Evangeline came forward nervously. "I am she. May I help you?"

The man in front pulled a piece of paper from his breast pocket and handed it to her. "We have a warrant for your arrest."

Miss Evangeline gaped at him as she unfolded the paper. "My arrest? What are the charges?"

"Child abuse and endangerment," he stated firmly and without emotion.

Liam and I gasped. Several children shrank behind their toys to hide. The two adult helpers looked utterly shocked.

My heart pounded wildly. There was no *way* what they were accusing her of was true. Miss Evangeline was one of the sweetest people I'd ever met, and she loved the kids as her own.

Miss Evangeline's eyes widened as she scanned the paper. "*Malnourishment?* Is this a joke?"

"You can bring it up at your hearing," the Task Force member told her. "Now, we can do this the easy way, or the hard way."

"These kids have never gone more than a few hours without eating!" Miss Evangeline protested. It was the loudest I'd ever heard her raise her voice. She shot a quick glance around the room and lowered her voice, like she didn't want the kids to see her lose it. "We keep records. I can show you." Her eyes darted across the page. "And what's this? *Mental and physical abuse?* I demand to see your evidence."

"It doesn't work like that, sweetheart," the Task Force member said. "It looks like we're going to have to do this the hard way."

He reached for her, and she screamed. "Ow! Please, not in front of the children."

"You should've come when you were told, then," he snarled.

He gripped tightly to her wrist and twisted it around her back. She cried out in pain. Several children had started to cry, and the other adults had frozen up. Her Familiar, a small hummingbird, dove for the Task Force member, but he merely swatted it out of the way. A wave of heat flashed through my body. I knew I was going to lose it at any second.

I shot to my feet. "Hey, take it easy on her!"

Liam was on his feet beside me in under a second. He grabbed my hand, as if to hold me back.

"Watch it," the Task Force member snapped as he pulled a pair of cuffs from his belt and secured it around Miss Evangeline's wrist. "Or you'll be next."

"Ow," Miss Evangeline cried. "That's too tight. You're hurting me. I'll come willingly."

"Stop resisting," he growled as he slapped the other side of the cuffs onto her wrist. He yanked on her shoulder, and she stumbled to the side. He must've took it as an attempt to escape, because he shoved her to the ground and jumped on top of her, squishing her face into the ground. "Are you done? Are you fucking done!?"

Tears streamed down Miss Evangeline's face, and my whole body quivered. I wanted to step in and help her, but I was no match against a dozen Task Force members— even if Liam and the few helpers stepped in with me.

"Stop it!" I yelled. "She said she'd come willingly!"

"You!" He pointed a gloved finger at me. "Shut your trap. And you." He leaned his face down so close to Miss Evangeline's that I bet she could feel his breath beneath his helmet. "You'll do as you're told."

"Okay, okay," she sobbed. "Please, just leave everyone else out of it."

He yanked Miss Evangeline to her feet and smacked her on the side of the head when she stumbled again. Terrified sobs from the children echoed throughout the room.

The main Task Force guy turned to his back-up. "You deal with the rest of them."

My blood ran cold as they scattered throughout the room and started grabbing children. "Wait!" I shouted at the one who made a beeline for Adriel. I threw myself between them. "What are you doing? The children have done nothing wrong!"

Then again, I didn't believe for a second that Miss Evangeline had done anything wrong, either.

"This home is being shut down," the Task Force member informed me. They had a higher voice— it might've even been a woman. "The children will be taken to a safe and secure facility while Miss White awaits her trial."

She reached down and grabbed Adriel by the elbow. "Come on, kid."

He screeched like he was in pain and kicked out of her hold. She grabbed for him again, holding him so hard he couldn't struggle away. The sound of Adriel's cries— mixed with that of the other kids'— made me want to hurl a fireball at the lot of Task Force members. It was like an arrow shot straight into my heart. I couldn't take it.

"You can't do this!" I shouted. I lunged forward to free Adriel, but Liam's arm caught me around the middle. I felt like I was being sling-shotted backward as my body slammed into his.

"Sophia, you can't stop this," he whispered in my ear.

"Sophia! Sophia!" Adriel cried as the evil woman dragged him away. He reached out toward me, but we couldn't reach each other.

"Liam, let go!" I shouted. I was ready to blow this whole place to kingdom come. Tears streamed down my cheeks. Esis was running back and forth at my feet, screeching and tugging on his ears.

"Sophia, you fight, and you'll be arrested too," Liam reminded me.

I glanced over and saw a Task Force member aiming a noxite gun at me. I stilled in Liam's arms, but my whole body quaked. I couldn't stop the flood of tears running down my cheeks. Meanwhile, Adriel was having a meltdown as the woman tried to drag him away. The man holding the noxite gun shifted the barrel and pointed it straight at Adriel.

"Do it," the woman sneered. She had Adriel by the neck now, obviously unable to hold on to him.

Suddenly, it felt like the whole room had gone silent. I heard the sound of the trigger and the *zip* as the dart sped across the room and into Adriel's thigh. It was like everything happened in slow motion— like everything was crumbling down around me.

"Adriel!" I screamed, the shriek echoing through my ears.

But he was gone before I could say goodbye.

My attention was stolen by a Task Force member who was shoving the young Familiars into cages. He tossed Baby inside with the others with no regard to their cramped space, then reached down for Esis. Esis snapped at him and growled.

"He's mine," I seethed.

The Task Force member backed off. I turned my face into Liam's shoulder as the sound of protests continued around us. The two employees who'd been playing with the kids were put into handcuffs and dragged away behind Miss Evangeline. Several other kids were shot with noxite guns for no reason at all.

Before I knew it, the play room had gone completely silent. The Task Force was gone— and they'd taken everyone associated with the home with them.

My knees buckled, and I slumped to the ground.

"Sophia! *Pawee!*" Liam placed his hand on the side of my face to help bring me back to reality.

I shook my head. I couldn't believe what I'd just seen. I blinked away they tears, but they just kept coming. "Liam, that was wrong. That was *so wrong*. Why didn't you let me fight back?"

"We can, *pawee*, but not here. Not like this," he said gently, though his voice shook. He was obviously horrified by what he'd just seen. "We can't fight for these kids from jail."

I nodded. I had to agree with his reasoning. It was good he was here so I didn't go all Koigni Bitch on their asses. They'd all be burnt to a crisp by now, and my ass would be in a cell not long after.

"It's not true," I whispered. "What they said about Miss Evangeline. She'd never hurt the kids."

"I know, Soph," Liam said.

"They made it up to take the kids," I accused. "It's those camps you heard them talking about. I bet they're doing it to divide the tribe— to use the kids as hostages so Biyami doesn't fight back."

"I think you're right, *pawee*," Liam agreed. "But—"

"No buts," I snapped so fiercely Esis jumped. "We keep waiting for some big battle to break out, but *I'm done*. This is the last straw."

I got to my feet as stone cold resolve washed over me. "Whatever their plan is, it isn't going to work. It's time we bring the battle to them and end this once and for all."

SEVENTEEN

Sophia had changed ever since Adriel had been taken away. She used to be terrified. She used to keep her head down and pray nobody would notice her.

Now a fire burned in her gaze whenever the Task Force walked by. A hard look came upon her face, and flames flickered upon her fingertips. Sometimes she shook. Her whole form quivered with slightly concealed rage— rage that was bursting at the edges of her being and begging to erupt.

She was fucking ruthless. Which scared the hell out of me. Now she and Imogen were both walking around like loose cannons. Both of them were about to snap. It was like they were looking for any reason to get back at the Elders and set things straight.

I couldn't blame her. Watching those kids get taken away by the Task Force was one of the most difficult things I'd ever been forced to do. I'd *never* seen Sophia like that. Her grief and wrath were beyond anything I'd ever imagined. Even I was afraid of her, in that moment.

I knew they'd taken the kids to the internment camps, but I didn't know where. No one did. So many Biyami, adults and children, were missing now. The only Biyami left, it seemed, were the ones at the school.

And the Task Force were definitely closing in. I couldn't explain it.

There was an underlying tension at Orenda Academy that had no name or face. Students, both Biyami and Defortai, were walking on edge. It was like all of us had predicted something big was going to happen, and nobody knew what it was.

Only that it'd be terrible when it did.

My instincts were screaming at me to get the fuck out. And ever since the group home had been raided, it was all I wanted to do. Jonah was right. We needed to leave. But how, I wasn't sure. It felt like we were trapped rats in a cage, and predators were closing in.

I didn't know if it mattered anymore that we didn't have a plan and had nowhere to go. All that mattered was we needed to stay alive. We'd helped so many people escape the castle. Now we had to escape ourselves.

I had a rotten feeling we'd waited too long. It was too late.

I was still running through multiple scenarios in my head days later, on Thursday at noon. None of the possibilities I came up with for getting out of here seemed plausible. We could escape through use of the Anichi dorms, but once we did, how would we survive afterwards? And how could I leave my family behind? They still needed me. If I left, I wanted them to come with me.

I was dropping off a paper for Baine and returning to the Biyami dorms when I got distracted. Biyami students were supposed to take the long way around school, as the Atrium was forbidden to them. But when I looked through the glass and saw that piece of shit Logan sitting on the fountain next to his lion Familiar, I couldn't give a fuck about the rules.

He'd messed with Sophia *twice* now, which was a bad move for him. It was time I put the bastard in his place.

I stormed through the Atrium and didn't slow my pace as I approached. People stopped talking, and eyes locked on my form. There weren't any Task Force around, but I couldn't care less if there were.

Logan's gaze narrowed, and his lion growled as I came near. His hand was still wrapped up, and the dick-shaped bruise was still prominent on his forehead where Sophia had hit him.

I hoped the fucker had a permanent mark. The world deserved to know what a dickhead he really was.

"Think you can threaten *my girl* and get away with it?" I challenged loudly. Logan stood up from the fountain— his lion crouched downward, ready to pounce.

"I don't see you doing anything about it," he threw at me. A fireball immediately conjured in his good hand, and the lion bared his teeth.

"How about I break your fucking neck?" I summoned water from the fountain he was sitting on, and it flowed around me in a rushing cyclone. The fire immediately grew around Logan's hand until it was running all the way up his arm. A circle of students had formed around us, holding their breath in anticipation.

Logan threw back his head and gave a mocking laugh. "You couldn't if you tried."

"Fucking bring it." I was going to suffocate this jackass. Let's see what kind of derogatory things came out of his mouth when his lungs were full of water.

Logan sneered. "After I get done with you, Henley's all mine. I'll make her come like you never have before."

My temper totally snapped. Logan and I both drew our arms back at the same time, but a sharp voice cut us off. "Mister Mitoh!"

Madame Doya stood merely a few feet away. Her face was burning and intense. Scarier than I'd ever seen it.

I wouldn't have hesitated to use my magic for anyone else. For some reason, her tone held me back from doing the worst.

Naomi was at her side, and she leapt forward. Her strong charge pinned Logan's Familiar to the ground. The lion groaned as Naomi snarled and immediately locked her fangs on to the creature's throat. The lion froze, terror in its eyes. He knew Naomi wouldn't hesitate to rip his neck open.

At the sight of Doya, Logan's eyes contracted. He immediately ran off. Naomi let Logan's lion go free, and the Familiar scampered away with a low whimper.

Doya's cruel gaze swept around the Atrium, and people dispersed. She gave a disgusted sniff as she looked at me. "Biyami aren't permitted in this area, Mister Mitoh."

That's what she fucking cared about? "I was merely protecting my own," I shot at her.

Doya's eyes flashed at that. "Sophia is not *your own*."

What was it with her? It was like she was possessive over Sophia or something. "Logan threatened to rape Sophia last week."

"I'm well aware of the situation, and dealing with it. I have made it clear to Mister Melborne that if he dares to harm Sophia, I will deal with him in a *very permanent* way. There is no need for you to get involved." Doya hesitated. "Though I do appreciate you defending her."

Holy shit, she actually thanked me for something. Count me impressed.

Doya raised a critical eyebrow and said, "You have already put Sophia in enough danger. I've got my eye on you, Mitoh, and I'm watching. Be careful where you tread. Before I deal with *you* as well."

Doya swept away, and Naomi prowled at her side. I was equally confused and offended. I knew Doya hated me— that much was obvious. Her dislike for me had only increased after she found out I was dating Sophia. Yet Doya had thanked me for protecting her... just before warning me to back off.

I wondered if proposing to Sophia would be enough to make me Doya's target. Dating was one thing— marriage was something else entirely. She'd probably try to kill me before the wedding even happened.

Like I cared. Doya could threaten me all she wanted. It wasn't going to stop me.

Well, that whole encounter ruined my morning. I was pretty pissed off. I needed to go for a walk and cool down. As I rounded an isolated corner, someone grabbed my arm. I immediately reacted, thinking that either the Task Force or a Defortai were fucking with me, but the water ball died in my hand when I saw that it was just my dad.

"What are you doing here?" I whispered. "And Dad... holy fuck."

He had a black eye, and a couple of bruises. Tatum wasn't here. What had happened?

"I've come to tell you plans have changed," he whispered. He glanced around to make sure we were alone before he said, "Madame Wells and I are specifically being targeted. Neither my word nor hers makes any difference anymore on the Elder Council."

"So what are you going to do?" My heart was pounding.

"I'm moving as much of the tribe as I can to another location. Kinpago isn't safe for the Toaqua anymore," Dad said.

"But I thought we were staying here to fight back?"

"There's another way," Dad said. "Ezra is rounding up the rest of the family as we speak. We leave tomorrow at dawn, to join the other Toaqua. Son, you need to come with us."

My mouth went dry. "I can't leave my friends."

"Bring all of them. There's enough room."

My eyes widened. "What are you saying? Have you been working on a place for the Water tribe to evacuate?"

"Yes. It was a last resort, one we unfortunately have to take." Dad seemed somber. The look on his face was tired— like he'd been up all night.

I wanted to find the person who'd given him a black eye and make them suffer.

"Where are we going? Is it far?" I asked.

"I can't explain anything here. It's too risky we'll be overheard." Dad's tone was completely serious. "Just know that you have to trust me. Gather your friends, and we'll meet at the house at midnight. Everything will be revealed."

Dad swept away. My mouth was dry, and my hands were shaking. Dad had a way out. We just had to get through today and tomorrow.

I needed to tell the others. Sophia was between classes, and I was betting the other two were at lunch. With luck, I found them clustered together in a ragged booth in the dining hall. Jonah and Imogen were leaning against each other. Sassy played mindlessly with a piece of potato, which Squeaks and Esis nudged back without much interest.

Nobody was eating. The food the school provided us was gross, and no one had much of an appetite these days. It was like we showed up for lunch out of habit more than anything else.

Sophia was sketching— writing— I don't know— furiously in a notebook she'd acquired. I didn't think it was for class. Her expression was hard and unforgiving as the pencil moved over the paper. She closed the notebook as I approached and shoved it in her bag with a rough vigor.

"We need to talk," I whispered. They knew what I meant by the tone in my voice.

We split up on our way to the Anichi dorms. It wasn't safe for us to walk in one big group anymore. It attracted too much attention. When we regathered in the safety of the Anichi dorms, I didn't waste any time. "My dad talked to me. He said he's moving the Water tribe to a safe location. He doesn't have any standing on the council anymore and is getting my entire family out. Ezra is helping them escape now. Dad told me that he wants us to come with him, and I think we should go."

Jonah's shoulders sagged in obvious relief. Imogen opened her mouth to say something, but Sophia got there first. "Liam, I want to go, but what about those children in the camps?" she asked viciously. "We can't leave now and let them stay there to rot."

"No one's saying that. I'm sure my dad has a plan to get them out, we just have to be patient," I responded.

"Like hell! I'm not waiting." Sophia's voice rose. "We have to storm into those camps and free those kids!"

"Soph, I want to do that, too, but the four of us can't take on the entire Task Force by ourselves," I pleaded. "Dad said he has a safe place. I bet it'll be easier to gather people to help us once we're far away from here. We need an army if we're going to shut those camps down."

Sophia fumed, but I could tell she agreed with me. "Fine," she said. "We get out of here, we get some Elementai around, and we fight back."

"We can fight back *here*." Imogen's hands were bunched into fists. "We can't abandon the tribe now."

"Im, doesn't it make more sense to get away from the problem and figure out how to deal with it then, instead of constantly being in danger?" Jonah asked. "We can't strategize if we're too preoccupied with always watching our backs."

Jonah's logic worked its way into Imogen's head. She gave a sigh of defeat. "You're probably right. But I don't like leaving the prophecy open. I wish we had enough time to figure out what this Air piece means."

"Won't it be easier to research the Air piece once we're safe, anyway? It'll be harder, but not impossible," I suggested.

"Maybe." Imogen tapped her chin. "Though we've exhausted every clue we could think of."

Something sparked in Jonah's eyes. "No, we haven't. I just thought of something."

"What is it?" Imogen asked in interest.

"Follow me to the library. It might be a dead end, but I want to make sure, just in case." Jonah looked to me. "Where are we meeting tonight, Liam?"

I wracked my brain for places to meet up. We could leave through the Anichi tunnel, but the woods there were being so heavily guarded lately I feared we'd get caught. We had to head the other direction. "The waterfall, seven o'clock tonight. Pack only what's necessary. We'll go to my parents' house from there."

Jonah nodded. He and Imogen left with their Familiars. I looked at Sophia and jerked my head. "Come on. I'll walk you to class."

"Why are we even going to class if we're leaving? Seems kind of pointless," she responded. Esis leapt into her arms and cooed.

"We don't want to raise unnecessary suspicion. Skipping classes makes it look like we're preparing to run," I pointed out.

"Good point." She hugged Esis closer to her. "Liam, I heard what happened between you and Logan earlier. What you did was sweet, but it's going to get you in trouble. You don't need to stick up for me. I can handle myself."

"Fuck that. I'll kill anybody who puts their hands on you," I spat.

Sophia gave a tiny smile. "Well, thanks for defending me."

"You never have to thank me. If anyone *ever* tried to hurt you, they'd have to kill me first. That's my promise, Soph."

Her smile faltered. "That's what I'm worried about."

I dropped Sophia off at Intermediate Koigni Magic. I wasn't scared to leave her there. With Doya around, nobody would touch her.

I had a few things to do before we left. My class wasn't until later on tonight. I knew I had to get ready to go, but I wanted to make sure things were taken care of here before I left.

When the Elders came to the school last week, Sophia had told me everything she'd overheard in Doya's office. Annette had threatened Doya, and said she was going to take Sophia's life. It wasn't going to stop, even if we were on the run. Which meant I was planning on taking her bitch-ass out first. We'd deal with Oleander later. But if I wouldn't be here to kill Annette, I needed to ask someone else to finish the job.

I'd been giving some thought on how to eliminate Annette, and figured poison was the best idea— some potions didn't leave traces behind in toxicology reports, and therefore, wouldn't arouse suspicion during an autopsy. But I wasn't a skilled alchemist, so I didn't know which ones to use.

Maddie was an exceptional alchemist for her age, but I didn't want to bring her into this. I didn't know who to ask for help.

"You need to back the hell up. Before I *make* you."

A familiar voice rang throughout the hall. I turned around. It was Mia. She was standing in front of a First Year girl, who was shaking and crying against the wall.

Mia's canine Familiar, Taryn, stood dutifully by her side. Directly across from her was Courtney— the bitch in my old Hawkei Leadership class last semester. Her large, rainbow-feathered bird snapped its beak at Taryn, who growled back.

Courtney sneered. "Why do you care, Mia? Willow's a Biyami. You shouldn't be defending her."

"Just because she's Biyami doesn't mean she has to do what you say," Mia snapped back. "Find someone else to kiss your ass."

Courtney's nose wrinkled. "What is your fiancé gonna think, you sticking up for a dirty Biyami?"

"I don't know. What's *yours* gonna think when I tell him you've been sleeping around with Gray Daniels?" Mia smirked.

Courtney's visage darkened. "You wouldn't dare."

"Try me." Mia's eyes narrowed.

Courtney looked to Willow. She backed away slowly and gave Mia a dirty look. "This isn't over. You're going down for being a filthy Biyami-lover."

"Tell Gray I said hi," Mia shouted loudly as she left. Courtney cringed and fled the scene.

Mia turned back around. Willow was still shaking. "Are you okay?" Mia whispered.

Willow sniffed and wiped the tears off her cheeks. "Yeah. I— I guess so."

"I'm sorry." Mia wrapped Willow in a hug. "You shouldn't have to go through that."

Willow sobbed again, then shook her head in an attempt to pull herself together. "Thanks for standing up for me."

"Don't worry about it. She comes at you again, you let me know. I've been praying for a chance to show Courtney she's not the toughest bitch in the room." Mia gave Willow a smile. She smiled back tearfully before scampering off.

It clicked in my head then. Mia. I needed her help. She was minoring in Alchemy. She'd know exactly what to give Annette to take her out.

I knew I was going against our voting policy in asking for her aid and revealing the Anichi dorms to her, but there was no time to gather a vote. Dad had told me to get ready to leave. We had hours. Mia hadn't helped us much with the smuggling missions, but she had been a pretty good informant as to who needed to escape school. She'd saved several people's lives. She hadn't turned us in, either, which meant we could trust her. She was in the halls defending a Biyami, for ancestors' sake. It was obvious she was on our side.

I was backed into a corner. I had to ask for Mia's help.

I caught Mia's eyes once Willow was gone. She immediately made her way over to me.

"I know that look on your face," she said. "What's going on?" Taryn barked in agreement.

I looked around, then gestured for her to follow me. I walked ahead of her in silence— she clutched her books to her chest, eyes darting from left to right.

"Where are we going?" Mia asked.

"I need to show you something," I whispered. It was a short walk to the tower from here. Mia asked no questions as we took the winding steps upward. At her side, Taryn remained quiet.

When we reached the top, Mia's mouth dropped open. "Wow." Mia turned in place. "This is amazing. Are these—?"

"The Anichi dorms," I finished for her. "There's a tunnel here leading to the grounds. It's how we've been sneaking people out."

Mia looked at me. "Why are you showing this to me now?"

"Because I'm getting out of here, Mia. My family and I are leaving town tonight," I told her.

"But the mission still stands. I need someone to finish the job."

"What's the mission?" Mia knelt and stroked Taryn's ears. "I'll help in any way I can."

I took a breath. "Chieftess Annette has to go. Something that won't draw suspicion to Toaqua. I was thinking poison."

Mia stilled. "Liam... you're asking me to commit murder."

"I know." I crossed my arms. "I wouldn't ask if I had any other option, but you're the only person who I know is smart enough to do it without getting caught. I know it's taking a life, but hundreds more will die if she's not dealt with. Her obsession with power can't be contained unless it's dealt with permanently."

Mia stared at the floor. "I know you're right. There are some poisons I can brew that would take care of her. Stuff the Task Force couldn't trace."

"So you *can* do it?" I pressed.

Mia bit her lip. "Why do you trust me with this? I cheated on you."

"That's all in the past. I don't care about that anymore," I said. "What's important now is doing what's best for the tribe."

Mia hesitated. "What do you need me to do?"

"Continue our work while we're gone. Keep smuggling people out," I told her. "And finish Annette. I wouldn't ask if I had any other choice. Otherwise, I'd do the job myself."

Mia waited a few long moments before she said, "Okay. I'm in. You can count on me."

"Thanks, Mia." It felt like a large weight had been removed from my shoulders. "I don't know how I'll ever repay you for this."

Mia avoided my eyes as she rose to her feet. "Where is your dad taking you?"

"If I knew, I'd tell you. But he's keeping it a secret," I said.

"It's probably for the best," she responded. "Good luck, Liam."

"You too." I felt terrible putting this on her. I didn't know how I could ask Mia to take a life.

But it wasn't like I had any other option. It was Annette or Sophia. And if that was the case, I'd always pick Sophia.

I just hoped Mia got away with it. I wouldn't forgive myself if she didn't.

&

I WAS COUNTING the hours until I met up with the others later so we could leave. Going to class felt pointless, but not showing up would draw attention, so I dragged myself to Professor Cheveyo's classroom for War and Negotiation at four o'clock just like any other Thursday.

The old warrior seemed more somber than usual as he prepared for today's lecture. A projection screen was set up at the head of the room, which Cheveyo was gathering slides for.

His Appaloosa Familiar was on high alert, and kept sending looks at the door, ears twitching as he listened intently. I sat next to Wyatt and Lira at our usual desk and tried to appear as casual as possible, but shit, it was hard. Only a few more hours and we'd be far away from here. Safe, for freaking once.

"You okay?" Wyatt whispered. Lira leaned in— she seemed similarly concerned.

I must've looked pale. "I'm fine," I said. "Just don't feel well today."

It was nice sometimes to use that as an excuse, even though more often than not it was true. I wanted to tell them I was leaving tonight, but I worried it might compromise my exit. I figured they were Toaqua, too, so maybe their families were involved in the exodus my dad was preparing and nobody wanted to say anything for fear of being overheard.

My answer satisfied Wyatt and Lira. They sat back in their seats, and the chatter in the room died down as Professor Cheveyo stood from his desk and began to speak.

"I suggest you all listen very closely today," he began. "This lesson will be on the exam."

A couple people groaned, but I caught something in Cheveyo's tone the others didn't. I didn't think this lesson would be on the exam at all. I think he wanted us to pay attention for entirely other reasons.

Cheveyo crossed his arms. "This semester, we've been learning about the various magical wars that have taken place over the centuries

— primarily the wars that the Hawkei have participated in. This lesson focuses on what is known today as the greatest magical conflict of our time."

Cheveyo turned off the lights and began the slide show. Images on the screen showed ruined battlefields— destroyed buildings and lifeless bodies lying on the streets. They didn't look too different from what I'd experienced in the riots.

Cheveyo stood near the screen. "Eighty years ago, there was a division among the magical community. Some within our supernatural world wanted to expose our kind to humans, so that we could live alongside them, and eventually, learn to control them. Others feared that this would be too dangerous, and that living in isolation would be safer for the supernatural community, as human technology was feared to be more powerful than magic. The opposite side argued that was exactly why the supernaturals needed to take control of the human threat; to stop human sciences before it became too late. This accumulated into a conflict called the Great Supernatural War."

More slides played across the screen as Cheveyo talked. It was hard to look at them— I saw too many similarities between the photographs of old and what was going on now. I tried focusing on my textbook instead, but the words blurred together as Cheveyo continued.

"The Arcanea— shifters and their sorceress mates— began the war by attacking the Miriamic Coven. The witches and warlocks fought back. That inciting incident was the spark that caused things to erupt in the magical world," Cheveyo began. "The Midnighters... the vampires and succubae... joined the Arcanea alongside the Celestials, otherwise known as angels. Meanwhile, the Atlanteans, mermaids, sided with the Miriamic Coven with the help of the Astromancers— talented enchanters."

Lira raised her hand. "What's the difference between an enchanter and a witch?"

"Enchanters are gifted with the potential to harness the abilities of space and astronomy," he replied. "They use the power of the stars and the zodiac to channel their magic."

Lira nodded. "That makes sense."

The slide changed. A photo of angels, vampires, witches, mermaids and enchanters took up the screen. Each of them were using their magical powers to try and win the fight. All I saw was people killing each other.

Cheveyo pointed to the screen. "The Arcanea, the Midnighters, and the Celestials all wanted to control the human world and gain dominion over it. The Miriamic Coven, the Atlanteans, and the Astromancers insisted that the magical world have no part in human affairs. So began a bloody conflict that lasted for six years, from 1939 to 1945."

"Those are the same years as World War II," Wyatt spoke.

"World War II was an excellent cover-up for the bloodshed happening between the magical races," Cheveyo said. "The Elementai did their best to remain uninvolved. We had friends on both sides, and didn't wish to make any enemies. But our involvement became necessary in 1941, when the Elven Union was exterminated."

I nodded. My grandfather had been one of the people who'd fought in the Supernatural War. He'd only been a teenager at the time. He hardly spoke of it, but when he did, he always mentioned the terrible atrocities the Elves had endured.

Cheveyo's frown deepened. "The Arcanea, Midnighters, and Celestials committed a terrible genocide against the Elves, who'd sided with the Miriamic Coven. They targeted the Elves directly and eliminated every last person in their race. It wasn't long before the Elven Union was completely wiped out."

Cheveyo began circulating the room. "After the Elves became extinct, the Elementai knew we could sit out no longer. Something had to be done, before the supernatural world collapsed. The Hawkei were nearly exterminated by humans long ago, and we refused to expose ourselves again. We sided with the Miriamic Coven, and fought for the right to conceal our magic. We eventually won the war in 1945. A treaty was signed, and all races agreed we would continue to conceal our magic as we had done in the past. So far, there has been peace."

So far. Who knew how long that was going to last?

"I'm confused. I thought the Hawkei were allies with the Arcanea. We trade with them all the time. Aren't they mad they lost the war?" Lira asked.

"Reparations were made after the war. There were countless negotiations on both sides to ensure everyone came out with a fair deal. The Hawkei and the Arcanea repaired their relationship, but sadly, the animosity between witches and sorceresses is still there to this day," Cheveyo answered.

He pointed to the slide. "The main focus of today's lesson is recognizing the stages of genocide, which are critically important so that atrocities against magical races, such as what happened with the Elves, never happen again. There are said to be as many as ten stages, but for today's lesson, we'll stick with the main eight."

The slide changed to show eight numbers on the board. Cheveyo began listing them off. "The first step is classification. A society begins to separate people based on the concept of *us* and *them*. That is, dividing groups of people into distinguishable categories."

As he spoke, gears started turning in my head, and I couldn't stop them. Classification— the division of the Houses.

"The second step," he continued, "is symbolization. Words and names are used to define the separate classes. Physical characteristics, such as skin color or face shape, along with dress or culture, are used to further segregate society. Later on, the targeted group is often required to wear an identifying symbol to show what classification they are."

The Biyami name. The tattoos.

Cheveyo moved onward. "Classification and symbolization are common operations in all cultures, but they become violent when combined with the third step; dehumanization. The targeted group is denied their humanity and shown to be *less than* when compared to the ones in power. They're referred to as *infestations, diseases,* or made to appear filthy somehow. This is an attempt to convince the masses as a whole that the targeted group doesn't deserve the same rights as everyone else, because they are *different* from all the rest. Usually, the argument is that the victims deserve what is coming to them."

I'd heard it so many times in the halls. *Dirty Biyami.* This whole lecture was making me sick. I thought I might puke. I wanted Cheveyo to stop, but he continued forward.

"Genocide has to be held by a hate group or a unified force, usually a state government. That leads us to our next step; organization."

Cheveyo's tone grew darker with every word. "In order for a genocide to take place, it must be organized and carefully planned. Genocide does not happen by random occurrence. It is a specific plan to eliminate a targeted group first by causing hatred and division, then through mass murder. It is directly connected to the next step; polarization. Those who oppose the discrimination and hatred are dealt with first, until society is forced to allow extremists to take over and there is no one left to oppose what is coming."

The Elders taking total control. Oleander dealing with those who opposed him and eliminating anyone who stuck up for the Biyami. The Task Force scaring the Defortai into submission.

Cheveyo cleared his throat. His voice was getting thick. "The sixth step is preparation. Lists of victims are created. People are taken from their homes and disappear. The property and personal items of the targeted group are confiscated. Internment camps are constructed, and transportation of victims into these camps starts taking place."

We were fucked. We were so, so fucked.

Cheveyo's words became quiet. Hopeless, even. "We come to the seventh step of the process; extermination. *Extermination* is the key word, here, because those murdering the targeted group do not consider their acts evil, because the victims are not deemed worthy of life. To them, it is the same as taking out pests, like insects or rodents. The targeted group is killed in large numbers, usually in horrific ways. Mass graves, mutilation, and burnings are common."

Cheveyo turned the slides off. He strode to the middle of the room. "And always— *always* after genocide happens is the final stage— denial. No matter how many are killed, or in what sick ways, deniers are always prevalent. No matter the case or how much proof is exhibited, there are those alive who refuse to believe what happened. There are still many magical people today who deny that the Elves were ever persecuted, despite there being none left today."

He rubbed his eyes, as if exhausted. "I expect all of you to be able to name and list the various stages of genocide the next time we meet. Anyone unfamiliar with any of the terms will fail. Class dismissed."

People got up to leave. The usual chatter resumed. Students laughed and smiled. There was a carefree vibe around the room which was eerie and bizarre. I caught bits of conversation about parties happening this weekend, who was dating who, and classes people were worried about failing. Even Lira and Wyatt didn't seem affected by Cheveyo's speech.

I felt like I was the only one who had truly gotten the message. How could anyone get up and go about their day after what Cheveyo had taught us? Didn't *anyone* see the similarities between what had happened with the Elves, and what was happening now? He'd practically given us a list of what had occurred in Hawkei society over the past few years. It was hard to swallow.

Yet nobody had listened. And if they had, they didn't care— or didn't want to. People didn't want to believe this kind of stuff happened in today's world. *Genocide* was a word for terrible things that happened in the past; stuff that couldn't take place anymore.

The sickening truth was staring us in the face, and the Hawkei couldn't face it.

But Cheveyo knew. That's why he was teaching us this. If I was the only one who'd learned anything today, I wasn't going to let it go to waste.

Extermination was the next step. Which meant I needed to get me and the people I loved the fuck out of here.

I hurried to the Biyami dorms. No one else was there when I arrived. The basement was empty. I hoped the others had packed their things already and were waiting for me at the waterfall. I grabbed my backpack and started throwing clothes in, along with my pills. I didn't care if the cameras caught me. It wasn't like I was coming back. I shoved the engagement ring into my pocket— the first chance I got, I was popping Sophia the question. I didn't care how. I just wanted her to be mine, and we both needed something to hold on to during times like these. The hope of a future together would keep us going. I abandoned everything else I didn't need and threw my backpack over my shoulder.

I tried not to think about leaving as I was doing so. Orenda Academy was my home, and I was abandoning it because I had no fucking choice. I didn't know when I'd come back to campus— if ever. It broke my fucking heart to leave it behind.

But better to have a broken heart than be dead. We should've left weeks ago. I was cursing myself out in my head for not seeing the light sooner.

I took the main road to Kinpago, but diverged into the woods before I hit town. I wandered through the trees I'd known my entire life, a forest that had been my childhood and everything else in between. Once we left Kinpago, where would we go? This place was all I'd ever known. I didn't know if I could live without it. I'd never been away from the reservation for more than a few weeks at a time. Could I really survive somewhere other than the land of my ancestors?

Noise broke me out of my thoughts. I heard dozens of voices up ahead. Pleading. The sounds of sobs. I pressed myself to a tree and crouched down behind a bush, so I'd stay hidden.

Through the leaves, I was able to make out an image. About twenty feet ahead was a line of people and animals. They were all ages. Many of them were crying. Some looked frantically for ways of escape, while others clutched their children or Familiars. They were Biyami, but if I had to guess, belonged to Yapluma House. All of them were lined up before a deep ditch in the ground behind them. It was one of the tar pits around the school.

A large group of Task Force members pointed noxite guns at them and closed in from all sides. There was nowhere for them to run. I looked at the ditch and pieced together what was going to happen. A noose of terror tightened around my neck.

"That is enough! I *demand* you stand down!"

Dean Alizeh stormed from the trees. Her thunderbird approached from behind her, and I breathed a sigh of relief. She was a Defortai with authority. She could stop this.

A Task Force member came forward. By the look of the uniform, I presumed them to be a captain. "We have official orders from Elder Oleander. Interference is breaking the law."

"Interference? How dare you!" Alizeh breathed. "You don't think I know what you're doing to all these people?"

"Step aside," the captain said coolly. "This is your final warning."

For as frightened and terrified as Dean Alizeh had been merely a few days before, she seemed to have reached her breaking point. "I cannot allow this to take place! I will no longer stand by like a coward and watch the people of my House be eliminated!" she cried.

"You've made your choice. Seize her!" the captain cried.

Dean Alizeh raised her hands to summon her Air powers, and lightning crackled off the thunderbird behind her. But before she could do anything, several officers shot her and her Familiar with noxite guns. Darts protruded out of their bodies, and their magic flickered. Officers strode forward to grab them both.

"What are you doing? Get your hands off me!" she yelled. She sounded terrified.

The officers ignored her. They threw Dean Alizeh and her thunderbird into the line of Biyami. Several people caught them. The officers lowered their noxite guns and raised their hands into the air. Elements grew within their fingers and waited.

"Fire!" the captain shouted. The firing squad began shooting. Fire, Water, Earth, and Air came rocketing out of the hands of the Task Force and connected with bodies.

A bolt of Earth hit Dean Alizeh in the chest. Her eyes rolled backward, and a large hole erupted in her middle just as her thunderbird was consumed by flames.

I knew she was gone long before she and her Familiar toppled into the pit.

I couldn't help it. I closed my eyes and leaned my back against the tree as people cried for mercy. I couldn't bear to watch, but I was forced to hear. The screams people made as they tried to avoid the firing squad, and failed, would be a sound I'd remember for the rest of my life. I listened to the sound of corpses rolling into the ditch as people fell, and the sound of elements as they ricocheted through the air.

I covered up my mouth so I didn't scream. If they found me, they'd kill me, too.

The silence afterward was the worst sound of all. Dead. Everyone was dead.

"Burn them," the captain said. "We move on to the others."

There was the crackling of fire. I smelled smoke, then the stench of burning bodies as the tar pit was set ablaze. I nearly gagged.

I was rocking myself long after the Task Force had gone. I needed to move, but felt paralyzed.

We'd lost our chance at getting a Storm Lord. Dean Alizeh, and dozens of other Yapluma, had been slaughtered.

Which meant the rest of us were next.

sophia
EIGHTEEN

I was on high alert as I traipsed through the forest that night as the sun began to set. Esis was huddled in the open zipper of my backpack, trembling. He'd insisted on nestling himself in there with the dragon egg. Esis didn't want to leave Julian behind, and I wasn't too keen on turning him back into the school, either.

I didn't have much with me. I'd managed to fit a few changes of clothes, a water bottle, and my camera in my backpack. I'd also snuck into the Survival Instincts classroom earlier and stolen a first aid kit, some rope, and a pocket knife from the supplies closet.

I had to leave my mother's scrapbook behind, but I'd managed to take a few photos— one of my parents with Doya, and another of my Grandma and Grandpa. It killed me that I couldn't tell my grandparents where I was going, but there was no time to go to the Koigni Village— and it would only put us at risk. I wanted them to come with us, but they were Defortai. They'd be safe. And I just knew they'd try to talk me out of it.

I pulled the zipper up on my fleece jacket. It was the beginning of April, and the weather was getting nicer, but the nights were still chilly. The sound of my heavy hiking boots sounded like drum beats in the empty forest. I thought I heard the sound of shrieks in the distance, but it must've been my imagination running wild on me.

I didn't walk the normal paths, but I'd been to the waterfall enough times that my feet knew where to take me. Finally, I heard the sound of rushing water cutting through the forest.

I broke through the trees, and my heart melted at the sight in front of me. Liam was knelt at the water's edge, looking deep in thought. His backpack lay beside him, and he was running his hands through the water.

The water swelled between the banks, creating a five-foot high dome that displayed a beautiful view of the fish inside. Above us, Fortune Fairies fluttered, creating a glittering display against the dark sky.

It was magical— like this was the one place where nothing bad could touch us. I could almost forget that we were running away.

Liam's head snapped up at the sound of a stick breaking beneath my feet. His eyes brightened, and he stood and rushed over to me. He wrapped me in a hug so tightly that my toes lifted off the ground. He spun me around, making me feel so light in spite of everything happening around us. I couldn't help smiling as my feet flew out in an arc and Liam's pine forest scent surrounded me.

He set me down and buried his face into my hair. "*Pawee.* I'm so glad to see you."

The tone of his voice made my body tense. I quickly drew away from him to look him in the eyes. There was relief within them— but something darker, too. "Liam, what's wrong? Did something happen?"

I glanced around frantically. "Where are Imogen and Jonah?"

"They're coming," he said quickly.

"Then what is it?" I demanded.

Liam took my hand and led me over to the water's edge. "I'll tell you when they get here. But first... there's something I want to do."

I took my backpack off and set it aside. Esis jumped out of it and scurried up a tree, batting at the Fortune Fairies above our heads.

Liam took my hands and gazed deep into my eyes. "*Pawee*, I know that everything around us is going to shit, but I wanted to do this before we left. I meant for it to be special, but I'm sick of waiting. So... here it goes."

Liam took a deep breath and reached into his pocket. I watched him curiously, wondering what he could possibly have in mind. I was kind of hoping it was another toy from the sex shop. It made sense that he wanted to work in a quickie before we went on the run. Who knew how long it'd be before we had another chance?

Liam cupped the object in his hands so I couldn't see it. "*Pawee—?*"

Squeee!

Esis jumped down from his branch, his arms spread wide like a flying squirrel. He landed on top of Liam's head. Liam lost his balance, and whatever was in his hand went flying. It landed in the water with a *sploosh*.

"Liam!" I cried as he fell to the ground.

I knelt at his side. He pulled Esis out of his hair, and Esis screamed in protest.

"Ow!" Liam complained. "Let go!"

Esis flailed his arms and legs. When Liam finally tore him away, a few strands of his hair had come out in Esis' hands. Esis pouted as Liam set him aside, but Liam's eyes were etched in fury.

"*Bad* Esis," he scolded.

He turned back to the water, staring into its depths hopelessly. "Are you fucking serious? This *can't* be happening right now."

I couldn't help it. I threw my head back in laughter and chuckled so loudly a few birds flew from their nests.

"*Pawee*, it's not funny!" Liam cried as he frantically scanned the river bottom for whatever he'd dropped.

"Yes... it... is," I snickered between laughs. "You should've seen... Esis— ancestors."

I was laughing so hard that tears were forming at the corners of my eyes. I wiped at them, welcoming the light, happy emotions.

"*Pawee*, you don't get it. I was going to..."

"Going to what?" I asked when he trailed off. *Fuck me like there's no tomorrow?*

Liam held up an index finger. "Hold on. I can salvage this. I just gotta find it."

He pointed his hands at the water and closed his eyes, concentrating hard. He spoke between gritted teeth. "There's so many rocks."

I placed a gentle hand on his shoulder. "Liam, it's fine. Whatever it is, I'm sure we can get another when all this is over."

"No, *pawee*," he said firmly. "I'm not letting this get ruined again."

I blinked a few times. "Again? What do you mean?"

"Aha!" Liam shoved his hands into the water, and a jet stream came up to meet him. He clutched the object tightly in his hand and turned to me on one knee. "*Pawee*, will you—?"

He cut off as he opened his hand. Inside sat a large golden key— an old one that looked as if it went to a treasure chest or something. It had a beautiful twisted design on the end, and there were various patches of green— like a penny that'd been lying in the rain for too long.

A moment of shock crossed Liam's face. He glanced back to the water, as if he couldn't figure out where the key had come from. Esis nudged him from behind, and he quickly relaxed.

Liam cleared his throat and pocketed the key. "Hold on."

He placed his hand back in the water, and it began to shape to his will. As the water twisted toward me, I gasped.

Between us, a stream of water had risen from the river. It was like a hand reaching out of the pool and controlled by his magic. At the very tip of it sat a beautiful silver ring with a teardrop diamond, little red and blue stones surrounding the shape.

My hand shot to my mouth, and tears rose to my eyes. My heart was pounding so hard I swore it shook the earth. Was this…?

Liam gazed up at me with a look I'd never seen before. It was so full of love and passion. "*Pawee*... will you marry me?"

The most amazing feeling of euphoria washed through me at that moment. It was so intense that I couldn't find the words. Liam Mitoh wanted to marry me! He wanted *me* to be his wife!

After a moment of silence, Liam's eyes went wide. He seemed terrified. "Ancestors, *pawee*, please say something."

"I— I," I stammered, still trying to find my voice. "Of course! Yes, Liam! Yes, I'll marry you!"

Liam breathed a sigh of relief. He reached for the ring and pulled it out of the stream of water. As soon as he stood, the water fell back into the river, as if it was never there in the first place. Tears streamed down Liam's face as he shakily placed the ring on my left hand.

A flood of emotions stronger than anything I'd ever felt before whipped through me all at once. I couldn't control the tears. I threw my right hand over my mouth again, then covered my eyes to keep him from seeing me cry. My shoulders shook involuntarily.

"What's wrong, *pawee?*" Liam's voice sounded more concerned than ever.

I dropped my hand from my face, letting the tears free fall down my cheeks. I shook my head as I gazed into his glistening eyes. "Nothing, Liam. I'm just so happy."

Liam swept me into his arms and squeezed me so tight I couldn't breathe. "Me, too, *pawee*. Ancestors, I can't believe it. You're going to be my wife."

He pulled away to take my face in his hands, then pressed his lips firmly against mine. I couldn't handle it anymore. There was so much heat on my skin that I thought I might explode.

"I need you. I need you now." I reached for the hem of Liam's shirt. His hands immediately went into the air, though he didn't stop kissing me. I drew away from him for only a second to pull the shirt up over his head. Meanwhile, Liam fumbled with the zipper on my jacket. The second he had the zipper undone, his cool hands were up my shirt, forcing the fabric of my bra aside. His hands ran over the swell of my breasts as he pressed his hips into mine. The heat in my body gathered between my thighs. The rush of emotion flooding through me, through us, was too much to handle.

I stripped my jacket off as fast as I could, then lifted my arms so he could remove my shirt. He tossed it aside in the grass. I parted my lips, and his tongue slid inside my mouth, drinking me in as if it were the last taste he was going to ever get. His arms came around me, and he unleashed the clasp on my bra. My breasts broke free into the chilly night air, and my nipples hardened beneath his touch.

I didn't know when it happened, but somehow we ended up on the ground while we were making out. I straddled Liam and started unzipping his pants, when he went rigid.

"What?" I asked in alarm.

Liam looked up to the trees above us. "We have an audience."

I glanced upward to see Esis hanging over a branch and watching us with big blue eyes. "Esis! Some privacy please!"

Liam laughed. "I've got this." Liam raised his hands, and the water from the river began to rise on all sides of us. He created a dome around us, trapping a few Fortune Fairies inside. The blinking lights from the fairies glittered off the swirling water. Above us, Esis was nothing more than a distorted white blob. I looked around in awe as fish of all colors swam through the walls Liam had put up.

"Liam," I breathed. "It's beautiful."

His voice shook. "I know you are."

I turned my eyes down at him to see he wasn't even looking at the water dome around us but was staring straight at me. My heart lifted in my chest. I couldn't tear my gaze off his face.

"Liam?" I said lightly.

"What is it, *my fiancé?*" He beamed at the words.

If I thought I couldn't get turned on any more than I already was, I was a damn liar. When Liam called me his fiancé, I thought I might come right then and there.

"Liam... make love to me."

A blissful look came over his face as he whispered, "Today, and every day after."

Liam grabbed me around the middle and flipped me over. He stripped off my shoes, then my pants. He took my panties in his mouth and pulling them down my legs.

Once I was lying naked on the ground, Liam undid his pants, setting his dick free. I spread my legs, and he positioned himself between them. In a single thrust, he slammed his way inside of me. I arched my back and moaned in pleasure.

Liam moved gently and with purpose. It was as if I could feel his passion pressing inside of me, deeper and deeper until I thought it might be too much— until I thought I was going to cry.

Liam Mitoh was my fiancé. We were getting *married*. Soon, I could call him my husband! It was everything I'd ever wished for and more. Being with him like this was my dream, and it had finally come true.

Liam trailed kisses down my neck as he moved inside of me. His body grinded against mine slowly, making every nerve in my body come alive. Every kiss along my collarbone sent shock waves through me. I wrapped my legs tightly around him and tangled my hands in his hair. He thrust in harder.

I gasped. "Liam."

He thrust deep again, sending a jolt of energy all the way down to my toes.

My breaths grew shallow. "Liam... my *fiancé*." I loved saying the words.

Liam pressed a kiss to the sensitive area just below my ear. My body tingled in exhilaration.

"I love it when you say that, *pawee*," he whispered.

"Fiancé," I repeated. "Liam, we're going to get married."

"Of course we are, Soph," he whispered into my ear. "You've always been the only one for me."

I inhaled another sharp breath as Liam increased his speed. Involuntary moans escaped my lips as he slammed into me over and over again. It was all too much, I was going to explode. One hand tightened in his hair, and the other clawed at his back. He let out a moan of pleasure as my fingernails raked along his skin.

He gasped in shallow heaves. "*Pawee*."

Pressure built up inside of me, gathering between my legs where his dick rubbed against me over and over again. I let him know I was about to go by tugging back on his hair. He took one last gasp of breath before we both spiraled into a mind-numbing orgasm at the same time.

My eyes shot open as I arched my back, so he could thrust as deep as possible as he came. All around me, the water dome pulsed in waves to the rhythm of his contractions. The Fortune Fairies' lights blinked on and stayed lit as they fluttered around above us.

It was all so magical I could hardly breathe.

Liam collapsed on top of me, pressing his face into my shoulder. It took both of us a few deep breaths to compose ourselves.

"I can't believe it," Liam whispered.

I stroked a few strands of his hair and stared up into the water. "Agreed. Who knew missionary could be so fun?"

Liam chuckled and drew away to look me in the eyes. "Any position's fun when you have the sexiest girl alive at your side. But that's not what I meant."

My cheeks blushed bright pink. "What did you mean, then?"

"I just never thought I'd be this happy," he said softly. "I've always wanted you to be mine, Soph, from the first time I saw you. Now you get to be mine forever."

His words caused a burning passion to erupt within me. He was right. I'd be his, and he'd be mine, always. We were making this permanent. I could've never dreamed when I made the decision to come to Orenda Academy, it would lead to this moment.

Though the world was falling apart, this was perfect. *He* was perfect. And we would create our own world, together.

A whistle cut through the momentary silence, and we both went rigid. Liam shot me a wide-eyed look.

"Hey, love birds!" Jonah's voice sounded from outside our bubble. We could see his and Imogen's blurry outlines outside the dome. "Finish your love making, then get your butts out here. We have stuff to discuss."

I threw my hand over my mouth and tried not to laugh. I wasn't succeeding.

Liam beamed, but he didn't take his eyes off me as he responded. "We'll just be a minute!"

"Ancestors, that's all it takes?" Imogen joked.

"You two can shut up now," I called back.

Liam made our dome bigger so we could stand up. We both put our pants back on, but our shirts were outside the dome. Liam reached through the water and grabbed my bra and shirt, then waited until I had them on before sending the water around us back into the river.

I straightened my shirt before turning to Imogen and Jonah. Imogen was wearing a huge backpack that stuck up higher than her head, and Squeaks was wearing a saddle bag. Sassy seemed coy, like she knew what had happened minutes ago.

Imogen narrowed her eyes at us. We must've been beaming, because she looked suspicious. "Is there something you two want to tell us?"

Liam draped an arm around my shoulder and smiled proudly. "It's official. Sophia and I are engaged."

Delight lit up both their faces. "*Squeee!*" Imogen bounced on her toes and flapped her hands. Beside her, Jonah brought his knuckles up to his teeth. His eyes went comically wide. He looked like an anime character or something the way his eyes sparkled.

"You finally did it!?" Jonah cried.

I looked to Liam. "Wait. They *knew* about this?"

Liam nodded. "They helped me pick out the ring."

I looked down to the ring on my hand and admired it. It truly was beautiful. "So *that's* why you guys have been acting so weird."

Imogen rushed forward. "Let us see! Let us see!"

Esis scurried down from the tree and hopped onto my shoulder to get a good look.

"*Oh em gee*," Imogen squealed when I showed her. "It's so pretty."

Jonah put a hand on his hip. "Okay, girl. So, for the dress, I was thinking big, poofy ball gown. We want you to look like a princess."

"Whoa," I said. "Slow down. We haven't discussed *any* details yet."

As happy as it made me to be engaged to Liam, I couldn't be thinking about wedding plans right now. There was too much going on.

"We need to be in a safe place before we get married," Liam said. "The wedding can come later."

When he said *get married*, butterflies ran through my stomach. This still didn't seem real to me. Jonah and Imogen groaned in disappointment.

"Right. So, what'd you guys want to talk to us about?" I asked.

Jonah's face fell. "Right. The thing is... we can't leave yet."

"What!?" Liam nearly exploded. "But my dad—"

"It's about the Air piece." Jonah reached into his pocket and shoved a piece of paper into Liam's hands.

Liam unfolded the letter and began scanning it with a furrowed brow. I peeked over his shoulder to read along. There were no names— just a message penned in quill ink.

I can't tell you how much I regret not listening to your concerns earlier. Events in Kinpago are far worse than I feared, and I can't sit around any longer pretending as if it's not happening. I wasn't lying when I told you I was not the Storm Lord. However, there is one piece of information I kept from you, as I feared for your safety and my own. I've just received troubling news that has confirmed my fears were misplaced. That is why I'm giving you this information now, in hopes that you can truly stop what's happening to our own brothers and sisters. The item you seek is hidden in the Air Kingdom, protected by a vicious beast. Tread carefully, for this is not a task you should take lightly. You put yourselves at risk if you go— but if you don't, the entire fate of the Hawkei is on the line.

I furrowed my brow as I finished reading. "What's the Air Kingdom?"

"It's a secret floating city known only to Yapluma," Jonah explained. "I'd forgotten about it until this morning— it's been abandoned for years, so it never crossed my mind to investigate it until now. Imogen and I were in the library, researching all we could on it just in case it had something to do with the prophecy."

Liam held up the sheet of paper. "Jonah, where did you get this?"

"It was tucked under my pillow. I found it right before we left, as Im and I were packing. Along with this." Jonah held up a large feather, that of a thunderbird— Alizeh's thunderbird.

"We tried looking for her, but she must've already took off like the rest of our professors," Imogen said.

Liam's face had gone so pale that he looked like a ghost. "She didn't leave... or at least, if she tried, she didn't make it."

My pulse quickened. "What do you mean?"

Liam closed his eyes and shook his head, as if trying to rid his mind of horrible images. "I saw..." He hesitated. "I saw the Task Force kill Alizeh."

My hand slapped over my mouth. Jonah and Imogen gasped.

"What happened?" Imogen asked softly.

Liam swallowed. "I was on my way over here when it happened. The Task Force lined them up... dozens of Biyami, even children... and they— they executed them. The police threw the bodies in a ditch and burned them all. I watched."

Both hands covered my mouth now. No wonder Liam had wanted to propose before he told me that. It was beyond cruel.

"But Alizeh's not Biyami," Jonah pointed out.

Liam shook his head. "No, but she came to try to stop it. So they killed her as well."

Imogen's hands balled into fists. "Then we have to do the same. We're following Alizeh's instructions before we leave."

"But we don't have a Storm Lord," Liam reminded us.

"It doesn't matter," Jonah stated. "We have to try. Come hell or high water, we're getting that Air piece. Tonight."

Liam
NINETEEN

There were screams coming from up ahead as we trekked through the depths of the woods. We'd left the waterfall behind as we followed Jonah to where he said the Air Kingdom was located. The four of us pressed close together in the forest — the noise was horrifying, even from this distance. It was a mixture of desperate pleas and breaking glass.

"Stay here," Jonah whispered. "I'm going to take a look."

Jonah went onward, Squeaks following. The rest of us remained silent and held back. A few minutes later, Jonah returned with a grim expression.

"The Yapluma village is being raided," Jonah said. "We need to go around."

"Task Force?" Imogen asked.

He nodded. "They're taking Biyami out of their homes and killing them on the streets. It won't be long before they start on the other villages."

"Fuck." I shook my head. "Good thing we're leaving tonight, then."

"Not without that Air piece," Imogen murmured.

Jonah turned and diverted through the woods a different way. As we walked hand in hand through the brush, I caught the glimmering of Sophia's engagement ring on her hand.

It gave me a total thrill. I couldn't believe this was really happening. She had said *yes*! Sophia and I were getting married. Though there was so much death and destruction all around us, I couldn't help but feel joy. After Nashoma died, I never thought I'd get married. I never thought that anyone would want me.

She caught me looking at the ring. I smiled and said, "It looks beautiful on you."

Esis chittered happily from her shoulder. Sophia glanced at it and said, "You picked the perfect ring. I can't wait to be your wife."

"I can't wait to be your husband." I nudged her shoulder. "Though asking you sure took long enough."

Her eyes narrowed. "What do you... oh!" Her expression brightened with realization. "The beach party at your house? And the lunar-fauna?"

"Both failed attempts," I confirmed. "Third time's the charm, I guess."

Sophia laughed lightly. "You tried. That's what counts."

"Jonah and Imogen convinced me I needed some grand proposal." I rolled my eyes. "My first mistake was listening to them from the beginning."

"They should know better. I'm not a flashy girl." She giggled. "Now they're going to be over the top in planning some huge wedding."

"I think we're both in agreement we should keep it simple." I paused. "As simple as they'll let us make it, anyway."

"Jonah will turn it into some big stage production." Sophia giggled, and Esis peeped in agreement.

"It's a wedding, not a play." My tone soured.

"I don't really care what happens." She kissed me on the cheek. "I just want to be married to you."

My heart warmed. "Me, too. As soon as possible."

Esis' eyes widened, and Sophia frowned slightly. "How, though? I mean, there isn't time to plan a wedding with all of... *this* going on." She waved her hand around.

I shrugged. "I don't know. But to be honest, I don't want to wait until after the war's over. Who knows how long that's going to take?"

"Or if we'll survive it," Sophia said quietly.

"Soph, stop." My voice became harsh. "Everything's going to be fine."

Sophia stroked Esis and frowned, like she wasn't sure.

"Quiet down, guys," Jonah called back. "We're almost there."

We fell silent. Jonah broke through the trees. We emerged into a flat clearing that was sparse and expansive. Above us were dozens of clouds that blocked out the moon. The area seemed dull and gray.

"So, where is it?" Imogen asked, putting her hands on her hips.

"Keep your panties on," Jonah shot back at her. "We've gotta go up. Hold on, guys."

Squeaks beat her wings and took off to the sky. Jonah raised his hands, and the rest of us began levitating off the ground. We slowly rose through the air, upward into the clouds. Imogen gave a little scream.

"Um, what exactly are we supposed to hold on *to*?" I asked in alarm.

In response, both Imogen and Sophia reached out and clung to me. Sassy paddled her way through the air and clung to my chest. Esis sat on my head and grabbed my hair, looking for a ride.

Like I'd be able to save them if we started falling.

"Relax," Jonah said lazily. He was lounging on his back and allowing the air currents to take us upward. "I've got you."

Moisture dotted our clothes as we entered into the clouds. Jonah allowed us to drop, and we landed on a hard surface. I looked down—beneath our feet was actual stone. Sophia and Imogen looked similarly confused. Sassy barked, and we turned around to face Jonah. Squeaks had bowed to us, and spread her wings out wide like she was presenting something grand.

"Welcome to the Air Kingdom," Jonah said. He floundered his arms in an elaborate, showy way, and the fog cleared.

The buildings were white, built with massive columns of stone and lined with silver trim. Large domes topped the columns that overlooked a large white wall around the city's perimeter. Towers stood on each of the four corners of the wall. Lion-like statues stood before a giant gate, one that was slightly propped open.

The moon overhead was only a quarter full. It illuminated the buildings, but didn't provide much light. Sophia ignited a ball of fire in her palm, so we could see better.

"Wow. This place is massive," Imogen said. Sassy barked in approval.

"Isn't it, though?" Jonah waggled his eyebrows. "By the way, don't tell anyone I brought you up here. To bring anyone to the Air Kingdom who isn't Yapluma is a capital offense to the Air Elders. They'll chop my head off."

"Yeah, we'll just put it in the paper tomorrow," I responded sarcastically. Jonah flipped me off.

Sophia's mouth was open as she approached the gates. "It looks like a Middle Eastern city," she remarked.

Jonah nodded. "The city itself was built by the descendants of oil sheiks who'd married Hawkei that explored their lands. It was a way to honor them."

I always thought Jonah's features looked more Arabic than Hawkei. We walked forward through the gates. Large arches stood next to long walls that held glimmering mosaics of Air creatures. Marble buildings towered beside statues of previous Air chiefs from long ago. There were elaborate fountains everywhere, but they'd been turned off. The city itself was crumbling into decay, and there were some places where graffiti and vandalism had taken place. Even with all of that, the splendor was barely concealed. I could only imagine what this place looked like at the height of its glory.

It was eerie. The city seemed so proud and majestic. For it to be completely abandoned by the people who built it was bizarre.

"So no Yapluma ever come up here?" Sophia's eyes roamed the buildings curiously, and Esis copied her as their heads swiveled from one way to the other.

"I mean... some Yapluma students fly here to goof around, drink and have sex," Jonah said. "And there are a few Yapluma archaeologists who come here from time to time to do some excavating and research. But overall, it's pretty empty. If the other tribes noticed Yapluma vanishing all the time, they'd get suspicious."

"How does the city stay afloat, with no Yapluma around to keep it flying?" Imogen asked.

"A long time ago, the Air Elders infused their magic into the city so it could float on its own— like what I did with the crystal," Jonah said.

"The buildings themselves actually have Air magic in them, along with the pathways and the rest of the architecture."

"So why was it abandoned?" Sophia asked.

"After Anichi was wiped out, the Air Elders decided intertribal communication needed to be a top priority," Jonah explained. "Isolating ourselves from the rest of the tribe would only create a deeper divide between us and the rest of the Houses. So Yapluma abandoned the Air Kingdom and focused on creating alliances instead. But we didn't tell the other Houses, just in case Yapluma ever needed to return to the city again."

Our footsteps echoed as we walked through the city. I was on edge, half expecting someone to jump out from behind a building and attack us at any minute. After all, we were chasing after some kind of animal in order to get the last piece. Who knew what it could be?

"I'm confused as to why it's called a kingdom. Hawkei don't have kings," Imogen said.

"It's called a kingdom because the Storm Lord was the literal king over it," Jonah said. "The Air Chief ruled the tribe on the ground, but in the skies, the Storm Lord had full authority. They were almost considered two separate groups; the Yapluma that lived on the earth and those that lived in the air."

"You sure know a lot about this place, Jonah. It would've been helpful if you'd told us about it a few months ago," I remarked.

"I literally *just* remembered all of this. It's not something I think about all the time," Jonah countered. "I haven't been up here since—"

Jonah cut off. If I had to guess, the last time he was up here was with Renar. No wonder he'd put it out of his head.

Imogen tapped a finger to her mouth. "Dean Alizeh said the Air piece would be here. The painting has got to be somewhere. But this place is huge. How do we know where to look?"

"She said the beast was guarding it," Jonah said. "If I had to make a guess, there's only one place it could be."

Jonah turned down a side street, and we followed. After walking for fifteen minutes, we came to a gigantic structure in the middle of the city. The towers and domes on this building were much larger than all the others. The building itself seemed to gleam underneath the light of the moon. Inside was what I could only guess were hundreds of rooms. It looked like a place where a sultan would reside.

"The Air Palace. That's where the Storm Lord used to live," Jonah said. "I'll bet anything the painting is in there."

"Let's go get it, then," I said.

We took the steps up to the main entryway. As we walked through the massive doors of the palace, we entered into an elaborate throne room with marble floors and a giant stone chair still at the head of the room. We had to maneuver around debris that had fallen from the ceiling, as well as furniture that had been left abandoned by Yapluma long ago. I sought for footprints in the dust, but there weren't any. There was no indication anyone was here but us.

The main floor of the palace was empty. We explored room after room, but the beast wasn't anywhere to be found. We passed many paintings, but none of them were the one we needed.

"It would sure help if we knew what we were looking for," Imogen said after we finished an extensive search of the kitchen.

"Something's here. I can feel the beast manipulating the air currents," Jonah said. "I think it's upstairs."

Sassy let out a low growl and hissed. She transformed into her kitsune form. Her fur glowed a harsher golden than I'd seen it before, and her vines poised to strike.

The other Familiars had a similar reaction. Esis hissed, and his fur stood on end. Squeaks jerked her head and pounded her hooves against the marble, like she was going to charge.

Jonah flung his hand out, as an indication for us to halt. "Do you feel that?" Jonah asked.

Imogen, Sophia and I looked blankly at each other. "No," I said.

"Exactly. Everything's stopped." He gestured for us to follow. The three of us kept close behind Jonah as he climbed the next flight up, while Sassy and Squeaks circled protectively around us. Esis kept his ears up, like he was listening.

"I think the beast knows we're here," Jonah said. "He's waiting for us."

"Like that isn't ominous," I grumbled.

The next floor was open to the elements. Most of the ceiling had given way, so that the moon could illuminate the area. The room was huge— three hundred feet long or more, and just as high. It was empty compared to the other rooms, with not much more than rubble and the occasional fallen stone to preoccupy the space.

Once we got to the second floor, we heard a guttural growling. Jonah immediately yanked us behind a huge square stone with his Air magic. We peeked around— my insides plummeted when I saw what it was.

The beast was fifty feet in length. It had the head and body of a lion, but bird's feet with massive talons. Two large wings rested on its back, and long canines poked out of its wide mouth. The creature's fur was light gray in color, and its mane was black. Lightning flashed in its blue eyes, and thunder could be heard every time it took a step. Small black clouds, flashing with electricity, gathered around it like a protective shield. It looked like it was created out of a literal storm.

This was a highly dangerous animal. A dragon couldn't take it down. This was going to be one hell of a fight.

"Holy shit. It's a *ugallu*," Jonah breathed.

"A what?" Imogen didn't even know what it was.

"They're storm monsters," Jonah whispered. "They're a huge part of Yapluma folklore. I didn't even know they existed. They're supposed to be a myth."

Just beyond the ugallu, on the other side of the room, was the painting. It was still covered up in a cloth, and leaning against the wall. The ugallu paced back and forth in front of it with its massive fangs bared. It was obvious we weren't getting to that painting without a battle.

"I don't understand. If it's so big, how did it get into your house to get the painting?" Sophia asked.

Before our very eyes, the ugallu transformed from a solid beast into a column of air. Though the creature was transparent, I could still see features. The beast was able to walk through statues and fountains in the room, like a ghost would. The ugallu changed back, and its form flickered twice before becoming solid again.

"Does that answer your question?" Jonah asked. His face was calculating. Squeaks glanced at him. He nodded before saying, "If the legends are right, ugallus are immune to every element except Air. Fire, Water, and Earth won't do a thing to hurt it. If this thing is going down, I've got to be the one to do it."

The three of us let out similar noises of protest. "Jonah, are you crazy?" I hissed. "You'll get killed out there if you try to take that thing on by yourself."

"I'm the only one who has a chance! You guys are going to get hurt," he insisted. "Ugallus are storm creatures, so the only way to bring one down is to create a storm that's stronger than he is. That's how you can get it to submit. If the stories are right, anyway."

"Let me help you. I can summon lightning," Sophia insisted.

"You haven't been able to conjure lightning in a while, Sophia. I guess now's a better time than ever for me to try," Jonah said.

"But you've never done it before," Imogen pointed out.

"So?" Jonah's expression was determined— raging. "Just stay out of the way. I can handle it."

"We're not going to let you take on this thing by yourself. We're coming with you," I insisted.

"No, guys. Why do you think *he* was sent to guard the painting? A Yapluma is supposed to defeat him— the strongest Yapluma of all. To get to the painting, we need a Storm Lord to defeat him. But we don't have one here, so I'll have to do." Jonah puffed out his chest. "I have to prove that I'm stronger than he is."

"But you're going to get hurt!" Imogen protested.

"I've got this. Just stay behind me."

Jonah dropped his bag. He emerged from the boulder and walked toward the ugallu with fists clenched.

Squeaks followed him with slow and intentful steps. Her head was lowered, and her wings were spread in a defensive position. She was getting ready to fight.

Imogen, Sophia and I looked at each other, as if asking if we were really going to let him do this, but we didn't have much of a choice. If our elements were useless, it'd only piss the creature off if we tried to fight it. But our faces were clear— if Jonah went down, we'd do whatever we could to get him out of there before the beast killed him.

The ugallu noticed Jonah coming. It snarled and faced him, but didn't make another move to attack.

Jonah stopped. "Hey. Um, we need something that's... right over there." Jonah pointed to the painting. "Would you mind being a dear and letting me grab it real quick?"

"Only the Storm Lord may pass," the creature responded in a heavy boom. It was using telepathy to communicate, like all Familiars did, but we could all hear it. For a creature to be strong enough to use that kind of magic only made me more scared for Jonah.

Jonah gave a nervous smile. "Well, you see, I'm the best you've got, boo. So are we gonna play nice, or—?"

The ugallu lunged toward Jonah with an open mouth. All of us screamed— Squeaks pushed Jonah out of the way. Jonah fell to the floor as the ugallu's jaws snapped right where he'd been only a few seconds before. Squeaks lashed out with her back legs and kicked the ugallu in the nose— the beast reared on its hind legs and growled as Jonah leapt to his feet.

"Okay," Jonah shouted. "You asked for it!"

Jonah rocketed into the air. His magic levitated him above the ground as the ugallu gave chase. Jonah threw blasts of Air magic back at the creature as he flew, but they hit the beast and bounced off without any effect. Jonah had to dodge and swerve out of the way as the monster's jaws nearly crushed him several times.

Squeaks spread her wings. She gave a galloping start, then leapt into the air. She lashed out at the beast's eyes with her hooves and attempted to draw blood with her beak, but the beast became transparent each time she drew near, only to change back to a solid form so it could lunge out when she got too close.

Squeaks barely avoided the beast's talons as she dove underneath its belly to distract it. Jonah sent a high-powered wind the monster's way. Such blasts were enough to cut a human being in half, but they only drew slight cuts of blood on the creature's side. Jonah cried out in frustration.

The ugallu was tired of being on defense. It wanted to go on the attack. The skies darkened above, and the black storm clouds collected around the beast's form began to grow.

Rain poured overhead from above. I tried to use my magic to stop it, but whatever forces the ugallu was using to summon the rain was out of my control. This water wouldn't listen to me.

As Jonah became drenched in the downpour, thunder crashed outward from the beast's giant feet. The thunder knocked Imogen, Sophia and I over from behind our hiding place.

Jonah was blasted out of the air, and so was Squeaks. The sound was so deafening it made my ears ring. Sophia shouted something to me, but her voice was lost to the thunder, and I was so dazed I couldn't understand anyway. It was like we were in the middle of a storm cloud.

That wasn't the worst of it. As Jonah and Squeaks got back up in the air, balls of electricity began glowing in the clouds surrounding the creature. They ricocheted outward as the monster fired them toward Jonah. Jonah and Squeaks managed to swerve away from the lightning balls. But as they hit the walls, they blasted huge craters in the side of them. I yanked Imogen out of the way as a lightning ball hit the stone. Half of the boulder gave way and was reduced to rubble, making our hiding space tinier than it was before. If Jonah got hit by one of those things, there'd be nothing of him left to take back.

"Jonah, look out!" Imogen shouted as a large lightning ball hurtled his way. Jonah whipped around at the last second to see the ball heading straight toward him— and Squeaks.

There wasn't enough time for him to get out of the way. He was going to be obliterated. Jonah's eyes flashed to his Familiar— like his first instinct was to protect Squeaks over himself.

As a reaction, Jonah jumped in the line of fire and put his hands out to block the lightning ball from hitting Squeaks. His eyes grew wide as the ball sailed directly at his chest, and the three of us screamed.

Then Jonah did something amazing. He *caught the lightning ball*. It was like this was soccer practice or something. Imogen and Sophia both let out gasps of shock.

Jonah seemed just as surprised as we did. His mouth was gaping, and his eyes were giant. Squeaks gave a cry of joy. Jonah snapped out of whatever stupor he was in to hurtle the lightning ball back at his opponent.

The ugallu tried to avoid the bomb, but it was too slow. The lightning ball hit the ugallu, and the monster was sent sailing backward as lightning exploded. As the smoke cleared, the beast got to its feet and shook its head— it wasn't hurt, but it was definitely stunned.

Before the beast could get up, Jonah weaved his hands and conjured a windstorm like I'd never seen before. The air around him became a swirling vortex that dragged the ugallu toward him. Jonah gritted his teeth, eyes closed in concentration. He forced his hands out, and the ugallu went slamming against several pillars. The windstorm smashed the ugallu into the walls, and the very palace shook as Jonah released his magic.

He fell to his knees with the effort of sustaining the windstorm. The beast's legs shook as it tried to get back on its feet.

As Jonah was recovering, Squeaks charged forward. Like she had during the Elemental Cup, Squeaks opened her mouth and screamed. From out of her beak came a whirling wind funnel that swept up the ugallu and slammed it into the ceiling at high speed. Squeaks pushed the wind tunnel up higher, until the ugallu was in the skies above and far out of our sight.

Squeaks brought her head sharply downward, and the beast came hurtling down from the sky. I heard stone crack as the beast slammed into the marble floor. The ugallu gave a groan of pain.

Squeaks drew back her scream, but only because she needed to catch her breath. As the ugallu rose up again, it seemed to gain a burst of adrenaline. It ran with its jaws open, fangs extended. Squeaks remained in place with a glint in her eye and her feathers raised in warning.

"Squeaks, no!" Jonah screamed.

As the ugallu closed in, Squeaks rocketed herself upward. She spread her wings and soared through the hole in the ceiling. Her form hovered in the clouds— she performed a swirling formation, and my mouth dropped open as I witnessed Squeaks change before my very eyes.

Squeaks' body became like the sky— silver and translucent, with wind swirling around her form. As she gave another scream, the clouds themselves moved at her command and took the form of hippogriffs. There were hundreds of them— stomping their hooves and beating their wings behind her.

Squeaks dove downward, and the collection of cloud-hippogriffs followed. The hippogriff herd slammed into the ugallu, and their hooves crashed into the beast as they trampled over it. The monster cried out while Jonah watched Squeaks control the herd with wonder.

As Squeaks turned around for another blow, the ugallu raised a mighty paw and knocked her out of the air. With the hit, the herd of cloud-hippogriffs vanished. She went tailspinning downward and landed on her side.

The fall was hard— I thought I heard something crunch as Squeaks went down, and she yelped in pain. Her hooves scraped against the marble as she struggled to get up.

"Squeaky!" Jonah cried out. He went to run to her, but another swipe from the ugallu's giant paw forced him to run the other way.

The beast's talons scraped against the floor as it clenched its paws in rage. The ugallu opened its mouth. Like a dragon breathing fire, strains of lightning emitted out of his open jaws. There were hundreds of strands that ignited the air as the ugallu literally breathed electricity. I grabbed on to the girls and pressed them against the rock. We didn't have time to look. The lightning pressed down around us, and we screamed as we felt the temperature in the room raise.

We were totally going to die. But hey, at least it was together, right?

Like I hadn't had that thought a million and one times before. This was just the newest escapade of shit in our collection of misadventures. I wondered if the ugallu liked its food chewy or extra crispy.

Then the lightning all around us stopped. We looked around the boulder to see where the lightning had gone.

A sense of pure disbelief ran through me as I saw the lightning crackling around Jonah's form. He was *controlling* it. Jonah could literally manipulate lightning!

The ugallu began to back away as thunder shook the room, but it wasn't coming from him. Storm clouds gathered around Jonah's form, and the rain coming in through the hole in the roof shifted to hail down upon the monster.

Jonah raised both of his hands, and two enormous lightning beams emitted from his palms and shot upward into the open air.

Imogen was jumping up and down and cheering. "Yes! Yes, yes, *yes!*"

This was impossible. How could Jonah do such spectacular things?

There was only one clear answer. Dean Alizeh hadn't lied. She never was the Storm Lord.

He'd been right in front of us all along.

Jonah gave a smirk and said, "Next time, don't mess with the Storm Lord, bitch."

In one motion, Jonah put both of his hands together. The lightning bolts collided and became one. He blasted the shot toward the ugallu. The lightning consumed the creature, and the beast roared in agony as it was slammed backward by the blow.

Jonah kept fueling the magical blast until the ugallu submitted— the creature fell to the floor, and didn't move as the magic slowly subsided. It was still breathing, but had obviously given up the fight.

When the beast was down, Jonah immediately ran to Squeaks. She struggled to her hooves before giving a happy chirp. Her wing was bent at a strange angle, but otherwise, she wasn't hurt.

The beast moaned. It shakily got to his feet and shook its head, but made no move to attack again. Instead, it bowed lowly to Jonah. *"Every Storm Lord throughout the centuries has had to first defeat me in order to claim the title, and you have. Welcome, new champion,"* the ugallu responded.

Sophia and Imogen both gave loud cheers of victory. I joined them with thrilled applause.

Jonah's smile was huge. His tone was laced with astonishment as he said, "I... I can't believe any of this. I didn't even know!"

"Storm Lords are not born. They are chosen. The ancestors have gifted you powerful abilities because you have proven the strength of your heart," the beast said. *"In these times, the Yapluma need a Storm Lord such as you to protect them."*

"But I don't have a thunderbird. My Familiar's a hippogriff," Jonah said as he stroked Squeaks' head.

"Many Storm Lords have had thunderbirds as their Familiars. But there are others who have not," the ugallu said. *"Being bonded to a powerful avian Familiar is proof of the power running through your veins."*

The ugallu eyed Squeaks' wing. *"I am impressed. Never has a Storm*

Lord fought me and had themselves or their Familiar come out with such minor injuries."

Squeaks gave a few happy noises, and Jonah added, "She says she'll bear the injury with honor. As a mark of her fight."

The ugallu inclined its head. "*You have earned what you came here for. Go now, and speak with the Storm Lord of the past. He shall help you along your journey.*"

The beast spread its wings. It took off and exited the room through the ceiling's opening, vanishing into the night.

Once the beast was gone, Imogen and Sophia ran out screaming from behind the boulder. They jumped onto Jonah in a group hug—Sassy wove around Squeaks' ankles while Esis climbed onto Squeaks' back. He placed a hand on her wing, and it straightened out immediately.

The three of them were jumping up and down in celebration. "Storm Lord, Storm Lord!" Imogen sang. "My best friend is the Storm Lord!"

"I *am* the Storm Lord!" Jonah squealed. "Wait until all those assholes at school hear about *this*! I can't wait to rub it in their faces!"

"Hold on," I said, and the three of them paused. "You know we can't tell anyone about this."

"Awww!" Jonah whined in protest. "Why not?"

"He's got a point," Sophia added. "If the Elders find out you're the Storm Lord, they'll totally take you out."

"I'll just fry 'em with my brand-new powers," Jonah said eagerly, and he took a stance like he was pretending to fire off lightning balls. "I'll be the King of Yapluma!"

"Sure you can pull that magic out of your ass whenever you want, *your highness?*" I asked.

"Obviously." Jonah rolled his eyes. "I wouldn't be the Storm Lord if I couldn't, right?"

"Okay. Do it right now." I crossed my arms.

Jonah tried. When he failed to make lightning appear, he made a face. "Okay. Maybe I need a *little* practice."

Squeaks chirped like she was amused. Jonah let out a dramatic sigh. "*Fine.* You ruin everything, Liam." Jonah pouched out his lip.

"Yeah, that's me, the chronic ruiner," I said. "But as much as I'm enjoying the fact you're a total badass, we might want to get back to what we were doing."

We turned around. The moonlight illuminated the painting on the other side of the room. The fabric it was under rustled slightly in the wind.

"The Air piece," Sophia breathed.

We were so close to getting answers. The last piece of the prophecy was only a few steps away.

TWENTY

Watching Jonah defeat the beast was beyond anything I'd ever seen. I'd never realized how amazing Jonah's powers were before. I bet it was why he was the only one of us who managed transference on the first try.

Jonah had this blissful look on his face, like he was completely at peace with being the Storm Lord. He was so full of himself. I could already tell this was all we'd hear about for the next month.

"Well...?" I pressed, gesturing to the painting.

Jonah straightened his spine. "Let's do this."

Jonah stepped forward, leading the way. The Air Kingdom was eerily silent. The only sound came from the soft pad of our feet and a gentle whistling of the wind. It was an ominous feeling if I ever felt one. Jonah stepped up to the painting and grasped the sheet in his hand.

"Wait!" Imogen cried.

All eyes turned to her.

She twisted the strap of her pack around in her fingers. "Before we do this, I want you all to know that no matter what the Air piece says, I love you all so much. Being friends with you..."

Imogen sniffled, and my heart sank. "Being friends with you has been the best experience of my life."

A light smile touched the corner of my lips. "Me too."

"And me," Jonah said.

We all looked to Liam. His lips twitched into a smile. "Yeah, yeah. Me too."

Imogen wiped at her eyes. "Okay, Jonah. Do it."

I held my breath. Jonah yanked on the sheet and revealed a breath-taking painting. I'd seen the copy of the portrait in the printout Imogen had shown us, but it was nothing compared to this. The painting was taller than I was, and incredibly life-like. Emmett Chang, the previous Storm Lord, was beyond talented. Each brush stroke was done with precision, and he'd used a rainbow of colors, some of which I felt I was seeing for the first time. I could practically see the clouds in the image swirling and hear the crackling of thunder. It was obvious he'd held deep love for his craft.

Everyone inhaled a breath at the same time and held it. Several seconds passed as we stood there, marveling at the magnificent Spirit Art.

Finally, Jonah broke our trance by lowering himself onto one knee. Squeaks bowed beside him, dipping her head so low her beak touched the ground. The rest of us followed suit.

Jonah's voice rang out through the hall. "Emmett Chang, Storm Lord and Elder of the Yapluma Tribe, I, Jonah Chanee, Storm Lord and... *badass*... summon thee."

I couldn't believe my eyes. Right in front of us, the paints began to swirl, as if the image itself was coming alive. Elder Chang's painted face twisted, until a nose grew out of the painting, then the rest of his face.

A figure identical to the one in the painting stepped straight out of the frame, until he took a full form. He crossed his hands and looked down at us with the kind of look a father might give his newborn. We were all stunned into silence.

"My child," Elder Chang said gently to Jonah. "You have summoned my spirit. How may I serve you?"

I knew Elder Chang was nothing more than a spirit— an imprint of his soul on the painting. But he looked so solid, like he was truly standing in front of us in the flesh. It was surreal, knowing he'd died so long ago.

Jonah gaped up at the former Storm Lord, but finally found his voice. "We were hoping you knew the wording to the prophecy, given by Showana Harjo."

Elder Chang held his head high and nodded once. "I do. The question is, Storm Lord, are you ready to hear it?"

"Yes," Jonah practically begged. "Showana split up the prophecy and gave a piece to every house. We've collected them all except the Air piece. Kinpago is in trouble, and we need this last piece to make sense of it all and save the Hawkei."

Elder Chang dropped his gaze and shook his head regrettably. "I'm afraid there's nothing you can do to save the Hawkei, my child."

We all exchanged a glance.

"Nothing we can do?" Jonah asked. "What does the prophecy say?"

He said nothing. After a beat of silence, Jonah added, "Please."

Elder Chang took a deep breath. Every muscle in my body went still as I awaited the long-anticipated reveal.

After several long seconds, Elder Chang finally spoke. "The prophecy states, *When the tribe divides in two and war has begun, the Hawkei have reached the point of no return. Smoke will blaze through the sky and signify the Hawkei's extinction.*"

I couldn't move. I couldn't breathe. It felt as if the Air Kingdom was shaking beneath us, though it was just my own body quaking. While I reeled, Imogen jotted the words down in a small notepad she'd brought along.

Point of no return? Extinction? Were we truly out of hope? Would my home be destroyed before I'd barely had a chance to save it? I could feel the blood draining from my face. My friends shared an equally hopeless expression.

"Are you sure that's what it says?" Jonah asked.

Elder Chang nodded. "Yes."

I shot to my feet. "No! That can't be right. We can change this. We *have* to!"

Imogen stood beside me. She clutched her notepad in her hand so tightly that the pages were crinkling. "Agreed. There has to be more."

I didn't know why I was still holding on to the hope that we could reverse Showana's prophecy. People had told me time and time again that prophecies always fulfilled themselves. But hadn't Showana said the outcome was up to me? How could I just abandon my people to let them perish?

Liam stood beside me and placed a gentle hand on my shoulder, to get me to calm down. But I didn't. My hands balled into fists, and I started pacing back and forth. Jonah got to his feet beside Imogen. Squeaks looked flustered while she watched him stand, as if wondering if she should keep bowing.

"Sophia," Liam said softly.

I shook him off. "I can't believe... This can't be right. Showana said..."

"This is all just more confirmation that we need to leave," Jonah pointed out.

"And abandon everyone?" Imogen cried.

"What about the children?" I added.

Jonah looked like I'd slapped him in the face. "Sophia, the tribe's *already* divided in two. Defortai and Biyami. There's no turning back. We're too late."

Liam pressed his fingers to his eyes, like he was tired of having this argument. He was supposed to be our leader... but at this point, he didn't have any words. Even he didn't know what to do.

"So what?" I snapped. "I'm supposed to help Defortai win!? I won't do that."

"So let's *leave*," Jonah begged. "Maybe that's the best way to prevent the prophecy. If you're not here, it can't be fulfilled."

"No. No. *No!*" Imogen raked her fingers through her pixie cut and started flipping through her notes frantically. "There has to be a way!"

Jonah grabbed her by the shoulders and forced her to look at him. "This isn't our fight anymore, Im."

Liam sighed. "Jonah's right. I want to save the tribe, too, but we need to take care of the people we love first."

I couldn't do it. I couldn't give up. I shook my head as I ran the pieces of the prophecy through my mind.

The fated Koigni child, born in the Summer Solstice in the Year of the Dragon,

Shall bring glory to the greatest House.

The future of the tribe is in Nivita's hands.
No Hawkei shall survive if the weakest refuse to bend.

When the tribe divides in two and war has begun
The Hawkei have reached the point of no return.
Smoke will Blaze through the sky and signify the Hawkei's extinction.

The prophesied one will bring death beyond comprehension.
It is she who shall cause Toaqua's darkest hour.

That's when it hit me. I couldn't bear to think of it, but maybe we really *had* reached the end. I spoke slowly, unable to believe the thought was coming out of my mouth. "Maybe... maybe I've already done my part."

"What do you mean?" Liam asked.

I swallowed. "The trial. It all started with us, Liam."

Liam reached out for my hands. "That's not true, *pawee*."

"But it is," I insisted. "Think of how many people have died since then. It's because of *me* that Defortai even exists. It's because of *me* that they're going to win."

"You don't know that," Imogen said in a reassuring tone.

"What does it mean, Elder Chang?" I spun to look at him, but I was shocked when my eyes met nothing but the flat painting. Elder Chang's spirit was gone.

"No!" I shouted. I raced toward the painting and ran my hands along the surface frantically. I checked the frame, like I might somehow find his spirit hiding within the canvas. There was nothing. I whirled back toward Jonah. "Bring him back! I have so many questions."

Jonah frowned. "Sophia, I think it's pretty clear what the Air piece means."

My fists tightened. "You don't know everything just because you're the Storm Lord."

Jonah's jaw dropped. "You need to calm down so we can figure this out."

I started pacing again. Esis tried to crawl up my leg, but I was too agitated to stop and pick him up. I nearly trampled him, and he jumped away. "How can I be calm? Our own people are about to die!"

Liam reached out and pulled me into a hug. I wiggled, but he only held me tighter.

Turns out, I really needed that hug. I relaxed into him. A single tear streaked down my cheek.

"I just wanted to save them all," I whispered. Images of the faces I was abandoning flashed through my mind. Lindsey. Miranda. My grandparents. Adriel. So many others.

Liam ran his fingers through my hair. "I know, Sophia. So did I."

Silence settled over the Air Kingdom. After a few moments, Imogen stepped forward and wrapped her arms around both Liam and I. The three of us rocked back and forth, and we all looked to Jonah.

"Come on, guys," he whimpered. "Don't make me cry."

Liam smirked. "Get in here."

Jonah joined in on the group hug. Our Familiars came close, too. Squeaks wrapped a wing around us, and Esis curled his tail around my ankle, while Sassy pushed her way between our legs and sat on our feet.

After several long moments of silence, I finally spoke. "So, what are we going to do?"

We all stepped away from the group hug. Everybody seemed lost.

Liam stepped in. "We're leaving, like we planned," he said. "But now that we have all the pieces, we can get a second opinion."

"From your dad?" Imogen asked.

Liam nodded. "Yeah. He might know what to do."

I hiked my backpack higher up my shoulders. "Okay. Then let's go."

We returned to the ground the same way we came. Jonah made a big deal about how now that he was the Storm Lord, he could've flown us all the way to Liam's house, but we knew we'd be seen from the skies. We crept through the darkness of the forest, being careful to listen for Task Force members, but it was silent all the way to the beach. My heart pounded the whole way back.

I breathed a sigh of relief when we reached the shore. The boat Liam's parents had left for us wasn't far from the trees. We glanced around, and when we saw the coast we clear, we went running through the sand and hopped into the boat. Liam used his powers to propel us along so we wouldn't be given away by the engine. I kept glancing around, waiting for the Task Force to step out of the trees or something and announce that we'd been caught, but the night was quiet.

Esis clung tightly to me as we pulled away from shore.

"I hope no one's worried," Imogen said, glancing at her watch.

"What time is it?" Liam asked.

"Almost one in the morning," Imogen announced.

"That late already?" Liam balked.

Jonah undid his hair tie and worked the strands back into a bun. "We must've spent a lot more time in the Air Kingdom than I thought."

Liam glanced behind us to the retreating shoreline, as if he expected someone to be following. I even noticed him look to the skies. I looked upward too, but there was nothing except the moon, stars, and some clouds.

"Are we safe?" Imogen asked, noticing Liam's intake of his surroundings.

"Yeah," Liam breathed. "I think we're safe for now."

It felt like an extra long ride, but eventually, the lights of Liam's house came closer and closer. We pulled up to the dock, and for a moment, I truly believed what Liam had said was true. The four of us and our Familiars were safe.

But it wasn't more than ten seconds that I'd stepped out of the boat and began tying it to the dock that two figures came running out of the house.

"Liam!" Ezra sprinted so quickly I was surprised he didn't fall on his face.

Everyone froze and watched as Ezra's silhouette came closer and closer. Dyami flew high above him, making circles in the sky. Ezra was followed by his mother, Haloke, though she wasn't as quick as he was. She seemed exhausted.

"What's wrong?" Liam asked breathlessly.

Ezra sprinted down the dock and reached Liam. He slammed into his brother so hard that Liam stumbled back. The two nearly fell off the dock as they embraced.

Liam squeezed him once, then grabbed his shoulders. "Ezra, what's going on?"

Ezra swallowed. "We thought you weren't going to make it. Where are Maddie and Drew? Are they with you?"

Liam shot the rest of us a wide-eyed glance, then looked beyond Ezra to their mother, who'd stopped at the end of the dock. "No, she's not. What do you mean? What happened to her?"

Ezra's expression dropped. "Dad hasn't seen her all day. He came back home to check, but—"

Liam's face fell. "Where is he?"

"He went out looking for you guys," Ezra said.

Liam clapped Ezra on the shoulder. "Get in. We're going back to help."

"Liam," his mother protested. Her tone was gentle, but it was enough to make Liam pause. "Let your father handle this."

Liam turned to her. "How long has he been gone? Long enough to send another search party?"

Haloke hesitated.

"Sorry, Mom," Liam said, "but we have to go look for Maddie. We saw the Task Force raiding the Yapluma village earlier tonight. If they finished, they might've moved on to the academy. Maddie's Biyami. She's a target."

Haloke steeled her gaze, and she stepped forward. The way she walked across the dock, you'd think she was walking on air. She was so graceful. She walked straight up to Liam and placed a hand on the side of his face. The moonlight shimmered off the water and into her eyes.

"Come home safely." She turned to Ezra and did the same thing to him by placing a palm on the side of his face. "Both of you."

"We will," Liam promised.

Liam and Ezra climbed back into the boat. I tossed the rope back in and jumped in behind them.

Ezra waved to his mother. "We'll be back soon."

"I'm holding you to that," she said.

No sooner had she said it than we were pulling away from the dock again. Dyami followed us from above. My fingers tangled in Esis' fur as I held him close. My hands were shaking. I hoped nothing bad had happened to Maddie.

When we returned to shore, the beach was just as quiet as we left it. It was almost eerie. The hair on the back of my neck stood up, though there was no reason for it. No one should be out here at this time of night, anyway.

We crept up the path and to the school. I was picturing the worst— Task Force members stationed at every exit, Biyami begging for their lives. But when we got to there, it was dead silent. We hid in the trees and looked to each other for explanation.

"If the castle wasn't raided, where could Maddie be?" Imogen thought aloud.

Moments passed. Imogen paused for a second before saying, "Yeah, that crossed my mind, too."

It sounded like she was talking to herself. I furrowed my brow and looked to Imogen. "Thought what?"

She shot me back a look that said I was crazy. "That if Maddie couldn't get out, she's hiding in the Anichi dorms. You *just* said that."

All eyes turned to Imogen.

"Uh... no I didn't," I said.

Imogen frowned. "You did. I just said, *Where could Maddie be? And* you're like, *The Anichi dorms.*"

"Imogen, I didn't—"

"Shh..." Imogen cut me off. She held a finger up and listened for several seconds. She spun around, looking deep into the woods. She raised her voice. "Who's there?"

Jonah pressed the back of his hand to Imogen's forehead. "No one's there, Im. Are you okay?"

She looked to the sky, then all around her. "Ancestors, that's *freaky!* Where's that voice coming from? And who the fuck are you calling *dipshit*, dipshit?"

"What voice—?" I started, but I was cut off when Imogen inhaled a sharp breath.

She looked down to Sassy, and the confusion on her face melted. It was quickly replaced by a heartwarming expression. "Sassyyyy!" she sang as she bent to pick up her Familiar, pulling her into a tight hug. "Oh em gee! You can talk to me."

"Finally," Jonah said with a sigh of relief. "I was wondering when you guys would start talking."

I felt a sting of jealousy hit me, since I'd never heard Esis speak before, but it was short lived. There were much more pressing matters at play.

Liam looked to the castle. "Well, if Sassy thinks Maddie might be in the Anichi dorms, I say that's the first place we check out."

Ezra placed a hand on Liam's chest before he could step forward. "Hold on. I'll send Dyami to check it out. He can fly over the glass ceiling and see if she's in there."

Liam nodded. "Okay."

Ezra signaled up to Dyami. We all watched as he soared around the castle. As he came in close to us, he shot Ezra the slightest of nods.

Ezra turned to the rest of us. "He says she's there."

Liam's shoulders fell in relief. "Then what are we waiting for? Let's go get her and bring her home."

"I'll go, bro," Ezra volunteered.

"No," Liam replied firmly. "We stick together."

Ezra's jaw tightened. "It'll be easier for one person to go. We're less likely to get caught by the Task Force. I'm Defortai, so even if I do get caught, they'll let me off."

"And if they see you with Maddie, a Biyami?" Liam demanded. "If we all go, we can fight back if it comes down to it. We won't get caught."

Ezra seemed to sense that there was no use arguing with Liam. "Okay. You're the leader."

Liam signaled for us to follow him, and we all hurried across the grass and to a door near the south stairwell. We slipped inside unnoticed and tiptoed up the stairs. Even Squeaks was abnormally quiet for herself.

We peeked into the hallway on the third floor. The hall was completely deserted, which seemed a little strange to me. We hadn't spotted a single Task Force member since we arrived.

"Where is everyone?" I whispered.

"I bet the Task Force is all preoccupied in the Yapluma village," Jonah guessed.

"Good point," I replied.

"A blessing in disguise," Liam muttered. "Come on. Let's go."

We stepped into the hall and rushed as quickly and quietly as we could to the doors of the Anichi tower. I worried that a Task Force member might turn the corner before we got there, but we slipped inside unnoticed. I blew out the breath of air I'd been holding, as did everyone else.

As we climbed the stairs, I couldn't help but wonder what drove Maddie to hide in the Anichi dorms tonight. Had there been too many Task Force members roaming the halls to keep her from leaving? Was she planning to stake it out until they did bed checks? Had she fallen asleep before she left? Did she know the halls were empty now?

We reached the top of the stairs, and my heart lifted in my chest when I saw Maddie sitting on one of the couches, safe and sound. We started toward her.

But my relief lasted a mere split second. Maddie's eyes went wide when she saw us.

She shot to her feet. "No! You shouldn't be here!"

"Maddie, what's going—?"

She cut Liam off. "It's a trap!"

My stomach plummeted to my toes as the sound of marching footsteps came from down the dorm hallway. All at once, Task Force members flooded into the common room from all directions. Our little group took a step back, pressing closely to one another. I glanced behind us at the entrance. Two Task Force members had already stepped in front of it, aiming their guns at our faces.

Esis screamed and clung tighter to me. Liam's hands curled into fists beside me, like he was ready to fight by any means necessary. Sassy turned to kitsune form immediately, and Imogen planted her feet firmly in a defensive stance. Ezra shot his gaze upward, as if checking for Dyami through the glass ceiling. Jonah threw himself in front of the rest of us and held his hands out like he was holding an invisible soccer ball. He probably thought he was going to conjure a lightning ball like he'd done in the Air Kingdom and knock these suckers on their asses, but nothing happened.

The beat of marching footsteps came to a halt as the Task Force members stood in formation. My eyes darted every which way, but all I saw were faceless, uniformed police. They had us completely surrounded.

Eerie silence passed for a beat, then came the sound of footsteps. They weren't like the march of the Task Force. They had a different rhythm, an angry, ominous beat that made my skin crawl.

When I saw who the footsteps belonged to, my body ignited with heat. I kept one hand at the ready, prepared to throw Fire if I had to.

Oleander stepped out of hiding, dragging a handcuffed and gagged Alric beside him. He held a pistol to Alric's head. I wasn't sure if it was filled with noxite bullets or real ones, but it was horrifying nonetheless. I half expected to see Baine being dragged behind Alric, but Baine was nowhere in sight, thank the ancestors.

Oleander grabbed Alric by the back of the shirt and shoved him forward. Alric yelped and tripped into the middle of the room. His forehead slammed to the ground, since his hands were bound behind his back. Oleander pointed the gun at Alric's head.

"What the hell is this?" Liam demanded.

Oleander chuckled maniacally. "Don't play dumb with me, Biyami. I know what you've been up to. I know all about your smuggling operation."

Liam gaped at him. "How?"

Oleander cleared his throat, and two figures stepped into the room.

Mia and Micah.

Damn it, Liam! I knew we couldn't trust her! The heat in my body grew by several degrees.

Mia cowered behind Micah. Her eyes were bloodshot, and she gave Liam one of the saddest looks I'd ever seen. I might've fallen for it if I wasn't so riled up. Micah, on the other hand, stood confidently with his arms crossed. He shot Liam a smug expression, like he was proud to be getting back at him after all this time. I bet he never forgot the time we confronted him in the alley when he caught him pushing Mia around.

Micah's horrid, lizard-like Familiar was even uglier than I remembered it. It stood beside Taryn, whose fur was falling out in patches.

"Please." Liam stepped forward. "Leave the rest of them out of this. It was my idea."

"Liam," I protested. "Don't."

He shot me back a pleading look. It was a look I'd never seen before — something that said this moment called for drastic measures beyond anything any of us could ever imagine. Whatever went down tonight, it was clear Liam would do whatever he had to in order to protect us. He'd vowed to keep us safe.

I was afraid of how far he'd take that promise.

Liam

TWENTY-ONE

We'd lost. We'd *so* fucking lost. The prophecy doomed us all to ruin and the tribe to extinction. Now my friends were in trouble. We'd been found out, and we were outnumbered. There was no getting out of this.

Oleander jerked his head. Eirakari was led in from one of the dorm rooms by two large alicorns. The ice dragon had chains around her muzzle and legs. She brayed for Maddie to help her. The alicorn kicked her in the face, and she lowered her head.

"Maddie, where's Drew?" Sophia asked calmly. Maddie gave a pitiful sob.

Oleander smirked. "The little girl's boyfriend was detained to make sure she cooperated. We'll release him once we're done here."

He was a right bastard. I could see the look in his eyes. He wouldn't give Drew back even if we complied with his demands.

Oleander moved forward. "I suggest one of you starts talking," he began. "Alric's fate has already been sealed, but some of you might escape judgement if you begin confessing."

It was clear what he was suggesting. He stared right at me as he said the words. For some reason, Oleander wanted me to give myself up.

I was the only bargaining chip we had. And we had to use it.

"This smuggling operation was my plan. Alric and I put it on," I said loudly. "We coerced the others and forced them to take part. I'm fully responsible."

"No!" Sophia rushed forward. "I won't let you do this!"

"This is the only way," I told her roughly. Couldn't she see I was trying to save her life? I'd do anything to save her.

"We'll all take responsibility!" Sophia was begging, and it was hard to watch. "We all took part, we're equally guilty!"

"Sophia, *stand down.*"

The tone in my voice shocked her. I'd never spoken to her like that, and I think it scared her.

Imogen and Jonah put their hands on Sophia's shoulders and pulled her back. Her nervous eyes shifted from Oleander to me as she tried to figure out what to do.

"Is that a formal confession?" Oleander asked.

"It is," I said firmly. "Judge me, but not the others. I promise to accept whatever punishment you give."

Oleander's eyes narrowed. "And why should we not prosecute the others? They've all had involvement."

"If you take me, and let the others go, I'll come quietly. I won't try to escape, and I won't hurt anyone," I said. "But if you don't, and try to arrest all of us... we'll fight. We'll fight back, and we'll do everything we can to take people down with us. We'll kill everyone in here if we have to. You won't take us alive. The choice is up to you."

Oleander grinned wickedly. "Deal. Take him into custody."

"*No!*" Sophia screamed. Two Task Force members moved forward. One forced my hands behind my back, while the other slapped on cuffs.

"The handcuffs are forged with noxite," the Task Force member said. "So don't be getting any bright ideas."

Yeah, right. I could feel my powers draining the minute they put them on. Oleander looked positively giddy as he said, "Liam Mitoh, you are hereby sentenced to death for high treason against the Elders. Your sentence shall be carried out at sunset tomorrow, before the entire tribe."

"Fine," I snapped. "Just get it the fuck over with."

"Liam," Sophia moaned. She was wailing in despair. Jonah and

Imogen's faces were streaked with tears as they helplessly stood by, unable to do much of anything but hold Sophia and each other.

"No! That wasn't our agreement!" Mia spoke for the first time. She strode forward in front of Oleander with her head held high. "You promised—"

"Agreements can be changed," Oleander spat at her. He gave a smoldering look to Micah. "Control your woman, before I take her into custody as well."

Micah grabbed Mia and yanked her backward by her hair. "Fucking behave," he snarled.

Mia fell silent, though absolute shock shone in her eyes. Micah pushed her down, and Mia fell to all fours in front of me.

"Liam," Mia gasped. "Please forgive me."

I couldn't even look at her right now. I was so disgusted with her. Sophia was right all along. That's what you get for trusting an ex. I'd been so fucking stupid. I'd put everyone in danger, and for what? All because I couldn't stop seeing the good in people.

There was no good left in Mia. Not after this.

"Bro," Ezra gasped. He was holding on to Maddie, who was crying into his shoulder.

"It's okay," I said quietly, though my voice shook. I needed to be strong for them. "It'll be all right."

Ezra was torn. His expression wavered. If he tried to save me, he'd be killing everyone else in the room. But by doing nothing, he was letting me die.

"You need to take care of the family, okay?" I told him. "That's your job now."

Ezra's face hardened, and he gave me a quick nod, though his lip trembled. It was too hard to watch, so I turned my back on the people I loved. I said nothing as the Task Force members escorted me out, painfully aware of the sound of Sophia's screams behind me.

"Take him to the dungeons," Oleander said. A Task Force member picked Alric off the floor and dragged him behind me. Oleander and the rest of the police abandoned my friends, and followed us downward. The stairs went winding in a spiral toward what felt like the pit of hell.

I didn't even know this school had an *actual* fucking dungeon. I thought the basement was it.

But if I thought the basement was bad, this was ten times worse. The only light was a few torches placed in uneven spaces along the wall. The floors and walls were stone, and the area was damp and musty. Cobwebs hung on the walls, and mice ran along the floor. The Task Force escorted me down a row of bars until we came to a small cell at the end of the block.

"Forgive me for departing so soon, but I have to prepare your execution," Oleander sneered in a delighted tone.

I was uncuffed and thrown into the empty cell headfirst. My forehead smacked against the stone as the guards walked away, and I gave a cry of pain. There was blood trickling down my forehead, but fuck it.

Oleander proceeded down a different hallway, and Task Force members dragged Alric behind him. The Head Dean didn't say a word, just kept his head down and his eyes closed— like he'd already accepted his fate. They vanished from sight. I heard the sound of a heavy iron door closing somewhere in the distance.

Where the fuck were they taking Alric? Paranoia that I'd been left alone down here was starting to take over. A small puddle in the corner gave me hope, but when I tried to summon my powers, the water didn't move.

I touched one of the bars and immediately experienced a buzzing sensation that was familiar. Bars were also noxite. Motherfucker.

I examined the walls for loose stone, the floor for cracks, anything that might give me hope this wasn't the end. But the cell was secure, and even if I could use my powers, there wasn't enough water in here for me to make an escape. The padlock was solid, and I didn't have anything to pick it.

There was no getting out of here. I really was trapped.

My back hit the stone wall, and I slid onto the floor. This cell had nothing— not even a bucket or a bed.

I was going to die tomorrow. I couldn't fathom that as a fact. I knew I'd been sentenced to die, but the idea that it was actually going to happen was comical. I'd tried to take my own life last year, but right now, all I wanted to do was live.

Whatever. I was glad for it. I'd sold myself to keep my friends safe. As long as they were alive, I didn't care what happened to me.

I didn't know how, but exhaustion forced me to get a few hours of sleep. When I woke up, there was a small ray of sunlight streaming through a window at the end of the block I hadn't seen last night.

I got off the stone floor and immediately cried out as a spasm went through my back. Every inch of my body wracked with horrible cramps and tremors. Sleeping on that stone had really fucked me up. I had to move gingerly to give myself time to adjust to the pain.

Hey, a bit of good news. If I was dead, at least I wouldn't have to deal with this shitty body anymore. My suffering was just about over.

A shadowy figure on the other side of the bars caught my attention. I pieced together features, and revulsion curled inside of me as I saw Mia cross her arms over her torso and hug herself.

"What are you doing here?" I snarled. "Fucking leave."

"I've only come to explain." Mia came into the light. Her expression was desperate as she observed me in the back corner of the cell.

"If you think I want an explanation from you, you're fucking nuts. You betrayed me. For the *second time*. And I was stupid enough to fall for your act."

"It wasn't an act. I really did want to help," she pleaded.

"I thought you changed. I thought you'd become a better person," I said bitterly. "Turns out you're still the same bitch who cheated on me and dumped me for a psychopath."

"You don't understand. In this new world, you have to do what you must to survive. Being Defortai doesn't mean you'll be safe."

"So you kill Biyami to save your own skin, is that it?" My knuckles cracked as I tightened them into fists. I was beyond infuriated. There weren't words for how mad I was. I was glad there were bars between Mia and I at that moment, because if there weren't, I was afraid of what I might do to her.

"Liam, I didn't think they were going to *kill* you!" Mia started crying. Tears poured down her face as she exclaimed, "Oleander promised he'd spare your life!"

"Oleander's a fucking liar!" I shouted. "How can you believe *anything* he says?"

"I had to do this for the sake of my family. It was the only way to keep us together." Mia's sobs grew louder. "Micah's been working for Oleander, but his performance has been disappointing. He's in trouble. If he failed the Elders one more time, he was going to lose everything, and they were going to dispose of him after. Telling Oleander about you was the only way to save his life."

"Forgive me if I think exchanging my life for that son of bitch is a worthy trade," I spat.

Her voice shook. "You don't understand. I can't have my child grow up without a father. Liam, I'm pregnant."

Mia's eyes overflowed as tears ran down her face. Some of my anger faded away at her confession. She put a hand on her stomach and took gasping breaths. "I didn't find out until recently. But this baby, it's every-thing to me. I'd do anything to protect him, Liam. Anything."

My insides soured. I'd do *anything* to have a baby with Sophia, but we weren't going to get that chance now— we never would. Even if we found a way to work around me being infertile and the tribe refusing our child, Mia had taken that away from us.

"Well, congratulations, I guess. Hopefully you'll treat that kid a hell of a lot better than you've treated me," I snapped bitterly. I couldn't help it. I hated her right now.

"This baby needs a stable life," Mia said firmly. "I was all for helping you rebel before I found out about him, but things have changed now. Overthrowing the Elders is impossible. This is the way things are. Micah and I have to do what's best for our child."

"Does he know?" I asked.

She rubbed her stomach. "Not yet. But I'm sure once I tell him, things will be different."

I gave a skeptical noise. "The best thing you can do for that baby is get yourself away from Micah. He's not going to be a good father."

"He'll change. This baby will bring us together."

"Please. He'll start abusing the kid right alongside you."

Mia's eyes grew wide. "He wouldn't do that."

"How many times did you think that before he started hitting you?"

Mia's eyes flashed to the side. I pressed myself against the bars. "You listen to what I'm saying. If that kid grew up with no father at all, it'd be a million times better than him having an abuser for a dad. What is that going to do to him, watching Micah hit you? What's it gonna do to him to let him get beat on?"

She shivered. "It won't happen. We belong together. This baby... Micah will love him."

Mia was a lost cause. She'd never believe Micah didn't have her best interests at heart. She had an addiction to a bad relationship, and she'd willingly bring kids into the situation if it meant keeping him around.

I'd wanted to rescue her so badly. But saving her had come at the cost of sacrificing myself. And I just couldn't do that anymore. I couldn't drown myself to keep her afloat. Whatever happened to Mia— and her child— it was in the hands of the Great Spirit now. I wanted no part of it anymore.

I just wish I'd made that decision months ago.

"You want to make up for this? Go get Sophia," I said. "You can get past the guards. Convince them to let me speak to her one last time. Then I'll forgive you. For everything."

Mia nodded. "Okay. I'm sorry, Liam."

"Yeah, sure. Sophia. Hurry."

Mia ran off. My legs were shaking, so I sat down on the floor again to get some rest. My eyes closed as I drifted in and out of consciousness. I was so tired.

They still hadn't brought Alric back. It'd been hours. I was terrified of what they'd done to him in the meantime. Or had they merely separated us? I didn't know.

Eventually, I heard another door open somewhere down the line. I heavy hiking boots slapped against stone as someone came running down the hallway. My heart lifted when my gaze connected with brown eyes. A Task Force member was near, and he seemed disinterested in what was going on.

Sophia fell to her knees when she reached my cell. The water soaked her jeans. I reached out through the bars and took her hands. The cell didn't permit us to do much else. Dried tear stains soaked her cheeks— it looked like she'd been crying all night.

"You've got five minutes," the guard said before he left us alone. Sophia broke down again. I reached up and wiped away her tears.

"Hey, hey, don't cry," I whispered. "It's all gonna be okay."

"Liam, you're going to die," she moaned. "I saw them building the execution ring. It's actually happening."

I felt like I was going to be sick, but the woman I loved was here and I couldn't fall to pieces in front of her. I changed the subject. "Where's Esis?"

"With Imogen. They wouldn't let me bring him down here." Sophia's frown was watery. "Liam, you look awful."

I forced a smile. "This isn't exactly a five star resort, you know."

Sophia gave a miserable laugh. "I don't know how you keep doing this," she said shakily. "I don't know how you stay so strong."

She didn't know it was because I didn't have a choice. Everything I did, I did for her, and I didn't want the memory of me breaking down before my execution seared into Sophia's mind for eternity long after I was gone. "What I feel doesn't matter right now," I said. "I care about you."

"That bitch Mia. I fucking hate her for giving you up." Sophia's voice was full of malice and loathing.

"She had a reason. Not a good one, but it's understandable," I said with a sigh. "She's pregnant with Micah's kid, and Micah was in hot water with Oleander. Giving us up was the only way to make sure he stayed alive."

Sophia's eyes cleared, and her features softened. For the first time, it looked like Sophia could understand Mia's actions. It was probably the mothering instinct in her.

"She needs to take that kid and run," Sophia whispered.

"It doesn't matter what she does now. She's not our concern," I insisted. "But Soph, you need to get the hell out of here."

"I'm not leaving without you." Her voice was firm and fierce. Her tears began to dry as she made the statement.

"You and I both know I'm not getting out of this one." I reached out and stroked her chestnut hair. I just wanted to run my hands through it, over and over.

"We've gotten out of some pretty bad situations," she said. "You've almost died how many times before? This one's no different."

"This time it's not just me who's in danger. It's all of us," I said. "You get Jonah and Imogen, and you leave. You understand me? *Leave*. Don't come back for me, don't try to play the hero. If you try to stop the execution, they'll kill you too, and my sacrifice will have been for nothing."

"You can't expect me to sit back and watch you die."

"I don't want you to watch. I want you to be long gone before any of that happens," I stated. "Take my family and go. Dad said he knows a safe place."

Sophia shook her head. "I won't do it. I'd rather die next to you."

"What is that going to do for me, huh?" I took her face in my hands. "Why would I want you to give up a single second of your life to try and save mine, when we both know it's not going to work?"

"I don't care. It's not worth living without you," she moaned.

"Don't ever say that." She was getting emotional again. My fingers combed through her hair. "Sophie, come on. You've gotta live your life and move on. You're gonna find someone else and have lots and lots of babies, okay? That's what you want. It'll make you happy. You've got to go on without me."

"I'm not doing any of that without you." Her fingers ran along my arms and over the muscles there, like she was painting, or sketching. I caught the glimmer of the engagement ring on her finger, and it was physically painful. "I want *your* babies."

"It's okay." I felt like I was saying that over and over, and it would never really be okay, but there was nothing else I could do. "You're gonna make it without me. You're strong."

"How can the ancestors let this happen?" Her heart seemed full of despair. "I don't understand why the Great Spirit wouldn't stop this."

"Sometimes the bad guys win, and there isn't anything we can do about it but leave what we lost behind and keep moving forward," I hushed. "The prophecy's done, Soph. There's nothing left for you to do. You can be free now. I want you to fly high, baby, and don't look back."

Sophia sniffed. I was aware of the guard's footsteps approaching.

"Time's up," he said. "Say your goodbyes."

"No. No, I want to stay with him!" Sophia screamed as the guard grabbed her by the forearm and yanked her to her feet. He pulled her in the direction of the exit as she cried my name over and over.

"Don't hurt her," I said feebly. Eventually, Sophia relented and allowed him to pull her away.

He dragged her out of my sight, and I heard the door close again.

Okay. She was gone, so now I was allowed to cry. I lay on my back on the stone floor and let the tears pour out of my eyes. I'd never see Sophia again, but she'd be alive. She'd be my last thought before the Elders got done doing whatever they had planned for me.

I just hoped to the ancestors whatever man came after me took care of her just as well as I would've.

But he'd never love her like I did. My passion for Sophia was incomprehensible. It went beyond feelings and could only be experienced at a soul level. If I had survived these past few years after Nashoma's death to lay my life down for Sophia, well... that was good enough for me.

Hours passed. There was nothing to do but sit back and contemplate my life, but the time passed ridiculously fast. It felt like I couldn't grasp on to enough minutes, enough seconds. I only had so many precious moments before my life was stolen from me, and they were determined to slip away. It felt horribly akin to my near death in the tournament, and it was traumatizing to relive it all over again.

When the light in the dungeons shifted, I heard the iron door that they'd taken Alric behind open. I watched a pair of Task Force members carry Alric down the hall as his feet dragged behind him.

His face was puffy and full of bruises and scars. His clothes were soaked with blood, and his head hung limply on his shoulders. Alric was hardly recognizable.

They'd tortured him for hours, and only just gotten done now. Why didn't they torture me, too? Didn't they think I had information to give?

The answer was clear. The Task Force knew Alric was hiding something beyond the smuggling operation— something he'd failed to tell me. I was certain it was the same thing Ezra and the rest of them were keeping from Sophia, Imogen, Jonah and I.

The guards opened the door and threw Alric into the cell next to mine. He fell face-first onto the stone and didn't move.

The guards left. I inched closer to Alric's cell and inspected his injuries. It didn't look like he had any broken bones, but he'd been roughed up pretty badly.

"Are you all right?" I asked. Alric painfully pulled himself to a sitting position. He leaned against the bars and breathed heavily, gasping for air.

"I'll be fine once they bring an end to this charade," he rasped. He looked longingly at the puddle in his cell, like he thought about trying to drink it, but didn't have enough energy.

"Where's Valda?"

"In the outer gardens, chained up," Alric breathed. "It's where they'll do it."

"Why haven't they executed us already? They've never hesitated to kill people before," I asked.

"Because they want to make it a show. We're examples," Alric said roughly. "They won't allow us to die without a public audience."

I was quiet for a moment before I said, "I'm guessing we'll be executed in a crueler way than is typical."

Alric gave a painful moan as he shifted. "Are you familiar with the phrase, *animorte ee kyra?*"

"Yes." It was an old Koigni way of execution. A victim would be tied to a pyre, and a small fire lit beneath them. It wouldn't create enough smoke for the victim to die by carbon monoxide poisoning, so they'd slowly burn for hours, the flames starting with the feet and working their way up. Some history books noted that the process could take days. It was the worst thing that could happen to a Toaqua.

"That's how you'll go. I'll be taken to a pool that's set up beside your pyre and submerged in increments. They'll hold me under until I'm struggling to breathe, then allow me to catch my breath before submerging me again. This process will continue, and they'll let me obtain shorter and shorter breaths each time until eventually, they won't let me up at all. It's a process that will take hours." Alric spoke casually, as if he was talking about the weather and not his own death. He'd totally given up. They'd broken him.

Horror crept over my bones and settled there. My gut twisted so badly it was actually agonizing. I didn't know how my tongue moved to ask the next question, because the rest of me was paralyzed. "What about your Familiar?"

"If Valda's lucky, her throat will be cut. But I don't see her going quietly."

The only sound that could be heard was that of Alric's labored breathing. I debated on asking my next question, but I was going to die regardless, so I figured it couldn't hurt. "What were they interrogating you about?"

Alric coughed. "Something that is none of your concern."

Rage festered underneath my skin and heated my core. "That's bull," I spat. "I've done everything you've asked me to without question. I've been there for everything, for everyone, and I know you're hiding something. You owe me an explanation."

Alric gave a tired sigh. "Liam, if I explained everything, you'd never forgive me."

"You can't let me go to my grave without telling me what's going on," I growled.

"What you must know is that there are things I purposely kept from you and your friends. I would not have done this unless there was no other choice."

"My brother knows. Some of our friends know. They're in on it," I insisted.

"Yes. And all of them have agreed that it was best to conceal certain things from the four of you. Trust me when I say that telling you everything would put Sophia's life in jeopardy— even now."

Fine. Alric could keep his secrets. Nothing was worth Sophia's life. It was obvious he wouldn't give up the goods, even at the end.

"I only wish I could see him. One last time," Alric whispered. He stared at the other end of his cell, as if he could see Professor Perot now.

I pitied Alric. I'd gotten to say goodbye to my love. Alric would never get to say farewell to Perot. He'd probably be dead long before Perot even got the news— wherever he was.

I tapped my fingers against the floor. "What I don't get... Oleander seemed pretty content to take me in the place of everyone else. He made it clear I was the one they were after."

"They never wanted you, Liam," Alric wheezed. "They're after your father."

I froze. "What?"

"Chief Mitoh disappeared a few days ago. Oleander ordered his death sentence. No one can find him," Alric said. "Your execution is to bring him out of the woodwork. They were going to use Maddie, but have considered this a better option. They have more evidence against you for the death penalty— not to mention Oleander wants to keep Maddie for himself, to use her gift for his own purposes."

My breath left my lungs, and my hands tangled in my hair. I sprang upward and started pacing my cell, looking for a way out— any way. Oleander had found out about Maddie's powers, and he was going to kill my dad. I couldn't let that happen.

"I can't sit here while they're planning to use me as bait. I have to get out," I insisted. I ran from corner to corner, grabbed the bars, shook them, but nothing did any good. I finally resorted to kicking and punching at the door, but it wouldn't budge. I felt like a trapped animal in a cage, the walls slowly closing in.

"Save your energy," Alric whispered. "You'll need it."

A growing terror encompassed my chest as I heard the sound of multiple boots clomping down the hallway. Twelve Task Force members, all holding noxite guns, marched in front of our cells. The lead guard stepped in front of my cell and opened the door. It made a resounding *clank* that echoed ominously in my ears.

"Sunset has come, kid," he said. "It's the end of the line."

TWENTY-TWO

Liam's words rang in my ears as the Task Force shoved me out of the dungeons. *You've gotta go on without me.*

No way in hell.

You're strong.

If I didn't find a way to stop this, I was nothing.

I curled my hands into fists and racked my brain for solutions as I headed back to the Anichi dorms, where my friends and I had stayed the night. We'd been granted our freedom, thanks to Liam's sacrifice, but the Task Force was still watching us closely. No doubt they were ready to strike the second we tried to retaliate. Like Oleander said, *agreements can be changed.* I didn't believe for one second he'd uphold his end of the bargain once Liam's execution took place. He had no honor.

Which meant I had to get Liam out of here one way or another, or we were all doomed. I wouldn't run like—

I yelped as a hand shot out from a dark classroom and pulled me into the shadows. I'd been so consumed in my own thoughts that I hadn't been watching my surroundings. I tried to scream, but a hand slapped over my mouth to stifle it.

"Shh, Sophia. It's me."

My eyes widened at the sound of that deep, rough voice. I grabbed his hand and pulled it off my mouth, then whirled around to face

Liwanu. He was wearing a bearskin rug on his back, like it was some sort of disguise, and held a bow with a quiver of arrows.

Liwanu must've felt the ring on my finger, because his eyes flickered downward, though he didn't look shocked. It was like he already knew.

At the sight of him, heat flared through my bones, so hot that my Fire threatened to escape. *This was all his fault!* If he'd been here to save Maddie, none of this would've happened. He'd failed his kids. Because of him, Liam was going to *die*.

Before I knew what I was doing, I swung my fist out, and it connected with Liwanu's jaw. Nearby, Tatum let out a low growl.

"Where *were* you?" I hissed. My voice was raw with devastation.

Liwanu rubbed his jaw. "I suppose I deserved that, didn't I?"

"Maddie was being held prisoner!" I snapped. "And now Liam's awaiting execution. You were supposed to be there for them, and you've been hiding like a *coward*! Some father you are."

Liwanu steeled his gaze, like the insult had no effect on him. If I hadn't been raging right now, I would've realized it was just a mask— one that a chief had to learn to wear in times like this.

"Please let me explain, Sophia," he begged.

I crossed my arms. "Fine. Where have you been all night? Where were you when Liam needed you?"

"Yesterday, I went to find Maddie, to tell her our plans to escape," Liwanu explained. "I couldn't find her anywhere. I returned to the house at midnight to see if Liam had gotten a message to her— that perhaps she was with you— but none of you were there. I ventured to the school to look for her and snuck around in this."

Liwanu gestured to his sorry excuse of a disguise. "I didn't know what had happened until I saw the Task Force taking Liam to the dungeons. I only learned about the Anichi dorms when I followed them to see where they were taking Liam. By the time I got to the dorms for the rest of you, they were so heavily guarded I couldn't get through."

"You could've used your magic," I spat.

"So they'd kill my son on the spot?" Liwanu asked. "I know how Oleander works, Miss Henley. Liam is only being held prisoner to bring me out of hiding. The council hasn't seen me for days— and I intend to keep it that way."

"So you'll risk your own son's life for your own!?" I exclaimed.

"Shh..." Liwanu shot a glance at the door and lowered his voice. "No, Sophia. Even if I come forward now, they won't pardon Liam. They'll kill us both. I've been waiting for an opportunity to speak to you. I intend to free both Liam and Maddie, but I need your help."

"Maddie?" I balked. "They still have her?"

We hadn't seen her since last night. I'd assumed Oleander had let her and Drew go per the agreement, and that either Liwanu had found them or they'd fled back to the island.

Liwanu frowned. "I heard the guards talking. Somehow, they found out about her gift. They're still holding her because of it."

My teeth gritted, but I was no longer mad at Liwanu. This just went to show Oleander would do anything to get his way.

"I'm in," I said.

Liwanu breathed a sigh of relief. "If we're going to work together, Sophia, there's something I must get off my chest first."

"Oh?" I raised an eyebrow.

Liwanu took a deep breath. "Sophia... I must apologize for how I've treated you in the past. Ancestors know the terrible things I have done, and the day will come when I must answer to the Great Spirit. But I see now how wrong I was. I always believed that Fire and Water couldn't mix— but you and Liam have proven otherwise, time and time again. Now I see that the only way to win this war is if Fire and Water come together."

His tone was genuine. It so full of sorrow that my eyes began to well with tears. Never before had I heard such a sincere apology.

"I guess what I'm trying to say, Sophia, is..." His eyes flickered down to my ring again. "Congratulations on the engagement, and welcome to the family."

Now I was crying for real. What the fuck? Tears streamed down my face as I took in his words. Liwanu had made amends before, but it wasn't like this. Back then, he was willing to accept mine and Liam's relationship because it was what made Liam happy, despite Liwanu's protests.

Now I saw no ill will behind his eyes. Liwanu wasn't just saying this for Liam's sake or some political move. He meant it. He wanted me to be his daughter-in-law.

I wiped at my eyes. "Thank you, Chief Mitoh."

Liwanu placed a hand on my shoulder. "Please, Sophia, call me Liwanu."

"Thank you... Liwanu," I said.

Then, before I knew what I was doing, I reached out and put my arms around Liwanu's middle— the way I used to hug my dad.

Liwanu stiffened for a moment before relaxing into the hug. Ancestors, he even smelled a little like my dad— like salt water and ocean breeze. We stood like that in silence for several moments, until Tatum came up and shoved his nose between us. I assumed he wanted to get in on the hug, but he was so big that he basically just shoved us apart. I scratched the grizzly bear on top of the head.

"Hey there, Tatum," I said. "You want some attention, too?"

The bear dropped his head, then looked back up at Liwanu with a melancholy expression. Liwanu's face fell. They shared a look I couldn't quite read.

"What is it?" I asked. "What'd he say?"

Liwanu stared at me with wide eyes— like he couldn't believe whatever Tatum had said. The strange look lasted only a second before he blinked and his face was back to normal. "Nothing, Sophia. It's time to rally the others and decide on our plan of attack."

"They're in the Anichi dorms," I told him. "But it's not safe there. The Task Force are watching."

Liwanu pressed a finger to his chin in thought. "Then we'll have to meet in another secure location."

I shook my head. "There aren't any in the castle anymore. The Anichi dorms were our best shot, and they've been discovered."

"There's another place," Liwanu said. "The four Houses still maintain control of their dormitories. Have Ezra lead you to the secret passageway to the Toaqua dorms. I'll meet you there."

"Wait," I said. "Where are you going?"

"You're a free woman for now," he reminded me. "But the Task Force still wants my head. I must not be seen."

"Okay. We'll see you soon."

I hurried out of the room and back toward the Anichi dorms. There were Task Force members at the base of the tower. They were walking around as if they were just passing by on patrol, but I knew they were there to watch our movements. Though we were free, Oleander was keeping close watch. I walked straight past them and up to the Anichi dorms.

Imogen was knotting her hands together in her lap, while Sassy spun around in circles like she was distressed. Ezra paced around and looked like he was about to punch something.

Jonah sat on one of the couches with his hands formed in a ball, like he was trying to conjure lightning. Squeaks was using her beak and claws to tear apart a pillow in fury. They all wore identical looks of worry on their faces.

Everyone's eyes darted toward me when I entered the common room. Esis jumped off the back of the sofa, where he'd been sitting next to Imogen, and bounded over to me.

"How's my brother?" Ezra asked breathlessly.

I caught Esis as he jumped toward my chest. He snuggled in tightly, like he'd missed me for the brief time I'd been away.

"Well, he's about to be executed, so you can guess," I stated flatly.

Ezra's lips tightened. "Yeah, I can see it clear as day. *Don't come after me, Sophia. Run away.*"

I raised my eyebrows. "Exactly."

Ezra huffed and crossed his arms. "Well, screw him. I'll do anything to save my brother."

"I would, too," Jonah said through gritted teeth, "if I could get these damn Storm Lord powers to work!"

Jonah shot to his feet and punched the cushion he'd been sitting on. Squeaks jumped from where she stood beside the couch.

Jonah growled. "I was gonna whip some shit up at the execution, get my best bud out of there, but I must've used up all my magical juice on that beast. I won't be recharged before this goes down."

I held up a hand to get Jonah to calm down. "We'll find another way."

"What's your plan?" Imogen asked.

I glanced around the room, as if I might spot a Task Force member hiding out in the shadows. Even if they hadn't stationed a spy up here, I knew this wasn't a safe place to talk.

"I can't say here," I said. "We need to pack our stuff and get going."

"How are we going to get past the Task Force without raising suspicion?" Imogen asked. "I bet they expect us to stay for the execution. Unless... are we taking the smuggling tunnel?"

I shook my head. "No. We're staying inside the school for now. But you make a good point. We'll leave our stuff here and come back for it later."

"If we have to make a quick break for it, Dyami can always fly through the glass ceiling," Ezra offered.

I nodded. "Take only your Familiars."

We left the Anichi dorms and walked by the Task Force members. I couldn't see their faces, but I caught them turning their heads, like they suspected something.

Ezra rubbed his belly. "I'm mighty hungry."

I elbowed him in the ribs, and he gasped. "Yeah, because *that* doesn't look suspicious," I hissed.

He shrugged as we entered the empty stairwell that led to the main floor. "It's not a lie. It's well past lunch time, and we haven't eaten all day."

I lowered my voice, even though there weren't any Task Force members around. "Then let's hope you can scrounge up some food for us from the Toaqua dorms. That's where we're headed."

Everyone furrowed their brows in unison, but Imogen was the one who spoke. "The dorms? Sophia, what's going on?"

"I can't say until we get there," I insisted. "It could put us all at risk. Ez, you need to get us into the secret tunnel that leads to the Toaqua dorms."

Ezra rubbed his hands mischievously. "You've got it. And food will be easy to find. I've got a stash of snacks hidden in that tunnel."

Jonah eyed me. "What kind of mission has Liam Baby got you up to?"

I ignored Jonah's question, because we exited the stairwell and there were two Task Force members walking down the hall.

Besides the Task Force, we only passed by a handful of students and one professor, but they paid us no mind. For a Friday, the castle was pretty quiet. The melancholy atmosphere might've had something to do with the recent raids and the execution blocks they were building outside in the gardens. But what did I know?

"Pst..." A voice came from inside one of the professor's offices. I almost didn't register it, until it came again. "Pst..."

Esis tugged on my shirt, and I backpedaled to glance inside the door, which was open only a crack. What I saw there made my heart stop.

"Maddie!?" I hissed.

Maddie didn't look at all like herself. Her hair was disheveled, and there was dirt all over her face and clothes. She looked like she'd spent a week down in the dungeons, not a single night. Everyone else stopped in their tracks.

Maddie opened the door wider and waved her hand. "Come inside, quick!"

We glanced up and down the hall, but the coast was clear, so the four of us and our Familiars ducked inside the office.

The office was nothing more than a dark room with empty shelves lining the walls. It must've belonged to one of the professors who left at the end of last semester. Eirakari took a step back into the corner to make room for everyone but with herself, Dyami, and Squeaks in the room, there was almost no space for the rest of us. By some miracle, Jonah managed to get the door closed.

"Ancestors, Maddie," Imogen whispered as she took in her appearance.

"We're so glad you're okay," I said, but I barely got the words out before Ezra shoved me aside.

He scooped up his little sister and squeezed her tightly. "Maddie, what happened to you? We thought you were released and went back home."

Maddie shook her head. "Oleander wanted to keep me locked up, but I escaped with Eirakari. I tried going back to the Anichi dorms, but the Task Force was watching like a hawk."

"Then why didn't you leave?" Ezra demanded. "They'll be looking for you."

Maddie wiped at her eyes. "They still have Drew. I have to find a way to get him out."

"No," Ezra said firmly. "They'll capture you again."

"Ez, this isn't up for debate." Maddie's eyes shone with determination.

"Yes, it is," he insisted. "Sophia has a plan."

All eyes turned to me.

I swallowed the lump in my throat. "Well... kind of."

"What do you mean, kind of?" Jonah asked. "Let's hear it."

"We have to get to the passageway," I reminded them.

Ezra glanced around the room. "This looks like a safe place to talk."

"Well, I can't tell you the plan, because I'm not the one who made it," I said.

They all exchanged a look of confusion.

"Then who?" Jonah demanded. "Where are you taking us, Sophia?"

"I told you already," I replied. "It's the only safe place to talk."

Imogen narrowed her eyes at me— like she suspected there was something I wasn't saying.

"I can't tell you in case someone's listening," I said. "But we have to get there, quick."

Maddie's tears had dried, and she faced me. "I trust you. I'm coming with."

"No, Mads," Ezra protested. "You could be spotted."

Maddie grabbed Ezra by the shoulders and looked straight into his eyes. "Ez, *I'm coming with.*"

He groaned. "Fine. It's not far. Let's go."

I didn't know how we made it through the halls without being spotted. We had a freaking ice dragon and thunderbird at our side. But there wasn't a single Task Force member in this part of the school. They must've been out raiding houses, or building the execution platforms. That, or the ancestors were watching over us today, because Ezra led us into another empty classroom without so much as spotting a Task Force member.

"This is where the secret tunnel is?" I asked, glancing around. It was just a normal classroom.

"Oh, you mean Ezra's sex dungeon?" Maddie joked.

Jonah nudged him with his elbow. "Dude, you have a *sex dungeon* and didn't tell me?"

Ezra frowned. "I prefer the term *hook-up hallway*."

"Yeah, yeah. Whatever," I said. "Show us the way."

Ezra opened a supply closet, and I glanced inside. There were shelves lined on either side, with potion vials filled with a clear liquid.

Ezra stepped into the closet and stood there for a few seconds with his arms at his sides and his palms held up.

"What's he doing?" Imogen asked.

"You'll see," Maddie said.

After a few moments, the liquid in the vials began to rise into the air. I realized that the liquid was nothing but water. Ezra controlled it so that it formed into a big ball in front of him, then he guided it to the stone wall at the back of the closet. The water moved to fill all the crevices between the stones, running like a river through them. The moment all the valleys were filled with water, a *click* sounded.

My eyebrows shot up as the stone wall slid to the side. It was a lock only Toaqua could open. *Clever.*

The door slid to the side all the way, revealing—

"Dad!?" Ezra cried.

A long hallway stretched in front of us, completely blanketed in darkness except for the small amount of light coming from the windows in the classroom. Liwanu leaned against the stone wall like he was exhausted. He stood up straight when he saw us.

"Inside, kids. Quickly." Liwanu waved, and we all hurried in. Dyami was so big that he barely fit. The door slid shut behind us, and Eirakari gave a low croon.

"Ow!" Imogen cried. "Jonah, that was my foot."

"Sorry," he muttered.

I cradled Esis in one arm and held up my free hand to light the passageway with my flame. Liwanu's eyes landed on Eirakari, then darted to Maddie.

"Maddie, you're okay!" he exclaimed.

Maddie threw herself at her dad and wrapped him in a hug. "I'm fine, Daddy. I got out by myself."

He pressed his nose into her hair as they embraced. "Good girl."

Maddie drew away from her father. "What's the plan? Sophia says you have one."

Liwanu cleared his throat. "Yes, well, first things first. Sophia— I want you to stay out of sight."

"What?" I gaped at him. "I thought you said you needed my help."

"That was before—"

"No excuses," I cut him off. "I will *not* stand back while the man I love is in danger. Nothing can stop me from helping you."

Liwanu hesitated. I must've sounded convincing, because he finally nodded. "Okay. But it's a priority to keep you safe. Ezra and Maddie, I want you to return home and get the family to the rendezvous point."

"No way," Ezra stated. "I'm helping you break out Liam."

"I'm not going, either," Maddie insisted. "They still have Drew."

Liwanu's features hardened. "My plan only requires one Toaqua, and I want to know you two are safe. For all we know, the Task Force is already at the island charging your mother with treason for hiding me away these last few days."

Ezra's face fell.

"Which is why, Ezra, I need you to go to them," Liwanu commanded. "Someone needs to protect them."

Ezra looked conflicted, but he knew he didn't have a choice. He couldn't abandon his mother and younger siblings in favor of his older brother, not when his father already had Liam handled.

"Okay," Ezra caved. "I'll fly Dyami to the island and get everyone off as quickly as I can."

Maddie crossed her arms. "Until we get Drew out, I'm staying."

"Maddie, I want you somewhere safe," Liwanu argued.

"In case you haven't noticed, *nowhere* is safe, Dad!" Maddie burst. "You just said yourself the Task Force might've gone after Mom. We each need to save someone— Ez goes after Mom and the kids, you go after Liam, and I go after Drew. Wouldn't you prefer to have a *naderei* at your side, anyway?"

Liwanu gaped at her. Maddie was always so soft spoken. I bet she'd never stood up to her dad like that before. For a moment, I thought I saw pride pass his features.

"Very well." Liwanu nodded firmly. "Maddie stays. As for the rest of us, here's what we're going to do."

&

EVERYTHING WAS IN PLACE. Liwanu's plan should work— in theory. But we only had one shot at this. If we didn't succeed— if things got out of hand— Liam's life wouldn't be the only one on the line.

The outer gardens were supposed to be a happy place. They were where Liam and I had shared that amazing kiss at the Elemental Ball, where we watched Imogen and Jonah give a fashion show, and where we shared so much laughter and love.

Now a dark cloud hung over the gardens, in both a literal and metaphorical sense. Practically the whole school was here, and I didn't think it was out of respect. I couldn't name a soul who'd want to watch this torture. No doubt the Task Force had incited fear into the students and faculty to force them to watch as their most beloved headmaster was put to death.

There was no better Hawkei for Oleander to make an example of. Everyone loved Alric.

I stood toward the front of the crowd near the fire. I wore a blue Orenda Academy hoodie I stole from the Lost and Found. The hood was up, concealing my face. It was the perfect disguise, considering all the other students were wearing similar attire. The evening wind was anything but pleasant. Most people wore hats and hoods to ward off the chill. Esis was nuzzled in the outer pocket, waiting.

Everywhere I looked, there were Task Force members. I'd never seen so many in one place at a time. Some had Familiars at their sides, which we hadn't anticipated. This wasn't going to be as easy as we thought.

Somewhere behind me were Jonah, Imogen, and Maddie, spread evenly throughout the crowd. It was all part of Liwanu's plan— rile the crowd and create a distraction so the Task Force couldn't stop us from going after Liam and Alric. Liwanu stood inside the castle, watching from out a window where the Task Force couldn't see him.

I scanned the crowd and noticed my friends. Lindsey and Miranda stood close to Vanessa. Each of them held one of her hands. Their Familiars stood in front and behind her, like they were protecting her and the baby. Aisha was on high alert, as if ready to fry anyone who came too close.

Vanessa's belly was huge now, and she was due within the month. I wished she could've stayed home.

The gardens were dead silent. Even the Familiars could sense what was about to happen, and not one made a peep. The only sound I could hear was the whistle of the wind through the trees. Dry leaves flew across the stone path at the front of the gardens, but besides that, nobody moved.

Behind the execution devices, Alric's Familiar, Valda, was being held down by chains. The amethyst dragon would be forced to watch as her Elementai was tortured to death. The entire Elder Council sat in chairs lined beside the water tank to observe. I tried to get a read on Madame Doya's expression, but she gave nothing away. The only hint of emotion I saw was when her eyes flickered out to the crowd. I followed her gaze to see Baine standing at the front, his hands crossed and features sullen.

Baine had been missing all day. I didn't know where he'd been. We needed him right now. Though he hadn't been let in on the plan, I hoped he joined in to help when things started getting crazy.

A drum beat sounded, marking the beginning of the execution ceremony. My stomach lurched. Soon, more and more drum beats came. They were slow and melancholy, like the music you heard in movies when they walked a line of prisoners to the gallows. Only this was worse.

I swallowed down the dry lump in my throat, just to make sure my body was still working.

The doors to the castle opened, and my stomach plummeted to my toes. Two Task Force members held Liam's shoulders and guided him into the gardens. His hands were bound in front of him by noxite handcuffs. His face had drained of all color and hope. Liam walked alongside the Task Force members willingly. He didn't fight them. He didn't try to get away. He just accepted his fate.

The Task Force members walked him onstage, to a device built over logs that I knew would be ignited minutes from now. It looked like a cross they used to crucify people on, except it was attached to a lever they could move up and down, depending on how much of his body they wanted to expose to the flames.

I felt sick. I could barely watch this. As they attached Liam to the device, two other Task Force members dragged Alric out of the castle. He stumbled. One of them grabbed Alric by the hair and pulled him back to his feet in a cruel manner. Several people in the crowd gasped. It was the first I heard anyone make a sound. Valda struggled in her chains, and her cries echoed to the mountains and back.

The Task Force forced Alric's arms up and tied them to a similar lever structure, hands above his head. As they did so, the sound of footsteps against stone echoed throughout the gardens. Oleander walked out of the castle and stopped between the two torture devices. He looked out at the crowd with an expression of regret, like he was truly sorry for what was happening here.

Manipulative bastard.

Oleander pulled a scroll from his pocket— a legit scroll, like we were in the fucking Middle Ages.

He began to read. "Caspian Alric and Liam Mitoh, you are both hereby charged with high treason."

He listed off their crimes, which made the two of them sound horrible. There were things on that list that went far beyond smuggling out "wanted criminals" from the tribe, as Oleander had put it. He suggested that the two of them had been working with Professor Fawn and Professor Costas, and were responsible for the plague that swept through the tribe last semester. He said they'd been plotting with Jaymin's people, and incited the riots that killed hundreds of Hawkei.

My hands curled into fists. I was ready to burn this fucking place to the ground. I'd had enough of these lies and was ready to get this over with— to *end* Oleander.

Murmurs traveled through the crowd as he continued to read the scroll. Half the crowd seemed to believe it and sounded pleased Liam and Alric were getting what they deserved. The other half were in shock.

"No, not Alric."

"Oleander wouldn't lie."

"There must be some mistake."

Oleander ignored the whispers. "The accused have been found guilty of masterminding the murders of over a dozen professors who disappeared after the riots."

"Ludicrous!" a voice came from the middle of the crowd. I recognized it as Jonah's. "Where's the proof? Where are the bodies?"

The murmurs grew.

Oleander acted as if he hadn't heard Jonah's outburst and continued to list off their crimes. "Caspian Alric has hereby been found guilty of illegally trafficking magical creatures in and out of Kinpago."

Illegal trafficking? I barely saw Alric around magical creatures, besides the dracavern I'd seen him with a few times. But he couldn't have been *trafficking* them. Oleander was grasping at every straw he could.

"We demand a trial!" Maddie's voice came from across the crowd.

A few people murmured in agreement.

"They've been framed!" Imogen called.

Task Force members stationed at the perimeter of the crowd could be seen looking for those shouting things, but it was so crowded they couldn't find the source.

Oleander rolled up his scroll and stuffed it back into his pocket. He turned to the Task Force behind him. From where I stood, I could see the vile look on his face. He wanted these two dead— and he'd find great pleasure in watching it happen.

Oleander said something to the Task Force members, then he took a seat beside the other Elders as the Task Force moved in to begin the torture. One of them lit the flames beneath Liam's feet, while another lowered Alric into the water tank. Liam flinched, waiting for the red-hot, searing pain to hit him.

Liwanu and I were ready. I killed the flames beneath Liam the same time Liwanu spread the water out around Alric, creating a pocket of air around him so he could breathe.

Liam's eyes shot open, and he looked downward in surprise. The flames were gone.

The entire crowd shared a collective gasp. No one was expecting the elements to misbehave.

Oleander shot to his feet. His nostrils flared as he scanned the crowd, as if to identify the culprit.

"You see?" Imogen shouted. "Even the ancestors don't want them dead."

A few people within the crowd agreed, but others began shouting protests.

"They're working together!"

"Someone's rigging it!"

Oleander looked shocked at first when he saw the fire go out, but now he smirked in satisfaction at the protests. He found pleasure in knowing there were idiots falling for his tactics.

Oleander held his hands in the air to quiet the crowd. "Fear not, fellow Hawkei. These traitors will get what they deserve. As for anyone found tampering with the elements, they will be prosecuted in the same manner."

"Find the traitors!" someone in the crowd shouted.

"Kill them!" another joined in.

"Spare the innocent!" Maddie screamed.

"Yeah," a voice I didn't recognize added. "How can any of these crimes be proven?"

It was a bit of a relief to know that we had part of the crowd on our side.

"The Elders need not explain themselves," Oleander spat as he returned to center stage. He must've realized he let his real personality slip through instead of the persona he put on for the masses, because he straightened his tie and changed his tone of voice. "As for those interrupting this execution..."

A Task Force member stepped forward and held a small black box out to Oleander. He opened it and pulled out an object I couldn't make out until he held it up to the crowd. *A compass.*

Oleander smirked as he placed it in his palm. "This is not just any ordinary compass. It is enchanted by the Arcanea to identify sources of magic. Which means that it will point to whoever was the last to use their powers."

Oleander's tone darkened, and my heart rate sped up. "This compass will show who is responsible for meddling with the Elder's sentence today."

My entire body froze as Oleander looked down at the compass. His eyes followed the arrow straight to me, and he pointed an ugly finger in my direction. "Get her!"

What the fuck!? This wasn't supposed to happen! All we wanted to do was rile the crowd. I wasn't supposed to be captured.

Task Force members ran at me at all angles. The earth shook beneath their feet, and wind whipped around me. I knew it was all thanks to Imogen and Jonah. A few Task Force members went down, but it didn't slow them all. They lunged at me, and I shot fireballs to protect myself. I glanced every way around me to find an exit, but I was completely surrounded.

Three Task Force members caught me at once, and I was slammed to the ground. Esis was almost squished in my pocket, but he scurried out of the way at the last second. Two Task Force members jumped him and held him down— because apparently it took two grown men to hold down a freaking kurble.

"Let go of me!" I screamed. I summoned heat to my skin to scare them off, but they must've not felt it through their gloves.

Something poked me in the back, and I knew on instinct that it was a noxite gun. "Move," one of the Task Force members growled from behind me.

My knees shook, but I did as they instructed. They dragged me up to the front and onto the execution platform. My gaze connected with Liam's, and my eyes began to water. I'd never seen him look as disappointed as he did in that moment.

Pawee, he mouthed.

I swallowed the tears back, only because I couldn't let myself cry in front of Oleander. If it were just me and Liam here, I would've been crying by now. The look he gave me was as if I'd just shot an arrow straight through his heart. I'd never meant to betray Liam— only to save him. And now I was going to be executed, too— and right in front of him, no doubt. He'd asked me to leave, and I didn't. In a way, I had betrayed my one true love.

The Task Force spun me around to face the crowd. Oleander reached up and snagged my hood down, ripping strands of hair as he did. I wished I could say the crowd was shocked, but it was if they expected this from me.

"Sophia Henley," Oleander sneered my name. "The evidence is clear. You are hereby sentenced to execution for interfering with the Elder's sentencing."

Two Task Force members stepped around me and placed a huge hunk of wood in front of me. It looked like a tree trunk. Another came forward, holding a giant ax.

What the fuck!? They were literally going to execute me medieval style via decapitation. What the hell was *wrong* with this administration?

"We had a deal!" Liam shouted at Oleander.

Oleander ignored him and just chuckled.

Doya shot to her feet, and Naomi bared her teeth. "This is absurd!"

"Sit down!" Oleander growled at her, before lowering his voice so only those on stage could hear. "You need to pick which side you're on, *Madame Doya*."

Doya's expression smoldered. His threat had made her hesitate—but at the same time, it didn't look like she was going to back down.

I narrowed my gaze at Oleander. "You had this planned all along, didn't you? You never intended to spare my friends, because you knew we'd step in."

Oleander spoke lowly so only I could hear. "I can't have anyone tampering with my message, now can I?"

That's all I was to him— a message, an *example*. We all were.

I smirked at him. "Good luck getting away with it."

Oleander cocked an eyebrow. "Believe me, Biyami rat. I can handle anything you throw at me."

The terrifying roar of a grizzly bear echoed throughout the gardens as Tatum ran out of the castle and barreled his way through the Task Force members lined up nearby. Liwanu rode on Tatum's back and let out a traditional Hawkei battle cry as they charged. Liwanu drew back a bow and aimed an arrow straight at Oleander's chest.

All Task Force members aimed their guns at the Water chief, but none of them shot, for fear that Oleander would be taken down with him. Tatum came to a halt at my side. Esis cheered in victory from the arms of one of the Task Force members.

The crowd gasped, but their voices were quickly silenced as they looked on in shock.

Oleander's features faltered. "Chief Mitoh. It's so nice of you to join us."

Oleander was playing nice, because he knew Liwanu was the one person in the tribe he couldn't make an example of. He couldn't take down one of the Elders so publicly, or people would surely turn against him. No one would believe it without a fair trial.

"Don't call me your chief," Liwanu growled. "You lost the right to call me that the day you split up the tribe!"

Liwanu kept his arrow trained on Oleander, but he addressed the crowd. "Oleander is not your ally! He and Chieftess Westfenix have been enemies to the Hawkei all this time. It was *her* idea to split up the tribe and incite a war, so she could gain ultimate power and put Koigni at the top. She desired that the Koigni would rule, instead of being treated as equals among all Houses. Oleander stole her idea and acted first, but he never had the best interests of his House at heart. All he cares about is getting to the top himself, and he'll take down anyone to get there."

"He's lying!" Oleander shouted. "The two-House system is what's best for the tribe!"

"Then where are all the Biyami!?" Liwanu snapped. "You've raided their homes, taken their children, and incited a genocide, all in the name of power!"

"I'm cleansing the tribe of criminal activity," Oleander sneered.

"You threatened the Elders and their families to go along with this, and look where it's gotten us!" Liwanu shouted, like he hadn't even heard Oleander's rebuttal. "You're killing our own!"

Oleander pointed a finger at Liwanu and turned to the crowd. "Lies! All lies! He's a traitor."

"Then let me ask you this," Liwanu screamed to the crowd. "Who would you rather lead the Defortai? Chieftess Westfenix, or Elder Oleander?"

It was in that moment that the crowd went fucking nuts. Liwanu knew what he was doing. The crowd was exclusively Defortai. Telling the truth about the Biyami genocide wasn't going to phase them. He had to hit them where it really hurt— pitting Annette's supporters against Oleander's.

"It was Annette's idea! She should be the one leading!"

"Oleander's a cheat!"

"At least he's a man. What does a woman know?"

"He's brand new to the council. He doesn't know shit."

"Oleander has honor. He speaks the truth."

Annette shot from her chair, seeing her opportunity and taking it. "Liwanu's right. Oleander is nothing but a fraud. *I* should be leading the Hawkei."

Annette cocked her head ever so slightly, as if giving someone a signal. The next second, a group of people that dressed like the ones from the riots came swarming into the execution area. They looked like Jaymin's people, but it was clear from Annette's subtle signal that she controlled them. She'd been ready for this— and she was going to pin it on Jaymin the moment it all went down.

Task Force members began shooting noxite darts into the crowd. Elementai and Familiars went down, but at least a dozen got past them and made a beeline for Oleander.

"Let go of me!" Oleander shouted.

"Not our chief! Not our chief!" they chanted as they dragged him over to the logs beneath Liam's execution ring.

I froze up as everything erupted at once. I was immediately taken back to the night of the riots, but this wasn't like the nightmares I'd been having over the last few months. This was far too real.

At least twenty fights had broken out among the crowd. Whirlwinds swirled around the gardens. The earth shook, and vines grew to wrap around people's legs. Toaqua were summoning water from Alric's torture tank to fight their enemies. The Koigni who'd grabbed Oleander had started a fire beneath Liam and had tossed Oleander into the flames. His deafening scream rang out through the gardens as his flesh burned.

The sound of a dragon's cry came from above as Eirakari swooped down from the sky. Maddie rode on her back to rescue Alric in the wave of chaos, joined by Imogen and Sassy. I thought I saw Baine rushing forward to help them, but there was so much happening that I couldn't be sure. Valda pulled at her chains, struggling to escape. I could see the chains straining to hold the dragon down.

Somewhere in all the chaos, Esis' scream tore through all the noise. That's what snapped me back to attention. A Task Force member was squeezing Esis tightly as he tried to struggle away.

I leapt into fight mode and ran over to him. I shot a fireball out of my hand, hitting the Task Force member square in the face. The fireball slammed into his helmet so hard that it shattered his visor. He dropped Esis, and my Familiar bounded over to me and jumped on my shoulder.

"Let's go!" I screamed.

I turned to Liam. Liwanu and Jonah were trying to get to him, but they couldn't get past the flames. I jumped straight over them and killed the ones around me with my magic while I reached up to untie the ropes binding Liam to the cross.

"*Pawee*, what did I tell you!?" Liam coughed through the smoke.

"I never made any promises," I shot back.

The deafening sound of shattering glass made the two of us flinch. I glanced behind me to see the water tank had broken. A tsunami of water was spreading out through the gardens. It met with the flaming pile of wood beneath my feet. A mix of steam and smoke rose on all sides of us as a chilling *hiss* drowned out most of the other noises.

"Sophia, save yourself!" Liam snapped.

"You don't have a choice," I growled. "I'm getting you out of here."

The ties binding Liam down broke free, and I caught him as he slumped forward. They must've not fed him a thing, because the weight he put on me suggested he could barely move his muscles. I'd never seen Liam this bad before. It was worse than when he'd been in the hospital with pneumonia earlier this year.

Esis placed a paw on Liam's arm as I dragged him out of the fire. Liwanu met up with me at the edge of it, but it was almost impossible to see. The fire had escaped the execution ring now and was burning the gardens to the ground. There was so much smoke it hurt my lungs, and I was Koigni.

Liam went into a coughing fit as I draped him over Tatum's back. Esis jumped on the grizzly, to stay close to Liam so he could heal.

"We need to get everyone out of here!" Jonah shouted above the roar of battle.

Liwanu pushed Tatum toward the doors of the school. "Get inside! All of you! We'll gather everyone in the Great Hall, then escape. Understood?"

Tatum began to run with Liam and Esis on his back. Jonah, Squeaks, and I raced into the school behind them. I prayed that the rest of our group would be there already with Alric.

But when we got inside the doors, it wasn't the safe haven we thought it'd be from the warzone out in the gardens. Curtains and tapestries were on fire, and the flames ate away at regalia displays and feathered headdresses. Right in front of our eyes, our beloved Orenda Academy was being destroyed.

My worst fear had come true. I was facing the riots all over again.

The only question was, how many of us would make it out alive?

Liam

TWENTY-THREE

ll around us was chaos. Students and Familiars were running everywhere, trying to escape the flames and trampling over each other to get out alive. I stirred on Tatum's back, slowly regaining consciousness. A few minutes ago I was tied to a freaking pyre. Now me and my friends were literally trapped in a matchbox that was going up in smoke.

"The Great Hall!" Dad shouted again. He charged forward. I slipped off of Tatum's back, so he could fight, and Esis jumped into my arms. Dad shot his bow into the crowd, and one of the arrows hit a Task Force member in the chest, bringing them down. Tatum roared and put his head down, barreling his way through the violence and clearing a way through. We ran toward the Great Hall, away from the flames that were slowly encroaching over the walls.

"Liam, are you okay?" Sophia screamed over the noise. Her worried expression clearly noted my poor health.

"I'm good!" I shouted back. I hadn't eaten and barely slept, but Esis' healing powers gave me the strength to stay on my feet. The adrenaline was pumping through my veins. I'd last until we were in a safe place.

Squeaks was helping Tatum clear a way through. A Task Force group ahead of us raised their noxite guns to shoot, but Jonah pushed his hand out, and a gust of air sent them smashing into the ceiling. We crossed through the hallway and entered into the Great Hall, and the noise increased tenfold.

There were already so many bodies. So much blood. Corpses of both Elementai and Familiars littered the floor as Task Force members and Hawkei battled for blood. Elements whizzed through the air, making the room look like it was igniting in fireworks. Meanwhile, Annette's assassins dueled Oleander's men, and it didn't look like either of them were gaining the upper hand. Yapluma flew overhead, and people dropped from the skies, bones shattering on the ground as noxite darts and elements took them out.

"Over there!" Dad pointed, and we followed his lead. Baine was waiting in the Great Hall with Maddie, Imogen, and Alric. Baine was holding Alric up, who was slumped over and looking half dead. Maddie had taken water with her from the pool, and shot it into the crowd before ordering the liquid to return to her hand so she could repeat the process. Imogen had manipulated the stone statues in the Great Hall to fight for her, and they prevented any Task Force member from coming too close. The statues knocked them down and ended their fight with a heavy blow if they dared to attack.

Sassy and Eirakari formed a protective barrier around the group. Sassy had transformed into her kitsune form. She lashed out with her vines at Task Force members and whipped them into submission. When a Task Force Familiar tried to charge her, Sassy wrapped her vines around the panther's form and tossed him across the room. The cat yowled as it slammed against the wall and struggled to get up. Eirakari spread her wings and shot daggers of ice into the crowd. When her snow breath hit Task Force members, they froze in place and became blocks of ice, immovable and helpless.

Valda had broken out of her chains. I could hear her from outside as she flew above the school, searching for Alric. The dragon's cries shook the walls, and the flags depicting the Defortai symbol fell from the ceiling at the weight of her screams.

Both of the doors to the Great Hall were open, but there was a Task Force barricade blocking the way out. They refused to let people through and shot noxite darts into the crowd madly, with no concern as to who their bullets hit. When people pressed against the barricade, the Task Force members raised their hands and sent lethal blows from their fingers, which hit the chests of those attempting to escape. Their bodies absorbed the magical impact and went cold, falling backward onto the floor. The wails of dying Familiars could be heard everywhere as their Elementai fell. Many magical creatures curled around their bonded partners in an attempt to defend their remains from desecration as they themselves slowly passed away.

They were killing their own people. Biyami, Defortai, it didn't matter. No one was an exception.

When Familiars tried to barge their way through the barricade, other magical creatures on the side of the Task Force prevented escape. Elementai dove out of the way as giant Familiars crashed together in the Great Hall, sending furniture flying. Gore poured from wounds as enormous reptiles ripped into griffins, direwolves, and pegasi. Unicorns had blood on their horns, and peryton battled to the death until their antlers were broken and lying in pieces on the floor.

We were trapped inside. There was nowhere else to go.

Squeaks grabbed on to a Task Force member in front of her and threw them overhead. We joined with the rest of the group in the middle of the Great Hall, but felt suffocated as Elementai started closing inward. We were going to be crushed.

"Back. Off!" Maddie screamed. She sent her Water magic out in a spinning disc, and it cut into the backs of several people, opening them up. They cried out as they went down, and Maddie's eyes sparked with tears. She didn't want to hurt anyone, but she had no choice.

"Give me some of that," I said. Maddie split the water she had and hovered it over to me. I maintained a steady flow of it around my hand as Dad turned in a circle.

"There must be a way." His eyes narrowed. "You all right, Caspian?"

Alric's head bobbed in a slow roll.

Baine grimaced. "We're outnumbered. No one's coming for us, Liwanu."

"They'll come," Dad swore. I had no idea who he was talking about, but I didn't have any time to ask, because he started barking directions. "The greenhouses aren't far. We'll make our way out through the dining hall, and then—"

Dad's voice was drowned out by noise as suddenly, one of the walls in the Great Hall gave way. People screamed and scattered as stone went flying.

Valda had broken through the wall. The dragon created a gaping exit in the castle that people ran through in an attempt to escape. As she stampeded through the wall, multiple stone bricks went flying, one of them as large as our group. It went sailing through the air toward us, threatening to crush us all.

"No!" Sophia flung her left hand out while tightly grasping the Spirit Totem around her neck. From her palm bloomed a visible, transparent shield, which she expanded outward. The white shield slammed against the stone brick, and the object shattered into pieces.

Sophia dropped her hand, wincing, and the shield died down with it. Multiple people around us stared at Sophia in wonderous horror, although most people were too busy fleeing to notice what she'd done.

Everyone around us who didn't know about the Spirit Totem gaped. Baine's face was particularly comical. "Miss Henley. How— how did you...?"

"Long story, this totem gives me Anichi magic," Sophia said. "I can make a force field. Not a strong one, but enough to help us."

"Marvelous!" Baine said, and a ray of hope lit up his face. "Can you keep one around us as we move?"

"I can't hold it for very long," Sophia explained quickly. "I'm still learning."

We didn't have time to talk further. The floor shook with the approach of dragon footsteps.

Alric stumbled out of Baine's arms and to Valda. The dragon laid down her head as he grew near, and Alric climbed on top of it. He sat on the crook between her neck and head, holding on to her horns as Valda charged forward.

"Caspian, don't try it," Dad begged.

"I have to make this right!" Alric called back. A fireball erupted in his palm, and Valda ran away from the group.

That sure sounded like he was going after Oleander.

As she left the ruins of the Great Hall, Valda's stampede was interrupted by a shadow approaching from the clouds. It was Oleander's Familiar— Skylis. He descended through the smoke that was quickly consuming the skies, red scales glinting in the flames that surrounded the area.

The dracash roared, and one of its heads shot down in an attempt to grab Valda by the neck. She lunged out of the way, and the dracash changed direction to circle back around again.

The dragon hybrid spurted jets of flame out of each one of his five heads. Alric redirected the flames so that they diverged into the air instead of hitting Valda. Skylis growled in frustration as he soared by. Valda rose up on her hind legs to snap at Skylis, but the dracash lunged out his claws, and they snagged on Valda's left wing. She gave a loud roar of pain and fell back down to the earth, creating a mini-earthquake. Alric tossed fireballs at Skylis while Valda recovered, though each of his shots missed.

Valda's wing was tattered and bleeding from Skylis' claws. She could no longer fly. She had to fight on the ground.

Skylis landed and swung his long tail at Valda. She ducked and lunged out with her fangs. Valda successfully managed to latch onto Skylis' tail, and she dug her teeth in. She wrenched Skylis around and flipped him onto his back before she climbed abroad him. Valda attempted to deliver a fatal blow to Skylis' chest, but she was unable to get at his heart with five heads to deal with. Alric could only keep two occupied at a time, while Valda was left to deal with three.

Eventually, Skylis launched her off, and the dracash was back on four legs again and charging at the female dragon. Alric held on for dear life as the two dragons battled for dominance, rising on their back legs to claw at each other with a horrific violence that went beyond the laws of nature. All of us were frozen in horror, too scared to get involved.

The dragons didn't care who they stepped on or hurt in their battle. Several people were smashed underneath the feet of the behemoths as their battle led back toward the Great Hall.

I couldn't move. My feet were stuck to the floor even as my heartbeat quickened in terror.

We had to get the fuck away from them, before we were all crushed.

"Elliot, go after Caspian!" Dad instructed. "I need to get the kids out of here."

Baine nodded. He moved faster than I'd ever seen him as he approached the advancing dragons. Baine gathered several strands of water from one of the nearby fountains, and wrapped bands around the heads of the monster. He tried to hold Skylis down as Valda and Alric attacked, though his face strained with effort.

I wasn't able to watch much more, because Dad grabbed my shirt and dragged me behind him. We were forced to turn our backs on Baine and make a run for it. The exit Valda had made was crowded with people and tough to get through, so Dad turned the other way and headed down the hallway in the direction of the dining hall.

As we ran, Squeaks and Sassy pressed in beside Sophia, as if they were protecting her. Sophia couldn't move two steps without the Familiars mirroring her movements. Esis scrambled out of my arms and jumped onto Sophia's hoodie. He snuggled into the pocket in front of her stomach and gave a low hiss, his hair standing on end.

"What's gotten into them?" Sophia screamed, completely baffled.

"Sassy won't say!" Imogen cried. Jonah gave a blank look and shook his head, like he didn't know either. The Familiars obviously knew something we didn't.

Maddie was slowing us down. Her head whipped from one direction to the other, hopelessly looking for Drew. I grabbed her hand and pulled her along, forcing her to keep up.

The cafeteria was just as chaotic as the Great Hall was. All the entrances were blocked once again by Task Force members, though they were having trouble controlling the crowd as the flames grew in intensity. The castle was really going up now. I struggled to breathe amidst all the smoke.

Friendly faces could be seen in the middle of the dining hall. Lindsey and Miranda were back to back, shooting off columns of flames from their hands at Task Force members and anyone else who challenged them. Their faces were panicked, like they had no idea what to do or where to go. Medusa bit anyone who drew near. She wrapped herself around the bodies of the people Lindsey dropped, crushing them with her strength. Evelyn, Miranda's kirin Familiar, charged and head-butted Elementai away with her horns.

On the other side of the room, Wyatt could be seen. He didn't have any water with him, so he resorted to punching people and Familiars who got too close. His knuckles were bloody, and red dripped from several cuts on his face. I didn't see his walrus Familiar anywhere. They'd probably gotten separated.

"Guys!" Imogen called, and she waved. The three of them recognized us, and their eyes lit up, but there were too many people blocking the way from us to them.

Then Evelyn stepped before the group and closed her eyes. A pulsing magic emitted from the kirin, and the sound knocked Hawkei off their feet, clearing a way through. The barrier died down as it swept through us, and I shivered as I felt the power of Evelyn's magic. Miranda patted Evelyn's neck as they approached, telling her she was a good girl.

"We were just looking for you," Lindsey said breathlessly, throwing her arms around Sophia. "It's a madhouse in here. There's no way out."

"There has to be a way," Dad said firmly. He was refusing to give up hope. But I didn't think the rest of us shared that sentiment. There were too many people, too many Task Force members. The chances of all of us making it out alive were dismal at this point.

"I don't know where Tuskin is," Wyatt said helplessly. "He could be anywhere."

"We'll find him," I said, but it seemed like a weak promise. Locating a missing Familiar in this mess was hopeless.

"Vanessa!" someone bellowed over the crowd. My heart dropped as I saw Bren, wretchedly calling his wife's name over the madness. "*Vanessa!*"

Bren's chimera Familiar tore into anyone that got too close. Kingston ripped apart Elementai and Familiars both who dared stray into his path. Many people gave them a wide berth as Bren recognized us and bolted our way.

"I heard the school had broken out into a fight. I came to get Ness and Aisha," Bren explained quickly. "Has anyone seen her?"

Lindsey quickly shook her head. "We lost Vanessa after the execution broke out into a panic."

"I need to find her. I'm not leaving without her," Bren vowed.

"We'll go with you," Miranda said quickly. "Where would she hide?"

"The Koigni dorms. She'd feel safe there," Lindsey blurted.

"Let's go," Bren said. He summoned a fireball in his palm and pushed a Toaqua to the floor who'd gotten in his way.

"It's crucial we stick together!" Dad objected, but no one listened to him. Bren, Miranda and Lindsey headed the opposite way in a vain search for Vanessa, their Familiars tailing at a run. Sophia went to follow, but Dad grabbed her wrist and held her back.

"We can't worry about them," Dad said quickly. "It's imperative we get you out of here, Sophia."

"Me!?" Sophia shouted. "What about everyone else?"

"I promise everything will be explained once we get there! Please, trust me," Dad pleaded.

Sophia blinked at him. She bit her lip as she watched her friends scamper away before she nodded.

"We go toward the center of the school," Dad said. "With everyone trying to find a way out, the battle will be weaker there."

"We could try escaping through the smuggling tunnel," Imogen suggested wildly.

"With the flames eating up the towers? I don't think so," Jonah shot back.

"I can calm the flames," Sophia said. "It'll give us enough time to escape."

"If you could do that, why don't the Koigni put the fire out?" Jonah asked.

"Because half of them are probably trying to do just that, and the other half are following Oleander's orders to erupt this place," Sophia responded grimly.

"It doesn't matter. We need to get out of this area. It's too dangerous," Dad said. "We'll come up with a plan when we're in a safer location."

He led the way out of the dining hall. It felt insane to be going deeper into the school, but it turned out to be a good idea. It seemed like the fires had mostly wrapped around the outer building and the core hadn't been affected yet. The air was clearer here, and it was easier for me to breathe.

As we neared one of the main staircases, a flood of Task Force members came out of nowhere. They began firing, but we dodged the noxite darts and shot off elements as fast as we could. There were so many. When one fell, another took their place. The Familiars pounced onto them and ripped out their throats as we fought to stay alive.

I heard a cry for help. Mia was cornered. She was curled up into a ball, her arms wrapped around her middle and screaming. Taryn was at her side, though the canine Familiar was limping and tired. A group of Task Force had cornered her, and were raising their hands to fire.

Out of the corner of my eye, I watched as Micah fled the scene. He'd abandoned her.

"Mia!" Wyatt shouted. His eyes had taken on a mad craze.

"She's a lost cause, forget it," I called, but fuck all if Wyatt listened. He charged into the group of Task Force members with raised fists and started punching anyone who was close.

The distraction gave Mia and Taryn enough time to slip by to safety. Wyatt was shot by a noxite dart, and carried off by the Task Force as Mia and Taryn ran away. It'd happened so fast none of us had time to interfere.

A hollowness grew in my core as one of my oldest friends faded from my sight. I didn't know if they'd kill him. I didn't know if I'd see him ever again.

"Keep moving," Dad said. He shoved me, and I stumbled forward. Jonah barely caught me as we headed to the center of the castle.

This was too much for me to deal with. It was too much. I couldn't handle this. My ears grew numb to the screams and pleas for mercy all around me, until it was just static. I felt desensitized. Dazed. Cold and unfeeling. The school that had been my home for the better part of four years had turned into a graveyard. It was more than overwhelming. It was unbearable. We passed so many places I recognized in a mad dash to escape. Sophia and I had fooled around in that closet. Jonah and I had gotten drunk in that empty classroom my sophomore year. Imogen and I had exchanged books in that library. We'd all gathered around that foyer just the other week and bitched about Doya. I'd watched my brother wrestle with Cade in that hallway, and took bets with Wyatt on who would win just last year.

Nashoma and I spent almost every day lounging on that bench right there. I'd throw my leg over the seat and he'd lay on top of it, neither of us with a care in the world. We'd sit there and people watch until Jonah found me, told me to quit being a loner and join everyone else in the Commons.

I used to avoid that corridor, because it reminded me of my Familiar, but right now all I wanted to do was stay. I could still remember how it felt when I ran my hands between his ears and buried my fingers in his thick black fur.

Orenda Academy was the only place I still felt connected to Nashoma. And it was dying.

As we rounded a corner, my heart stopped cold. Oleander stood in the middle of a long hallway, a line of Task Force behind him. All of them had their hands raised, elements glowing within. Horrible burn marks marred Oleander's features.

Oleander wasn't fucking around this time. Forget the noxite. He was going to kill us.

A wide smile spread across his face. "Maddie. I was hoping I'd find you here."

"Don't speak to him," Dad said immediately, casting a glance my sister's way. But Oleander chuckled.

"I think you all realize the situation is quite hopeless," Oleander said. "Don't you, Maddie?"

His voice was like a sickening lullaby, drawing my sister in. Maddie shivered as she said, "What do you want?"

"There doesn't need to be any more bloodshed." Oleander extended a hand. "Come with me, girl, and your family goes free. With the exception of Miss Henley, of course."

"What do you want with Sophia?" Maddie asked nervously.

"Both of you girls show extraordinary power," Oleander cooed. "I only want to put that power to good use."

"To hurt people, you mean," Maddie snapped.

"To make a better world. You and Miss Henley should've never been categorized as Biyami. A poor mistake. The two of you are much too strong," Oleander said. "I'm only trying to make the tribe the best it can be."

Oleander's eyes locked on Sophia. "Miss Henley, what do you want? Don't you think it's time people stop dying for you?"

Sophia took in a ragged breath. Oleander's words cut into her. I didn't want them to have any effect, but they did. Sophia didn't want anyone else to get hurt.

I caught something in her eyes. She was going to do it. She was going to give herself up to save us.

"I'm not going with you," Maddie proclaimed. Her loud voice broke the connection between Oleander and Sophia. Oleander's attention flickered back to her.

"Maddie, imagine the good we could do together. The kind of tribe we could create," Oleander said. "With your knowledge of the future, there wouldn't be a need for any more wars. We could put a stop to the violence, once and for all."

I saw the greedy glint in his eye. Oleander had an obsession with learning about the future, and he thought Maddie could give him all the answers. He didn't understand nor care that her gift didn't work like that. He wanted a prophet, and she was his only chance at getting one. He'd kill all of us to capture her alive.

When Maddie didn't respond, Oleander made a *tsking* sound. "That's too bad. I was hoping we could come to an agreement, but it looks like I'll have to tell your little boyfriend you're not interested in saving him. He was crying out for you when last I left him."

Maddie's lip quivered at the mention of Drew. Before Maddie could give an answer, there was the sound of marching boots behind us.

Oleander's face blanched. I turned and witnessed a line of Koigni approaching in unison, each of them female. They were led by Chieftess Annette, who was flanked by Haley. Annette's phoenix, along with Anwara, hovered over the brigade.

Annette curled her mouth into a nasty smile and said, "There you are, you little snake. I've been looking for you."

Oleander gave a nervous laugh. "Now, Annette, let's not get carried away."

"The title of High Chieftess belongs to *me*," Annette snarled. "It's time you got out of my way."

Annette raised her hand simultaneously with her assassins. I realized that there were two different sides pointing elements at us, and we were stuck in the middle.

"Get out of the way!" Dad pushed Sophia to the side, and all of us dropped to the floor as elements raced overheard. Fire met with Water, Earth, and Air. The only thing we could do was cling to the stone tile while Annette and Oleander waged in a war for power.

"Don't hurt the *naderei!*" Oleander screeched. The two lines broke, and individuals raced forward to combat opponents individually. We scrambled to our feet and pressed to the wall to avoid the battle, but currently, there was nowhere for us to run without getting caught in the line of fire.

Annette fired column after column of fire in Oleander's direction, but the coward had taken place behind a group of Task Force members and was using them as shields to protect himself. It was obvious Oleander was becoming quickly overwhelmed. His gaze locked on Maddie before he gave a rage-filled snarl and turned to flee.

Annette had Oleander in her sights. With one more fireball, she could easily take him down.

But there was one person who was in her way. Sophia. Annette's eyes shone with joy at the thought of taking two birds out with one stone. She could eliminate her rival and the girl who'd caused her so much trouble, all in one blow.

Sophia was too far away. I couldn't get to her. Sophia turned just as Annette was gathering her magic. She didn't have enough time to make a counter attack. She was going to die.

Ancestors, no, not her! Anyone but her, I screamed inwardly, giving a desperate prayer that erupted in the very core of me.

"Sophia!" Dad pushed her out of the way before Annette and charged, putting himself in the way of the fireball. He knocked Annette down, and the fireball ricocheted toward the ceiling instead. Embers went flying everywhere.

Annette screamed with rage as she got off the floor, but by this time, Oleander was already gone. Dad scrambled away before Annette could retaliate. The Task Force members broke off, and Annette's remaining assassins gave chase after Oleander.

But they weren't the only ones.

"Drew!" Maddie screamed. She raced after Oleander. Eirakari roared and ran forward after her Elementai. Maddie swung herself onto Eirakari's back, and both of them disappeared around the corner in an anguished search for Drew.

"Mads, no!" I shouted, but it was too late. None of us could keep up with a charging dragon.

"I'll go after her," Dad said quickly. He pulled himself onto Tatum and looked directly at me. "Meet me at the statue of the rearing pegasus outside the Atrium. If I'm not there by the time you arrive, *get yourselves out.*"

Then Dad was gone. It was just the four of us, plus our Familiars. Sophia tugged on my arm. "Liam, the statue!" she cried.

But my eyes were locked on a skirmish in the hallway. Haley was having trouble keeping up. Two Task Force members had cornered her, and though Anwara had taken one on, Haley couldn't defeat the other. Her magic was countered each time by her enemy, who avoided her Fire powers and used their Water magic to combat her moves.

Looks like Haley couldn't handle picking on someone her own size. Served her fucking right.

Annette noticed that her daughter was struggling and stomped over. With one fluid movement, Annette cast a wall of fire over the two Task Force members, and they screamed as her magic burned them alive.

As the bodies of the two Task Force members hit the floor, Annette whirled on Haley. Haley was left quaking before her. "I'm sorry, Mother," she belted out. "I'll do better next time."

"You're *weak!* You've always been weak," Annette screamed as her face turned red. "We would've caught Oleander by now if we didn't have to wait for you to keep up!"

"I didn't mean it," Haley stammered. Above her, Anwara let out a pleading coo. I'd never seen Haley look so vulnerable and small.

"You don't have what it takes to lead the tribe," Annette snarled. She advanced on Haley and launched a fireball. The fireball collided with Haley's cheek and sizzled, burning off skin. Haley screamed with pain, cupping a hand to her eye. A large burn formed over her eye and bloomed on the side of her face from her mother's magic.

What happened next... I don't think any of us saw it coming. Haley cast a resentful look toward her mother, and Anwara dove toward Annette's phoenix, screeching a war cry.

The elder phoenix was there to meet her with open claws, but Anwara didn't fly into them. Instead, she swooped around and opened her beak. A cannon of flame erupted from Anwara's belly and streamed out of her mouth, enveloping Annette's phoenix in flames. The elder bird wailed in agony as the flames encompassed his body. His wings beat frantically in an attempt to escape, but the effort was futile. Anwara kept the flames sustained, and the other phoenix fell out of the air.

The charred corpse of Annette's phoenix hit the floor with a harsh *thud*, ashes peeling off of its burnt husk.

Annette's phoenix didn't move. Annette fell to her knees, her entire form quivering. She crawled on her hands and knees to her Familiar's body and pulled him onto her lap.

Anwara wasn't bothered. She hovered over the scene with an impassive expression no one could deny. The Familiar was clearly glad the other phoenix was dead.

But Haley was completely shaken. She stared wide-eyed at her mother as Chieftess Annette clung to the corpse of her Familiar.

"You've killed me," Annette rasped, tears streaming down her face. It was only then that two shocked tears dripped out of Haley's eyes, too.

"Liam, come on!" Sophia was still pulling on my arm. I snapped out of it. We left Haley and Annette behind, though the memory of what Anwara had done was seared into my mind forever.

As we passed a staircase, Sophia's face drained of all color. "Julian!" she shouted, realization flickering across her features. Jonah and Imogen both looked sick at mention of the abandoned dragon egg.

"Where is he?" I forced out.

"The Anichi dorms. All of our stuff is up there," Sophia burst out.

"I'll go get him. Get to the statue." Before anyone could stop me, I started climbing the staircase. On any other day, it would've taken me ages to climb three flights, but there was no time to dawdle. I'd suck up the repercussions of my illness later, if I made it out alive.

When I got to the Anichi dorms, I had to put the top of my shirt over my face to act as a filter. I immediately went to the doorway that led through the smuggling tunnel to see if it was safe to use, but once I opened it, smoke came billowing out. It burned my eyes and immediately hit my lungs. I slammed the door and gasped for air as my lungs contracted, praying to the ancestors I wasn't having an asthma attack.

As my mind reeled, I searched the common room for our stuff. Sophia's backpack was in the corner. I could see the red shell of the dragon egg as it peeked out the top.

I grabbed the backpack, but with a quick look inside, my insides tightened with dread. Thin lines ran throughout the egg. I could hear tiny sounds as the dragon inside rapped against the egg shell, trying to get out.

The egg was hatching. Perfect fucking timing, as usual.

I zipped up the backpack and flung it over my shoulder, hoping Julian could wait until we got the hell out of here. There wasn't any time to grab the rest of the luggage. We'd have to leave with the clothes on our backs.

I found Sophia, Jonah, and Imogen waiting by the pegasus statue near the Atrium, though my stomach bottomed out when I saw that Dad and Maddie weren't there with them. Squeaks gave a loud caw as I approached, and Sassy joined in with a few quick barks.

"I found him," I said breathlessly as I skidded to a stop. "But the Anichi dorms are going down. The fire's taken over up there."

"What about the tunnel?" Imogen gasped.

"We can't escape that way," I said, shaking my head. "The smuggling tunnel is blocked up with smoke. We'll suffocate if we try, even with Jonah's magic."

Jonah punched the stone statue, frustrated. His knuckles bled, but he didn't act like he cared. "Okay, so what do we do? Your dad told us to leave if he wasn't here by the time we arrived."

The four of us looked helpless. We knew what we'd been *told* to do, but none of us wanted to leave without Dad or Maddie.

It was Sophia who made the decision for us. "We don't have a choice. We have to do what your dad said, Liam. He obviously knows what's best."

A cold lump grew in my throat, but I forced it down and said, "You're right. Come on. We can try the northwest corridor. There's a back entrance that way."

The back entrance was usually locked, but with luck, we might be able to force our way through. Once we got there, however, we found the area overwhelmed with Task Force and students. Everyone had the same idea. Students tried to squeeze through the small opening all at once, while Task Force shot noxite into the crowd.

"What do we do, Liam, what do we do?" Imogen clung to my shirt, her voice wrought with despair. Jonah and Sophia looked to me, their eyes pleading for some sort of direction.

But I couldn't lead in a situation like this. What was I supposed to tell them? To lie down and wait to die?

"I can help." A deep voice broke in through the insanity. A muscular man with a strong jaw and wavy blond hair towered before us. His enormous gray hippogriff stood behind, head held high. Out of all the panicked faces, this guy seemed like the one person who was still calm.

I recognized him. He was the giant who'd left Alric's office last semester. They'd gotten in an argument about something, though I didn't know what. The only reason I remembered him was because he was the only person I'd seen who was taller than Jonah.

"Who the hell are you?" Imogen squeaked.

"A friend," the stranger said. He looked to Sophia and said, "Miss Henley, I am relieved to have found you."

"How do you know my name?" Sophia breathed.

"*Everyone* knows your name, Miss Henley," he replied. "And it's very important we get you to safety."

The floor rumbled. More Task Force members came flooding in. The gray hippogriff turned to face the horde and gave a fierce call. The man's eyes narrowed.

"Jake, we have to go!" a woman cried near the staircase. Her eyes were focused on the stranger's before she shot a gust of wind up the staircase, knocking several Task Force members over. It was a valiant effort, but more kept coming. Jake's knuckles cracked. The wind around him picked up, ruffling the hippogriff's feathers.

"Sabor and I will hold them off. Go to the Atrium. Liwanu should meet you there," Jake said quickly. His Familiar, Sabor, cracked his beak and looked thrilled at the prospect of violence.

"You know my dad?" I asked, astounded.

"Yes! Leave quickly, before there's no chance."

Before we could say another word, Jake ran in the opposite direction and joined the Yapluma girl at the staircase. He flung his hands out, and a whirlwind erupted, smashing the staircase to bits. The Task Force members that weren't swept up by the whirlwind were stuck at the top of the staircase, unable to get down without finding another way. Jonah looked impressed.

"Go, now!" Jake commanded. "While you still have time!"

Imogen, Sophia and I hesitated. We didn't know this guy at all. Was it all a trap?

"Guys, I feel like we can trust him!" Jonah shouted over the noise, and Squeaks nodded in agreement. "We should do what he says!"

"Jonah, just because you think he's cute doesn't mean he's on our side," Imogen snapped.

Jonah's cheeks turned pink. "I do *not* think he's cute."

"We don't have a choice. Look!" Sophia pointed down the hallway. An onslaught of Task Force members were marching toward us. Jake, Sabor and the Yapluma woman were the only thing standing in their way.

"Well, looks like we're following directions. Come on!" I shouted. With my decision, the group followed me. We abandoned the corridors and changed direction, toward the Atrium.

Once we got there, I was relieved to see my dad standing outside the glass doors of the inner courtyard... though my heart seized when I saw my sister wasn't with him. Only Tatum was at his side.

Dad's eyes cleared when he saw us coming near. "Thank the ancestors. I hoped Jake would find you."

"Maddie?" I asked, my throat tight.

Dad shook his head. "I don't know where she is." His voice seemed devoid of all hope. "She could be anywhere in this mess."

"We can't abandon her," Sophia protested.

"I'm not going to. But the four of you need to leave," Dad said firmly.

The sound of voices emitting from inside the Atrium cut him off. Dad pulled us behind a wall. Through the windows surrounding the Atrium, we saw Elder Malison enter into the room with a dozen Task Force members behind. He was ordering them to search the area. It wouldn't be long before we were found.

Dad's voice lowered. "Listen to me. There's a secret passageway not too far from here. Remember the statue of the dancing sprite? If you press down on her hand, the wall will open up. It'll take you to the gardens. From there, you'll have a better chance."

"What about you?" I asked hoarsely.

"Forget about me." Dad put his hands on my shoulders. "You need to take care of your family, understand? That's what's important now. They come first."

I didn't get it. *He* was my family. So was Maddie. I didn't know what he was talking about. Did this have something to do with Sophia and I being engaged?

"Liam, listen to me," Dad said. "Whatever happens, don't interfere. It's not important now. It'll be all right."

Dad's voice was clear and soothing. I felt like I was six years old again and he was trying to comfort me after I was sure there was a monster under my bed. I was a grown man, but the world had never seemed more frightening.

I felt like he was passing me the torch. And I didn't like that feeling.

"I'll distract him," Dad said. "Go."

Dad headed through the glass doors of the Atrium to face Malison and the Task Force. Jonah and Imogen looked anxiously down the hall, but my eyes were glued on Dad's back as he and Tatum strolled toward Malison.

"Liam, let's go!" Sophia hissed.

But I didn't want to. I couldn't leave— not like this.

"We have to stay and make sure he's okay," I begged. "Don't make me leave now, Sophia. We'll watch. Just for a few minutes, to make sure he escapes."

Sophia's expression twisted. She glanced at Imogen and Jonah, like she didn't know what to do, but no one said anything. Squeaks' hooves danced nervously on the stone, and Sassy whimpered lowly as I pressed myself to the wall and dared to peer through the window to watch.

A few of the windows had been broken, so I could hear Dad when he said, "You were the worst mistake I ever made with the council, Malison."

A couple of Task Force members laughed. I heard Malison cackle with them and reply, "We've been looking for you for days. Where's your boy?"

"Far away from you," Dad lied. "I suggest we stop talking and get this over with."

"You always wanted things your way, but this time, I have to agree. No noxite darts," Malison announced. "You heard Oleander. He wants Chief Mitoh dead. Let's finish what we started."

The Task Force began firing elements, but Dad had already moved. He threw aside his bow and wove his hands in an intricate fashion. The water from the koi pool, the waterfall, and the fountain inside the Atrium created a huge wall of water that caused all other elements to fizzle. Malison tried to manipulate the water himself, but his magic wasn't as powerful as Dad's, and the element wouldn't listen to him. In a colossal show of magic, Dad moved the water so that it created a spiraling cylinder and swept up the Task Force members that approached. The cylinder changed into a wave that crashed from one end of the Atrium to the other.

Tatum changed. As Dad grew the wave's intensity, Tatum morphed into it and became a bear of water. His size grew until he rivaled the wave. The water bear stampeded throughout the Atrium, crashing into Task Force members and crushing them underfoot. Malison scrambled to get out of the way, taking refuge behind a pillar as Dad's magic rushed throughout the inner courtyard.

But those Task Force members weren't the only ones. More kept coming. Dozens of police came in through the doorway Malison had entered. When Dad took down one, two more came in to take their place. I watched his eyes grow frantic as he and Tatum struggled to fight them off. Malison's cruel smile was growing wider and wider with each passing second.

Dad couldn't handle all of them. Even with his power, there were too many. He was horribly outnumbered.

Then a rock slammed into his back by a Nivita, and Dad cried out in pain. I tried focusing my powers on stopping Malison's heart, but I couldn't do it. Not from here. I was too weak.

"Soph, expand the forcefield around my dad," I begged.

"I can't," Sophia said. Her expression was strained as she attempted to cast the forcefield at a distance. The shield flickered once or twice around him, like it was in danger of going out.

She was tired. All of us were tired. Even Sophia's powers had limits, and we were at the brink of them.

I went for the door, but Jonah grabbed me and held me back.

"Let me go, dammit!" I cried. My voice was loud, but the battle in the Atrium was so loud, no one heard me scream.

"Liam. We need to leave," Jonah said firmly. He tried to yank me in the direction of the sprite statue down the hall, but I wasn't budging.

"We need to help my dad!" I kicked out, but my feet met nothing but air. Imogen and Sophia observed, unsure of what to do.

"Your dad told us to leave! We need to obey his orders!" Jonah snapped roughly.

"Let. Me. *Go!*"

I did the only thing I could. I hurt Jonah.

I still had a fist full of water that I'd taken from Maddie earlier. I froze it, then brought my fist slamming backward into Jonah's face.

Jonah let me go and staggered away, holding on to his nose. Blood spurted everywhere. I darted for the door again, but Imogen cried out for Sassy, and the kitsune's vines wrapped around my legs. I fell down, then grabbed the vines around my legs and kicked them off before Sassy could tighten her hold on me. Imogen flung her arms out, and the stone floor wrapped around my feet, but I used the water in my hand like bombs, shooting jets downward to shatter the stone. Squeaks tried to get in my way, but I shot an icicle in her direction. She jumped out of the way, shocked I'd actually attempt to hurt her.

I didn't want to hurt anyone. But I'd do anything to anybody if it meant stopping this.

At a loss for anything else to do, Imogen and Jonah threw both of themselves on me, taking an arm each. Squeaks grabbed the back of my shirt, and Sassy held on to my pant leg with her teeth. But still, even with all of them holding me back, the magic pumping through my blood and the terror of what might actually happen kept moving me forward.

Sassy couldn't hold me. Jonah couldn't. Neither could Imogen. Or Squeaks.

I was inches away from the door. If I broke through it, Malison and the Task Force would know we were here and would probably kill us all. But I wasn't thinking straight. In that moment, I didn't care if I lived or died. All I wanted to do was save my dad.

"Sophia!" Jonah desperately cried, but it was a useless attempt. The entire fucking world couldn't hold me back right now from saving my dad if it tried.

But there was one person who was stronger than I was. And she was the love of my life.

"Liam, don't make me do this," Sophia begged. She raised her hands slowly. Her eyes were wet, and Esis gave a warning cry from inside her sweatshirt.

I didn't care. My fingers reached for the handle.

Sophia closed her eyes and turned her face away. She gave a sob, and tears streamed down her face as her magic enveloped me in a column of flame.

Imogen, Jonah, Sassy, and Squeaks let go. I gave a harrowing cry of pain as Sophia's flames began licking up my arms. I could hear skin as it bubbled and cracked, feeling my body melting under her power. I nearly passed out from the pain. Her flames were so incredibly intense that I didn't have time to think. My forearms blackened before my very eyes. I didn't realize that the animalistic screams of pain were coming from me until my knees hit stone.

Sophia only pulled her magic back when I'd fallen to the floor. The flames died instantly. The pain had vanished, as the flames had killed the nerves. She'd only burned my forearms, leaving my clothes and face untouched, but her Fire had completely ruined my hands. I was unable to do anything but lay there and breathe. Every breath felt like agony.

I heard tiny nails scrabbling on the floor, and saw Esis standing next to my head. I watched, dazed, as third-degree burns began knitting my flesh together into new skin.

As Esis worked his healing power over me, I watched through the glass as the fight continued. Tatum and Dad were pressed against a wall. Tatum was back in his grizzly form, and the Familiar was acting like a cornered animal. He swiped out with his paws and roared for the Task Members to go away, yet they advanced closer and closer.

Then the glass ceiling of the Atrium broke open, and one of Skylis' heads crashed through. The dracash dove one of his heads downward and enveloped Tatum within his teeth before the bear could retaliate.

The dragon hybrid clamped his jaws down, and a sickening *crack* could be heard throughout the Atrium as Skylis broke Tatum's spine.

My mind went blank then. I raced for explanations. For hope. I'd outlived Nashoma. Dad could do the same thing with Tatum, right?

But Dad wasn't me.

As Tatum's lifeless body fell to the floor from the jaws of Skylis, Dad cried out in grief. He put a hand to his heart, as if it physically pained him to remain upright.

Malison grinned— he held up a hand for the Task Force, and they stopped advancing. They remained a still half-circle as Dad panted from the loss of losing Tatum only seconds before.

"Looks like this one's done for," Malison seethed. "We have other matters to attend to. Let this traitor spend his last miserable hours in anguish."

Malison left. He took his Task Force members with him, and the room became empty. Skylis, satisfied with what he had done, spread his wings and took off.

Dad was the only one left in the inner courtyard after mere minutes. He stood blankly over Tatum's body, like he couldn't believe what had happened. Sophia, Imogen and Jonah stood completely still. I struggled to get up— my arms shook with the effort of trying.

I had to go to Dad now. I had to tell him he would be okay. That he could do this without Tatum.

Then another figure advanced from the shadows. She knelt down and took an arrow from Dad's discarded bow, which was still lying on the ground. Her advancement from behind was so quick, I didn't see it coming until it was too late.

Before I could cry out a warning, Chieftess Annette raised the arrow and plunged it into my father's back. It speared through his chest, right through his heart.

All hearing faded away. If I was screaming, or crying, I didn't know it. Time itself had stopped.

From here, I could see Annette's lips move as they mouthed words. *You cost me everything.*

Dad collapsed. Annette staggered backward— she made it a few more steps before she tilted against a column. She sank down it slowly, her nails gripping the sides, until her form crumpled on the ground and the light faded from her eyes.

Dad broke the arrow off in his chest and pulled it out. He gave a gasp as blood poured out from the wound— his eyes widened, and he slumped across Tatum's body.

He gave a few quick, short breaths before he slowly stilled... his eyes remained glossy, mouth open like he was still in shock.

His lungs gave a shuddering noise, then he became quiet.

I slowly rose to my feet. No one stopped me as I gently opened the glass door of the Atrium. I walked toward Dad with quiet steps. This couldn't be real. It was just a bad dream.

"Dad?" For as loud as it had been only moments before, now it was deathly quiet.

When I came to where he lie, I fell down next to him. I rolled him over so that he was on his back instead of his stomach and shook his shoulder. His glass eyes stared blankly up at the ceiling, and not at me.

"Dad, come on." I shook him again. "Dad. I want to go home."

I knew something was wrong when I heard Imogen sobbing behind me, but I didn't know what.

Dad continued to gaze at something I couldn't see. I shook him harder this time.

"Dad, please. Get up. You have to get up." I had to be crying, because my face was wet. But I didn't want to admit it. This couldn't be true. My dad couldn't really be...

Sophia collapsed next to me. She flung her arms around my shoulders, and Esis curled up on my lap.

This felt like a shitty repeat. The agonizing feelings pulsating across my chest were all too horribly well-known. I knew what this emotion was, but I didn't want to face it again.

"Dad," I whispered one last time. "Don't go."

Too late. I remembered I'd begged the ancestors to take anyone but Sophia. I didn't know they actually would. They'd answered my prayer in the worst possible way.

Toaqua's darkest hour had come. The Water tribe had no chief, and my dad was gone.

sophia
TWENTY-FOUR

I couldn't move. I couldn't speak. The end to the prophecy was here. It'd come true.

It is she who shall cause Toaqua's darkest hour.

Liwanu's death. *I'm* the one who caused the riots. *I'm* the one who stopped Liam from saving his dad. I'd killed him.

Oh, God! I'd burnt Liam! I could hardly wrap my head around what I'd done. I'd hurt him to save the rest of us. The only way to stomach it was knowing Esis had healed him afterward, but putting him through that kind of pain...

I hated myself for it. The memory of watching the love of my life be burned alive by my flames was pure hell. And there was no escaping from it.

"We have to go!" Jonah shouted, pulling me back to attention. He was tugging on Liam, trying to pull him off his dad, but Liam wouldn't budge. Tears ran down his face, but other than that, he didn't react. He was like a statue.

I glanced upward, wondering if we could make it out of the shattered ceiling, but Jonah's powers still weren't recharged, and Squeaks couldn't handle all of us at once.

Through the windows of the Atrium, we could see Task Force

members running down the halls and shouting orders at each other. If we didn't get out of here *now*, we didn't have a chance.

"Liam!" Imogen joined Jonah in pulling him off his dad. Squeaks grabbed Liam's shirt in her beak and tugged hard. Between the three of them, they dragged him away.

Liam just stared at his father's lifeless body, like he was nothing more than a shell of a human being... like a piece of himself had died with his father. He didn't fight as Jonah shoved him onto Squeak's back.

Seeing him like that made me want to fall to pieces alongside him.

Imogen and Jonah looked to me for guidance. That's when it hit me. I didn't have time to fall apart. I had to be strong now. With Liam out for the count, I had to step up and be the leader of the Reject Team. Otherwise, we were all dead.

"We have to get to that sprite statue Liwanu talked about," I said firmly. "This way."

I headed in the opposite direction of the Task Force and led my friends out of the Atrium and back to the main halls of the school. Jonah cleared the air of smoke in front of us, but it barely helped. Smoke billowed all throughout the school and filled our lungs. The roaring crackle of fire could be heard from every angle as it ate away at any burnable material it could find.

We came to a T at the end of the hall, and I pointed to our right. "This way!"

But when we rounded the corner, my heart stalled in my chest. The first thing I saw was Valda standing at the end of the wide corridor. She'd stepped in front of Alric to protect him, but he pushed past her.

Alric was worse for wear than I'd ever seen him. His hair was in complete disarray, and soot covered his face. His clothes were torn and hung off of him in strands, and he clutched his stomach like he'd been injured.

Madame Doya stood with her back toward us. Naomi bared her teeth at Alric. The two faced each other. Neither noticed us.

I looked around for Baine. Last I'd seen him, he was going after Alric to help him. I didn't see him anywhere now, which scared me.

"You know what I have to do," Madame Doya said, flatly and without emotion.

Alric took a step forward, but he grimaced as he moved. "Then you know, Eleanor, that I will fight until my very last breath."

I couldn't see Doya's face, but I imagined it turning into a sneer.

"Very well, Caspian," Doya said in that same stoic, unfeeling manner. "You give me no choice."

Doya flicked her wrist, and I gasped as long wisps of flames shot from the walls and in Alric's direction. He waved his hands, and the flames separated and redirected on either side of him. Valda crouched down low and let out a terrifying roar. Naomi growled, then sprinted toward the dragon.

It all happened so fast that I didn't realize what was happening right away. Doya... against Alric?

It sounded insane. But after Doya had stuck up for me time and time again— after she said she wanted me to be chieftess— I really thought that she was on her side. I was starting to think her apathetic nature was perhaps a mask for the Elders.

But standing here now, watching her attack Alric, I knew that I was wrong. The fun-loving, adventurous girl I'd seen in my mother's photo album had died long ago. As much as I held on to the hope that she might still be in there somewhere, she wasn't. Doya must've been lying when she said she wanted me to be chieftess. She would always be a cold-hearted woman, driven by anger and a thirst for power. It was clear now she'd always been on Oleander's side, and she'd do anything to get her way— including killing the Head Dean.

Naomi leapt onto Valda's back and sank her teeth into the dragon's neck. Valda reared back on her hind legs, slamming her head into the ceiling as she cried out. She swiped her claws at Naomi, but the fire lion jumped out of the way and began tearing her claws into Valda's wings. Doya continued to shoot flame after flame at Alric while he did all he could to defend himself.

Alric wasn't weak by any means. There was a reason he'd been Head Dean. But after everything he'd been through these past few days — being held prisoner and tortured, not to mention the fights he'd already been through with Oleander's Familiar— he didn't stand a chance.

"What do we do!?" Imogen cried. Tears filled her eyes as we watched in horror. "We have to save him!"

Imogen and Jonah looked to me. We all knew it; if anyone could save Alric, it had to be a Koigni. There was too much Fire racing through the air for anyone else to get involved.

I hesitated. Doya was my mentor. She was far stronger than me.

That moment of hesitation was my mistake.

Before I could process it, Alric had created a wall of Fire that spanned from one wall to the other, blocking our view of him. It shot toward Doya at an incredible speed, so fast that if she'd blinked, it would've slammed straight into her.

But Doya was ready for it. She lifted her hands, and the wall of Fire stopped dead only inches from her. If she took a step forward, she could touch it.

Doya swirled her hands, and the wall of flames began to shape to her will. The flames transformed into a huge Fire tornado that took up the entire corridor. Flames from all along the walls swirled into the tornado, until there was nothing left but scorch marks on the walls and fragments of tapestries. She'd gathered every last bit of flame into the twister.

The roaring cries of the dragon and lion echoed down the hall, but I couldn't see them past the flames that reached to the ceiling.

In the blink of an eye, Doya thrust her hands forward, and the Fire tornado swirled down the hall at lightning speed.

"*No!*" I screamed, but it was too late.

The tornado whipped Alric off his feet. Torturous screams echoed down the hall, and all I saw was the shadow of a burning corpse as Alric fell to his knees. Doya's flames consumed him, wiping out everything in their path— including Alric's life.

Doya heard my cry and whirled toward me, but I barely noticed as my eyes turned toward Valda and Naomi. Valda's gaze darted down to Alric's burning body. She let out a mournful cry that made my guts twist.

It was the single distraction Naomi needed to lunge at Valda's throat.

Naomi's sharp teeth sank into Valda's flesh, and the dragon roared in pain. Naomi's strong jaws clamped down harder on the dragon's throat, and then... *rrrrrip!*

Naomi yanked her head to the side, and flesh tore from Valda's neck. Scales and blood went flying as the lion ripped Valda's trachea straight from her body. Valda stumbled, and hot blood poured out of her body as the dragon sank to the floor, dead.

I thought I was going to be sick, but the nausea didn't compare to the red-hot rage blazing through my body at that moment. Doya was a traitor! A *murderer*! She'd killed Alric!

I couldn't hold my Fire back. Everything came rushing out all at once. I shoved Esis onto Squeaks' back and ran forward. A scream ripped from my lungs, and I aimed my hands at Doya. A jet of flame larger than anything I'd ever conjured before shot from my palms straight at the woman who'd protected me time and time again.

No matter how many times she'd saved Sophia Henley, she couldn't run from Kyra Koignichi. My spirit name meant *Blazing Firespirit*, and that meant I would stand and fight for the people I loved. *No one* got away with murdering my headmaster, my leader who'd smuggled so many good people to safety. Madame Doya would have to answer to me — and she would pay for what she did.

Doya's magic pushed against my own. It felt like I was aiming my Fire at a brick wall. The harder I pushed and the more Fire I conjured, the more she pushed back.

"Sophia!" Doya screamed past the sounds of the raging inferno around us. The flames had returned to eat away at the school again, and smoke was filling my eyes and my lungs. "You don't want to do this!"

Doya threw her arms apart, and my flames split straight down the middle. Her fiery red hair billowed around her as flames rushed past on either side of her. She wore that tight expression I was so used to, only it was ten times worse. Doya stared at me in a way that should've lit me aflame.

"You killed him!" I shouted.

"I had to!" she screamed. "You don't understand!"

"I understand perfectly," I spat. "You're on Oleander's side. You always have been!"

Tears began to stream down my face, but the flames shooting from my palms didn't slow.

"You knew the prophecy wasn't as it seemed," I accused. "You knew it was talking about Defortai. That's why you protected me all this time. You wanted Oleander to win!"

Doya's features shifted into an even more terrifying gaze. Her nostrils flared, and I could've sworn I saw smoke puff out of them. "You have *no idea* what I want!"

Doya thrust her arms outward, and the flames I'd been conjuring shot straight back at me. Somehow, Doya had taken control of them. They hit me, knocking me off my feet.

My back slammed into the flaming wall. I bounced off of it and landed on my ass on the ground. I gasped for breath as Doya advanced on me. She held a fireball in her hand and stared down at me in disgust. "Sophia, I—"

The sound of Naomi's growl cut her off. Doya's gaze snapped in Naomi's direction, and her face fell. I didn't know what Naomi was saying to her, but it was obvious they were having a conversation.

Doya turned her wide-eyed gaze back to me, and her lips curled back into a sneer. There was a mixture of surprise and disgust on her face. "Sophia... how could you?"

I had no idea what she was talking about, but whatever Naomi had said to her, it distracted Doya for too long. A loud squawk sounded through the corridor, and Squeaks jumped between me and Doya. She reared up on her hind legs and smashed her foot across the side of Doya's face.

Doya screamed and clutched her cheek, but that was all I saw before Esis jumped in my lap.

Liam's face swam in front of my vision. He wrapped his arms around me and pulled me close, rocking me from side to side. But he must've still been in shock, because he didn't say anything. He just held me.

"Come on!" Jonah roared. He reached out and grabbed Liam and me by the shoulder and dragged us to our feet, using what Air magic he had left to help us up. "Imogen!"

"Hold on!" she shouted. "I'm buying us time."

Around us, the castle rumbled as Imogen used her Earth magic to control the stones. Doya shot fireball after fireball at Squeaks, but Squeaks dodged them all, advancing on Doya like she was about to rip her throat out. Sassy jumped forward, her vines snapping in all directions.

"Squeaks! Come on!" Jonah shouted.

Squeaks squawked so loud it vibrated the castle. Then she whirled around and followed Jonah's command, coming back to us. Imogen screamed as she brought her hands together, and the stone around us crumbled. The ceiling caved in, sending dust flying everywhere. Smoke billowed up through the hole above us.

I stared wide-eyed at the barrier between us and Doya. I couldn't see her, but I heard Naomi's growling and Doya screaming my name as we sprinted in the other direction. Doya couldn't follow us past the stones.

My heart hammered. "We'll have to go around!"

I led everyone down another hall and used my magic to kill as many flames as I could, but it was getting worse by the second. Jonah manipulated the oxygen in the air, but it wouldn't be much longer before we couldn't breathe anymore.

Finally, we rounded the corner and reached the sprite statue. I pressed down on her hand like Liwanu had said, and the sound of stone grinding against stone met my ears. I hurried around to the back of the statue. I saw that a tunnel had opened in the wall, just big enough for us to crawl through.

"Everybody in!" I demanded.

I planned to wait for everyone else to get in first, but Squeaks nudged me, pushing me in first. Esis scurried along at my side. I crawled forward quickly to make room for everyone else. Liam crawled in next. He was coughing up a lung, though he still hadn't said anything since his dad had died. He had this blank look in his eyes that just told me he was confused, and lost.

I don't think he even knew where we were right now.

When I saw that everyone was inside the tunnel, I turned and guided everyone to the end, where we found an opening between two huge bushes in the gardens. They were nothing more than a shell of what they used to be, with dying embers glowing at the ends of the branches.

I killed the embers with my magic to let everyone through. Behind us, the castle continued to burn, the flames eating away at everything in their path. Parts of the forest were on fire, too, from where it'd spread from the gardens.

There was no turning back now. We started toward the mountains, which was the only clear path from the fire. Esis stood on my shoulder, sniffing the air.

As we entered the woods, my heart stalled. Two figures took shape through the trees. I noticed they were followed by a small feline and a white goat.

"Grandma! Grandpa!" I shouted.

I thought I was seeing things. Maybe I was hallucinating from all the smoke inhalation. But when they ran forward and surrounded me in a hug, I knew it was real. I pressed my nose into my grandpa's shirt and inhaled a deep breath, enjoying the clean air.

I drew away from their hug. "What are you two *doing* here!?"

"We saw the flames from the Koigni village," Grandma said in a rush. "We came to find you!"

Grandpa took me by the shoulders. "Sophia, we need to get you and your friends out of here."

"I know—"

A squawk sounded through the forest, though it hadn't come from Squeaks. In fact, I'd never heard such a terrifying bird call in all my life. My blood ran cold as two people sauntered out from behind the trees. A cockatrice and a god-awful ugly swamp creature called a bunyip stood at their sides. The bunyip was the same size as the cockatrice, but had green and brown fur, and horns instead of eyes.

Renar and Mallory.

Renar clicked his tongue. "I can't let you do that. Oleander wants Sophia, and she's not leaving."

Grandpa threw himself in front of me. "Like hell she's not!"

Grandma crossed her arms and joined my grandpa in front of me, her head held high. "You're not taking her."

Renar shrugged. "Have it your way."

He cocked his head, and the cockatrice followed his command. Before my grandparents could conjure Fire— before I could even blink — Alvarice snapped his beak forward. He caught my grandmother around the throat, and sliced his sharp talons across my grandfather's chest.

Grandma didn't even have a chance to scream before her throat was slit from the cockatrice's razor-sharp beak. Grandpa went down, clutching his chest and crying out in pain. Mallory's evil cackle echoed through the forest, like she was *amused* by the slaughter.

Horror tore through me like a sword. I barely had a second to process what had happened before Alvarice tore my grandmother's stomach open with his beak. He began ripping her innards out, splaying them on the forest floor. A warm liquid sprayed upward into my face, and it took me a second to realize it was her blood.

My grandma's cat hissed at Alvarice, but one swipe of the cocka-trice's claws, and Thelma's head went flying off her shoulders. Blood splattered across the tree beside my grandmother's Familiar.

My hands shot to my mouth in horror as I screamed in terror and grief. It all happened so fast that I could hardly process it.

I couldn't believe it. My grandparents. They... they...

Jonah stepped in front of me, and Imogen's fury-filled eyes locked on Mallory. The earth began to rumble beneath our feet. Sassy's vines snapped, and the trees began to rock and sway.

Jonah stepped toward Renar. Lightning crackled in his hands for the first time since we left the Air kingdom.

"You're going to pay for that," Jonah threatened.

Renar chuckled. "I'm *so* scared."

Jonah threw his hand out, and lightning struck the tree beside Renar. Renar and Mallory's laughter died instantly, and Imogen and Jonah moved in to attack.

I didn't see what else happened, because I rushed over to my grandpa with Esis at my side. My grandma was already gone— I couldn't save her, but maybe I could save him. Liam froze in place beside me— like he couldn't stand to watch any more people die after the massacre we'd seen tonight. He couldn't tear his eyes away from Thelma's severed head.

The sounds of fighting faded through the trees as Jonah and Imogen chased Renar and Mallory off. My grandpa gasped as I took one of his hands. He clutched the other to his chest, but more and more blood kept coming out between his fingers. Alvarice had nicked his heart.

"Sophia," he struggled to say through ragged breaths. "There's something I need—"

"Shh... Grandpa," I whispered. "Esis is going to help."

Esis placed a paw on my grandpa's stomach, but blood pumped out of him so fast that I feared there may not be time. I bit down hard on my lower lip to silence my doubt.

Grandpa shook his head while his Familiar wailed from beside him. The Dall sheep's cry was unbearably heartbreaking.

"Sophia, you have to know." Grandpa squeezed my hand tighter, struggling through the pain to speak. I leaned down close so that he could whisper in my ear. "I'm not... your grandfather."

My heart stopped, and tears streamed down my face. "What? No."

My voice cracked. Why was Grandpa using his last breath to lie to me?

His bottom lip quivered. "I love you like my own, Sophia, but Lucy and Anthony aren't your real parents. There were *two* children born on the night of your birth. Our biological granddaughter died in childbirth with Lucy. Your mother gave you to us to raise, but we sent you with the Henley family. To protect you."

I shook my head in disbelief. This couldn't be real. Why hadn't they told me this before?

"You must find your real parents," Grandpa whispered. "Promise me, Sophia."

I gaped at him. Holy shit. He wasn't suffering from some dying delusion. He was telling the truth.

"Who?" I asked through the tears. "Who are my real parents?"

Grandpa's eyes clouded over, like his vision had gone. "I don't know who your father is, but your mother... your mother is..."

Grandpa's hand went limp, and the life drained from his eyes as his lungs gave a dying shudder. I felt his heartbeat fade until it wasn't there at all.

"Grandpa, no!" I screamed, slamming my fist against his shoulder. "No!"

My whole body felt heavy and empty at the same time. An invisible force squeezed me tighter and tighter with each passing second. I gasped for breath that wouldn't come.

"Grandpa, come back!" I pleaded. Sobs tore through my chest like a blade. "Who is my real mother? Who is she?"

In the distance, the sound of marching feet could be heard. "They escaped into the trees!"

My head snapped upward, and I pulled my trembling, blood-covered hands off my grandfather's body. My sobs quieted as I listened to the voices in the night.

"Don't let them get away!"

My adrenaline spiked, bringing me back to reality. Beside me, Liam's eyes went wide.

"Fuck," I muttered under my breath. "The Task Force is coming."

Just as I said it, we saw the first of them burst through the trees. They were coming at us so fast, and there were so many of them.

I hesitated, but the Task Force just kept coming. Liam gasped, and that's when I knew what I had to do. I shot to my feet. Fire burst of my palms, raining down on the trees in front of us and creating a huge wall of flame to hold the Task Force off.

"Sophia! Liam!" Imogen's voice came through the forest in the opposite direction.

I scooped Esis up in my arms, then grabbed Liam's hand. "We have to go."

I tried to usher Grandpa's Familiar along with us, but he wouldn't move. He curled up next to my grandfather's body, whimpering.

Liam stared down at the helpless creature and swallowed. I knew we were thinking the same thing, and I could hardly bear it. With my grandpa gone, his Familiar would soon follow. There was nothing more we could do.

We had to leave the mutilated bodies of the grandparents I loved behind. And that nearly killed me.

Liam tugged on my arm, and we ran toward the sound of Imogen's voice. Esis screamed in protest, holding his paws out toward my grandpa like he wanted to go back and help, but he was already gone.

Imogen and Jonah hurried through the trees toward us, Sassy and Squeaks by their side.

"Did you get Renar and Mallory?" I asked breathlessly.

Jonah shook his head sadly. "They got away."

"The Task Force is coming," I warned them.

"Then let's get our asses out of here," Jonah said.

We ran up the mountain as fast as our feet could carry us. It was surprising how quickly we moved, considering how worn we were from everything that had happened. But I guess when your life is on the line, you're willing to push through anything to save it.

Even grief.

The whole time, my mind raced as I tried to accept what just happened as reality. How could my grandparents be gone? Why had they been so foolish and tried to come find me? How could they have *lied* to me all this time? Did I even know them for who they truly were?

Did I even know myself?

We didn't stop until we were halfway up the Ancestral Mountain and were confident we'd lost the Task Force. We stopped in a clearing. I remembered it from when Liam told me about the ancestors my first semester here.

My friends all sat on the ground to take a break, but I just stood there, unable to move as I looked back the way we'd come. Through the darkness of the night, all I could see was Orenda Academy ablaze. Everywhere I looked, there was fire consuming the castle I once called home. Not a tower was left untouched. The bright red flames were in stark contrast to the dark sky, and even from this distance it almost hurt my eyes. And yet, I couldn't tear my gaze away.

There was no *home* anymore. My family was gone. I didn't even know who my real parents were, and the one place I belonged in this world was burning to the ground. I was lost.

All I could hear were the words of the Air prophecy echoing in my mind.

"*Smoke will blaze through the sky and signify the Hawkei's extinction.*"

The prophecy had been fulfilled.
We had no hope left.

Liam

TWENTY-FIVE

"Come on, buddy. You gotta get up."

Jonah yanked on my arm. I'd been sitting against the totem pole in the mountain clearing for a good forty minutes, though it felt more like decades had passed. I'd aged years since this morning. I'd grown up in the span of a few seconds.

Annette stabbing Dad.

Alric burning to death.

Blood pouring from Betsy's throat.

Thelma's head rolling from her shoulders.

Alan being torn apart before my very eyes.

It was too much to handle. Their deaths repeated on a playback reel, over and over in my mind. I was afraid to shut my eyes, for fear I'd see the whole thing once again.

I knew how this went. I thought I'd escaped it forever, but I never would. I relived Nashoma's death in my dreams for months. I'd watched my father die. I'd seen Sophia's face as her grandparents were torn apart by a cockatrice right in front of her.

These were things that'd be holes in my spirit for the rest of my life. If you could call it a life. My limbs were so leaden and heavy, I couldn't move.

"Bud, let's go." Jonah didn't take no for an answer. He forcibly hauled me to my feet. I swayed, but Jonah put his hands on my shoulders to steady me.

"We can't stay here," he said firmly.

I just stared back at him. It was like I didn't know how to speak English anymore. The words were confusing and jumbled. What did he mean? I didn't know.

"Liam, you have to say something," Jonah pleaded. His shoulders slumped forward, and Squeaks gave a quiet coo.

I hadn't said a thing since my dad had died. I was unable to make words come out of my mouth. Talking seemed like something the living would do.

"Guys, Sophia's gone," Imogen said in a rush. She came out of the bushes in a panic. Sassy was at her heels, yipping. "She walked off by herself."

That got my fucking attention. It was like I came rushing back into my body. "Where'd she go?"

"I don't know." Imogen took deep, gulping breaths as she tried not to panic. "I swear she was just there a minute ago."

The three of us split up and began calling for Sophia. I headed down the mountain as fast as I could— which wasn't very fast. I was weak, tired, and worn, but I forced my body to keep going. If Sophia was lost, we needed to find her before the Task Force did.

I saw Esis. He was sitting at the base of the mountain. His head was tilted, and his ears perked. He gave a helpless squeak. It sounded like the noise of an animal that had been left behind.

Ahead of him, Sophia had staggered down the mountain path. Her steps were slow and wobbling. She moved like a zombie. She was walking like her soul had been broken and there was nothing left in her.

"Sophia!"

When I called her name, she turned around and gave me a deadened look. Ashes and soot were streaked across her face. Tracks of tears made thin lines within them.

I'd never seen her look like that in my life. She'd been completely led astray.

People weren't meant to be put through hell like this. Humanity couldn't endure the things it did to each other.

Sophia turned her back to me and continued down the path. She didn't have anywhere to go, but still, she walked.

I scooped up Esis and jogged in front of her. I put out a hand to stop her. "*Pawee*, stop. Where are you going?"

"Somewhere. Anywhere," she replied. "Far away from here."

Esis crawled out of my arms and into hers. He clung to her chest. Sophia wrapped her arms around him and snuggled her face into his fur. Esis hugged Sophia with all his might and curled his tail around her cheek.

Footsteps on the trail signified Imogen and Jonah had caught up. They stared at us for a moment before Imogen came beside me. "We have to leave."

"Where?" Sophia whispered. "Where in the world is safe now?"

"We know a way. Follow us," Jonah said.

Squeaks led the way around the mountain and through the brush. When we got to the woods, Imogen and Jonah wove a way around thick vegetation that I'd never been before.

"Guys, where are we going?" I asked. I kept my arm tightly around Sophia, half because I was worried she'd run off again, and half because if I didn't hold her right now, I was scared I'd have a breakdown.

Sophia's bag was still over my back. I could feel Julian's egg as it bounced between my shoulders. He hadn't hatched yet. That was the only blessing we'd received this night.

"You all know there's a cave system under Kinpago," Imogen said. "Jonah and I found an entrance to one of the caves. It leads out of here."

"We found it months ago," Jonah said. "We've only been back a few times since."

We came to a huge stone wall. It was ten feet tall, and definitely looked like it'd been built by Nivita. I expected Jonah to lift us up over it, until Imogen grabbed on to one of the stones to start climbing.

"The wall's got a magical ward around it. Our powers won't work. Bottoms up," Jonah said.

He started by helping Imogen over the wall. I tried to lift Sophia, but

I was too tired. I ended up falling down. Jonah got her over before he gave me a boost. Squeaks flew Sassy and Esis to the other side.

Once we were over the wall, I looked around. Imogen headed into the trees, and my jaw dropped as we entered into a clearing. Rabbits with deer antlers and small wings hopped and flew around. When they saw us coming, they ran for cover, though a fat one got stuck in the hole to his warren and a friend had to push him through.

"Wolpertingers!" Sophia shouted. The smallest bit of light had come back into her eyes.

"Told you they were real," Imogen grumbled sourly. Sassy peeped in agreement beside her.

"And burlangers," I said. Imogen was right after all. These creatures did exist. Tiny puffs of fur, with huge eyes, curly antennas and fuzzy feet rolled around the clearing, making cheering noises. They bounced off the trees and up and down on the grass. They looked like fluffy tennis balls come to life.

"And lillybats," Imogen said, pointing. Nesting in the trees were bats. They had wings that looked like the white petals of lilies. As the moonlight touched their forms, they spread their wings in unison. The colony took off, probably in search of bugs to eat.

"We didn't tell anyone about this place, because we wanted to protect the endangered creatures here," Jonah said.

"This place really is magical," Sophia hushed. "With these creatures running around, and Esis, it gives me hope that some of the Anichi creatures that are supposed to be extinct are still alive somewhere."

We watched the colony of lillybats disappear before moving on. The wolpertingers were hiding, but the burlangers didn't seem afraid. They bounced around our feet and ricocheted off Squeaks as we walked, like they were enjoying the company.

The burlangers scuttled off as we came to the mouth of a large cave entrance. Imogen jerked her head. "Come on. This is the way out."

Jonah shivered, but he started toward the cave with a steely expression. "Well, let's get this over with."

We entered the cave. Sophia lit a light in her hand, but it wasn't fire. It was a white glow— her Anichi light.

She'd obviously had enough of Fire tonight. Our echoing steps were the only thing that could be heard as our group proceeded down the damp and twisting tunnel.

"Do you guys really think this leads to a way out?" Sophia whispered.

"I've walked it a few times, though I've never gotten to the end. It's too long. One of the shorter tunnels leads to a highway," Imogen said. "We have stuff there waiting."

"What?" I froze. "You mean... you were *planning* for this?"

"Don't ask, Liam," Imogen begged. "Wait until we get out of here."

Her tone was suspicious. But I was too exhausted to argue. Imogen kept her eyes focused on the ground, like she was looking for footprints or something.

"The first time we were down here, we ran into an orthus— a two headed reptile," Imogen said. "I'm looking out for it."

"Yeah, and it nearly bit my head off," Jonah complained.

"You're exaggerating." Imogen rolled her eyes. "We think it's safe now, though. Last time Jonah and I checked, there weren't any signs of life down here."

"When was that?" I asked.

"Only a month ago."

"Im, what aren't you telling us?" I growled. My arm tightened on Sophia. Imogen and Jonah looked at each other.

"Just hold on, Liam. I promise I'll explain everything," Imogen whispered.

I kept my mouth shut, but I was kind of peeved Imogen and Jonah had been keeping secrets. Jonah practically ran through the cave to get out of it as quickly as possible, but the rest of us slowed him down. He let out a huge sigh of relief as the end of the cave same into sight. It was shielded with pine tree branches.

"So what's waiting for us at the end?" I asked, hoping to the ancestors it was a way out of here.

"My parents didn't get *all* my money," Jonah said. "I used what I had left to buy this."

Jonah parted the trees. Ahead of us was a brand new grey pick-up truck— one of those monsters that sucks up a ton of gas.

Jonah's chest swelled with pride as we approached the vehicle. "I upgraded everything on it. It's lifted, has a turbo-charged engine, a cold-air intake and an aftermarket exhaust system." He slapped the hood, and Squeaks did an excited dance. "The tank's full. It'll get us a few hours away before we'll have to stop again."

"You can't be fucking serious," I said. My shoulders dropped as I watched Jonah open the driver's side door. I wasn't a fan of human-built machines. I didn't have a problem with vehicles as long as they were made by supernaturals— like my dad. He'd built my bike.

Thinking about my dad hurt. So I tried not to.

"Look, this is our one way of escape. Squeaks can't carry us all, and we don't have a carriage," Imogen snapped. "Just get in."

Whatever. It was that or walking. And I don't think I could take another step. I reluctantly climbed into the back of the truck, and Sophia got in beside me. Jonah started up the engine. Sassy hopped onto Imogen's lap up front, while Esis fastened the middle seatbelt around him next to Sophia and snuggled happily in his seat.

Outside the truck, Squeaks spread her wings and took off into the skies. She'd follow us at a distance from above, where she wouldn't be seen in the cloud cover.

I grabbed on to the door handle as we started moving. Sophia noticed that I'd gone pale and took my hand. "Liam, relax."

I took a deep breath and blew it out. I really didn't like cars. They were rolling death traps. I knew that was ironic, because I rode a bike, but my bike was *magical*. It was totally different.

Imogen reached into a cooler up front. She passed out granola bars and bottles of water. "It isn't much, but it'll hold us over until we stop."

I didn't feel much like eating. The thought of it made me want to throw up. But at the same time, I hadn't consumed anything in well over forty-eight hours. I'd be in for a serious health crisis if I put off eating any longer.

Sophia bent forward and ruffled through her backpack. She gasped when she saw the lines moving through Julian's egg. "What's going on?"

"He's hatching. But it could take a few more hours," I said. "He's not ready to come out yet."

She nodded, and moved the egg aside to dig at the bottom of the bag.

I was shocked when she deposited three pill bottles into my hand, as well as my inhaler.

"I put some of your pills in my bag when you were imprisoned, just in case we made it out," Sophia said.

"You're a lifesaver, Soph." They wouldn't last me long, but at least they were something.

We traveled down the road for fifteen minutes in silence before I said, "Okay... it's time to tell us where we're going. Imogen?"

Jonah glanced at her. She turned around in her seat to look at Sophia and I. "Guys... there's something I've been meaning to tell you. About my tournament winnings."

I'd been wondering what had happened to them. When Sophia and I didn't respond, Imogen confessed, "I bought a house."

"You *what?*" Sophia and I asked at the same time.

"I purchased it before we left on the *Hozho* for vacation," Imogen said quietly. "Just in case we needed a place to go."

"But... you wanted to stay and fight the most," I said.

"I know." Imogen's eyes grew misty. "This was supposed to be a last resort."

She wiped at her face. "That's what I told myself, anyway. I knew I was lying to myself and that we'd have to leave eventually. I just didn't want to."

"So you've had this place ready for *months* and you didn't tell us?" Sophia snapped.

"I know. I should've told you guys." Imogen shook her head. "I just wanted to get revenge on the Elders so bad. I was so concerned with getting vengeance I put you all in danger. And I'm so, so sorry."

"I can't believe you, Imogen." Sophia crossed her arms and fell back against her seat. Imogen bit her lip.

I said nothing. I didn't know if it would've changed anything if we'd left sooner. We were supposed to leave with my family. Neither plan had really worked out.

"Don't be so hard on her, guys," Jonah said softly. "We're all each other's got now."

Sophia's face softened. "What about our families? What about my parents and Amelia? Your parents and brothers, Im? Liam's—"

Sophia cut off at the mention of my family. My throat tightened. Ezra was probably waiting for us with Mom and the rest of our siblings somewhere, wondering why we hadn't shown up yet with Dad or Maddie.

Dad had been murdered. I didn't know if Maddie was dead or alive.

"What matters is getting us to a safe place," Jonah said firmly. "We can search for our loved ones once we know we're out of Oleander's reach. He's never gonna stop looking for you, Sophia. Trying to find our families now is just going to put ourselves and them in danger."

Sophia didn't respond. Her eyes were fixed on the trees whizzing by the window.

We all knew Jonah was right. Didn't make the truth any harder to swallow.

My eyes were too tired to stay open anymore. I passed out less than half an hour into the trip. I was aware of Sophia as she curled up next to me, and Esis' tiny snores below us.

"Jonah, we should pull over." Imogen's voice woke me up a few hours later. Sophia and I had fallen asleep against each other. It was still dark out— probably early morning.

"We have to keep going." I could hear the fatigue in his voice. Imogen put a hand on his arm.

"You're going to fall asleep at the wheel. We need to take a break."

Jonah sighed. He pulled off the road. He drove the truck into the woods, and off-roaded until we came to a spot where the trees were too close together for the truck to get through. Jonah parked the car behind a group of trees to hide it, then we walked until we found a clearing.

It was cold out. I shivered as I gathered wood and built a fire. Sophia lit it, and Jonah pulled logs around the fire for us to sit on. Squeaks came down from the skies and curled up by the fire. Her eyes shut immediately, and Sassy curled up by her side. Esis nestled in Sassy's tail and watched us with his wide blue gaze.

This felt horribly like the Elemental Cup. And I'd thought that had been the worst of my life. Psh. I had no idea.

Imogen began setting up a tent, and Jonah went to help her. She unrolled sleeping bags from the back of the truck, and passed around portable meals for us to cook and eat.

Everyone was tired, but no one wanted to sleep. We sat on the logs by the fire long after we'd gotten done eating and just stared at the flames.

Sophia hugged herself. "Guys," she said. Her eyes watered. "You need to help me find my parents."

Imogen's eyebrows furrowed. Jonah sat up. "What do you mean?"

"My grandpa told me before he died that Lucy and Anthony Greyson weren't my real parents," Sophia rattled off in a monotone. "There were two children born the night Toaqua attacked Koigni, but one of them died. I survived. The woman who's my real mother— she gave me to my grandparents, to keep me safe. Then they gave me to the Henleys."

"You didn't get a name?" Imogen whispered.

Sophia shook her head. Her voice was choked. "No. I have no idea who they could be."

She wiped away tears with the heel of her hand. "All I know is they have to be Koigni, because I have Fire magic. But other than that, I've got nothing."

She sniffed. "I need to know where I come from. And I feel like once I know who they are, all the questions I have about myself are going to fall into place."

Jonah got up. He laid a hand on Sophia's shoulder. "We'll help you find your real parents, girl. They're out there somewhere." He smiled. "Hopefully they're a hell of a lot better than mine."

I wrapped my arm around her waist. "You know I'll always be here for you. No matter what. You deserve to find your family. I know they're out there somewhere, waiting for you."

Sophia gave me a soft kiss. Imogen popped right up from her seat. Her hands were bunched together into fists, and her voice cracked when she spoke.

"I don't know where my parents or brothers are. I've lost my home, my school… everything. But I know I have my family right here," Imogen said. "Wherever you guys are, I'm home."

Jonah flung an arm around Imogen's shoulders. "You guys are a better family to me than my own ever could be," he said. "Sophia, Im, you're my true sisters. And Liam, you're my brother. As long as we've got each other, we can do anything. We can get through this. And we'll come out stronger for it. I have a feeling better days are coming."

Sophia and I rose together. "I don't know my parents, but I know who I am," Sophia said. "We might've lost everything today— all of us— but it won't be in vain. We're going to make a better world together, in honor of the people we lost and what they sacrificed for us to get here. We're going to make our ancestors proud."

An idea came to form quickly in my head. "We'll make a new tribe," I said. "It'll be a tribe of our own. We don't need the Elders. We just need each other."

"Then let's make a pact. Right here, right now," Imogen said quickly. "We're going to rebuild. We'll find our families, and we'll make a tribe that will represent everything the Hawkei should've always been. It'll be unified. One tribe."

"*One tribe*," the group of us said together. The words sounded... I don't know, magical. There was something about them that said nothing would ever be the same.

From this moment on, everything would change. The four of us would make a new world. Together.

The group turned as we heard a cracking sound. Sophia's backpack was wriggling. Julian was breaking free.

Instinctively, I dove toward the backpack and pulled the egg out of it. I sat down on the log and placed the egg on my lap. As I did, the shell exploded— little bits of egg flew everywhere as a newborn fledgling dragon stumbled free.

The dragon had four legs, and his red scales were as scarlet as the egg shell had been. Silver spikes ran all the way down his spine and ended in an arrowhead tail. Two straight horns protruded from his head, and fiery eyes flashed when they landed on mine. Julian was no bigger than my forearm, but already, he looked fierce.

"Oh my gosh! He's beautiful!" Imogen burst as my friends crowded around me.

Julian gave a low growl in his throat that sounded more like a chirp. He looked up at me as if searching for guidance.

When our eyes locked, a warm feeling grew in my stomach. I lifted a hand and ran it over Julian's scales. He squeaked in pleasure, then charged into my shirt. Julian cuddled himself against my torso, his little talons scratching at my jeans as he rubbed against me.

"No way," Jonah said. He sounded awed. "Liam, he *just* imprinted on you."

"Uh... so does he think I'm his mom or something?" I asked as Julian's chirping sounds grew louder. He was really loving this. He bumped against my hand, like a cat would, and I scratched his back so he'd calm down.

"Do you realize what this means?" Sophia said in excitement. She gave a dance behind me, and Jonah cheered.

"No." I hadn't taken Dragonology, so I didn't know what they were talking about.

"Dragons don't bond with anyone after they've imprinted on an Elementai," Imogen breathed. "Liam, he's yours."

Mine? Julian was *mine?*

Julian let out a puff of smoke before he gave a contented coo and curled up on my lap. A rush of love and attachment overcame my heart just then, and I had to hold back tears.

I couldn't believe it. I thought it was impossible. I never believed I could have a magical creature again. I didn't think one could ever love me, but here Julian was, acting like I was the only person he needed in the world.

He'd never replace Nashoma— never be my Familiar. But he didn't need to be. I had a companion now, one that had bonded with me. I didn't have to be alone anymore. No matter what, Julian would always be there. Magical creatures came to you at your lowest point, and Julian had arrived when I'd needed him most.

My old life had died today. It had to, in order to give me a new one. All of us would grieve for what we'd lost and everything we'd suffered.

But life would move on. Nature demanded that. We were still alive, and by the ancestors, we were going to give Oleander and the Task Force hell. We were going to show the Elders they couldn't keep us down. No matter what, we'd always get back up for one more round— even if the odds were stacked against us.

Sophia and I would get married. We'd have our wedding, and we'd find her real parents. We'd bring our families back together again and reunite with our friends. The brightest morning always came after the darkest night, and the greatest rewards always came after the most painful trials.

We were going to make a new beginning. And somehow, someway, we'd get our tribe back.

END OF BOOK FOUR

Turn the page to read a special excerpt from Book Five: *The Elemental War!*

HIDDEN LEGENDS

Read more from the Hidden Legends universe! Each Hidden Legends series takes place within the same world, but in separate and unique societies. Every series stands on its own, and they can be read in any order.

SHIFTERS, FAE, & SORCERESSES

University of Sorcery by Megan Linski

WITCHES, DEMONS, & REAPERS

College of Witchcraft by Alicia Rades

SUPERNATURAL PRISON

Prison for Supernatural Offenders by Megan Linski & Alicia Rades

Never miss a new release! Join our newsletter at www.hiddenlegendsbooks.com/fanclub/

THE ELEMENTAL WAR
CHAPTER ONE

Liam

Son. You need to open your eyes.

Everything ignited. The landscape around me dipped and folded. Each tree and plant had been demolished to cinders. There was nothing left around me but an empty desert that went on for miles and miles, far past the horizon. The ground was cracked, raw and devoid of life except for the ashes that littered the area. Blackened, charred ground met with an orange-yellow sky. The smell of smoke and fire was everywhere, surrounding me and closing in. It was suffocating me, and my throat gasped for air.

Breathe. I needed to breathe.

It's okay, son. Hands reached out and steadied me through the blazing darkness. Once they touched me, the smoke scattered and dispersed in columns that went rushing upward. The harsh sunset illuminated a tough face and a grim exterior.

My entire body quivered with relief as I recognized the stern expression and familiar features that were so much like my own.

"Dad," I choked out. Relief rushed through my veins like a harsh stream. I never thought I'd see him again. Ancestors, I missed him so much.

I reached out for him, but my hand glided straight through his spirit. He could touch me, but I couldn't touch him. Horror grew in my lungs, and I took a breath to let out a scream. The twilight welled, and the temperature shot up several degrees. We were standing at the cusp of the Ancestral Lands, and he was on a plane of existence I couldn't reach.

Because I wasn't dead. *Why* wasn't I fucking dead?

Dad reached out and put his hands on my shoulders. *Listen to me,* he said roughly. *There isn't much time. You need to get Sophia to a safe place.*

"Where?" I asked. "Where is safe anymore?"

She has to come first now. Do you understand? Dad's eyes bored into mine with an intensity that I'd never seen before. *You protect her with everything you have. You need to be her leader and guide. If you don't, everything's at risk. Your whole life has come down to this.*

"I'm trying," I pleaded. "I'm trying so hard."

I'm sorry, but you don't have time to fall apart, Dad growled. *Your family is counting on you. Be there for them, Liam. They're your responsibility.*

"I don't know what you mean," I stuttered. "What am I supposed to do?"

Dad said nothing more— just vanished. I stumbled forward, and his spirit melded into the colors of the sky, a grizzly bear running with the vibrancy of the wind.

"Dad? Dad!" My voice grew into a panic as I searched for him. "Dad, don't leave me! I need you!"

It was too late. He was gone again.

I had to find him. I was nothing without him, without his guidance. I couldn't face this world alone. I couldn't be the man of the family. That was his job, not mine.

I started running. I bolted through the desert as fast as I could. My body couldn't labor me here. I was merely spirit energy, so I didn't feel any pain. But no matter where I ran, it seemed like I remained in the same spot.

The ground beneath my feet began to split. Large, cavernous holes opened up in the earth, and lava bubbled at the bottom. I looked down and saw with a horrible fall of my stomach that the pits beneath were five-hundred foot drops... and they were growing around me, leaving me nowhere to go.

I wasn't in the Ancestral Lands at all. I was in *Aiya Nocshun...* the Mighty Darkness. The Hawkei's literal hell. I'd been sentenced here because I'd failed to save the people I loved. My ancestors had turned their backs on me. I had committed too many sins. I was no longer worthy to join them in the afterlife.

A wretched screeching caught my attention. A red baby dragon, no longer than my forearm, was running from the caverns opening up in the ground. He slid as the rocks tilted backward, chirping for someone to save him.

My heart plummeted. Julian had been damned along with me? Ancestors, what had I done?

"Julian, come here!" I called out to my dragon.

Julian spotted me on the edge of one of the caverns and gave a cry of relief. Julian ran, avoiding the gaping holes in the earth that were threatening to swallow him whole, and leapt into my arms. The newborn dragon shook as he cuddled against my chest, burying his head in my jacket.

"It's all right," I forced out as I stroked the dragon's back, but I was certain it was a lie. The lava pits were closing in, and any second now I'd tumble into them, sending Julian and I headfirst into eternal torment.

We had to move. There were small round platforms of earth, around five feet across, that I could jump to in order to escape the caverns and get to the other side safely. I leapt from platform to platform, avoiding the lava and keeping Julian close to my chest. I didn't want him getting hurt. I needed to get him out of here. If I couldn't save myself, there had to be a way to save my dragon. I wouldn't let him suffer because of me.

Finally, I reached solid ground, and I staggered away from the bubbling pits. Eventually, Julian and I made it back to... somewhere... and the lava pits behind us disappeared.

I trembled as I clung to Julian. Water. I wanted water. Just a drop. I wanted to use my powers again, one last time.

I wouldn't get it. I was being punished. I'd never be able to use my element again. I'd be stuck in this horrible world of flame, constantly scared and uncomfortable as I was beaten down and tortured by my opposite element.

"Liam!" A deep voice interrupted my alarmed thoughts, and I spun around. Fear pierced my chest as I saw Jonah on his knees, his hands and ankles bound with noxite cuffs. True fear shone in his eyes as he cried out for me.

No. No, this couldn't be happening! I couldn't have *dragged* my friends down here with me!

"Help me!" Jonah cried. "Why aren't you doing anything?"

I completely froze. Julian scrambled in my jacket, his nails tearing at my shirt. Jonah struggled as he tried to get out of his cuffs, but he couldn't break free.

"We need you!" Another voice broke into my mind. Imogen had appeared beside Jonah. She too had noxite cuffs binding her limbs, and she couldn't move.

I glanced behind them and saw the lifeless bodies of Squeaks and Sassy. The hippogriff and fox lay immobile, bodies broken and shattered as they stared out into the endless night. Jonah and Imogen hadn't noticed their Familiars had been killed— all they had eyes for was me.

I still couldn't move. I was too afraid. I was a coward, and that's exactly what had gotten us down here. It was all my fault.

"You're supposed to be our *leader*! Do something!" Jonah barked. Their faces tightened with rage as I remained passive.

I couldn't. I was wholly incapable. I couldn't be the leader my father demanded I be. I wasn't half the chief he was. *Helpless* felt like a term of strength, compared to how weak I was in that moment.

It was then that two spears came flying out of the black clouds. The first one pierced Jonah's neck. It severed his spine and punctured his throat, ending all hope of life. He fell to the side, and his body landed with a sick *thud*.

The second spear sliced Imogen's chest. She gave a few ragged breaths, and tears of blood fell from her eyes as she stared up at me hatefully.

"You've killed us, Liam," Imogen whispered in a dying breath, then she slunk forward. The spear stuck out of her back as she collapsed forward and didn't move again.

I'd killed them. I was a *murderer*.

I had to get out of here. I ignored the wild protests from Julian inside of my jacket as I sprinted, trying to get away from this nightmare. As I did, I passed mountains of bodies. Mom's face stared out at me in a blank expression. Her body was draped over Maddie's and stuck full of arrows, as if she'd been trying to protect her. Maddie was already gone, her throat cut and insides opened up. A cockatrice fed on her remains, its beak dripping blood as it gave me an ominous warning to stay back.

I could hear my other siblings crying somewhere, but no matter which direction I turned, they weren't there. I didn't see Katie, Christian, or Jackson, though they screamed for me relentlessly.

The scariest thing of all was that I could neither see nor hear Ezra. I searched everywhere for him, but I couldn't find my little brother. I didn't know what had happened to him, and the fear of what he could be enduring broke me.

Without warning, the mountains of bodies vanished. All the corpses disappeared, and I was left by myself in the twilight, desert landscape, only the smell of death for company.

"Julian?" I looked inside my jacket, but he was gone, too. He'd been stolen away from me. A lump grew in my throat at the prospect of being totally alone in this land, forever.

Death was a total ending. And here I was. I'd earned every bit of it.

"Liam!"

My heart simultaneously leapt with hope and clenched in fear as I heard the most beautiful voice in the world behind me. It was Sophia who had shouted my name. Her arms were wrapped tightly around her stomach. Her face appeared horrified, a torturous reflection of my own terror. Esis wasn't with her. I had no idea where he'd gone, but I hoped he was safe. I didn't want Sophia here with me— didn't want her to experience this world— but at least I hadn't been abandoned completely.

"*Pawee*," I wept. I surged forward and wrapped her in my arms. I held her tightly and rocked her back and forth as I cried. Sophia hugged me back and rested her head on my shoulder, a light smile on her lips.

She didn't smell like herself. She didn't *feel* like herself. It was like I wasn't even touching her, though she was right here in my arms. Something was way off.

"Sophie, you need to get away from me," I begged. I forced myself to let go of her, and although it was painful, it was the right thing to do. "I'm no good for you. If you stick with me, you'll end up like everyone else."

"It's going to be okay. We'll make it through this together," she insisted. She put her forehead to mine and brushed the hair back from my face before she took a step back.

"I have something to tell you," she began. "I'm—"

She never got the words out of her mouth, because an ax came swinging downward. The blade wasn't held by anyone or swung by anything, but it met its target. It sliced through Sophia's neck, decapitating her and severing her head right off her shoulders.

Her blood splashed onto my face, and I gave a wailing cry of grief. I fell to my knees as her headless corpse crumpled against the ground. I watched as her head went rolling away, coming to a stop several feet away. She still wore a shocked expression, mouth open in surprise.

I put my head in my hands and rocked back and forth. I didn't want this to be real. It couldn't be real.

This isn't real, a low, kindly voice growled. *You need to wake up.*

I knew that voice like I knew the sound of my own. I refused to raise my head out of my hands, but I felt a wet nose nudging at me, and saw black fur from between my fingers.

Liam, you don't have time. The Task Force is coming. Your family is in danger, Nashoma growled. *Wake up!*

I was aware of someone's hand on my shoulder, shaking me awake, and the sound of my name as the hellish landscape faded from my sight.

As my eyes opened once more, I took in a gasp of breath. Reality crashed upon me like a wave, but what I'd experienced stuck with me as I came back to the land of the living.

I was afraid of hell... but it was already here.

Continue The Elemental War to discover the fate of the Hawkei!

BONUS OFFERS

Find coloring pages, games, quizzes, and bonus content at www. hiddenlegendsbooks.com

Join *Orenda Academy of Magical Creatures* on Facebook to talk to other Elementai about upcoming books in the Hidden Legends Universe!

Never miss a new release! Join our newsletter at

www.hiddenlegendsbooks.com/fanclub

Check out the *Academy of Magical Creatures Official Playlist* on Spotify!

About the Authors

Megan Linski (left) and Alicia Rades (right) are two best friends and the authors of the *Academy of Magical Creatures* series. Both are USA TODAY Bestselling Authors and award-winning novelists for teens and young adults. Megan Linski is a disabled author who loves laughter, adventure, and fantasy worlds. She is a proud member of Koigni House. Alicia Rades is a mother who enjoys exploring paranormal realms and trying new recipes. She is a champion from Toaqua House. Both girls love nature, animals, sexy romances, and eating cheese.